Cold talons pinched his skin

"Dean…" someone said, and he couldn't believe how much it sounded like Krysty.

Something shimmered into being on his right. It was impossibly close, near enough to reach out and touch him. He'd have seen anyone or anything that had come that close to him.

Then he saw the face, made out the features. She was indistinct, as if he were seeing her through a heavy fog

"Krysty?" Dean said, not believing it

"Your father is coming for you. Look for him." The words sounded as if they were coming from a long distance, then she was gone. Before the boy could puzzle over her appearance and what it meant, the door burst open. Framed in it was a nightmare figure Dean remembered well: a giant mutie pig, its beady, merciless eyes nearly buried in wrinkles of scarred gristle.

Before he could draw the Browning, the beast started for him, squealing shrilly in anticipation of an easy kill.

THE DEATHLANDS SAGA

This world is their legacy, a world born in the violent nuclear spasm of 2001 that was the bitter outcome of a struggle for global dominance.

There is no real escape from this shockscape where life always hangs in the balance, vulnerable to newly demonic nature, barbarism, lawlessness.

But they are the warrior survivalists, and they endure—in the way of the lion, the hawk and the tiger, true to nature's heart despite its ruination.

Ryan Cawdor: The privileged son of an East Coast baron. Acquainted with betrayal from a tender age, he is a master of the hard realities.

Krysty Wroth: Harmony ville's own Titian-haired beauty, a woman with the strength of tempered steel. Her premonitions and Gaia powers have been fostered by her Mother Sonja.

J. B. Dix, the Armorer: Weapons master and Ryan's close ally, he, too, honed his skills traversing the Deathlands with the legendary Trader.

Doctor Theophilus Tanner: Torn from his family and a gentler life in 1896, Doc has been thrown into a future he couldn't have imagined.

Dr. Mildred Wyeth: Her father was killed by the Ku Klux Klan, but her fate is not much lighter. Restored from predark cryogenic suspension, she brings twentieth-century healing skills to a nightmare.

Jak Lauren: A true child of the wastelands, reared on adversity, loss and danger, the albino teenager is a fierce fighter and loyal friend.

Dean Cawdor: Ryan's young son by Sharona accepts the only world he knows, and yet he is the seedling bearing the promise of tomorrow.

In a world where all was lost, they are humanity's last hope....

JAMES AXLER

AFTERMATH

A GOLD EAGLE BOOK FROM

W🌐RLDWIDE®

TORONTO • NEW YORK • LONDON
AMSTERDAM • PARIS • SYDNEY • HAMBURG
STOCKHOLM • ATHENS • TOKYO • MILAN
MADRID • WARSAW • BUDAPEST • AUCKLAND

First edition March 2006

ISBN 0-373-62407-7

AFTERMATH

Some say that men love games
Some say that war's a game
And from the Roman days
The red god sets the pace

Mars, it's always Mars
With Venus in his arms

Don't they know the real arena
She draws blood to stoke her love
And the Reaper shows his bones
Shedding kindness like a cloak

Mars, his nights of bliss
Venus and her blood-red kiss

—from the Liar cycle
the rock group Polo Heads

CONTENTS

THE MARS ARENA

It was the moon that gave the brushwooders away, hanging against the sable sky, as white and bright as a man's skull just carved clean.

Ryan Cawdor stifled a curse as he moved through the shadows and silence of the forest, quiet himself so the stalkers wouldn't know he was among them. The Steyr rifle that had seen him out of so many tight spots across Deathlands was hard and sure in his hands.

Jak Lauren had noticed the brushwooders first, even before the sun had dropped like a burst heart against the leaden evening sky. But Ryan's combat sense had been prickling the back of his neck an hour before that.

Ryan held his breath as he watched the brushwooders, not wanting the thin gray fog to give away his position. The pursuers had broken into at least two groups that he could identify, and walked up the broken terrain in a staggered line. It was a pincer movement, as old as war itself.

The one-eyed warrior had used it a few times himself, and he knew it would be deadly effective. He and his companions were outnumbered at least seven to one.

The sky was clear at the moment, but against the mountains the weather could change in an instant. The wind came out of the north and carried a wolf's bite. Ryan had dressed warmly, wearing a heavy coat he'd found after he and his companions had raided deserted houses along their trek in from the gateway among the Western Islands. But he'd had to shed the coat to double back on their would-be attackers because the material was too light colored.

He felt as if he were freezing on the outside, but inside his survival instinct was burning him up. He was a tall man, a couple inches over six feet, broad shouldered and clean limbed. His dark curling hair held a frosting of snow from the flurries that appeared suddenly over the Sierra Nevada along the Cific Ocean.

Most women would have called him handsome, if not for the black leather patch that covered his left eye, and the cruel, puckered scar that ran from the corner of his right eye, down his cheek to just above his jawbone.

Two pointmen, one the head of each group of the pincer arms, met and knelt to examine the ground in the light of the full moon. Ryan knew they were following footsteps his group had left in the damp earth underneath the crust of snow. Given the weather conditions, it was hard to pass unnoticed even as practiced as his people were.

They'd seen the brushwooders earlier in the day without being seen themselves, not many hours after they'd made the jump through the mat-trans into the area. It had taken Ryan only a few minutes of observation to figure them for the raiding parties he'd been told about. The companions had encountered a group of farmers in the early evening and learned that brushwooders had fired several farmhouses and killed a dozen people. It was part of a spree of violence that had been going on for days.

Violence was nothing new in Deathlands, or to the companions. The fleeing group of farmers had also warned Ryan that the weapons they carried would be highly prized by the brushwooders. Their leader had designs on consolidating his hold on the area and killing anyone who stood to oppose him. Adding to his armament was necessary to achieve his goal.

Ryan had kept his people clear of the roving hands of brushwooders, but their search for a pass through the mountains had brought them here, and within sight of one of the brushwooder patrols. Now they were running through the darkness for their lives.

Rising, his nose tilted up and forward as if he were taking in the air like a hunting hound, the pointman nearer to Ryan turned to his group and pointed toward the east, where the terrain grew steeper. He moved on, moonlight glinting from the blaster in his hands. He'd torn branches off trees and stuck them inside his clothing for camouflage, as well as down the neck of his coat and in the sleeves. Other branches were pinned against his chest and shoulders.

Footfalls crunched into the snow behind Ryan. He whirled, bringing up the Steyr to cover the lone shadow twenty feet away.

"Me," J. B. Dix whispered.

"How many?" Ryan asked.

"I counted forty-two," J.B. replied, closing the distance between them without being spotted, "then I gave up. It's bastard cold out here, and I'm not happy about them not being sociable enough to fall for our little trick back at the other camp."

When they'd found out they were being followed, Ryan had kept his group moving, ready to defend themselves. Once he'd seen the brushwooders were willing to wait, he'd guessed they were waiting to ambush the travelers while they were sleeping rather than risking an all-out confrontation. Tense minutes had passed before they acted as if they were making camp not more than three miles back.

"Could be they did," Ryan replied. "Mebbe they waited until the campfire we left died a bit, then crept down to where we left those rocks piled up under blankets and realized we'd already gone."

"Didn't have any trouble picking up our trail," J.B. observed, taking off his steel-rimmed glasses for a moment to clean them. When he put them back into place, he reached up and gave his battered fedora a tug, making sure it was settled into place.

"I figure Krysty and the others are a hundred yards ahead of the pack," Ryan said.

"Yeah." J.B. glanced at his wrist chron. "It's been long enough."

"This bunch of coldhearts have got their noses opened up for the chilling they're expecting to dish out," Ryan said, nodding at the rear of the two pincer movements. "They aren't going to expect us to come up on them from behind."

"We want to introduce ourselves fast or slow?"

"Slow," Ryan answered. "They aren't interested in moving quick, and they're getting spread out. If we put a few of them down, it'll only add to the confusion when they start running into their own dead backtracking us after the wheels come off."

J.B. looked up at the dark sky. "The way this snow is picking up and sticking so quick to what's already here, we could buy a few minutes. By the time they get them-

selves regrouped, the footsteps going up that mountainside will have disappeared."

"Mebbe we'll have disappeared right alongside them."
Ryan flashed his old friend a grim smile. "I got the left."

J.B. nodded, then faded into the shadows.

Ryan went in the other direction.

WITH THE STEYR slung over one shoulder, Ryan slipped the
panga free of its sheath. The eighteen-inch weapon sported
a wicked blade that he kept honed to razor sharpness.

He crept up on the man walking drag on the left pincer movement, moving easily and quietly. The brushwooder had stopped briefly to adjust his pack.

Ryan stepped forward without hesitation, the panga
pointed up from his fist. He clapped a hand over the
brushwooder's mouth, then sliced the edged steel across
the man's exposed neck.

The blade bit deeper than Ryan thought it should have,
then hung up for just a second. The man jumped in his
grasp as the wound spewed hot blood over Ryan's arms. The
brushwooder tried to force a scream past the hand over his
mouth, then drew in another breath through his nose to try
again, letting Ryan know the windpipe hadn't been severed.

Glancing down, Ryan saw the man had evidently been
scratching at his bearded throat when he'd raked the panga
across. The blade had sliced off three of the man's fingers,
the stubs shooting blood into the air, but the panga had
gotten trapped in the middle joint of the index finger.

Ryan changed his leverage and pulled more forcefully
on the panga. The blade separated the last finger a heartbeat before opening a wound in the man's neck. He held
the kicking, dying man until only spasmodic quivers were
left, then shoved the corpse into a stand of brush. He

took the man's coat, glancing over his shoulder to make sure he hadn't been seen.

In the moonlight, and supported in the brush, the dead man looked as if he were about to commit an ambush. As a final touch, Ryan propped up one of the corpse's arms and leveled the man's blaster in front of him. Both dead eyes remained open, catching the moonlight reflected up from the patches of snow around them.

Ryan knew it would be enough to fool most folks.

RYAN FELL IN behind the pincer movement again, pulling on the dead man's coat as he ran. The garment was snug across the shoulders, too small to be properly closed. But the stains from his bloody hands blended right in with the accumulated dirt that soiled the coat.

The sounds of his footsteps were lost among the shushing and tramping the brushwooders made. Marked by muddied snow, their trail was easy to track. The next two men in line were together, their heads close as they talked.

Ryan closed the distances then. He held his pace, gazing ahead of the two and spotting the man in front of them. He couldn't act yet, but a dip in the terrain was coming up. If he could move fast enough, he could take them both out before anyone saw. He tightened his grip on the panga.

The dip arrived, and Ryan lunged between his two targets and knocked them off balance. He thrust the panga through the first brushwooder's throat, the point skidding along the vertebrae for an instant, then plunging through the other side.

The brushwooder dropped to his knees, hands seizing the panga impaling his throat. Strained gurgling bubbled from his mutilated throat.

The second one turned, leveling a blaster at Ryan's

chest. The brushwooder's face was pale, unravaged by time or circumstance as yet—and feminine.

Ryan swung an arm out, chopping at the wrist behind the blaster. There was enough time for him to draw his 9 mm P-226 pistol and shoot, but the noise would have alerted her companions.

His arm connected with the wrist solidly, and the blaster went spinning away.

Her mouth opened for a scream, and she tried to step away and rake his face with a handful of jagged nails at the same time.

Ryan slapped the arm away, then stepped in and punched her in the stomach. Only a wheeze of pain escaped her lips. Moving into her again, he used his greater weight and size to tackle her and send them both crashing to the ground.

Grabbing the woman's shoulder and maneuvering his weight, Ryan landed on top, keeping his face and eye just out of her reach as he put a hand over her mouth.

Her lips smeared wetly against his palm as she tried to sink her teeth into him. Angry tears brimmed in her pale eyes, then slid down her face.

Ryan had no real mercy in him for hostile strangers, and none at all for people intent on making sure he caught the last train West. But for a moment, looking down into her face and feeling her struggle for life, he paused. He didn't feel anything for her. She was just a predator who'd taken on a bigger and more efficient predator. Her death was a natural progression.

Something in her face reminded him of Dean. Not a resemblance, because he'd marked his son with his own features most, despite Sharona's contribution to the gene pool. Though this was a young woman, clearly no more a child, she possessed that same spark of vitality, the same brash disbelief that anything could ever harm her.

Dean was the reason the companions had come to the Western Islands. Over the past few weeks, the nightmares about the boy had wakened Krysty from sleep a handful of times and left her shaking with dread. Thinking of his son, Ryan let out a slow breath that became a gray cloud, mixing with the air escaping through the girl's nose.

The girl moved quickly, taking advantage of her respite. She shook her arm, and a long-bladed throwing knife popped into her hand from a spring-loaded sleeve sheath.

Only Ryan's quick reflexes, honed by a lifetime in the courtship of sudden death, saved his life. He shifted to one side and felt the stinging kiss of the blade as it slithered along his ribs, unable to find real purchase. The folds of the heavy coat prevented the girl from drawing the knife back and using it again immediately.

Closing his hand more tightly over her mouth and lower jaw, Ryan grabbed a fistful of hair at the back of her head. She kicked under him, trying to dislodge his weight. He rode out her efforts, then twisted her head in his hands just as she managed to work the knife free again.

Vertebrae shattered in her neck as her skull popped free of her spine. The damage robbed her immediately of her motor skills. The knife fell from nerveless fingers.

Her eyes were already dimming when Ryan released her. He forced himself to his feet and ran a hand inside his coat. His fingers came away covered with bright scarlet from the wound along his side, but his touch revealed its clean edges, only a couple inches long and not bleeding seriously.

"What the fuck is going on here?" a man's deep voice demanded.

Ryan was already in motion, his legs driving him. His

peripheral vision revealed the man standing at the top of the hill that had cut off the violent business from the rest of the brushwooder attack teams.

Instead of breaking and trying to run away from the man, Ryan raced straight at him, his hand grabbing the throwing knife that still had his blood on it.

The brushwooder hesitated for a moment, stunned by Ryan's apparent suicidal play. He raised his rifle when the one-eyed man was less than fifteen feet away and closing fast.

Ryan drew back his arm and let the knife fly. Jak Lauren was by far the best hand with a blade Ryan had ever seen, but working for the Trader had provided an all-around education in the arts of death. The knife sailed like a steel dart, barely passing above the muzzle of the leveled rifle.

Ryan dived to one side as soon as the knife left his fingerprints. He hit the ground on his wounded side and stifled a cry of pain from the impact. He rolled at once, clawing the P-226 from its holster.

Coming up on his knees, the blaster before him, Ryan watched as the brushwooder struggled to remain on his feet. The rifle remained unfired. His mouth was open, the haft of the knife jutting from between his lips.

Ryan kept the SIG-Sauer trained on his adversary as he approached the man.

Harsh gagging croaks issued from the man's bloody lips, cut up by the passage of the sharp blade. He tried to bring the rifle around, but Ryan grabbed the barrel and yanked it away. He then pulled up the knife, bringing the man's face toward his own.

The brushwooder tried to scream, but the sound came out his nasal passages as a drawn-out whine that announced his death.

Holding on to the haft, Ryan kicked the corpse free. He cleaned the blade on the man's clothes, then noticed the case over his back. Inside, neatly stored, was a fiberglass bow in three pieces that screwed together, and a quiver of arrows.

Ryan drew out one of the shafts and studied the big, triangular hunting arrowhead at its end. It showed signs of use, like the bow, but appeared in good shape.

He tossed the case to one side, then maneuvered the dead man into the trees. It took only a few minutes more to retrieve and clean the panga, and to arrange the other two bodies.

Moving at a trot, warm now from his exertions and from the adrenaline pumping through his system, Ryan adjusted the case containing the bow and arrows and followed the brushwooders.

KRYSTY WROTH PUT the thought of the pursuing brushwooders as far out of her mind as she could, concentrating instead on the broken terrain. The full moon was both a blessing and a curse.

Without it, they'd have been dead for sure. Chasms opened up unexpectedly, covered by shadows.

"No torches, no muzzle-flashes," Mildred Wyeth said beside her. "And that's the good news. The bad news is that Ryan and J.B. could already be chilled and we just don't know it yet."

"No," Krysty said. "If Ryan was dead, I'd know."

Pressing on, the red-haired beauty followed the narrow path that Jak had taken only minutes ago. The ledge was only a couple feet wide, and wisps of snow trying to cover its surface made walking only a little tricky. She thanked Gaia, the Earth Mother, that the wind was too cold to let the flurries cling to the stone. Conditions could have been much worse.

Krysty felt her hair coil tightly against her scalp. Her hair was deep crimson and prehensile, products of her mutie blood. She was a couple inches short of six feet, with generous curves and emerald green eyes. The dark blue Western boots she wore weren't made for hard climbing, but they were what she was used to, and anything else would have made it even harder.

Navigating another area of loose rock, she concentrated for a moment, trying to *feel* her lover's presence. Besides the sentient hair, her mutie heritage bequeathed her other things. The limited prescience she sometimes experienced had been working overtime of late, mostly about Dean. And maybe only then because the boy was so much a part of Ryan.

Mildred nearly slipped, and Krysty watched as the woman righted herself and pressed against the stone face of the mountain. Her coat whipped around her.

"Damn wind," the black woman said. "Caught me by surprise. I'm not as aerodynamically correct as you are."

Of medium height, Mildred was stocky. Her face was almost covered by the hood she wore, but a few of the beaded plaits of her hair hung out on either side of her chin. A Czech-made ZKR 551 .38 target revolver was in one of her gloved hands. She'd learned to shoot more than a hundred years ago, and her skills had been good enough to win her a few medals.

Born on December 17, 1964, Mildred was still in her thirties. Three days before 2001 had been rung in, she'd gone to a hospital in her hometown of Lincoln, Nebraska. The operation was supposed to be somewhat boring to those in the medical field: exploratory abdominal surgery, nothing life-threatening at all.

Instead, she'd had a reaction to the anesthetic and gone into a coma. In order to save her, the surgeons had placed her in cryogenic sleep. She'd slept on for a hundred years, through the death of the world and of everyone she knew. Ryan Cawdor and his companions had rescued her.

"Usually I rather enjoy a brisk walk in cool weather. And mayhap a little adventure, as well. However, as we come to the end of this injurious little excursion, I shall be vexed to end up without a cup of tea to cap off a rather exciting evening."

"Doc," Mildred said, "as long as you're flapping your lips the way you are, I know you aren't too put out."

"My dear Dr. Wyeth," Theophilus Algernon Tanner said, "your erudition is beyond reproach. However, the skill you exhibit in expressing yourself can be a tad bit lacking for one of the medical calling."

Mildred had been a medical doctor in her day, specializing—ironically—in cryogenic research and development.

Like her, Doc Tanner had been displaced in time, though his removal from the century he'd been born into had been achieved by means Krysty understood even less than cryogenics.

Doc was tall and thin, which gave his long arms and legs even greater reach. His silver hair normally fell to his shoulders, but was now whipped into a frenzy by the wind. He'd thrust his ebony walking stick through his belt, the silver lion's-head handle protruding through the part in his coat. The collar of his stained and faded frock coat was visible above the collar of the thermal jacket he wore over it.

Born in a small hamlet in Vermont in 1868, Doc had been hauled into the twentieth century by the white coats of Operation Chronos. He had proved ungracious and difficult by his own reckoning, and had been dead set on returning to his beloved wife and children. As a result of his rebellious actions on several occasions, the powers behind Operation Chronos had shoved him a hundred years into the future, into the sprawl of savagery that had become Deathlands.

"Blow it out your ass, Doc," Mildred said.

"Indeed," the old man replied. "Your words ill become you, dear lady."

Krysty ignored the bantering. Camaraderie took many forms. Some were more noisy than others.

The ledge turned right at nearly ninety degrees. She took it gingerly, keeping her weight toward the stone face.

The snow flurries swirled into her face now, making it hard to see. She blinked stinging tears from her eyes. Her hands felt numb, and she had to wonder how much longer she could trust them.

"Are you sure about the pass, Doc?" she called back over her shoulder.

"My dear Krysty," Doc said, a smile framing the shocking white perfection of his teeth, "my certitude is based wholly on the fact that I trust John Barrymore's skills with that minisextant of his, even though we're operating on knowledge gleaned from an exercise in cartography that is only a modest hundred or so years old and did not enjoy the opportunity of conforming to a vastly violated topography in this region."

"You're making my head hurt," Mildred complained.

"You have," Doc said in simpler words, "my best guess. Admittedly we appear to be betwixt a rock and a hard place."

Krysty silently agreed and went on. The ledge ended abruptly. Without pause, it vanished right into the side of what looked like a sheer rise of fifteen feet or more.

She scoured the wall in front of her and on the right. Nothing was there.

"What's wrong?" Mildred asked.

"Dead end," Krysty replied. She looked over the ledge to her left, feeling the pull of vertigo. The flying snow vanished into the shadows that lay stretched against the mountainside. She couldn't see the bottom.

"What about Jak?" Mildred asked.

Krysty shook her head, not feeling the albino teenager anywhere. "I don't see him."

Mildred scraped a foot across the stone ledge. "Awful damn slippery here."

Doc came up beside them, one hand on the mountain behind as he balanced and peered over the edge. "Oh, dear," he said in a quiet voice. "The poor lad."

Catching the lower limbs of an oak tree, Ryan climbed ten feet up. The branches shook, littering the ground with snow that fell from the green leaves, but none of the brushwooders took notice. Despite the wintry feel of the night and the snow, it was only early fall. The nukecaust had screwed up Nature's rhythms a hundred years earlier, and the earthquakes and the active volcanoes in the area affected the weather, as well, seeding the air from dozens of radioactive hot spots.

Trader had talked about the strange atmospheric conditions hovering over the region. Ryan knew for a fact that farther north the land had turned to frozen ruin, and the volcanoes stretched in between, with some of them way to the south. With the volcanoes spouting rad-blasted waste into the air on a regular basis, anything could come falling out of the sky and he wouldn't have been surprised. He'd stopped really smelling the sulphur stink hours ago, but he remained aware of it.

He nestled in among the boughs, gauging the strength of the pincer movement spread out around him with a trained eye.

His and J.B.'s efforts hadn't gone unrewarded. The steady advance of the brushwooders had been broken, and a few milled around waiting for the rearguard to catch up. Word was evidently spreading up the line that a number of them weren't coming. Ryan could see even the point-men were holding their position some 120 yards away at the foothills that led to the steep mountain trail where Krysty and the others had gone.

Clouds scudded over the bright moon, laying patches of darkness over the broken land. But against the growing white islands of drifting snow, the brushwooders stood out as good targets.

Ryan didn't intend to miss the opportunity to add to the confusion. He opened the case containing the bow and quiver of arrows. The three sections easily screwed into one another. Fitting the string was tricky while standing in the tree, but he managed.

Voices reached his ears now, letting him know the brushwooders were abandoning the stealthy approach.

The arrows felt heavy enough for proper chilling. He was more at home with a handblaster or the panga, which was an old friend, tried, trusted and true. But he knew his way around a bow. His father, Baron Titus Cawdor, had seen to the education of all his sons. The barony at Front Royal hadn't been easily won, nor easily held. A knowledge of weapons had been necessary.

He nocked an arrow, drew it back to his ear and sighted through the opening between the branches. Releasing half a breath, he let it fly. As the arrow jumped from the bow the string twanged, but not loud enough to be heard from more than a few paces.

Less than forty yards distant, the arrow pierced a man's inner thigh, and a primal cry of pain suddenly rent the chill air.

The man stumbled, bent double and hovered over the fletched end of the arrow. The other brushwooders stood frozen, wondering how one among them could have been wounded without sign or sound of an attack.

"Fireblast," Ryan cursed. Shooting one of the men and dropping him dead in his tracks had been the plan. Maybe he'd have been lucky enough to down another one or two before they'd have even known he was among them. Wounding the man and letting him scream spun events into the sudden rush of near death.

He sighted on another target, reminding himself to aim higher with the bow because the trajectory had proved wrong on the first shot. He let out half a breath, then released the three-fingered hold he had on the string.

This time the feathered missile flew true, biting deeply into the chest of a brushwooder taking cover behind a lightning-blasted tree at the wrong angle. The man went backward, hands wrapping around the shaft as he was driven by the impact, and stretched out across a patch of snow that quickly turned dark.

Blasters roared, muzzle-flashes visible among the trees in a semicircle of fire.

None of the bullets came close to Ryan. He drew back another arrow and released it, leading a figure sprinting across an open space. Though he'd aimed at the center of the body, the shaft went low, taking the brushwooder in the thighs from the side, fixing them together. The man fell headlong to the ground.

Bullets whacked into the oak tree, ripping leaves and branches free. A collective cry rose up from the brush-wooders as more and more of them spotted the source of the arrows.

Ryan abandoned the bow, letting it drop through the branches below, and reached down to grab the barrel of the Steyr. Slipping the sling from his shoulder, he brought the rifle on target as three men broke cover and streaked for the tree.

His finger stroked the trigger, two shots per man. Three corpses dropped in a tangled sprawl before the last one could break away.

"He's in the tree!" a woman yelled.

"Over here!"

"Get him!" someone yelled. "Blow the son of a bitch out of the tree!"

Ryan emptied the Steyr's clip rapidly. He knew he brought down three more men scattered beneath the trees, and one of them for sure wouldn't be getting back up again.

A bullet cut through Ryan's sleeve as he worked his way into a clear area between the branches on the rear side of the tree. He stepped out over the ten-foot drop and let go.

He bent his knees to get himself loose for the hard landing. At the bottom of the fall, he let his weight go with the pull of gravity, then pushed himself back up.

Out of the corner of his eye, he noticed the shadow along the bole of the tree that didn't fit. It was man-shaped and held a blaster.

"FUCKER'S REALLY PUT his foot up the ass of Satan this time."

As he gazed through his Starlight binoculars at the one-eyed man in the oak tree calmly fitting another arrow to the bowstring, Hayden LeMarck said, "I'll give you five to two that he comes out of it alive."

"I'll take your jack," Wallis Thoroughgood replied, "and be man enough to stand you a beer at Dripping Sal's when we get back to Jakestown." He was a blocky man, crowding sixty if he was a day. Dressed in a coat and insulated coveralls, only the man's round face showed, the features resembling those of a demented cherub.

The rattle of bridles and the creak of saddle leather sounded behind LeMarck. "Keep those damn horses still. You don't, and we could still end up hip deep in goddamn brushwooders."

"Yes, sir," someone replied.

As one of the head sec men for Baron Sparning Hardcoe, LeMarck got respect. He was a tall, lean man with fair hair and muttonchop whiskers that ran deep auburn. A hawk's bill of a nose jutted over a thin-lipped mouth.

The brushwooders had raided some of the outer farms around the little ville of Angeltears less than a week earlier. Representatives from the ville had sailed north to Jakestown ville, the biggest community in the seven villes under the control of the Five Barons, and talked with Baron Hardcoe himself. Hardcoe had made it LeMarck's job to track down the brushwooders and punish them, and assigned twenty men to go with him.

Angeltears was the smallest of the seven villes. As such, it was the least productive and the least developed. Any of the other four barons would have ignored it and let the people in Angeltears work out their own problems.

Hardcoe cherished every bit of his temporary empire, though. Even if he had to relinquish it to one of the other barons at the end of the Big Game in eight days.

In the day and a half he'd been tracking the brushwooders, LeMarck had found out the group had grown to nearly a hundred strong. He'd gotten his information from three brushwooders he'd tortured the previous night. The different groups had united under a man named James Ball Daugherty, who'd blown in from somewhere across the big desert if the stories were to be believed. No one had known how successful Daugherty had gotten at organizing the brushwooders until the raids on Angeltears had left so many dead farmers in burning fields. It was the biggest mob of them that had ever been seen in the history of the villes.

After learning how many enemy they were truly facing and knowing they'd be taking them on in their turf, LeMarck's team had wanted to pull back and call on Hardcoe for reinforcements. With all that the baron had going on in Jakestown, LeMarck had been reluctant to do that until he couldn't see any other way clear.

That was why he'd been tailing the brushwooders. If Daugherty was to get himself suddenly dead through an assassination attempt, LeMarck figured the big group of brushwooders would break back down into smaller, more-manageable units that could be exterminated at the proper time. Their threat would have been removed.

The sec man was in his late twenties, and his closest experience to a father figure had been Hardcoe. There wasn't anything LeMarck hadn't done or wouldn't do for the man. He knew Hardcoe was concerned about losing the seven villes to one of the other barons through the baronial charter, and LeMarck had been up late nights thinking about how to ensure Hardcoe retained control.

That was why he'd been playing with the idea of trying to take Daugherty alive after hearing about the man. Arriving in Angeltears the day before yesterday, though, he'd heard about the way Daugherty ran the brushwooders like barbarians. There was no finesse about the man, no real cunning. The only thing that stood out about him was that he had a genuine taste for blood.

Before, the brushwooders had scavenged from the outlying farms, not killing unless someone tried to stop them. They were thieves, and a menace only to people who traveled among the seven villes. Of the Five Barons, Hardcoe was the only one who organized sec parties to ride shotgun on trade caravans. Of course, to get the protection, the caravans also had to fit in their schedules with Hardcoe's, which caused problems for those people selling perishable items.

Now LeMarck figured it was only a matter of time before Daugherty got to thinking about taking one of the fat caravans in the next eight days. The people of the seven villes knew about the Big Game, too, and the fact that they might be changing barons again. And if Hardcoe did lose out, there would be no more caravans.

It would be Daugherty's last chance at a big score worth a lot of jack.

LeMarck had come into the forest with the intent of not letting that happen. But watching the one-eyed man work his team ahead of the brushwooders and double back on them, the sec boss got to considering his rejected plans for Daugherty.

The brushwooders' leader wasn't as cunning and smart as LeMarck had hoped. But the one-eyed man was a thriller on wheels, the kind of man Hardcoe could use for the Big Game. He'd like to give the baron some good news when he joined his sec men on the ride to Vegas.

Still, the brushwooders outnumbered the two men they were stalking. Just in case he had to tip the scales in the one-eyed man's favor, LeMarck reached for his rifle and kept a keen eye on the advancing brushwooders.

JAK LAUREN MOVED instinctively, rolling to his left, already wary since the blaster had erupted down the mountainside. He swiveled his head, trying to figure out what had attacked him. All he'd noticed on some subliminal level was an explosion of movement from the snowbank ahead of him.

Broken terrain ranged all around him. Some of it looked smoothed over by the drifting snow, but it was deceiving. A step on unsafe ground meant a twisted or broken ankle for an unwary traveler. Twice he'd found areas where the snow had covered cracks in the mountain big enough for a body to plummet through. The first one ended in a shattered death's-grin of rock thirty feet down. He never had seen the bottom to the second.

A sibilant hiss ripped through the air.

To Jak, it sounded like a man stropping a razor, working up a proper shaving edge. With the wind blowing, it was hard to tell exactly what direction it came from.

He wore a long coat over his regular clothes, but he shucked out of it. Even with the drop in the temperature and the howling wind, he knew he could stand the cold for a few minutes—especially if those minutes added to his life expectancy.

He drew the .357 Magnum Colt Python from his belt and a pair of his leaf-bladed throwing knives.

The hiss cut through the air again, followed by immediate movement. This time Jak got a better look at the creature.

It shot up from the ground as if fired from the mouth of a blaster. Diamond shaped and at least a foot and a half across from opposing corners, the beast sailed through the air straight at Jak's face.

The teenager ducked and spun, bringing up the .357.

From the brief glimpse he'd caught of the creature, Jak knew it was white and had two deep aquamarine eyes set close together. A thin, barbed tail almost four feet long trailed out behind it.

When it hit the snow, the beast vanished, blending in like a chameleon.

Jak fired three shots that ripped through the snow and hammered rocks into pieces. At first he'd figured the creature was albino, but the way it vanished into the landscape let him know it had control—at least to some degree—over its coloration.

Albinos he knew about. He himself was bone white and had ruby red eyes. His long hair was the color of fresh milk. At something short of five and a half feet tall and built whipcord lean, he didn't look like the deadly efficient killer that he was. He'd been born and bred in Cajun country in the south of Deathlands, but he'd ranged far and wide, going up against his share of predators.

With the sibilant cry, the creature rocketed at him again. The tail whipped in readiness as it took to the air, and a large, fanged mouth opened on its underside.

Considering the aerodynamics of the mutie beast, Jak figured that it scooted along the snow until it built up enough speed to get airborne. It didn't need much room or time in the winds. And evidently it knew how to best use those winds to its advantage.

The beast cut through the air, streaking for Jak's neck, flipping sideways to lose altitude and change direction suddenly so it approached from an arc.

Instead of dodging this time, Jak took three running

steps toward the creature, which didn't break off its attack. The tail whipped forward under its flat belly.

At the last moment, Jak leaped high into the air, using his innate acrobatic abilities and spring-steel muscles to their fullest. He put out a hand, and his fingertips lightly grazed the slick, oily membrane of the animal's body.

The mutie beast shrieked in anger, flapping its sides to change direction. With the wind against it, there was no way it could turn, but it became a more challenging target.

Jak flipped over the creature, coming around with his feet over his head and facing in the direction of the creature's glide path. No more than five feet from his target, he pulled the trigger through the remaining three rounds in the heavy blaster. As he continued his flip, he twisted to land on his feet facing the mutie beast.

Two of the hollowpoints slammed into the creature, ripping it apart. It collapsed to the ground, a bloody mass of meat.

The teenager put his knives away, then shook the empty casings from the Python and reloaded.

"Jak!" Krysty called.

"Here." The albino walked to the dead creature and picked it up by the barbed tail. He crossed to the edge of the cliff face he'd climbed.

Krysty, Mildred and Doc gazed up at him, worried looks on their cold-pinched faces.

"Dear lad," Doc said, "we thought you'd fallen to your demise."

Jak shook his head. "I fall, I'd scream. Let you know not safe."

"Of course you would. How foolish of me to think otherwise. Forgive the awkward ruminations of a man aged by experience."

"Sure." Jak shrugged. More weapons were being used down the mountainside. He saw the bright sparks leaping among the trees.

"What was the blasterfire?" Krysty asked, her attention divided between Jak and the action behind them.

The albino lifted the dead mutie beast, then dropped it onto the ledge among them. "This. See one, better chill quick. Otherwise, chill you."

"How'd you get up there?" Mildred asked.

Jak knelt and pointed, wanting to go back for his coat. But it would be better to wait, in case there was another of the gliding creatures. The next person up could cover his back.

"Step there," Jak said. "Careful. Skin knees, if go too sudden like. Then step there." He pointed again. "Get up this far, help pull you up."

Krysty went first, managing the climb with difficulty. "Did you find the pass?"

Jak shook his head. "Not yet. Mebbe out there. Not look everywhere yet. Shooting started, I got back here."

Krysty stood beside him, her pistol in her fist. Her attention shifted back to the forested lands farther down.

"Shooting good sign," Jak said as he reached for Mildred's hand. "Ryan and J.B. dead, nobody to shoot at."

Ryan squeezed the Steyr's trigger before he had the rifle quite to his shoulder. When it fired, the recoil made the Steyr jump in his hands.

The bullet caught the brushwooder full in the chest and knocked him back. The man's blaster discharged into the ground more than a yard from Ryan, tearing up a fist-sized clod of snow-frosted earth. Already dying, with blood spitting up over his lips, the brushwooder stubbornly tried to bring his weapon to bear again.

Ryan shouldered the Steyr and aimed at the man's head. Before he could squeeze off another round, the familiar boom of J.B.'s Smith & Wesson M-4000 shotgun filled the clearing beneath the tree.

A nasty hornet's nest of the Remington fléchettes belched out by the 12-gauge shotgun tore into the man's face, shoulders and chest. The impact bared white breast-bone and bounced him against the tree bole. The few fléchettes that had missed the man embedded in the tree and stuck out like steel spurs.

"Close one," the Armorer commented as he sought a new target.

"Been closer," Ryan answered. He pushed the dead man from the tree and used the trunk for cover.

J.B. stood fast and worked his way through the shotgun's magazine, spitting out death. The swarms of fléchettes chopped into the brushwooders and stripped them of their sudden courage. "You about ready to get out of here?"

"I'm done." Lifting the Steyr, Ryan quickly picked off two men who were within his range. "You take the lead, and I'll close the back door."

Renewed gunfire broke out behind them. Turning, his back to a boulder almost as big as a wag, Ryan glanced at the trees and brush where they'd left the dead brushwooders. The advancing brushwooders had gone to ground under his fire and were shooting at the corpses. Bullets hitting the dead brushwooders caused jerky movements, drawing even more intense fire.

"Hold your goddamn fire!" someone yelled. "Those people are dead!"

"That'll slow them for a minute. Let's get out of here," Ryan said.

The Armorer took point, moving in a broad semicircle that would bring them to the foot of the mountains.

Driving his legs hard against the muddy earth, Ryan hoped Krysty and the others had found the pass they'd been looking for. If the storm front kept moving in and trapped them in the mountains, it could mean their deaths.

"GREN!" J.B. called out.

Ryan went to ground at once, sliding in behind the thick trunk of a felled tree.

J.B. pulled the pin on the explosive and lobbed the bomb toward the small knot of brushwooders defending the foothills that led to the ledge climbing into the mountains. "A little something extra I took off one of the brushwooders while I was punching their tickets for the last train West."

Ryan hunkered down against the tree, both hands gripping the Steyr.

Someone tried to yell a warning, but the effort was torn apart and lost in the detonation of the gren. Shrapnel sliced through the trees overhead, and the concussion hurled small rocks and gravel in all directions.

"Company's coming up from behind real fast," J.B. said into the silence that followed the blast.

Ryan spotted the shadows shifting through the trees behind them. No longer trying to keep their presence a secret, some of the brushwooders carried lanterns and torches.

"There's not going to be an easy way of doing this," Ryan called out.

"Then it'd be best to get it over with quick so we don't have time to obsess on it," J.B. replied without hesitation. "The coldhearts behind us know we're in a tight spot."

Already bullets were starting to clip branches from the trees overhead and slam into the bark on Ryan's side of the dead oak.

"On three, then," Ryan said, knowing the brushwooders nestled in the foothills could hear them. He drew the SIG-Sauer with his right hand and held the rifle in his left.

"On three," J.B. repeated.

"Three!" Ryan pushed himself up and into a run. There was a lull as the brushwooders were caught by surprise.

Spotting two men who shared cover behind a big
squared-off rock that came up to their chests, he brought
up the SIG-Sauer and snap-fired two rounds. Both 9 mm
hollowpoints caught the man on the left in the chest over
the heart and drove him backward. As he spun, bringing
the blaster to bear on the second brushwooder, Ryan saw
the other man's head jerk backward.

Ryan never broke stride. A second later he reached the
rock in time to spot a hard-faced woman kneeling at the
side of a tree. She had J.B. in her sights less than a dozen
paces away.

Ryan fired three rounds into the woman's belly, blowing her guts out. The woman started to scream, forcing more of her intestines outside her body.

Ryan left her to it. The screams might prove distracting and hold off the other brushwooders for a few seconds more.

J.B. finished up with the last man remaining in between them and the path leading to the ledge. Expertly he moved his Uzi subgun in a tight figure eight that chopped his target down.

Ricochets whined off the square-cut rock as Ryan knelt to examine the second brushwooder who'd been standing there. He kicked the man over onto his back, surprised there was no exit wound from whatever had hit him.

The silvery chill of moonlight bathed the dead man's face. A neat, round bullet hole was centered between his wide, staring eyes.

The gut-shot woman finally died, and all her painful shrieking died with her.

"Problem?" J.B. asked, ducking behind the rock.

"He's been chilled." Ryan dropped the head. "But I didn't chill him."

"It could have been an accidental shot, what with all these rounds flying."

"Square between the eyes like that?" Ryan shook his head, then raked his gaze over the ridges surrounding the forested valley. The distance was too great and the shadows drawn too deeply to allow him to see much. And getting more adventurous in looking wasn't a good plan; the brushwooders were hitting the square-cut stone regularly now. "I don't think so."

"Me, neither," the Armorer stated. He leaned over and put his fingers on the dead man's face. "Big round. Thirty-aught-six mebbe. And for it not to penetrate the head, means it had to have been a subsonic round." He flinched from stone splinters driven from the rock by a fresh salvo of bullets. "Hanging around here has about run its course."

Ryan nodded, his mind still working at the man who lay before him. He didn't care for mysteries or puzzles. He broke for the path leading to the ledge.

"ANYTHING?"

Ryan shook his head, scanning their backtrail along the climb while they took a breather. "Brushwooders are coming up behind us, but they're losing ground."

"How many?"

"Thirty, mebbe."

Kneeling beside him, J.B. lifted his fedora and brushed an arm along his forehead. He grimaced at the sweat stains on his coat sleeve. "We keep moving like this, sweating this hard, we're due for a bad case of hypothermia."

Ryan nodded. Through the binoculars he could occasionally see the line of brushwooders winding around the turns. Sniping would get a few of them, but then they'd have his position, too, which might make it bad all the way around.

He pushed himself to his feet. "Let's go."

The cloud cover had wiped away the moon, dimmed the light they had to move by. If it wasn't for the reflective quality of the snow, they wouldn't have been able to see in the dark at all. Their progress had slowed considerably.

"The ones who don't fall and kill themselves on the climb, or we don't shoot if they come up on us, the storm may take," Ryan declared.

The wind had picked up, and it had turned colder.

"Their man isn't a leader," J.B. said. "He gets enough of them chilled tonight, they'll turn on him. They must be good and afraid of him to come this far."

Ryan kept a hand in contact with the stone wall at his side as he pressed forward. The snow flurries increased, burning cold into his face except where the scar tissue had robbed him of sensation. Though he couldn't feel his face so much anymore between the old injuries and the fanged cold, he couldn't keep his teeth from chattering like a desert rattler in full threat.

Without warning, his boot skidded out from under him. The edge of the abyss to his left yawned open suddenly. Wrapping around him like a demanding lover, the wind sucked at him, trying to pull him from the wall.

"Fireblast!" he swore, getting his balance back enough to fall against the wall behind him.

J.B. reached for him.

"Got it," Ryan said. The hunger and the cold had hollowed him out enough that he knew he was running on adrenaline. He pushed himself up, feeling the dark anger moving around inside him. Dying quiet, frozen to death on some mountain, had never been in the cards for him the way he had it figured. When he caught the last train West, it'd be with a blaster in his fist and his blood mixing with that of an enemy.

"We can rest," the Armorer said.

"We can rest when we're dead. Something here." Ryan scraped at the ground with his boot. Thin black liquid covered the stone in odd-shaped clots. As they tore under his boot, some of them turned red.

"Blood," J.B. commented.

Ryan nodded. "Somebody's." His eye lit on the awkward shape at the bottom of the sheer rise in front of him. The wall ahead bore one of Jak's signs, letting him know to keep going straight.

The shadow turned out to be a dead beast that had been blown apart by bullets. The eyes had dimmed, but there was no mistaking the deadly way the tail was barbed. One of Jak's leaf-bladed knives was thrust between the creature's eyes.

"You ever seen anything like this?" Ryan asked.

"No."

"Trader always said a man could live out his whole life in Deathlands just looking at what there is to see and never see it all. As soon as a man passed on, mutie genes tickled by all the radioactivity breezing across the Deathlands would make up something new."

"And more than likely it'd be something hungry," J.B. finished.

Ryan pulled the throwing knife from the dead mutie beast. "Guess Jak left this as a message."

J.B. grinned. "It isn't hard to understand. You see any of these, kill them quick."

Ryan slung the creature out over the abyss and let go. He never heard it hit bottom. He cleaned the knife with the snow and put it in his gear. "Step careful around the blood. I'll help you up first." He put the Steyr against the wall and made a stirrup of his hands.

J.B. stepped into Ryan's hands and scrambled up as he was pushed along. He reconned the top, then gave Ryan a thumb's-up. "Ace on the line. We're clear." He offered his hand down.

"In a minute," Ryan said, unbuckling his pants. "Got something to take care of." It was almost too bastard cold to piss, but he managed. His urine smoked as if it were on fire, splattering the ground in a wide puddle. When he finished, he buttoned up his pants again, then took the hand the Armorer extended.

At the top of the wall, Ryan looked back down on the puddle of piss. It was barely noticeable under the cover of shadows.

"A few minutes at this temperature," J.B. said, "that's going to freeze up real nice."

"Hope so. Be a nice surprise for the first brushwooder or two who happen up on it. If we get lucky, mebbe it'll take out the ramrod."

He found Jak's next mark, then turned his steps in that direction. Krysty and the others couldn't be much farther ahead.

Krysty pushed herself against the wind as fast as she could, taking time only to make sure each footfall landed on solid ground. They were up in the crown of the mountains now, and the crevasses that had resulted from the quakes and the volcanic pressures cropped up more frequently.

Jak and Mildred had gone off in a northerly direction to check out another route open to them. She still had fifteen minutes before they were supposed to return to report their findings.

The valley between the gap-toothed peaks she was using as her compass points suddenly split into two again. She turned up the collar of her coat. The thought of Ryan out there unprotected against the elements didn't sit well.

"Gaia watch over him," she said, "because I've never loved anyone more." The wind whipped her words out of her mouth, battered them into nothing.

"What's that, my dear?" Doc asked from behind her.

"Wishful thinking."

The old man came up beside her, his head pulled down into his coat and his hands jammed into his pockets. He held his walking stick up under his arm. The butt of his .63 Le Mat blaster stuck out from between the buttons of the coat. "Not upon a star, though, I see. It comes to mind that with the seeming scarcity of the mercury's ability to hit the scarlet field at all upon this night, and with the stench of sulfur from the volcanoes so like brimstone, one could truly say it is as cold as hell upon this mountain."

Krysty ignored the comment and considered the two options before her.

Both chasms led through the rock, angling down.

"Pardon, dear lady, I know your mind is not entertained a whit by my self-indulgent observations."

"Not your fault, Doc. I'm just worried about Ryan."

"Think not upon that. He'll be along in short order, I'm sure."

Krysty knew Doc was trying to make her feel better, but he was also sincere. She let out a tense breath. "I know. Mebbe I'm just more worried about us getting trapped up here."

"We've options open to us yet that remain unexplored." Doc gestured at the narrow defiles standing dark and empty before them.

"So which way?"

Doc peered at the two trails. "Neither of them appear to be heavily trod thoroughfares. But the one on the right beckons because it appears rather bleaker and even more deserted."

"Let's get it done." Krysty pulled out her blaster. "Double red, Doc. We haven't run into any more of those flying things Jak turned up, but that doesn't mean they're not around."

"Sally forth, brave lass, and know that I stand at the ready in your service."

Krysty headed forward, crunching her boots over loose, broken rock. She kept the .38's hammer eared back, and her eyes shifting back and forth to pick up any movement with her peripheral vision.

The mountain quivered unexpectedly, like an old dog staving off its death throes one more night. But it was enough to knock Krysty from her feet.

"By the Three Kennedys!" Doc roared, tumbling to land on the stone.

Krysty threw herself to the ground and covered her head with her arms. Rocks rained all around her, some of them thudding painfully into her body.

As quickly as they came, the tremors stopped.

The woman raised her head, tasting blood inside her mouth from a split lip. Dust hovered in the air around them, dirtying the snow and mixing with the flurries. She was grateful to find that she hadn't lost her blaster in the confusion. She glanced at her companion.

The old man lay very still on the ground, partially covered with rock and dirt.

"Doc!" Krysty shoved her way up from the debris.

"I'm quite all right, my dear Krysty. I was just lying here, gathering my thoughts and making sure I remained yet anatomically correct. I do feel of a piece, but not the piece that I was. And I seem to hurt in every place near and dear to me, and a few that I'd not been aware of. I shall choose to view that as a good sign."

Krysty crossed over to him and took hold of his jacket in her free hand. She helped him to his feet, keeping watch over the two of them.

"Thank you for your concern, but I assure you I'm well enough to stand on my own." Fastidious as ever, Doc took a moment to brush at his clothing.

As Krysty shifted around, trying to peer through the haze filling the defile, rock rushed down the incline and shot through the fissure in the ground only two yards away. Evidently the quake had done some damage to the underlying strata, because the fissure was now three feet across when before it had only been inches.

Among the thuds and splats of rock and earth tumbling over the side, there was also a decidedly metallic sound.

"And how are you?" Doc asked, gazing at her with some worry.

"Shh," Krysty said, cocking her head to listen.

The sound repeated in a series of rapid basso beats.

Intrigued, Krysty crept closer, going down on her belly at the edge of the fissure. She peered down into it but could see nothing. "Did you hear that?"

"Indeed I did. These old ears are still sharp as a bat's." Doc went prone at her side, then stretched out a hand. "Do you feel it?"

Krysty stretched her hand out over the fissure, careful not to put it too close in case something predatory came roaring up with snapping fangs. The breeze coming up from the fissure wrapped itself around her fingers. "Warm air."

"Exactly." Doc peered down into the gloom, sticking his head in a little farther than Krysty felt was safe. "Mayhap the shivers we felt but moments ago opened up a new artery into the heart of the volcanic region that holds the roots of this mountain range." He extended both hands out. "Ah, and it's enough to warm an old man's bones."

His movements sent a fresh pile of rock and dirt cascading into the fissure. More bonging sounded.

"Something else is down there. Volcanoes don't make bonging sounds," Krysty argued.

"No, they do not."

Krysty pulled out one of the short torches she carried in her pack. Holding it only a little way inside the fissure, she set it on fire with a self-light. The oil caught slowly but spread fast, casting golden streamers of incandescence above and below.

The fissure hollowed out nearly three feet beneath the surface. The shattered stone understructure of the mountain held a chamber that showed signs of old growth; twisted, dead trees and bushes gathered against low spots where the rainwater runoff evidently flowed through into even lower recesses.

The warm air that pushed up into Krysty's face smelled of stringent sulfur and bacteria-laden loam. Her hair relaxed around her head, fanning out a little to better absorb the extra heat. She used her gift, trying to sort out any threats that lurked below. From the looks of things, she judged that nothing under the rocky crust lived.

"In past times, mayhap even stretching back as far as the nukecaust," Doc said, "that area below was once the top of this mountain."

"It isn't anymore." Krysty moved the torch, about ready to give up on the search. If the chamber did open up into the volcanic substrata, that definitely wasn't a course she wanted to pursue. Warm air would come in useful, though, if they had to stay on the mountaintop to ride out the storm.

"Wait," Doc said, "I thought I saw something."

"Moving?" Krysty brought her blaster forward.

"No. A vehicle possibly."

Krysty moved the torch again. The flames jumped and remained burning bright yellow in the steady supply of oxygen. The chamber was almost twenty feet across and thirty feet deep. Flaming bits of the torch dropped the intervening distance, and some of them landed on a metal surface halfway buried in the mountainside.

Canted on its side, the blue-and-white fuselage lay crusted over by boulders and dirt that had worked its way from the top of the mountain to the hidden chamber under the fissure. The rear propeller was missing, as was much of the tail section, and the main rotor held one bent blade stretching up. The others were buried somewhere under it. The Plexiglas bubble was almost covered, as well, but enough of it showed that the multiple fractures threading through it were apparent.

The facet of the craft that most interested Krysty was the word Rescue lettered on the door.

She looked around the fissure opening and thought she might be able to make the climb. "I'm going in," she told Doc.

The old man looked at her. "I don't wish to offend you, my dear Krysty, but the idea of you in that cave harbors no good thoughts in this weary old head despite the present temperature, which has undoubtedly slowed the flow of blood through my brain."

She handed him the torch and shrugged out of her backpack. "Good thoughts or not, that was evidently some kind of rescue airwag. There could be medicines and dressings inside that we can use."

"Then I beg of you, let me go there in your stead."

She gestured with the torch, pointing down as far as she could. The flames wrapped around her fingers for just an instant but not long enough to burn. "That's pretty steep. Do you think you could make it any better than me?"

"I would surely give it the effort," Doc replied.

"Doc," Krysty said, "I'm in better shape than you for this sort of thing. If anything happens down there, I'll need you up here."

The old man covered her hand with his and looked at her solemnly. "As you wish. I am yours but to command."

Krysty clambered into the fissure, her nasal passages and throat burning as she fought the gag reflex against the sulfur smell. Once inside, she fashioned a mask over her nose and mouth from a handkerchief, then took the torch from Doc and started down.

The grade tilted steeply. She took a tacking course, not heading straight for the helicopter, but rather making for the other side of the flattest section of stone she could find a few inches below her initial position. She made two more angled passes before she got close enough to the aircraft to touch it, scooting on her butt part of the way so she wouldn't start sliding.

In the center of the chamber, the torch pretty well illuminated her surroundings. Craggy walls seemed to pulse in on her with jagged teeth as the torchlight ebbed and flowed, and a dark crack opened up beneath the helicopter.

Resting her hand on the craft gingerly, Krysty peered into the crack under the helicopter. The blackness extended a long way. She shoved the torch farther into it but still couldn't see the bottom.

Shifting a rock with the toe of her boot, she nudged it over the edge. The rock hit the sides of the crack as it passed, making loud whanging noises as it dropped farther away. She finally gave up on it when she realized her breathing had gotten louder than the impacts.

"Are you all right?" Doc called down.

"Just eyeballing things before I go any farther," she replied. Still moving slowly, she went to the front of the helicopter and peered inside.

A skeleton that had gone gray white in death sat strapped into the pilot's seat, dressed in a red short-sleeved shirt and gray slacks. The material hung in shreds, worried at by insects and beasts, faded and ravaged by time. Layers of dust and dirt caked the dead man and the inside of the helicopter.

Krysty's hair tightened against her neck. Reminding herself of the potential booty that might lie inside the craft just for her taking at a time when the companions might need it, she thrust the torch forward.

Reflections of the flames danced in the webbed lines of the Plexiglas. Shadows wavered around the corpse like dark things that had been disturbed from their rest—or feeding. The hollow eye sockets seemed locked on Krysty as she took another step forward.

The door opened easily, creaking with the decades of disuse. A fresh shower of dirt and pebbles rolled down the incline in an earthen wave.

"Krysty!"

"I'm okay, Doc." She glanced up at the old man, peering anxiously into the gloom. "I'm going to take a look inside."

"Be careful. I do believe friend Ryan would be most vexed should I allow anything of ill nature occur to you."

Krysty turned her attention back to the aircraft. The helicopter had a low ceiling, which didn't give her enough room to stand. But it held seats for the dead man and one other, as well as space behind for cargo.

She pulled herself in through the door, pausing a moment as she felt the craft wobble under her. Metal shrieked in long, low notes, then it stopped. Evidently the helicopter was wedged firmly.

She held the torch as high as she could inside the cockpit. Upon closer inspection, she saw that the front of the dead man's skull was broken, smashed in completely along the right cheek and temple.

She grabbed the corpse's shirt and shook it. Dust and dirt fell away from the material, and a chunk of it came away in her fist. She smoothed it out on the empty seat, keeping the torch raised high. The pockets held an assortment of coins, a penknife and a few butterscotch candies in individual wrappers that had turned black.

Satisfied there was nothing of use in the cockpit, she went into the cargo area.

A stretcher clung to one wall, halfway covering a red fire extinguisher. Shallow metal racks covered the other wall, filled with narrow drawers that looked almost as big as bread loaves.

All of the drawers were marked with names. She knew only some of them, but they all had to do with pharmaceuticals or surgical equipment. She opened the drawers in succession, working quickly.

In minutes she had filled her pouch and pockets and every empty space on her person. It pained her to see that so much remained they could use. Once she got back with the others, they could arrange another raiding party.

She took up the torch from the fire-extinguisher mounting and headed back toward the cockpit. As she passed through, she felt something burn along the back of her hand. When she examined her hand, a long scratch dripped blood.

Using one of the packages of gauze she'd left in the supply bins, she wiped at the scratch to make sure it wasn't anything to worry about.

Her mutie ability kicked in with a force she'd seldom felt when not actually threatened with physical harm. Her senses swam, taking her into the bloody splotch on the back of her hand. It felt as though her heart had stilled.

The crimson smear expanded, drawing Krysty as if into a tunnel, eclipsing her surroundings. A magnetic force with unbelievable power pulled her inside.

Dean was in there with her. She felt him, then called out to him but he didn't answer. Shadows gathered around her, and she could almost see through them. Images changed and darted about, hinting at shapes or things she was familiar with.

Mother Sonja had mentioned experiences similar to the one she was having now. She'd seen trouble coming at times, and been able to warn the family members whom she saw in her visions.

But Mother Sonja had also said all her visions pertained to those who were related to her by blood.

Dean was Ryan's child, not Krysty's, born to another woman. Maybe that was why the vision was so unclear. That it existed at all was testimony to her love for Ryan.

Another deep breath, and clarity came to the vision.

She stood alone in a room that looked like a concrete bunker but felt like something else. Broken conduit pipes ran across the low ceiling overhead. Tables lay overturned in the center of the room, cards and multicolored disks spilling from them and littering the floor.

Corpses littered the room, as well. Some hung over the chairs and tables, and others lay across the cards and disks. Many of them were years dead and missing parts from greedy insects and animals, but at least two of them still glistened with their own fresh blood. All of them had died violently.

A shadow lurched against the wall to her left and made hacking noises.

Krysty turned, her hand dropping automatically for the butt of her .38. But somehow she wasn't able to reach it. In her frustration she started to lose the vision.

"Concentrate," a woman's voice ordered. The words sounded nearly empty, as if the speaker had used her last dying gasp to deliver them. "You don't need a weapon here. You are not here. Find the boy. He must know what you have to say."

Krysty tried to ask who was talking to her.

"Do not waste this time. They will die if you do."

Going forward, Krysty stared hard at the shadow. Strangely colored lights caressed the high points of the young man's face and the armor that he wore. In the darkness, she believed the armor was a full-length bulletproof vest that covered the young man from his shoulders to his crotch.

He gasped, blood trickling from the corner of his mouth, and kept his handblaster pointed toward the door. The barrel wavered, taking all his flagging strength attempting to hold it level. Even in the darkness she could tell that he was blond and light eyed.

It wasn't Dean. Krysty felt relief wash over her.

"Wait," the woman's voice advised.

Watching the young man, Krysty saw the pattern of the colored lights change, winking and shifting to track across the dark skin. A shadow suddenly filled the doorway behind the young man, leaner but with a dangerous air of self-assurance.

The young man obviously heard some kind of noise and whirled to face the doorway. His blaster roared.

The shadow jumped out of the way as the bullet smacked into the door frame.

"Shit, Louis, put that blaster down before you hurt somebody you're not supposed to," a young man's voice directed.

Krysty recognized Dean at once. She tried to call out to him as he crossed the room to the wounded boy.

"Save your strength," the woman's voice said. "You'll get your chance to speak with him if you work with me. And you'll have to speak with him if you're going to save his life—or that of your mate."

"Who are you?" Krysty demanded. She tried to find the source of the voice, using her gift.

Abruptly Dean started to fade away.

"Concentrate!"

Krysty returned her attention to Dean.

The boy looked at Louis, then pulled at the straps holding the body armor. Blood smeared Dean's fingers as he worked.

Reluctantly the body armor separated with a sucking sound. Dean peered under the armor, his face wrinkling in fear and anger. He still looked like a little boy, not yet twelve, but Krysty felt the need to comfort him, too.

"Those shitters!" Dean yelled. "They shot you bad, Louis! They shot you real bad!"

Without saying a word, the taller boy suddenly slumped forward. His face went slack as crimson-stained spittle threaded from his mouth.

Dean went down under Louis's weight. "Louis, you can't die! You can't leave me here alone! Louis!"

The querulous snuffling of a large beast sounded outside the room. Then it came closer. Split hooves rang on the concrete floor.

Dean heaved himself from under the dead boy. Blood, old and new, stained his green armored vest. He leveled his Browning Hi-Power before him, back against the wall.

"Talk to him!" the woman's voice urged.

"He can't hear me," Krysty said.

"Now," she stated, "now he can. Your mind will know the words."

Krysty stepped forward and reached out to touch Dean, who still gave no indication that he saw her. Her hand passed right through his shoulder, but for an instant there was the sensation of an electrical discharge.

The shuffling of the beast in the hallway sounded loud, letting her know it had to have been huge.

"Dean," she said, trying to talk normally.

His head swiveled in her direction, and he made an effort to focus. "Krysty?"

She wanted to tell him to run, that there was nothing he could do for his dead friend. Instead, she said, "Your father is coming for you. Look for him."

Before she could try again, the woman snapped, "Come, there is still much to do."

And Krysty's mind was overwhelmed by the darkness.

DEAN CAWDOR WAS on an adventure. It wasn't a grand adventure like the ones they talked about or read from books in his literature class. There was no Roland here, no Beowulf, no Tom Sawyer or Huck Finn.

But it was an adventure anyway.

"Dean!" Calgary Ventnor whispered. "Come on!"

The boy moved carefully, picking his way through the brush till he reached Calgary.

"Did you see anybody?" Calgary demanded, cutting his eyes in all directions.

"No," Dean replied.

The Nicholas Brody School hunkered on the gentle swell of land coming up from acres of vegetable gardens. Beyond the cultivated lands, the forest began again.

The school had its beginnings in an old stone farmhouse. Rooms and additions had been constructed with concrete blocks, then matted over with adobe bricks. Rifle slits were cut in along the walls, with thick steel shutters that could be pulled closed and bolted down inside.

"It's two-fifteen," Calgary said. "If we don't hurry, we're going to miss seeing it."

Dean laid a hand on the other boy's shoulder and held him back. "If we hurry too much, we're going to get caught. And then where will we be?"

Calgary made a face. He had fair hair, a squat, heavy build, some of the whitest skin Dean had ever seen aside from Jak Lauren's, and big ears that stuck out at right angles to his round head. He sucked at his teeth, a habit Dean had noticed in the other boy whenever he got nervous.

"Kicked out, that's for sure," Calgary said.

Dean figured that was about the size of it. But he couldn't resist the adventure that lay before them. He said her name just to build his courage: Phaedra Lemon.

"You keep talking like that, and the headmaster's night sec crew are going to catch us for certain."

"Is," Dean said automatically.

"What?"

"Is," Dean repeated. "The night sec crew *is* going to catch us."

Calgary's eyes widened. "You really think so?" He started to stand up. The brush was no more than waist high, and he would have been revealed at once.

At that moment the guard they'd been timing came around that side on the catwalk behind the wooden palisades built to withstand cannon fire, as well as the elements.

Dean tackled Calgary and dumped him to the ground, sliding a hand over his mouth. "Shh. And be still or I'm going to bop you one! I mean it!"

Calgary stopped struggling and stared hard at Dean.

Dean let him go once the guard had moved on.

"What the hell did you do that for?" Calgary asked angrily.

"You were going to give us away."

"You're the one who said we were going to get caught!"

Dean gave up. One thing he'd learned about Calgary Ventnor in the past few months was that the boy never admitted when he was wrong.

When it came to test grading and Calgary fell just a few points shy of a C, the boy would just naturally start arguing with the instructors. Dean had been amazed to see him in action. On the surface Calgary looked just like what he was: a preacher's kid getting a little bit bigger view of the world before going back to Leadville to take over his father's flock when the time came.

The thing that attracted Dean to Calgary was the fact the boy was good in his books. Something that escaped

Dean in one of the classes, especially math, where the teachers put out word problems that sounded like something Doc would have rambled on about, Calgary just understood easily. Calgary refused to study, but he'd help Dean when asked.

Of course, Dean usually had to work some kind of trade-off and give Calgary something he wanted. Most of the time what Calgary wanted was easy enough, getting shown a wrestling hold he'd seen Dean use in phys ed, stories about some of the things Dean had seen while traveling with his dad, Krysty and the others and sometimes just to hold one of the knives Jak Lauren had left with him.

What Calgary had wanted for helping with the frog-dissection test had been different. At first the boy had been kind of cagey about telling Dean what he wanted. He'd helped Dean track frogs in the little creeks around the vegetable acreage, nail them to boards they salvaged from the carpentry shop, then cut them open and name all the parts.

Dean had seen the insides of lots of things, living and dead, but he'd never thought about naming what was in there. On a frog, as with most things, there were parts he'd eat and parts he wouldn't eat. Sometimes, when things had gotten really desperate for the group, there'd even been parts that he'd rather not have eaten but did anyway.

Almost a dozen slow and luckless frogs came and went, some in more pieces than others as Dean got better at naming the parts and got better at cutting really carefully, and Calgary still didn't say what he wanted in exchange.

Dean had even asked, as if he were just curious.

Calgary hadn't said.

Then the test came and went.

Dean asked again, telling him he didn't know why he was keeping all closemouthed about it.

Calgary said to wait.

Last week the test results had come in. And though Dean didn't figure himself a scholar, and biology wasn't all that interesting anyway, he'd made an A on the test. He was proud, but at the same time he knew Calgary would be figuring Dean owed him big.

Of course, Calgary had. And when he'd told Dean what he wanted, down in the root cellar of the school putting away canned vegetables on their rotation, Dean had had to ask him to repeat himself.

"Phaedra Lemon," Calgary had said, "sleeps in the nude. I have it on good authority from some of the girls I know."

Dean hadn't thought it was a big deal. Nudity was just something that happened to folks when they didn't have their clothes on. He couldn't see why Calgary would be so interested in seeing a naked girl.

"Because," Calgary had informed him in a strained voice, "I've never seen one."

"Oh," Dean had said. Evidently Mr. Ventnor was really strict, because Leadville had gaudies where a woman could be seen naked for very little jack.

Since the quest to discover whether Phaedra Lemon really slept in the altogether involved some subterfuge and breaking of school rules, Dean's interest had been piqued. And he'd made the plan that had brought them here tonight.

"Keep your head down," Dean admonished the boy, "and follow me."

Calgary grabbed Dean's ankle. "I've changed my mind."

Dean couldn't believe it. "What?"

"I don't want to go." Calgary sucked on his teeth and couldn't meet Dean's eyes.

"It's all you've talked about for a week."

"I no longer think this is a good idea."

Dean had noticed whenever Calgary got stubborn, his diction improved. "Fine. Suit yourself. Now that I'm out here, I think I'm going to go have a peek."

Calgary grabbed his arm. "You can't do that!"

"Why not?"

For a moment the boy seemed stumped. "Why, because I don't wish for you to."

Dean shook his head. "I'll be double-damned for a mutie stupe if I've made this trip all for nothing."

"You just want to look at her," Calgary accused.

"No." But Dean knew it might be true. In order to set up tonight's little foray, he'd had to find out which one of the girls' dormitories Phaedra Lemon was in, which part of that building she bunked in and—finally—what she actually looked like. It wouldn't have been good at all to go creeping around in the wrong girl's bedroom.

And he especially didn't want to end up in Edna Royerer's bedroom by ill luck. The old dormitory supervisor, it was said, had a habit of sleeping on a shotgun loaded with salt rock.

As the days had gone by, though, he'd discovered the adventure had taken on some aspects that he hadn't quite counted on. Phaedra Lemon, for some unknown reason, had become more beautiful during the past week than any girl he'd seen at Nicholas Brody School or before. The past couple of nights had passed by probably as uncomfortably for him as they had for Calgary. He just couldn't help wondering if Phaedra really did sleep naked.

Dean grew more irritable. "Cal, look. You have some choices here. You can stay out here tonight and sleep on the cold, wet ground and slip back into the school when the gardening shift comes out. Or you can join me in climbing those walls with this rope—" he held up the coils of hemp "—sneak by Phaedra Lemon's room long enough to find out if those stories are true and then get the rest of the night's sleep in your own warm bed."

Calgary sucked on his teeth and glanced up at the timber wall.

"Now, what's it going to be?" Dean asked.

Ryan and J.B. found Jak and Mildred just after the teenager started to pull the dead man from the collapsed overhang of snow and rock. Mildred lowered her pistol when she recognized them.

"How'd you happen on him?" Ryan asked. Keeping the Steyr in one numbed hand, he wrapped his arms around himself in an attempt to hold in his escaping body heat.

"Didn't chill him," Jak said. "Found him. Arm sticking out. Saw it."

The man wore a long coat, high boots and a thermal cap so furry the dead eyes under the bill looked like a taxidermist's glassy marbles. A backpack remained strapped on his shoulders. Ryan guessed that the man was probably in his late fifties and had been in robust health, judging from the broad shoulders and leaned-out build.

A cottony pallor had set up under his skin, washing it of most of the pigmentation. When Ryan moved the man's arm with his boot, just testing what he'd seen when Jak was moving the corpse, the limb moved fairly easily.

"Fresh dead," Jak announced, squatting next to the deceased. "Broke neck." He pulled down the man's collar and exhibited the bruised throat, then twisted the head from side to side.

Ryan knelt, hopeful that the coat might fit, and started to pull the dead man from it. He noticed the curious tattoo on the inside of the man's left forearm near the inner elbow. A big dark blue dot was in the middle, echoed by concentric rings in lighter blue that got bigger and bigger around it, like the ripples made from a stone dropped into a pool. A double strand of orange bars and lines ran through it.

"Did you find the pass?" the Armorer asked as he put on his coat. Mildred had been carrying it for him.

"No," Mildred said. "The ridge Jak and I were following petered out into a drop-off that we'd need climbing gear to get down."

Chilled to the bone, Ryan shrugged into the coat, which cut some of the wind. When he spoke, his teeth still chattered. "Where's Krysty and Doc?"

"Split up," Jak answered. "Thought mebbe better chance two directions. Ain't heard, though."

"Are they supposed to meet you anywhere?"

"Back along the way you and J.B. probably come," Mildred replied. "If they were there, you'd have seen them or they'd have seen you." She stood close to the Armorer, one of her gloved hands in his. Though they were somewhat reticent about showing their relationship because of their respective taciturn natures, the commitment between them was deep.

Ryan turned up the coat collar. He thought he'd never be warm again. "When?"

"Overdue." Jak flicked out one of his leaf-bladed knives and sliced through the backpack's shoulder straps, then yanked it out from under the dead man.

"How long?"

"Eight minutes." Jak opened the backpack and pulled out a largish bundle of foil-colored material. He turned it over in his hands, inspecting it.

"What do you have, Jak?" Ryan asked.

"Therm tent." The albino shoved the bundle at Ryan, tapping the instructions printed on the foil surface. "Good for heat, good for cold. Got snap-together poles." He flexed his hands around the material hard enough to show the skeletal rods. "Got self-heats, ring-pulls and maps in here, too."

"The man came prepared for some hard living," Ryan said. "Take the food, water and the tent. Let's see the maps."

Jak passed them over, then started transferring items to his pack. There wasn't much, but it added to the small stores they had.

"Mildred," Ryan said, unfolding one of the maps, "take a look at the tattoo on the inside of this guy's arm. Tell me what you think."

Mildred hunkered down beside the dead man while J.B. took up guard.

Ryan unfolded the map carefully because it was old. Long strips of plaster tape held it together and repaired tears in different areas. Purple marker, looking almost black in the thin light reflected by the snow, stained the map, tracing routes across California, Oregon, Idaho and Montana.

Ryan passed the map to the Armorer. "Can't tell if he was coming or going."

J.B. took the map and looked it over.

"The dot," Ryan said to Mildred, referring to the tattoo, "I figure is the sun. The concentric rings around it are the solar system." He'd seen pictures in astronomy books he'd found in different places around Deathlands. "The corkscrewed ladder I don't know. Seen it on some doors in a few of the redoubts we've been inside."

"I think it's supposed to be a representation of DNA," the black woman replied, "building blocks of the universe. But why it would be overlapping the solar system like this so intentionally, I have no idea."

Ryan picked up one of the corpse's limp hands, cold as the stone around it, and felt the fingers and palm. "He didn't do much honest work. Hands are too soft. No calluses. Big man like him, he'd be showing something of his life in his hands if he did anything physical. You have to wonder what brought him out here."

"I'm guessing," J.B. said, "but I think this guy come down from Montana."

"What makes you think that?" Ryan looked up at his friend. He felt a little warmer in the coat now. Thoughts of Krysty and her welfare kept tumbling through his mind. The dead man was proof of the dangers that waited on the mountain. Ryan was ready to move, but what he learned here might help them all, so he made himself be patient.

"This place—" J.B. touched the map just east of their present position "—is marked with one asterisk. There's a plotted line that leads down to it."

"That map is well drawn," Ryan commented. "Whoever did it took the time to make it neat. But the coastline's wrong. We know that from our trip up."

"Yeah, but it's bastard old. Paper's even gone yellow with age. Mebbe when it was first drawn, it was more accurate. Things could have changed along the Western Islands. Hell, they're changing now."

Light suddenly flared in Jak's hands, bright white and concentrated in a narrow beam. "Flashlight."

The light didn't have the finished machine look of some of those that Ryan had seen in the past.

"Homemade," Jak stated.

"Let me borrow it," J.B. told him. He took the flashlight when Jak passed it over, then shone it over the map. "Here."

Ryan stood up to look, joined by Mildred and Jak.

The Armorer traced the purple line north with his forefinger, careful to keep his arm out of the light. The line ended at a point lettered Heimdall Point in the lower southwest quadrant of Montana. "This is where he must have started out."

"I've never heard of Heimdall Point," Ryan said.

Neither had anyone else.

"Norse mythology mentions a guy named Heimdall," Mildred said. "Guarded Bifrost."

Jak looked the question at her.

"Bifrost was a bridge," Mildred explained. "Supposed to be made of fire, water and air and colored like a rainbow. Asgard was the home of the Norse gods. Bifrost stretched from Asgard to other parts of the world, or worlds depending on your interpretation of how things were. Way the story's told, Heimdall had gold teeth and ears so sharp they could hear grass growing."

"Sec man to gods," the albino said.

"Pretty much sums it up. Heimdall carried a trumpet and blew it every time the gods came or went." Mildred's brow knitted. "The stories also mention that Heimdall was supposed to blow that horn the loudest to announce the end of the world. A time they called Ragnarok."

"The end of the world's come and gone," Ryan said,

"unless these people got something more planned. Or know something we don't."

"A DNA strand overlaying a picture of the solar system," the black woman mused. "That doesn't sound like they're preparing for the end, or even believe that it is."

Ryan looked at the dead man. "However it was, his story died with him."

"There's probably still people out here who were with him," J.B. countered.

"Does he have a weapon?" Ryan asked Jak.

The albino held up an empty holster. "Did. Gone. Mebbe lost in snow when tremors come."

"No long blaster?" Ryan was wondering if the dead man might offer part of a solution to the subsonic rifle shot that had maybe saved his life.

Jak shrugged. "Mebbe lost, too."

"There's a pair of asterisks here," J.B. said, tapping an area beyond the pass they were looking for. It was south and east of Carson City. "I'm betting this guy was headed there next."

"Does it say what's there?" Ryan asked.

"This notation's new, marked on top of a piece of tape so nothing's lost underneath." J.B. squinted at it through his glasses. "Shostakovich's Anvil. Sounds Russian."

"Could be some kind of Russian settlement there, come drifting down out of the north."

Ryan didn't like not knowing what the man had been doing there, and how come he ended up with his neck broken. "And these people found out about it and were going to visit?"

"Way past asking," Jak said.

"Yeah, but it's an ace on the line this man wasn't out here on his own." Ryan headed off in the direction Jak had said

Krysty had taken. They needed to be moving off the mountain if they could, or take shelter from the storm if they couldn't.

KRYSTY OPENED her eyes and found herself in a hallway that stank of death. Ahead of her Ryan—clad in a scarlet armored vest—moved through shifting shadows and a cloud of dust.

Her lover carried the Steyr rifle in his hands. The knuckles of his left hand were skinned; blood trickled between his fingers, spattering the floor beneath his steps. His beard growth looked days old, and his eyes had dark hollows under them.

"Ryan!" she called out.

As with Dean, though, the big man didn't hear her. Before she could move to one side of the hallway or the other, he walked right through her.

"Where's Ryan?" she asked, following along her lover's backtrail.

"It's not time for you to know," came the older woman's voice.

"This isn't happening now?"

"No."

Krysty felt the world shift around her, opening up slightly, and she suddenly realized she couldn't feel the rocks beneath her feet. "When?"

"Concentrate," the older woman snapped. "If you lose him, then I lose him, and it could be that you'll lose him for all time. Do you want that?"

"No." Krysty focused on Ryan, abruptly noticing she was no longer able to hear his footsteps against the rock-strewn floor. Even his edges had grown indistinct.

"Follow him."

Krysty started forward, surprised at how hard it was to move now. His long stride outdistanced hers. She put more effort into her steps, wishing she could run.

"You grow tired," the woman's voice said. "It's not your fault. This is very demanding. Especially for you, the focus point."

Ryan hesitated at the next door, letting the Steyr lead him around the corner. It gave Krysty almost enough time to catch him. She reached out to touch him, expecting her hand to go through his back, and it did. It looked as if her hand had been amputated at the wrist and thrust inside Ryan's back. When her lover took a step forward again, her hand reappeared as if by magic.

Ryan walked up a short flight of stairs. At the top a small doorway let into a room that held splintered shards of the same multicolored light Krysty had seen during her visit with Dean.

"Close enough," the woman said. "Get ready to talk to him."

Krysty moved closer as Ryan stepped into the room. A lumpy shadow tore itself free of the ceiling only a few feet in front of him, then came hurtling down. She tried to cry out a warning, knowing it was already too late.

Ryan moved fast. Ducking under the lumpy pile of multilegged flesh, he brought the Steyr's butt around in a wicked arc. The splat of the impact filled the small room.

The creature shrilled in pain and went scuttling away, hiding under the dilapidated bed. A broken mirror across from it held dozens of images.

Ryan drew the SIG-Sauer and pumped three rounds into the bed, searching for the mutie creature.

The whining it made became even more shrill and pained. Without a sign of its movements, it shot out from under the bed, its legs clawing for Ryan.

"Fireblast!" the one-eyed man snarled, but the word sounded out of sync to Krysty, slow and ringing. He pushed the blaster into the creature's face and pulled the trigger.

Momentum kept the mutie beast flying at him even after he'd killed it. Blood and ripped pieces of flesh thudded against him. Some of it stuck to the armored vest. The main portion of the creature's corpse dropped in a twisted heap at his boots.

"Now," the woman urged.

"Ryan," Krysty called.

He turned toward her, raising the blaster automatically until it centered on her face. His knuckle was whitening on the trigger before he squinted, then his eye widened in startled recognition.

"Krysty," he said. His voice was choked, thick with emotion. "I thought they chilled you." He reached a hand out to her, but it passed through.

"I'm not really here, lover," she said, then tried to explain what she was experiencing. But the words wouldn't leave her mouth. Instead, she said something else. "Dean's here with you. Find him."

"Dean?" He shook his head and called to her.

She tried to reach back for him even though her fingers would surely have passed through his anyway. Almost, they touched.

Her eyelids closed.

"You've done well," the woman said. "Now it is up to them, up to the chain of events you've helped set into motion. Destiny is written in the stars, but sometimes we can nudge them a bit in one direction or the other. Hopefully this will be enough."

"Enough for what?" Krysty tried to open her eyes but couldn't.

"Enough to let both father and son live." The woman's voice faded. "You must look to your own needs, my child. Your path remains rocky yet, as well. Take care. And do not tell Ryan, no matter how much you might wish to."

WHEN SHE OPENED her eyes, Krysty discovered she was still in the helicopter, leaning heavily against the empty copilot's seat. All she wanted to do was sleep; she didn't care where. Somehow she had managed to hang on to the torch, which was dying down rapidly now. Smoke filled the interior of the aircraft, stinging her eyes and making her throat burn.

Then she could hear Doc bellowing for her.

She pushed herself up, trying to find a more comfortable place on her shoulders for her bulging pack. She stepped outside the helicopter and waved the torch. "I'm here, Doc."

Her companion waved down from the open fissure. "So you are, my dear, so you are. I was on the verge of becoming greatly concerned when I saw your torch stop moving about. I thought perhaps you were having some kind of problem and had been incapacitated by something. Believe me, an overactive imagination is a curse of considerable magnitude."

"What about the others?"

"They have not as yet joined us. Perhaps they ran into Ryan and John Barrymore, and are even now plotting our course from these dire straits."

Poised on one knee, still a little down and forward of the helicopter, Krysty felt the beginnings of another tremor. At first she thought it might be her imagination, maybe her stomach jumping around because she was so done in.

When pebbles started skittering and falling down the incline, bouncing all over her in their rush to fall into the fissure behind her, she knew it wasn't her imagination.

Metal creaked as the helicopter slipped free of its grave. In a moment it was loose and sliding at her.

THE MARS ARENA: 09

After throwing the knotted rope they'd swiped and prepared over the garrison wall, Dean went up it as quick
as a monkey. Calgary struggled behind, huffing and
puffing.

"Keep your head down!" Dean told Calgary in a hoarse
whisper. "If we get caught, it'll probably go bad for us, but
it'll go bad for the people pulling sec rotation, too."

Chastised and afraid, Calgary dropped his head to the
hard wooden surface and watched Dean.

Sitting there in the darkness, contemplating the area he
needed to cross to get to the girls' dormitory, Dean couldn't
help wondering how his dad was doing. Only a few minutes ago, he'd felt really close to Krysty—almost as if he
could just reach out and touch her. Once he'd even
thought he'd heard her voice.

"Dean," Calgary whispered, "are you just going to sit
there?"

"Until the guard makes the corner, stupe." Dean watched the distant shadow. "Get ready."

"I think I hurt my leg."

Dean heaved a sigh. "Calgary, you wanted to see a naked girl tonight. Or at least find out if she is naked. Now get up off your ass."

As the guard hit the corner, Dean moved off at once, staying low. He felt the vibration of Calgary's heavier steps echo along the wooden timbers.

At the end of the catwalk, the rooftop of the girls' dormitory they sought was only a seven-foot jump out, almost on the same level. Probably the original buildings hadn't been that close to the perimeter walls, but the school had grown over the years and the walls hadn't. Dean took the jump in stride.

Calgary hesitated, freezing on the catwalk like one of the gargoyles Dean had seen in a history book. He waved to the boy. "Come on."

Eyes closed, which Dean considered to be triple stupe of the first order, Calgary jumped. He made the distance with no problem, but tried immediately to remain standing straight up. The incline of the roof threw him off.

"Oh, shit!" Calgary said, waving his arms wildly.

Dean grabbed him by the shirt and helped him find his balance. "You hit this rooftop like a sack of guts hitting the butcher's floor," he whispered, pulling the boy down to the roof. "You better hope everybody in this damn building is a sound sleeper."

That was one thing that Dean had found true; people inside the school's heavy walls slept more soundly than he'd have ever thought about doing when he was with his dad. At school, it was a totally different way of living. He threw an arm around Calgary's shoulders and held him down until the sec guard passed.

"We're pretty close to her, aren't we?" Calgary said.

"Ever notice that vanilla scent she wears?" Dean asked.

Calgary hesitated a moment, then shook his head. "I've never been that close."

"Trust me," Dean said, "she wears it. Get your nose open a little bit, and you'll probably be smelling it in the next few minutes. Then we'll find out if vanilla scent is the only thing she wears at night." He grinned. Finding Phaedra was no longer just for Calgary and the thrill of doing something he wasn't supposed to. There were mysteries to be solved that he hadn't even known he was interested in.

Dean led the way across a third of the rooftop, staying below the ridged top so the sec people wouldn't see him. Calgary trailed at his heels, complaining that they were moving too fast, until Dean told him to shut his mouth or he'd make Calgary carry his own shoes between his teeth.

Leaning over the eaves, Dean counted windows. When he found the fifth one, he scooted across the rooftop on his stomach, using his fingers and toes. With his head lower than the rest of his body, the blood rushed to fill his brain and face, making it feel that it would explode. His heart hammered inside his chest, too.

"Is that her room?" Calgary asked.

"It's her room." Hauling himself over the edge, Dean looked into Phaedra Lemon's bedroom.

The room was small, holding only two beds, a chest of drawers and a trunk at the foot of each bed. Boys slept four to a room in bunks, but the girls only doubled up and had single beds. There were fewer girls, and Mr. Brody had mentioned that at one time only boys were allowed at the school.

In the moonlight slanting through the window, Phaedra Lemon's long hair shone like spun gold, spread out on her pillow. She slept with a blanket pulled to her shoulder and her fist under her chin. At fifteen, she had curves under that blanket.

She also had her mouth open, innocent like. That one detail almost made Dean feel guilty enough to shuck the whole adventure and go back to his room.

"Can you see anything?" Calgary asked.

Dean swiveled his head, finding the other boy hanging off the eaves almost as far as he was. Calgary's face was so suffused with blood it looked like a melon about to burst.

"I see that she's sleeping under a blanket," Dean replied.

"But is she naked under it?"

"Stay here." Dean handled his weight on his arms, gripping the eaves with his hands as he turned himself over. The ledge out in front of the window was no more than three or four inches, barely enough for him to put the ends of his shoes on. He managed and soon found it would hold his weight.

"What are you doing?" Calgary asked in a frightened whisper. "You're going to get caught!"

"Only if you don't shut your mouth." Quiet as he could be, Dean pressed his fingers against the windowpane and pushed up.

The window slid easily, only having a few rough spots. Nicholas Brody made sure craftsmanship went into every aspect of his school. Thinking about the old headmaster was troubling to Dean, because it was sort of betraying the trust the man had placed in him by accepting his enrollment. Of course, his dad had also placed a lot of jack in Mr. Brody's hands along with responsibility for his son's tutelage.

But Dean wasn't exactly thinking things through that night. Somehow he wasn't able to. Seeing Phaedra lying there under that blanket, all curvy and unaware, had numbed the guilty pangs.

Light-footed as a cat and just as sure, he crept into the room. He glanced at the other bed and saw the girl sleeping there, her head thrown back, snoring softly. He knew her, too, but he couldn't remember her name. He didn't even care.

He moved closer to Phaedra's bed, eyes running along the womanly body under the lightweight lavender blanket. At least, it looked lavender in the moonlight. She smelled of vanilla, too, just as he knew she would.

He'd always known women had different shapes than men. Rona had been beautiful and he'd bathed with her, and Dean was aware of the stares Krysty got whenever they were around men.

The time was magical for Dean in ways that he knew he'd never be able to put into words. It was one of those pictures he knew he'd carry around in his head forever. Except for the sight of Calgary Ventnor's head hanging down in view of the window like some ugly fruit, it was perfect. The boy motioned for Dean to hurry.

Gently Dean reached out for the edge of the blanket, took it between his finger and thumb and began to pull it down. He hadn't done more than reveal one bare shoulder when he noticed that Phaedra Lemon's eyes were open and she was staring right at him.

The girl's mouth started to round out, opening, and she took a deeper breath.

Figuring she was going to scream, Dean dropped a hand to her face and covered her mouth, wondering what had driven him to be stupe enough to get caught in her bedroom.

Ryan spotted Doc leaning down into a hole in the ground. Then he heard the old man shouting Krysty's name. Another big tremor hit, nearly knocking Ryan from his feet as he redoubled his efforts. He skidded across a boulder, shaving skin from both palms.

In five more long strides over the wobbling ground, he was beside Doc. "Where's Krysty?"

"There!" The old man pointed.

Squinting his eye, Ryan peered into the fissure. It was dark inside, but he could just make out the dying embers of a torch as it skittered over the side of another, widening crack in the earth. For an instant the torch flared to new life, no longer battered by the stones it rolled across.

In the sudden light, Ryan saw Krysty as the wreckage of a helicopter emerged from the cracking stone wall above her, disgorging its trapped prize like a heifer giving birth. Krysty was struggling to maintain a grip, but Ryan knew the falling helicopter would rake her from her precarious perch the instant it ripped free of its earthen womb.

Then the torch disappeared into the yawning abyss below, not scattering in all directions from an impact. It simply kept falling, drawing farther away. Everything went dark. The scream of tortured metal continued, letting him know the helicopter was still in motion even though he couldn't see it.

Ryan glanced over his shoulder and saw that J.B. was already tying a rope around an outcrop nearly six feet from the lip of the fissure.

"I volunteered to go down in her stead," Doc said, his face pale and drawn. He didn't move from the edge of the fissure. He gazed back down into the dark hole. "I truly did, but she would have none of it. I am very sorry, friend Ryan."

"She's not dead yet, Doc."

Ryan grabbed the free end of the rope. "Jak, get that light shining into that hole. I need to see."

The albino quickly moved into position. The flashlight came on with a burst of incandescence as he pointed it into the fissure. "Help's coming," he yelled down to Krysty. He couldn't throw her the rope; she was using both hands to hang on.

"How much rope are you going to need?" the Armorer asked.

Ryan peered into the hole, trying to gauge the distance from the fissure's mouth to Krysty's position. "Give me twenty-five, thirty feet beyond the lip."

"Fifty-foot rope," J.B. said. "I get you shored up good and proper, that's going to cut it close to what we've got to use."

Ryan nodded.

"Lover," Krysty called. Her voice was almost calm, but

Ryan could hear the fear in her. "Give it up. I can't make it. There's no sense in losing both of us."

Working the end of the rope around his boots, Ryan watched Krysty as she scrambled along the moving incline and tried in vain to find purchase. She fell, and for a second he thought it might be the end of her. But she made it back up, just in time for the helicopter to take away another foot of precious space.

"Hold on, dammit!" Ryan shouted. He cinched the rope around both boots, just above the ankle. There was no time to try a controlled hand-over-hand descent.

The tremors subsided for a moment, long enough for Ryan to think they'd quit completely. The helicopter kept sliding, breaking out bigger sections of the wall that had held it for so long.

"Ryan!" Krysty called.

He peered over the edge, then rolled down to hang from his hands. The rope dangled in a loose coil between his tied feet, looping back up and out of sight. He was still twenty feet from Krysty, another ten in horizontal distance. "J.B."

"You're tied on," the Armorer said. He poked his head over the edge, face tense.

"I can't let you do it," Krysty told Ryan. "I'll jump off the edge myself before I let you get killed, too."

"You jump off," Ryan told her, smiling with a cockiness he definitely didn't feel, "hell, you'll only be making it harder, not stopping me."

"I don't want you to die, lover."

"I'm not going to die, and I'm not going to let you die, either."

PHAEDRA LEMON bit Dean's hand.

"Shit!" he whispered. "Don't be biting me!" He used his

other hand, pulling at that gold hair from behind to turn her face up to his. The vanilla smell of her swarmed around him and clouded his mind. Most of the fear inside him went away as he realized he'd unconsciously covered her body with his.

She tried to bite him again, her saliva running across his palm. Twisting in the bed, she tried to escape him.

Dean was all too aware of the soft flesh just on the other side of the lavender blanket, almost trapped in some tantalizing fashion beneath his body. "Hot pipe!" he croaked.

He threw a leg over her, trying to keep her from squirming off the bed. It was a miracle, he decided, how that blanket stayed in place.

Without warning, she brought a small hand out from under the blanket, curled it tight into a fist, then slammed him on the nose with it.

Dean stifled a curse and grabbed his nose. It hurt like hell. He held out his free hand to ward off another blow. He didn't know which hurt worse—his bitten hand or his nose.

"Stop!" he said in a forced whisper. "I'm sorry!" He was fully expecting the girl to bash him again and start to scream bloody murder.

Instead, she gripped the blanket with one hand and kept it tucked under her chin, maintained a fist poised to strike and scooted away from him. She looked at him, blinking, her nose flaring. "Dean?"

Looking at her face, Dean wondered why he'd never noticed what a cute nose she had. He took his hand away from his face and checked his fingers for blood. Only a few crimson stains colored his fingertips. "Damn, that hurt!" he said.

"Quiet!" Phaedra insisted in a whisper.

Dean blinked at her. "Quiet?"

"Yes, you jackass. You'll wake Bitha." She gave him a look that informed him he should have known that.

"I will?" Dean was confused.

"Whisper!"

He lowered his voice. "Sorry."

"That's better."

He looked at her, scrunched up against the headboard as if she were afraid he was going to jump at her again. He felt bad about that. "Didn't mean to scare you."

"What did you think you were going to do creeping around in my room like that?"

"I—"

Across the room, Bitha rolled over in bed, talking in her sleep.

"Shh!" Phaedra hissed.

Bitha reached out to the small bedside table and took up a glass there. She drank deeply, then crumpled back into her pillow all without looking at them for an instant.

"She's a heavy sleeper," Phaedra whispered, "but she gets dry at night."

Since she was turned to face him, Dean knew Phaedra didn't see Calgary Ventnor hanging upside down from the eaves. He nodded, not knowing what else to do, wondering how the hell it was that he was having a conversation with the girl when she should have been yelling her head off. And there was still the mystery of what lay beneath the blanket. The heady aroma of vanilla surrounded him.

"Now," she whispered in a harder voice, "you were going to tell me what you're doing in my bedroom."

TEARS GLINTED in Krysty's eyes as she watched Ryan hang from the rocky lip above her. She wouldn't let him see her cry, not because she was afraid.

"J.B.," Ryan called out.

"You're tied on," the Armorer called back.

Krysty's arms shook from the effort of hanging on, the muscles burning as they writhed under her skin. Gaia, if she'd only fallen before Ryan had reached her, he wouldn't be here putting his life on the line.

"You look at me," Ryan ordered, putting steel in his voice.

She lifted her head and looked into the volcanic blue of his eye. The scars on his face were part of the man, not artificial things at all. She couldn't imagine him without them. He was the handsomest man she'd ever seen.

"We've been through too many things, me and you," he told her as he gripped his way around the fissure mouth for a more feasible purchase point, "for you to just give up on me now."

"You and I," she corrected automatically. The fissure behind her shook again, opening another three or four feet.

"You and me," he repeated. "That's how it's going to be. You and me getting out of here."

"What are you doing?" she asked.

Hardly before the words were out of her mouth, the helicopter finally shrugged itself free of its subterranean tomb and came skidding at her. There was nothing she could do to avoid it. The aircraft gained speed and grew larger, sparks jumping out from under it as the metal skin scraped across stone.

And Ryan leaped from his hold on the fissure's edge, falling.

"CAME TO SEE YOU," Dean answered.

"Me?" Phaedra's eyes lifted in surprise.

"Yeah."

"Why?"

"I don't know." He felt stupe saying that, but it sounded better than giving her the real reason.

"You don't know?" Her question became a challenge.

For some reason, knowing he shouldn't have but feeling it and giving in to the emotion all the same, Dean got angry. "That's right!"

"Shh!" Phaedra uncoiled her fist and put her forefinger to her lips.

They both glanced at Bitha, who slept on.

Dean swiveled his head back to Phaedra, gazing at her lips and wondering why he hadn't noticed how ripe and full they looked. He breathed in again, deep, but trying not to let her know what he was doing. The scent of vanilla filled his nostrils, and he knew he'd never forget it.

"Don't sit there smiling," Phaedra chastised.

"Was I smiling?" Dean put on a serious face.

"You still are."

Dean tried not to let his gaze linger too long on the rounded breast almost visible under the lavender blanket. He'd never known lavender could be so attractive, either. "I always look like this."

"Uh-uh." Phaedra shook her head, her gold locks flying. "Usually you've got a bored look on your face." She smiled, her eyes narrowing. "You don't look bored now."

"Getting punched in the nose kind of knocks the boredness right out of you." He moved his nose as if he were worried about it. In truth, he'd almost forgotten about it. Probably he would have, except for the occasional throb.

"So what brought you to my room?" Phaedra asked.

Guile was second nature to Dean, having been raised for so long by Rona to protect his father's identity and keep things about himself secret. "I didn't know this was your room."

She raised her eyebrows, the smile dimming only a little. "Oh, and who else's bedroom have you been prowling around in the dead of night?"

"I didn't say I'd been prowling around in anyone else's bedroom." Dean was feeling mad all over again because she was being so accusing about everything. Maybe it would have been better if Phaedra had just screamed. Talking to her wasn't something he really wanted to do. At least if the dorm sec people got hold of him, they'd ask him what the hell he thought he was doing and he could just say "I don't know," shrug and be done with it.

But then he'd have Nicholas Brody to contend with.

The prospect made him think maybe talking to Phaedra might not be as dire as he believed at the moment.

"You got in here by accident?" Phaedra's tone took on heavy sarcasm.

Lying, he sensed, would only have brought out the big blasters. "No," Dean said.

"Whisper!"

"I am."

"Then get better at it!"

Dean's face flushed and burned.

"If you didn't get here by accident," Phaedra said, "then you planned to be here."

But not caught, Dean wanted to say. He nodded. "I've got to go."

Phaedra frowned at him. "You just got here."

"This isn't exactly a visit," Dean said.

"Then why are you here?"

"Will you—?"

"Shh!" Phaedra's forefinger zipped to her lips, and the blanket slid down to reveal a bare shoulder.

Dean waited.

In her bed Bitha stretched, yawned and rolled over the other way.

"She gets restless," Phaedra explained in a whisper. "Usually when her period is coming on."

Dean also decided he could have done without that bit of information. "I've got to go."

"You can't go."

Dean smirked. "Look, you might have surprised me with that punch to the nose because I wasn't expecting it, but there's no way you can keep me from going." He stood.

Phaedra glared at him. "I can scream."

With the way the light was hitting her, Dean thought he could see the outline of one pointy nipple jutting out from her breast. That one little bump of flesh tonight intrigued him more than all the naked breasts he'd ever seen. "Why would you scream?"

"Why not?"

Frustrated, Dean sat on the edge of the bed. "You're confusing."

"I'm confusing?"

"Yes, and you're turning everything you say into a damn question. I feel like I'm in the middle of one of Coco Copeland's math exams."

"I'm confusing?" she repeated, irritation weaving through her voice as sure as a stickie had suckers on his butt.

Dean let his own irritation show. "Yes. First you're yelling at me for being here. Now you're threatening to yell at me if I leave. That's confusing."

"I'll let you go," she said, "if you'll tell me why you were here."

Dean took a deep breath, decided that he was doomed for sure, surer even than a triple-stupe mutie who'd wandered one time too many into a rad-blasted area following a vision. "I came to find out something."

"What?"

"Something about you." He couldn't just blurt it out. His face felt hot again, and the electricity was back squirming in his groin as he looked at that little nubbin of flesh poking at the lavender blanket. Glancing over Phaedra's shoulder, he looked at Calgary hanging there like some kind of stupe bat. Silently he wished the boy's head would explode. During the confusion of all the flying bloody matter and what little brains Calgary actually had, judging from tonight's little adventure, Dean was certain he could make an escape.

"What about me?"

"I heard that you slept naked." Dean watched her. There, he'd said it.

She looked at him, her mouth going open but no sounds coming out, as if she were a fish drowning in the air. She worked her jaw a few times.

Dean wondered if he had time to make a dash for the window before she started yelling. Or hitting.

Before he could move, she found her voice. "You came up here to look at me naked?"

That one he could dodge. "Actually just to find out if you were."

Her face went crimson, blushing dark in the shadows gathered in the room. Without her body moving enough to give a hint of what she was about to do, she punched at Dean again.

Before he could get away, the blow landed against his nose hard enough to start stars flashing behind his eyeballs.

RYAN FELL. Illuminated from above and behind by the flashlight Jak held, he skimmed across the hard rock leading down to Krysty.

Her face was turned from him, focusing on the approaching bulk of the wrecked helicopter.

The skeleton dressed in rags sitting in the cockpit jumped and jerked behind the controls, looking as though it had come to life and was piloting the wreckage of his craft with insane glee. The Plexiglas nose slid straight at Krysty.

Ryan hit the steep incline more than eight feet from her. His stomach lurched inside him when he knew he was going to reach her too late. Forgetting the rope around his ankles, he tried to push himself up and run. Unable to, he dug his boots in and leaped forward, skidding down the tilted rock, trying to navigate an interception path using his hands, ignoring the pain that was inflicted.

Rock and dirt came shooting after him, overtaking him, swirling up inside his mouth, nose and eye. He blinked, closing on Krysty.

But the helicopter was nearer. She put her hands out as if to hold it back, took a final look at him and went over the side, bulldozed by the helicopter.

"Krysty!" Mildred yelled from above.

Ryan watched as Krysty fell, captured in the beam of the flash Jak held. Heaving himself over the side, Ryan plunged into the abyss after her. Hot sulfuric fumes pressed into his face, burning his nose and eye. He spotted Krysty ahead of him, on the other side of the helicopter. Her eyes were still focused on him.

Ryan prayed the rope wouldn't come up short.

In her desperation Krysty grabbed the helicopter as it tipped over the ledge. She got one hand around a helicopter skid. For a moment, despite the piles of rock and sand shoving up behind it, the aircraft teetered on the edge of the precipice.

Before it fell, Ryan was there. He wrapped his arms around Krysty, pulling her into him. The rope kept playing out, and they fell past the fissure's edge.

"Ryan!" Krysty screamed, taking his face in her hands. Her sentient hair coiled protectively around her scalp.

"It's okay," he said, reaching around her to hook his fingers in the thick leather belt at her back.

Just as he was beginning to think something had gone wrong and J.B. hadn't gotten his knots tight enough, the rope yanked up fast around Ryan's boots. The force bruised his ankles despite the leather and despite the elasticity of the nylon weave, and the rope felt as if it had cut into his flesh.

He came to a sudden stop.

While the rope held him, giving enough to keep his legs from popping out of his knee or hip joints, he was the only thing holding on to Krysty. He growled with the pain of it all. His legs, his back and his arms and shoulders suddenly felt as if they'd been subjected to the fiery kiss of an incendiary gren.

Before he could recover, the helicopter was on them, batting them aside like a piÑata as it nose-dived into the abyss. An instant later they were slammed against the side of the fissure.

The rough rock bit into Ryan's back, but he didn't think there were any skin abrasions, since the dead man's coat provided padding. He bounced a couple of times, twisting along the rope's trajectories, swapping sides with Krysty, then came to a rest against the underside of the second fissure.

"Fireblast," Ryan said weakly as soon as he was able to draw a breath. He kept his arms locked tight. Krysty sagged in his arms, not quite limp. "Krysty?"

"Here, lover." With effort she lifted her head and met his gaze. "I'm right here."

"Don't let go," he warned. "Don't know how much I

can trust my arms." They felt weak and numb all at the same time—a bad combination for a man needing his best from them.

"Ryan!" Jak called.

"We're here! Haul us in! Careful!"

Krysty shifted her grip, grabbing fistfuls of Ryan's coat and putting some of her weight on the garment instead of in his arms. "Thank you. I thought I was dead and done for, lover."

He shook his head, finding the unconscious movement difficult under their present circumstances. "Not as long as there's a breath left in me and I see a way clear."

J.B., Doc, Mildred and Jak pulled them up, keeping the tension on the line steady, moving them along. Ryan and Krysty scraped along the fissure wall until they were raised above it. With the line unanchored, they twirled out of control until they reached the lip of the top fissure.

J.B. grabbed Krysty's arm and helped her onto solid ground. The echo of the tremors from the last wave of the quake still vibrated through the mountain.

"Truly, my dear Ryan," Doc said as he offered his hand, "that was one of the most outstanding exercises in courageous gallantry that these old eyes have ever beheld."

"Speak for yourself, Doc," Mildred said, flicking out a knife and cutting the rope from Ryan's ankles. The knots were drawn up too tight from the fall to ever untie. "I nearly wet my pants when I saw them both go over the edge."

Ryan kicked out of the cut rope, gritting his teeth against the pain in his ankles, legs and back. Everything still seemed to move when he wanted it to, which was a good sign.

"Thought lost for sure," Jak added. "Glad not."

"Me, too." Ryan took Jak's hand and forced himself to his feet.

A harsh, spitting bolt of snake-tongued lightning suddenly fried the sky above them, leaving the harsh, acrid smell of ozone behind.

Ryan glanced up just in time to watch a second jagged streak of lightning blaze across the sky. "Brushwooders'll probably hole up in this if they're smart."

J.B. nodded. "They'll probably be thinking we'll be doing the same thing."

Ryan bared a feral grin. "If we had a choice, we'd more than likely do that. I think mebbe a little farther on, we could find a better place to set up that tent Jak found. Distance is a weapon we got right now, and we'd be better off using it."

Mildred was the only one who voiced an objection. "With the temperature dropping like it is, we're going to be risking exposure out here."

"Exposure to hostile blasters and us without cover," Ryan replied, "I figure that would kill us some quicker." He made decisions for the group, and they all knew it. And when they had something to say, they spoke their minds and he thought about it. Democracies didn't survive in Deathlands, because they took too long to react to changes in the given situation.

"You're right," Mildred said. "I was just thinking maybe you and Krysty might take it easy after all you've been through."

Krysty touched the woman's shoulder. "I'll be okay. Ryan took the worst of it."

Ryan shrugged on his pack, feeling the deeper pain of his ordeal hovering around him, warded off by the adrenaline still pumping through his system. "I'm going to walk," he said, "until I find a place safe enough or I can't walk anymore. Anything else would be double stupe, and put the rest of you in danger, as well." He turned to the albino. "Jak, which way?"

The teenager pointed with his chin. "Ahead."

Turning up the collar of his coat, Ryan moved out. "You got point, Jak."

The albino nodded and vanished into the snow flurries within a half-dozen steps.

"J.B.," Ryan said, "you're walking drag."

The Armorer dropped out of the single-file line forming behind Ryan.

"Doc, you're the man next to him." He forced himself up the slight incline already covered with a layer of snow. He kept the Steyr in one hand and used the other to help balance himself as he went over the uneven terrain. He could no longer see Jak, but his combat senses allowed him to feel the teen's presence somewhere up in front of him.

Pain nagged every step Ryan made, but he knew it was nothing permanent. A good night's rest, possibly two if it could be managed, and he'd be as good as new. He pushed the accumulated aches and discomforts aside, falling into the easy rhythm of movement he'd become accustomed to.

"DAMMIT!" DEAN YELLED before he could stop himself. He was almost certain Phaedra had broken his nose this time. Red dots exploded in his vision. He put both hands in front of him to ward off another blow.

The bed shifted as Phaedra drew back her arm. "You triple-stupe mutie jackass! You bastard pervert! Your mother probably lay with the ugliest, foulest boar she could find to sire you!" She launched another blow.

Dean batted it aside, angry himself now, and fearful of taking another direct hit to the nose. Phaedra was three or four years older than he was, an inch or so taller and probably near the same weight because she carried a woman's figure instead of a girl's.

"Stop it!" he yelled at her.

She struck at him again.

Dean took the punch on the outside of his arm and moved it away.

Phaedra howled with frustration.

"They're going to hear you," Dean said, his voice not much above a strong whisper.

"I don't care! I hate you! I'm going to scratch your eyes out, then I'm going to stomp them into jelly, put them onto pieces of sourdough bread and give them to the rats!" She flailed an open hand at him, and he caught it on his shoulder, the smack echoing in the room.

Dean grabbed her wrists out of self-defense. Over her shoulder, Calgary Ventnor was waving frantically for him to leave the room. "Stop it!" he told the girl. "I thought you weren't going to scream if I told you!"

"I lied!" Her eyes blazed at him. "You're insufferable! I can't believe I let you sit on my bed!"

"You didn't let me," Dean said. "I slipped in here and let myself." The blanket had dropped even farther, to where the material clung only by the nubbin of her nipple to protect the last shreds of modesty. His breath felt thick in his throat.

Calgary Ventnor mouthed Dean's name in wide pantomime. The boy slipped, a white look of terror crossing his animated and blood-filled features.

For a moment Dean thought Calgary was going to fall and had mixed feelings about the other boy's survival. He kept his hands around Phaedra's wrists and forced her back on the bed, where she couldn't gain enough leverage to break free. One leg coiled around his waist in an effort to move out from beneath him. With all the flesh showing, Dean was suddenly and certainly sure that the girl wasn't wearing panties, either. He was watching the expanse of flesh increase, hypnotized, stopping just short of her sex, but not short enough to keep the blond wisps of her pubic hair hidden.

Dean swallowed hard, amazed at how all the air seemed to have gone from the room.

Phaedra jammed a thumb in the corner of his eye.

"Dammit, dammit, dammit!" Dean said, struggling to keep his voice low despite the flash of pain. Blood swam across his vision.

"Sick bastard!" Phaedra snarled.

Dean couldn't believe no one was coming to beat down the bedroom door. In a desperate move to shut up any more outbursts from the girl, he put his mouth over hers. It wasn't a kiss; it was just a seal of flesh against flesh.

Phaedra fought hard for a moment or two, wrapping her bedclothes around them. Then all the fight drained from her. Without warning, her lips sought Dean's.

Thinking maybe it was a ploy designed to win his confidence, Dean kept his mouth in place. The kiss happened without intention. Somehow he just wasn't able to keep his lips together. Then he wasn't able to keep his teeth together as Phaedra's tongue invaded his mouth.

He felt as if he were on fire, suddenly swollen up too big to fit inside his own skin. Not just in his crotch, but all over. He even felt light-headed. But he didn't for an instant believe he would be able to stick his tongue outside his own mouth without having it bitten off.

At length Phaedra broke off the kiss and lay quietly under him, her eyes closed. When she opened them, however, she said, "You're bleeding!"

Dean had noticed the liquid seeping from his eye, running down his face to moisten her cheek. He'd figured it was tears from his injured eye, but the injury hadn't seemed important at the time. Nor had the pain.

"Did I do that?" she asked, suddenly all innocence. She tried to pull her arms free.

Dean squinted the injured eye closed and tried to ignore the hurt again. It was definitely harder now, and the eye pained him badly, too. "I don't see anybody else who's been hitting me."

"I didn't mean to do that."

"You going to tell me you didn't mean to hit me in the nose, either?"

"I meant to do that."

"Oh."

"I didn't intend to hurt your eye." Pink strands of watered-down blood streamed from her cheek to her pillow.

Dean gazed down at her, letting his uninjured eye take in the sight of the creamy flesh open for his inspection. He looked at her breast, the nipple standing so proudly, flushed with blood and dark against the strawberry areole. "You're pretty," he said before he had much time to think about it.

"Thank you."

He looked back into her face, noting that she didn't act embarrassed at all with his looking. "You kiss good, too."

"Thank you again. You kiss pretty good yourself."

He shifted on her, knowing she had to be noticing how excited he was against her leg, feeling kind of embarrassed about that himself. His dad had mentioned such things were natural; otherwise, what would bring men and women together long enough no matter what the hardship or circumstance to bring babies into the world? Of course, his dad had also said that bringing babies into the world generally wasn't on most people's minds at those times. But it was nothing to be ashamed of.

Still, Dean didn't feel comfortable.

"Have you been kissed before, Dean?" she asked.

"Sure." His response was automatic, defensive. He started to add that he'd been kissed lots of times even though that wasn't exactly true. Then he remembered that every time he tried to answer more than just the question on the table, he'd ended up in trouble. He wasn't stupe, so he kept his mouth shut.

She seemed happy enough about that. "Did you like it?"

"Yeah."

Her face darkened.

"But not as much as this time," he added.

"Why?"

He was confused. "Why what?" He was also aware of Calgary Ventnor struggling on the eaves of the house, either because he couldn't get his balance or because he was trying to better peer into the room.

"Why didn't you like it as much as this time?"

Dean wished he had more time to think. Hell, he wished he didn't feel so confused by everything his body was telling him that he *could* think. Telling her that he didn't know didn't sound like a good move.

"It was you," he said, hoping that was a safe statement. It also made clear that he thought all the responsibility, for good or evil, should be hers, which might be chancy.

She smiled at him. "You know, Dean Cawdor, looking at you all rawboned and unkempt sometimes, and hearing about how you fought so dirty out on the school ground, I didn't think you'd be such a romantic."

Dean raised his eyebrows, which made his bad eye hurt.

He hoped Jak never heard about this, because he'd never live it down.

"If you'll let go of my wrists, maybe I can make your eye feel better. I can at least clean it up."

Gingerly Dean released her, pushing himself back.

Phaedra started to sit up, unmindful that the blanket had gathered at her waist, revealing her breasts to him. "Can't believe we didn't wake somebody up with all that noise," she said with a grin.

Dean couldn't, either. He was also aware that Calgary had edged down farther on the eaves. "Uh, mebbe you need to keep covered up." He didn't want the other boy to see.

"Why? You embarrassed? After all, it was you come stealing into my bedroom."

Dean watched Calgary suddenly come loose from the eaves over Phaedra's shoulder—and fall.

Calgary screamed, loud and high-pitched like someone being torn apart by stampeding horses. A muffled thud ended it.

"Shit," Dean said, wondering if the boy had accidentally chilled himself. Bad enough to be caught in the girls' dorm, but triple bad if Calgary ended up dead. He pushed up from the bed, one hand clapped over his injured eye because the moon seemed too bright for him.

"What was that?" Phaedra demanded, yanking the lavender blanket around herself.

Dean stuck his head out the window and peered down. Calgary was squirming around, trying to suck in air like a man come near to drowning and finally back on dry land.

"That's Calgary Ventnor," Phaedra said, shoving through the window beside Dean.

"Yeah," Dean replied, wondering how the hell he was going to explain the other boy's presence. Telling Phaedra that the jaunt into her bedroom had been at Calgary's instigation seemed tantamount to slitting his wrists the long way. But he couldn't think, not the way his head was hurting and with the vanilla scent of Phaedra standing so close coming into his swollen nose with every breath.

She looked at him. "Calgary must have followed you up here."

Dean blinked his good eye at her, then didn't hesitate at all. "That's probably it."

"He's a pervert," Phaedra declared. "He's been caught two, three times peeking through glory holes he's carved through the girls' shower room."

"Phaedra?" a voice behind them said.

They turned together, Dean bumping his head on the window frame and creating a new onslaught of pain that nearly swept his senses away.

Bitha was sitting up in her bed. Her eyes widened as they locked on Dean. Then she screamed, an ear-piercing shriek that would have moved the dead.

Phaedra grabbed Dean's arm and pushed him at the window. "Get out!"

"What?" Before he knew it, she almost had him out the window.

"If they don't catch you, they won't know who you are," Phaedra said in a desperate whisper. "Bitha can't see shit without her glasses. If you don't get caught, neither one of us has to explain what you were doing in here."

"That's a long way down," Dean protested.

"Yes, well, Calgary Ventnor is still alive, isn't he?" Phaedra pushed again, shoving Dean through the window. "If he can make the jump, so can you."

Footsteps sounded at the door, and a man's voice demanded, "Are you girls all right in there?" A heavy hand beat against the door rapidly, shaking the heavy timbers.

Dean glanced at the door, one leg over the window frame and barely finding purchase on the narrow board below. Bitha was still screaming, the covers pulled over her head.

"Go!" Phaedra ordered impatiently. She put her shoulder against Dean with more force than he'd expected.

Off balance and hanging precariously, Dean had no chance to keep his grip. He plummeted, waving his arms wildly in an attempt not to land on Calgary. An instant before he hit the ground, he managed to get his feet under him. On impact he crumpled his legs and breathed the air out of his lungs, letting his body be its own cushioning system. He went forward into a roll and came up on his feet, none the worse for wear. The drop had been no big challenge, but it had looked bad because of the night shadows draping the landscape.

Peering up, he saw yellow light invade the bedroom behind Phaedra. Bitha was still screaming, and Dean couldn't believe the pitch she was getting, not to mention the lack of wear and tear apparent on her vocal cords. The girl should have been in choir.

"Sorry," Phaedra called down in an excited whisper, still holding the blanket over her breasts.

"Dean," Calgary said, "help me. I think I broke my leg." He reached a hand up, tears streaking his face.

"You're lucky you didn't break your bastard neck, you stupe." Dean took the other boy's hand, unwilling to leave him there.

"I think it was a pretty near thing." He hiccuped as he tried to suck in another breath.

A big arm swept Phaedra out of the window. She cursed

and hit the man attached to it. The man shoved his flashlight outside and held it aloft to light up the grounds.

Dean knew they were drawing entirely too much unwanted attention. He moved Calgary by force, pulling the boy along behind him at almost a dead run.

He kept them moving, dodging between the girls' quarters and the stable. Horses whickered inside, woken by the shouts of alarm starting around the perimeter of the school.

Dean ran Calgary headlong into the corral fence, getting behind the other boy with just enough shoulder and strength to start him over the top rail.

Calgary wasn't happy about the turn of events at all, groaning as Dean muscled him over the railing and pulled him down into the tromped earth. It had rained a couple days earlier, so the ground was still soft in most places.

The flickering torchlight from one of the school's sec guards on the ground illuminated the rails but didn't reach far into the muddy areas beyond. Men yelled to one another, calling out clear areas.

There was no sound, no warning. Then a light but firm hand shoved against Dean's shoulder as he lay on the ground and watched two sec men go wandering by with flashlights in their hands.

Dean came around quick, curling up and ready to spring to his feet. As he made the effort, responding to the shadow leaning over him, the hand shifted from his shoulder to the center of his chest. A strong push sent Dean tumbling to his ass again.

"Don't," a man's voice warned. "Damn kid. You're already in it up to your neck."

Peering through the gloom, Dean recognized Jake. The sec man had been the first school resident Dean had met. "I'm sitting," the boy grumbled.

Jake glared down at him, then looked at Calgary and back again. He wore a sun-bleached and battered brimmed hat, a gray work shirt and blue jeans tucked into scarred work boots that had never seen an honest day of rest. The way he held the Browning 71 rifle in his hand, it looked as if flesh, bone and steel never parted company.

"That you up in the girls' dorm?" Jake asked.

"No," Calgary answered quickly.

Dean returned the man's penetrating gaze. "Yes, sir."

"He went in," Calgary said, pointing at Dean with one hand and trying to brush shit off with the other.

"You was just hanging around on the rooftop," Jake said, pinning the other boy with his gaze.

Calgary didn't have anything to say to that.

Jake canted the rifle over his shoulder and pushed his hat back with a gnarled thumb. He looked at Dean, his face stern but his eyes full of mischief. "I ain't gonna ask you what you was doing inside that dorm."

Dean felt relieved.

"But Brody, he's gonna want to know. You might want to think on that."

"Yes, sir," Dean said.

Jake nodded. "Let's go. You boys caused enough of a stir tonight."

Dean got up and followed the sec man, knowing he'd probably just blown every chance he had of finishing out the term at the school. He figured his dad was going to be real disappointed.

RYAN DIDN'T BOTHER checking his chron to find out how long the march took them to get to the pass. He stayed in the lower reaches of the narrow trail that twisted through the broken slabs of rock that had tumbled into their way, evidently from the latest earthquake.

Jak ranged ahead of them, a ghost on a field that looked beyond the pale.

Another few minutes saw them clear of most of the debris. When Jak turned, Ryan waved him to the north side of the pass near what appeared to be the entrance, or exit, depending on how a man was making his way through the mountains.

"I'm going up," Ryan said. "I'll take a look around above us and make sure there isn't any rock waiting to come tumbling down when we least expect it."

"Be careful, lover," Krysty said.

Ryan shouldered the Steyr, found some handholds and started up. Jak went with him. Below, J.B. and Doc started to set up the therm tent out of the wind in the protected areas afforded by the stone wall.

Arms aching, Ryan pulled himself up the final few feet and found himself on a small plateau that quickly fell away in all directions. Jak was at his side a heartbeat later.

Ryan shaded his eye against the swirling snowflakes and peered around. A carpet of white covered the land, interrupted in a lot of places by trees and treetops that made islands of green. There were no signs of fires or of the brushwooders in the areas open to him.

"Anything?" he asked Jak.

"No."

"Let's hope we're right."

THE TENT WAS IN PLACE when Jak and Ryan returned. Ryan smelled the aroma of a freshly opened self-heat even before they'd finished the descent. His stomach rumbled, reminding him how many hours it had been since he'd last had a meal.

J.B. sat hunkered down with his back against a wall a little up from the rounded dome of the tent. From his position he could see over the tent and all approach paths for at least fifty yards in any direction. The Armorer held a steaming self-heat in his hands, eating slow so he could savor the warmth of the container for a bit, too.

"Here, lover." Krysty handed him a self-heat when she emerged from the tent.

Ryan took the container gratefully. He figured his stomach might revolt later, but for now it put some warmth in him and got a good start on filling up all the hollow spaces.

"Go on inside the tent," J.B. said. "I got this watch."

Ryan nodded. "Wake me in an hour and a half. I'll take that one."

Ryan entered the tent, followed by Jak, Mildred and Krysty, who zipped the flap closed again.

"Not much room," Mildred said, sitting cross-legged in a corner, "but it does take a body out of that wind."

Ryan stretched out as much as he was able. The tent wasn't very big, so they were all touching one another. But that way they'd also be able to share the warmth. He finished the stew and put the container aside, laying his head on his arm. His eye drifted closed when he felt Krysty's hand on his brow. Her fingers felt soft across the areas that weren't nerve damaged from the injuries he'd taken over the years. Moments later he fell asleep.

"Wake up!"

Ryan cracked open his eye and closed his hand around the SIG-Sauer. Jak was nowhere in sight, but it had been the albino's voice. He got to his knees, feeling Krysty moving beside him. "Jak."

"Yeah."

"Trouble?"

Doc, Mildred and J.B. awakened, as well, all of them reaching for weapons.

"Burning daylight," Jak called back. He sounded irritated. "Figured you people up by now."

Ryan pushed through the tent flap, surprised by the brightness and warmth of the sun hanging low in a mass of purple clouds to the east. He left his coat open, knowing he wasn't going to need it for the slight chill that remained from the storm last night.

All around him was the sound of running water. Snow

melted at an incredible rate, pouring down tracks already worn through the rock and soil. Steam curled up from the ground, rolling in gentle fogs across the countryside.

"I didn't expect this, lover." Krysty came up beside Ryan and put her hand in his.

"Don't see how you could have," Ryan replied.

"It probably has a lot to do with the underlying volcanic activity and the atmospheric conditions in regards to the debris that regularly shoots into the upper stratosphere," Doc stated, putting a hand to his forehead to shade his eyes.

"Feels like a cold sauna out here," Mildred said.

J.B. looked at the drenched ground. "There's a good chance we're going to leave a trail wherever we go."

Ryan nodded, surveying the terrain around them. "We stick to the rocks so we don't leave tracks."

"Yeah, but that's going to put us working the high ground. Better chance of the brushwooders seeing us."

"We get a few more miles behind us, they won't have a chance at all."

"Downhill," Jak said, "mebbe melting snow wash away all tracks." The albino teenager sat tending a slow cook fire nestled between a ring of rocks he'd evidently placed. He turned a long spit that held four animals that had roasted nicely.

"And mebbe we'll end up trying to cross some awfully flooded lands," Ryan added. "Up top we should be able to get a better lay of the terrain. Pick a good spot to cross at instead of being chased into a bad one."

"Where'd you get breakfast?" Mildred asked.

Jak waved an arm. "Little animals kept sticking heads up not far away. I pitched rocks. And I got these." He poured out a pouch that contained bright red cherry tomatoes and dark purple berries.

"Growing wild?" Ryan asked.

Jak nodded. "Have to look some. Color was pretty easy to see this morning against snow."

"By the Three Kennedys!" Doc hunkered down and picked up one of the tomatoes, which was about the size of his thumb. "Jak, lad, have I mentioned lately how valuable an asset I consider you to be?"

The albino just looked at Doc, then turned the spit another notch.

"I find myself constantly enthralled by the vagaries and mysteries of Mother Nature even in these godforsaken lands." Doc rolled the cherry tomato between his fingers, as if savoring the taste by touch. He tilted his head and glanced at Mildred. "Concerning all the volcanic activity and radiation residue, would it be wise to partake of this repast?"

"Those fruits could be holding in some radioactive waste," Mildred admitted.

"If do," Jak said, "can't be much." He waved at the roasting meat. "They eating it."

"Then let's eat," J.B. said. "Small as they are, if there was anything in them going to kill a body, they'd have died off."

Ryan squatted long enough to pull off a haunch. The animal looked like a ground squirrel of some type, but was the size of a chicken. Surprisingly there was a fair amount of meat on the bones.

He dropped the Steyr over his shoulder and took up a handful of tomatoes and berries. There appeared to be plenty of both. He walked to a nearby outcrop and unlocked his knees until he was in a squatting position that wouldn't allow him to be easily skylined against the mountain.

Krysty came up behind him, her hands as laden as his.

Ryan looked at her, seeing the pinched worry lines over the bridge of her nose as she stared out beyond the pass. "Did you have any bad dreams about Dean?"

She hesitated, then shook her head. "I don't remember dreaming at all, I was so tired. I know I stood watch, stayed away during the whole time, but I don't remember that too clearly, either."

Ryan knew something was bothering his red-haired lover, but she also knew he wouldn't ask. When she was ready to talk about it, she would. It was how things were between them.

Scanning the eastern horizon, Ryan said, "It's been a long time. I need to see him again."

Krysty put an arm across his back and hugged him. "I know, lover. We've all missed him."

"I have to ask myself, though, if he's going to be ready to leave the friends he's made at that school and take up this hard traveling life of ours again."

DEAN WAS READY to be anywhere in all of Deathlands except where he was right at that moment. He sat in one of the straight-backed chairs outside Nicholas Brody's office, arms crossed over his chest and fidgeting. He couldn't seem to find a comfortable place to put his hands.

Jake sat across from him on the small desk where the secretary kept all the records and bits of school business intact and organized. A spray of dried flowers from one of the gardens filled a light green blown-glass vase from the art department.

The door opened, and Dean's heart leaped to the back of his throat.

Phaedra Lemon stepped into the outer office, wearing

the light-colored blouse and denim skirt that were the school's uniform for its female students.

Dean's jaw almost dropped. He hadn't expected her there.

"My dear," Nicholas Brody said in that officious way of his, "I certainly appreciate your willingness to involve yourself in reporting this case of scandalous behavior on the part of these young men. Rest assured, then, that I will do my utmost to resolve these conflicts straightaway."

Phaedra started to say something.

Brody shushed her with an uplifted hand. "My dear, really. I've troubled you for enough of your time."

"Yes, sir." Phaedra dropped a short curtsy, then turned on her heel and walked to Dean. "I did my best to explain to Mr. Brody that you were only returning an earring of a friend's that I'd lost. I told him I thought it was a most gallant thing to do."

"Uh, okay." Dean gazed at her and blinked. Suddenly hot, he pulled at his shirt collar, thinking it had to have shrunk since he'd put it on that morning. He glanced at Brody.

The headmaster stood in the doorway, hands locked behind his back in a familiar pose. His broad face was unreadable.

Phaedra left without another word, her vanilla scent lingering after her.

"Mr. Cawdor," Brody said. "If you would, please." He stepped aside and waved inside his office.

Dean pushed himself out of the chair and swallowed hard. Muties or stickies, he thought, a dozen of them or two dozen, and him armed only with a pea shooter, that would be better than walking into that room.

But he went.

"Tracks," Ryan told J.B.

The Armorer walked forward, automatically unslinging the S&W M-4000 scattergun. Behind the round lenses, his hawk-sharp eyes surveyed the broken terrain. The sun blazed down, growing hotter and melting the snow even more rapidly.

Ryan touched the indentation of a boot that had slipped off a shelf of rock and made a J-shape in the soft earth. Then he pointed out the muddy impressions the boot had made along the rocky trail they were following.

"Fresh," J.B. said.

"Yeah." Ryan ran his fingers through the smear of mud. It was still damp. "Mebbe less than an hour old."

"We could find another way. Down there looks like mebbe we could cross without getting mired too bad."

Ryan studied the bowl-shaped valley nearly a hundred yards below. "That's a pretty wide stretch. If the brushwooders come up on us suddenly, we could get royally fucked."

"We've got to be leaving them behind," J.B. said. "They'd have to be flat traveling to match the pace we've set."

Ryan flicked his eye over the rocky shelf. Here and there were other mud smears. "Whoever it was, he wasn't alone."

"No, but there couldn't be many of them."

"We'll keep on going the way we were." Ryan decided that partly because staying with the rise of stone seemed safest and the least traceable, and partly because he was curious. "Pass the word."

J.B. nodded and went back along the trail.

Carrion eaters circled lazily in the blue sky, their wings dead still. Ryan chose not to view that as an omen, because he wasn't a superstitious man.

"HAVE A SEAT, Mr. Cawdor." Nicholas Brody indicated one of the three straight-backed chairs in front of his desk.

"Yes, sir." Dean sat, dropping his hands into his lap.

Brody's brows drew together. "I await elucidation, Mr. Cawdor, with a calm demeanor yet a certain sense of purpose."

"Yes, sir." Dean had learned early on that when an instructor at the school spoke, it usually meant kitchen duty or mucking out the stables for not being prompt with an answer.

"Aren't you going to say anything?"

"Yes, sir." Dean let out his breath, maintaining eye contact with the older man with difficulty. "I'm sorry." He was bastard sorry he'd gotten caught.

"Your feelings in this regard are both noted and appreciated. But that in no way begins to clarify how you came to be on that structure."

"I climbed, sir."

"Of course you climbed," Brody snapped. "I know very well that you're incapable of sprouting wings like some Icarus. What I endeavor to comprehend is what motivated you to go up there in the first place."

Dean had been dreading that question, but he was prepared. "I don't know, sir."

"Did Miss Lemon invite you up?"

Suddenly Dean felt hot again, his mind preoccupied with the idea that maybe Phaedra was in the habit of asking other boys up to her room and he didn't know about it. That had to be why Brody asked. The possibility made him angry for reasons he wasn't certain of. Maybe her explanation of the earring was to clear herself and not him at all. Confusion followed closely on the heels of his anger.

"No, sir, she didn't," Dean answered truthfully.

"She didn't know you were coming?"

"No, sir." Now Dean wanted to know if Phaedra had asked other boys up to her room on different occasions. Maybe she'd even started the rumor of her sleeping naked herself, just to entice unsuspecting boys to her room so she could push them out windows. "Have I been the only one caught in her room, Mr. Brody?"

The headmaster scowled, not at Dean, but at the thought. "You mean there have been others?"

Dean's stomach rolled over. He was only making matters worse. Surely he would have heard about any others. Everyone had heard of him today. "No, sir."

"Do you know of any other boys who've visited Miss Lemon's room after lights-out?" Brody demanded.

"No, sir."

"Would you lie about that, Mr. Cawdor?"

Dean considered the question, thinking about the

classes in philosophical reasoning he'd had. It hadn't been much, but it had given him a grasp of certain concepts. "Excuse me, sir, but if you have to ask that question, my answer's not going to be worth shit."

"I remind you about your use of bad language, Mr. Cawdor."

"Sorry, sir."

"I want to understand what took you up on that rooftop," Brody said. "This is a serious infraction of the rules of this school."

"Yes, sir."

Brody sighed. "Dean, I am in a hard way here. If your father was someone local, I could call upon him, seek his advice in this matter. At least have some avenue to pursue concerning your punishment. I would not want to see you ostracized from the student body and be rendered a virtual prisoner on these premises. Tell me, young Cawdor, in your own words, why it was that you scaled that building and transgressed into Miss Lemon's bedroom. Give me something upon which I might build a case for your defense, seeing as how you remain unable to defend your actions yourself."

Dean tried, but the words just wouldn't come out. Just saying he went there because he wondered if Phaedra slept naked sounded totally stupe.

"Evidently Miss Lemon feels some allegiance for you," Brody stated. "Otherwise, she'd have been the first clamoring for your head on the proverbial pike. Instead, she marches herself into my office this morning in an effort to clear you. Her explanation of this missing earring is manifestly balderdash. I'm quite certain she realized I believed not a word of it, yet why would she defend you?"

Krysty fell into step beside Doc. "You and I have talked about my powers before."

"At length upon occasion," Doc replied. "As I recall, I have evidenced more real curiosity about your abilities than you yourself. You have always appeared predisposed to accept them on faith."

"That's true." She gazed ahead, spotting Ryan walking point, J.B. strung out behind him a hundred yards at right flank. Watching him, so far away from her if something happened, made a chill run down her spine.

"I assume you have not brought up the subject simply for the prospect of idle conversation."

"Everything I tell you, Doc, you can't tell Ryan."

"That man is savagely keen, dear lady. Mayhap he'll learn just as much from what I omit as he would from what I told him."

"That's the way it has to be," Krysty said. "To protect him. And mebbe Dean, as well."

"You're sure?" Doc's face showed he was troubled, as well as intrigued.

Krysty reached out and took Doc's hand briefly, squeezing it to reassure him as much as herself. Then she told him about the vision she'd had down in the chasm.

"You believe in my powers, don't you, Doc?"

"Believe in them, my dear, without a doubt. My ability to understand them is lacking. Though there were definite experimental studies being done within the Totality Concept, based loosely on scientific research. I never got too close to them. Speculation you cannot adequately quantify is something I never took to very much."

"I have a theory."

"That, my dear Krysty, is a phrase every scientist loves to hear. For with the existence of such a hypothesis, a catalyst may be introduced whereby events may be suitably weighed and measured. Of course, it is possible that your theory will be disproved, putting you squarely back where you started."

"I have to ask myself a couple of things. First I have to ask myself if seeing them mebbe kill each other in that place was the only event that vision really showed me."

"What do you mean?"

"Suppose I saw them, but I couldn't do a thing about it. Couldn't stop it. Suppose my mind couldn't handle seeing such a thing and just created the parts where I went to them and talked to them."

"Ah, my dear, you have truly twisted this puzzle. Was the whole event a fabrication, or were parts of it? If so, which parts?"

It sounded worse coming from Doc.

"So it could be that Ryan and Dean are going to face off

against each other, the one never knowing the other was there, and mebbe kill one or both," Krysty said.

"Or possibly you have managed to intervene in some fashion," Doc said. "Or will."

"It's just as possible, though," Krysty replied, "that the reason I won't be at Ryan's side when this happens later, is because I can't be." She turned and went farther up the mountain, avoiding the chasm Ryan had walked around. "It's just as possible that I could be chilled by then, and no help to him at all."

"I shall make you a promise, my dear," Doc stated in a gentle voice. "As long as I yet live, nothing shall harm you until we see the truth of this vision. I shall become your shield and buckler, and may all that remains holy in this accursed land keep my strength unflagging."

Krysty looked at him. "You're a good friend, Doc."

"It is simple to be a good friend," he replied smiling, "when you're in the company of good friends."

When Ryan went down suddenly in front of her, Krysty at first thought her lover had fallen over a piece of the broken terrain. Then the sound of a blastershot rolled over her.

The only thing that warned Ryan the sniper had a bead on him was the glint of sunlight against glass. But it only amplified the feeling that something predatory was eyeing him. He went down to his right, throwing himself at a stand of grayish green rock jutting up from the broken earth.

The heavy bullet whizzed in, big enough to sound for an instant like incoming artillery. The round smashed a misshapen rock the size of a pumpkin into fragments where he'd been standing.

"Fireblast!" Ryan yelled as he slammed up against the outcrop. His back took the brunt of the impact, but his right ear bumped up against the stone surface hard enough to rip flesh. When he reached up to check it, he found the ear still in one piece but bleeding profusely. He rose to a kneeling position behind the rock.

The second bullet clipped a fist-sized chunk from Ryan's cover and sent stone slivers stinging into his face. He narrowed his eye instinctively. Sinking back behind the rock, he looked to his rear. "J.B., do you know where he's at?"

"Got a perch up there about four hundred yards away. At eleven o'clock."

Ryan checked back along the trail. "Anybody hit?"

They all answered back in short order, letting him know they were intact.

Slithering around the rock, Ryan went lower, staying on his belly against the hot stone. Peering around the corner of his cover, he studied the horizon.

Another glint sparked like white fire nestled on the dark of the stone perch J.B. had to have seen. Ryan moved his head back an instant before another heavy bullet cracked against the rock with enough force to cause a vibration.

"Fireblast!" Ryan said. "Bastard must be up there with a damn cannon." He readied the Steyr, adjusting for the distance.

"Unless I miss my guess," the Armorer called up, "that's a Sharps .50-cal buffalo rifle."

Ryan was familiar with the weapon. In the hands of an expert, the Sharps was capable of making clean kills out to a thousand yards.

On the other side of his cover, the one-eyed man dropped the Steyr against his shoulder and squeezed off two quick rounds. Both of them hit the sniper's position, but he doubted either one hit the man. Still, it gave the shooter something to think about.

Ryan rolled behind cover again and looked back along the mountainside. Below and to his left nearly seventy yards, treetops scrubbed against the side of the defile. The drop might not kill them, but there was every chance someone could break a leg or an arm. Neither prospect would leave them in good shape to escape the brushwooders.

The mountain ridge to the right promised only more heights with not much in the way of protective cover. Every minute they were pinned down brought the brushwooders that much closer, as well. Ryan had no doubts that the shots had been heard.

Pushing himself up against the rock, Ryan yelled, "Stop shooting!"

"Fuck you!" a man's voice yelled back. "You didn't seem to have a problem shooting at us!"

Us meant more than one. Ryan wondered exactly how many more. "That's because you shot first! Wanted you to know we could do this the easy way or the hard way!"

"You people just hold your position! You will not be allowed to reach a greater proximity!"

"What the hell do you want us to do?" Ryan asked.

"Go back the way you came!" The voice echoed off the higher position, rolling across the mountainside.

"Can't do that!"

"That will be your preference, but I assure you that inclination will categorically lead only to your demise!"

"Talks like Doc," J.B. commented.

"Do you see him?" Ryan asked.

"No. He's got himself set in good. Got more sense than to move, either."

"You figure one guy?"

"Mebbe. Bullets come kind of slow. That Sharps is a breechloader. One round at a time at that."

"If we give him multiple targets, he's going to be hard up against it trying to get us all," Ryan said.

Ryan scanned the terrain for the albino teenager, who was nowhere to be seen. "Jak?"

A pebble thudded softly against Ryan's right arm. He turned in that direction and barely made out the youth lying like a second layer of dirt over the stone shelf little more than ten yards away.

"If I give them a target," Ryan said, "do you think you can get up in there behind them without being seen?"

"Daylight makes hard. Mebbe. Drop into trees, could get around."

"J.B."

"I heard you," the Armorer said.

"When I go left, you break right. You get somewhere safe, bang a couple rounds at them to let them know we're still knocking at the door." Ryan spared a last glance at Jak, then pushed himself up from the ground and ran.

He dived behind a low hill of fresh-broken earth, then kicked his feet, pushing up flush against the earthen ridge.

A bullet slammed into the ground and tore away a piece bigger than the palm of Ryan's hand. He pulled the Steyr to his shoulder and fired two rounds at the sniper's perch. Then he was running again, his mind automatically figuring the time it would take a man to jack another round into the Sharps buffalo rifle.

Jak had already disappeared.

"It wasn't Phaedra's fault we were there," Dean said, shifting in his chair and wishing his voice didn't shake the way it did. He hurried on before Brody could say anything. "Calgary come to me—came to me—a couple days ago. He'd done me a good turn, so I owed him. He wanted me to climb up in that dormitory with him, kind of help him along because he couldn't figure a way to do it himself."

"And Miss Lemon didn't invite yourself or young Ventnor into her room?" Brody asked.

"Mr. Brody," Dean said, looking at the headmaster, "you make a big deal here at the school about fair play and honesty. I'm being honest. I'm sorry I broke your rules, I truly am, especially if I'm gonna get kicked out over it. But if you're even thinking for a minute about blaming Phaedra for any of this, well, then, I don't think my dad knew exactly the place he was leaving me at. If Phaedra gets punished and her not guilty in any of this, I'll have to kick my own self out, because I don't want to be part of no place that does that."

Silence filled the room when Dean finished speaking. He couldn't believe he'd talked so much. If he hadn't been mad, he wouldn't have.

Brody broke the silence. "Thank you, Dean, for bringing my responsibility in this matter to the forefront of my mind. And for your forthrightness."

Dean shoved out of the chair and started for the door. He was scared, but he kind of felt good all at the same time.

LESS THAN A MINUTE after they'd started their moves against the sniper's position, Ryan and J.B. worked out a rhythm. The Armorer would snap off a few rounds with his Uzi, splattering the rocks around the unseen gunman, and Ryan would bolt into motion. It took the sniper five or ten seconds to get up the courage to crank off a round. By that time Ryan had usually found his next bit of cover.

Flinging his hands in front of his face as he counted silently, Ryan threw himself forward. He hit the hard ground and slid behind a broken shelf of rock. A .50-caliber round dug into the earth only a few inches from his left boot, leaving a hole he could almost put his fist into.

The next bullet came before Ryan was ready for it, shattering a blocky stone in front of him and sending pieces of it thudding into his legs. He lost his balance and fell, rolling to the side to protect his rifle.

"Ryan!" the Armorer yelled.

"I'm okay." Ryan shoved himself to his feet and took shelter beside an outcrop from the ridge beside him. "Move up while I cover you." He shouldered the Steyr, putting the cross hairs over the sniper's perch. "Go!"

He squeezed off a half-dozen rounds as J.B. broke cover and ran. Even at 250 yards, the shots could have been centered on a pie plate when they struck the sniper's position.

J.B. came up beside him, breathing deep. "It'll work better if we leapfrog it. First me, then you."

Ryan nodded. He glanced back toward the area where Krysty, Doc and Mildred lay waiting. He'd told them to stay put. With too many targets taking the field, the sniper would have had a better chance to get one of them. "Ready?"

"As I ever was," J.B. replied.

"Do it."

The Armorer sidled up to the corner and burned another short burst toward the sniper, then broke cover and ran.

DOWN IN THE BAYOUS where he'd been born, there were stories told around campfires that Jak Lauren could sneak up on mutie gators and take the teeth from their jaws before they knew he was among them. The albino had never contributed to the stories, except by doing things others were too afraid to do or weren't able to do. To Jak it had all been about survival.

And it was survival now that drove him from hiding into an assault up the narrow chimney of rock where the sniper hid. The climb through the tops of the trees at the edge of the cliff face had been simple compared to the vertical challenge in front of him.

The rock chimney stood almost forty feet up, looking like some kind of turret on a castle he'd once seen in a child's faded fairy-tale book. A trail curled around it like a dog's tail wrapped around itself.

The trail was tempting, but Jak knew it would leave him open to anyone keeping watch over it. The only other way to reach the sniper's perch was straight up.

The Sharps rifle banged loudly again, the report echoing in the narrow press of mountaintops surrounding the sniper's perch.

The albino slipped from the cliff's edge and sprinted across the fifteen yards separating him from the stone chimney. He stood at its base, listening intently, trying to hear the slightest scrabble overhead that would indicate he'd been seen or heard.

Satisfied he had escaped notice, he unlaced his boots and stepped out of them. He flexed his toes as he tested the chimney for his first handhold, then took one of his leaf-bladed throwing knives and placed it between his teeth. Leaning into the rock and digging his fingers and toes into the cracks and crevices, he started up.

"Do you see Jak?" Ryan asked, raking the sniper's position through the Steyr's scope. The cross hairs settled comfortably between the albino's shoulder blades, thirty feet up the sheer wall under the overhang.

"Yeah," J.B. replied, punching fresh bullets into the Uzi's magazine. When he put the last one in and shoved the clip home, he doffed his hat long enough to wipe his brow on his shirtsleeve. "Going to have to be careful and not hit him."

"If we stop coming in on the sniper, he's going to know something's wrong."

J.B. nodded. "If Jak runs into trouble, we're not going to do him much good way the hell out here."

Ryan squinted his eye and stared hard at the chimney rock. "You see a trail behind that rock?"

"I was thinking mebbe," the Armorer said. "The distance and the dust, it's hard to make out."

"When he gets to the top of those rocks, I'm going to

make for that trail. If Jak has a real fight on his hands, you take out whoever you see on that ridgeline and leave Jak free."

"Sure."

Ryan readied himself, ignoring the cramp in his left calf that came from the constant dodging and powering into sprints. The chimney rock was still nearly 130 yards away.

The brushwooders had seriously cut their lead, though, and were drawing closer by the minute.

"Go," J.B. said, opening up with the Uzi.

Even as the machine pistol belched an angry snarl of death, Ryan shoved himself from behind cover and ran, counting.

CLINGING TO THE SIDE of the chimney rock, Jak saw the long barrel of the Sharps buffalo rifle stick out over the lip of the ledge. It was still beyond his reach.

Sweat from his efforts and the residual humidity in the air drenched his clothing. His arms and legs trembled slightly with the constant strain he'd expended crawling the past thirty-five feet.

He moved his left hand, prying for his next handhold, precariously balanced on his right foot and holding tight with his other hand. He pressed his left knee against the stone, finding enough of a grip to feel confident about searching for the new hold. Going down at this point would be harder than continuing up.

Shoving his fingers into the small crevice as hard as he could, he heard the definitive bang of the Sharps as the round was touched off. The hold he'd discovered was a good one. He eased his weight around, searching for a foothold and found it.

Jak shoved himself up, gaining nearly two feet this

time. His right shoulder blade spasmed, and he nearly let out a foul curse before he caught himself.

The barrel of the Sharps nosed over the lip of rock above him.

Just as he was getting ready to shift his weight again, the irregular notch of stone he clasped in his left hand gave way. Bits of rock tumbled down the side of the stone chimney.

Swinging wildly for just a moment, Jak helplessly stared at the ground nearly forty feet below, hanging by his other hand as first one foot, then the other slid free. An effort of iron-willed determination kept the fingers of his right hand in place, supporting all his weight.

The big rifle banged again, and the echoes cracked against the open spaces where Ryan, J.B. and the others were pinned down.

Slowly, and in agony, Jak pulled himself back into place. Once his feet were on firm footing again, he pushed himself upward, not wanting to give his muscles a chance to cramp up. Fire burned through his limbs and back.

Bullets from Ryan's Steyr slammed into the rock beside the sniper's position, stone splinters raining in a sudden hail.

Jak narrowed his eyes against it and kept moving. When the Sharps thundered again, he was ready. As the big .50-caliber rifle pulled back and the breech opened, the albino shoved himself onto the ledge. He caught Ryan's sudden breakneck run from the corner of his eye.

Then Jak could see nothing but the bottom of the ledge as he pushed himself up with both hands. Saliva leaked down over his chin from carrying the knife, cool in the winds that rushed over the chimney top.

The man with the Sharps rifle spotted him first.

"Bernsen!" The man with the Sharps was a scraggly old man who looked as if he'd been worn whipcord tough by a hard, adventurous life. His gray beard was tangled, cut square at the bottom only a few inches below his chin. His silver hair was pulled back in a single stand that hung on his bony shoulder like the tail of a dead animal. He wore hiking boots, jeans and a black-and-red-checked flannel shirt that had the sleeves rolled up enough to reveal the same orange-and-blue tattoo on his inner forearm that had been on the dead man. He fumbled, trying to insert another cartridge into the Sharps.

"Get down, Hoyle!" Bernsen yelled. He was a few years younger than his companion, broader built and softer by the look of him. A paunch settled gracelessly into his lap, and he didn't seem certain of the long-barreled Dan Wesson .41 Magnum blaster he held in both hands. However, he brought the weapon around quick enough.

Jak slipped the leaf-bladed knife from his teeth and flipped it at the man, deliberately missing the man's head only by inches. Ryan wanted them alive if it could be managed.

Bernsen ducked, rolling with a lack of coordination to another area behind his partner's position, and yelped in fear.

Still in motion, Jak leaped at Hoyle. The old man had the cartridge in the breech and was pulling the lever closed. Fisting another knife from the top of his boot, Jak batted away the barrel of the Sharps with his free arm. The rifle exploded as the hammer fell, sending the bullet ricocheting from the rock behind the ledge.

Closing on the man, Jak shouldered Hoyle in the stomach hard enough to knock him off balance. Before his opponent could recover, Jak stepped in behind him and seized his ponytail.

Bernsen tracked them with the .41 Magnum blaster. "Get down, Hoyle! You're in the way! Give me a clean shot!"

Hoyle struggled to get away, throwing his weight to one side and swinging back with the butt of the Sharps.

Already expecting the move, Jak shifted with the man, staying behind him and avoiding the rifle butt. Jak brought the knife to the man's throat, yanking back on the ponytail to bare it even further. The keen edge lay over the jugular.

Bernsen fired anyway, the bullet whizzing less than a foot from Jak's head. Awkwardly the heavy man thumbed back the hammer.

"Stop," Jak ordered in a harsh voice, "or die!" He nicked Hoyle's neck with the blade to emphasize his point. Three bloody tears wept from the small incision and trickled down the man's sweaty neck.

Instead, eyes wide and round with fear, Bernsen leveled the blaster to fire again.

Ryan found the trail behind the chimney rock and threw himself into an assault on the steep downgrade at the same time the big rifle roared from above. He didn't hear J.B.'s Uzi chatter into life, so he knew the Armorer hadn't had a shot.

Keeping the Steyr across his chest, his attention divided between the loose stones under his feet and the narrow corkscrew leading up into the chimney rock, he ran as hard as he could. Spots danced crazily in his vision.

A blaster—some large caliber—boomed only a few paces ahead of him.

Ryan came around the corner in time to see the heavy man taking up slack on the weapon's trigger a second time. Jak was covered by the man standing in front of him, the guy pressed into service by the knife blade held at his throat, but there was every possibility that the bullets would pass through the human shield and hit Jak.

Bringing up the rifle, Ryan fired four quick rounds, spacing them in an uneven line only inches above the blaster-wielder's head. The man ducked instinctively and brought around his weapon.

Ryan threw himself forward and chopped down with the Steyr's barrel, cracking the man viciously across the wrists as the blaster went off. The bullet sped by only inches from Ryan's head.

The man screamed in pain and dropped the heavy weapon. Before he could make an attempt to recover it, Ryan kicked it away, then booted the man in the side.

The man raised his hands in defense and buried his face in his arms. "Don't! Please don't hurt me any more!"

"Go ahead and kill us," the man Jak held said, "or leave him alone. He's not been out in this mean world overmuch. Not used to rough handling."

The man's words made Ryan curious about what had brought them to the Western Islands area, but not overly so. He picked up the revolver and stuck it inside his belt. Two backpacks with aluminum frames leaned against the stone wall, out of sight beyond the ledge.

"Stay away from those packs," Ryan growled.

Keeping his head buried, the man nodded.

Ryan looked at Jak.

"Hoyle," the teenager said, releasing his hold on the man's hair. "That one's Bernsen." He leaned down and picked up the Sharps.

Ryan stepped to the ledge overlooking the mountainside. Moving so he could be seen, he waved to Krysty, Doc and Mildred. Immediately the three began to move up.

The brushwooders weren't far behind, almost within rifle range, as a few of them proved by firing rounds that fell less than thirty yards behind Krysty's position. The companions had lost whatever edge mobility had given them in the long minutes they'd spent being pinned down by sniper fire.

"You got them?" Ryan asked Jak.

"Do now." Jak had his .357 Magnum blaster in hand as he waved Hoyle into place beside Bernsen.

Reluctantly, acting as though he was just waiting for an opportunity, the bearded man sat.

Ryan fixed both men with a harsh look. "Up to you now if you live or die." He reloaded the Steyr and slung it. "Me, I don't much care. Easier to chill you than watch you." He glanced at Jak. "If they try anything, chill them both, then push them over the edge and let the vultures have them."

"Okay." Jak squatted, his pistol resting easily on one thigh.

"I'm going to take a look around and be back in a couple minutes." Ryan started up the grade at the back of the chimney rock. Simply outrunning the brushwooders was no longer an option. It remained to be seen what was left.

"Get down!" J.B. yelled.

Ryan stepped into the cave mouth he'd found at the back of the rock chimney an instant before the explosion shook the ground. He gazed down the long dark throat of the tunnel spearing out in front of him as debris slammed into the ground around him. He couldn't see the other end and had no inkling of what might lie in wait.

"Fireblast," he swore as small-arms fire opened up above. He turned and shoved his way back up the steep path that had led him to the cave.

The companions were spread across the crest of the chimney rock when he doubled back, seeking cover where they could find it. The Armorer had taken up the Sharps buffalo rifle.

Black smoke wafted up from somewhere below the edge of the rock, and a wave of heat washed over Ryan as he threw himself down beside J.B. and brought the Steyr forward.

"They've set up a mortar," the Armorer said, pulling the butt of the Sharps into his shoulder. The original peep sight had been replaced with a telescopic lens. J.B. fitted himself into the eyepiece. "Got close."

"We can't hold this position," Ryan said. "I found a cave back there."

J.B. coolly took up slack on the trigger. "Any idea where it goes?"

"I was figuring on asking our company."

The Sharps banged, slamming against the Armorer's shoulder. Immediately the wiry man levered the action and reached for a bullet in the bandolier they'd removed from the prisoners.

Down on the incline, one of the brushwooders manning the mortar yelped and went down clutching his thigh.

Ryan crept back to the prisoners, staying low, and stopped in front of Hoyle. Bernsen kept his arms wrapped over his head and mewled piteously. Doc kept cautious watch with his Le Mat blaster.

"The cave," Ryan prompted. "That's where you were headed."

Hoyle hesitated, his lower lip pinched tight against his teeth.

"They've got another one away," J.B. called.

Before the words trailed off, a second explosion rocked the vicinity, throwing up a fresh shower of pebbles and stone splinters. The detonation caused momentary deafness.

"Getting closer," J.B. warned. "Another round or two the way they're improving, they'll put one right on top of us."

"Talk," Ryan grated. "Either way it goes, we got no

choice but that cave. If you hold back on me, I'll dangle you over the edge of this rock and drop you down to those brushwooders. If you get lucky, mebbe you'll connect with a mortar round before you hit bottom."

"We were going to the cave," Hoyle admitted grudgingly. "There's a river down below. Runs underground for a time."

"Then why try to chill us?"

"We checked earlier. River was too high to try. We were waiting for it to go down. We got a raft down there."

Ryan glanced at the rest of his group. "Jak, Krysty," Ryan said, "you two take point. Double yellow. I didn't hear anything, but that doesn't mean it's clear. Doc, give me a hand with the prisoners." He grabbed the shoulder of Hoyle's jacket and hoisted the man to his feet. "J.B., Mildred, you've got our backs."

Together the group moved toward the cave. Before they reached it, another mortar round impacted against the chimney rock nearly a dozen feet above their heads. A great tumble of split stone came slithering free, scattering across the rocky shelf under their feet, nearly knocking them to the ground.

"Get up and move," Ryan growled, yanking his prisoner to his feet. Hoyle had taken a stone ricochet to the side of his head. Streamers of twisting crimson ran down his temple and jaw, tracking across his neck before being staunched in his shirt collar.

Jak and Krysty vanished into the gaping maw of the cave. Bullets pocked the sides of the opening, spitting small shards that bit at Ryan's face. He hustled Hoyle inside the cave, moving the man forcibly. A blur of movement triggered instinctive reflex action on Ryan's part.

He shifted hands with the Steyr, then cleared leather with the SIG-Sauer. Snap-firing, he aimed the 9 mm blaster at the four men who'd climbed the trail up the side of the chimney rock and pulled off successive rounds as quickly as he could. He wasn't sure if he hit anything, but the bullets sent most of the brushwooders scurrying for cover.

One of the men leaned forward with a scattergun. Ryan lifted the SIG-Sauer, tracking on to his attacker. A heartbeat before his finger pulled through the trigger, bloody mist evacuated the side of the brushwooder's head, sucking away chunks of his skull and blobs of brain matter.

Ryan put another round through the man's left eye, yanking the head around almost 180 degrees. When he glanced to the side, he saw Mildred standing there, the Czech target weapon held securely in both her hands.

J.B. drew his lover into the crook of one arm and started her toward the cave. Bullets beat a deadly tattoo against the rock surfaces in their wake.

As the Armorer and Mildred raced across the open space, Ryan triggered a fusillade of bullets that ripped across the tops of the rocks the brushwooders were using for cover. Foul oaths cracked the air over the din of the blaster as the men ducked into hiding and remained there.

J.B. unbuckled the Smith & Wesson M-4000 scattergun from his back and tossed it to Ryan. "Close quarters like this, if those brushwooders try shoving into the cave, it'll be just like a gren going off in their faces."

Ryan readied the weapon and raked his vision across the dark inner recesses of the cave until he spotted Hoyle. Doc was moving Bernsen along at a fair clip. "Go," Ryan ordered.

Hoyle moved out at once.

The trail leading down into the cave was twisting and narrow. The heat rolled into the opening after them. In short order, though, the temperature started to drop rapidly. The perspiration that had settled under Ryan's clothing suddenly turned to mobile ice beads that tracked shivers along his skin.

"I hear running water," Mildred said.

Ryan heard it, too, a rapid splashing that sloshed wetly against stone. He blinked his eye in an effort to speed up the change to night vision. The rock floor split into a V, widening rapidly. In the mouth a raging torrent gushed from an underground schism and overfilled the space left between the legs of the V. Water twisted and spilled over the rock ledges on either side of the river, making the way chancy, its roar rendering conversation difficult.

The incline grew sharper, tilting down into the shadows that swallowed up the other end of the cave system. Debris choked the river in a handful of places, flotsam and jetsam from civilization in the form of timbers, chairs, bits of clothing and toys, all of it knitted together by clumps of weeds and tangles of branches, some of them still carrying leaves.

Ryan glanced over his shoulder and saw Mildred and J.B. working their way after him. "How much farther to the raft?" he asked Hoyle.

"Fifty yards mebbe. Hard to tell in this."

Gunfire flashed near the mouth of the cave. The men standing in front of it were skylined by the sunlight beyond, broken shadows against the darker and deeper silhouettes of rock. The positions of others were given away by muzzle-flashes.

J.B. cut loose with the Uzi and zipped a line of deadly demarcation in the middle of the group. There were at least six shadows, maybe more.

The next turn in the tunnel caught Ryan by surprise. One instant Hoyle was moving in front of him, light against the black rock, and in the next the man had disappeared.

The breaking wave of whitecaps smashing against the

ledge gave Ryan an indication of where the turn was. He pressed in close against the rock and followed it. Water swirled up to his knees, fighting against the gravity and the insistence of the force spewing it out of the underground crevice.

"Lover."

Squinting, Ryan peered past Hoyle and spotted Krysty standing under a low overhang of rock. Jagged fangs thrust down from the rooftop, closing the cave up like a man dying of lockjaw. Scarcely four feet remained above the surface of the churning river.

The black water spread across thirty or forty feet of the cave opening, well out of the regular channel it had carved over decades. Judging from the way the white waves crashed against the walls with dulled roars, then swirled madly back in on themselves, the water level wasn't dropping. It was rising dramatically. The cave widened out at this spot, at the bottom of the incline. A bowl-shaped depression created by the regular fall of water over the years had left worn rings in the pale alabaster of the limestone. The shaft where the river continued was eight or ten feet across. The water roared into the spillway like a thing possessed.

"Dark night!" J.B. breathed.

"Hasn't gone down," Hoyle said. "Only a crazy fucker would try to go down that river in the shape it's in."

"Where's the raft?" Ryan demanded.

"You can't be serious." Hoyle stared at him wide-eyed. "We'd all die."

Krysty walked through the water with difficulty to join them.

"If we stay here," Ryan told him, "we're dead for sure. With a raft mebbe we got some kind of chance. That water's going somewhere, bastard quick."

"It goes underground."

Without warning, a large wave of water rolled forward, drenching them. A scream sounded behind them, then a brushwooder came hurtling over the fall, limbs flailing in the weak light as he shot out into empty space for an instant. The man hit the water and sank in the churning depths. A moment later he reappeared, yards from where he'd gone under, only long enough to suck in a breath as he was swept toward the bottleneck. Then he went under again and didn't come back up.

Hoyle stared with grim fascination at the bottleneck where the brushwooder had disappeared.

"The raft," Ryan repeated coldly. "Otherwise, I break both your knees with a rock and toss you in the river."

"Over here." Hoyle peered at the cave walls for a moment, then got his bearings. He made his way carefully along the ledge to a spot where a triangle of rocky spikes jutted from the wall. "I'll need some help." He put his hands on either side of the area around the three rocks and started to pull.

Ryan stepped forward and added his own muscle to the effort. The section of rock came out slowly, with a grating sound that ripped through the swish and swirl of the raging river and a vibration of friction that ran through Ryan's arms.

"Hiding place for emergency rations and our gear," Hoyle explained. "We've used this river before."

"You didn't come up it," Ryan said.

"No. Usually we use it to go down. Sometimes we can travel two, mebbe three days by river. A lot faster and easier than going overland."

The block of stone came out faster at the end, nearly tumbling Ryan off balance. Dropping the heavy weight into the water moving just below his ribs now, he reached out and caught a fistful of Hoyle's shirt as the man nearly slid back into the torrent threatening to pluck them from their perch.

Krysty reached into the opening and dragged out an olive oval of thick plastic and vinyl. She held on to it with difficulty as the river fiercely tried to take it away from her.

"I've got it," Hoyle said, closing his hands over the vinyl with Krysty's.

"Ryan," J.B. called.

Even as Ryan turned to look, bullets lanced into the whirling caldron of water filling the basin. At least two men clung to the ledge above them, shooting blindly down into the water in an effort to take out their targets. J.B. triggered two 3-round bursts at the men, but they'd moved back into the rock and made difficult targets. They were also evidently wearing body armor of some type, because the Armorer's rounds knocked dust from their clothing.

Ryan raised the S&W shotgun to his shoulder and squeezed the trigger. At the distance, with the choke adjusted, the razor-edged fléchettes spread into almost a man-size pattern.

They slashed into the two brushwooders and sliced them from their position, cutting easily through whatever body armor the men might have scavenged. Their screams of pain ended suddenly when they dropped into the raging water.

When Ryan looked back at the raft, he saw that Jak had joined Krysty and Hoyle in trying to maneuver it above the water. The oval's size made it awkward; the footing made the efforts treacherous.

Hoyle reached into the center of the oval, snaking a hand through the folded wrinkles, then yanked. As he withdrew his hand, the oval started to unfold on its own with a prolonged hiss.

"Compressed air," Hoyle said. "It'll fill the raft. Scavenged this emergency raft and a couple like it over the years from ships and boats that went down around Vancouver a few years back when I was working on trade and barter for my next home-cooked meal. When I signed on with the Heimdall Foundation, I figured one of them might come in handy one day here." He shook his head. "I sure do hate being right when it comes to shit like this."

The raft continued to flop, and the dimensions became clear. It would be a tight fit, but Ryan thought they would all squeeze in. The way he figured it, if things got tight, the Heimdall Foundation men were ballast.

"What's this you were saying about the Heimdall Foundation?" Doc demanded over the roar of the river.

"Place I work for," Hoyle answered. "Bernsen knows more about it." The man struggled to hang on to the raft as the current tried to rip it from him, Krysty and Jak.

Doc turned his attention to the man he was keeping watch over. Bernsen had turned green in the dim light, his attention focused on the bottleneck of cave walls. Doc shook the man and began to question him.

Ryan ignored the conversation. The level of the water had risen, leaving precious little more than three feet beneath the cavern ceiling where it plunged through the orifice leading out of the basin. From the looks of things, the water was going to fill all the space within minutes.

Ryan took a length of rope from his pack and cut off a ten-foot piece with the panga.

"Watch it with that knife," Hoyle shouted. "You cut a hole in this raft, and we got no chance at all."

Working quickly, Ryan slid the panga back into its sheath, then tied one end of the section of rope to a loop on the raft. Checking the wall at his side, he found a notched rock that would allow him to tie the other end.

"When we start loading people into that raft," he explained, "we're not going to be able to hold it. This way we can keep it steady until we're prepared."

He cut another ten-foot length and passed it to Jak. "The side, not the other end. So we'll be able to cut it away."

Jak tied the rope on to the raft without comment, understanding at once.

In seconds the raft was as stable as they could make it. The vinyl craft jumped on the water, now at least a couple inches higher, and pulled at the tethers.

At Ryan's command, the companions loaded into the raft one at a time. The additional weight made it sink even more into the water, and the river's pull on it grew stronger.

Ryan pulled himself into the tangle and press of bodies. Krysty took hold of his clothing and aided his efforts. Even as Ryan tried to find a comfortable position, a small knot of brushwooders took up a line along the ledge leading down to the basin. A spark flared in the hands of one, then caught and became a miniature crimson star that threw off a spitting pink light to quickly fill the tidal cavern.

"Flare," Jak said.

Mildred raised her pistol and pulled through a round just as the brushwooders spotted the raft. With the way the raft bobbed and twisted, it was impossible to hit anything she aimed at. Her shot went well wide and high of its intended mark.

The brushwooders brought their weapons to bear.

Ryan ripped the panga from his hip and grabbed the forward lip of the raft, hauling himself over Hoyle. "Jak, cut away!"

The albino had one of the leaf-shaped throwing knives

in his hand in an eye blink, the keen edge sliding through the stabilizing rope at the side of the raft. Immediately the craft jumped like a fish hitting the end of a line after a long run. Incredibly it lifted partially out of the water, threatening to turn crossways in the chop of the swirling currents.

Bullets plopped into the water from the brushwooders' guns, the sharp reports of the weapons punching through the steady roar of the rising river.

Ryan slashed with the panga. Off balance aboard the writhing raft, he parted the rope less than two inches from the vinyl air pocket forming the side. There was no time to brace himself against the sudden lunge the raft took. He felt Krysty's hands at his back, taking hold of his belt and adding her weight to his.

"Hold on, lover," she called.

The river took them, shoving them at the bottleneck at an unbelievable rate of speed. They missed the bottleneck opening by several feet and slammed into the wall. The raft rode the trapped current up out of the water, crashing the left side and a large portion of the bottom against the immovable rock.

Ryan grabbed one of the tie-downs and threw an arm across Krysty's shoulders, pulling her close to him. There was nothing else any of them could do. The river had them at its mercy, and it was a toss-up as to whether the raft would remain on top of the water or plummet into its black depths.

Twisting suddenly, the raft came around, shifting ends and plunging down the dark throat of the tunnel. The light of the flare vanished behind them, though the brushwooders' bullets hammered into the sides of the tunnel for a few seconds more.

Ryan kept his arm tight around Krysty and took a quick head count before all light left them. Everyone had made it.

The dark water sucked away all vestiges of light from the flare and left them in darkness. Ryan hung on fiercely, riding out the fight the river was giving them so effortlessly. Though he tried not to consider it, he knew that it would only take one sharp rock to rip out the side of the raft.

Abruptly a light flared into life at the front of the raft, splashing against the cavern roof not more than two feet above their heads. In the forward end of the raft, Jak swung the flashlight he'd freed from his gear downriver.

Ryan shifted a little, rising but not getting too close to the low ceiling of rock. They were traveling fast; the way the water-worn limestone passed them above and on both sides told him that. The stone looked green in the yellow light of the flash, tracked in horizontal layers that showed years of formation. The rough edges announced the damage that had been done by the monster quakes and passage of water over the decades since skydark. It was possible that some of the cavern had been in existence even before the world had ended.

The raft continued to bob and jump, following the irregular path of the tunnel. Jak held the flashlight, shifting it to illuminate the way.

"How far before we slow down?" Ryan yelled to Hoyle.

"Don't know. I never got on the water when it was like this." Hoyle's gaze remained transfixed on the dark water before them.

The tunnel took another twist, almost falling back on itself and causing the raft to ride high enough up on the side to slam into the low ceiling. When Jak got the flashlight turned in the new direction, there was barely enough time for any of them to register the sudden drop-off facing them before they were shooting through it.

Ryan's stomach twisted in protest at the sudden feeling of weightlessness, then tried to pull through itself when the raft slammed back into the water.

"By the Three Kennedys," Doc exploded, "I should not like to be forced to endure that inauspicious travail again!"

Ryan silently agreed, but he could tell by the lurch of the raft that they were already picking up speed. He watched as Jak brought the light around. The raft swung sideways slowly in current, pulled faster still by the river.

For a moment it looked as if the river channel was widening and deepening.

Then the blank wall rose before them without warning. The water smashed up against it, cresting six or seven feet to the broken stalactites above it. Bats fluttered in the beam of Jak's flashlight, bits and pieces of shadows startled from their resting places.

"Oh, shit!" Mildred exclaimed.

Then there was no more time. Ryan buried himself in the raft, drawing Krysty down with him. The water wasn't filling the chamber; it was being drawn away completely underground. But he had no way of knowing how far it went. He had one brief hope that the raft might somehow manage to stay afloat on the river without being drawn into the undertow. If it did, there was a possibility they could wait out the time it took to drain most of the floodwaters from the river.

The raft smashed into the wall hard enough to jar Ryan's teeth and his eyeball in its socket. He felt the pitch and yaw of the raft beneath him, then it overturned and started taking on water.

"Let go," Krysty told him.

Ryan released her, knowing she was right. There was no way to stay together in the deluge. He squeezed her hand, then released her. He had time to suck in most of one deep breath before the undertow reached out for them and yanked them under. There was no way to fight against the pull. Concentrating on survival, Ryan went with it.

The chill of the river coiled around him, filling his senses with a rush of confusion. He spotted Jak ahead of him, the albino highlighted by a nimbus of weak yellow light from the flashlight he still held. The youth's other hand was wrapped tightly in one of the equipment loops.

Ryan didn't know if the albino was hanging on to the raft on purpose or if he'd been trapped by it.

With greater width and breadth, the raft acted like a kite caught in a strong wind, moving ahead of the rest of the companions quickly.

The bubble of light surrounding Jak faded with the distance, but held long enough to show the underwater exit for the river. Ryan watched the raft and Jake slide into the huge hole, then they disappeared.

He let himself go, riding out the current, remembering how the rest of the companions had been spaced out around him, all of them caught up in the river. The current pulled him deeper still, and even colder water ran rampant there, an ice wall that slammed him through the outlet. His left hand slapped into the edge of the opening with enough force to create a blaze of pain, followed almost immediately by numbness.

The water picked up speed, shooting him forward with greater intensity. He covered his head with his arms, hoping that he didn't go up against the tunnel's side. The impact would probably be enough to kill him. It would probably also be enough to kill any of the others. But they were all out of choices, and the ace was on the line.

GAZING THROUGH his binoculars, Hayden LeMarck watched the brushwooders walk away from the chimney rock. None of the outlanders appeared to be in their midst.

"Mebbe they got away," Wallis Thoroughgood said. "Even if they'd killed the outlanders, the brushwooders probably would have brought out the corpses."

LeMarck studied the brushwooders. All of them looked haggard and worn. None of them had any of the outlanders' weapons, giving him even more reason to believe the group had managed another escape. That possibility, however, was also daunting because this final escape might have taken them from him, as well.

"Don't appear to be as many of them as there was," the sec commander said.

"Three, four," Thoroughgood replied, "mebbe five of them are missing. Probably means they ran into the outlanders somewhere up in those rocks."

"And the outlanders got away." LeMarck dropped the binoculars into his pack. "Renstell, given that there's a point of entry to the river in those rocks, where do you figure they'd come out topside again?"

Renstell narrowed his eyes against the sun as he looked out across the broken landscape. "Four or five miles away. But they'd be fools to try that river now, sir."

"Why?"

"That blizzard last night, come this morning with the sun melting it all down the way it did, that river's gonna be raging. There're places in the tunnels where the river goes that fill up sudden when a man least expects it. They went into it, there's every chance they're going to drown like rats before they get through it."

The sec boss watched the brushwooders making their way across the land almost three hundred yards away. He wished he knew what was going on inside, hoping that Renstell was wrong about the outlanders' drowning.

LIGHT PENETRATED the water above Ryan's head. Weakened from lack of oxygen, battered by the river current and the stone channel it rushed through, he forced his body to work. He stroked for the surface, kicking as strong as he was able.

Long seconds later, stubbornly refusing to give in to the

need to breathe, his head came up out of the water. He allowed himself two breaths, swiveling around to get his bearings.

The river was quieter here, but continued to exert a steady pull. It was also much wider, sixty or seventy feet at least. But it was still contained in a cavern. Stalactites lined the uneven rooftop nearly twenty feet above. Cracks opened the dome in places, allowing thin streamers of yellow light to pour in and give the cave a semblance of twilight at best.

He took another deep breath, then plunged under the water, angling down. There was enough light to see a few yards in all directions. Fish darted past him, some no longer than one of his fingers, and others greater than the length of his arms. Even though chilled by the cold river water, he still felt an arctic kiss thrill along his nape as he thought about what might be in the river with him.

When he surfaced, Ryan saw J.B. and Mildred less than twenty feet away. They managed on their own, hacking, coughing and spluttering up river water. Hoyle bobbed to the surface behind them.

"Dry land's over that way," Ryan called out, knowing it would take a few seconds for their eyes to adjust to the dim lighting. He pointed.

J.B. looked around, managing to hang on to his fedora while he floated. "Where's Doc, Jak and Krysty?"

"Don't know." Ryan went down again, kicking violently, knowing they were running out of time. He met Krysty, who was coming up, pulling the slack form of Doc after her, barely illuminated in the ghostly water.

Grabbing a shoulder of the old man's frock coat, Ryan helped Krysty swim to the surface. "Let me have him," Ryan said when they were up.

Krysty nodded, breaking away and treading water. She

gasped, the sound echoing over the flat planes of the water and reverberating in the cave over the movement of the river current.

Ryan levered an arm under Doc's chin and started for shore.

Dean lay on his back on his bed in the boys' dorm, his hands clasped behind his head. On the top bunk, he was almost lifted from the general hubbub from his room-mates, and from the din oozing in from the hallway and the other rooms on that floor of the building.

He focused on a fly clinging to the ceiling. Maybe it wouldn't have been so bad to have been born a fly. And flies, Dean noted, seemed to be happiest when they were face deep in a pile of shit, which was exactly where he figured he was.

A heavy step trod on the wooden floor of the dorm, causing boards to creak.

"Uh-oh," someone said, signaling a mad dash that got all of them cleaning up their bunks. Paper swished as it was put away, and books made leaden thunks dropping into footlockers in front of the beds.

Dean didn't move. There wasn't any way he could get into more trouble.

"Boys," Nicholas Brody's deep voice rumbled, "I'd like to pass a few moments with Mr. Cawdor if I may."

Dean sat up on the bed, his bare feet dangling over the edge. He'd showered that morning, and his hair was still damp. He wore only the school-designated T-shirt and his underwear.

His three roommates moved back to their beds, looking at Brody but trying desperately not to meet the man's glance.

"Alone," Brody said.

Immediately the three boys jumped up and herded out into the hallway, relief evident in the way they carried themselves.

Brody closed the door behind them, then reached into Dean's footlocker and brought out a pair of pants. He tossed them to Dean. "In proper decorum, if you please, Mr. Cawdor." He turned to face the window, hands locked behind his back as he stared out into the courtyard where the flag waved in the breeze from the pole.

"Didn't know you were coming," Dean said as he shoved one leg into the trousers, "or I'd have been ready." As much trouble as he was in, not getting dressed as asked would have been the least of his problems. But he had respect for Nicholas Brody.

"I really wish you had not ventured up onto that building, Mr. Cawdor," the headmaster said tiredly. "Really, I wish you had not."

"What's going to happen to me, sir? For what I did."

The headmaster grimaced. "That remains to be seen, lad. I am faced with a most difficult situation. Mr. Ventnor was summarily excused from the rest of his classes this year, over his father's insistent arguments and hostilities. He'll not be returning to this school without due attention in regards to this situation, nor without an official apology to this institution and to Miss Lemon. But that was due in part to his own licentious behavior and how he handled the whole affair, as well as his father's bullheadedness."

"Is that what's going to happen to me?" Dean felt his stomach lurch. He didn't realize how much he was going to miss the school, or how much the idea that he could get kicked out sickened him.

"I find myself in quite a quandary in regards to you." Brody's gaze was bright, direct. "You lied to me by omission, telling me you knew not what led you to stray to that building this morning. Surely the response of an irresponsible and churlish boy. Yet you stepped forward when Miss Lemon's integrity was in danger of becoming forfeit. An act of a young gentleman who knows there must be a recompense for actions foolishly taken, as well as the primacy of innocence being protected and a sense of fair play. Neither Mr. Ventnor nor his progenitor handled the situation with even a fraction of the courage you exhibited."

"Will I be allowed to stay?"

Brody shook his head. "I don't know, lad. I'll have to think on it. Punishment in these regards must be strictly adhered to, else the student body at this institution will run amok and even more stringent measures will need be applied to bring them into line once more. I set those standards, and I don't mean to see them broken."

"Yes, sir." Dean wished he could break eye contact, but found he couldn't.

"Keep your chin up, Mr. Cawdor. However it turns out, you've kept at least a portion of my respect today. A most important portion, I might add. And maybe earned self-respect in your own eyes that you will see once we are days past this present encumbrance. I shall try to get word to your father by the means I have open to me, and we shall see what must be done. Until then, you'll be confined to your quarters."

"Yes, sir."

Brody left.

As soon as the door closed, Dean tossed himself back onto his bed. He felt like crying, something he hadn't allowed himself to do in a long time. At the same time he felt like kicking down the walls of his room. Instead, he lay on his back and threw a forearm across his eyes to block out his vision.

"Cawdor."

For a moment Dean was unsure if he'd actually heard the voice or if it was his imagination.

"Dean Cawdor."

Dean unwrapped his arm from his eyes. He craned his head around and looked at the doorway.

Ethan Perry, tall and muscled, a blue-black undercoating of beard and mustache still showing through fresh-shaved chin, stood looking in at him.

"What do you want?" Dean asked.

Perry smiled. He had the easy confidence of the natural athlete. Some few months short of eighteen, Perry was the most gifted of those in the phys-ed class at the school. Whenever a game was played—football, baseball or dodge ball—everyone wanted to be on Perry's side.

"Heard about what happened this morning," Perry said. "I know Ventnor's too gutless to do something like that, so I figure it was you who put together the raid on the girls' dorm. Pretty clever."

Dean just looked at the other boy, hardly breathing. He

and Perry had shared some differences out on the playing field. Perry had a group of ten boys that he ran roughshod over. They were the best the school had to offer when it came to sports. They ate together, slept in the same dorms and did their studying together. When one of them scored low on a test, the others pitched in to help him study harder so the group remained unbroken. No other team the school fielded was ever able to defeat Perry's team.

The reason Perry didn't like Dean was that in individual effort, Dean bested several if not all of the ten boys. Sometimes that included Perry himself.

Perry leaned against the door and stuck a toothpick in his mouth. The other boys who belonged in the room stayed out in the hallway. "Me and my buddies are doing some exercises tonight with Mr. Solomon. Thought mebbe you'd like to join us."

Solomon was the new phys-ed teacher. At least, he was new by the school's standards. Payton Solomon had only been with Nicholas Brody's staff for the past seventeen months. During that time, the phys-ed teacher had helped mold Perry's group into the unit it was.

"Why me?" Dean asked.

Perry shrugged. "Mr. Solomon thought it might be a good idea. Me, I don't think we need you, but he was pretty insistent. Conover busted a rib this morning during one of our martial-arts sessions, and Mr. Solomon wanted you to fill in tonight."

"Doing what?"

Perry shrugged again. "Does it matter?"

Dean was silent. Really it didn't. It was a chance to get out and do something. "Does Mr. Solomon know I've been told to stay in my quarters?"

"Probably." Perry made a show of looking around.

"Doesn't appear to be anybody gonna make sure that's what you do. So I guess whether you stay or go is mostly up to you."

A well of resentment opened up in Dean. He'd been more or less abandoned at the school by his dad, even after he'd voiced an objection to coming there. He'd minded most of the bigger rules, his mostly minor infractions more inconsiderate than rebellious. It wasn't until he'd gone to see Phaedra Lemon that things seemed to come apart.

And Phaedra hadn't appeared all that angry about his coming to see her.

So he couldn't understand how Brody had a real bone to pick with him.

"If I get caught, will Mr. Solomon talk to Mr. Brody for me?" Dean asked.

"Fuck that," Perry said. "None of us are gonna get caught." He smiled. "We'll even teach you to be more sly than you were this morning."

Listening to the other boy made Dean feel better. Maybe something good had come out of getting caught sneaking around after all. Of all the student body, Perry and his group seemed to be the most like Dean. They were fierce, hard, rough and feared throughout the school. They weren't pampered kids at all.

Used to being a loner, Dean hadn't tried overly hard to take up with the group. But he wouldn't have objected to an offer of friendship or interest on their behalf. Mr. Solomon had never before tried to pair any of Perry's group with him.

"So what's it gonna be?" Perry asked. "If you don't want to do it, I gotta ask somebody else."

"What time am I supposed to be there?" Dean asked.

Perry smiled. "I'll come get you when it's time. Mr. Solomon said it'd be after dark, and to try to sleep this afternoon if you could because we're gonna be out most all night."

"Okay," Dean said.

Perry left without another word.

Dean lay back on the bed, excited and scared at the same time, and wondering what Mr. Solomon had in mind. Skulking around in the dark, though, sounded good to him no matter what the excuse. He closed his eyes and, after a time, slept.

A pair of skikes came up out of the water in tandem, breaking the choppy gray surface, and streaked for Ryan. Hoyle had identified the creatures. Ryan moved to the side quickly, his blaster already in his hand. The five-foot wide section of graveled earth that formed a natural berm for the river didn't give him much room to work with.

The wedge-shaped bodies arced fluidly, bringing the barbed tails around into attack positions. There wasn't much air current in the cavern to allow the skikes to maneuver gracefully. Once they'd launched themselves from the river, they were more projectiles than fliers.

"Goddamn!" Hoyle shouted. The man went to ground, taking cover behind an outcrop, seizing two stones in his fists.

Ryan brought up the SIG-Sauer and cut loose two rounds at the lead skike. Only one round hit the mutie creature, but it punched through the skike's chest, blowing its heart and backbone through its dorsal surface.

The skike died with a shrill cry that ululated throughout the cavern. Writhing out its death throes, the creature plopped to the ground in front of Ryan, the barbed tail sticking out into the river.

The second skike hit the cavern wall over Ryan's head. The mutie creature seemed hardly dazed at all by the sudden impact against the wall. Flexing its sides, it scooted across the gravel, heading back to the river.

"Kill it!" Hoyle yelled. "Kill the bastard thing before it gets the chance to tell the others we're here! Those shitters hunt in packs."

Ryan kicked the dead skike out of his way as he pursued the live one. Shrilling now, the skike planed across the shallow water, obviously waiting until it reached a deeper part of the river before diving. Taking deliberate aim, Ryan squeezed the SIG-Sauer's trigger three times.

The skike possessed an uncanny skill for dodging while in the water, changing course a half-dozen times in an eye blink, rolling its membrane to feint in still other directions.

All three rounds missed the creature. Then Krysty's weapon boomed, too, throwing up geysers of water around the skike. Taking a double-handed grip on his weapon and wading into the cold water, Ryan fired in a steady roll, working a pattern around the skike that allowed for forward movement, as well as to either side. The water was the creature's element.

He'd almost run his clip dry when he scored his first hit. Ears ringing from the concussions of his weapon, he saw the plume of blood jet up from the creature's left side. The membrane curled in on itself slightly, trying to cover the hole near the bottom. The skike kept moving, pulling to the right and starting to go under.

Ryan fired his last two rounds. The slide blew back into the locked and empty position at the same time he spotted the sudden cloud of blood churn the water and erase the skike from view. He replaced the clip, storing the empty in his pocket.

He waited, tense. Krysty had a hand over Bernsen's mouth, and the man was only able to make small, plaintive noises. She prodded the back of his skull with the barrel of her weapon to freeze him.

"You got it," Hoyle said breathlessly.

Ryan glared the man into silence. A moment later the skike's dead and mutilated body surfaced in a diamond of bloody flesh. It floated upside down, blue-gray belly turned up against the ceiling of the cavern. Ryan waited a little longer, until he was sure nothing else was coming after them.

"HOW FAR ARE YOU GOING to go looking for the boy?" Hoyle asked.

Ryan had the lead, and Krysty covered his back. Neither of the two men had been allowed weapons. "As far as it takes," he answered.

"Him holding on to that raft like he was, he could be anywhere. Hell, if he drowned, he might not be stopped yet."

Ryan knew that was true. Linked to the raft, Jak had been at its full mercy. "I'll take that chance."

"Leaving your friends back there wasn't any too smart, either, if you ask me."

"Didn't ask."

"Those skikes will be all stirred up from the floods,

swimming around all hot up from being in rut. They won't hesitate about attacking those people back there."

Ryan kept moving, ducking under an overhang of crooked, lichen-covered rock that jutted from the cavern wall. The cavern was continuing to widen slightly, allowing more light in from cracks across the ceiling. The river appeared to be moving slower, but still at a steady clip.

"They haven't been attacked," he said.

"How do you know?"

"J.B. would have blasted anything that tried," Ryan replied. "Would have heard that."

"What do you intend to do with us?" Bernsen asked.

"Depends," Ryan answered. Along the sides of the river, trees and branches and other detritus had hung up in the scattered shallows, seining still more refuse from the current.

"'Depends'?" Bernsen echoed. "What kind of answer is that? My God, that's no answer at all."

"It's the only one I've got for you," Ryan said. "You and your friend here know this river, and I can use knowledge like that."

Ahead and to the right, a scarecrow figure in jeans and a green flannel shirt lay draped over a broken red-and-white-striped sawhorse that had seen its last good days years ago. Ryan approached it long enough to make sure the albino teenager wasn't covered over by the corpse.

He grabbed the corpse by the hair and lifted it. The woman was days-old dead, her throat cut straight across. Other cuts marred her face, showing she'd died hard and her killer hadn't been successful on the first try. Or had carried a grudge.

Jak was nowhere around.

Ryan dropped the woman's head back into the water,

disturbing the small minnows that had been feeding on the soft parts of her face. In another few hours she wouldn't be recognizable at all. He walked back out of the water and kept on going.

"How far does the cave system go?"

"This one?" Hoyle responded.

"Yeah." Ryan kept his gaze moving. So far they hadn't been attacked by any more skikes, though they had seen a handful of the creatures skimming by underwater. There'd been no gunfire from farther back in the cave where they'd left J.B., Doc and Mildred, so it was a good bet they were still safe.

"This one goes on for a couple miles more. Then you have some daylight for another fifteen miles or so. Another cave system after that where you have to make a decision about where you want to go. The river forks in three directions and continues on for various distances."

"As far as Colorado?" Ryan asked.

Hoyle nodded, then asked, "What's in Colorado?"

"My son," Ryan replied. And he gave the man that, just enough to let Hoyle know he wasn't going to brook any arguments later when answers were called for. "Mebbe you want to tell me what you're doing up here." There was enough edge to Ryan's words that Hoyle would know taking a pass on the question wasn't a good idea.

"Working a job."

"What job?"

"Guide."

"For Bernsen?"

"And his friends."

Ryan followed the turn of the river, going cautious, the SIG-Sauer blaster covering the terrain ahead of him in case there were any lurking skikes. Only parts of the cavern lay in shadow, and beams of sunlight from crevices in the ceiling glinted silver off the unsettled river. "How many friends?"

Hoyle made the story short, saying that the men were scientists and all of them had been killed but Bernsen. Three of them had been chilled during an encounter with the brushwooders a couple days earlier. Two had died by skike poison after they'd gotten away from the brushwooders. And Mellelan had fallen to break his neck only the day before when they'd been hurrying through the mountains trying to beat out the approaching storm.

"Saw a tattoo on Mellelan," Ryan said when the man had finished. "Spotted one on Bernsen, too. And you."

Hoyle scratched the inside of his arm absentmindedly. "They got a thing about identifying each other. In some places they ain't too welcome. Ten, fifteen years ago old David Napier tried telling a few folks up north to be on the lookout for certain things. Some of those folks took objection to what he was preaching, called him a heretic and strung him up. Made the other people of the Heimdall Foundation kind of shy about being noticed."

"Heard mention of that Heimdall name, but what is it, this foundation?"

"You'd have to ask Bernsen to get the real particulars of that," Hoyle said. "Basically these people use telescopes and stare up at the sky all night long. They got books, vids and some comp progs that talk about all that stuff up there. Call it astronomy."

"All that looking, they got to be looking for something."

"Falling stars," Hoyle answered.

"That what brought you from Montana?"

Hoyle narrowed his eyes. "How do you know about Montana?"

"Mellelan had a map. Heimdall Point was marked on it."

"Now, that's a fool thing to do." Hoyle spit in disgust. "I hope you took up that map."

Ryan nodded.

"Don't need something like that falling into unfriendly hands. The Heimdall Foundation ain't set up proper to repel an attack." Hoyle shook his head. "These poor bastards, they been in their damn little towers too long looking up at the sky if you ask me."

"That's not what I asked you," Ryan said in a harder voice.

"Yeah, yeah. I've been guiding these assholes around a few places, going here and there for the last four years. Pay's good. I get some jack at the end of every trek successful or not, and I manage to steal enough predark stuff along the way to hock through some friends I got in a few places to keep myself living comfortable."

"Get to it."

"Over the last few months they took a special interest in a star they started calling *Shostakovich's Anvil*."

"Twisted name for a star."

"That's what I thought. But they don't ask me before they go naming them. And the way they talked, it sounded like somebody else had already named this one."

"Might not have such an easy job when you get back there," Ryan stated, "with a few scientists short."

"Hell, ain't none of us loose yet. I figure we won't be clear of the reach of the Five Barons for a while."

"Who're the Five Barons?"

"Now, that's a story," Hoyle said.

THE HISTORY Hoyle gave Ryan was concise but complete.

In the beginning there'd been a gathering of small villes

along the Cific coast. Each had clung to ideals and traditions handed down from those who'd survived the nukecaust or had migrated there afterward to be near the ocean. The aquatic life in the area had been less harmed than the land-based creatures, and as Hoyle stated, a man had to eat.

The villes hadn't gotten along well together. Each had staked out territorial claims that had been disputed over the years. Several villes had split off from the original ville. One of those had died out from an epidemic that created a natural southern boundary.

After that, things remained peaceable—until the arrival of the barons.

"Any of them barons you ask about," Hoyle told Ryan, "you're going to hear a different story about how and why they came to be trapped out in the deserts the way they were. Only them and their Maker and a handful of their close sec people know the right of it."

All of the barons, six of them at the time, had wandered in from the desert, drawn by tales they'd heard of the villes and how robbing was easy there because the people in the seven villes were too busy raising stuff to eat and fishing to worry about learning to fight.

When the barons got among the villes, greed had set in. The villes were too close to allow for expansion by each separate baron. They tried splitting them up, but none of them were men who wanted to share.

"They went to war with each other," Hoyle went on. "Fighting, killing and sabotaging, the like of which none of the people of the seven villes had ever seen before. Oh, they'd had their scraps over the years, but it wasn't nothing like what the barons could dish out against each other.

"But with the barons killing one another and reducing

their manpower down to something that wouldn't allow them to stand firm against the mutie bands wandering in the desert if they had to return there, they struck a bargain.

"Only one of the barons could comfortably run the seven villes at one time," Hoyle said. "So they decided a competition was in order to figure out who was going to get control without killing each other. All of them were so aligned that if any one of them swore out a blood feud against another, the others would step in and stop it. A shift in the balance of power wasn't tolerated. Jink Masten, the old sixth baron, was the only man all five of the others couldn't stand. They killed him three years ago, and became known as the Five Barons."

Ryan listened, knowing the savagery that had to have gone on between the barons. The history was a familiar story to him.

"They got together and created the Big Game," Hoyle went on. "Found a place out in the desert, somewhere that held a lot of meaning to it at one time. A place where luck and chance came together, they tell me. I never seen it."

"What do they do there?"

"Choose up teams. Kidnap folk and use them to fight for them. Control of the seven villes for the next year goes to the baron whose team wins."

"What does the winning team get?" Ryan asked.

"Killed, mostly. Except for one man. Or woman. Or mutie. The barons ain't particular. They don't want anybody to get a chance at getting together an experienced team, you know."

"So why do those people fight?"

"Don't give them much choice at the time."

Ryan turned the story over in his head as he walked through inches-deep water where the river had completely filled the cavern. "Which baron is in charge now, and who's his sec boss?" Ryan asked.

"Baron Hardcoe," Hoyle answered. "LeMarck's his most loyal man, but not the only sec boss. Hardcoe probably has a half-dozen of them. Got a lot of men with him."

"And they've got control of the seven villes?" Ryan's mind flipped the details around, keeping them mentally accessible while he put everything together.

"For now. The Big Game will decide who's going to get control of the seven villes for the next year."

"That was LeMarck out there behind us?" Ryan was thinking of the mysterious rifle shot that had nailed one of the brushwooders before he and J.B. had caught up to their companions.

"Behind you and the brushwooders," Hoyle confirmed with a nod. "Spotted him through the telescopic sights of that Sharps."

"And you'd know him?"

"Met him last week. Sort of. Bernsen and his friends thought that star was going to drop somewhere near the seven villes. I explained to them that nothing went on in that area unless it was okayed by the barons, so they marched into Jakestown pretty as you please and asked Hardcoe for permission to stay for a couple days. I've always heard he was interested on predark learnings, and I guess it must be so, because he not only let them stay, but hell, he even put 'em up."

"Why would Hardcoe be up here?"

"The last I heard, Baron Hardcoe assigned LeMarck to bring in the brushwooder leader. Daugherty's been raiding some of the farmers in the villes, and Hardcoe takes his business serious."

"So he could have been after Daugherty?"

"Mebbe, but from what I saw, he seemed to be showing a lot of interest in you people."

Ryan didn't have an explanation for that, but he let it drift around in the back of his mind while they walked.

Nearly an hour later, they found Jak.

Ryan spotted the raft first, tucked up mostly out of sight behind and under some driftwood. Jak was just one shadow among myriad others, until he stepped out into view with a leaf-bladed throwing knife in one hand and his .357 Magnum in the other.

"Knew you come soon," Jak said, grinning a little. "Waited. Too damn hard pull raft back up river alone."

By the time they reached the part of the cavern where they'd left Doc, Mildred and J.B., Krysty ached all over. She hadn't rested well the night before, and she'd taken a turn at pulling the raft partway, which had started out easy then gotten to be serious work as they approached the faster-running water still pouring into the river.

Doc was sitting up when they arrived, drinking some soup from a self-heat, and his color looked better.

"Ah," the old man croaked in a voice that sounded more like him than his earlier weak whisper, "there they are now."

"Anything happen while we were gone?" Ryan asked J.B.

The Armorer adjusted his fedora and shook his head. "River seems to be slowing some. Saw no sign of anybody who was looking for us. Unless you count a body that come through about an hour ago. Looked like a brush-wooder, but I didn't wade out to go check. Those damn skike were all over it. Things got bastard sharp teeth."

"We have another problem." Ryan squatted, waving at Jak to put the prisoners against the cavern wall almost ten feet away. He told the companions about Hoyle's sighting of Hayden LeMarck, the seven villes and the Five Barons. The picture Ryan painted of the villes was grim.

"Mebbe the brushwooders gave up," Ryan said at the end of it, "but mebbe LeMarck didn't."

"Didn't see him along trail," Jak said. "He there, I know."

"If he was tracking the brushwooders," Mildred said, "could be he found us then. We weren't able to take in everything going on behind us."

"But why get interested in us?" Krysty asked. "We've never even been through those villes."

"Don't know," Ryan said.

"Mebbe LeMarck and his sec men aren't looking for us at all," J.B. said. "Reckon they could have been on the trail of these two people just as much as they were after the brushwooders."

"Yeah, but why?" Ryan probed. "We found nothing in either one of those men's equipment that looked valuable."

"Perhaps their interest lies in the cartographic discovery we made in the dead man's pack," Doc said. "This Heimdall Foundation sounds intriguing. Mayhap Baron Hardcoe thought so, as well."

"In Montana?" Mildred asked. "That's way the hell out of his usual beat, sounds like to me."

"True," Doc said, "but follow my mental perambulations for a few moments if you will, while I digress. We've established from Mr. Hoyle's testimony that the Heimdall Foundation is without a standing army, yet has an abundance of foodstuffs and creature comforts that might sound desirable to Baron Hardcoe should he lose his bid at this Big Game a few days hence."

"You're saying instead of being turned back into the wastelands bordering the seven villes, mebbe Hardcoe has his eyes set on taking over the Heimdall Foundation?" J.B. asked.

"It would be," Doc argued, "a place to go."

"Makes sense," Krysty agreed.

"That does," Ryan said. "What doesn't is why Hardcoe didn't just capture the Heimdall Foundation scientists when they were in his ville and be done with it."

No one had an answer to that.

"Mebbe the falling star," Jak suggested.

"Mebbe." Ryan looked up at Bernsen. "Get over here."

"Me?" the man asked.

Ryan nodded.

Krysty knew part of Ryan's willingness to question Bernsen stemmed from her lover's own innate curiosity. Ryan Cawdor was a wanderer, a man who had to look beyond strange horizons.

Bernsen sidled over to the group, not looking happy about it at all.

"Tell me about *Shostakovich's Anvil*," Ryan ordered.

The scientist glared at Hoyle over his shoulder. "I don't have to answer you."

"No," Ryan said in a level voice. "Mebbe we'll see how the skike like you."

The man dragged a hand over his round face, sweating profusely from fear, exertion and the humidity trapped in the cavern. "*Shostakovich's Anvil* is—was—a Soviet space station. It was put up before the nukecaust and was supposed to collect data. And aside from the knowledge collected, it's also interesting if you remember the chaotic nature of the world at that time, nations aligning themselves with the two superpowers."

"Yes, it was a competition out there, too, just like on the planet," the Armorer said.

"Yes," Bernsen responded. "However, both the Americans and the Russians knew that forewarned meant being forearmed. Not everyone believed that aliens who came back to the planet would be friendly."

"As I recall," Doc said, "there were plenty of numbers in either camp who believed aliens would be mankind's greatest friend, or its most loathsome enemy."

"Yes, all-out struggle for supremacy. And then bang! We almost encountered *the* end—but our ancestors survived the nukecaust," Bernsen said, "and they started the Heimdall Foundation. Most of the electronic equipment at that time was exposed to the electromagnetic pulse from the nuclear weapons. Nothing worked. They struggled together and managed to find enough telescopes and comps to survey the night sky and to record their findings. They also added to their treasure trove with books, comp progs, vids and buried government files."

"You've been tracking these falling satellites," Ryan said.

"When we could find them." Bernsen mopped his damp face with his shirtsleeve.

"If you were tracking them, what were you doing in the seven villes?"

"We've acquired conflicting data over the years," Bernsen said, "and even with the comps we've put together, we're in no way able to do the space monitoring they did in the predark times. Where the Soviet space station was going to land was open to conjecture. But we narrowed it down to two places."

"Jakestown," Ryan said.

The scientist nodded. "Depending on atmospheric conditions, which we're not too exact on."

"Where's the other place?" Ryan asked.

Bernsen seemed hesitant, but in the end he answered. "About forty miles north and slightly east of this position, there's a lake."

"Pyramid Lake," Hoyle cut in. "Should be on any maps you've got."

J.B. opened his map and traced the surface with a forefinger. "Got it."

"How did you plan on getting there?" Ryan asked.

"This river," Hoyle said, "goes most of the way. Got mebbe a twelve-mile hike over some rough country in Smoke Creek Desert."

"How rough?"

"Man's got no water, he's dead. Got no fire at night, he's dead. You burn to death during the day, and freeze your goddamn ass off at night."

"What about the water in the lake?"

"I'd purify it before I drank it. Drank it before and I'm still here."

"Any game along the way?"

"Precious little," Hoyle replied. "Country's still carrying a taint of rad-blasting from farther east."

Shifting his attention back to Bernsen, Ryan asked, "When's the space station going to come down?"

"Two days from now. An hour or two after nightfall."

"How sure are you?"

"I came out here to see it," Bernsen said. "Six other people from the foundation died getting this far. We're pretty certain."

"Everybody get your gear together," Ryan ordered. "We're leaving in five minutes."

"YOU'RE GOING after the space station, aren't you?" Krysty asked.

"Yeah," Ryan replied. "Only a day, mebbe two out of our way. Keeping the raft and staying with the river as much as we can, we should make the time up okay." He studied her.

Krysty knew the strain she was under showed to him. There weren't any real secrets between them anymore, except the ones Ryan knew she didn't want to know about—and the vision she'd had yesterday.

"You think we should do it another way?" he asked.

That he would ask rather than simply leading the companions let her know he was concerned about her. She reached up and softly stroked his face. "Kind of thinking about the people mebbe closing in on our backtrail bothers me. It'll pass."

He nodded and started moving gear toward the raft.

Krysty picked up one of the backpacks they'd been fortunate enough to keep throughout the flood and started after him. At least, with Ryan headed up to the site of the falling space station—whether it landed there or not—it would give him something to think about instead of why she was being so quiet. It would also give her more time to figure out what the vision actually meant. She hoped.

The moon was hidden behind a cloud bank when Dean joined up with the rest of Perry's group in the forest beyond the school's cultivated fields. Mr. Solomon, tall and angular, with a long, thick mustache that curled down from his upper lip, stood in front of them. He was dressed in black, as well, but had double pistol holsters with revolvers shoved into them.

"You're late, Mr. Perry," Solomon said in a low voice that carried.

"Won't happen again, sir."

Dean instantly rebelled against the man's military bearing as he fell into line with the other boys. Authority didn't suit him, and Solomon was more by-the-book than any of the teachers at the school. There were some rumors that Solomon had a background in sec work somewhere farther west, maybe even as far as the Cific Ocean coastline.

Solomon flicked his dead gaze on Dean. "Glad you could join us, Mr. Cawdor."

Dean nodded.

"I hadn't planned on the unfortunate incident that removed Mr. Conover from our midst this morning." Solomon crossed the space to stand in front of Dean. "Tonight's activities, though, required ten players. I've never seen you operate in the dark. How good are you?"

"Okay," Dean said.

"I guess we'll have the truth of that in short order." Solomon walked back down the line, his hands clasped behind his back, his spine rigid and his shoulders squared. He met each boy's gaze in turn. "Tonight's exercise requires cunning and stealth. Follow me."

Dean went with the others and trailed after Solomon.

The phys-ed instructor came to a stop on a small promontory overlooking rugged terrain filled with trees, brush and hills. He pointed at five of the boys, then presented them with black handkerchiefs. "Put those in your belts, loose enough to pull out but not loose enough to fall out on their own."

The five boys tucked the handkerchiefs in their belts, testing them for tightness.

"The exercise works like this," Solomon said. "The five of you with the black flags will be given a minute head start. Your goal is the tree out there." He pointed.

Dean followed the phys-ed teacher's finger, spotting the tall Colorado blue spruce nearly a half mile away. A white banner fluttered near its top.

Solomon went on. "Then the others will follow. I want you to use stealth, not speed traversing that terrain. Some of you could run that distance in three, four minutes. Shadows are all over the place out there. One misstep and you could end up with a broken leg or a broken foot. Or worse. I don't want to get anyone hurt out there and screw up this team any more than it has been after this morning. Is that clear?"

"Yeah," Dean said, right along with the other boys.

"Those of you who are pursuing the flag bearers, your assignment is to take their flag," Solomon said. "By whatever means you have at your disposal."

"How physical can we get?" Perry asked.

"Short of permanent damage," the phys-ed teacher answered. "Bruises and small cuts I can explain. You do anything more than that, and this unit and its status will be in danger at this school."

"What do we get for reaching the tree with our flag?" Hercules Moxen asked. He was close to six feet tall, almost a head taller than Dean, and had fiery red hair. Not all of his substantial weight was muscle, but there was enough to give most grown men pause. Coupled with the fact that Moxen loved to fight, he was a bad guy to have cross words with.

"You don't have to do the extra PT the others will for failing to catch you."

"What do we get if we catch them?" The question came from the other side of Dean.

Looking down the line, Dean saw the speaker was Louis McKenzie. Of all the boys in Perry's group, Dean liked Louis best. The boy always had a smile and a gentle way about him if he cared to show it. He was blond and had light green eyes that belonged on a cat, and he was a little taller than Dean but built in the same lanky fashion.

"Then they get extra PT," Solomon replied. "Some incentive both ways. After we do this once, we'll do it again, and the pursued will become the pursuers." He looked down the line of boys. "Everybody ready?"

"Yes, sir," they answered.

Solomon paired the boys off, giving each of them a target.

Dean got Hercules Moxen. The other boy smirked and shook his head as if he couldn't believe it.

"See you at the tree, small fry," Moxen said. "When you're doing the extra PT, think of me."

Dean didn't say anything. Talk was just talk; his dad had taught him that. He drew in deep breaths, pumping up his oxygen level. Despite Solomon's warning not to simply head for the tree, Dean figured Moxen would try to reach the tree as quick as he was able.

"Go!" Solomon said.

The first five boys launched themselves into the darkness, feet swishing through the underbrush.

"Stand ready," Solomon ordered the other boys, checking his wrist chron.

Dean watched Moxen until the boy vanished behind a triangular pine tree. He kept on breathing, waiting. The minute passed slowly.

"Go," the phys-ed teacher finally said.

Dean bolted, already moving at top speed, trusting his night vision and reflexes to keep him from serious damage. He pumped his feet against the ground, swinging his arms at his sides. It felt good to be out, testing himself against someone else, deep in the wild where his primitive senses could take care of him instead of social skills that he didn't feel as confident about.

He ran, convinced he was closing the distance.

His breath sounded loud in his ears and burned along his throat as he ran through the brush. He used every skill he'd ever been taught, skirting plants, trees and bushes that would have warned of his passage had he touched them. He tried to listen for Hercules Moxen but couldn't hear the boy.

The terrain was uneven and dangerous because the cloud-covered moon cast no light. Still, he increased his speed, not giving in. If the other boy had covered this much ground, he would be tired when Dean caught up with him, giving Dean an edge that he needed to overcome Moxen's strength.

He was two steps up the rise before he knew it. Gravity pulled at him, sucking him off balance. He put his hands against the rough ground, slithering them through a painful tangle of brush as thorns tore at his flesh. When he got to the top of the ridge, the world opened up to him again, letting him see the small valley on the other side of the rise.

Moxen sprawled facedown at the bottom of it, arms flung out to his sides, one leg twisted over the other.

"Shit," Dean said, continuing down into the valley. It was just his luck. Remanded to his room, and here he was finding Moxen probably dead.

He threw himself to the ground beside Moxen, not even thinking for a moment that the bigger boy was just fooling him. Moxen's legs were too twisted for that, and it had to be painful. If nothing was broken, it had been a close call.

Dean grabbed the boy's shoulder, turning him gently, wanting to make sure there was no chance Moxen would smother with his face pressed against the earth like that.

The youth rolled over loosely, dirt smeared against his pallid cheeks. The boy's eyes were halfway open, glinting dully in the weak moonlight. Drool oozed out of one corner of his mouth, mixing with the weak traces of blood. He blew out white bubbles of spittle and moved one arm, struggling to speak.

Dean knew that if Moxen had been knocked out, he'd

have come to quicker than he was. And that white spit looked like evidence of a bad reaction to something he ate.

"What's wrong?" Dean asked, leaning closer. Then he spotted the small feathered dart stuck deep in Moxen's neck. A chill slid down Dean's back. He tried not to act as if he'd seen it. Then he heard the pad of a soft footfall behind him.

Throwing himself to one side, Dean dived and rolled, coming up on his feet so he could look back in the direction he'd heard the footstep. He was breathing hard, his heart hammering.

A dark figure, barely discernible in the black clothing and standing in the tree line less than forty feet away, took aim with a long-barreled blaster. A ruby dot appeared at the top of the pistol, sending a beam forward that stabbed into Dean's right eye.

Dean dropped, squatting and placing the palms of his hands against the ground. What sounded like two huge bugs whipped by over his head, missing him by inches. Shoving himself up again, he ran, heading back toward the starting area. Dean didn't recognize the man, but evidently he had been waiting for the boys to come breaking through the brush.

Or he'd come after them.

The new thought didn't sit well with Dean as he ran, making him more cautious. The sound of footsteps pursued him. His shoulders tightened up, expecting to feel one of the darts pierce his skin.

Yells from some of the other boys, scattered over the terrain, let Dean know the man hadn't come alone. He reached out for the slender bole of a pine tree and swung himself in a tight curve to point himself in an altered direction. While he had his hand on the tree, he felt a feathered dart sink into the rough bark between his fingers.

He stayed with the pine trees, knowing the branches would be heavy enough to deflect the darts. Then he was all out of trees, with the ridgeline leading back at the starting point seventy yards away. He zigzagged, risking a glance over his shoulder that showed his pursuer breaking out of the brush twenty yards behind him. His lungs burned from the sustained effort and fear, knowing the man following him could come faster simply by maintaining a straight line that Dean couldn't risk.

He made it to the top of the ridge and saw Mr. Solomon standing there in the shadow of a tree and holding binoculars to his face.

"Mr. Solomon!" Dean gasped, sprinting toward the phys-ed teacher. "Something's gone wrong! There are men out there shooting us!"

Solomon turned his head, dropping the binoculars to his side. "I know."

Dean stopped his forward progress at once, reading the coldness in the teacher's answer. "You did it! You betrayed them, betrayed all of us!"

"Yeah," Solomon said. His fist came around suddenly, filled with one of the long-barreled pistols. The ruby light gleamed, splashing across Dean's chest.

Before Dean could move, a trio of whispered coughs sounded, followed immediately by three bursts of pain across his chest and stomach. Incredulous, he glanced down at himself. Three feathered darts stuck out from his body. He reached for them, feeling the pain already going away as a numbness spread throughout his torso. Then his legs wouldn't hold him anymore, and he fell to the ground.

A WAVE OF SUDDEN NAUSEA jerked Krysty upright in the raft. She clapped a hand over her mouth and swallowed a ball of bile that had risen to her throat.

"Krysty, my dear," Doc said, leaning forward to take her free arm, "are you all right?" His face showed concern, his brows pulled tight together.

The woman couldn't answer; her stomach still rolled. She kept her hand over her mouth as she struggled to the side of the raft. Trees lined the riverbanks on both sides. Jak and Ryan were scouting at the top of the nearby hill to get their bearings.

"Need some help?" Mildred asked.

Hoyle and Bernsen parted and made room for Krysty. J.B. aimed the Uzi at them, just to let them know they didn't dare make a move on Krysty or try to take her weapon.

She kept her lips together until she had her head over the raft's side, then spit, trying to get everything out of her mouth that she could. She shivered, goose bumps pimpling her skin. She felt suddenly drained of strength.

"Krysty," Mildred said, slipping a hand over her forehead and wrapping an arm around her shoulders to help support her, "what's wrong?"

"Don't know."

"Something you ate?"

"Ate out of the same batch of self-heats as everyone else did. No one else seems sick."

"You don't have a fever."

"I don't feel hot," Krysty said. "Just sick. My head hurts, my vision's blurry and that ringing— Do you hear that ringing?" She wiped the back of her hand across her mouth again.

"No ringing. Do you feel dizzy?"

"Some." She reached into the brackish water, cupped a handful, then smeared it over her face. It cooled her a little, but not enough to take the real edge off the flush she felt.

Mildred continued to support her friend. Without the other woman's help, Krysty didn't think she could have stayed up at all. She felt boneless, totally lethargic.

"How's your hearing?" Mildred asked. She sounded very distant.

"I still hear ringing." Krysty shook her head to clear her ears but succeeded only in triggering another stomach spasm. She stopped and cupped a second handful of water to splash on her face. When she blinked the droplets from her eyes, she thought she saw something centered in the ripples spreading out from the raft.

Focusing her vision with effort, she breathed shallowly, trying not to put too much strain on her protesting stomach. The image cleared, riding the crest of the wave.

Even as it started to get lost in the distance and the darkness, Krysty recognized it: Dean. His face was slack, empty and pale. The boy's eyes shone dully, like the eyes on people Krysty had seen who had advanced cataracts.

"Oh, Gaia," Krysty said weakly. The sick feeling slammed into her stomach again, but there was nothing for it to purge. She tried to hang on to the vision, make it clearer so she could see where the boy was. From what she'd been able to glimpse, Dean didn't appear to be anywhere in the school. He was outside, surrounded by brush, long grass under his head.

"What is it, my dear?" Doc asked.

"It's Dean," Krysty said. "He looks dead. Gaia, Doc, he looks dead!"

As quick as it had come, the nausea left Krysty. All she felt now was cold and empty. She wrapped her arms around herself in an effort to keep warm, her teeth chattering.

Mildred took a blanket from one of the backpacks Hoyle and Bernsen had been carrying, then draped it around the woman's shoulders.

"Oh, Mildred, I saw him. Saw Dean dead," Krysty said, rocking slightly and trying to clear her head, trying to think.

"Maybe. Or maybe it was something else."

"What?" Krysty asked, looking at the woman.

"I don't know."

"Then you can't say that."

Mildred's face hardened. "You just get it together, girl. This is no place for someone who's lost her head."

"I know." Krysty dropped her chin onto her chest and closed her eyes. That was a mistake, because the image of Dean came swirling back into her head, all mixed up with the visions she'd had the day before. "But what else could it be, Mildred? Give me something I can believe in."

Mildred shook her head. "I can't do that. You're going to believe in whatever you want to believe in."

"If I may…" Doc interrupted.

Krysty looked at the old man, seeing him raise an eyebrow at Mildred.

"Go ahead," the doctor said.

Doc leaned in closer, his eyes locked on Krysty's. "Are you sure Dean was dead in your vision?"

"He looked that way."

"Then he could have just as well been asleep."

"Not asleep," Krysty argued. "I've seen him asleep. It wasn't anything like this. He was too pale, barely breathing. And he was outside somewhere."

"Then mayhap he was sick and you saw him at that time. It might not be something that is going on now at all."

Krysty wanted to believe that. At least it was something better than believing he was dead, a chance to get to Dean before it was too late.

"You might be able to find out," Doc said.

She looked at him, knowing what he was going to say. "I don't know if I can do that. I lost him, and I couldn't hang on to that image anymore."

"Don't try for an image," Doc said. "You yourself have said if anything happened to Ryan you would know. And you believe that tie goes beyond just yourself and Ryan."

Krysty nodded, not feeling so lost. It was a thought to hold on to.

Doc reached out and took one of her hands. "To allay your feelings and fears, you should try to reach out to Dean."

"But what if I can't feel him?"

"That's not the question you should be asking yourself," Doc admonished. "You should instead be asking yourself what if you *can* feel him."

She nodded, feeling her fear shove icy tendrils through her brain. "I know you're right, Doc, but I'm still afraid."

"The only thing to fear is the unknown," the old man said. "Not the truth. I know not what happened to my own family, and I would give anything to have that peace of knowing for sure. There comes a time when what you're supposed to do is lay down the burdens you've been carrying. And fear, dear lady, is a huge burden to bear. You've been given enough of them of late."

Reluctantly Krysty closed her eyes and concentrated on Dean. She built his face in her mind, the way she'd seen it thousands of times, so like Ryan that she could see part of what her lover had to have been like as a child. Despite Ryan's irritation with Dean over behavior on occasion, there wasn't so much separating the father and son.

Electricity grazed her mind, sharp and insistent. Then Dean was there, his presence not as strong and as vibrant as it normally was, but that might have been because of the distance and her own fatigue. She reached out to him, felt his aliveness.

"Krysty," Doc said.

"It's okay, Doc." Feeling weak, Krysty wiped a shirtsleeve across her face to dry the fresh tears. "He's there."

"Alive?"

"Yes."

"And you're sure?"

"Yes. The only thing I really felt in him was tiredness and that he was afraid."

"Kind of sums up a normal day for a youngster if you ask me," J.B. commented.

Doc patted Krysty's hand. "Just you rest easy, dear lady. Ryan will return in a short while, and things will seem better."

"Guess so." Krysty pulled the blanket around her tighter, trying to stave off the chill still threatening to consume her. A headache dawned in the back of her head and lingered as a dull throb. She kept her gaze focused on the dark and forbidding forest around them, afraid to close her eyes because of what she might find there. "Gaia," she whispered, "stand by me. I don't know what you're trying to show me, don't know what it all means. But keep me strong enough to endure. And hold dear to you all that I hold dear, please."

"I CHECKED, Baron, and the boys appear to be all right. No permanent injuries, nothing that would keep them from being of service to you."

Full consciousness returned to Dean slowly, flickering in by dribs and drabs. His head hurt, and he could feel his heartbeat throbbing in his ears and his neck.

"All ten are there?" a deeper voice asked.

"Yes."

Dean slitted his eyes open. He could already tell he was lying on a hard surface—not the ground, though. As he let the dim yellow light filter into his vision, he opened his hand on his side opposite the one the men talked on. He splayed his fingers, sliding them across a smooth wooden surface that held only a few nicks and rough spots.

"You say this group has been trained together, Solomon?" the deep voice asked.

"For just short of ten months," Solomon answered.

"This one looks kind of skinny." Something hard pressed into Dean's side, and he closed his eyes, clamping his lips shut against a cry of pain.

"Don't worry about him, Baron," another man said. "Bastard kid there is quick as lightning. Had him in my sights, and he wheeled on me as I was squeezing the trigger. Disappeared like a fucking ghost and was gone before I could draw another bead."

"So he can run," the baron said. "Don't need a runner. Need a fighter."

"He can fight," Solomon said. "He's a chiller."

"Know that for a fact, do you?"

"If that boy had gotten his hands on a weapon, you might not have all your men back out of the brush," Solomon replied. "If he hadn't trusted me just long enough, I wouldn't have bagged him for you. And I think he was already figuring out that I wasn't on his side."

Dean slitted his eyes open again. This time he saw the wall of bars separating him from the speakers. Solomon was talking to a gruff-looking man in road leathers, the right side of his face spiderwebbed with tattoos, a rifle resting easy in the crook of his arm.

"Moves like that, Baron," the gruff man said, "you can't teach. Boy's been around some."

Beyond the trio of men, another dozen were making final preparations on the wags that had formed a loose circle around the area.

"Give me that light," the baron ordered. He took a cylinder from the man beside him, switched it on and fanned the lens out into a broad cone.

With the extra light, Dean could see that he was in a wag of some type. The sides were covered by canvas over a rib cage of bars just like the ones covering the back end, converting the wag to a cage on wheels. Slavers used vehicles like these when they could.

His heartbeat sped up. Solomon had sold them out to

slavers. The other boys were scattered around him. A few moved, struggling to throw off the effects of the trank dart they'd been hit with.

The baron strode to the end of the wag, then stepped up on a platform mounted there. The wag shifted as it took on the man's weight.

Framed in the light he directed at the top of the canvas-covered cage, the baron looked fierce. His face was scalpeled by hard living in mean times, scraped free of any softness or empathy. Long black hair framed his face and ran down past his shoulders. A mustache and goatee almost disguised the old knife scar that ran across his cruel lips. Another scar started from the bottom of the goatee and trailed down the side of his neck, showing how close he'd come to death.

He wore jeans with wraparound black chaps over them, a body-armor vest with a death's-head painted over his heart, a deep turquoise silk shirt with a high collar under that. Feathered earrings thatched with blue-jay quills hung from either side of his head. A cut-down Mossberg Bull-pup 12 shotgun rode in a hand-tooled breakout holster that ran the length of the man's right thigh, the butt sawed off and replaced with a fold-out metal stock. He carried a Detonics .45 in shoulder leather.

"I'm Baron Vinge Connrad," the man declared. "That probably don't mean a thing to most of you."

It didn't mean anything to Dean. Scoping out the other boys without moving his head, he figured it didn't mean anything to anyone else, either.

"What does matter," Connrad continued, "is that I own you as of this minute. You can live or die right now." He slipped the Mossberg free of the thigh holster and held it in one hand. "What's it going to be?"

None of the boys said anything.

"I better damn sure get an answer," Connrad growled, leveling the Mossberg. "Otherwise, I'm going to shoot me some fish in a barrel."

"Live!" Ethan Perry said, blood tracking a split lip. The other boys took up the cry.

Dean, who'd said nothing, found himself being prodded with the shotgun muzzle. He thought about trying to grab the barrel but decided against it. Even if he managed to get it away from the man, there was nowhere to go.

"What about you, kid?" Connrad demanded.

"I want to live," Dean answered.

Connrad flashed him a cruel grin, eyes shadowed by the night's darkness. "Smart kid." He withdrew the Mossberg.

Dean sat up, sidling out of reach of an arm through the cage. "What do we have to do to live?"

"Chill a few people. Nothing big."

"Who?"

"Does it matter?" Connrad's gaze was direct and forceful.

Dean dropped his arms over his folded knees. "Not really."

Connrad looked over his shoulder at Solomon. "I like this kid, Payton."

Solomon nodded. "Knew you would. Like to talk about the jack you owe me for training these kids for you."

Connrad waved a dismissive hand, turning his gaze back to Dean. "You're kind of the runt of the litter, kid. Way you heard from Solomon, I paid him some good jack for finding ten of you here at the school and putting you together as a team. Promised him more when he delivered you." He grinned. "Been thinking about that, though. Saunders!"

Instantly the gruff man beside the phys-ed teacher put a gun to Solomon's head, then quickly relieved him of his weapons. "Put your hands up and keep them there," Saunders ordered.

"What the hell is going on?" Solomon demanded.

"Got to thinking about it," Connrad said. "You don't want to go to Vegas with us, and that leaves me kind of exposed. You might tell some of Brody's people about this transaction. Mebbe old Brody is an ornery enough cuss to send somebody looking for us. Can't have that."

"Wait a minute," Solomon said. "If I sell you out, I'm writing my own death sentence." Desperation filled his face. "Even if you didn't hunt me down, Brody or one of those townsfolk would."

"Mebbe. And mebbe you'd cut some kind of deal if you got caught getting out of this territory. Townsfolk get kind of soft, forget those hard roots that got them as far as they are. If you came with us, I'd know you got free of the situation. But you didn't want it that way."

"I'll go!" Solomon said in a strained voice. "I'll go with you! It's not that big of a deal!"

Connrad fixed Dean with his stare. "You believe him?"

Dean looked deep into the phys-ed teacher's eyes, thinking about the way Solomon had betrayed Nicholas Brody, the school and the nine other boys sitting in the cage behind him. "No."

Connrad smiled, honest pleasure showing. "Lad after my own heart. You figure ol' Solomon would up and split the first chance he got?"

"Yeah."

"So do I." The baron glanced at the teacher. Solomon was pale, shaky. "You think I should just shoot him and be done with it?"

"Up to you," Dean said.

Connrad abruptly passed the flashlight to another man,

then worked the shotgun's slide to eject five shells. "Got one left in there. You hard enough to shoot Solomon for what he done?"

Dean returned the baron's flat gaze full measure. Nothing stirred inside him; it was all about survival now. "Yeah."

"Cawdor!" Ethan Perry exploded. "You can't do that! You coldhearted little son of a bitch!" The boy erupted from his seat and came at Dean.

Dean rose to his feet to defend himself.

"Sit down!" Connrad barked. He wielded the Detonics in his other hand, pointing it directly at Perry's head. "Or I'll blow your bastard head off!"

Other boys, including Moxen and Louis McKenzie, reached up for Perry and pulled him back down. Perry put up a struggle, but it was mostly show. There wasn't any way he was going to go up against the baron's pistol.

Dean smelled the raw stink of fear filling the wag cage.

"Want to do it?" Connrad asked Dean.

"Up to you. You're in charge." Dean tried to play it the way his dad would, imagining his father in his shoes, willing himself to step into his dad's way of thinking. It was all about here and now, living to take one more breath and not regretting what he had to do to take it.

Connrad passed the Mossberg through the bars.

Dean took it, keeping his hand out of the trigger guard. The gun felt solid, dependable. He thought about the one round in the magazine, wondering if it was really there.

"Go ahead and do it," the baron urged, pointing the Detonics at Dean.

Slowly Dean brought the shotgun to bear on the baron's chest. He peered intently at the man over the barrel, neither of them backing off.

Dean continued to stare across the length of the shotgun at Baron Vinge Connrad, not letting himself feel anything. Several of the baron's sec men started forward, drawing their weapons. He ignored them; they would all be too late.

"Stay back!" Connrad ordered.

The men froze at once.

"What are you going to do, kid?" the baron asked.

"Depends."

"On what?" Connrad didn't seem afraid at all. The pistol stayed on target, not moving.

"Whether you're a slaver," Dean replied, struggling to keep his voice from breaking. "I got no wish to be a slave. Rather die. Guess we could find out who's faster."

"You'd be dead."

"And free."

"If you believe in any kind of life after this one," Connrad said. "Do you?"

"Don't know. Mebbe if I'm fast enough, we could go see together." Dean forced himself to keep from shaking. His finger stayed away from the trigger.

Connrad laughed. "God, but you're a mean kid. I could have sired you myself. I'm no slaver. Got some chilling work for you to do. After that you go free. My word on it."

"If I told you to open this door, would you?" Dean asked.

Connrad shook his head. "No. I didn't get where I am giving in to other people."

Dean nodded. "Didn't think so. But I wanted to make my point." He shifted the shotgun back to cover the phys-ed teacher. "Move your man back. Way you got this barrel chopped off, spread's going to get him, too."

Connrad waved Saunders off. The sec man stepped backward, but kept his pistol lined up on the phys-ed teacher's head.

Pulling the metal stock into his shoulder and thrusting the abbreviated muzzle through the bars, Dean covered Solomon. There was still some question whether the weapon was actually loaded. It might all be a setup to scare the phys-ed teacher. Dean prepared himself all the same, knowing he was willing to take the man's life for how he'd betrayed them.

He curled his finger around the trigger.

Solomon broke and tried to run.

Dean squeezed the trigger, riding out the recoil. The double-aught buckshot erupted from the muzzle and caught the man in midstride, knocking him flat at once, ripping his flesh to shreds.

"You killed him!" Ethan Perry screamed as Solomon kicked out his final few seconds of life. "You crazy bastard!"

Still in motion, Dean swung the shotgun on Connrad, catching the man by surprise. He squeezed the trigger, aiming directly at the man's head. The hammer fell with a click.

Connrad didn't even flinch. "Empty."

"See that," Dean said.

"Even if there'd been a shell in the chamber, you wouldn't have gotten out of the cage alive."

Dean made himself smile. "You said there was only one round. Had to find out if your word is worth anything. If it wasn't, better to get the dying over with now."

Connrad shook his head and laughed. "You got balls, kid, I'll give you that. You and me are going to do just fine." He held out a hand for the shotgun.

Dean passed it across, glancing briefly at Solomon's corpse. He felt something, but he didn't let the feeling grow. He was going to have to stay hard, mean, if he wanted to live.

"You other boys," the baron said, "listen up."

Perry kept screaming angry curses.

"Shut up," Connrad ordered, "or I'm going to blast you through the mouth, see if that don't cut down on the noise."

Shooting Dean angry looks, Perry quieted.

"Better," Connrad said. "Got an announcement I want to make before we leave here." He pointed at Dean. "Anybody so much as lays a hand on this boy, that person's going to answer to me. Then that person's going to die. That's a promise. Any questions?"

There were none.

"Saunders, shut up this wag and make sure everything's secure." Connrad stepped off the platform behind the cage, already thumbing loads into the Mossberg.

Once the flaps had been dropped to cover the bars, Dean sank to his haunches and tried not to be sick. It was one thing to kill a man or mutie that was trying to kill him, or kill an animal for food, but it was another to shoot a man just standing there looking at him. His stomach rolled threateningly. His dad would have done it, though, and for just the same reasons he had.

"You feel better, you bastard?" Perry demanded. "Does killing an unarmed man get you off?"

Dean poked his fingers through the bars, finally able to get his whole hand through. He reached for the edge of the tarp covering the cage, trying to separate it.

"Ease off on him," Louis McKenzie warned.

"Fuck you, too," Perry said. "If they put a gun in that bastard's hand and told him to chill us, what do you think he's going to do?"

"What the hell's wrong with you, Ethan?" Bobby Handley asked. "You have a soft spot for old Solomon? Seems you always was his favorite, and he liked looking at you in the shower."

Perry lunged up, hands reaching for Handley's throat. Several boys worked together to put Perry down, piling on top of him.

"That it, Ethan?" Jordie Ferguson asked. He was blond and blue eyed, his long hair spilling down his back. "Old Solomon feeding you sausage in the can?"

A cry of inarticulate rage split Perry's lips.

"Mebbe you already forgot how Solomon sold us out," Chanz Montoya said. "Me, I wasn't going to forget. Ever. If Dean hadn't killed Solomon, mebbe that man would have never got caught. Wouldn't have wanted to see that happen."

"I'd have killed him," Enrique Green stated.

Perry calmed down. "Dammit, let me go."

Louis fixed him with a hard gaze that Dean could read even in the darkness. "Word to the wise, Perry—

don't try that again. Not to Bobby, not to Dean, not to any of us."

"And if I do?" Perry growled.

"Then we'll chill you ourselves," Louis stated.

Perry looked around the group. "You think you're talking for all of them?"

"Yeah."

His fingers on the edge of the tarp, Dean hesitated. Boots still showed at the back of the wag. He waited, not wanting to risk getting caught and catching someone's wrath. He turned his attention to the boys at the other end of the wag, watching the shift of power from Perry to Louis.

"He is," Moxen declared, quickly followed by the other boys.

Dean was surprised. Louis had always been the quietest and most pleasant of Perry's group. He hadn't seemed like leadership material.

"You okay with that, Dean?" Louis asked, not breaking eye contact with Perry.

"Yeah," Dean answered.

"I put this group together," Perry argued. "You're not going to just push me out like that."

"Solomon put this group together," Louis corrected, "and he named you leader." He gestured at the cage bars around them. "I, for one, am not too happy with where that has taken us."

"You're going to give me grief," Perry said in a disbelieving voice, "and Dean just chilled Solomon?"

"I did it for a reason," Dean said, feeling pressure to have his say. Some of it was so he could hear himself, maybe even convince himself.

"Why?" Perry demanded. "Revenge?"

"Works for me," Moxen said. Green echoed the sentiment.

"They took us down with those trank guns," Dean argued, "and didn't make any sound that carried. A shotgun blast might have been heard back at the school. Especially if Jake or Joel was on duty. Thought mebbe they might come looking."

"Then you should have missed Solomon," Perry snarled.

Dean gave him a cold look. "I didn't want to. Mebbe we aren't coming back from wherever they're taking us. I didn't want Solomon getting away with chilling all of us." He paused. "I had another reason, too. We're going to be noticed missing in the morning. Somebody'll come looking for us. If Connrad and his people leave Solomon's body where it is, it'll give whoever comes looking a chance to start searching in the right direction."

Louis looked at Dean, a slight grin on his lips. "Slick. I wouldn't have thought about that."

Dean parted the tarp after the boots moved away. All the boys except Perry crowded around him, peering through the tarp, as well.

Outside, a sec man held a lantern while two others lifted Solomon's body and threw it onto the wag.

"Guess they thought about it, too," Conor said glumly.

Dean let the tarp drop. "Mebbe. But there's the blood. Be harder to see, but they can't clean it all up. Not after what that shotgun did."

The wag lurched forward, banging the boys around. They spread out, everybody staying away from Perry.

Settling back against the side of the wag and getting as comfortable as he could, Dean forced himself to relax and not think about chilling Solomon.

"You think Brody'll send somebody?" Moxen asked Dean.

"I don't know. If Brody gets word to my dad," Dean said, "I know he'll be there as soon as he can be." And he hung on to that thought for comfort, not daring ask himself how far away his dad might be at that moment.

"WHAT ABOUT DEAN?" Krysty asked. She sat astride her lover on the riverbank behind a copse of trees, within shouting distance of the other companions as dawn colored the eastern sky rose and gold. Neither of them had any clothes on, pressing flesh against flesh, a blanket beneath them. Their weapons were within easy reach.

Ryan looked up at her, his hands kneading her full breasts, tweaking her nipples until they stood fully erect. "Can't lead these people to him. And that's assuming LeMarck doesn't overtake us. It's in our best interest to change courses."

While they'd been up on higher ground, he and Jak had spotted LeMarck. The seven villes sec commander had linked up with more troops.

Krysty loved the feel of her lover's hands on her, hot and insistent. She ran her own hands against his chest, pushing to roll her hips against his. His hard erection lay between the lips of her sex, not yet penetrating her. She had to make herself think, to keep the thread of conversation.

"I had a vision about Dean last night," she said, staring into Ryan's cobalt blue eye. It was red and bloodshot, mute testimony that he hadn't been getting enough rest. None of them had.

Ryan paused, waiting.

"In that vision Dean looked sick, out somewhere in the open so he couldn't be protected."

"Was he still at the school?"

"I don't know. Couldn't see that. I'm worried about him, though."

Ryan pulled her down to him and kissed her tenderly, then held her tight against him. "We'll get to him, Krysty. That's what we're all out here for. Just can't see a way clear to do it yet. The river goes on another fifteen, twenty miles before it switches back to the north and joins up with the Humboldt River according to Hoyle. It might take us the wrong direction, way the hell off the route we want to go."

"I know. I looked at the map, too, when you and J.B. were going over things. We could hole up somewhere and hope LeMarck and his baron miss us."

"We could," Ryan agreed. "But if we get caught out here, there's no defensible place we could hope to hold. Our best bet is movement. We'll catch a few hours' sleep here, then push on before noon. Hoyle says the impact area where the space station is coming down is about fifteen miles from here, according to J.B.'s minisextant. We can make that by nightfall, mebbe set up camp, see what we're left with next morning. Chron's ticking against Hardcoe and LeMarck. They got to be getting on to this Big Game of theirs. Once they do, we'll be left alone."

"We could be late getting to Dean," Krysty protested.

"I know." She saw the fear in him, then, and knew that no matter what he did, even though it looked as if he were directing the companions on a course that would take them far from his son, Ryan cared deeply about Dean. "But it's all I can think of to do."

She kissed him, feeling warmer toward him because of the softness she knew lurked in his savage heart. Ryan Cawdor was a true product of the Deathlands: hard, un-relenting and willing to spill any blood that wasn't his own or that he didn't want to look out for. But he intended to save Dean.

And that's all she could expect of him.

"To get to him any sooner without getting captured," Ryan said, "we'd need a mat-trans."

"I know." Krysty started moving on top of him, rubbing her slick sex back and forth across his erection, finally drawing it into herself with her vaginal muscles. She pushed all the insecurity and fear that the visions had seeded within her out of her mind, concentrating on the pleasure she was giving and receiving.

She felt Ryan hard and deep within her, his erection stabbing up into her belly, stretching her tight and making her feel so full. She pressed herself up again into a seated position, her hands shoving against his chest as she lifted her hips and slammed them back onto him, taking him even deeper.

His fingers burned hotly across her bare flesh as he seized her ass and cupped her into him, meeting her stroke for stroke. She let herself go with the pleasure, waves of it cresting inside her, building to something even bigger. She concentrated on the here and now, not thinking about the dangers that still faced them.

Nicholas Brody sat behind his desk, staring across his steepled fingers at Jake. "You're sure someone was murdered?"

The sec man occupied one of the chairs in front of the desk, his hat in his hands. "Yes, sir. That much blood, had to be someone killed there."

"And what makes you so certain? That blood you found up in those hills could have been where someone shot an animal, hopeful to provision their larder."

Jake shook his head. "No." He opened a fist and displayed several bits of black fabric spotted with rust-colored blood. "That's from clothing, Mr. Brody. Shotgun pattern killed whoever was up on that ridge and tore bits of cloth from whatever he or she was wearing. We found pellets in the trees."

Brody glanced out the window at the school grounds. He couldn't believe something like this had happened. Never in all the years that his institution had been established had something so untoward occurred. "Was it school clothing? From one of the missing boys?"

"Hard to say."

Brody returned his gaze to the man. Jake had been out searching since that morning's roster showed the ten missing boys. "Your best guess, then."

"Sir, with all respect intended, ain't no way I can tell you that. What I can tell you is this—the wag tracks on top of that ridgeline are fresh. Still got green plants crushed up in the clods they turned out of the earth. I'm guessing, but mebbe there were as many as six or seven wags."

"That sounds like more than someone would need to spirit away those boys," Brody said.

"Yes, sir. I'm thinking so, too. Got a feeling we don't know the half of it. All them wags, they got themselves a regular convoy."

"Do you think the boys went with them willingly?" Brody hated asking the question. It made him sound uncertain of himself.

Jake passed over a small object.

Brody took it, examining it carefully, noting its needle-shaped end and the feathers that were obviously there for guidance. "A dart?" He adjusted his glasses, looking toward the sec man for elucidation.

"Trank. Shoot someone with it, knocks them out for a while. Mebbe minutes, mebbe hours, depending on what it's carrying. Found that one in a tree around the blood site."

"You're suggesting the boys were abducted."

"Yes, sir. Come to find out that Mr. Solomon is missing from the ranks, as well."

Brody didn't keep tabs on the staff as tightly as he did the students. If an instructor became remiss in his or her duties, that was duly noted and addressed. He referred to the list of the missing boys. "All of these boys were a part of Mr. Solomon's pet group, were they not?"

"Yes, sir."

"Except for Mr. Cawdor."

"Only kitten in a litter of skunks," Jake agreed.

"Have you talked to Mr. Conover? I believe he was hurt yesterday morning."

"Talked to him. Told me Mr. Solomon was running some special maneuvers last night with his group."

"Without my authorization?"

"If you didn't authorize it, he did it without your authorization."

Brody placed his hands flat on the desk. "I didn't authorize it. Could you attempt to track these people down, Jake, and would you be willing?"

"Yes, sir," the sec man answered. "On both counts. But it's going to take considerable from the sec crew here, and I'll probably have to hire in some help from Leadville. Got some hardcases there do odd jobs when the jack's right."

Brody didn't like the idea of dealing with fiddle-footed ruffians, but circumstances had left him lacking in choices. "I'll defer to your esteemed judgment in that matter, Jake, and I'll place whatever amount of jack you need at your disposal whenever you say. As far as the sec around this institution, we'll limp along without you for the time it takes. Just bring those boys back safe and sound."

The sec man nodded and clapped on his hat. "I'll see it done, sir."

Brody watched the man go and tried not to think of what might be happening to the missing boys. God forbid that he should have to tell any of their parents that he'd failed to protect them as he'd promised. Especially Dean

Cawdor's father. He'd heard numerous stories about the way the man had left Leadville after dropping off his son.

The man wasn't forgiving, Brody knew. Rather, Ryan Cawdor was the epitome of a mythological Greek warrior camouflaged in flesh and blood.

SUNDOWN HAD BEGUN in earnest as Ryan reached the foothills of the low mountains surrounding Honey Lake. The dry heat of the Smoke Creek Desert had sapped him all day long, drawing the moisture from his body. Now, with the long shadows of night coming on, the wind blew cold, erasing the desert's heat.

The sound of chanting off to his left, brought to his ears by the wind, sent him diving for cover. He waved the rest of the companions to cover behind rocks and boulders.

The chanting grew steadily louder, filled with ululating wails that seemed a cross between agony and ecstasy. Dozens of voices, male and female, young and old, took up the hue and cry.

Ryan took out his night glasses and trained them in the direction of the chanting. The land fell away from his position, settling into a bowl-shaped depression where a handful of campfires burned embers against the night. Tens of dimly lit figures surrounded the fires, chanting, none of them really hitting a harmony or a tempo. All of them were gazing up at the starry sky.

"Muties, lover," Krysty said, crawling up on her elbows next to him.

Ryan nodded, trailing his night glasses over the rad-blasted stick figures clad in tatters of human clothing and animal pelts. Many of them were nearly bald or were patchy from the radiated lands they'd spent years in. None of them had any weapons beyond a club or a knife, though some wore cow and buffalo skulls on their heads as armor. A few others had worked rib bones into decorative chest protectors.

All of them were misshapen from leftover nuclear bombardment, covered with scabs and weeping, open sores that leaked vile green pus. Most of them looked to be scabbies, but there were a few stickies among them.

"Odd to see so many different kinds of muties gathered together in the middle of nowhere," Krysty whispered.

"Yeah," Ryan replied quietly. "And causing all this noise seems out of place, too. Draw down the bigger predators on them in no time." He glanced back toward the others and waved them forward, signaling to Jak and J.B. that they were to come quietly.

In seconds the companions and the Heimdall Foundation members were hiding behind the ridge overlooking the depression filled with muties. All of them kept their weapons at the ready, and the two prisoners took time to pick up stones to defend themselves.

"By the Three Kennedys!" Doc exclaimed in a hush. "They look like they are in the throes of some mystical epiphany!"

"What's set them off like that?" Ryan asked, his curiosity aroused. There'd been no sign of pursuit by LeMarck's group of raiders all during the day. With the muties gathered as they were in the area, that could work to their advantage, as well. Where he and his group might hope to slip through and escape notice, the wags would definitely draw attention.

"I do not know, Ryan." The old man pointed. "As you can plainly see for yourself, they are not spending any time communicating with one another. Rather, they seem to be attempting to placate or seek acknowledgment from a being higher than themselves."

"Muties with religion?" Jak shook his head. "No such thing, Doc."

"That we have seen thus far, dear boy," the old man corrected. "And might I remind you that we have seen many strange and wondrous things on our journeys."

"Not religion," Krysty said, "fear. They're afraid of something, and they came here because they thought they might be protected."

"From what?" J.B. asked.

Krysty shook her head. "It's all mixed up. I don't have an image. I'm not sure that they know what's driven them here."

"The space station?" Ryan asked. It was the only thing they knew that was going to make this night different from any others that had taken place in Smoke Creek Desert.

"I don't know, lover. Mebbe."

"Primitive instinct," Mildred said.

"What do you mean?" J.B. asked.

"Those muties live on an intellectual edge barely higher than most animals," the woman stated. "I think we can all agree on that." The declaration passed without objection. "Back in the twentieth century, before California was nuked and collapsed off the face of the planet, scientists had already been studying the effects of natural phenomena on animals."

"Don't understand," Jak said.

Mildred turned to him slightly, but included all the companions in her conversation. "Earthquakes. Flood. Storms. Extrahard winters. The lack of game. All things that take place in Nature that humans have a hard time detecting, animals seem to know about ahead of time. Like they have an extra sense that humans forgot about or never developed."

"This is true," Doc said. "Even after the invention of the seismograph, an observation of animals, especially their migratory habits, was maintained. Often the animals reacted to unknown stimuli that warned them sometimes as much as days before data-gathering devices would report activity."

"You think those muties can sense the space station coming down out of the sky?" Bernsen asked. He barked a short laugh. "That's preposterous. It took the teams at the Heimdall Foundation months to track *Shostakovich's Anvil*."

"And you people got it wrong once already," Mildred said in a hard voice. "Or else you wouldn't have been up around the seven villes. I see these muties sitting here now, waiting for what you say is going to happen."

The fat scientist's face colored slightly.

"Would you then," Doc asked, "care to venture a hypothesis concerning the presence of the muties at this particular location at this precise time?"

"No," Bernsen admitted after a moment.

"How far are we from the area where it's supposed to come down?" Ryan asked.

J.B. took out his minisextant and did his calculations.

While the Armorer was busy, Ryan kept watch over the muties. They were growing more agitated, shifting individually and in small groups, not really noticing now when others encroached on their space. Some of them added more wood to their fires. Ryan knew that wood was scarce in the area. The companions had experienced some difficulty themselves in obtaining it in hopes of having a campfire to warm themselves at some point in the night.

The muties had come prepared with bundles of sticks, branches and driftwood tied by strings.

"About three hundred yards north and west of our position," the Armorer announced.

Ryan turned his night glasses away from the muties and looked toward Honey Lake. The body of water was much larger than indicated on the map they'd been working from. It glistened, dark and oily, in the distance, acting like a mirror for the stars and moon above. The reflection resembled a piece of sky that had fallen and taken root in the desert rock and sand.

Then a flare ignited, reflected on the lake's surface as it skipped between the stars like a rock skimming waves. Ryan glanced back up, knowing what he was actually seeing was in the sky.

"There," Krysty said, taking him by the arm and pointing to the east.

Ryan stared at the orange-white burn streaking across the sky. It looked only inches long, but he knew what he was looking at was actually several miles in length.

"It's reentering the atmosphere," Bernsen said in a reverent voice.

"On fire?" Jak asked. "Be burned time gets here. Waste to come if does."

"Dear boy," Doc said, "the space station itself might not be burning up. What you're seeing is the friction of the station battering against the air."

"It could still burn up before it reaches the ground," Mildred stated. "Space stations weren't designed as reentry vehicles."

"No, not as a general rule," Bernsen said, his eyes glued to the action in the heavens, "but this one was built to withstand a hell of a beating—meteors, satellites and space weapons if it was ever under attack. There was so much the Russians hoped to gain from the recording equipment aboard it. They built it to last."

Below their position the muties were all pointing skyward. Their chanting and ululation had increased to almost deafening proportions even over the distance separating them from the companions. More wood dropped onto the campfires, making the flames reach even higher.

Ryan watched, a thrill going through him. Looking at something no one had ever seen before was always exhilarating.

The space station, if that was what it truly was, fell quickly. The orange faded to yellow as the heat increased, then turned white. Streaking earthward, the space station's trajectory abruptly changed.

"It's breaking apart," Ryan said.

"No!" Bernsen screamed, almost starting over the ridge. J.B. grabbed the man by the shirt collar and hauled him back. "It can't break apart! It's not supposed to do that!"

"Stay put," the Armorer warned, "or you'll never get the chance to tell anyone you saw this. I'd sooner kill you than let the muties have a chance, because they'd take us right along with you."

Bernsen stuffed his fists against his mouth, shaking his head from side to side.

Ryan watched as the space station broke up into at least four pieces. He thought he might have seen a fifth go spinning away to the south, but whatever trail it might have made disappeared quickly against the harsh light of the reentry burn.

The light was so bright it reduced the night's shadows to pinpricks against the uneven ground, almost blinding in its intensity. The largest piece continued along its trajectory toward Honey Lake. The lake's surface blazed with white fire, shimmering across the surface, only a few pockets of darkness left where debris shoved up through the water.

"Dark night!" J.B. exclaimed as it got closer, approaching with increasing speed as bits and pieces of the space station were torn off or burned off and streamlined the craft. "Damn thing's so big it's going to fall on top of us!"

"Stand your ground," Ryan advised. "If we start moving, we could end up right under it, or the muties will see us."

The companions all dug into the ground, watching the falling space station's final approach. It slammed into the ground 150 yards from the mutie campsite, sundering the rock and scattering sand before it like an ocean wave. Tremors shook the earth.

The chanting broke as the sand washed over the muties, knocking dozens of them to the ground. A moment later the space-station wreckage rolled over them, pulping them against the desert floor. The closer ranks of muties broke and ran, coming up the grade toward the companions.

Behind them, red-hot and throwing off heat waves that could be felt even along the ridgeline, the chunk of space station skidded toward Honey Lake. In seconds it shot out over the black depths and sank, glowing eerily until it disappeared.

The screaming muties didn't stop their flight, moving on a direct course to overrun the companions' position.

"Move back!" Ryan roared, bringing the Steyr to his shoulder. He fired in quick succession, a rolling thunder of five shots that mowed down five muties, bullets driving deep through their chests and faces.

Corpses dropped in front of the charging crowd, but the

other muties gave them little attention, trampling over them. The line broke only for a moment, the momentum unstoppable. Recognizing a threat they could deal with, the muties raised clubs and axs, bared blades and spears and continued to run.

J.B.'s Uzi snarled into angry life. The rounds cut a swath in the ranks of the muties. He ducked behind a boulder to change clips. "Ryan, we aren't going to be able to hold them back."

The one-eyed man silently agreed. The muties were a stampede of frightened flesh. Whatever had drawn them there, they'd been betrayed.

Sparing a glance over his shoulder, Ryan watched as Krysty guided Doc farther back into the broken landscape, Bernsen at their heels. Jak was covering their backs, the .357 Magnum pistol in his fist banging out death.

Hoyle was cut down in midstride less than fifteen yards away. A hard-thrown spear took him in the back, sliding into his heart, then burst through his chest. The Heimdall Foundation guide halted his run, crumpling to his knees. He grabbed the spearhead protruding from his chest in disbelief, then toppled forward.

His rifle reloaded, Ryan exchanged looks with J.B. "Time to go."

"Ready," the Armorer replied as he pulled the shotgun around. "Follow my lead?"

"Do it," Ryan said. He was no more than ten feet behind J.B. when they broke into a run. The muties were almost within clawing distance, and a spear sailed over Ryan's shoulder, dropping point first into the inclined terrain ahead of him.

Krysty was over the top of the next ridge, coming around with her .38 in both hands as she took advantage of the cover offered. She opened her mouth, screaming a warning.

Ryan couldn't read the words, but he knew the intent. He cut hard left, his hearing only now starting to return from the concussive force of the space station's impact. A grinding groan echoed around him.

"Fireblast!" Ryan cursed as he saw the rectangular shape of the wag crest the ridgeline to the left of Krysty's position. He had no doubt to whom it belonged. "J.B.!"

"I see it!" the Armorer shouted back.

Heavy machine guns mounted on the wag started blasting away. Tracer rounds flared purple against the velvet night. Fifty-caliber death drummed into the muties, spinning them, dumping them from their feet, knocking them onto their backs. Then the withering fire whipped on, turning toward Ryan and J.B., smacking into the earth only inches behind them.

Ryan went to ground behind an outcrop as the wag switched on its lights. He brought up the Steyr and put rounds through the driver's side of the windshield. One of them cratered the hood over the engine, ripping through the metal with a shriek and scattering sparks across the hood.

The driver turned away. If he was hurt, it wasn't enough to interfere with his driving. The wide bumper caught muties mercilessly, the tires rolling over them where they dropped.

Other wags joined the first, the wheels digging into the ground, throwing out huge rooster tails behind them. Their lights blazed over the sudden battleground.

One of the armored vehicles suddenly zipped out of the formation. As the headlights came around, Ryan spotted Mildred trying to outrun the wag. The driver must have recognized her, because he stayed with her without running her down.

"Millie!" J.B. shouted. He switched back to the Uzi and rattled a trio of short bursts across the front of the vehicle, the slugs hammering the metal but failing to penetrate. The autofire also failed to break off the wag's pursuit of Mildred.

For a moment Ryan lost sight of the action as more wags cut off the woman's escape route. He picked his targets, sighting carefully, then taking up the trigger slack. He put bullets through the heads of two men who swung free of the blocking wags and attempted to seize Mildred. The woman stood her ground fearlessly, willing to sell her life as dearly as possible. Every time her pistol cracked, a sec man or a mutie went down.

Abruptly the wag trailing her slewed sideways. Two men in back who'd been manning the machine guns whipped out a section of heavy netting equipped with weights. The net flew true, unfurling in midair until it dropped around Mildred.

She went down hard, trying to shake the empty brass from the Czech-made ZKR and struggle up from the folds of the net. Before she had a chance to finish the reload, at least six men pushed her back to the ground. When they cleared off her, she wasn't fighting anymore.

Ryan couldn't believe the woman was dead, but any kind of rescue was next to impossible. J.B. worked the Uzi calmly and dispassionately, raking short bursts across the wag personnel and the handful of muties who hadn't quit the area.

Ryan dropped one of the two men who'd thrown the net. The Steyr's round blasted the man backward over the side of the wag. Despite the supposed orders not to kill, the other machine gunner opened up on Ryan's position. Clods of dirt and rock ripped loose around him. He sank back into cover. Slinging the rifle, he drew the SIG-Sauer.

J.B. was already moving in on Mildred's position. Two

3-round bursts knocked down two of the men trying to lift the woman from the ground.

Ryan took that as a sign of hope. If they'd killed the woman, they'd have left her there. He broke cover, moving in from the other side, backing J.B.'s play. It was possible they could recover her if they got control of one of the wags and put the others out of commission.

He ran toward the nearest wag, the SIG-Sauer raised before him. The sec man on the passenger side noticed him first, yelling a warning to the men in front of him. Both had their hands full with muties determined to take their lives.

Ryan fired two rounds. Bright scarlet blood, illuminated by the lights from the other wags, splashed against the fractured windshield inside the wag's cab as a sec man dropped inside the vehicle. The driver had a chance for one quick, terrified glance at Ryan, then a bullet took him squarely between the eyes, snapping his head back.

Slipping his free hand onto the door latch, Ryan triggered it and started to yank it open. The sec man's body tumbled to the ground as a hail of bullets punched through the door.

Having no choice, Ryan abandoned his position. He dived toward the back of the truck, spotting one of the saddle tanks. He threw himself under the wag and unleathered his panga. Three quick thrusts opened holes in the gas tank. Liquid spilled out the holes, pooling rapidly in the sand.

The sec men cautiously approached the side of the wag.

Ryan scrambled through on the other side and saw J.B. cutting away at the net that held Mildred. The Armorer glanced in his direction once, hand sliding back for the Uzi. When J.B. saw who it was, he turned back to his task.

Rocks lay scattered across the ground. Ryan seized two that looked as if they had heavy mineral content. He hoped some of it was iron or flint. He tossed them under-handed toward the broad pool of gasoline beneath the wag. When they landed, he fired immediately.

The 9 mm rounds struck the rocks, knocking sparks from one of them. The sparks proved enough to ignite the gasoline. Flames spread across the pool, then started leaping up the torrents pouring from the ruptured gas tank.

"Cover her!" Ryan yelled at J.B. "There's going to be a blow!"

An instant later the gas tank under the wag exploded from the built-up vapor inside. The vehicle jumped in its tracks, the tank reduced to shrapnel that blasted in all directions. Several pieces ripped the sec men to shreds, and two of the wag's rear tires went flat.

Ryan pushed himself to his feet. Alerted by movement in his peripheral vision, he yelled a warning to J.B. just as a shadow stepped around the front of the wag that had come up behind Mildred.

The Armorer was deadly and quick, rounds from the Uzi chopping into the man standing there.

Ryan added two shots of his own, blasting the man's face apart. Then he watched as J.B. turned and fell to his knees. He dropped the Uzi before Ryan covered the distance.

Once he was close enough, Ryan saw the fletched darts buried deeply into the side of J.B.'s neck and cheek. "Fireblast!" he swore. Managing Mildred while unconscious would have been difficult enough even if they'd been able to commandeer a wag. With the Armorer out of the picture, the remotely possible had become decidedly impossible.

"Go!" J.B. whispered hoarsely, struggling to remain on his knees and failing by degrees. "They don't want us dead right now. Mebbe we got some time. As long as you and the others are free."

Ryan looked at his oldest friend. "If there's a way, J.B., I'll be there for you."

"Know you will." J.B was almost prone on the ground, his hand reaching for Mildred's. He almost made it before the drug in his system shut him down.

A bullet cut the air only inches from Ryan's eye, galvanizing him into action. He snapped off shots, emptying the SIG-Sauer's magazine. As he changed clips, he headed on a tangent that would take him across the fire burning the tarp from the back of the wag he'd left crippled. He knew that for a moment he'd be as clear a target as he could imagine, but after that, whoever had been watching him would lose their night vision.

It was a good plan, the best he could hope for under the circumstances. But he hadn't planned on the small wag that rocketed at him before his own vision could completely clear.

He glimpsed it for only a second, trying to pinpoint the sound. Then the wag was on him, skidding in the sand and the loose rock as the driver tried to avoid a head-on collision. Ryan's own footing was treacherous as he suddenly changed directions. His ankle turned under him painfully, costing him inches.

Unable to totally clear the vehicle, he twisted and put his hands out before him, cushioning the impact. When contact was made, it felt as if his arms were going to tear out of their sockets. The SIG-Sauer left his hand, lost from sight before it hit the ground.

He arced his body onto the wag's hood so he wouldn't go down under the four-wheel-drive, all-terrain tires. Out of control, he smashed up against the windshield, fracturing the glass with his bodyweight. He recognized Hayden LeMarck's face on the other side of the spiderwebbed windshield, mouth moving as he shouted orders to the driver.

Breath knocked out of him from the impact, Ryan pushed himself from the hood as the wag came to a halt. His legs almost wouldn't hold him as he forced himself to stand. He managed only trembling steps. Angrily he ripped the panga free of its sheath as LeMarck climbed out of the halted wag.

Ryan went at the man full tilt, knowing if he could buy himself only a few more seconds, he might be able to function better. His ribs ached and his ankle throbbed, but nothing seemed broken.

LeMarck was taken by surprise, but the sec boss's reflexes were quick enough to dodge the deadly panga.

Ryan drew back to try again, then felt the sharp bite of trank darts pinning him from his knees to his neck. Stubbornly he stayed awake to make one more slash at LeMarck, missing the sec boss by more than an inch. He didn't remain conscious long enough to feel the impact he made against the ground.

WHEN RYAN WENT DOWN less than sixty yards from her position, Krysty started for the top of the ridge, snapping the cylinder of her .38 closed after reloading. Her attention remained focused on her lover, and the man standing above him.

The mutie ranks had been broken, existing now only in retreating clumps. Some of them fought on from behind cover, directing their vengeance on the sec team. Snipers deployed at the sec commander's instruction and began to mop up the muties who chose to fight rather than flee.

Before Krysty reached the top of the ridge and was seen, Jak wrapped his strong arms around her. He clapped a hand over her mouth and put his face close to her ear so he could whisper without his voice carrying far.

"Do Ryan no good, go running out there," he said.

Krysty gave up the struggle almost at once, anchored in the harsh realities of the situation. It was almost too much for her: the visions, the not knowing if they really were the future or if they were just bad hallucinations, the secrets she was keeping from Ryan, and the suspense of what was happening with Dean. She pulled Jak's hand away and made herself exhale.

"It's okay," she said, going back to ground behind the ridgeline, "I'm not going out there."

"It would be a very brave thing to do," Doc said sincerely, putting a hand on her shoulder.

"It would be stupe," Krysty replied. "There'd only be one more person to rescue, and one less to help."

"Yes," the old man said quietly. "Dear Krysty, having a care toward our own freedom is how we may best serve our fallen companions."

Krysty knew that, but it didn't assuage any of the feelings of guilt that assailed her. She holstered her weapon. Below, sec men surrounded Ryan and carried him to the back of a wag. She watched until she couldn't see him anymore.

"Follow," Jak said. "Best make tracks away from here before they see us and come after. Then no one come rescue."

"We're going to find them," Krysty said so there'd be no mistake.

"Yes, dear lady," Doc agreed, "we shall. And it appears we have at least some time on our hands. The Big Game in Vegas is not until six more days."

But Krysty also knew transportation would be a problem. The wags could go much faster than they could. Crossing the desert on foot to Vegas would be almost impossible. Even if they made the distance, and on time, they'd be in no shape to help anyone.

"Gaia, help me find a way," Krysty prayed. She followed Doc, while Jak kept point, motioning to Bernsen to keep up with him. They weren't followed.

"GOT THREE OF THEM," Wallis Thoroughgood said, gazing into the back of the wag where the three captured outlanders lay caged and still unconscious.

LeMarck gazed around the battlefield. Everything was a flurry of activity as the sec teams secured their gear, tended to the few wounded and made what repairs were necessary to the wags. Two of the vehicles appeared destroyed. The first had been set on fire by the one-eyed man, and the resulting explosions had killed four men and burned the wag badly. He'd given the order to drain the surviving tank and leave the wag behind.

The second wag was lost when a group of muties had rolled a huge boulder at it while it had been going down the hillside. The boulder had smashed into the wag and buckled the vehicle's frame and drivetrain, flipping it onto its side. The driver's side had been buried in the sand, and it would have taken too much time to attempt a recovery of the saddle fuel tank on that side, so only the one on the passenger side had been tapped.

Both of the wags were being jettisoned. They didn't dare try to haul them across the desert because it would have reduced their top speed if they were attacked. And pulling them would have increased gas consumption, as well as announcing to the other barons that they'd undergone a hardship.

LeMarck looked at the three captured outlanders. "There are still three of them out there."

"I know it," Baron Hardcoe said, running a hand across his broad face. "But how many men is it going to cost us to try to dig them out?"

LeMarck nodded.

"Cut our losses here," Hardcoe said. "Three of them, from what I've seen, are going to tip the odds in our favor in the Big Game. Mebbe we ought to be satisfied with that much."

"All six would have been better," LeMarck remarked.

"I think so, too. But we got three. Let's work with that."

"Yes, sir."

"Get your men ready," Hardcoe instructed. "I want to shake the dust from this place in ten minutes or less."

LeMarck went to see that it was done, but he ordered men to keep an eye on the ridges around the area just in case. And he could always hope the other three would find a way to follow them. If they arrived in Vegas before the representing teams were dropped into the pit, they could be added. The thought gave him hope.

KRYSTY AND THE OTHERS waited almost an hour after the sec teams left before coming down out of the mountains. The muties had left, too, going back to wherever they'd come from.

They split up, reccing the area to see what the sec men had left behind. Bernsen went with Doc, since the two of them were more mechanically inclined.

Bodies lay everywhere, muties and sec men. Hardcoe and LeMarck hadn't bothered with their dead.

Krysty and Jak prowled through the interior of the overturned wag. She kept her mind occupied on what she could find and off what might be happening to Ryan, J.B. and Mildred.

"Got gas in outside tank," Jak said. "Slapped it. Sounded full. Got four tires still whole that side, too. Take lot of work to dig out."

Krysty found two boxes of .38 ammunition and a box of 9 mm in the sliding drawer under the driver's seat. Sand had spilled in through the open window, and she had to dig to get at it, then pry it open with a crowbar Jak dug out of the toolbox in the back.

"Got shovels," Jak said, holding up one of the folding trenching tools. "Some other things."

"Keep it in mind." Krysty put the ammo in her backpack. "Mebbe we'll find a use for them." Netting caught her attention, hanging from a hook above the door and disappearing under the mound of loose sand. She dug patiently, following the netting, getting to the bottom and finding a half-dozen self-heats in the bag. She took them out and stored them, too. They'd lost some of their food when Ryan and J.B. were taken. Mildred had been carrying half of the medicine Krysty had turned up in the helicopter.

"Krysty!" Doc bellowed.

Standing up awkwardly between the seats, Krysty looked through the shattered passenger-side window. Doc and Bernsen were under the raised hood of the burned wag. It had still been burning in places when the companions had arrived. They'd thrown handfuls of sand onto the flames until they died away.

"What's wrong, Doc?" she asked.

"Actually, my dear," the old man replied with a white-toothed grin, "things have the appearance of being very right." He turned to Bernsen. "Hit it."

The scientist leaned under the wag's raised hood with a screwdriver. Sparks flashed, then the wag's engine started with a throaty snort. It ran for only a few seconds before dying.

"The good news," Doc said, "is that this engine is capable of running in spite of the fire. The bad news is one tank was ruptured by an explosion and the other was drained of fuel."

"We've got fuel over here," Krysty replied. "It'll take some digging to get to it."

"By the Three Kennedys, then we shall give this the proverbial old college try. Repairs also necessitate replacing some of the fuel lines, but that appears possible, as well."

"Get on it," Krysty said. "Jak and I will get the fuel."

"Capital!"

She walked to the rear of the wag, sliding around the seat. Jak waited for her, handing her one of the trenching tools he held. "Got can, too." He pointed at the empty jerrican in the back. "Looks usable. Get under tank, puncture mebbe with knife, drain into can and carry to Doc."

"Sounds like a plan." Krysty took the shovel and walked out the back of the wag. Rounding the vehicle, stepping over two muties who'd almost been eviscerated by heavy-caliber rounds, she scanned the ridges, wary of anyone who might be waiting.

"Nobody," Jak said. "Animals starting creep back into area. They feel safe, we feel safe."

Krysty took the youth's word for it. Her senses weren't as sharp as Jak's, but they registered no threats waiting in the shadows. She put her foot on the rolled shoulder of the shovel blade and rammed it deeply into the sand. The sand moved easily, but there was a lot of it. She kept working as Jak fell in beside her, concentrating on the effort, knowing every shovelful put her that much closer to Ryan.

"Welcome to Las Vegas," Mildred said, pressing her face against the bars covering the sides and back of the wag. The sun was going down, setting in ocher and amber behind them as they traveled east.

Ryan roused himself from semislumber against the cab of the wag and joined Mildred. J.B. got on the other side. The wag continued on across the bumpy road, jarring the occupants as it rolled along at forty or fifty miles per hour.

The remains of the entertainment city lay like a dying neon rose in the parched sand of the desert. Dozens of colors sprayed across the broken buildings jutting from the landscape, and seemed to be centered in the heart of the city.

"Skydark was hard on this burg," Mildred said. "It used to be something to look at."

"Been here?" J.B. asked.

Mildred nodded, her gaze glued on the city as they came down off the long, sweeping hills surrounding

Vegas. "A couple visits. First time was when I was a college freshman. Sort of to get the bridle in my teeth and prove I could do anything I wanted to do."

Ryan ran his eye over the wreckage of the city, which hadn't taken direct hits from nukes like some of the larger metropolitan areas during the war. But the nukes that had claimed nearby silo sites had created enough particle drift to kill off most vegetation and animal life in the days and weeks that followed. Very little had crept back into the area to begin the struggle against the desert and leftover rad spots. The terrain so far had been dull, echoing a depressing monotony.

The city was far more interesting. There were some tall buildings among the shorter ones, but the majority of space was taken on the horizontal rather than the vertical, not like Lantic Ocean coastal villes. At some point decades past, quakes had riven Vegas, splintering it and leaving huge, gaping cracks in the streets. The tectonic pressures had also tumbled down most of the taller buildings.

Ryan glanced at the line of wags ahead of them, then the few that followed. In the six days they'd been traveling, there'd been no sign of Krysty or the others. Not all of the six days had been necessary to make the trip, but Hardcoe and LeMarck had made certain they were used. There'd also been limited interaction with LeMarck, and none at all with the baron. The sec commander treated them like valuable livestock.

"How well do you think you remember your way around the ville?" he asked Mildred.

"Depends on where we go. Vegas is built on a strip where all the action stayed. Provided the pit is located somewhere in that, and the landmarks weren't too screwed up by the quakes and whatever scavengers there might have been, I can find my way around."

"Gives us an edge," Ryan said.

"Mighty slim one," J.B. acknowledged.

Ryan nodded. "Going to have to work with what we have." He stayed at the bars, studying the ville as the convoy drew closer. According to LeMarck and what Ryan had learned from the Heimdall Foundation men, the chilling was scheduled to begin at midnight. He'd wondered about that at first, trying to understand how they'd be able to wander around in the dark and tell who was chilling who. But seeing the way the neon lights lit up the ville's inner core resolved that mystery.

All that remained was the living and the dying.

"Is that the wag housing our companions, Krysty?" Doc asked.

From their vantage point up above the narrow road that led down into Vegas, the red-haired woman adjusted the magnification on her binoculars. She brought the first few wags into focus, not recognizing anyone.

The first wag slowed to cross a narrow wooden bridge that linked the cracked remnants of the highway on either side of a twelve- or fifteen-foot fissure that looked almost as deep. Twilight made it harder to judge distances.

She moved back, scanning each wag in turn. She knew LeMarck by sight. During the last three of the six days they'd spent pursuing the convoy, she'd marked the sec commander's face, knowing him from the description Ryan and Bernsen had provided, the latter confirming it visually on one occasion.

The initial three days of the pursuit, the companions had traveled hell-bent for leather, having to circle around a few times to pick up the convoy's trail. A map of the southwestern United States, found in the overturned wag, had helped them considerably, but had been misleading at times, as well. When they'd caught up with Hardcoe's convoy, they'd had to slow down, waiting for an opportunity to free Ryan, J.B. and Mildred. It hadn't happened. The baron's sec men had kept too tight a rein on things. So Krysty and the others had remained tantalizingly close, but had been given no opportunity to steal their friends away without getting captured in the process.

Jak had come the closest to breaking into the camp, but even he had almost been found out before he could get within a hundred yards of the wags. Sec men in hiding had sprung their trap too early. Jak had gotten away, but the episode had let them know Hardcoe's men considered Ryan and the others as bait, as well as a prize.

A few wags farther down the convoy, Krysty found their captured companions. She focused the binoculars on Ryan, his face visible to her. By his features she knew he was plotting and planning. He hadn't given up at all.

"It's them," she announced to the others. She wished she could tell her lover that they were there, at the very least offer him some words of encouragement. She put those thoughts from her mind and turned to what she could do.

"Ville pretty with lights. Baron must have lots gas and generators," Jak said. "Not know only chilling waiting inside."

"Well, against yon walls and phantasmal faery illuminations," Doc said, "we shall test our mettle and discover if we should be found yet wanting in purpose and desire."

Jak nodded and looked at Krysty. "Sec tight on bridge. How we cross?"

Krysty put the binoculars away. "On foot. There's no

other choice. We'll carry as much gear as we can. Darkness should cover us well enough."

"We're just going to get caught," Bernsen said gloomily.

Jak popped the hood on the wag and took the starter coil, pocketing it. Krysty understood enough about mechanics to know that the wag couldn't start without the coil.

"Leave you here," the teenager offered.

Bernsen's mouth opened, and his eyes looked dead. "No." He mopped his forehead with his sleeve. "No, I'm afraid that won't do at all."

Krysty gazed at Jak and Doc. "Strip down your gear. Keep the weapons and medication, anything that will help once we reach Ryan and the others. Everything else we leave here."

"You realize someone may find the wag," the scientist interjected.

"Mebbe," Krysty said. "And mebbe they won't find it until the Big Game is over and we have the others out. Have to take the chance."

"This is, I've heard," Doc said, gazing at the ville of lights spread out before them, "certainly the place for taking chances and hoping for long shots to come through."

The stripping completed, Krysty asked Jak to take point and Doc to keep Bernsen under guard. Then they moved off into the night.

INSIDE VEGAS, the wag carrying Ryan, J.B. and Mildred split off from the others and rolled down the cracked and crumbled streets. A contingent of pedestrian sec men fell into a jog beside the wag, their gear rattling as they moved. Most of the street signs were up, and Mildred read them off with growing confidence. Several of the streets were too cracked up to be passable by wag. Two-by-twelve boards lay across the cracks, supported by piles of rock and bricks that had been gathered from the debris left by the tumbledown buildings.

The wag slowed as it made its way across the makeshift bridges. The boards creaked under the weight.

"I know where we're at," Mildred said.

"Where?" Ryan peered forward. The brightness of the neon lights increased and the range of colors incredible.

"South Las Vegas Boulevard," Mildred replied. "Back in my day, they called it the Strip." She pointed. "See? Over there is the MGM Theme Park."

Ryan peered in that direction, barely making out the framework of the building. As his eye grew used to the darkness to their right, he spotted the massive statue of a lion toppled over in the street in front of the structure. The huge head had broken off and was separated from its body by dozens of yards. A scar tracked its right cheek, deep and irregular enough to have been caused by a mortar round.

On the north side of the building, perhaps as much as fifty feet of railing stuck out from the ground floor and traveled due north. Weeds, trees and brush had scrambled up between the cracks of the broken streets and structures, filling the neon-lit ville with clumps of forest.

"What's the railing?" he asked.

"Monorail," Mildred answered. "Used to run people from the MGM to Bally's and back again. They made plenty of places for tourists to drop their money."

Ryan fell silent again, keeping watchful. Opportunities for escape would present themselves if he remained patient. There was no way to force it. He read the signs of the places and streets they passed, listening to Mildred talk to J.B. about the things she'd seen over a hundred years ago.

A huge building with a glittering entranceway stood on

the edge of a precipice. Neon lights announced the name as Bally's. Ryan figured it was the one Mildred had been talking about, especially after he saw part of the monorail sticking out from the side.

The wag swerved off the street, following a path beaten through the growing brush and over built-up patches filling the cracks in the ground. Ryan shifted, holding on to the bars with one hand as he watched a steel door in the wall before the wag. The steel door wasn't part of the original building. It had been added sometime later. Rust covered the facade, blending the dents and tears into a rugged sameness.

With a rough rasping of chain links rolling over a drum, the steel door went up in jerks. The wag driver came to a near stop, then edged forward until the door cleared the top of the vehicle. Inside the parking area beyond, Hayden LeMarck had a full complement of sec men armed to the teeth.

Light came from fluorescent tubes on the high ceiling, supplemented by oil lanterns hanging on the walls and carried by some of the sec men. LeMarck rushed over to the wag, calling out to his men and gathering them around him.

A large, burly man with hair sprouting across his shoulders leaped onto the back of the wag. He fitted a key into the lock and removed it, then whipped the door back. "Out," he ordered. "And if you try anything, we'll gut shoot you and leave you to die while some of those rabid mutie animals we've got penned up eat you."

Ryan led the way out of the wag. The steel door came down with a rush of chain and a clanging thump against the remnants of royal purple carpet over the concrete foundations. He signaled to J.B. with his fingers, telling the Armorer to stand and observe.

LeMarck stopped in front of Ryan, remaining out of easy reach. "Are you ready?"

Somewhere beyond the concrete wall in front of them, the sound of drums beating echoed into the room, accompanied by wild yells and the sound of animal cries. There were also mechanical noises, groaning and hissing that Ryan couldn't recognize.

"I have a choice?" Ryan asked dryly.

LeMarck smiled, but it wasn't a confident effort. He turned to one of the other men. "Get them suited up."

LESS THAN TEN MINUTES later, Ryan had been outfitted with a scarlet armored bodysuit that covered his chest, stomach and groin. He also had his holster, though empty of the SIG-Sauer P-226, and pouches and pockets for ammo and other gear.

The guards took Ryan, J.B. and Mildred up three flights of stairs and down two different hallways until they found Hayden LeMarck. The room was large, a public meeting place of some kind, lit by oil lanterns hanging on wall hooks that left soot patterns on the decorative walls. Ryan reckoned it had been a gaudy of some type at one time, judging from the shelves, remnants of mirrors and free-standing bar against the back wall.

LeMarck stood in front of the opposite wall, which had taken heavy damage in the past. Sledges had been used to knock out sections of it, and glass panes had been puttied in, creating a ten-foot-wide and six-foot-tall window that looked out over some of the worst carnage in Vegas.

It looked as though a giant had stomped a footprint into the center of the ville just beyond Bally's. Keeping his sense of direction even after he'd been brought into the building had been second nature for Ryan. He knew they were facing north.

The neon glare of the ville was strongest at this point, teeming with dozens of colors of differing intensities. The lights slammed against the windows, all of them offset from the others, and created prism effects that spun out over Ryan, J.B., Mildred and the nearest sec men. LeMarck looked as if he were standing in front of a burst rainbow.

He addressed them with a military bearing, hands clasped behind his back. "You people have been given a great honor," he stated, "to be selected as Baron Hardcoe's champions."

J.B. spit on the floor. The spittle splattered over the sec commander's boots.

Color rouged LeMarck's face, but he maintained his calm and ignored the act. "In a few minutes you're going to be released into that pit." He pointed through the glass wall. "Quakes dropped the center of this area years ago. The barons all worked together to build the restraining wall around the outside of the pit area and to rebuild some of the things inside. Like the neon lights."

Ryan could barely make out the metal wall created from pieced-together slabs of concrete and sections of metal.

"You can't get over it," LeMarck said. "It's forty-feet tall. Barbed wire strands circle the top another six feet over that. Concrete was poured on top of the wall beneath the wire, and glass, nails and shards of metal were mixed into it. Even if you found rope and a grappling hook, and could throw it that high, the rope would be cut by the glass and shards on top of the wall. Not to mention the fact that you'd be perfect targets for the snipers along the outer perimeter."

Staring back through the window, Ryan glimpsed two

of the guards in the foreground, obviously walking predetermined areas.

"Whose guards?" Ryan asked.

LeMarck smiled, obviously pleased. "Thinking, are you? Good, I like that. Knew the survival instinct would kick in along the way." He glanced out the window. "The guards are from all the barons' camps, with overlapping fields of fire, on the pit fighters, as well as one another." He shifted his attention back to Ryan. "In years past one of the barons had the idea of using a couple of his wall guards as snipers. They had silenced weapons, thought they wouldn't be noticed. But they were. And they were shot. For every man they shot, one of that baron's men was shot. The two that were left over didn't last long."

"You said there'd be ten of us," Mildred stated.

LeMarck nodded. "And there will be. I wanted to talk to the three of you. You're used to working as a unit. Got a lot of hard miles on you, from the look of you. Saw how you went through those brushwooders. The other seven aren't going to be much help, I'm afraid. Unless you can convince them to listen to you."

Ryan didn't say anything.

"I figure it'd be a waste of time," the sec commander said. "They're going to be scared, not wanting to listen to anyone."

"What's in the pit," J.B. asked, "besides the other teams?"

"Muties—scabbies and stickies," LeMarck answered. "Animals, some of them mutie and some of them not. Four-legged. Snakes. Got some water traps in there with poisonous eels, piranha, anything nasty that could live and kill in that environment."

"If we win," Ryan asked, "we're going to be set free?"

LeMarck lied without hesitation, Ryan not seeing a flicker of guilt in the man's eyes. "Yes."

"How much do you know about the Five Barons and the seven villes?" the sec commander asked. He checked his wrist chron.

"Man whose team wins this," Ryan said, "gets control of the seven villes for a year." He didn't give a damn about any of the history of the Big Game. Hoyle and Bernsen had provided enough of it. Once he stepped out into that pit, it was chill or be chilled.

"What about Baron Sparning Hardcoe?"

"I was told he's one of the more efficient chillers in the group," Ryan replied. "Runs second to Baron Connrad in numbers of his private army."

"There's more to Baron Hardcoe than that," LeMarck stated.

"Yeah," J.B. said. "I can see how he'd give folks that impression, what with the way he invites some of them to play this game for him."

The sec commander looked angry and defensive. "The baron is building docks and boats in the seven villes. Building up trade along the northern Cific coastline. People are moving into the villes now, instead of working to stay away from them. There's work there, homes, mebbe a future if they all pull together."

"And he's doing all of this out of the goodness of his soul," Mildred said sarcastically.

"I'm trying to give you something to fight for. What's at stake is bigger than just the people in this room. I want you to see that."

Ryan fixed him with a harsh stare. "If you believe in what Hardcoe's doing so much, why don't you go get nine other people who can fight and believe in the baron as much as you, and you jokers take a dive into that pit tonight."

LeMarck's lips tightened as though he'd just bitten into a sour lemon. He didn't try to answer.

"Got plenty to fight for," J.B. added. "Our lives are on the line here. That's enough for us. And when you boil it down, that's what's good enough for most people. I don't give a rat's ass about docks or boats or trade. Hardcoe's planning on making plenty of jack out of the deal or he wouldn't be doing it. And it's the jack he's got a greedy eye turned to, not the people you say are going to benefit by it."

LeMarck's face hardened. "Move out. Only got a few minutes before they start releasing you people into the pit."

A SHORT WALK LATER, through musty hallways outside rooms that were filled with wrecked furniture, overturned gambling tables and skeletons that had died of rad-drift, Ryan stood in the center of a smaller room lined with metal walls.

LeMarck and his men left them there, bolting the door behind them.

The ceiling had been torn out, leaving an upper level where people could look down on them. A short railing covered with wrapped lengths of razor wire surrounded the opening. In a short time LeMarck was at the railing gazing at them.

A net was suspended from the ceiling above the sec boss, a length of steel cable running through a pulley system holding it in place.

"Our weapons," J.B. said.

"That's right," LeMarck replied, raising his voice to manage the distance. "Figured you might give a better accounting of yourselves if you had the tools you were most familiar with. You'll find they've been well taken care of, and there's ample ammunition for all of them."

"What happens when we run out?" Mildred asked.

"Hopefully you'll be sparing with it and pick your targets," LeMarck told her. "Along the way you'll find you can pick up more from the other teams. Assuming that you've killed them. And there are caches where more ammunition has been placed."

Ryan stared at the double doors in front of him that undoubtedly led into the pit. He crossed the distance and pushed against them. Neither moved.

"Bring the rest of them in," LeMarck ordered.

A moment later seven men entered the room. All of them had a look of hardness, but it was the black giant, his hair tied with bits of cloth, who captured Ryan's attention.

The black man's eyes held yellow madness, like someone who had traveled too long in the rad-blasted lands. His hands were secured behind him. One of LeMarck's sec men moved in behind him and keyed open the cuffs. Giving no warning, the black giant turned and backhanded the sec man.

The man flew through the air and crumpled against the wall by the door, unconscious or dead. Blood trickled from his ears.

"Black Michael!" LeMarck yelled.

The giant ignored the sec commander and leaped to the door, trying to pry it open with his thick fingers. The other six new arrivals quickly put distance between themselves and the big man.

"Stop, you bastard, and move away from that door, or I swear I'll chill you myself." LeMarck drew his side arm.

Black Michael growled insanely. "Do that and you'll be a man short."

"Mebbe."

Ryan wasn't fooled. LeMarck meant his threat, but there was some hesitation in the sec commander.

Black Michael barked laughter, but moved away from the door just the same. He reached up to his shoulders and started pulling on his armor's straps. The vest he wore hadn't been intended for a man of his girth. The outfitters had obviously had a hard time finding something he could wear. The red paint looked fresh.

"Leave that on," LeMarck ordered.

"Fuck you," the giant roared. The straps gave with long tearing noises, and the body armor dropped to the floor. His naked chest, shoulders and abdomen rippled with sweat-slick muscles. "If I'm gonna die, I'm gonna die my way. Shirt makes too much color in the night. Like this, no one see me."

LeMarck said nothing, stepping aside as five men moved into view at the railing. One of them Ryan recognized as Hardcoe. He guessed the others were barons, as well. All of them had bands tied around their left biceps. Hardcoe's was red. The other colors were purple, orange, green and blue.

"I count nine in your color, Hardcoe," a baron with green on his arm stated. Blue-jay feathers hung from his earrings, and his face looked carved from angry stone.

"The tenth man refuses to wear his armor, Baron Conn-rad," LeMarck said.

"Rules say the champions are supposed to wear their color," Connrad said. "Keep down confusion on who's who."

"No," Hardcoe said coolly, "the rules don't say that. As to confusion, take a look at this man. I don't think there'll be any confusion with him."

Connrad scowled but said nothing more. The group passed on.

LeMarck looked relieved. At his command two men stepped into the room and grabbed the man Black Michael had hit, pulling him out.

Grinning, the giant crossed the room to Mildred. "Black, like me," he said, looking down at her.

"Black," Mildred agreed, not backing away, "but not like you at all."

Black Michael raised a hand as if he were about to slap her.

"No," J.B. said, stepping forward into a combat stance, his hands loose and ready before him.

Laughing, Black Michael turned to face the Armorer. He dwarfed J.B. in height and in build. "You think you mean enough to take me, little man?"

"Up to you whether we find out," J.B. replied.

"Break you in half like a stick."

The Armorer didn't make a reply, slowly reaching out and moving Mildred behind him out of the big man's zone.

"This man something special to you?" Black Michael asked Mildred.

She didn't answer.

"You don't have to tell me," the giant said. "I can see in your eyes. Mebbe I'll catch up to you and him out there in the dark and those pretty lights. I twist his head, and you can hear how his neck cracks and see him jump when he dies." He laughed again, an evil sound that filled the small room.

J.B. continued guiding Mildred away from the man, never turning his back to Black Michael.

"Wait for me out in the dark, little man," the giant promised, "and I'll be there soon."

"Ryan," the Armorer called, wrapping an arm around Mildred. The woman shuddered against him.

"Extra baggage," Ryan said in a flat voice. "See no sense in taking it along."

J.B. nodded.

Black Michael ignored them.

Up above, LeMarck's sec team raised two sheets of see-through plas and braced it with four-by-four beams, booting them together in an L-shape.

"Lower the weapons," the sec commander ordered.

The cable creaked as it was fed through the pulley, and the net descended into the room. Ryan, J.B. and Mildred were the first to reach the net as it came within grasp. The other men came swiftly, shoving at one another to claim their weapons.

J.B. reached into the net and pulled his S&W scatter-gun from the collection. Black Michael surged forward, swatting men out of his way without a care. Moving quickly but without mistake, the Armorer opened the shotgun's receiver. Ryan spotted the red casing of the round sliding home as J.B. released it.

Ryan took up his own P-226 and worked the slide, stripping the first round into the chamber. As he watched,

Black Michael picked up a huge revolver. From the size of it, Ryan guessed it was a remake of a .454 Casull, large by any standard, but looking small in the ebony giant's fist.

Without warning, J.B. shoved the shotgun's muzzle into Black Michael's face, and pulled the trigger.

The ebony giant's pistol hand had been moving toward the Armorer, but when the explosion of fléchettes slammed into his face and ripped away the flesh, diving in through the eye holes, the nasal cavity, and the mouth, emptying out his brain pan in a crimson-and-gray rush, the hand flopped lifelessly away. The Casull clanked as it hit the floor.

"What the hell are you doing?" LeMarck demanded.

The blast from J.B.'s shotgun was still echoing in the room.

Ryan fired two shots, aiming for LeMarck's heart. He wasn't surprised to see them leave splintered fractures across the surface of the plas but not penetrate.

Two sec men stepped around the edges of the plas, only exposing enough of themselves to aim their weapons into the room below.

"No!" LeMarck screamed, raising his weapon.

J.B. fired another round. A few of the fléchettes became embedded in the plas, but the majority of them caught the sec man in the shoulder and arm, spinning him, his flesh in tatters.

LeMarck blew out the back of the other sec man's head. Brain matter splattered across the plas in a red gush. Most of the remaining sec men appeared confused.

"Leave them alone!" the sec boss ordered. "Any man raises a weapon against them dies by my hand!"

The sec men calmed down grudgingly.

"What the hell do you think you're doing?" LeMarck demanded.

"Man wasn't going to work with us," Ryan said. "Figured we weren't going to let him work against us, either."

"You stupe son of a bitch!" LeMarck roared. "You've got one less man to fight for the baron!"

"Tell the baron he's always welcome to join in, fight for himself," Ryan replied. Then he turned to the other six men, ignoring the sec boss. "How many of you want to take a chance on getting out of here alive?"

Two of them answered immediately, while the other four remained silent. After a moment one of them asked, "Why the hell should we join up with you? Way I understand it, it's every man for himself out there."

"Mebbe," Ryan agreed, "but if you aren't working with me, then I'll put my sights on you when I see you. Work with me, mebbe we can find a way clear of here."

"Have you seen that wall?" the man asked. "Fuck, ain't no way we're going to climb that."

"In or out?" Ryan asked. Though he kept the barrel pointing down, he swiveled the SIG-Sauer in the man's direction.

"Don't give a feller much choice," the man stated.

"Choices ended the minute Hardcoe's people dropped you in this hellpit," Mildred said. Her own Czech target pistol was in her hand.

"Lady's right, Owen," one of the other undecided men admitted. "If we don't throw in with him, it mebbe means going up against him in the end. Seems to know his business all right. Mebbe with him we'll have a chance of getting clear of this once and for all with a whole skin."

Another man agreed after Owen nodded.

The fourth man said, "Fuck, that still leaves us going up against him in the end." He glanced around at his comrades. His words carried weight.

"Don't have to be that way," Ryan said.

"You see any other way for it?" the man asked.

"Yeah," Ryan said tightly. "All of us getting out of here."

"Mister, I don't know where you're from, and don't even give a fuck, but you got to know one thing from the get-go. Ain't nobody never escaped from the pit once they were shut up in it."

Ryan regarded the man. "You mean, nobody yet."

"He's got brass, Fielding," Owen said. "Got to give him that." He turned to Ryan. "I'm Owen. This's Fielding. Two skinny jaspers in the back are Tyler and Taylor Thompson. Twins, if you ain't made that out yet. Heavy guy's Moosh Whandell. And that leaves Clingdon."

Ryan quickly introduced himself and the others.

"You people know each other?" he asked when he'd finished.

Owen shook his head. "The twins knew either other. The rest of us met on the wag. Knew Black Michael's name 'cause the sec guards were always having a hard time with him. Heard he bit a man's cock off in Jakestown before they put him on the wag and brought him out here. Bastard sick son of a bitch."

"Know what we're up against?"

"Some of it. Sec men liked trying to scare the shit out of us telling us stories."

"Start off figuring it's all gospel," Ryan said, "we'll find out the truth of it as we go along. We're going out there together. You move when I say move, where I say move, and you move damn fast."

"You know something we don't?" Fielding asked. "That why you were getting such special treatment?"

"Hell," Ryan said, "I'd never even heard of the villes or the Big Game little over a week ago."

"So this is all new to you," Fielding said. "Why should we listen to you?"

"This pit's new to me," Ryan said, "but chilling isn't." He made his voice hard, abrasive. The other men could be an advantage, and he wanted to win them over. "There's a certain safety in numbers."

A siren ripped through the cavernous upper floor, startling several of the sec men who'd been peering anxiously down into the lower floor.

"Open the doors!" LeMarck said. "It's time!"

Chains ratcheted in their housings as the wheels above were turned. The double metal doors drew apart by inches at a time. In short order the light from inside the room spilled onto the wreckage of buildings soaking up the neon glamour of the Five Barons' private killing ground.

Ryan stepped forward, the SIG-Sauer in his fist as he scanned the edges of the wall less than ten feet higher than his present position. Moonlight and neon reflected from the keen edges of the razor wire looped around the poles set on top of the wall surrounding the quake-sunk area. Other patches gleamed, as well. Upon closer inspection, Ryan identified them as glass and sharp bits of metal.

Even with the brief running start that was possible from the lip of the room jutting over the grounds below, Ryan knew he'd fall short of the wall, and not get the height he needed to grab the top. He glanced at the ground. The terrain had been shaped over the years, falling away as much as fifteen feet in a direct fall, then sloping away to the floor of the pit.

He raked his gaze around the pit and thought he could see two other groups making the jump into the battlezone to the west of them. He also spotted some bulky shapes moving casually through the dark, and some feline ones, as well. Something hungry snarled out its warning, building up its courage.

"Get outside!" LeMarck yelled.

"Fucker can't make us do that," Fielding said.

As if he'd heard the man, the sec commander made a show of pulling a pin on a gren, counting down, then dropping it into the room. It smacked against the concrete floor.

"Move!" Ryan ordered as he stepped off the edge of the building. He dropped fast, landing on spongy ground, his knees giving as he dealt with the sudden stop. Mildred and J.B. were on his heels. The other six men dropped only a heartbeat or two later.

Then the gren blew, spewing forth chunks of Black Michael that rained all over the terrain. Something in a pool of water only a few yards away reared up, seized one of the ebony giant's hands in its sharp teeth and pulled it into the mud-colored liquid.

Overhead the doors closed, cutting off any hope they might have had about using the room as an escape hatch later.

Ryan watched, waving his group back while the rectangle of light coming from the room closed off and disappeared. He looked at his friends, perspiration already making his skin slick under the armor.

"J.B.," he said, "you've got a point. Mildred, you're behind him, leading these men." He made sure Fielding and the others heard. "I'm walking slack."

They all nodded.

"Weapons out," Ryan said. "Safeties on until I tell you otherwise. We're going to keep a low profile for as long as we can. Kill quick and kill silent if we get the chance. Those other teams can take each other out for a while.

They do it proper and really work on it, mebbe they can cut down the odds for us."

When there were no questions, Ryan gave the order to move out. They sank into the shadows, listening to the first of the firefights break the natural rhythms of the night creatures gathered in the pit.

Ryan stayed ten yards ahead of his group, panga in his right hand. Screams echoed all around him, punctuated by single shots and by short bursts from automatic weapons. Residual heat contained in the pit, whether from atmospheric conditions or from some other source, covered him with perspiration. His clothing stuck to his skin. Insects, including some of the largest mosquitoes he'd seen since his trek through Minnesota, swarmed him, darted at his eyes, danced on his exposed flesh and penetrated his clothing not covered by the armor.

Most of the neon lights were mounted on the buildings on either side of the cracked street twenty yards to their left. A few of the buildings were whole, but most of them were smashed. Whoever had put the lights back into operation had known something about electrical work. Fields of brightly colored illumination overlapped one another, creating even more tints, ripping away even the blackest shadows.

Glancing up at the wall forty feet above him, twenty feet above the nearest and tallest tree, Ryan saw the perimeter guards walking their assigned posts. Killing them from the distance was simple enough, especially with the Steyr slung over his back. But it didn't give them a way out.

He moved on, looping around a collection of busted and rusted wags. Something shifted inside, giving Ryan the only warning he received. He backed away a half step from the vehicle as a serpent's head shot out of the dark recesses.

The snake's mouth was open wide, jaws distended and fangs glistening bone white.

Ryan raked the panga through the thick neck behind the wedge-shaped head, decapitating it. Operating on nerve reflex, the rest of the snake's thirty-foot body came coiling out of the burned wag. Bleeding profusely from the stump, the serpent's body writhed on the ground, leaving black splatter patterns.

"Ryan!" Mildred called.

"I'm okay," he called back, scanning the wag for any further movement as the snake continued to flop around. Nothing else appeared. He took up point again, then noticed the shifting shadows under a series of forked branches from a fifteen-foot-tall spruce.

The back of Ryan's neck tightened, feeling eyes on him now. A gleam of metal flickered, picking up a purple and then a turquoise haze from the neon lights surrounding them. He reached down for the SIG-Sauer, moving sideways so his blaster hand was away from them.

Then branches cracked over Ryan's head. A massive feline head shook as the big animal regained purchase and leaped at him.

Clearing the blaster of leather, Ryan barely had time to yell a warning to the others before he was dodging, trying to get clear of the big mutie cat that was determined to drop on top of him.

DEAN GLANCED UP at the second story through the hole that had been chopped through the ceiling of the first-floor room he was in. Baron Vinge Connrad's sec teams poured liquid into the room from a fifty-five-gallon drum. It sloshed and sparkled in noisy glugs as it splashed against the wall and the floor.

The sharp, sweet odor told Dean what it was in a single drawn breath. "Gasoline!" he yelled to the other boys. They all retreated to the farthest wall.

Perry had drawn back, separating himself from the rest of the group even though he wore the same green armored vest as the rest of them.

Dean pressed against the double doors that would open onto the pit area. He was tired from seven days of travel, of constantly looking along their backtrail to see if his dad or some of Brody's sec people were following. In all that time he'd seen no one. Now his nerves were stretched tight as catgut on a bow. Adrenaline surged inside him again, though, as the gasoline pooled around their feet.

"Dirty fuckers!" Louis railed, his blond hair plastered to his skull by the heat that had stifled them in the room. "You brought us all this way just to set us on fire? That it?"

Dean felt like yelling, too, but he knew it would have been just out of fear, and he didn't want to give them that. He leveled his Browning Hi-Power. Solomon had stolen it out of Nicholas Brody's safe, proving that the phys-ed teacher hadn't planned on going back to the school after the transaction, and had given it to their captors with an explanation that it was Dean's personal weapon. Vinge Connrad had been pleased to discover that Dean had such a weapon, and had made returning the weapon a presentation just before the other boys were armed.

Squeezing the trigger, Dean fired at the sec boss now brandishing an unlighted torch. The bullet plunked into the see-through plas sheet on a tangent that would have put it squarely between his target's eyes.

The sec boss nearly fell over himself trying to get away, then glared at the misshapen chunk of lead hanging in front of him.

"What the hell do you think you're doing?" Ethan Perry demanded. He pushed himself off the wall and came at Dean.

Shifting the blaster to cover Perry, Dean said, "Don't." One word, delivered hard, gave the implicit understanding there'd be no negotiations.

"Back off," Louis ordered, moving into position beside Dean, his pistol in both hands but not pointed at anyone.

Perry made a move to pull his own blaster.

"No," Louis said to Perry. "You do it and I'll put you down myself."

"Stupe fucker's going to set off the gasoline shooting that damn gun," Perry complained.

"He does, they do," Louis said, "you really give a shit which way it goes?"

Connrad's sec boss laughed. "You little boys got more sand in you than I'd have thought. Mebbe the baron did have the right idea."

"Ceiling up there is made of metal and concrete," Dean whispered to Louis. "Bullets'll bounce pretty damn good. Figure the angles right, that bulletproof glass won't do dick for them."

Louis gave him a tight nod. "Better than dying in here with nothing done." He raised his voice.

"Moxen?"

"Yeah?"

"Cover Perry. He moves, tries to pull his blaster, gun him down and be done with it."

"You got it." Moxen lifted his .45 and pointed it at Perry's chest. An evil grin tightened the big youth's round face.

Dean went one way, his boots slapping through the gasoline, leaving Louis circling around the other. When he had the angle he wanted, Dean fired the Browning rapidly, zipping rounds past the empty space not covered by the heavy bulletproof plas.

The sec man laughed, pointing down at the boys. That stopped when one of the sec men caught a flattened and slowed bullet that cored through the side of his head and tore his jaw off. The others were in shock, watching as the dying man collapsed against the plas with blood spraying from his ruined face. The man tore the plas sheet from the grips of the men who were struggling to hold it stable. Released, the plas came crashing down into the lower room, sending up geysers from the inch-deep gasoline pool that had gathered across the floor.

Dean continued firing, driving the sec men back, taking down two more of them. The other boys joined them in blasting the sec team.

Curses and screams of pain rewarded their combined efforts, the blasting and the voices almost covering over the shrill buzz of the siren. The double doors abruptly jerked open just as Vinge Connrad appeared behind the single remaining plas sheet. He had his blaster in hand and was scowling down into the room. His eyes locked with Dean's.

"You arrogant little whelp!" the baron snarled. "I might have known you'd be ringleading this!"

Dean exchanged his empty clip for a fresh one, careful to place the expended one in his pants pocket. His dad had been a stickler about saving anything that could be used again. Especially if it was hard to come by. He thumbed the slide release and stripped the first round into the chamber.

The double doors gaped completely open. Gasoline dripped over the edge, then began a cascade even though the drum had emptied.

Raising his blaster, Dean put three rounds into the plas sheet in front of Connrad's face.

The baron grinned, not worried at all that the bullets might penetrate. "You do me proud, boy. Truly you do. Now you haul ass out there and kill everything you can. Don't let your guard down even for a moment, because they're all going to be out to kill you."

Dean sidestepped, keeping up the Hi-Power, finding a new angle to bounce bullets. He started firing as soon as the muzzle cleared the plas sheet. Bullets skidded from the walls and whizzed through the ranks of the sec men, driving them to the ground again. Out of his peripheral vision, Dean watched the hot brass drop into the gasoline, make the liquid sizzle just a second, then sink.

"That's it, boy," Connrad said. "Keep that spirit." He took out a self-light, scratched it to life on his jeans, then applied it to a torch he got from one of his sec men. "Get moving. Fly or fry."

The torch caught easily. The baron let it burn for a moment, giving the flames time to grow stronger.

"Dean," Louis said, "time to go." Some of the other boys were already dropping over the side. Perry was among them.

Stubbornly Dean tried to manage a new angle, reading the way the walls and ceiling were set up.

Without another word, Connrad pitched the torch out into the open. Sparks peeled back off it as it dropped, smoke coiling in the trail it made through the empty air.

Dean turned and ran for the double doors. Louis was waiting, his face pale with fear, eyes reflecting the falling torch.

As Dean reached the double doors, blinking his eyes trying to get some of his night vision in place, he was aware of the gasoline bursting into fiery movement behind him. He turned his head only slightly, pounding his feet hard against the concrete floor and trying not to think about slipping and falling into the gasoline.

A wave of blue flames, turning yellow on the ends from the richness of the fuel, trailed him to the double doors.

Louis leaped from the edge out into the night.

Dean had a brief impression of buildings, concrete sidewalks and streets that seemed to be choking on underbrush. Then he launched himself out into space, fear causing his heart to bang against his ribs as if it were going to tear through his breastbone.

Gravity took over and he fell. Before he made it to the ground, the flames rushed through the double doors after him. Coiling, the fire followed the stream of gasoline from the doors down the fifteen feet to the ground. Along the way it ignited spatters in the air, turning them into fizzy comets. Most of them died out before hitting bottom.

The flames also set Dean's gasoline-saturated boots on fire. He felt the heat flare up around his calves, scorching his pant legs.

When the fire hit the ground, it instantly spread across

the gasoline pooled at the base of the room at Bally's, lighting up the area at once.

Seeing his flaming boots, Dean landed hard and stamped them, trying to put out the fire. Ahead of him and a few yards to his right, he spotted a bowl of water nearly three yards across. He ran to the water, knowing it would be only seconds before the flames exhausted the gasoline clinging to his boots and started burning the footwear itself. There was no way he could do without boots.

He didn't stop running until he was almost knee-deep in the pool. White smoke curled up from the surface as the fire extinguished with hisses.

A bullet whizzed by Dean's head, sounding like a large buzzing insect. A heartbeat later the sound of the initial shot cracked over them. By then the second bullet was already on its way. Enrique Green howled and went down on his butt, grabbing at his left leg.

Dean whirled, changing clips in his blaster. He hunkered down in the water, wanting to make sure there was no chance the fire on his boots would restart.

Green was on the ground holding his left leg, bright blood staining his left thigh while Moxen and Louis grabbed his arms. Together they dragged the boy to cover behind a stand of trees. Bobby Handley already had a strip of cloth torn from his own shirt ready to make a compress to cover the wound.

"Anybody see the son of a bitch did this?" Louis demanded.

"I got him," Jordie Ferguson announced calmly. The boy lay behind a wag lying on its side, a sniper rifle extended before him, snugged into his shoulder. "Tree out there. How far?"

Still low in the water, his backside almost touching the

surface, Dean glanced at the tree Jordie was talking about. It was obvious, because a bright muzzle-flash blinked on and off again. The third round dug a hole in the muddy ground near Green's position.

"Hundred and twenty, hundred and forty yards," Dean called out.

"Which one?" Ferguson asked, working the range marking on his telescopic sight.

"Split the difference," Louis yelled, "and knock that guy's lights out before he kills one of us!"

Ferguson lifted the rifle, then squeezed off a shot, quickly working the bolt action and readying another round. The second bullet wasn't necessary. In the distance the sniper dropped from the tree without a sound.

Dean started to move from the water, but something rubbery and strong wrapped around his leg and wouldn't let him move. Glancing down, he heard a snuffling of loosed breath breaking through water, then a gray body rose up, pulled along by the arm-leg gripping Dean.

It was a mutie of some kind. That was all Dean knew for sure. The thing had five rubbery limbs nearly six feet in length at first glance. Then he realized one of the limbs had eyes, three of them, spaced in a triangular shape. In the center was an algae-covered shell that looked whole, then opened up into a teeth-filled mouth big enough for Dean to shove his head into.

Two more limbs roped around the boy's left arm and his neck, pulling the mouth toward his abdomen. Jaws extended, filled with razor-sharp ivory, reaching for Dean's flesh.

Raising his blaster, the boy felt his breath lock tight in his chest. He fired several rounds, blowing chunks of the shell away from the creature, sending the jaws retreating. As the limbs withdrew from their tight embrace, he put three more rounds through the appendage with the eyes.

The mutie beast screamed as it released Dean and slid back into the dark water. Blood floated on top of the water like an oil slick, throwing off patterns that picked up the garish neon lighting surrounding the pit.

"Hot pipe!" Dean said, backing out of the water with his blaster pointing at the pool. He was shaking, but tried to get over it quick. He wished he knew if the thing were still alive, then decided it didn't really matter, because he wasn't going close to any more basins. He joined the other boys.

Louis was staring intently at the terrain. "Remember how Solomon used to say that every battlefield was like a chessboard?" he asked.

Dean didn't remember, so he figured it was something the phys-ed teacher had talked about with the ten original members of the team. But the others nodded.

"Always said the best place to take was the high ground," Louis went on. He stabbed a finger through the darkness. "That, I figure, is about the highest ground we could take."

Following the direction the blond youth was pointing, Dean made out the red neon lights proclaiming The Mirage. More glittering sputtered in front of the immense building. He squinted his eyes, not daring to believe what he was seeing, then recognized that his eyes hadn't played tricks on him. Five, possibly six stories up on the building, water gushed out, creating falls that fell somewhere in front of it, lost in trees and foliage.

"Place is huge," Conor commented. "Be hard to hold."

Louis nodded. "We're not going to try to hold the whole thing. We'll just find a place inside it that we can hold, wait things out and make them come to us."

"Supposed to be chilling these people out here," Green said, his face showing the pain he was in.

Louis looked at him. "That what you want to do, Enrique? Start wandering around finding people and things to chill? This isn't a shooting gallery. Me, I'm just wanting to get out of here with as much of my own skin intact as I can."

"Said they'd chill us if we didn't fight." Green indicated the wound in his leg, then jerked a thumb back at the gasoline fire still coiling out of the room they'd been forced to evacuate. "I believe them."

Louis made his face hard, sweeping the faces of his friends with his gaze. "I don't figure they're planning on letting any of us out of here. And that's the truth. We never even heard about these Five Barons and their seven villes until a few days ago. Hell, we didn't know anything about Solomon, either. If they let us go, they'd know they were in for some trouble from mebbe our parents. Mebbe us on down the line. Safe jack's just to kill us and be done with it."

"You got a mean way of putting things," Bobby Handley said.

"Mean world," Louis replied.

"Best way is like Louis said," Dean spoke up. "Chill anybody we have to, but keep an eye out for a chance to get out of this place."

Louis nodded. "Anybody want to do it another way, they're welcome to pick up and leave."

No one said anything, but most of them shuffled nervously, flinching when they heard a sudden spurt of gunfire to the east of them. For a moment Dean almost thought it was his dad's SIG-Sauer blaster. Then he shoved the idea away. It was just a hope that he had no business nursing along. His dad was a long way from this place.

Hayden LeMarck stood behind Baron Hardcoe's chair and stared out the bulletproof window. His hand rested on his Glock blaster, the restraining strap already popped open enough that a yank would have it in his hand. Wallis Thoroughgood stood at his side, eating a turkey drumstick from the kitchen that had been set up outside the room.

The other barons sat in chairs in front of the window, as well, two sec men allowed in with each of them.

The window gave a view of the pit that had been created of the quake-stricken area. LeMarck watched the sporadic gunfire dispassionately, making himself breathe regular enough to appear calm. For the past handful of years, he'd remained on watch in the room during the Big Game. No experience was ever the same as a previous one.

"Boys?" Baron Dettwyler drawled, pausing to glance at Vinge Connrad, who was safely out of arm's reach. "You sent boys into that pit, Vinge? Were you addled when you made that decision?"

Connrad hoisted a glass filled with a native beer Hardcoe had brought from the seven villes in weather-beaten casks. Though the barons had separate views on how rulership of the villes should be managed, they all kept the beer makers and wine presses moving right along, no matter in whose hands the villes were.

Taking a long drink, Connrad wiped the foam from his beard with the back of his hand and belched loudly. "You haven't seen those boys in action. Trying to get them out into the pit, they chilled four of my men in that room, injured seven others before we chased them out with burning gasoline."

"They shot bullets through the plas sheets?" Dettwyler asked. He was a huge, fat man with a bald head, and many people, LeMarck knew, made the mistake of thinking Dettwyler soft or simple. Neither was the truth. The fat disguised hard bands of muscle, and Dettwyler had a preference for biting out the throat of anyone he fought in hand-to-hand combat. A black silk half mask covered the right side of his face. Years back the baron's head had been forced up against a boiling-water container in a mutie encampment. The metal had contained some dangerous rad, hanging on from the nukecaust. The burn had opened Dettwyler's face, and the rad that seeped into it caused chronic cancers that had to be cut out, leaving a raw, bleeding area that never healed properly.

"Not through the plas," Connrad corrected. "Little bastards bounced bullets off the wall."

"I've never seen or heard of that being done." Francis Giskard's youthful face broke into a delighted smile. He raised his glass. "I must compliment you on your choice of champions this year. They appear to be most industrious."

Connrad lifted his glass and drank the rest of its contents.

"Where did you get them?" Giskard asked.

LeMarck kept track of the conversations, but his eyes remained focused on the pit area. One of the wall sec men near the old Las Vegas Convention Center raised a flash with a purple lens cover, signaling twice. They had thermographic binoculars and could see a person's body heat through the walls of buildings. Special rad buttons inside the body armor, treated so they reflected different levels of light, announced the color of the person they looked at.

"It appears that you've lost a couple more men, Giskard," Deke Ramsey, the remaining baron, said. He was tall and ruddy, his rust red hair shot through with gray and thinning on the top. "That brings your total lost to what? Five?"

"Four," Giskard said easily. "And might I remind you, I need only one to win." He leaned forward and slid two more purple beads across the free-standing abacus on the low table in front of him. "Connrad, I await your answer."

"You can wait on it," Connrad growled. "It's my secret."

LeMarck flicked his eyes toward the pit, searching the valleys cut through the shadows by the strings of neon lights. He got only a glimpse of the boys in their green body armor, then they faded under the tree coverage. It was no great feat of intellect that they were on their way to the Mirage. He smiled to himself, knowing they would find plenty of surprises in the building. Connrad, who was the only baron among them who hadn't had to shift a bead yet, would be doing that in short order. Perhaps it would be a lot of beads. LeMarck waited in anticipation.

"Usually the mortality rate runs much higher at this

point of the game," Dettwyler said. "Perhaps we didn't include enough beasts and muties this year."

"There's plenty," Hardcoe replied. "People we've got out there, they're better chillers than most."

All the barons nodded, then Dettwyler yelled out for more pitchers of beer to be brought.

"Something I want to ask you, Giskard," Connrad said.

"Ask away, my friend."

"Assuming that you by some freak of accident manage to win, what do you plan on doing with the seven villes?"

"I plan on living a life of luxury for a year," Giskard replied. "I'm painfully overdue, as you're well aware."

"Wasn't talking about that," Connrad said. "I was talking about the construction that Hardcoe's managed this year."

LeMarck felt a tremor of anxiety thrill through him. The statement confirmed that Connrad did have spies among their people at the seven villes. And he hadn't found all of them. He cursed silently.

"An intelligent man would take what I've started," Hardcoe said in a soft voice, "and keep on building."

Connrad whipped his head around. "That's what you think?"

"Yeah."

"You saying I'm not an intelligent man?" Connrad demanded.

LeMarck shifted in response to the new stances assumed by the sec men behind Connrad. His hand closed hard around the butt of the Glock.

"Didn't say that," Hardcoe said flatly.

"I think you did."

Hardcoe shrugged. His pistol was in his lap, LeMarck knew, barely covered by a red cloth napkin with white dice showing black pips on the faces. "Up to you what you think."

Connrad showed wolf's teeth, a rictus devoid of anything near human emotion, showing only cold calculation. Then he laughed raucously. "Better hope you win, Sparning, because I'm going to burn you out if you don't. And that's a promise."

Out on the wall, a sec man raised a flash with a red lens. It blinked on and off.

LeMarck surprised himself by holding his breath, waiting for the lens to flash again. But it was only the once. Hardcoe leaned forward and slid over another red bead on the abacus on the table in front of him.

"Your second casualty," Connrad stated.

"Only my first in this Mars Arena," Hardcoe acknowledged. "It's sure a fit place for that old god of war. But the Big Game is young yet. Don't count your victims before you see them stretched cold on the slabs in the morning."

Connrad laughed loudly, sure of himself.

LeMarck hated the sound, but his thoughts turned instantly to the red team out in the pit, wondering which among them had been lost. He hoped it wasn't the one-eyed man.

RYAN WENT TO GROUND, rolling over twice to put more yardage between himself and the big mutie cat.

The huge animal's shoulders stood almost as tall as Ryan's armpit. The eyes spit green fire, rolling in the weak moonlight, threaded with brilliant crimson blood lines burning in the yellowed whites. Its fur was night black, and white fangs stabbed free of purple-gray lips, drooling crystal-clear strings.

The cat landed with a loose thump in the area where

Ryan had stood. Spitting out a wicked, irritated cough, the animal sprang after him.

J.B.'s Uzi ripped a spray of bullets against the trees and through the brush where it had been standing, but the mutie cat gave no pause at all.

Ryan squeezed off two rounds, faster than he'd wanted to because he knew he didn't have the shot he needed. Both bullets creased the raised muscle mass surrounding the cat's neck; neither did any permanent damage.

"Get back, Ryan!" Mildred yelled. "Get back and give me some room!"

Her last words got tangled up in the sudden screams and yells of the stickies breaking out of the brush. Gunfire broke out in earnest as the other members of the group opened fire. Even with a number of them going down, the stickies rushed forward, waving clubs and stone-sharpened knives made of whatever metal scraps they could find.

The cat's shoulder smashed into Ryan. He barely managed to avoid the snapping jaws, but the impact knocked the SIG-Sauer from his hand. There was no time to bring up the Steyr because the mutie cat wheeled around instantly.

Whipping its head forward again, the cat tried to sink its fangs into Ryan's throat. Even focused on the animal as he was, he was aware of the stickies getting closer.

J.B. and Mildred raced forward to take away the no-man's-land that separated the stickies from Ryan and the cat, grabbing cover behind trees and rocks where they could. Spears sailed through the air, followed by a few stone axs and squared-off hammers that split or broke off pieces of the rocks they slammed against.

Ryan caught the cat by its dish-shaped ears, halting the wedge-shaped head. It howled in pain and surprise. Instantly changing tactics, the cat curled up backward and tried to bring its claw-studded hind legs into play.

Already expecting the move, Ryan wasn't there when the claws slashed through empty air. He moved to the right, feeling that he was moving in slow motion next to the cat's quickness.

Before the animal could come around, Ryan grabbed a fistful of the loose hide at its neck. With a lithe jump, he bounded onto the cat's shoulders, he gripped the fur-covered flesh he had hold of as tightly as he could, then locked his legs around in front of the cat's forward legs so it couldn't rip him to shreds with its hind claws.

The cat snarled and spit, twisting and turning to rid itself of its burden.

Ryan held on, putting his body on top of the cat's, weighing down the animal's head. Making the cat work the larger muscles of its body to support him and try to throw him off would cause the beast to use up oxygen more quickly, slowing and weakening it. Ryan still believed the creature could outlast his own strength. He leaned forward, biting into the animal's neck in an attempt to forge one more point of attachment.

He ripped the panga free and used his left hand to work the big knife. Reaching under the mutie cat's neck, he stabbed it in the chest. The beast quivered as though an electric shock had hit it.

Drawing the panga from its flesh sheath, Ryan stabbed again, burying the weapon as deep as he could, then twisting it to tear the wound open as wide as he was able. The cat snapped its jaws as he pulled the knife free again, barely missing sinking its ivory fangs into his arm.

The exertion of hanging on, avoiding the cat's snapping jaws and being on the offense took its toll. Ryan had difficulty breathing, choking on the wet, smelly fur in his mouth, the smell of fresh blood clogging his nostrils.

He took a fresh grip on the panga, shifting the blade. Knowing he couldn't hang on to the cat much longer, feeling the burning ache throbbing deep in his shoulder, his lungs working hard to suck in air he couldn't breathe, he drew the panga hard against the mutie cat's throat, pulling with everything he had left. The effort unseated him from the cat's back, but not before he felt the cascade of hot blood spill in waves across his knife arm.

Ryan sailed backward, flailing for something close to control of his fall. The cat had already turned, searching for its tormentor, scarlet frosting its purple-gray lips and black fur of its throat.

Landing hard on his side, Ryan felt the breath spurt out of his lungs. He forced himself to roll over and get to his feet as the big cat padded toward him. "Fireblast!" he cursed. He spotted the SIG-Sauer on the ground, but it was to the mutie cat's left. Getting it was impossible without coming too close to the injured animal.

"Ryan!" J.B. yelled from his position behind a young oak tree.

It was the only warning Ryan got about the stickie that exploded out of the brush with a spear held at waist level. Reacting to the attacker, Ryan shifted his body, letting the triangular spearhead slide past him, ripping along the scarlet armored vest. He chopped down with his hand and grabbed the forward haft of the spear, watching a look of surprise spread across the stickie's rad-burned features.

Continuing to use his weight and strength to push down the spear, Ryan buried it point first into the ground. He used the added leverage to flip the stickie toward the mutie cat.

The stickie shrieked as it flew upside down, smashing

against the beast's snarling face. The cat closed its jaws over the stickie's head and shoulders. Bone crunched as it chewed. Breath rattled and made sucking noises as it passed through the animal's ravaged throat.

Still hanging on to the spear, Ryan ran to the mutie cat's side. It spit out the dead, nerve-quivering stickie and turned to face him. Before it had time to respond, Ryan moved in close, both hands gripping the spear. He chose his spot, then rammed it in behind the cat's foreleg, aiming for the heart.

The cat lifted a paw and swatted at Ryan, who was already in motion. The claws came close enough to shear his hair and break the skin along his forehead. Warm blood slipped across his face.

The paw slapped against the embedded spear, snapping the haft as if it was a straw. It took a step at Ryan, who'd moved off to recover his SIG-Sauer. By the time he'd scooped up the blaster and raised it, he saw death claim the cat.

The animal's hindquarters shivered, then dropped out from under it. The eyes were already glazing before its head slammed against the ground.

Breathing hard, his throat feeling as if it were on fire, Ryan raked a hand through his curly hair and moved it back out of his face. He kept his blaster pointed in the direction the stickies had attacked from.

Only a few of them were in view, and they were headed back into the brush, some of them limping or holding hands over bleeding wounds. The rest of them were dead, lying in all kinds of poses between the tree line and where J.B., Mildred and the others had held the line.

Waiting for his heart rate to slow to somewhere near normal, Ryan used the slack time to reload the partially spent magazine in his blaster, then do the same to the clips he'd used inside the holding area. "Everybody okay?"

"Not everybody," J.B. said quietly, nodding back and to the right where one of the Thompson twins lay on the ground, a short-hafted ax jutting from his cracked skull. The other twin knelt beside his dead brother, holding his sibling's bloody hand.

Ryan crossed to the younger man, making himself hard. He put a hand on Thompson's shoulder and shook it. "Got no time for grief. We need to be pushing on."

"Fuck you, mister," the twin said hoarsely, his eyes filled with tears. "My brother needs burying."

Ryan met the man's rage and sorrow head-on. "You plan on staying to bury him?"

"It's the Christian thing to do," Thompson replied. "I don't feel good about just leaving him here. Like this."

"You're not supposed to," Ryan said. "But it's got to be done if you're going to have a chance to tell your kids about their uncle. Only way he's going to live on."

Tenderly laying his dead brother's hands across his chest, Thompson stood. His jaw tightened, becoming a hard line as he gripped the haft of the ax and pulled it from the dead man's skull. The blade came free with a sucking noise. He tossed it away.

Ryan adjusted his gear. "Then let's get moving." He looked across the tops of the trees and brush. "See that building there, Mildred?" He studied the red neon lettering on its side.

"The Mirage," the woman said.

"You figure on making for the Mirage?" J.B. asked.

"Highest vantage point," Ryan answered. "We get inside there, mebbe we don't have to worry about the animals or the muties so much."

"We aren't going to be the only ones thinking like that," Mildred warned.

"Kind of planned on that," Ryan said, breaking into a ground-eating stride. "Some of the other groups will think of it eventually. Be best mebbe if we were already set up and waiting for them. I don't think any of the Five Barons have made any converts tonight. Could be we can offer to let them throw in their lot with us. The Mirage is close to the wall on that side."

"Mebbe," J.B. said. "Even if we made a way across the wall, chilled our way through the sec men keeping watch there, we'd still have to find a wag and get enough of a head start on the barons that they couldn't catch us."

"I know." Ryan nodded. "But Trader always said no matter how many beers you drink—"

"—you can only take one piss at a time," the Armorer finished.

Mentally Ryan plotted a course toward the Mirage that would take advantage of as much cover along the way as possible.

A FEATHERY WARNING brushed the back of Krysty's skull. She halted, Doc and Bernsen just behind her, ducking in the jagged crack they were using to creep up on the Las Vegas Convention Center. Her hand stayed tight around her .38 as she scanned the uneven terrain for any sign of Jak or whatever had tripped her psychic alert.

Jak had been less than twenty yards in front of them, but he'd disappeared as quick and traceless as morning mist getting hit by full sunlight.

Thirty yards away the convention center looked as if it had been through a war. Bullets and rockets from past encounters had left scars and gouges on the cracked exterior. If any of the windows had survived intact, Krysty wasn't able to see them.

The thing that made the convention center attractive was its proximity to the eastern wall surrounding the sunken center of the ville. She'd already spotted the men making the rounds on top of the wall, armed with blasters. The sounds of battle and dying, the crash of weapons and the growls of beasts, the smell of foliage thick and sweet with blossoms and otherworldly scents filled her physical senses.

Boots crunched on the rocky terrain only a few yards away.

Freezing into position, knowing sudden movement caught a person's peripheral vision faster than anything, Krysty waited, barely breathing. She saw the sec guard only a few heartbeats later, then he was gone, and the feathery touch inside her head disappeared with him.

She let out a tense breath, surveying the grounds in front of their position again. Three wags were parked near the entranceway to the convention center. She guessed that some of the sec men on top of the wall had driven over, then went up stairs on the inside.

Looking back over her shoulder, she waved on Doc and Bernsen. From the repeated scans she'd made of the sec men on the wall, their interest was primarily on what was going on in the pit.

Jak rose up out of the darkness by the first wag as Krysty reached it. Tense and nervous, she put the .38 on him before he realized who it was. Her finger had taken up the trigger slack.

"Me," the teenager said. "Was inside for a bit."

"What's it look like in there?" Krysty asked.

"Empty," Jak answered, coming closer and speaking in a whisper. "Most sec watching pit."

"Is there a way to get to the top?"

Jak nodded. "Way to get to top. Way underneath, too."

"Underneath?"

"Yeah. Place to park wags. Lots of dead wags already there."

"We'll take a look," Krysty said. "See what we have to work with. Let's check the wags out here first."

They split up. Doc and Bernsen went through one of them while Krysty and Jak took the other two. All of them held ammo and assault rifles, supplies and spare jerricans of fuel.

Jak's wag turned out to have something extra tucked away in a large red toolbox. "Krysty."

She crossed over to him, watching him drop the toolbox on the ground. Someone had put a lock on it, but the youth had gotten rid of it by simply slicing through the plastic grooves. When he opened it, she saw small grease-paper-wrapped blocks placed neatly inside.

"Plas ex?" Krysty asked.

"Yeah." Jak took out one of the small packages, juggling it easily in his hand. "Got detonators, too. Some timers, some distance. Batteries look okay."

"Help me put this stuff into the bags," Krysty said, kneeling quickly and beginning to shove it into her backpack. "Ryan and the others are going to need a back door. With this, I think we can make it."

Ryan took up a position behind an overturned truck nearly a hundred yards from the Mirage. Over the years trees had thrust insistent branches, trunks and roots through the wag's body, anchoring it to the ground while at the same time pushing it inches upward.

The Mirage was incredible. Small falls, probably less impressive than they were before the nukecaust had claimed the ville, jetted from the fifth floor, pouring into cracked basins that held some kind of return system that was only partially working. Lit by sporadic underwater neon lights, the white frothing overflow leaked out into the jungle.

It had taken the group long minutes to cover the distance. In that time they'd had three encounters and had lost Clingdon to a slimy, tentacled creature that had been wrapped up on a spit of land trailing from a broad pond on the east side of Las Vegas Boulevard. Fielding had died during an ambush by members of the blue team coming up from behind and to the side. The companions had dropped three enemy gunners before they'd managed an escape.

"How do you want to handle this?" J.B. asked. He slipped off his wire-rimmed glasses and cleaned them quickly on a handkerchief that looked miraculously dry.

Ryan mopped sweat from his brow and looked back over his ragtag army. Mildred, like the Armorer, was calm and collected, but the three remaining men appeared shaken, on the verge of spooking at every sound around them.

"Front door looks inviting," Ryan said, taking his binoculars from his gear, "but there're already some takers on it."

J.B. lifted an eyebrow. "Missed them. Damn, they must be good."

"Lots of other entertainment going on," Ryan commented dryly. "Missing them is understandable. And they are good."

Turning to face the building, J.B. put his glasses back on. "How good?"

"Good enough that I've only managed to lock on to their shadows a couple times."

"What's their color?"

"Green. Mebbe. They've made themselves hard to see."

"If they're green," J.B. said, "they've got no casualties that I've noticed."

Ryan nodded. The Armorer had been the first to notice the different-colored lenses used by the sec men on top of the wall. When they'd left the dead Thompson twin behind, a harsh, bright light had shone onto the area a few minutes later, splashing the corpse. Shortly after that, J.B. had pointed out the sec man waving the flash with the red lens, aiming the beam back at the big window in Bally's where the barons watched the game.

J.B. had been keeping count automatically. By his count, the purple team had taken the most damage with seven people gone. With four of their teammates dead, Ryan's red team was running a close second in casualties.

"Mebbe they're better than I was thinking." Ryan focused the binoculars and got a chance to watch the last three green-team members race into the Mirage. "They're boys."

"Boys?" J.B. echoed.

Ryan nodded. "From the looks of them. Saw some faces that time. Young. Mebbe early twenties, but I'm putting my jack on them being teens. No later."

"What are boys doing out here?" Mildred asked. "The blue team had some young among them, but they were all men."

"Don't know." Ryan kept careful watch over the entrance, but didn't see any of the green team again. "But they move like a unit. Solid. Working point, wings and slack, everybody keeping covering fire over everybody else."

"Just like Trader set up his operations," J.B. stated. "One of his commandments on War Wag One. 'Thou shalt cover thy neighbor's ass.'"

"Sec squad?" Mildred asked.

"From the look of them," Ryan answered.

"Don't see them as volunteers," Mildred replied. "Unless they got some kind of special arrangement that's going to get them out of here."

"We were promised," J.B. said. "Mebbe they got promised, too, and believed it."

"Stupid if they did," Mildred said. "But they're young. Maybe they just don't know any better."

Ryan put away the night glasses and took up the Steyr. "Two reasons that group went into the Mirage. One, they're hunting the high ground like us, mebbe going to take a chance at that wall if they can. Two, they've got something waiting for them that their baron set up."

"There's only one way to find out," J.B. said.

"Yeah." Ryan stood and pointed at a window on the second floor. "We go in from the side. Second floor. We've already seen some of these buildings are booby-trapped. That one's an obvious choice."

J.B. silently agreed. "What about those boys?"

Ryan kept his face hard. "If they get in our face and raise their weapons, blow them away. No other way about it. Them or us. Me, I'd prefer it be us." He stepped into the nearby shadows and moved toward the building.

DEAN FELT AS IF he'd stepped into another world. His clothing was still damp from the short run through the cascading falls spraying down from the fifth floor of the Mirage. He ran a hand through his hair and brushed it back in wet curls.

Conor still walked point, a rifle cradled in his arms. The boy craned his head, taking in the sights.

Dean knew it wasn't safe to be gawking, but he didn't blame the other boy for it, either. After walking through the entranceway, they were confronted by another jungle that had evidently overgrown its boundaries in the decades since the skydark.

Paths twisted in different directions between the trees and foliage. Some of them were just ruts made by small animals able to get under the lower branches of the trees. Others, though, were man-made, tall and cleared out, the ground pounded bare of grass in patches.

A few of the trails had been tramped down recently. Dean spotted the machete marks on the tree trunks and saw the amputated branches that still showed meat in places. The trees themselves weren't indigenous to the area. Dean recognized them as banana trees and palms. But they were mixed in now with spruce and oak.

The ceiling was eighty or ninety feet overhead, and it was hard to see through the darkness. Occasional brief movements let him know the branches held winged night predators.

"Tighten it up," Louis called out. "Conor, cut your lead to about ten yards and hold up at corners. That way we can back you up if you need it."

"Right."

Dean kept his blaster before him in a two-handed grip. If someone or something jumped out from behind the trees, getting the pistol away from him would be harder with both hands on it.

A few yards farther on, they came in sight of the front desk. Dean had stayed in motels before, from honest-run little places operated by a family, to bigger establishments that held roomers in the second or third floor over the stage areas where gaudy sluts pandered their wares. He'd never seen a front desk as big as the one he gazed at.

Lazy tendrils from dozens of plants crawled across the pitted surface of the desk. Behind it, track lighting with subdued illumination played over the huge glass front of an aquarium. Dean was certain it measured over fifty feet.

Dean shivered as he stared into the cold, menacing eye of a small fish that coasted against the glass wall. Whether it was physically possible or not, he had the feeling the eye was staring right back at him, could see him in the dark and gazed with a chill and hungry limited intelligence.

"Bloodthirsty little bastards," Green said. "Did you see the teeth on that one?"

Curiosity partially satiated, the group moved on under

Louis's command. The hallway closed them in more tightly, and none of them saw the trip wire.

Conor's foot caught it. "Hey," he started to protest, almost stumbling over the wire.

His next words were swallowed by a deafening blast. Dean struggled to maintain his balance, watching Conor fly through the air, the closest of them to the explosion that ripped the front desk to shreds and smashed the front of the aquarium.

Tons of water shot out of the broken glass wall, splashing over all the boys in a tidal wave of soaking force. Dean went down, losing traction and his footing at once. His hand slipped across the wet carpet, but he managed to get a finger hold on a hole that had been worn through the material down to the concrete foundation.

As he tried to shove himself up to his feet, a sharp agony started in the side of his neck, lighting a flame in his brain. He reached up to just above his collarbone, searching for the source of the pain. His fingers slid over a small, scaly body that wiggled fiercely in his hand.

Dean's stomach twisted in sudden sickness at the realization of what had him by the neck. He pulled, but the teeth were clamped on tight, making his flesh come with it. Blood spilled down the side of his neck, then tracked down onto his chest beneath the vest.

"Bastard biter's got me, Louis!" Moxen yelled. "Help me!" One of the carnivorous fish had fastened onto his face. Scarlet lines trailed down his cheek and across his lips. His eyes were wide, filled with fear.

Holding on to the fish with one hand, Dean holstered his blaster and reached for the knife he'd been given. One swipe, and he hacked the fish apart just behind its oversize jaws. The teeth remained embedded and fixed.

Louis crossed over to Moxen and sliced the fish off, inserting a knife blade just behind the bulging eye and twisting it. The jaws popped open, releasing Moxen's face. Louis tossed the dying fish away.

After removing the fish head from his neck, Dean surveyed the other boys. Many of them were screaming and cursing in fright. A chill ran through Dean as he realized how deadly the fish could have been if they'd remained in their own element.

Enrique Green shuddered on the floor as if he were having some kind of fit. The boy's mouth gaped open in a silent scream. The wound in his leg released a spreading pink stain into the inch-deep water littered with flopping fish.

Dean crossed over to Green, intending to help the boy to his feet. When he rolled him over, a sucking noise caught his attention. He glanced down and saw three fish working at the boy's side. They'd opened a large wound just below the rib cage.

Managing to grab one of the fish, Dean watched in horror as another one ate its way into Green's insides. "Oh, shit," Dean said, throwing the first fish away. He cut the second fish off, leaving the head and ignoring the sudden streams of blood squirting out that showed arterial flow.

He tightened his fingers and rammed them into Green's side, tearing the flesh with the pressure he exerted. He touched the sharp fins of the fish's tail, gained almost an inch on it as he watched the ridge of flesh that showed the fish's passage inside Enrique, moving across the boy's stomach. Another surge, and the fish was lost to him.

"Damn, Enrique," Dean cried in frustration. He felt a scaly body slip next to his leg and drew away. Tears filled his eyes, brought on by the helpless rage he felt.

The fleshy ridge turned abruptly, crawling up to Enrique's chest. It slowed when it reached his solar plexus.

"Dean," Green stammered, blood gushing from his mouth, spraying with his words, "it hurts. Hurts bad." Before he could utter another word, convulsions seized him. He died, choking and heaving, trying to get up. Then his head relaxed, and his eyes remained open wide.

"Fuck," Perry said.

Dean looked up and found the youth standing only a few feet away. The rest of the boys appeared bloodied but intact. Conor looked the worst, bleeding down the side of his face from a large gash across his forehead. Moxen and Handley were stomping fish still flopping in the shallow water.

"Dean," Louis said quietly, "he's dead."

"I know it," Dean said. "Fish got him."

"Got to go," Louis said. "No place for us to stay here."

Dean nodded. He picked up his strewed gear and arranged it for quick access, certain he was going to need it. He felt bad about leaving Green lying there, but it had to be done.

"Conor, do you feel up to taking point again?" Louis asked.

The boy hesitated just a moment. "Don't see how you could trust me after that. Got Enrique chilled, too."

"Did you see that trip wire?" Louis asked.

The boy shook his head.

"Neither did the rest of us. Shit happens. All we can do is our best. I don't think you'll get any complaints from us." He looked around the group meaningfully.

All the boys shook their heads.

"Can you do it?" Louis asked.

"I can try," Conor replied.

Louis nodded. "That's all we're asking. Ready when you are."

Conor took a deep breath, raked his gaze around the others looking for any last-minute changes of mind, then turned and took up his position.

Dean followed reluctantly, feeling that no matter where they went in the building, none of them were safe.

The convention center's underground parking garage was a sargasso of rusting and stripped wags. Remnants of the yellow lines that had once separated the vehicles lay along the dust-covered concrete floor, brought into sharp relief by the oil lantern Jak had stolen from farther down the hall.

The albino held up the lantern and turned up the wick. More of the shadows in the garage peeled away. "Wall," he said.

Krysty looked a few feet ahead of him and saw the solid concrete wall that ended their tangled journey through the steel husks. They'd gone down the emergency stairs on one side of the main lobby and followed them into the garage. The elevators didn't work, nor did any of the other lights in the building.

Evidently whatever the power source the Five Barons had tapped into to establish their private killing ground, hadn't been used to illuminate the convention center. Perhaps they didn't have the power to spare. In either event, the decision worked in the companions' favor.

"Doc?" Krysty said.

"This is the wall, dear lady," the old man replied. He came forward with the small notebook he'd liberated from Bernsen's pack.

On the sheets of paper, he'd carefully penciled in an outline of the building and the path they'd taken to get to the garage. Measurements—as close as he could approximate them by stepping off the distance—were tagged between marked arrowheads.

Doc tapped the paper. "I am sure this is it, Krysty, unless I am totally addled and cannot remember simple spatial and cartography skills. This building is not much of a challenge."

"This section," Krysty said, "overlooks the pit edge we spotted from the upstairs window?"

"A moment to confirm that, please." Doc left her briefly, sliding through the rows of overturned cars.

Sentient hair at the back of Krysty's neck coiled defensively. She turned, looking at Bernsen, who'd crept considerably closer while she'd presented her back to him.

"Don't even think about it," she warned, moving her hand to the butt of her blaster. "I'd kill you before you could touch me."

"I wasn't doing anything," Bernsen said with the most innocence he could muster, but his shoulders dropped in dejection. He stuck out his lower lip and backed off a few feet.

Doc returned a moment later. "This is definitely the location, dear lady."

Krysty approached the wall Doc had indicated and looked at the cinder blocks it was made of. Some of the mortar had cracked and worn away in places. Hunks and bits of it snapped and popped under her boots as she ran a hand along its surface to get a feel for it.

"Won't take much," Jak said. "Little plas ex probably make big hole." He came up behind her and stood at her side.

"Think you're right. Let's get to it."

Jak unhooked his backpack and started rummaging through its contents for the blocks of explosive.

Krysty kneaded the plas ex slightly before pushing it against the rough, uneven surface of the wall. When she had enough little balls in place, she stabbed a remote detonator into each.

"You sure Ryan inside now?" Jak asked as they finished blocking out the circular patch of the wall they'd chosen.

"Yes," she said. Even though her mind swirled, threatening to conjure up all kinds of possibilities about what the near future might hold, she was convinced of her lover's presence.

"Know where?"

"Feeling I'm getting from him, I can track it."

"Dean there?"

"Him, too." She didn't even try to figure out what was going to happen between father and son out on the killing ground.

"Where?"

"I don't know, Jak. I just know they're close."

"Confusing in dark. Could be trouble seeing the other."

"I know. Dammit, I know." She inserted the last detonator, then walked back to the nearest empty wag.

Jak followed her. "Sorry. Stupe of me. You'd already thought that."

Krysty studied the wag. In the past someone had taken the engine and transmission, stripping other parts out of the inside. The windshield was cracked, two holes knocked into it big enough for her to fit her hand through. The tires were flat, but at least they were there.

"Give me a hand," she told Jak, "and let's see if we can move it." She grabbed the steering wheel while the teenager slipped in behind the wag.

The vehicle creaked and popped in protest, then grudgingly started to move. It took a lot of work to put the wag in front of the area they'd mined with the plas ex. Once they had it there, Krysty looked at the space, figuring it would only take one more wag and at most two more to block the brunt of the blasts against the wall. That way the explosion would be concentrated, hopefully opening up the wall.

If it didn't, escape would be even more difficult.

RYAN REACHED DOWN and gave J.B. a hand up into the window on the second floor of the Mirage. Mildred and the others were already behind him, lined up on both sides of the door.

The room had once been a storage area of some type. Racks that held barren clothes hangers shared space with cabinets, display counters and shelves.

Moosh Wandell, Thompson and Owen guarded the door, anxiously peering into the darkened hallway. The echoes of the explosion had died away less than two minutes earlier.

J.B. slithered in over the sill. "Saw a green light a minute ago."

"One of the boys is dead," Mildred commented.

The Armorer nodded. "Looks that way."

Ryan scratched his stubbled chin, thinking about it. "All the green team was inside the building. Means they've got a way of seeing through the walls."

"Unless they've got the windows staked out," Mildred said. "Maybe a sec man just looked in and saw the boy down."

"And confirmed him dead?" Ryan shook his head. "They've got buildings open all over the pit. Hadn't thought about it before, but they'd probably want a way to check on anybody inside them."

"Haven't seen any vid equipment," J.B. said. "Starlight scopes would take away the night, but they wouldn't allow the sec guards to see through the walls. Something else might, though."

Ryan looked at his friend.

"Thermographic sights," J.B. said. "They register body heat if things between them aren't too dense, or don't carry too much of a heat signature themselves. A barn would have to have serious jack to afford that kind of equipment. Hard to find."

Ryan didn't like the idea of the sec guards being able to spy on them at any time. "What about a heat signature?"

"Man," Owen whispered harshly, "we're sitting ducks standing in one place like this. That explosion, you know those green-team guys aren't going to stay put. They'll be moving. And with them moving, they're liable to run smack into us."

"With us moving," Mildred argued, "there's no less risk."

The man shifted nervously. "Moving around some would just feel better."

"When the time comes to move," Ryan said in a hard voice, "I'll let you know."

Owen's gaze burned for just a moment, then he looked back into the hallway.

"Heat signature of the human body is 98.6," the Armorer said. "Nothing else around us burns that hot."

"What about the neon lights?" Ryan asked.

"No."

"But if we got a good blaze going somewhere… "

J.B. nodded. "It'd blind the sec men's sights for a while, but when we moved from the fire, they'd find us again."

"It would buy us some time, though."

"Sure."

Ryan shouldered the Steyr. "Good to know. There'll come a time we may need to buy a few minutes." Drawing the SIG-Sauer, he started for the hallway. The skin across his neck and shoulders was tight. It wasn't pleasant thinking about the boys roaming around inside the building with them. But they were killers; they'd proved their ability. If it came to it, he'd put them down and walk over their bodies without a second thought if it would put him one step closer to his freedom.

PEERING THROUGH the thermographic sniper sights, Hayden LeMarck saw the human-shaped heat signatures of the green team walk away from the dying ember of the team member they'd left behind in the Mirage entrance. The dozens of piranha that had splashed across the floor after the explosion glowed steadily brighter as their body temperature escalated. Some of them still flopped weakly.

"Confirmed kill on one of the green team," LeMarck told Hardcoe. "His body temp's dropping." He looked at the baron.

"The green team is inside the building?" Hardcoe asked.

"Yes, sir."

Hardcoe smiled, then rubbed his hands together. "Wallis."

"Sir," Thoroughgood replied.

"Get a message to tell Phibes to let them go."

"Sir?" Thoroughgood looked confused.

LeMarck was confused himself. He'd known Hardcoe and Phibes had been working on the traps for this year's Big Game, but none of the details had been released. Phibes was renowned in the seven villes for his vicious, bloodthirsty ways and appetites.

"Just get him the message," the Baron said. "He'll know what I mean."

Thoroughgood left, moving quickly.

Hardcoe looked at Connrad. "It appears good fortune has turned the other cheek on you."

"One death," Connrad growled, reaching forward and sliding a bead across his abacus. "You've suffered four."

"Not as many as young Francis's team," Hardcoe answered good-naturedly.

Giskard made a mock woeful face, then reached for a fresh drink.

"What is it you sent your man for?" Connrad demanded.

"You're familiar with Phibes?" Hardcoe asked.

Connrad gave a short, impatient nod. "Calls himself a physician. A worse joke was never made."

"He is somewhat—coarse and ill-tempered," Hardcoe agreed.

"The man," Giskard said definitely, "is sick and perverted."

Dettwyler leaned forward. "Wasn't he the man who tried to bring life back into corpses, create some kind of army of the undead?"

"Yes," Deke Ramsey replied. "He was partially successful from what I was told."

LeMarck recalled the incident and shivered. The shambling monstrosities that Phibes had raised were mockeries of men, women and children, torn from the fresh womb of the grave and pieced together in various ways. Mercifully the things had only experienced near life for a matter of minutes and had appeared in no way under control of themselves, much less Phibes's control. They'd been burned so that no one would attempt to figure out what the man had done to raise them from the dead.

Hardcoe waved the comment away, not answering. "Phibes is a genius."

"The way I heard it," Connrad said, "he's got access to certain predark materials."

"I don't ask," Hardcoe responded.

"But neither do you deny knowledge of such a thing," Giskard countered.

"Forget that," Connrad said. "What is he loosing into the pit?"

Hardcoe smiled, a cold effort genuinely without humor. "In his travels in recent days, he came across an interesting strain of beasts created before the skydark. From somewhere along the upper Cific coastline."

"What kinds of beasts are they?" Dettwyler asked.

"Monkeys," Hardcoe answered.

"Monkeys," Connrad scoffed. He slapped his knee. "As a baron, you have a right to include whatever traps you deem necessary in the pit. How the hell can you expect monkeys to be a threat to armed men?"

"They've mutated," Hardcoe answered, "just as the big cats we found roaming this burg have."

"In what way?" Giskard asked.

LeMarck was interested, as well. He didn't like getting cut from the information loop, but he knew it was necessary at times.

"I didn't know this at the time," Hardcoe said, "but most primates are carnivorous to a degree."

"Primates?" Dettwyler asked.

LeMarck knew the term had come from Phibes, and Hardcoe had picked it up. Hardcoe liked appearing educated.

"Any kind of monkey or ape," Hardcoe replied. "These are meat eaters by choice. For the last seven months, Phibes has been working with them here—feeding them, making them angry and fearful, starving them sometimes until they almost went insane. Twice they started fighting among themselves, killing four of the weaker ones and devouring them. Over the years Phibes said they've been inbred until insanity is less than a stone's throw away for them."

"Get to it," Connrad said.

"For the last two months the monkeys have had a constant feeding area," Hardcoe replied.

"The Mirage," Giskard guessed.

"Exactly." Hardcoe smiled. "They haven't been fed in the last four days and have been secured in a soundproof room near the top of the Mirage. Phibes has an electronic door opener. Those monkeys have been released into that building by now."

"They're still just monkeys," Dettwyler snorted. "Not much threat in that."

"I seem to recall that you weren't impressed with the piranha in the fish tank at the Mirage's entry," Hardcoe returned. "One of Connrad's prize team members is now dead because of it."

"Only one." Dettwyler still didn't appear impressed.

"True, but now that team is running scared. They thought to take the high ground, as other teams before them had planned on. Only now they're not as safe as they believed they were going to be. They're going to run into those monkeys." Hardcoe leaned forward in his chair and lowered his voice, drawing in the others to his story. "Those monkeys are meat eaters, as I've said, but they're also little more than a foot and a half tall, much stronger and faster than they appear, and have wings."

"Winged monkeys?"

LeMarck looked at Dettwyler. The baron definitely looked impressed now.

"Can they fly?" Giskard asked.

"Not fly," Hardcoe said. "However, they can glide pretty damn good. I've seen them do it myself."

A quick, covert glance at Connrad let LeMarck know the baron wasn't receiving the news with the confidence he'd had before.

"Something new, eh, Vinge? That's what we wanted for the pit." Hardcoe grinned. "And no matter how well drilled those boys you managed to gather up are, there's no way they could have prepared for this."

Connrad didn't say anything; he just lifted his binoculars.

LeMarck raised the thermographic lenses to his eyes again, scanning the topmost floors of the Mirage. In a matter of moments he managed to locate the monkeys, dimly outlined by their shape as they scuttled across the floor. They were a horde, their body temperatures considerably elevated from a human's, and even slightly higher than a mutie biped's. It was a certain sign of rad-influenced mutation.

The monkeys moved quickly, seeking out the empty elevator shafts and sliding down between the levels to the bottom floor. Some of them unfurled wings almost twice as broad as they were tall, and glided down, bouncing off the walls.

"You've never said how many monkeys there were," Ramsey said.

"Dozens," Hardcoe replied. "The green team won't get out of that building alive. I'm afraid, Vinge, that your seasoned troops—with their training and their intent to take the high ground—are going to find that those tactics have ultimately chilled them all."

Connrad paused for a moment before answering. "Getting down to the nut cutting, it's going to matter who's the best chillers. Just like it always has."

"A man who's a believer until the bitter end," Giskard said. "Very good of you, Vinge."

LeMarck moved the thermographic lenses around, picking up other hot spots. He felt better about the outcome. The green team appeared the only ones who could give the one-eyed man and his party any serious competition.

Abruptly he ran the lenses across a heat signature that read human. He brought the lenses back slowly, finding what he was looking for on the second floor.

He leaned down to Hardcoe's ear. "Sir."

Hardcoe listened.

"Our team is in the building, as well."

"Where?"

"Second floor," LeMarck answered.

The muscles along the baron's jawline tightened. "If they've got the sense we've given them credit for, as soon as they hear the monkeys take the green team, they'll leave the building."

LeMarck straightened again, hoping it was true.

WITH JAK WATCHING her back, Krysty put the last plas-ex charge in place against the ceiling. On the top floor now, she knew the sec men were only a few feet above her. The only things separating her from them were the crawl space, ceiling, roof and whatever duct work was in place.

"Done," she said to Jak.

He stepped out of the shadows beside the room's door. He nodded, then turned and led the way into the hall, followed by Krysty.

They went down the emergency stairs in a matter of minutes, returning to the first floor. Doc remained in the underground garage with Bernsen, who'd become increasingly nervous as he figured out what Krysty and the others were planning to do.

The man might become a problem. In Ryan's place, Krysty thought she might have chilled the scientist then and there to protect the other companions. They owed Bernsen nothing; the man had even tried to kill them.

But she wasn't Ryan. So she'd taken the chance that Doc could handle the man.

On the first floor, Jak went through the double doors leading out into the main hall. Another two turns put them into a large meeting area. Rusted metal folding chairs were thrown haphazardly about, partially buried by the chunks of ceiling that had fallen over the decades.

They stopped at one of the large plate-glass windows overlooking the pit area.

Looking through the glass, Krysty saw intermittent gunfire flash yellow and white against the foliage and the neon burn spots.

"Ready?" Jak asked.

Krysty took a deep breath and nodded. The visions she'd had while in the airwag still made no sense, but her mutie powers told her definitely that Ryan was still in the Mirage and that Dean was probably in there, as well. Her power tweaked suddenly, and the sense of imminent danger for Ryan suddenly increased. "We need to go."

Jak removed the window. He'd loosened it earlier, working the dried putty from the framework with a knife. He spit on his hands, then rubbed them against each other.

The glass was a three-foot-by-four-foot rectangle. Jak placed his hands against it, using the friction of his moistened palms to draw the window back and prevent it from falling from his grasp when he drew it farther away.

Krysty caught the edge of the glass and helped him put it against the wall on the floor. She kept her ears cocked for the sound of a sec guard's shoe brushing against the carpet outside, but didn't think it would really happen. The sec men were too interested in the death being dealt in the pit.

Jak shook loose a length of climbing rope with a small grapple already attached. He hooked it to the window's lip, then threw the rope outside.

When there was no immediate gunfire in response, he clambered out after it.

"Go," Krysty said. "I'll be right behind you."

Looking down, she spotted Jak already on the ground forty feet down. He looped the rope around his waist, bracing it for her descent.

Breathing a quiet prayer to Gaia, Krysty slid down into the waiting death arena.

The rope burned Krysty's hands and she bit her lip to endure the pain. Seconds later her boots hit the ground.

There was no choice but to leave the rope where it was and hope it wouldn't be spotted. If it was found later, it would be too late to matter. She hoped.

Jak turned and took the lead, running toward the foliage forty yards distant.

Krysty followed, drawing her weapon. If she had to use it, she'd only be one more shooter among the dozens left in the pit area. The only things she worried about were the bare places between the buildings, the forested areas and the wall. Care had been taken to keep them separated.

She ran, trusting Jak's woodcraft skills and her own persistent mutie powers to put her on the path to Ryan.

THE ONLY WARNING Dean and the other boys got was the heavy rustle of what sounded like leather on fabric behind them. They turned together, bringing up their weapons.

Dean's eyes burned, trying to sort out the shadows from reality over the sights of the Browning Hi-Power.

Several shadows were in motion, though. He peered at them intently as they approached. Then they started jabbering hostility.

"Monkeys!" Bobby Handley called out. "Just a bunch of monkeys! There's no reason to be scared!"

As the shadows went away and the moonlight leaking through the building fell across the monkeys, Dean saw that they weren't ordinary beasts of their kind.

These monkeys looked leaner, their legs more proportioned with their arms and upper bodies. Their heads, however, were half again as large as they needed to be, and they were filled with teeth and bright, burning eyes. The lower jaws held more teeth than usual, and the bottom canines thrust belligerently upward, curving dangerously, fangs that almost reached the eyes.

At first Dean thought the monkeys were humpbacked. A moment later he saw that the abnormality on the creatures' backs was folded wings.

Louis stepped forward, dropping his rifle into position. "Monkeys or not, fuckers might be dangerous. Wouldn't put it past the people running this show to infect them with rabies." He burned a blast a couple feet in front of the advancing wave of monkeys.

Instead of retreating or coming to a stop, the monkeys instantly went on the attack. Some of them leaped into the air like ungainly birds, the wings flapping hard enough to crack the air.

"Shit!" Moxen cried out. "Chill them!" His weapon was already up and firing.

Dean joined in, trying to pick his targets to make sure of the kill. The monkeys were too densely packed to miss, but a wound would probably serve only to make them angrier than they obviously were.

The attempt to hold the line was over in seconds. The monkeys came on too fiercely, none of them appearing to be frightened by the gunfire exploding around them.

Dean backed away, the Browning's slide blowing back empty. He changed magazines, ducking under the gliding attack of one of the creatures. The fierce jaws snapped closed only inches from his left eye, hot drool splashing against his cheek.

"Run!" Louis yelled. "Break off and try to find a place to hole up!"

Slamming the fresh magazine home, Dean fought his way free of the clutches of three monkeys who'd seized his legs. To his right he saw Moxen go down under at least a half-dozen of them. Moxen screamed shrilly.

Dean started forward, wondering how he was going to help the other boy.

Abruptly Moxen stopped screaming. His body quivered, then relaxed. When it started to move again, it was due to the monkeys piled on top of him stripping the flesh from his bones in bloody gobbets.

Dean turned and ran, finding he was nearly the last of them to move out.

The monkeys continued to scream shrilly and raced after them, at a disadvantage because of their shorter legs. But the disadvantage wasn't much.

"Outside!" Handley yelled ahead of Dean. "We'd stand a better chance outside, Louis!"

"No way!" the youth called back. "We get outside in the open, these bastards would chew us to bits in no time!"

Without warning, something clipped Dean's shoulder and nearly toppled him from his feet. He managed to maintain his balance and watched in horror as a group of the winged monkeys flew into the boys.

Four of them landed on Handley, knocking the boy forward and to the ground, blood covering his features immediately. The monkeys clawed his back and buttocks, tearing through the clothing to get at his flesh.

"No!" Dean cried out hoarsely. He turned and brought up his blaster, so scared he had to fight to stay alive, fight to keep moving.

"Forget him!" Louis ordered, suddenly coming up hard against Dean. His momentum was enough to propel them both into a hallway splitting off the main corridor. "This hallway's smaller!" Louis helped Dean stay on his feet, kept him moving. "Mebbe we can cut down the number that come at us!"

More boys screamed out in the main corridor. Dean couldn't even recognize the voices. He got himself organized and started to match Louis's pace, not wanting to slow the boy and get them both chilled.

The hallway ended abruptly. Dean stared at the wooden door ahead of them. The plaque, its white letters barely visible against the black in the shadows, read Gentlemen.

"Bathroom," Dean said.

"Go through it," Louis ordered, looking over his shoulder. "We got no choice."

Looking back, Dean saw the monkeys approaching them, some of the mutie animals unfurling their wings to launch into a glide. He fumbled for the door and got it open. Louis followed him inside.

The only light falling into the room came from the weak illumination reflected from the hallway. Once Louis shut and bolted the door, even that went away.

Dean heard the monkeys' claws scratching against the door. The sound grew steadily louder, coming quicker and quicker.

"WE'VE GOT INTRUDERS inside the pit," Wallis Thorough-good said as soon as he entered the room.

"Who?" LeMarck demanded before anyone else had time to react to the announcement.

"Don't know." Thoroughgood pointed through the glass down at the pit. "They came through the window of the old convention center, slid down a rope and are hauling ass."

Connrad looked at one of his sec commanders. "Get word out to the wall guards. Tell them I want these peo-ple killed."

The man nodded and rushed out of the room.

Hardcoe gave the same order to Thoroughgood, who promptly vanished outside again.

LeMarck felt the tension in the room suddenly increase as all the barons leaned forward with their glasses in hand. He knew they were all thinking the same thing: if any of the barons had been behind the insertion of extra troops, that baron was a dead man.

The situation didn't make for casual conversation.

LeMarck trained his own glasses on the wall by the convention center and spotted the rope immediately, then he picked up the thermographic lenses and began to search for the intruders. In seconds he had their heat sig-natures. Neither of them showed the special ID buttons that were in the body armor of the team members.

He grew cold inside, because he figured he knew who

the intruders were, and there was no way Hardcoe wouldn't be blamed for it. Death hovered over the room, waiting to be released. He dropped his hand to his Glock.

THE SHRILL SCREAMS and echoing thunder of blasters drew Ryan to a halt along the stairwell that led from the second floor to the first. Weak light dribbled in from the mesh windows in the doors to the emergency stairs.

"Not after us," J.B. said quietly behind him.

Ryan eased forward, the SIG-Sauer at the ready, hammer locked back so it would take only a two-pound squeeze to touch off the first round. He peered through the scarred, metal-ribbed glass, feeling the Armorer's breath light against the back of his neck.

The light was better outside. Scanning the scene before him, Ryan felt his hackles lift. Four of the green team were down, scattered along a couple corridors and almost buried under dozens of creatures that looked like things from a mat-trans chili nightmare.

"Dark night," J.B. breathed.

"Back," he told J.B. "Before these bastards get our scent." He signaled to Owen and Mildred, backing the group up the stairs. It had been Ryan's intention to identify the green team, isolate them from his group's own movements and chill them if it came to that.

"Looks like the green team's almost fresh out of members," J.B. stated.

Just as they started up the second set of steps, something smashed into the emergency door below.

At the tail of the line, Ryan peered back at the door. A monkey's face almost filled the rectangle, then two others popped into view, shoving the first beast away.

"Move!" Ryan ordered. "They're onto us!"

The door rattled, the knob turning slowly. Excited monkey screams filled the space.

"Bastards can work the knobs," Mildred said as she moved up the steps.

Ryan sighted along the length of his blaster, then put two rounds into the monkey's face. The screams of the animals increased, quickly reaching a frenzied stage. The bullets left holes in the glass, one of them snipping through the wire mesh. More monkeys suddenly clawed at the door.

Before Ryan reached the second landing, he heard the door below open, then the rapid padding of monkey feet against the steps.

"THEY'RE MAKING for the Mirage!"

LeMarck looked at Connrad's sec man. "Are you sure?"

"Yes, sir!" It was obvious the sec man was panicked, knowing it appeared that his own baron had at least a fifty percent chance of culpability in inserting extra champions. Otherwise, he'd have never responded to LeMarck's question.

Dettwyler pulled a blaster and pointed it in Hardcoe and Connrad's direction. "One of you two bastards is trying to pull a fast one on us. I want to know which one it is."

Quietly and quickly, LeMarck pulled his Glock and kept it out of sight by turning his body.

"You don't pull a blaster on me," Connrad warned, "unless you're going to use it."

"I'll use it, all right," Dettwyler said, "if I find out you're behind this."

"Then you'd better be fast enough to kill me, too," Hardcoe said. "Because I'll kill you right after you pull that trigger if you fuck around anymore."

Dettwyler grinned nervously. "Thought you and Conn-rad were enemies, Hardcoe."

"Hasn't changed a bit. If I had the chance out away from here and I thought I could take him, mebbe I'd find out if I could." He paused. "But not here. Not now. The truce between us will be honored in this place. It's the only thing that keeps the peace between us. I won't see it broken. By anyone."

Giskard calmly stretched out his hand. A small derringer popped into his palm. His fingers closed around the blaster as he shoved the blunt muzzle behind Dettwyler's ear. "I'm more of a gambling man," the young baron said cockily. "I think I can pull the trigger on this little pocket cannon before you manage to squeeze through that one. Want to see?"

"Get the blaster away from him," one of Dettwyler's sec men ordered, pulling his own weapon and pointing it at Giskard.

LeMarck took a step toward Hardcoe, intending to use himself as a shield to protect the baron if it proved necessary.

Giskard laughed. "And isn't this a fine how-do-you-do, Dettwyler?" He shook his head, moving the derringer slightly but keeping it in contact with the fat man's jawline. "As soon as you pull the trigger—or mebbe even only *look* like you're going to, why, mebbe all the people in this room are dead men."

Dettwyler didn't say anything.

"What I suggest," Giskard said, "is a moment of reason. You pulled the first blaster. By rights I think it should be you who first puts his away. Don't you agree?"

Face contorted with anger, Dettwyler complied.

With a sigh of relief, Giskard lowered the derringer's hammer. The barons ordered their men to follow suit.

LeMarck let out a long breath as quietly as he could, trying to appear indifferent to the whole situation. But his heart pounded inside him.

"Vinge," Hardcoe said, "I'll not see *you* make an attempt on Dettwyler, either, not while we're here."

"No man pulls a blaster on me and lives," Connrad said. The feathered earrings shivered with the fury moving the man.

"What you do away from here," Hardcoe said, "is none of my business. Here, I've had my say on."

"What we should all be doing," Giskard said, "is taking care of those interlopers, before they further interrupt the Big Game and we have to declare it a null effort. Then we'll be faced with leaving things as they are until next year and playing again."

Connrad eyed Hardcoe. "If that happens, it seems like things could turn out in your favor."

"I didn't put those people in there," Hardcoe stated.

"Mebbe we should go find out." Connrad turned to his nearest sec boss. "Pass the word along to those wall guards to get some people into the pit, track those two people down, kill them and identify them. I want their bodies brought out of there. And get some guards off the wall near the Mirage and into the building. Get some men in there with flame throwers. I don't want any of our people hurt by those monkeys before they have a chance to put down the interlopers."

"Yes, sir." The man left at once.

Hardcoe pushed himself out of his seat, his movements followed at once by Connrad. "I'm not going to stay in here and watch this. I want to be out there where I can see things for myself."

"Then so do I," Connrad said.

LeMarck took up his position and went with them. Never before during a Big Game had the barons left the security of the safe room. He didn't like the way the night was shaping up.

And if he was right about the identity of the two people out there in the pit, he was near to liking it even less.

"I DON'T KNOW what you're doing with these people," Bernsen said to Doc. "You're a man of science, hardly their ilk at all."

Doc sat against the opposite wall from the one Jak and Krysty had spent time salting with their explosives. He shook his head, listening to the frantic crack of weapons overhead, and offered a silent prayer to his Maker for his friends left so unprotected and outmanned in the pit.

"Are you acquainted with the works of the Bard?" Doc asked.

"William Shakespeare?" Bernsen looked puzzled.

"The very man," Doc agreed with a nod.

"He was no scientist."

"On the contrary," Doc said, "I believe he indeed was. And his spheres of investigation were the vagaries of the human heart versus the morality of civilization using power as a catalyst."

"Perhaps I'll look upon his works in time," Bernsen.

Doc wasn't fool enough to think the man was sincere. It was only an effort at placating him. "As the Bard said in his work *The Tempest,* 'Misery acquaints a man with strange bedfellows.' I've found that, in my years, to be a most apt statement."

"But we have a chance to get out of here," Bernsen said. "Those people are going to get caught. In the process they're going to get us caught, as well."

"You cannot say that. These people are very good at what they do. You have not seen even a fraction of the perils they've faced together during their travels."

"Fool's luck." The scientist shook his head. "You, my friend, are guilty of a most destructive false pride."

"That shall remain to be seen, and I shall have a front-row seat."

"THAT LOCK'S not going to hold them long."

Dean knew that, listening to the way the scratching of the monkeys filled the bathroom. "There's not going to be another way out of here, either. One way in, one way out."

"Got to be," Louis replied.

A self-light flared in the darkness, illuminating first Louis's features, then spreading across the interior of the bathroom.

It was a big room, perhaps the biggest of its kind that Dean had ever seen. His heart pounded in his chest, causing blood to rush through his ears.

Stalls lined the wall to his left, flanked by urinals. Shattered mirrors clung haphazardly to the tiled walls. Bugs fled across the tiled floor, retreating from skeletons that were decades old and corpses that may have only been weeks in decaying.

"Up," Louis said, holding the self-light toward the ceiling. "Mebbe some crawl space we can get through." He cursed when the self-light burned his fingers, and dropped the flaming stick to the floor.

Dean hated being left blind in the darkness. His skin

crawled at the sound of the monkeys' nails scratching against the door.

Louis struck another self-light, then pushed his way through one of the stalls. He stood on the toilet and shoved one of the acoustic tiles out of the metal frame that formed the ceiling. Glancing down at Dean, he said, "I think we can get through here. Hurry."

Dean hauled himself up beside Louis and caught the lip of the metal frame. It took a lot of strength to pull his body up inside. The collection of dust and odor sent him into a sneezing fit as he lay against the top of the ceiling. The floor of the next level was scarcely more than two feet above him.

"Dean," Louis called.

Looking back, Dean saw the other boy struggling to pull himself up. Reaching down, Dean caught the vest of Louis's body armor and yanked him through. As he passed through, Louis dropped the flaming self-light to the floor.

"See anything?" Louis asked.

"There wasn't time," Dean replied, choking as the dust filled his lungs.

Another self-light flared into being. Perspiration dripped down Louis's face, glowing like pearls. "Over there."

Dean looked, seeing the access shaft in front of them. He started for it immediately. Before he reached it, Louis dropped the self-light, but finding the entranceway to the access shaft was no problem. Dean crawled inside, then found it shifted straight up within a few feet.

Louis lit another self-light. "Can we make it?"

"I think so," Dean said. "Be a hard climb."

"Beats the hell out of staying down here."

The sound of the door finally crashing inward filled the bathroom and echoed through the crawl space. An instant later brown hairy hands gripped the sides of the metal frame where Dean and Louis had come up through.

"Smell us," Dean said.

"Not for long," Louis promised. "Get moving." He retrieved a gren from his pack and pulled the pin. Turning, he lobbed the bomb back onto the acoustic tiles.

Dean went up the shaft, bracing his back against the side with his palms extended in front of him, shoving his way up with his feet. Louis was right below him.

When the gren blew, it sent a flash of light stabbing into Dean's eyes. Monkeys screamed in terror and in rage. Dean kept climbing, feeling the wave of heat pass over him. Wherever they were headed, it had to be better than where they were.

Ryan was the last man through the door on the second level. Monkeys filled the landing below, their eyes glowing ruby red. He paused for a moment, squeezing the SIG-Sauer's trigger as rapidly as he could until it was empty.

Monkeys flopped backward, chilled by the full-metal-jacket rounds.

He stepped back to reload, and J.B. stepped forward.

"Grens," the Armorer said, showing Ryan the spherical objects in his hands. J.B. pulled the pins with his teeth, then tossed the bombs into the stairwell.

When the explosion sounded so quickly after, Ryan thought for a moment that J.B. had miscalculated the time and blown them all to hell. Then he realized that the other explosion was farther off.

The two bombs the Armorer had launched erupted right after he pulled the stairwell door closed.

"Might have discouraged them some," J.B. said, adjusting his hat, "but they're still plenty interested."

Ryan took the lead. He sprinted down the hallway, past elevators with sagging doors torn from their tracks. Moonlight poured in through the windows at one end of the corridor and filtered out the set at the other end. They crossed two intersections before the monkeys came boiling out of the stairwell, screeches and blood-curdling howls reverberating throughout the corridor.

Taking the first left at the next intersection he came to, Ryan slapped at doors, kicking them open. The locks had been broken or shot out over the years. All of the rooms were bedrooms of some type, though the furniture had been stolen or torn to pieces.

None of them offered any hope of escape.

"Those were winged monkeys," Mildred said, her words broken up by her struggle to breathe during the exertion of running.

"Yep," J.B. agreed. "Big teeth for monkeys, though."

"All we need," the woman said, "is for a green ball of fire to drop from the ceiling and suddenly proclaim, 'I am the great and powerful Oz!'"

Ryan didn't have a clue as to what Mildred was talking about. He sucked in air through his nose, keeping his lungs charged with fresh oxygen as he focused on surviving the trap that had been sprung inside the Mirage.

He took a right at the next intersection, spotting the huge plate-glass window at the end of the hallway. "J.B." He lifted the SIG-Sauer and started to fire rounds at the glass, which starred but didn't shatter.

"Take the glass out," Ryan ordered. "We'll go over the side, get back into the forest. Mebbe lose ourselves. We can't hold this building."

J.B. lifted the S&W scattergun to his shoulder and fired. The fléchettes struck the window already weakened by Ryan's rounds and blew out nearly the whole section.

Ryan stopped at the window, looking around warily for snipers posted outside. He knocked the ragged chunks of glass from the bottom track of the window with the barrel of the SIG-Sauer blaster.

Mildred touched his shoulder as she came up beside him. She pointed. "Look."

Ryan followed her line of direction and saw two figures dashing through the forest less than a quarter mile away. He reached into his pack and took out his binoculars. Focusing them, he made out Jak and Krysty just as they slipped under low tree branches. He kept tracking them until he saw them come out on the other side only a few feet from a large pond surrounded by a raised bank.

Muzzle-flashes burned hot against the shadows and foliage behind them, marking the course of their pursuers.

"Fireblast!" Ryan snarled, watching his lover as bullets cut through the brush around her.

A dozen riders on horseback galloped toward Krysty and Jak's position, circling slightly to get through the tangled brush. Ryan lifted the SIG-Sauer and banged out a handful of rounds. At that distance the rounds weren't effective against the riders, but they did warn Jak and Krysty. Two rifle rounds struck fragments from the brickwork near Ryan's head, driving him to cover.

Spotting the riders, Jak and Krysty turned suddenly and headed for the pond. Bullets ripped into the ground where they'd been. Tracer rounds scattered sparks in their wake. In seconds they were gone from view.

"Go," Ryan told J.B.

The Armorer didn't wait to be told again, hoisting himself up immediately through the window and launching himself outward. Mildred followed, trailed by Moosh Wandell and Thompson.

Ryan wheeled in the direction of the approaching monkeys and started to fire. His bullets had little effect on the phalanx of hairy and winged bodies, as the beasts' anger kept them moving.

While the monkeys were still ten feet short of the final intersection that would bring them less than thirty feet from Ryan's position at the window, two men stepped out forward wearing some sort of sec uniform. Both men carried what appeared to be homemade flamethrowers.

Huge gouts of roiling black-and-orange liquid fire jetted from elongated tubes and flowed over the front line of monkeys. Gurgling hisses filled the corridor, followed immediately by the agonized dying cries of the animals. The smell of burned fur and feathers became an overpowering stench.

Ryan held his fire, hoping they'd escape unnoticed while the sec men were involved with the monkeys. Owen was now clambering through the broken window.

"There!" an armed sec man shouted, pointing at Ryan and Owen. A green armband marked him as belonging to one of the barons. Evidently someone was going to use the confusion to whittle down the odds on Hardcoe's team of warriors. Ryan grinned to himself, already in motion, knowing if it had been him, he'd have done the same thing. Why chance it when a victory can be made certain?

Instantly the men with the flamethrowers came around, both of them firing.

Ryan shouted a warning to Owen, then threw himself farther down the side corridor the companions hadn't traveled.

Orange-and-black fire coursed along the wall, blistering paint and peeling paper, which started to burn a heartbeat later when it reached flashpoint.

Owen was caught in the window by both flaming streams. He screamed the last few seconds of his life away as his body caught on fire. He fell from the window with flames wrapped around him, finally becoming mercifully silent.

With a last look at the fire-filled window, Ryan pushed himself to his feet and raced down the corridor. There was no way he could make it through the swirling inferno. Behind him he heard the shouts of the men who'd taken up the chase. He ran, searching for a way out of the maze, knowing there was little chance that Jak and Krysty could escape from the situation they'd been in unless J.B. and Mildred were able to get into position to help. Even at that, all of their lives might still become forfeit.

"CALL THEM OFF, dammit!" LeMarck yelled at Connrad. Through the binoculars he'd seen the men with flamethrowers attacking Hardcoe's champions. He knew he was stepping way past the boundaries that had been established regarding how underlings spoke to barons.

"Shut up, boy!" Connrad snarled. "Your team lost its immunity when they fired upon my sec guards!"

Atop the tall wall overlooking the pit, LeMarck turned to face Connrad. His hand dropped down to his pistol. Immediately two of Connrad's sec men lifted their own weapons. At least if he laid his life down taking out Connrad, maybe the blame wouldn't fall on Hardcoe.

"No," Hardcoe said, stepping in front of LeMarck, "not this way." He reached out and stilled his sec boss's hand.

His eyes remained locked on LeMarck's, he raised his voice. "Vinge."

"Yeah."

"Saying I agree with your view on that team of mine down in the pit," Hardcoe said, "and saying that I sit by and don't raise a hand while your sec men mow them down, let's also say that if your team joins mine and tries to win free of the pit, they're also forfeit and will be executed accordingly."

Peering over Hardcoe's shoulder, LeMarck saw Connrad run a big hand over his face.

"I said they're also forfeit," Hardcoe stated in a harsh voice. "Do you agree?" Satisfied that LeMarck wasn't going to move, the baron turned to face his foe.

"Yeah," Connrad answered, but LeMarck could tell it wasn't an answer he wanted to give.

LeMarck let out a tense breath. The die had been cast. Now it only remained to be seen who exactly came up with snake eyes.

THE AIR SHAFT BENT again another ten feet up. Dean followed it with difficulty, aided by the adrenaline surging through his body and urged on by Louis cursing at his heels.

He crawled another seven or eight feet, then his forward hand encountered a mesh screen tightly set into place. "It's blocked," he called back to Louis. The shaft had also narrowed, barely passable even if Dean flattened himself.

A self-light flared to life, throwing slashes of illumination over Dean's shoulder. The vent in front of him was about two feet wide by eighteen inches high. The self-light framed most of the rectangle on the carpeted floor on the other side of the vent.

Tables and chairs were scattered across the room, joined by a few skeletons dressed in the tatters. Rodents and insects scattered at the sudden illumination.

"Get the damn thing out of the way!" Louis ordered. "Those monkeys will be here any second!"

Now that he could see what was blocking the way, Dean slipped a long-bladed hunting knife free of his belt and shoved it under the vent frame next to one of the top screws. Once the knife was in place, he twisted with all his strength. The screw popped with a screech.

Before Dean could slide the knife beside the next screw, he heard the double *whumpf* of grens going off somewhere nearby in the building. He twisted the blade, popping off another screw. One more and he had the top of the vent loosened.

"Hurry, Dean!" Louis urged. "They're having trouble getting up the shaft, but I don't think it's going to hold them very long!"

When the two side screws had been popped free, Dean put the knife away, then rested his shoulder against the vent and put his weight into it. The self-light went out as the vent popped loose. It banged on the carpet below, lost in the darkness.

Dean slithered through, falling out on his head but managing to block the impact with his hands. Louis came out right behind him.

Monkey feet drummed against the sides of the shaft, the screeches and jabbering growing louder.

"Go!" Louis said, reaching out in the darkness and shoving his companion forward.

Dean made his way as quickly as he could across the debris-strewn floor, nearly tripping over unidentifiable objects. He caught himself four times before he made it to the opposite wall where he'd seen the door.

Light burned to life in Louis's cupped palms. The boy's

blond locks were plastered to his head, his cheeks red-dened by blood. "Damn door's got to be here somewhere."

"There," Dean said, spotting the door five feet from their position.

The first monkey dropped to the carpeted floor.

Dean spun and brought up the Hi-Power, banging out three shots. The bullets hit the monkey, and bounced it backward against the wall. "Go on," he yelled. "I'll fol-low you."

Louis didn't waste time arguing. He needed both hands to keep the self-light alive.

Shifting his aim, Dean pumped rounds into the vent area. A couple of the large eyes winked out. Two more monkeys dropped from the vent and charged forward. Dean heard Louis open the door behind him.

A third monkey launched itself from the vent, wings spread out to catch the air.

"Dean!"

Turning, the boy raced for the door.

Louis held it open. Weak illumination from the hallway windows took the place of the self-light Louis dropped at his feet. The boy had his pistol in hand and was firing over Dean's head and shoulders.

Once in the corridor, Dean helped Louis slam the door shut, both boys resting their weight against it as the flying monkey slammed against it hard enough to open it almost an inch. The monkey slid blunt, hairy fingers through the crack, angling to gain enough purchase to shove the door all the way open with its incredible strength.

"Bastard!" Louis growled, pressing against the wooden surface.

Dean unsheathed his knife, then ran it down the side of the door, neatly slicing off all five of the monkey's fingers. Blood squirted from the injured appendages as its hand disappeared back inside. Shifting his grip on the knife, Dean rammed the blade into the jamb near the top of the door. He slipped a second knife into the jamb near the bottom.

"Hold them for a little while, mebbe," Dean said.

Louis took the lead, trotting across the worn and stained carpet in the corridor.

Dean sucked in air, wishing his lungs weren't so empty because he knew he was making too much noise. The sounds of combat were all around him now, and the open spaces were filling up with the haze of smoke, as if the building had caught fire somehow. He wondered where the others were, how they were doing—if they were still alive.

Abruptly two bulky shadows stepped around the corner of the intersection ahead of them, little more than twenty feet away.

Then Dean noticed the wavering fires captured in the barrels of the misshapen pistols they carried in their gloved hands. Hoses curled from the weapon and around the men's legs.

"Shit!" Louis said, backpedaling at once and streaking for the other end of the corridor. He bumped against Dean, pushing him back in that direction, as well.

Dean ran as hard as he could, understanding now where all the smoke had come from. He glanced over his shoulder and spotted the sudden mushrooms of orange-and-black flames suddenly gush from the spouts of the flamethrowers. A partially open door ahead of them only a couple steps on the left caught Dean's attention.

He slammed into Louis, knocking them both through the door as the boiling fire rushed through the corridor, filling it. The two boys fell to the floor.

Gazing around the empty boxes on the nearly depleted storage racks, the stainless steel gleaming in the sudden glare of the flames, Dean realized there was no other way out of the room.

"Back out," he told Louis. "It's the only way."

They got to their feet and poised by the door, checking their weapons as they waited for the flames to die down. When the flamethrowers ceased spitting fire, Louis took the lead around the doorway, breaking into a sprint at once across the corridor carpet. Fire pockets blazed on the walls and on the floor, some of them clinging precariously to the acoustic tile overhead.

Dean trailed after the other boy, sweating profusely, more scared now than at any time that he could ever remember. The corner of the next intersection was fifteen feet away when the harsh crackle of blasterfire started behind them.

Louis staggered abruptly, almost losing a step. Blood spread in a widening pattern below the armored vest on his left side, just above his hip.

As they turned the corner, Dean saw the other boy was definitely losing his stride.

"Go on, Dean," Louis gasped, holding his side. His face was white with pain. "I can't run much farther. Mebbe I can give you some more time."

"No," Dean answered. He hooked the boy's arm over his shoulders. "We're going to get out of this together." Taking part of Louis's weight, he guided the boy toward a door on the left.

Inside, the walls had been stripped to concrete. The low ceiling held broken conduit pipes and shattered fluorescent tubes. Overturned tables were in the center of the room, broken chairs all around them. They were metal and wouldn't burn, which was the only reason Dean could figure they hadn't been taken. It looked like a private gaming room for small groups.

"Stay in here," Dean told Louis. "Try to find someplace to hide. I'll see if I can't get them away from us."

Louis nodded, leaning against the back wall that dog-legged and took it out of immediate view of the door. Blood streamed out the side of his mouth. Wordlessly he offered Dean his rifle, indicating he only had the strength to manage his handblaster.

"I'll be back," Dean said. "I promise. Just hold on." Slinging the rifle, he sprinted back out of the room and into the hallway, listening to Louis hack and cough until the door closed and cut the sound off.

He also heard the running footsteps coming up the hallway they'd just turned off.

"I shot one of the sons of bitches," a man growled. "Know I did. Saw him stagger when the bullet took him."

"If you did," another man replied, "we'll find him soon enough."

"Not soon enough for me," a third man grunted. "Those bastard monkeys are dangerous. Did you see what they did to those boys below?"

In the distance Dean saw another intersection. With luck the sec men would think he and Louis had made it that far. Instead of racing in that direction, he holstered the Browning, then ran a few short steps and jumped for one of the metal crossbars in the ceiling overhead. A number of the acoustic tiles were missing, making a checkerboard of the ceiling.

Scrambling quickly, Dean hauled himself up into the darkness and lay along the crawl space. He positioned himself so he could see down into the corridor, then slipped the assault rifle over his shoulder and snapped the safety off. He pushed the selector to full-auto, snugged the rifle into his shoulder the way his dad and J.B. had taught him, and waited.

The sec team talked briefly below. Dean didn't look in their direction, not wanting to be a moving shadow above them. He'd gambled everything, his life and Louis's, on the play that was about to go down. His breath came forcibly.

"Must not have been hurt as bad as you thought, Clement," someone said. "Fuckers have already made the next corner."

The sec team went forward at a cautious jog.

Dean watched them come into view. He slid his finger over the rifle trigger, taking up slack. When the five men came into view, staggered out a little across the corridor, he dropped the rifle's open sights over the flamethrower tank on the back of the man on the left. He pulled the trigger, running through ten shots that struck the tank, then shifted to the other man with the flamethrower just now turning around to see where the shots had been fired from. Dean caressed the trigger, running the magazine dry.

Before the last shot cycled through the rifle, the fuel propellant in the flamethrower tanks blew up. Wet orange flames jetted everywhere from the explosion, curling against the windows on the opposite wall and filling them with a layer of soot. The wall on the interior caught fire in dozens of places, creating a stench that floated everywhere. Men screamed and writhed in agony until their lives ran out.

LeMarck watched as the sudden flare of the propellant washed away the scene of the green-team member who'd gunned down the sec guards. He dropped the binoculars and glared at Connrad, whose face seemed to become carved of stone.

"They're forfeit," the sec boss said in a voice loud enough for them all to hear.

"Kill them," Connrad growled. "Kill them all."

Around them the sec men rushed toward the rope ladders that would allow them to get into the pit. Death was coming.

And this time LeMarck didn't think even the one-eyed man could escape.

BLINKING AGAINST the spots that suddenly dotted his vision from the exploding fuel tanks, Dean reloaded the rifle, then dropped through the roof to the corridor floor. He felt good, then, more certain that he and Louis would find a means of escape.

He returned to the room, pushing through the door.

Louis spun suddenly, more quickly than Dean would have thought possible. The blaster in his hand went off, throwing out a foot-long muzzle-flash.

Dean jumped to one side of the doorway, the bullet barely missing him as it smacked into the door frame. "Shit, Louis, put that blaster down before you hurt somebody you're not supposed to." He walked into the room.

"What about the men behind us?" Louis asked. He held his hand to his side.

"All chilled," Dean said. "My dad always told me to take advantage of a situation if I could. Those flamethrower tanks strapped to their backs like they were, those bastards were just walking grens waiting to have their pins pulled. I pulled them."

"I don't think I'm going to make this one," Louis said. In the feeble light coming through the partially open door, his face was as pale as ivory, streaked with perspiration, and his eyes were starting to film over.

"You'll make it," Dean said confidently. "Come this far, I am not going to let you die on me now." His fingers worked the boy's armored vest, becoming bloody almost at first touch. When the body armor opened up, he peered under the armor and saw that Louis was right.

The bullet that had hit him in the lower back had passed through his groin, then deflected off the body armor covering his crotch and tore its way through his upper body, as well. The spent bullet lay a couple inches above his right nipple, a dark spot just below the freshly bruised skin that looked like a nest full of maggots.

"Those shitters!" Dean yelled in angry frustration and fear. "They shot you bad, Louis! They shot you real bad!"

Without another word, Louis toppled forward as if the bones had gone out of his legs. Blood leaked from his mouth below his sightless gaze.

Dean tried to catch the dead boy, but the sudden loose weight was too much. He went down under Louis, panicked all over again. "Louis, you can't die! You can't leave me here alone! Louis!"

The absence of the boy's breathing seemed like an impossible vacuum to Dean. Then it was filled by the snuffling of some large beast just outside the door. Hooves rang on a concrete patch out in the corridor.

It felt as if cold talons suddenly pinched the skin on the back of Dean's neck, pulling it way too tight. Forcing himself up, the boy drew the Browning, barely breathing as he watched the door.

"Dean," someone said, and he couldn't believe how much it sounded like Krysty.

Something shimmered into being on his right. It was impossibly close, near enough to reach out and touch him. He'd have seen anyone or anything that had come that close to him.

Then he saw the face, made out the features. She was indistinct, as if he were seeing her through a heavy fog.

"Krysty?" he said, not believing it.

"Your father is coming for you. Look for him."

Her words sounded as though they were coming from a long distance, then she was gone, just like some kind of ghost. Before he could puzzle over her appearance and what it meant, the door burst open.

Framed in it was a nightmare figure that Dean remembered well: a giant mutie pig, its beady, merciless eyes nearly buried in wrinkles of scarred gristle. The wicked tusks curled up on either side of its mouth.

Before he could get the Browning, the beast started for him, squealing shrilly in anticipation of an easy kill.

The corridor Ryan turned onto was filled with fire. A roiling ball of it wavered back and forth in front of him, seeking oxygen, threatening to collapse in on itself from the lack of fuel.

He had eluded his pursuers for the moment and was aware that the Mirage was showing potential for burning down around his ears. The sec men with the flamethrowers had been generous with their attentions, leaving burning areas and dead monkeys in their wake.

The group at the bottom of the inferno hadn't been so lucky.

Eyes stinging from the heat and the smoke, Ryan couldn't tell how many of them there were, or what exactly had killed them. With the way at least temporarily impassable, he turned back and took one of the other hallways that he'd passed up.

He sucked at the knuckles of his left hand, which he'd

skinned badly when he'd thrown himself away from the flamethrower at the window. He spit out a mouthful of blood, hitting a small fire that clung tenaciously to fragments of the worn carpet in the hallway.

When he was halfway down the new corridor, glancing to the sides to check the doors of what turned out to be more hotel rooms, he felt a chill gust through him, and even thought he'd smelled Krysty's scent next to him. He didn't look; if Krysty was still alive, she was outside with the others.

Servos whined through the hall, but he didn't know what they came from. There were other men searching through the ruins of the Mirage, as well. He'd seen them. And he'd seen one more dead boy in green. At the most, only five of them remained.

Farther down the hallway, he found a door that had a short flight of stairs behind it. The brass plate on the door announced Hotel Staff Only. The lock had been shot through.

With the Steyr in his hands, his back and side pressing against the side of the stairwells for cover, he went up. His ears monitored all sounds. A slight whisper of movement came from the top of the stairs.

At the landing, he paused, looking back the way he'd come and wanting to make sure retreat was still open to him. Satisfied no one was closing the gap behind him, he put his hand on the doorknob and turned. It wasn't locked, and the door opened easily.

Inside the room, slashes of neon lights danced around carelessly. The wall to his left held only glass from top to bottom. A bed occupied a space to his right, tucked in beside a desk that held a comp. The broken mirror covering a big section of the wall on the other side reflected the furniture, making it look as if another room were just next door.

He looked for the source of the noise, his senses at full peak. He stepped into the room, then ducked under the attack of the winged monkey that had been clinging to the space between the door and the ceiling. Unable to get off a shot, he swung the Steyr and felt the meaty impact as he struck the monkey with the rifle's butt.

Shrilling in pain, the monkey scuttled under the bed.

Drawing the SIG-Sauer, Ryan touched off three rounds across the bed, trying to find the mutie creature.

With a scream of pain and rage, the monkey came out from under the bed in a rush. Its mouth was open, showing its deadly fangs, the black talons reaching for Ryan's throat.

"Fireblast!" Ryan shoved the blaster into the monkey's face and pulled the trigger. The 9 mm round punched a hole through the beast's mouth and exited through the back of its head. Some of the flying matter stuck to his armored vest, while the majority of the creature landed in a disjointed confusion of limbs and wings at his feet.

"Ryan."

He was moving, turning, lifting the blaster as he recognized the voice. His finger already rested on the trigger when he said her name. "Krysty." His voice came out hard, disbelieving. "I thought they chilled you." He reached a hand out to the one she had extended. Instead of flesh, he felt a chill similar to the one that had passed through him in the corridor down below.

"I'm not really here, lover," she said.

Ryan's mind whirled with the multiple meanings of that simple declaration. His heart suddenly felt like a stone, cold and as distant as her voice.

"Dean's here with you. Find him."

"Dean?" He shook his head, struggling with everything being dealt to him.

She started to fade, winking out of existence like a dying star.

Ryan reached for her again, called out her name, but felt even the chill of their contact melt away from him as she disappeared.

The only thing that remained was the pull he was suddenly aware of inside his head. "Dean," he breathed, walking over to the wall of glass.

He peered through it with difficulty. Soot grimed it over, layers deep from the fires burning below. At one time, judging from the way the room was laid out, it had been a sec office looking down over the casino below.

The main door held tropical plants Ryan recognized from the jump to Amazonia. They had overgrown boundaries previously established by the building's architects, and had even thrust branches and new growth through the wall.

Once, it looked like a ville had been built inside the gaming room. Tables, chairs and slot machines were toppled over, chaotic. Dead people littered the floor. Some of them were dressed in old-style clothing, while many of the others wore much cruder dress.

Sec guards moved below, as well, searching through the debris, shooting at the monkeys still living.

The pull didn't come from that direction, Ryan knew. He turned and went back down the stairs, getting more sure as he followed the sensation.

He couldn't keep his thoughts from Dean. He'd missed much of his son's younger years, but he didn't begrudge that happenstance. The things he'd done, the places he'd gone, Dean would have been dead.

But he was determined not to lose the boy now, not to the pit creatures, muties or other chill squads. Not to the barons.

He fed the anger inside him, working it until the fatigue dropped away and his nerve and reflexes were as sharp as they ever were.

Out in the second-floor corridor, he turned, going farther into unexplored territory. The pull grew weaker. Realizing his mistake, he turned and went in the other direction, the SIG-Sauer in his fist.

The pull in his mind led him around the corner where the fire had been. It still burned, flames licking almost to the ceiling where acoustic tile smoldered.

A dark shape shoved at one of the doors on the other side of the fire. He squinted, peering through the heat wave given off by the flames, and recognized the shape as one of the wild pigs the companions had encountered before. There'd been plenty of them in the pit.

In the next second the wild pig thrust its way through the door.

Ryan took a few running steps and launched himself through the flames, covering his face with one arm. He felt the heat and smelled his hair singe. Then in the next moment he was through it, racing for the door as the pig disappeared into the room.

Reaching the entrance, Ryan threw himself to one side of it, the SIG-Sauer clutched firmly in both hands.

Shots rang out, changing the pitch of the wild pig's squeals. Impacts against flesh sounded wet and meaty.

Ryan peered around the door and watched as the pig bore down on a boy in green body armor who stood against the wall. Another boy, obviously dead, was at the feet of the first. The wild pig remained on its feet, running at the boy with the blaster flaming in his hand. The muzzle jumped with every rapid shot, but the boy brought it immediately back on target.

The pig careened against the wall as the boy adroitly shuffled out of the way. But its shoulder brushed against him hard enough to knock him to the floor. Recovering immediately, pushing himself one-handed into a sitting position, the boy stuck the blaster's muzzle into the pig's ear and pulled the trigger twice as the insane beast turned its head toward him, fangs snapping within inches of the boy's arm.

Then the pig shuddered, splaying out its legs, and died.

Ryan stepped part of the way around the doorway, knowing he was backlit by the flames in the corridor so that none of his face showed. The boy noticed him at once, lost in the darkness himself, and started to bring up his blaster.

"You make a move to pull that trigger," Ryan said, "and I'm going to chill you where you sit. Name's Ryan Cawdor. I'm looking for my son, Dean." He took up slack on the SIG-Sauer, knowing the boy might be too fearful to even hear him.

As he registered the words the man spoke, Dean recognized his stance, the way he held his head, the way he held the blaster.

His throat felt all closed up, but he forced his voice to work. "Dad?" He worked to shove the dead pig from his leg where it had him trapped, keeping his grip on his blaster. "Dad!"

The deadweight slid away, and Dean pushed himself to his feet, running toward his father with open arms.

Recognizing his son, Ryan rushed forward, grabbing the boy in his arms, his feelings running rampant. He couldn't remember a time when he and J.B. hadn't been friends, trusting each other with their lives. Opening up to Krysty had been hard after the experiences he'd had with most women.

And Dean—it had been a true puzzle to sort out exactly where to put his son in his life.

But in this instant, with death surrounding them and actively hunting them, Ryan was glad to hold the boy next to him, glad to see that none of the blood on him seemed to be coming from any serious wounds. Dean hugged him back, stronger than Ryan had remembered. For the moment this was the perfect place for Dean to be.

KRYSTY SWAM beneath the surface of the pond, trying not to leave a ripple in her wake, struggling not to imagine what might be in the water with them. Jak had her by the arm, and she had no choice but to trust his instinct for direction; the water was too murky to see through.

Just when she thought her lungs were going to burst from lack of oxygen, her hand encountered thick mud that felt greasy and cold. Jak guided them up a moment later.

"Breathe easy," he whispered in her ear as he gently guided her out of the water. "Hard not breathing fast, but got to. Otherwise get chilled."

Krysty started to turn her head, taking in her surroundings. Jak had brought them up in a nest of reeds and cattails. Some of them were broken off, stabbing uncomfortably into her neck and chin. At least, she hoped it was broken stems and not an insect or water creature. The pond was big, deep and cold, nestled into land that had been bermed at some point. One side of it still held chunks of pavement from a street, a stop sign and the rusted remains of a once colorfully painted trash container.

Jak put his hand on her head from behind. "Be still. They watch for us."

Krysty froze into position, noting the horses and their riders winding through the trees. All of the men had guns. Only a few of them carried bull's-eye lanterns, shining light across the surface of the pond and turning it almost mirror bright.

"What does that thermographic sight show?" they heard one of the riders demand.

"Nothing," another rider replied. "Bunch of water. What'd you expect?"

"What about the Mirage?" the first rider asked.

"Hard to say. The lower two stories are pretty much blazing. That much heat, hard to get any kind of reading at all."

"Did anyone see them jump into the pond?"

A chorus of negatives came back.

"There's a possibility they made it to the Mirage," someone said.

"Mebbe," the first rider agreed. "Let's stick it out here and see if we can turn up anything in the water. Beats the hell out of going up there and getting your nuts toasted."

Krysty freed her .38 from the soaked leather holster and set herself to move.

"Wait," Jak cautioned. "I go first. I kill silent. When shit hits fan, you move."

"Okay," she replied.

Jak reached into the shallow water and lifted up a fistful of black mud, which he smeared over his face, through his hair, then over his arms. When he finished, he was no longer as pale as milk. He looked like a black, wild-haired demon sprung whole from the night's shadows.

Jak crept out of the water as the riders went into motion, staying just outside the tall reeds and cattails. In less than a dozen steps, he'd disappeared soundlessly from Krysty's sight.

The riders split into two groups and went around the pond in both directions. The group to Krysty's left would reach her first. She kept the .38 in her hand, certain her skin was turning blue enough to match the water. Her sentient hair clung to her head.

Less than two minutes later, one of the riders directed his horse through the cattails and reeds toward where Krysty was hiding. His mount didn't like stepping through the mud and the water, shying away and nickering.

Krysty held the blaster, waiting, her heart thumping.

"Hey, Lloyd, what the hell's wrong with you?" someone demanded.

There was no answer.

The man in front of Krysty halted his horse and looked back over his shoulder, less than ten feet from her position. "You want to stop shouting like that?" the man asked.

Behind him a rider suddenly toppled to the ground, clawing at his throat.

"Hey!" the man in front of Krysty shouted. "Somebody just chilled Harris and Lloyd! Both of them are laying on the ground over there with knives through their throats!"

"I see him!" another man cried out.

Gunshots rang out.

Coming up out of the water just as the man in front of her tried to bring his mount around, Krysty grabbed the bridle.

The horse reared up in fear, its eyes rolling white.

Unprepared, the rider fell into the muddy water.

Krysty didn't hesitate about shooting the man twice in the back of the head before he could get to his feet. His body collapsed face forward into the murky water.

Knowing she wouldn't be able to calm the horse without letting it get out of the water, Krysty kept hold of the bridle and ran along at the animal's side, waiting for an opportunity to get into the saddle. The horse also served as a temporary shield, blocking sight of her from most of the other riders.

Up on the bank, her feet under her more solidly, she reached up for the pommel while never breaking stride. With a lithe leap, she pulled herself up into the saddle. Another moment spent taking up the slack in the reins, and she was in control of the fear-maddened horse.

She cut it in a tight half circle, searching the shadows for Jak.

He came up off the ground with no warning. One of the two horses that had belonged to the men he'd killed was tied to a tree, stamping its feet and fighting the bit in its mouth. Apparently one of the riders had gotten down to check out a suspicious area.

Racing across the ground, Jak approached the tethered horse from behind. Before it knew he was there, the albino placed his hands against the horse's rump and vaulted into the saddle. Bullets cut through branches and leaves above his head as he reached forward, staying low against the horse's neck, and untied the reins. He brought the animal around and kicked it lightly. The horse exploded into a gallop.

The other horse streaked for the trees, heading in a westerly direction that would take it toward the Mirage. Another horse was also free, galloping in the same direction.

"Get horses!" Jak called.

Krysty nodded, pulling her mount's head around and kicking it into motion. Bullets whizzed around her as gunfire split the night. Glancing ahead and to the right, she could see flames coming from the first and second floors of the Mirage.

Behind them the surviving sec-team members were already putting a posse together.

Cutting around a tree, Krysty halted her mount for a moment and looked back. Jak rode low in the saddle and fired his .357 Magnum blaster at the men less than forty yards behind him.

Krysty raised the .38 and thumbed back the hammer. The distance from herself to the first rider was less than seventy yards. She centered the muzzle over the man's chest, then squeezed away the slight pull. The .38 banged in her fist.

The lead rider slapped a hand to a spot where his throat joined his chest, then fell from the saddle.

Thumbing the hammer back again, Krysty lined up her second shot and emptied another saddle. Jak was almost on top of her when she fired her remaining round. The bullet went inches wide of its target. Krysty kicked her horse back into motion, barely taking a lead over her companion.

Seven men still remained in pursuit.

She swung the cylinder open and dumped the brass. Fishing shells from her shirt pocket, she tried to refill the cylinder and keep an eye on the frightened horse, as well. It took eight bullets to finally reload the blaster because she dropped three of them.

Jak was having the same problem.

Abruptly a shadow moved ahead of Krysty. Her horse noticed it before she did, sidestepping fast enough to almost throw her from the saddle. She pointed her pistol at the shadow, then saw that it wore J.B.'s beloved fedora and steel-rimmed glasses.

"Keep riding," the Armorer said. "Mildred and I will take care of the posse."

Krysty nodded, then kicked her horse in the sides again,

closing on the animal in front of her. Jak drew abreast of her, pointing to the other one, then himself.

"I'LL TAKE THE ODD ONES," J.B. said, lifting his Uzi as the posse closed on their position. "Leaves you the even ones." He stood in the shelter of a blue spruce, the stiff needles scratching at his face.

"I got them," Mildred said calmly. She held the Czech target pistol balanced in both hands.

J.B. knew the wait wouldn't be long; the drumming sound of the horses' hooves grew louder. He was a patient stalker, but he knew the work would be bloody and quick.

Moosh Wandell and Thompson were farther back in the brush, set up to cover their retreat if any of the riders survived the ambush.

Listening to the hooves strike the ground, J.B. timed his move, stepping out when he knew they'd all be between the narrow defile leading through the brush. The rider didn't have a chance to register J.B.'s appearance before the Armorer caressed the Uzi's trigger and sent a 3-round burst into his face. The man's head came apart instantly, and he vanished under the hooves of the horses behind him.

The animals reacted badly, trying to avoid contact with the corpse tumbling under their feet.

Mildred remained in the brush, firing between the branches.

The next four riders dropped from their frightened mounts in quick succession. The woman worked to get the sixth rider, managing a hard shot uphill as the man took off in that direction.

The lone surviving rider retreated behind a row of trees, heading back to the area around the pond. A line of 9 mm bullets from the Uzi tore bark from the trees that he took cover behind.

"Gather up the horses that you can," J.B. told Mildred. He reached out with quick hands and grabbed the pommel of a horse passing by. "I'll be back."

"Be careful," Mildred called after him.

Hauling himself into the saddle, the Armorer reached for the reins, then took control of the animal. He brought it around sharply, almost causing the beast's legs to collapse under them. Then the horse recovered its footing, charging back down the trail when J.B. put his heels to it.

He stayed to the trail, his horse leaping over the corpses when it came to them. Through the brush he saw the last rider trying to wend his way among the trees and bushes to a clearing.

The sec man glanced at the Armorer through the forest, eyes going big with fear.

They came out into the clearing at the same time. J.B. lifted the Uzi one-handed, guiding the horse with the reins in the other.

To the rider's credit, he wheeled his mount toward the Armorer and lifted his own blaster, firing immediately and screaming at the top of his voice.

J.B. cut his horse toward the man but held his finger poised over the Uzi's trigger until he was certain of the kill. By his own estimate, he had between two and eight rounds left in the 30-round magazine.

Less than twenty yards remained between them when the Armorer cut loose. The 9 mm rounds smashed the sec man out of his saddle, the riderless horse streaking past.

He went after it, catching the animal's reins in seconds and wrapping them around the pommel. Grinding engine noises drew his attention north. Through the trees and along the skyline in the distance, he saw the headlights of wags rolling through the pit toward the Mirage. Even the remnants of the streets that had once been Vegas were rough, causing the vehicles to jump and jar.

"Dark night," he said out loud. Reining his mount to the side, he kicked its ribs and sent it galloping back along the trail.

When he reached the spot where he'd left Mildred and the two surviving members of the red team, he saw that Jak and Krysty had returned, as well. Between them they'd captured nine of the horses. Moosh Wandell and Thompson were pulling themselves into the saddles.

Mildred saw his face and immediately knew something was wrong. "What is it?" she asked.

"Wags are coming," J.B. replied, "fast. And plenty of them!"

"Where's the rest of your team?" a harsh voice demanded.

"Don't know," a boy replied. "Probably dead. Like everybody else."

"How many are dead?"

Ryan moved silently toward the voices, Dean at his heels. The boy showed more coordination and patience than Ryan could remember from past times. They walked along the corridors of the first floor trying to find a way out of the Mirage. The snipers along the perimeter walls of the pit had to have been put on the alert for any more window jumping. Ryan had nearly had his head taken off by a round while breaking out soot-covered glass along the second floor.

Coming around the corner opening onto the area by the front desk, Ryan saw dozens of big-toothed fish lying dead in the pools of water across the floor. One of the dead boys was there, as well, staring up at the black ceiling.

Farther back, near the line of foliage that had swept into the entranceway from the atrium, three sec guards stood over two boys wearing the green-armored vests.

The sec guards made no move to harm them, but they kept their rifles ready in their hands. The boys knelt on the floor, their hands tucked behind their backs.

"All of them are dead," one of the boys said.

"You know that for a fact?" The speaker was a grizzled man with a potbelly. His face bore the scars of past wars.

"No."

"How many do you know rightly for a fact, boy?"

"Six," the boy said. "Six for certain. Fish got one of them. Five others were killed by those damn monkeys."

"Hate those fucking monkeys," one of the other sec men said.

Not seeing anyone else around, Ryan lifted the SIG-Sauer and stepped out so he was in the clear. Without a word he shot the grizzled man through the side of the head, showering his brains over a broad-leafed fern of some type. Before the first man had time to drop, Ryan shifted his aim.

The second sec guard had his rifle up and was stitching a crooked pattern across the floor, leaving pockmarks where the bullets struck.

Shooting from instinct, Ryan put three rounds into the man's head. The third guard had a blaster in both hands and got off two shots before Ryan could pick him up.

Both rounds slammed into Ryan with bruising force despite the armored vest, but the bullets didn't penetrate. He shot the man four times across the crotch area. At least one of the rounds bounced off the bulletproof armor covering the man's cock, but the force was devastating. The other three bullets gouged into his thighs.

The sec man went down screaming. He tried to maintain enough presence of mind to keep his blaster on target.

Ryan walked over, squeezing the trigger as he neared the man, and put two rounds through the man's wide mouth.

The two boys in green body armor tried to go for the dropped weapons.

"No," Ryan cautioned in a hard voice. "Not until we reach an understanding about what's happening here."

The boys froze.

Dean came forward out of the shadows.

"You know these boys?" Ryan asked his son.

Dean nodded. "Ethan Perry and Conor. Don't remember his last name right now. If I ever knew it."

"Who the hell is this?" Perry demanded. His features were disheveled and bloodstained, carrying a multitude of scratches.

"My dad," Dean answered.

The smaller boy, Conor, looked up at Ryan. "You come here to get Dean out?"

"Didn't start out that way," Ryan replied, "but I'm aiming to see it done."

"What about us?" Perry asked.

"Free country," Ryan said. "If you can keep up, you can come along. If you don't carry your weight, you get left behind."

Both boys nodded.

"Arm yourselves," Ryan said. "We're pulling up stakes. Now." He strode toward the atrium, seeing the dark outline of the entranceway framed behind the trees and plants.

Dean stayed close behind him, and the other two boys fell in, as well.

"Louis?" Conor asked.

"Dead," Dean replied.

"Oh."

Senses alert for any sign of danger, Ryan came to a halt at the entranceway and peered around its edge. He saw the wags heading toward the Mirage, almost obscured in the white smoke drifting off the burning building. "Fireblast," he swore quietly.

He signaled to the boys and took off around the corner of the building, watchful of the snipers along the top of the wall on the other side. He skirted the edge of the outside swimming pool, counting on the falls streaming from the fifth floor to help cover them from easy view. He wondered where Mildred and J.B. had gone.

Hooves beat against the ground, the sound coming from the west.

Turning in that direction, Ryan watched a group of riders approach at a fast gallop, staying under the canopy of trees as much as possible. Then, under a bright shaft of moonlight, he spotted red hair on the rider of the lead horse.

Krysty brought the horse to a stop at the edge of the swimming pool, her eyes focused on him, guided more than by just her vision.

"Time to shake the dust of this place from us, lover," she called across the water.

Bullets from the guards on top of the wall suddenly sheared through the trees over the riders and horses. J.B. swung up a rifle he'd liberated from someone along the way. The Armorer cracked off expert shots, dropping two of the sec men from the top of the wall. One of them fell onto the top of the hotel, and the other took the forty-foot plunge into the swimming pool. The rest of the sec guards went into hiding as Jak, Mildred, Krysty, Moosh Wandell and Thompson added their fire to J.B.'s.

"Go," Ryan told Dean.

Without a word the boy dived into the water and began to swim briskly, followed by Conor and Perry.

Holstering the SIG-Sauer and pulling up the Steyr, Ryan picked off two snipers, further demoralizing the sec crew overhead. He dived into the water, staying under for a time to cut through it more swiftly. When he surfaced, he was barely two strokes behind Dean and ahead of the two other boys.

He reached the bank at the same time Dean did, then took the reins Krysty offered. "Good to see you again," he told her as he swung into the saddle. "After seeing you when I was in the Mirage, I wasn't counting on it."

"I know," Krysty replied. "Wasn't sure I'd be here myself."

Puzzled by her words but knowing he didn't have the time to investigate them further, Ryan reached out briefly to touch her hand. He wanted to know for sure she was real, was there. Her fingers twined with his, strong, sure and permanent.

She leaned forward in her stirrups and brushed a kiss against his lips. "We get the time, lover, I'll show you how real I am."

Ryan smiled at her in spite of the situation and the restless horse tramping the ground beneath him. "I'll hold you to that." Then he reined the horse around. "Which way?"

"West," she replied. "There's a wall there separating the pit from the old convention center."

"I remember the convention center," Mildred said, "but I don't see how it's going to help us."

"It has an underground garage," Krysty said.

"Just another wall," Mildred replied.

The flame-haired woman pulled out two remote-control detonators. "Remember that old Christian story about the walls of Jericho? Well, I've got a couple of Gabriel's horns here."

The next few minutes were a hurried blur for Ryan. He stayed in the saddle, one hand filled with the SIG-Sauer as he kicked the horse's sides and kept it at a full gallop. He shot at everything that moved: muties, creatures and surviving members of the barons' teams.

They stayed within the trees as much as they could, taking advantage of the cover offered. With the rough terrain the wags were struggling to close the distance, not able to gain much on the horses.

The horses, however, were only flesh and blood. All of them were sweat-flecked from their exertions, looking as if they'd been dipped in soapy water. Ryan knew if they had to run them much farther, they'd burst the animals' hearts.

As the group took a final sweep through the remaining forest, Moosh Wandell caught a round in the side of his head that dumped him from his saddle.

The others didn't slow their mounts for an instant. If the man wasn't dead, he was certainly too wounded to keep up with them.

Ryan fired a half-dozen shots at the tree less than a hundred yards away. He concentrated on where he'd seen the muzzle-flash that had claimed Moosh. A few seconds after the rolling thunder had died away, a body tumbled from the branches.

"Good shooting," J.B. said.

"Lucky," Ryan growled.

Jak reached out and captured the riderless horse's reins. "Doc has own mount now."

Another moment through the treacherous forest and uncertain footing of the terrain, and they were at the edge of the brush in front of the wall that Krysty had guided them to.

There was also a phalanx of sec men bunched together on top of the wall. They fired at will, chipping branches and bark from the surrounding trees.

"Fireblast," Ryan said, staring at the army assembled before them. "We ride out into that, we're going to get seriously chopped up."

"Mebbe not," Krysty said without explanation. "Could be those sec men have picked the wrong place to be." She took out one of the detonators, wincing slightly as a bullet ricocheted from the elm tree just above her head. "Jak and I didn't just mine the wall."

"Better do what you have to do," Ryan said, twisting in the saddle and peering over his shoulder. "Those wags are getting closer."

She slid her thumb over the red detonator button, then pressed it.

DOC'S ATTENTION was focused primarily on the sudden and definite increase in shots cracking from the sec men's stations above him. He didn't hear Bernsen come up behind him until it was too late. Only the slight scuff of a shoe against concrete alerted him. He spun.

The scientist held a chunk of stone in either hand, turning both his arms into hammers that could crush Doc's skull. "You're a fool," he grunted, "and you're going to die a fool. I'm not going to die with you." He swung the rock in his right hand.

Pain exploded along Doc's jawline. As he went backward against the wall beside him, stars swam into the old man's vision, taking away the weak light coming from the lantern Krysty and Jak had left with him in the underground parking garage.

"With your background," Bernsen berated him, "you know you shouldn't let emotion get involved with your work." He swung the chunk of stone in the other hand, intending to smash Doc's skull.

By the time the blow arrived, Doc moved his head. The rock smacked into the wall, shattering and scarring the cinder blocks.

"I must insist, Doctor," Doc said, "that you control yourself. Otherwise, I fear your choice of actions will lead only to ill fortune."

White spittle framed Bernsen's mouth, and madness gleamed in his eyes. He swung again, this time succeeding in knocking the Le Mat blaster from Doc's grip.

"The only ill fortune will be yours," Bernsen said, "for ever thinking you could hold me here against my will." He swung the stone again.

Senses still reeling, Doc dodged another blow and slid the sword stick from his belt. Without thinking, he twisted the lion's head and drew the concealed sword in a practiced and easy gesture.

Before Bernsen could avoid it, the tip of the steel blade flicked out and carved another mouth from one side of his neck to the other. He let go of the stones, reaching up to his throat and making drowning sounds. Crimson sprayed from his mouth and the slash across his throat.

"I will not be dissuaded from my post," Doc said vehemently. "Nor do I accept being killed while at it. May God have mercy on your soul."

Bernsen toppled forward, the light going out of his eyes.

Then the convention center shuddered like an arthritic dog being struck with cold shivers. The sound of the explosion hammered into the underground garage only a moment later.

"By the Three Kennedys!" Doc exclaimed as he glanced toward the section of wall that he expected to go flying, as well. Instead, a barrage of broken rock trembled from the ceiling. He braced himself against the wall behind him, wondering if the stories above might suddenly collapse and come crashing down on him, reducing him to a protein paste.

HAYDEN LEMARCK WATCHED as the center of the wall of the convention center blew apart. The explosives that ripped it to shreds were cunningly placed. The rooftop was ripped loose, then fell back in on itself, taking a thirty-foot section with it—as well as the sec guards trying to snipe the one-eyed man and his companions.

"Son of a bitch!" someone roared.

"Is someone inside the convention center?" Vinge Connrad demanded. The baron held his rifle in hand, his eyes wild and hot.

No one seemed to have an answer.

"Devil take all of you!" Connrad yelled. "I want a team down there now who can report the truth to me!"

LeMarck didn't figure anyone was inside the convention center. Whoever had entered the pit had mined it on their way in. Getting rid of the sec teams on top made sense, but he didn't know why the one-eyed man had returned to this site with his companions. There was no way out.

He peered through the scope, searching for his quarry. For a moment he thought he might have spotted the one-eyed man among the trees. His finger slid around the sniper rifle's trigger and took up slack. He let out half a breath, then held it. He thought he might have a shot, but also figured the bullet might have been deflected from the branches.

LeMarck also found himself of mixed emotions about killing the one-eyed man. Of all the champions in the Big Game, the one-eyed man and his group deserved most to live.

"Hayden."

The sec commander recognized Baron Hardcoe's voice at once. "Sir?"

"Do you see them?" The baron came to a stop beside them.

LeMarck hesitated only a moment. No matter what else the one-eyed man might represent, he was a danger to Hardcoe if he chose to follow a path of vengeance. "Not clearly, sir, but I'm hoping for a shot."

"Good man." Hardcoe set his Ameli 82 on the fence line. "Mebbe I can flush them out for you." He settled in behind the machine gun and opened it up.

"Dawson, Hughes!" Connrad roared. "You people are with me! Now move your asses!"

Out of his peripheral vision, LeMarck watched Connrad grab a home-built grenade launcher along with a small bag of bombs, slinging both over his shoulder.

"You can stay up here if you want," Connrad told Hardcoe, "but I'm going down to ground level and fuck those bastards over royally. You can sort through the pieces later."

"You've got men down there, too," Hardcoe said.

"Then mebbe we both lose," Connrad said. "Mebbe we'll do the Big Game over in the next few weeks, or mebbe Giskard just gets lucky this year. Either way, those skanks die in the next handful of minutes. You can take an ace on the line on that."

Connrad led his men down the metal staircase that had been welded together to reach the ground, their boots ringing against the steps.

LeMarck looked back through his scope, sorting out the blacks and the greens until he found part of a face. Memory told him the fedora and steel-rimmed glasses belonged to one of the men among One-Eye's group. He let out his breath and steadied for the shot as Hardcoe's machine gun howled in unrestrained carnage.

Then the building shuddered again, letting him know there had been a secondary set of explosives.

Peering over the edge, he saw the bottom of the convention center come spewing out. "Shit!" Glancing back up, he saw the line of riders gallop out of the trees. He turned and used the stairs Hardcoe and his sec crew had taken.

Ryan fought his horse as the plas ex went off in the building, showering the trees with concrete chips and debris. Watching the wall fronting the underground garage, he saw the hole take shape, yawning open to a mouth of darkness almost twelve yards across and nearly as tall.

"Ride!" he told the others.

Krysty took the lead since she knew the interior of the garage, followed by Mildred.

J.B. held back, manhandling his frightened horse. Specks of blood glowed on the animal's muzzle, sprayed out through its nostrils. "These animals don't have much more to give."

Ryan nodded in agreement. "Mebbe they got enough, though."

When the last of the riders took off, Ryan kicked his mount in the sides. Bullets hit the ground in front of him and on both sides, striking sparks off rocks. The snipers on top of the wall were getting their nerve and the range back.

J.B. took a slight lead over him as they neared the rock-strewn incline leading to the hole in the underground garage.

Ryan stayed low over the saddle and the horse's neck as he passed through the hole. His eye had problems adjusting to the darkness in the underbelly of the convention center.

Wags had been blown haphazardly around, tumbling over one another. Even rusted ones showed new scratches and dents, whole patches of oxidized metal rubbed raw again.

On the other side of the garage, Jak had stopped the extra horse for Doc. The old man appeared shaken up but whole. Jak had to assist him in getting a boot into the stirrup, then reached down and grabbed Doc's waistband, helping pull him into the saddle.

Krysty navigated the stairway leading to the upper floors. The horses' hooves rang on the stone, echoing hollowly in the cavernous vault. Mildred was behind her, trailed by Thompson, Conor, Perry and Dean.

Coming up behind Doc, Ryan looked down and saw Bernsen's body nearly buried in refuse that had tumbled from the ceiling. His throat was cut, clots of crimson covering the front of his shirt.

"What happened to him?" Ryan asked.

Doc grabbed the reins from Jak. "Thank you, my dear boy. I fear I am somewhat shaken about, and my equestrian skills are not as sharp as we would prefer." He shifted his attention to Ryan. "He suggested, very strongly, that I be remiss in my friendship. I corrected his oversight."

"For once and for all, it looks to me," J.B. noted.

"Yes."

Ryan slapped Doc's mount on the flank and got it moving. Doc guided it up the stairs, the horse's breath blowing out in steamy clouds as it clopped up the steps.

Glancing out the hole made by the plas ex, Ryan spotted the sec wags only a few yards away.

"They might get them in here if they're lucky," J.B. said, clamping down his fedora more tightly. "But even if they get them through that maze of wrecked wags, there's no way they're going to get them up these stairs."

Ryan nodded, glancing up. Jak was already navigating the landing. "Mebbe some waiting outside." He waited expectantly for blasterfire, but none came.

"Had wags outside," Jak called down. "Took coil wires." He held them up. "Got time, we make them ours."

Following J.B., Ryan urged his horse up the stairs. The saddle rocked violently under him as the animal found a gait that would allow it to climb the incline. Passing through the landing required a little more skill.

He caught the door at the top of the stairs as J.B. passed through, then the next one that opened up onto the main lobby. The horse's breath was loud in his ears, rasping back and forth like a bellows.

Dust filled the lobby, swirling in gusts that were lit up by the lanterns hanging on the walls. The horses' hooves striking the concrete under the tattered carpet made the building sound hollow, empty.

The smack of a bullet hitting flesh and the vibration under his thigh was the only warning Ryan had about snipers in the room. He wheeled his mount to the right, felt it stumble for a moment under him and spotted three men firing from entranceways across the foyer.

Over half the horses were already out the door. Ryan

glimpsed the night sky beyond, filled with bright, daz-zling stars.

Facing the men head-on to present a smaller target with the horse, Ryan lifted the SIG-Sauer and squeezed off rounds. Bullets plucked at his clothing, one of them burning a furrow across his temple above his left ear.

He put the sights over the lantern on the wall by the man on the right. Squeezing off a pair of rounds, he watched the lantern come apart, drenching the sec man in oil. The burning wick fell more slowly, but when it touched the man, it wreathed him in flames.

The man started to scream, distracting the other two gunners nearby.

Maintaining his stance, Ryan shot the next man in the head, then fired the blaster's magazine dry, hitting the last man in the chest and the throat, knocking him down.

J.B. held the door for him.

Ryan kicked his mount and ducked under the door frame. It was immediately cooler outside. In the moonlight he could see the blood dripping from his horse's nostrils, letting him know at least one of the bullets that had hit the animal had cored through one or both lungs. It was dying beneath him. He took the empty magazine from the SIG-Sauer and rammed a fresh one home, thumbing the slide release so it snapped closed.

The Armorer had his shotgun in his hand. "No time to make for the wags." He nodded upward. "They're already regrouping."

"Then we make do with the horses," Ryan said. "Get out into the forest as far as we can. Mebbe we can find a way to lose ourselves. They may be regrouping, but it looks like they're starting to fight among themselves, as well."

Across the top of the wall, some of the sec men had

turned their fire on one another. One man fell from the side, screaming the whole way, until he crashed against the ground less than three yards away.

J.B.'s horse spooked. Wrestling with the reins, the Armorer headed the animal in the right direction. "See you on the other side."

Ryan nodded, wondering how much more his mount had to give. Before he could kick the horse in the sides to get it going, he saw an open-topped wag come around the side of the convention center, throwing out rooster tails of dust and rock behind it.

He squinted his eye to make out the men inside it. The only one he recognized was Vinge Connrad. The baron's blue-jay earrings fluttered in the slipstream coming in over the wag's shield.

As Ryan watched, Connrad raised a tube to his shoulder and flipped up the sights. His target was J.B., but the others would follow. There was no way the horses could outrun the wag, and with the homemade rocket launcher, Connrad only had to get close to kill them all.

Ryan kicked his horse in the sides. At first it was sluggish, then gained speed rapidly. The animal didn't appear skittish about the wag. Ryan figured it was too far over the line of death to even realize where it was headed. Blood came from its nostrils in streams now, spraying across Ryan's pant legs.

Twenty-five feet from the wag, Ryan opened up with the SIG-Sauer, firing as rapidly as he could. Most of the rounds scored on the vehicle, and he managed to get the guy manning the heavy machine gun mounted on the rear deck.

As the gunner fell, Ryan rode out the end of his interception course just as Connrad turned the rocket launcher on him.

Five feet out, the horse plunging at breakneck speed toward the front of the wag from an angle, Ryan pulled his feet from the stirrups and crouched on the saddle.

A moment before impact, the horse suddenly realized where it was. But it was too late to avoid the collision. The horse gave a gurgling whinny of fear.

Ryan leaped forward, hoping he had enough momentum and strength to clear the wag. He tumbled over in midair, just as Connrad's rocket jetted free of the launcher to impact against the convention center. The warhead exploded a new hole in the side of the building.

As he continued to turn, seeing the ground coming up at him fast now, Ryan got a brief glimpse of the horse smashing into the wag. At the last moment it had tried to leap over the vehicle.

The horse never came close to clearing the vehicle. The front of the wag struck the horse at the legs, breaking all of them. Lifted by the low bumper, the horse bounced off the hood and crashed into the windshield. The driver had time for one short-lived scream before the horse's body smashed into him and killed him.

Then Ryan lost the wag briefly, going loose a moment before he struck the ground hard enough to knock the breath from his lungs. He made himself hang on to his blaster despite the pain of the sudden stop. He forced himself into motion, his reflexes working to get his lungs to function again, building a burning pressure in his chest.

He turned, getting his bearings, looking for the wag.

Connrad had kidnapped Dean and brought him to the Big Game. Ryan knew that from the brief conversation he'd had with his son back in the Mirage. He felt the anger work within his flesh and bone. His breath came back, and his legs worked just fine as he sprinted toward the wag.

Out of control, the vehicle had smashed against the bole of an ancient oak tree, gouging the bark. Steam sprayed from the broken radiator, throwing hissing puddles on the ground under the chassis. The horse was lying on the ground behind the wag, torn open and already dead, its intestines wrapped around the dead driver and the rear deck where the machine gun had been mounted.

For a moment Ryan thought Connrad might be dead, as well. Then the baron surged up from the passenger seat and got out.

The baron spun to face Ryan, his hand clawing for his blaster. The only thing he touched was an empty holster.

Ryan grinned coldly. "Looks like you lose the whole hand this time. Guess they'll be talking about the four barons from now on."

"Fuck you!" Connrad yelled. He reached into the back of the wag and took out a machete, then charged at Ryan.

Lifting the SIG-Sauer, Ryan squeezed the trigger, then noticed the slide had blown back empty. When he'd been shooting at the wag, he'd emptied the magazine and hadn't realized it.

"Got to have bullets for your blaster if you're going to kill me with it, stupe!" Connrad screamed, taking a two-handed grip on the machete handle. "I'm going to make you into twins!"

Tripping the slide release, Ryan closed the empty blaster and shoved it into his holster. Just as the baron started his swing with the machete, Ryan cleared leather with the panga. Knowing he couldn't stop the heavier blade without risking breaking his weapon, he used the smaller knife to parry the machete.

Metal screamed against metal and sparks flared when the keen edges met and slid against each other.

Ryan felt the anger burning in him.

Connrad closed on him, trying to use his greater weight to an advantage. "I'm going to break you, little man, but I'm not going to kill you. For that, I'm going to use a slow fire. Cut a piece of you off at a time and let you watch that piece burn. Then we'll move on to the next piece. Death's going to be a long time in coming."

"No," Ryan said calmly, "that's not going to happen." The one-eyed man whipped his free hand up suddenly, driving it into Connrad's unprotected chin.

The baron groaned in pain and shoved back, getting more distance between himself and his opponent. The big man swung the machete again, slashing sideways this time in an effort to shear his adversary's head from his shoulders.

Ryan ducked under the effort, but felt the keen edge shear a few dark curls from the top of his head. He kicked at Connrad's knee from a squatting position.

The kneecap shattering sounded like the crack of a gunshot. Even hurting as he was, Connrad tried to swing the machete again as Ryan came back up to a standing position.

Sweeping his left arm up to block the baron's weapon arm, Ryan rammed the panga's point into the underside of the bigger man's jaw. The blade slid home easily, gliding through flesh until it was stopped by the back of Connrad's skull.

The baron heaved convulsively, collapsing first on his broken knee as life left him. The machete dropped to the ground.

Ryan yanked his weapon free and let the corpse drop to the ground. He turned around and found himself confronted by Hayden LeMarck.

The sec boss had his rifle leveled, standing less than twenty feet away. "I hadn't counted on you killing Connrad. That's going to create problems, unless I shoot you myself and bring you in. Mebbe then the other barons will believe Hardcoe didn't have anything to do with Connrad's assassination."

Ryan breathed hard, giving in to his body's demand for oxygen. The panga was still clutched in his hand, and the empty SIG-Sauer was in its holster. The only chance he had was for the Steyr.

"Man come out here looking for trouble. I didn't go looking for it." Ryan paused. "Seems like you come out here hunting it, too."

LeMarck nodded back at the pit area. "You see all that fighting going on up there?"

"Yeah."

"You caused that. You and your friends. Thrown everything that was balanced between the barons into a frenzy. Going to be a lot of chilling before things settle down again."

"With Connrad dead, Hardcoe should have an easier time of claiming the villes."

"Mebbe. Be easier to do if I chill you here and take your body back."

"Be difficult to drag a man when you're dead yourself," a hard voice said.

Looking over LeMarck's shoulder, Ryan saw J.B. on his horse in the shadows, his shotgun raised to his shoulder.

"Your friend with the hat?" LeMarck asked. He didn't move the rifle's sights from Ryan's head.

"Yeah."

"I'll tell you something," the sec boss said, raising his voice, "if you thought you could have taken me without getting your friend chilled, you'd have already done it."

"True enough," J.B. admitted.

"But you don't think you can shoot me and keep me from shooting your buddy."

"Got a better than average chance," J.B. replied. "shotgun's loaded with twenty razor-edged fléchettes. The impact of them shredding flesh from bone is going to stagger you some."

"But will it be enough?" LeMarck was smiling.

"I guess that remains to be seen, doesn't it?" Ryan asked. "One thing's for certain—we can't hang around here to think about it much."

"Agreed," LeMarck said. "I get myself chilled, I figure Hardcoe's going to have an even harder time hanging on to the seven villes. How do you want to handle this?"

"Start walking backward," Ryan said, "toward the wag. You can keep the rifle on me. Before you get behind it, you throw out the rifle or my friend takes your head off with the shotgun. Sound fair enough?"

"Fair enough," LeMarck said. "But I'd rather see you dead. Don't want to have to get sleepless at night wondering when you're going to be coming back our way."

"Revenge isn't all that high on my list," Ryan told him truthfully. "I see a chance to get it, walk away clean, I'll do it. I'm more interested in a whole skin. Cut my losses here. But I will tell you one thing—if I see you anywhere around me again, I'll chill you on the spot. No questions asked, no warning given."

"I'll keep that in mind." LeMarck started to back up, reaching the corner of the wrecked wag.

"Far enough," J.B. called. "Throw out the rifle."

After only a moment of hesitation, the sec boss did as he'd been told, moving swiftly behind the wag.

Ryan ran toward J.B. The Armorer kicked a foot out of the stirrup on Ryan's side. Hooking his boot in the stirrup, Ryan hauled himself up behind his friend. The horse jostled around, adjusting to the weight.

Pulling on the reins, J.B. backed the horse to the trail leading into the forest. Ryan rammed a fresh magazine into the SIG-Sauer, then pointed it at LeMarck's position.

"Okay," Ryan said. "I've got him covered."

J.B. wheeled the horse and kicked it into a full gallop.

LeMarck moved at once, coming up over the edge of the wag with a blaster in his fist.

Ryan fired, scattering bullets all around the sec boss and sending the man to cover again. In a heartbeat the wag and the convention center were out of sight.

Less than two hundred yards farther on, with the horse giving out beneath their combined weight, Ryan saw the clearing up ahead where an armawag sat like a mythical beast, its ugly cannon snout pointed toward the ruins of the ville.

Remains of Vegas's former glory still thrust above the trees and grass around and behind the wag, letting Ryan know they hadn't yet cleared the area where the ville had once stood. Most of the buildings were smaller now, mainly private dwellings and scaled-down shops. A lot of the area hadn't had much in the way of development. A sign nearly hidden by a blackberry bush read Las Vegas Country Club.

Saddles and bridles littered the ground in front of the armawag.

"What the hell?" J.B. said, pulling the horse up short and guiding it behind a stand of trees.

Ryan slid down, refilling the hand blaster and holstering it so he could take up the Steyr.

Abruptly the armawag's hatch opened, and a man pushed himself into view.

Ryan recognized the weathered features of Jake, one of Nicholas Brody's chief sec men.

Jake touched the brim of his hat. "Cawdor, you know me?"

"I know you," Ryan replied. "Just don't know what you're doing here." He put the telescopic sights over the man's heart.

"Brody sent me for the missing boys," Jake replied. "Took me a while to round up some able-bodied men and come running, but we're here now. Dean told me him, Conor and Perry are all that's left."

"Yeah."

Jake let out a breath. "Don't reckon Mr. Brody's going to be overly fond of hearing that."

"Probably not."

"I got the rest of your people aboard this wag and others," Jake said. "I'm offering you a ride back to the school if you want. Don't figure on anybody back there bothering us too much if we come outfitted like this."

"I'd say you're right," Ryan replied with a grin.

"So I'm asking you now. You want to ride back or you want to fight your way out of this forest?"

Ryan slung his rifle. "If it's all the same to you, I'd rather ride."

THE MARS ARENA: EPILOGUE

Days later, rested from sleeping in beds for two nights and their wounds cleaned and tended, Ryan and Krysty sat at one of the patio tables sharing a breakfast that had been made in the Nicholas Brody School. There were melons and hash browns, fresh-cured bacon and breakfast steak, eggs any way a person wanted them, warm biscuits and coffee that was real coffee and not coffee sub.

During their stay, Ryan had found the headmaster to be reclusive, suffering more from the sickness that plagued him. Mildred had spent some time with the man, offering a treatment plan and some of the medicine Krysty had recovered from the airwag in the mountains.

Even with the deaths of seven children hanging over the school, evidenced by the flag in the center courtyard flying at half-mast and the black armbands on the student body and teachers, the situation Nicholas Brody had created with his dream seemed idyllic.

Farther down the hill, Mildred and J.B. stood side by side in a field, getting the companions' weapons travel ready again. Doc had spent some time lecturing in a few of the science classes, much to the chagrin and irritation of the teachers, and Ryan figured the old man was there now, talking elegantly of how important knowledge was. Jak spent his time in the woods with Jake, tracking down venison and other meats for the school's larder.

"I figure on moving out tomorrow morning," Ryan said, pushing his plate away, finally unable to handle anything more to eat. He was still sore in a few places, but the level of pain was a comfortable, familiar one.

"This is a nice place," Krysty said wistfully. "Mebbe we could spend a few more days here."

He reached out and took her hand. "But it's not our place. Me, Jak and J.B., we fly in the face of everything Brody's trying to teach these young people. Death sits down at the table with us, and they know it. You and Mildred and Doc, you're not so far gone that you can't fit in with these surroundings. They look at us, they know we're one step out of the grave."

"I know, lover. What about Dean? Is he going with us?"

Ryan glanced back toward the picnic area where Dean and Phaedra Lemon sat at one of the wooden tables. "I'll have to ask him."

"He seems to be quite smitten with Phaedra, lover."

"She's a cute girl," Ryan allowed. "Seems to like him, too."

"I'd say so," Krysty replied with a small smile. "Wouldn't it have been nice if we could have met like that? Shared some of our innocence awhile?"

Ryan looked at her grimly and told her the truth. "I don't remember ever being innocent. And if we had met, mebbe we wouldn't have cared at all for each other. It's the travels we've had this far that's brought us together and kept us that way."

"Gaia's will that it'll always be so. My heart has never been bound to anyone the way it has been to you, Ryan Cawdor."

He tried to say something, but the words refused to find their way into his head.

Krysty touched his lips with her fingers. "Shh. I know what's in your heart. It's enough for me."

Leaning forward, Ryan kissed her. When they parted, he glanced at Dean and saw his son was getting kissed by Phaedra.

"Like father, like son." Krysty laughed.

And the sound was pleasant enough to Ryan that he didn't feel any embarrassment at all.

IT WAS A FEW HOURS LATER when Ryan caught his son alone. They'd spent quite a bit of time together over the past few days, but Dean had made time for Phaedra, as well.

The boy was standing on the catwalk around the inner palisade wall, a piece of straw between his teeth as he gazed out over the land spread before him.

"Mind if I come up?" Ryan called.

Dean looked down, startled. "I can come down."

"Rather come up if you don't mind," Ryan said. "Been inside these walls all day. Be good to look out some."

Dean nodded.

Ryan scaled the ladder easily and clambered up beside his son. "See anything you like?"

"Everything. I haven't gotten out much in the time I've been here. Field trips occasionally, camp-outs over-night even less. Still not used to having walls around me all the time."

Ryan grinned and tousled his son's hair. "Know how

you feel." He stood beside Dean and looked out over the world, feeling the wanderlust calling to him, making him want to roll on to see what he could see. "We're clearing out of here tomorrow morning."

"I thought it would be sooner."

"If we hadn't been through everything like we were, might have been sooner." He looked at Dean. "Got to ask you what you want to do, though."

Dean returned his gaze, eyes wide. "What do you mean?"

"I talked it over with Brody. He says you're welcome to stay here if you want. Instead of kicking you out of school for prowling, he's willing to work out some other punishment that'll allow you to stay in your classes if you'd rather."

Dean looked a little disappointed. "Good to know."

"He says you're a good student, showing some real potential."

"I've been studying hard."

"I know that, too."

Dean looked deep into Ryan's eyes. "What if I asked to come with you?"

"Then you'd have to have all your gear packed and be ready to move out at daybreak."

It took a moment for the words to penetrate, then a broad smile lit Dean's face. "You mean it?"

"Yeah."

"I didn't do the whole year."

"You did enough," Ryan said, "for now. You want to come back later, we'll see about that, too. I just thought right now it might be difficult for you to leave with Phaedra hanging around and such."

Dean shook his head. "She knows, Dad. She told me that I'd be leaving soon as I could. Said she could see it in my eyes. Went on to tell me I'm not a domesticated bird. I'm born to the wild. But that doesn't mean I can't come see her if I get back this way."

"Sometimes a woman knows a man's heart more than he knows it himself, son. Man gets too used to living by his wits, and stopping to feel things slows that down."

"I guess so," Dean agreed. "You mind if I go tell Phaedra?"

"Go ahead," Ryan said.

Dean grabbed the sides of the ladder and wrapped his feet around them, creating just enough friction to let himself slide safely down the ladder. When he hit the ground, he took off running.

"Dean!" Ryan called.

The boy turned around, eyes full of mischief and a big grin on his face.

"One other thing."

"What's that, Dad?"

"When I get up in the morning," Ryan said, "I don't want to hear about you being caught on top of the dorm in the middle of the night again."

"Don't worry about that," Dean called back. "Nobody's going to catch me."

Ryan turned quickly, before his son could see him start to laugh. He saw Krysty out in the vegetable gardens, going through plants and vines with students, her hair flame red in the bright sunlight.

He thought about her and him, and how things might be if they had a place of their own. Krysty would love the children they had, bring them up in gardens like the one out there, be content in a small house.

Ryan couldn't see it happening any time soon. But the thought was pleasant enough. After a few more minutes, he went down to join Krysty, to share in one more peaceful afternoon before they once again took up their journey through Deathlands.

ICEBLOOD

When Man's blood is of the broth of ice,
  his life is measured by a wanton throw of the dice;
In the midnight hours he broods in a lonely state
  with spirit dead and desolate.
                              —Justin Geoffrey

The Road to Outlands—
From Secret Government Files to the Future

Almost two hundred years after the global holocaust, Kane, a former Magistrate of Cobaltville, often thought the world had been lucky to survive at all after a nuclear device detonated in the Russian embassy in Washington, D.C. The aftermath—forever known as sky-Dark—reshaped continents and turned civilization into ashes.

Nearly depopulated, America became the Deathlands—poisoned by radiation, home to chaos and mutated life-forms. Feudal rule reappeared in the form of baronies, while remote outposts clung to a brutish existence.

What eventually helped shape this wasteland were the redoubts, the secret preholocaust military installations with stores of weapons, and the home of gateways, the locational matter-transfer facilities. Some of the redoubts hid clues that had once fed wild theories of government cover-ups and alien visitations.

Rearmed from redoubt stockpiles, the barons consolidated their power and reclaimed technology for the villes. Their power, supported by some invisible authority, extended beyond their fortified walls to what was now called the Outlands. It was here in the hellzones that humanity survived, living with chemical storms, hounded by Magistrates.

In the villes, rigid laws were enforced to atone for the sins of the past and prepare the way for a better future. That was the barons' public credo and their right-to-rule.

Kane, along with friend and fellow Magistrate Grant, had upheld that claim until a fateful Outlands expedition. A displaced piece of technology…a question to a keeper of the archives…a vague clue about alien masters—and their world shifted radically. Suddenly, Brigid Baptiste, the archivist, faced summary execution, and Grant a quick termination. For Kane there was forgiveness if he abandoned his friends and pledged his unquestioning allegiance to Baron Cobalt and his unknown masters.

But that allegiance would make him support a mysterious and alien power and deny loyalty and friends. Then what would be left?

Kane had been brought up solely to serve the ville. Brigid's only link with her family was her mother's red-gold hair, green eyes and supple form. Grant's clues to his lineage were his ebony skin and powerful physique. But Domi, she of the white hair, was an Outlander pressed into sexual servitude in Cobaltville. She at least knew her roots and was a reminder to the exiles that the outcasts belonged in the human family.

Parents, friends, community—the very root of humanity was denied. With no continuity, there was no forward momentum to the future. And that was the crux—when Kane began to wonder if there was a future.

For Kane, it wouldn't do. So the only way was out—way, way out.

After their escape, they found shelter at the forgotten Cerberus redoubt headed by Lakesh, a scientist, Cobaltville's head archivist, and secret opponent of the barons.

With their past turned into a lie, their future threatened, only one thing was left to give meaning to the outcasts. The hunger for freedom, the will to resist the hostile influences. And perhaps, by opposing, end them.

ICEBLOOD: PROLOGUE

The Byang-thang Plateau, northwest Tibet

Clots of frozen blood glittered like rubies dropped from a broken necklace. They stretched back over the hard-packed snow as far as Grigori Zakat could see, swallowed by the shadows cast by the titanic peaks of the Cherga Mountains.

His booted feet had barely left their imprints on the hoar-frost overlaying the crust of snow, but the drops of blood left an unmistakable trail in crimson for his pursuers.

Zakat stumbled, a rushing wave of dizziness engulfing him. He sank down to the snow, supporting himself by his left arm, keeping his right hand pressed tightly against the pressure bandage taped over the throbbing wound beneath his ribs. Blood oozed around the edges.

He shook his head and remembered he had only one pursuer now, and that was death itself. Boro Orolok and his Mongol clan-brothers were at least a thousand miles behind him and could no longer threaten him with their *bundhi* daggers.

Zakat didn't know what had turned the followers of the Tushe Gun against the Russian garrison in the Black Gobi, but he suspected the three Americans who had accompanied Colonel Sverdlovosk were somehow responsible. He didn't know what had happened to his superior officer, either, but whatever influence the colonel exerted over Orolok's clan had come to an obvious and decisive end.

Zakat slowly pushed himself to his feet, despising the tremor in his legs, silently enduring the wave of vertigo. He refused to voice a cry of pain as the raw lips of his wound pulled and stretched. He was more than just a major in the Internal Security Network or even an operative of District Twelve—he was an ordained Khlysty priest and he knew pain was only of the body and could thus be controlled.

He began walking again, concentrating on placing one foot ahead of the other. He had no destination in mind; he wanted only to put as much distance as possible between himself and the wreckage of the Tu-114 cargo plane.

Zakat wasn't sure how much time had elapsed since the huge aircraft had crashed onto the mountain plateau. He could remember only the snowcapped peaks coming up fast, then a splintering shock, a grinding, relentless screech of rupturing metal. Something fell on him and knocked him unconscious.

The sound of crackling flames, the stench of burning oil and scorched flesh woke him. His back was hot, and he looked around to see flames filling the interior of the ship. Fortunately the fuel tank was nearly drained so it didn't explode, but oil and other flammable lubricants were aflame. The fire was intense enough to consume the bodies of the two troopers in the passenger compartment.

Not bothering to examine Kuryadin, slumped over in the pilot's chair with a razor-edged fragment of the foreport embedded in his throat, Zakat unbuckled the safety harness and climbed out through the port, heedless of the lacerations he received. He cut himself several times in the process.

The broken-backed aircraft was afire from the wings back, so even if there were useful items in cargo, he couldn't reach them. He staggered away, his body a screaming mass of agony, but the most pain radiated out from the stab wound in his midsection. He stumbled across the frozen snow and forced himself to continue for hours upon hours.

The air, though bitingly cold, was quiet and still. So far, his heavy topcoat, fleece-lined gloves and insulated boots had kept him from freezing. He knew, however, that once the sun dropped behind the distant peaks, the temperature would plummet. He would have to find shelter or perish of exposure. Even the superhuman vitality granted to him by his faith had its limits.

He recalled the details of the martyrdom of Saint Rasputin, how he had survived poison, multiple gunshot wounds, blows to the head and near drowning. At last, he had succumbed to the freezing temperature of the waters in Moika canal.

Zakat fumbled beneath his blood-stiffened woolen shirt to finger the token of his faith hanging from a thong around his neck. He touched the tiny wooden phallus and caressed the stylized crystal testicles affixed to it.

The emblem symbolized Rasputin's penis, cut off by one of his assassins, then recovered and preserved in a velvet container by his devoted followers. Upon his initiation into the priesthood, Zakat had been permitted to glimpse but not touch the blackened, desiccated holy relic.

As he staggered onward, Zakat mouthed Rasputin's last words, "I will not die. *I will not die!*"

He continued whispering the mantra in an under-the-breath singsong as he had been taught. Even someone near him wouldn't be able to understand the hymn hissing from his lips.

No one, not even his superior officers, suspected he was a Khlysty priest. The few members of his sect who held high posts in the Russian government had helped him to dodge the rigorous background checks prior to his assignment to District Twelve, the ultrasecret arm of the Internal Security Network.

Zakat was his Khlysty name not his birth name, but no one questioned it, even though it meant "twilight." The few people who had glimpsed the pattern of wealed, raised scars on his back, the result of numerous flagellation rituals, had kept their curiosity in check. In the Internal Security Network, it was considered bad form to question a comrade, and even quite dangerous to make personal inquiries of an officer. It hinted at ambition. Primarily because he didn't appear to be ambitious, Grigori Zakat had advanced rapidly as a District Twelve officer under the command of Sverdlovosk.

Zakat went to great lengths to present the image of an aesthete, an effete intellectual who wrote charming verse for his own amusement in his off hours. Tall and slender, with a high pale forehead beneath sleek black hair and a languid manner, he didn't look as if he entertained any ambitions more taxing than rising by noon.

But of course he did. He couldn't be a Khlysty priest otherwise. He approached the obstacles to his ambition differently than other men. His approach relied on an offhand comment made to a superior officer regarding rivals, the discreet planting of black market contraband among their possessions or, if they were particularly impressionable, a campaign of subtle suggestions that they were being treated unfairly, passed over for advancement. When his competitors filed their complaints, they tended to either disappear or be reduced in rank, and Zakat easily stepped into the power vacuum.

He had achieved the rank of major less than a year ago, after he arranged matters to make General Stovoski believe he had been seduced by his middle-aged, oversexed wife. Zakat managed to smile at the memory of Stovoski's face when the general stumbled into the parlor to find his wife kneeling before him, clawing at his trousers, oblivious to his pious protests.

The stupid cow of a woman, her brain saturated with vodka, had been childishly easy to manipulate, never realizing that the strength of Zakat's will had overwhelmed hers. And if his mind was exceptionally strong, his body complemented it. None of his comrades or even the surprisingly perceptive Sverdlovosk knew he had the strength in his delicate-appearing hands to throttle a man to death, something he had done as part of the ordination ceremony.

Much of his Khlysty training revolved around camouflage, infiltration and deception. Through years of long practice, he could make his gray eyes reflect nothing but a mild, dull disinterest in his surroundings.

His eyes glinted now with flinty sparks of a fierce determination not to die on this desolate waste. He knew he could survive a long time without food, sustained only by his faith and the power of his convictions.

"I will not die," he chanted. *"I will not die!"*

He trudged on, the terrain steepening gradually. Sometime toward late afternoon—he guessed it was late afternoon, since his wrist chron had been damaged in the crash—clouds thickened over the face of the sun.

At first he was grateful because the cloud cover reduced not only the glare from the hoarfrost but also the chances of contracting snow-blindness. Then a wind sprang up and slashed at him with icy talons.

Sleet began slicing across the rocky plain, turning his surroundings to formless, misty shapes. Zakat squinted against the stinging ice particles and kept moving, uncomfortably aware he could be only a few steps from a bottomless crevasse. The blood on his clothing froze hard as a sheathing of metal.

Tearing a strip from the lining of his greatcoat, he tied it around his eyes so his lids wouldn't freeze together. The driving sleet rendered him almost blind anyway.

He forced himself to concentrate only on what lay ahead, to plod through the swirling curtain of white. His body lost all sensation, even pain, numb to anything other than putting one foot in front of the other. Then, he put one foot in empty air.

Fanning his arms, Zakat plummeted straight down, lips clamping tight over the scream forcing its way up his throat. He didn't fall far or long before his plunge turned into a head-over-heels tumble, his body plowing through banked snow like the prow of a ship. His thrashing descent ended, and he lay motionless, breathing shallowly through his nostrils.

He continued to lie there, noting how pleasantly warm his limbs began to feel. That spreading warmth galvanized him into a floundering rush to hands and knees. He knew he was freezing to death, with the subzero wind wailing around him like the sound of distant violins.

The fall had dislodged his blindfold, so he experimentally opened one eye. For a moment, he saw nothing but white and wondered if he was snow-blind, despite his precautions. A strong gust of wind ripped a part in the sleet curtain, and he saw the dark bulk of the monastery.

Buildings reared above him, constructed so closely together they appeared to be pushing one another off the cliff. A courtyard barely a hundred feet squared was jammed between the monastery storehouse and a mountain wall. The roofs of the buildings looked of Chinese design, but the architecture was careless and crude.

Struggling erect, he forced his legs to carry him toward the entrance between two tall bastions of snow-covered rock. He no longer felt his feet at all.

A figure wearing a soiled yellow cloak and a red cowl materialized between the two rocks. With a prayer wheel spinning in his right hand and a brass bell clanging in his left, the monk shouted a warning into the courtyard behind him, then a challenge to Zakat.

The Russian smiled humorlessly. The monk probably thought he was an earthbound Dre, a malign messenger of death that figured prominently in Tibetan legend. He lifted his left hand and gestured to the monk. His right closed around the butt of the Tokarev holstered at his waist.

The monk's eyes narrowed to barely perceptible slits in his face as Zakat approached him, palm outward to show he was unarmed. The monk's eyes focused on his left hand. With a long-legged bound, Zakat sprang to the small man, planting the short barrel of his Tokarev pistol against the monk's jaw. He didn't speak, assuming the monk understood his actions.

The bell and the prayer wheel flew in opposite directions. The bell gave a final, feeble chime when it struck the frost-encrusted flagstones. Gathering a fistful of soiled robe in his left hand, Zakat pushed the monk ahead of him through the monastery's gate, into the courtyard.

As he entered, he heard the bellowing of a great brass horn and a clangor of bells from the walls. A small man in yellow robes emerged from a door on the far side of the courtyard. Worked in yellow thread on the breast of his black tunic was a swastika running to the left, the symbol of the Bon-po religious order. Like most Bon shamans, he was starkly dressed. Beneath a dark leather turban, his black hair was tied back with a clip made of a human finger bone. Oddly pale, finely textured skin stretched tight over prominent cheekbones and brow arches. Behind the round, steel-rimmed lenses of thick spectacles, his huge, fathomless eyes glittered like those of a raptorial bird.

A bloodred baldric extended across his torso from left shoulder to right hip. A coiled whip hung from it. Tucked into the baldric was a short, curving *ram dao* sacrificial sword. The oak hilt was extravagantly designed with ivory and gold inlays.

The Bon-po priest was followed out the door by a group of six excited men. Their red armbands and soot-blackened faces marked them as Dob-Dobs, the monkish soldiery. In their sashes, they carried iron cudgels shaped like oversize door keys. Rawhide thongs were looped through the handles, and already several of the Dob-Dobs were whirling them overhead. When released, the cudgels struck with deadly, bone-breaking force.

Zakat only briefly considered triggering his pistol. Perhaps he could kill three of the monks, maybe four, but he saw no point to it. Either the Dob-Dobs would crush his skull with their crude weapons or he would perish out on the plateau. He released the monk and stood motionless, angry shouts filling his ears. His head throbbed in rhythm to the gibbering cacophony.

The black-turbaned man gracefully stepped through the howling Dob-Dobs, and Zakat was struck by his fluid, danceresque movements. His jet-black gaze swept over Zakat, then focused on him, staring unblinkingly through the lenses of his spectacles. His almost inhumanly large eyes widened, his lips moved and a whispering, altered voice came forth.

Zakat met that stare, transfixed, unable to tear his gaze away. Although his Khlysty training revolved around a form of psionics, of imposing the force of one will upon the other, he knew the black-turbaned man was a master. With a distant sense of dread, he realized the Bon-po sha-

man was invoking the *angkur,* the powerful one-pointed-
ness of thought, and directing a blade of *tsal* energy into
his mind. He felt it as a sensation of a cold, caressing cobweb brushing his brain.

If he hadn't been exhausted and weak from blood loss,
Zakat knew he stood a good chance of deflecting that
blade, even turning it on its wielder. As it was, he could
only stand as the shaman's eyes filled his field of vision,
then his mind. He tried to erect a barrier around his
thoughts, visualizing an impenetrable brick wall.

A ghost of a smile creased the shaman's thin lips, and
the edges of Zakat's vision blackened. The insubstantial
cobweb ensnared his mind, capturing his dreams, his desires and most secret yearnings like a fisherman would net
a school of fish. He felt the black-turbaned man examining them as they wriggled and thrashed.

Then, for an instant that felt like a chain of interlocking eternities, his mind meshed with the shaman's. A tsu-
nami of raw, naked ambition crashed over him, the
undertow dragging his conscious mind into dark, cold
depths. Suddenly, Zakat felt trapped, his spirit locked forever with a black yet somehow shining stone, its facets cut
to form a trapezohedron.

The sleet-blurred sun seemed to reel in the sky. Zakat
was only dimly aware of falling, first to his knees, then on
his face, stretching out on the snow-encrusted flagstones.
Right before he sank into the warm embrace of uncon-
sciousness, he heard a deep voice bellowing commands.
He didn't respond to it, assuming he was delirious.

The language the voice spoke was Russian.

"Easy," the voice whispered. "Easy."

Grigori Zakat grunted and opened his eyes. He was a little dismayed by how much effort it required and even more dismayed when he saw nothing but a dark, blurred shape looming over him. Still the shape spoke in a language he knew.

Clearing a throat that felt as though it were lined with gravel, he managed to husk out, "Russian. I thought I dreamed hearing it."

A deep, slightly mocking laugh boomed from the shape, and the rich odor of wine wafted into his nostrils. "Perhaps you are dreaming still, no? Perhaps you are freezing to death out on the plateau. The mind plays cruel tricks on the dying."

Zakat blinked several times, and the laughing shape slowly resolved into a more or less human outline. A big man beamed down at him. Although burly, with a massive belly straining at a blue-and-gold satin tunic, he didn't look fat. A thick gray beard spilled over his chest, and his small brown eyes, bagged by flesh pouches, twinkled with amusement.

Squinting around the small stone-walled chamber lit by torches sputtering in sconces, Zakat became aware of the overpowering smell of rancid yak butter drifting in from the corridor. The only decoration in the room was provided by a hanging tapestry, covered with geometric forms. The central one, worked in black thread, appeared to be a trapezohedron.

"Where am I?" he asked.

"Directly above the center of the Earth," the bearded man replied. He unsuccessfully swallowed a belch. "Tibet.

You are enjoying the hospitality of the Trasilunpo lamasery. I am the high lama here. My name is Dorjieff."

The name rang a distant chord of recognition in Zakat's memory, but it was so faint he didn't care to seek it out. He shifted on the hard cot, and flares of pain blazed all over his body. Lifting his trembling hands in front of his eyes, he saw they were swathed in bandages, soaked with a foul-smelling unguent.

"Frostbite," Dorjieff said. "I believe you'll recover without the loss of any extremities."

Lifting the blanket, Zakat saw his naked body was covered with blue contusions and raw abrasions. Many windings of bandages encircled his midsection. He kept his expression blank, even when he noticed that his Khlysty emblem was no longer around his neck.

"You were blessed, all things considered," continued Dorjieff. He pinched the air with a forefinger and thumb. "That sword thrust missed your vitals by *this* much. I was able to suture the wound without complications. Internal bleeding was slight. You'll bear a rather unsightly scar, I fear."

"You are a doctor?"

Dorjieff shrugged. "Necessity has forced me to act in many roles during my life."

"How long have I been here?"

"Your second day draws to a close." Dorjieff's hair-rimmed lips quirked in a smile as he added, "Father Twilight."

Zakat did not react. He only gazed up at the bearded man with a mild question in his eyes. Like a street conjurer performing before an audience of urchins, Dorjieff made exaggerated passes through the air with his hands. When he opened his left hand, the tiny wooden phallus dangled by its thong from his forefinger, the crystal testicles reflecting the torchlight.

"A Khlysty cross," Dorjieff murmured. "I was under the impression the sect was outlawed in the motherland, much like the Skotpsis."

Zakat couldn't disguise his distaste at the comparison. Skotpsis were among the most ancient of Russian sects, true enough, and savagely persecuted. An all-male cult, its followers paradoxically swore fealty to the pagan goddess Cybele. The primary expression of their worship was the surgical removal of their penises and testicles.

Dorjieff noticed his sour expression and chuckled. "I did not mean to insult you. I was under the impression the Skotpsis were a breakaway group of the Khlystys."

"A common misapprehension," Zakat murmured.

"I understand that Khlystys practice a so-called communal sin," Dorjieff said. "An indiscriminate sexual orgy among the male and female apostles. A ceremony difficult to participate in if the males have had their tools put away."

Dorjieff's gentle smile disappeared. "However, what is not a misapprehension, common or otherwise, is that for an officer of the ISN to be a Khlysty priest is more than a conflict of interest—it is a firing-squad offense."

As much as he wanted to, Zakat did not reach up to take the talisman. In a low voice, he said, "We are far from the motherland."

Dorjieff gusted out a sigh overlaid with the smell of wine and dropped the emblem onto Zakat's chest. "And from District Twelve."

Zakat covered his astonishment by hiking himself up on his elbows and slipping the thong over his head. "You are now a Buddhist?"

The bearded man shrugged noncommittally. "As I said, necessity has forced me into many roles. Soldier, doctor, holy man. Guardian."

Zakat was puzzled by the remark, but he didn't question the man. Swinging his legs over the edge of the cot, he tried to sit up, but his head swam dizzily. Dorjieff put a hand under his elbow and steadied him until he had planted both feet firmly on a woven-reed floor mat.

"I took the liberty of looking at your identification papers and orders," Dorjieff said. "That is how I know your name and your affiliation with District Twelve. Or at least, the name you currently use. I suppose you have played many roles with just as many affiliations."

As the vertigo ebbed, Zakat saw the torchlight reflected in a pinpoint from a ring on the middle finger of Dorjieff's left hand. Made of thick, hammered brass, in its setting was a single stone, cut in a confusing geometric pattern. It took him a moment to recognize it as a trapezohedron.

"How do you know of District Twelve?" Zakat asked.

Dorjieff combed a hand through his beard, smiling crookedly. "Many years ago, I was an operative. I was dispatched here to establish an intelligence network in the Himalayas, just in case our old friends, the Chinese, tried to reclaim Tibet."

His smile became a broad grin. "You might say I went native. I found higher rewards here than any Mother Russia could offer. My intelligence network is still intact. A sherpa brought to me the tale of your aircraft crash. And of its one survivor, struggling through twenty miles of rugged snowfields in subzero temperatures. An endurance born of your Khlysty training?"

Zakat nodded. "The power of the mind controlling the limitations of the flesh."

"You intrigue me, Father. We may perhaps be of some use to each other. Tsong-ka-po, the lama who founded the Trasilunpo order many centuries ago, made a prophecy associated with a man much like you."

That piqued Zakat's interest, and he lifted his head to stare into Dorjieff's eyes, searching for indications of deception. He saw only a glaze from imbibing too much wine. He didn't stare long, as two figures appeared in the arched doorway on the far side of the cell.

One was a diminutive girl of perhaps sixteen years, wearing the black shirt and baggy red trousers of a Tibetan peasant, her glossy black hair intricately braided on both sides of her head. Even in the dim light, Zakat noticed her firm breasts swelling beneath the coarsely spun fabric. The other figure was a man, not much taller than she.

Glancing over his shoulder, Dorjieff said, "Come in, Trai. Gyatso, our visitor appears to have recovered from your ministrations."

The black-turbaned Bon-po shaman stepped into the room, a thick yellow robe folded over one arm. The girl held a pair of sandals. Her black almond eyes were cast downward. Gyatso fixed an unblinking stare on Zakat as he approached him.

Zakat tried to meet it.

Dorjieff chuckled softly, and said, "The secret of Bon training consists of developing a power of concentration surpassing even that of men like yourself, who are the most gifted in psychic respects."

Dorjieff turned to Gyatso. "This is Father Zakat," Dorjieff told him genially. "He will be staying with us for a little while."

Gyatso nodded. "Yes, Tsyansis Khan-po."

Trai placed the sandals on the floor mat and, not raising her eyes, backed out of the room, head bowed. Gyatso laid the robe on the foot of the cot. His fingers were exceptionally, almost inhumanly long, the middle ones nearly the length of Zakat's entire hand.

As he shouldered into the robe, Zakat said quietly, "I know a little of this dialect, Dorjieff. Tsyansis Khan-po translates as 'the king of fear.' A title you assumed or earned?"

Dorjieff shrugged negligently. "A bit of both over the years. The question of the moment is what to do with you."

He belched loudly, and Zakat caught the swift, disgusted glance Gyatso flicked toward Dorjieff.

Standing up, knotting a sash around the robe and stepping into the sandals, Zakat chose his words carefully. "You might look at me as a fellow expatriate seeking asylum."

Dorjieff threw back his head and laughed. "This lamasery is not a sanctuary. It is more of an embassy…or a guard post. If it had not been for Gyatso's intervention, the Dob-Dobs would have slain you on the spot."

Zakat glanced quickly at Gyatso and once more experienced the sensation of a cold cobweb wisping over his mind. "Why did you intervene?"

Dorjieff stated, "He is a priest, like ourselves, but of the old Bon-po religion. He is also an emissary, a hereditary ambassador. Therefore, his whims are given a certain deference."

Zakat eyed the slightly built, bespectacled man. "Emissary from what nation?"

"A group of nations, actually, known by different names in different ages."

Dorjieff seemed inclined to continue, but when Gyatso cast him an unblinking stare, he coughed self-consciously. "You will learn more," the bearded man said, "or you will not. The decision is not mine."

Zakat steeled himself and fixed his eyes on Gyatso. When he felt the caressing mind touch, he didn't flinch or blink. In a soft, lilting whisper, he inquired, "Is the decision yours, my myopic friend?"

As if mocking him, Gyatso answered in the same tone, "You owe your life to me, Father Zakat. Do you pay your debts?"

Zakat allowed a smile to slowly crease his lips. "Always," he answered. "And sometimes, with a great deal of interest."

Gyatso nodded. "Then we have much in common. And much to share."

ICEBLOOD: 01

Five months later

Kane lowered the compact set of binoculars and hissed out a slow, disgusted breath. "Now, isn't *this* just what we need."

"What do you mean?" asked Brigid Baptiste.

Wordlessly, Kane handed her the binoculars. She elbowed closer to the crest of the ridge and peered through the eyepieces, adjusting the focus to accommodate her own slightly astigmatic vision. The microbinoculars' 8x21 magnifying power brought the details of the distant Indian village to crystal clarity.

The settlement of tepees, looking like upside-down cones, were arranged in two loose circles, one surrounding the other. She caught the faint whiff of wood smoke. To one side of the village, she saw a herd of hobbled horses and on the other were wooden racks upon which animal hides were stretched. Women in fringed buckskin smocks labored over the frameworks, scraping away fur from the hides.

"The camp of the Sioux and the Cheyenne," Brigid said. "So what? We knew they were here."

"Look a little to your left," Kane directed grimly.

As she complied, she heard a faint yell from the outer perimeter of the lodges. In a clear area, she saw bare-chested men cavorting around a tall wooden pole. Their long black hair was bedecked with sprays of colorful feathers, and their bodies were painted a variety of bright hues and confusing patterns. They canted their heads back so they could stare at the round object topping the pole. She couldn't quite make out whether the object was a stone or part of the pole itself.

"Some kind of ceremony," Brigid commented, unconsciously lowering her voice.

"Keep looking."

Brigid did as he said. After a moment, the cluster of men around the pole separated, and her breath caught in her throat. Auerbach lay staked to the ground, his legs spread-eagled, his wrists bound tightly to the base of the pole. A pyramid of dry twigs rose from the juncture of his naked thighs. She saw how sweat glistened on his face, how his eyes were wide with terror. On the pale skin of his bare right shoulder spread a great blue-black bruise.

Sweeping the binoculars in a slow scan over the village, Brigid tried to make a head count, but the people milled about among the tepees.

"I don't see Rouch anywhere," Brigid murmured, lowering the binoculars. "I wish I knew if that was good or bad."

Kane sighed, running an impatient hand through his dark hair. "Why break with tradition? Let's assume it's bad."

She imitated his sigh. "What do you want to do?"

Kane began inching backward from the top of the knoll. "What I want to do is turn around and go back to Cerberus. But I know I'll end up doing what I *don't* want to do."

Brigid paused a moment before following him, loath to give up the springtime sun driving the last of the early-morning chill from her body. She tried to enjoy the warm air, rich with the smell of new growth. Under other circumstances, she would have enjoyed the two-day hike from the foothills of the Bitterroot Range. She liked being outdoors, away from the sepulchral silences and cold vanadium confines of the Cerberus redoubt. But neither she, Kane nor Grant was on a nature hike.

She joined Kane and Grant at the bottom of the slope. "Just like we suspected," Kane said to him. "The Indians have them. They're working up to roast Auerbach's chestnuts."

Grant winced, then his dark face contorted in a scowl of angry frustration. "How many of the opposition?"

"I couldn't get a clear idea," Brigid said. "But if you're asking whether they outnumber us—they definitely do, by at least a five-to-one margin. And that's a conservative estimate."

"What's new about that? We're always outnumbered." A very tall, very broad-shouldered man, Grant's heavy brows knitted, shadowing his dark eyes. A down-sweeping mustache showed jet-black against the coffee brown of his skin. His heavy-jawed face was set in a perpetual scowl. Impatiently, he tugged up the collar of his black, calf-length coat.

Brigid shrugged. She didn't deny Grant's statement but said, "We don't know if Auerbach and Rouch might have offended the Indians, broken one of their taboos. We should practice a little diplomacy first. They're our nearest neighbors, after all."

She was a tall, full-breasted and long-limbed woman, and Brigid Baptiste's willowy figure reflected an unusual strength without detracting from her undeniable femininity. An unruly mane of long, red-gold hair spilled over her shoulders, framing a smoothly sculpted face with a rosy complexion dusted lightly with freckles across her nose and cheeks. There was a softness in her features that bespoke a deep wellspring of compassion, yet a hint of iron resolve was there, too. The color of emeralds glittered in her big, feline-slanted eyes.

Kane glanced toward her, a wry smile playing over his lips. "I don't think what they're doing to Auerbach is part of a 'welcome to the neighborhood' routine."

An inch over six feet, he was not as tall or as broad as Grant, but every line of his supple, compact body was hard and stripped of excess flesh. He looked like a warrior—from the hawklike set of his head on the corded neck, to the square shoulders and the lean hips and long legs. Kane was built with the savage economy of a gray wolf. His high-planed face, normally clean shaved, bristled with a couple days' worth of beard stubble. Though his mouth held a smile, his narrowed gray blue eyes were alert and cold.

"Anybody got a suggestion of how to play this?" Grant asked dourly.

After a thoughtful moment, Kane replied, "I think you should stay put, be our ace on the line."

Out of the pocket of his dark tan overcoat, he withdrew his trans-comm. Thumbing up the cover of the palm-sized radiophone, he pressed a key. "I'll keep the frequency open. Monitor my channel."

The range of the comm devices was generally limited to a mile, but in open country, in clear weather, contact could be established at two miles.

Clipping it to the underside lapel of his coat, he continued, "Another option is just to leave Auerbach and Rouch where they are. It'd be simpler all the way around."

"Safer, too," Grant rumbled. "For all we know, it's how the Indians deal with slaggers."

Brigid knew they weren't serious, so she didn't respond to their comments. Still, it was a reminder that Grant and Kane had spent their entire adult lives as killers—superbly trained Magistrates, bearing not only the legal license to pass final judgment on slaggers, or lawbreakers, but the moral sanction, as well.

She couldn't deny their anger was justifiable. Four days ago, Auerbach had volunteered to make the trek from the mountain plateau housing the Cerberus redoubt to the foothills to perform routine maintenance on a motion sensor on the road. The only pass to the plateau had been blocked several months ago by a C-4 triggered avalanche, and the old blacktop highway remained completely impassable by vehicles.

Auerbach served the redoubt as a medical aide, not as a tech, and his eagerness to jockey a Land Rover down the treacherous path to perform a mechanical task had struck everyone as odd, particularly Kane. The fact that Beth-Li Rouch was willing to accompany him seemed even stranger, but no one questioned it. Kane figured they were entitled to their whims, assuming they were suffering from redoubt fever, chafing at being cooped up inside the installation now that spring had arrived.

The journey from the plateau to the foothills usually required several hours, so Auerbach and Rouch weren't expected to return until late the following day. When it drew to a close, with no sign of them, no one in the redoubt was overly concerned. The signals transmitted by their subcutaneous biolink transponders showed no indications of stress. The transponder, a nonharmful radioactive chemical that bound itself to the glucose in the blood and a middle layer of epidermis, transmitted heart rate, brain-wave patterns, respiration and blood count. The signal was relayed by a Comsat satellite to the Cerberus redoubt and could be employed as a tracking device.

The telemetry showed that Auerbach and Rouch had left the foothills, crossing the tableland on foot, for reasons that none of the redoubt's personnel could fathom or even guess at. They had far exceeded the range of the trans-comms, so Kane, Brigid and Grant commandeered the Sandcat fast-attack vehicle and set off in pursuit.

They discovered the Land Rover parked at the edge of the rockfall. Grant found their trail in the grassy plains, which left no choice but to track them on foot. The only settlement within a hundred miles of the Bitterroot Range was a small one consisting of Amerindians. After the nukecaust, many of the surviving Plains tribes had reasserted their ancient claims over ancestral lands, and the group of Sioux and Cheyenne had done the same with this region of Montana. The atomic megacull had been a blessing to most Native peoples, the "purification" of prophecy.

The Indians never ventured into the Bitterroot Range, or the Darks, as they had been called for over a century. They attributed a sinister, superstitious significance to the mountains' deeply shadowed ravines and grim, gray peaks.

The nearest the tribesmen had come to the range was on the same day the pass had been blocked, when they were pursuing a roamer band that had attacked their village and carried off captives. One of the Indian warriors had glimpsed Kane, and so it was assumed they knew this part of Montana harbored other human beings.

After a day of trailing Rouch and Auerbach across the grasslands, Grant, Brigid and Kane came across the prints of unshod horses around the cold ashes of a campfire. The conclusion was inescapable, though they were able to take a small comfort in the lack of blood or signs of a serious struggle. They'd followed the trail to the Indian village, where Auerbach—and Rouch, presumably—were held captive.

Kneeling beside his backpack, Kane reached into a pouch and removed a small M-60 gren.

Uneasily, Brigid said, "Do you think you'll need that?"

"I haven't thought that far ahead," he answered curtly. "Do you think you can speak their lingo well enough so I won't have to?"

She paused a moment, thinking. Some months before, she had found a Lakota-to-English dictionary in the Cerberus database. Due to her eidetic memory, she had no problem recalling what she had read, but the Siouxan language relied on tones, as well as phonemes, and she had only once heard it spoken.

She murmured, *"Hota Wanagi."*

Kane straightened up, squinting at her quizzically. "What?"

"Hota Wanagi," she repeated. "That's what the warrior who shot Le Loup Garou called you, remember?"

Kane did and his lips quirked in a mirthless smile. "Gray Ghost, right?"

Brigid nodded. "Right. Maybe he'll remember you."

Kane doubted that very much, recollecting how he had been coated from head to toe with gray rock dust during the knife duel with the roamer chieftain, Le Loup Garou.

"He saved your life," said Grant. "Maybe he's a man of some standing in the village."

Kane pocketed the gren. "Maybe. But more than likely, he was concentrating on chilling Le Loup, not on saving me."

"He saw you fighting him," Brigid argued. "It's not much of an ace, but it's the only one we have to play."

Kane grinned at her use of the slang she had picked up over the eight months of her association with him and Grant. Because of her precise manner of speaking, it sounded incongruous.

He inspected his Sin Eater, holstered at his right forearm beneath the sleeve of his coat. He tested the spring-release mechanism by tensing his wrist tendons. The handblaster leaped into his hand, the butt unfolding and slapping into his palm.

Less than fourteen inches in length at full extension, the Sin Eater featured a magazine that carried twenty 9 mm rounds. When not in use, the stock folded over the top of the weapon, lying along the frame, reducing its holstered length to ten inches. The forearm holster was equipped with sensitive actuators that controlled a flexible cable in the holster and snapped the weapon smoothly into the hand, the stock unfolding in the same motion. Ingeniously designed to fire immediately upon contact with the index finger, the Sin Eater had no trigger guard or safety. Since the gun fired upon touching the crooked finger, Kane took pains to keep his finger straight and outstretched.

Brow slightly furrowed, Brigid watched as Kane pushed the blaster back into its holster, adjusting his coat sleeve. Then she unslung the mini-Uzi from her shoulder and placed it next to her pack.

"What are you doing?" demanded Grant.

She shrugged. "If we want the Indians to believe we mean them no harm, it's best we don't stroll into their village weighed down with musketry."

She opened her jacket, showing a flat, razor-keen knife in a sheath stitched to the lining. "I'll have this."

Grant lifted an eyebrow. "Domi's idea, right?"

She only nodded. Domi, the outlander girl, was a well-spring of sneaky inventiveness. At Lakesh's request, she had stayed behind at the redoubt, in case she had to rescue the three of them.

"If she was here," Grant continued, "she could flank the settlement."

Brigid refrained from mentioning that Domi had expressed an extreme dislike of Beth-Li Rouch, and more than likely wouldn't put herself in jeopardy to rescue a woman she despised.

Kane buttoned up his coat, wishing it were his Magistrate-issue Kevlar-weave garment, a twin to the one Grant wore. He had abandoned his own protective garment a few months before when he was forced to take a swim in the Irish Sea.

Eyeing the position of the sun, he announced, "Well, if they're going to take our scalps, we might as well give them the chance while it's still daylight."

Grant took out his trans-comm and keyed in the frequency of Kane's unit. He put one finger to his nose in the wry one-percent salute as they started off around the knoll. It was gesture reserved for those undertakings with a very small chance of success. Kane deliberately didn't return the salute, not calculating the odds at such a low number.

Before following him, Brigid spared a moment to glance back at the distant gray peaks of the Bitterroot Range shouldering up from the horizon. Clouds wreathed them, and snow still patched some areas. Winter lingered a very long time at such high altitudes.

Kane walked with a self-assured, long-legged stride, and Brigid's swift, almost mannish gait helped her keep pace with him. They walked directly toward the jumble of tepees, noting a lack of sentries on the perimeter.

They didn't speak as they walked, but the closer they came to the village, the more Brigid sensed a change in Kane. With every step, he slipped deeper into his Magistrate's persona, walking heel-to-toe as he entered a potential killzone, his passage barely rustling the high grasses. He moved swiftly, as gracefully as a wraith. His long months as an exile had not dulled the edge of his instincts.

Kane observed wryly, "I guess everybody is too occupied with Auerbach's cookout to post guards."

Brigid repressed a shudder. "Where do you think Beth-Li is?"

Kane's shoulders moved beneath his coat in a shrug.

"Maybe she got away," Brigid suggested.

After a moment of thoughtful silence, Kane replied, "Maybe. She's resourceful. Probably more so than Auerbach."

"So I've been told." Try as she might, Brigid couldn't blunt the edge of sarcasm in her voice.

Kane detected it, cast her a swift slit-eyed glare, but said nothing. Brigid regretted the comment, but she doubted Kane had been seriously stung by it. She knew more about Beth-Li Rouch and Auerbach's relationship than he did, but she kept that knowledge to herself.

They reached the outer perimeter of tepees before they were seen. A yelping outcry arose, and the onlookers clustered around the pole whirled, then several men surged forward. They wore buckskin leggings and breechclouts with feathers in their long braided hair. Paint distorted their coppery faces into fearsome masks. They shouted angrily.

Brigid hesitated, but Kane side-mouthed, "Keep walking. Brazen it out."

Into the trans-comm, he whispered, "We're about to make contact."

Grant's filtered voice responded, "Acknowledged. Moving up."

The warriors rocked to a halt and started whooping. He saw no blasters, only knives and tomahawks, though one beefy man carried a long lance. Kane guessed they were yelling of what they were going to do to the interlopers and he figured it was just as well he didn't understand their language.

The man with the lance swaggered toward them, his gait almost a provocative strut. Painted vermilion stripes criss-crossed his blunt-jawed face.

Brigid and Kane continued walking, doing their best to keep their expressions composed.

Shaking the lance, the warrior howled, *"Hoppo, wasi-cun! Hoppo!"*

"I think he's telling us to go away," Brigid whispered.

Kane didn't reply. Instead, he swiftly assessed the man's broad chest and heavily muscled arms. He looked to be strong, more than capable of hurling the lance right through either one of them. His jet-black eyes darted back and forth between the two people, then fixed on Kane.

With a shrill cry, he rushed at Kane, swinging the butt of the lance in a whistling arc toward his face.

Without breaking stride, Kane lifted his hands, crossed

his wrists and caught the end of the wooden shaft between them. Grasping it tightly, he pivoted, thrust out his hip and tossed the warrior over it. The man crashed full-length onto the ground with a thud everyone heard.

Kane released the lance and it dropped across the warrior's lap. As the warrior struggled dizzily to a sitting position, Brigid stamped down sharply on the steel head and the shaft jumped up, connecting sharply with the underside of his chin. Wood cracked loudly against bone, and the warrior fell over onto his back.

Instantly, Brigid and Kane were at the hub of a wheel of enraged people, many of them with knives in their fists. They shouted and pointed their blades, closing in. Kane readied his hand to receive the Sin Eater, but Brigid raised her arms and shouted, *"Mita kuye cola! Hota Wanagi!"*

The enraged outcries dropped to a mutter, but the Indians didn't lower their blades. A man's voice said forcefully, *"Hota Wanagi?"*

A warrior shouldered his way through the throng. He had strong Amerindian features, wide cheekbones with yellow lightning bolts painted on them and shiny black hair plaited in two braids that fell almost to his waist. Behind his right ear, a single feather dangled, as white as one of the cirrus clouds overhead.

He wore a loose vest of smoked leather and a pair of boot moccasins. Around his waist was a heavy, brass-studded belt that carried, in loops, a knife, a set of pliers and a polished chunk of turquoise. His erect carriage exuded a quiet dignity.

Narrow, burning eyes bored deeply into Kane's. *"Hota Wanagi.* Gray Ghost. I didn't recognize you."

Both Brigid and Kane were surprised into speechlessness for a long moment. The man's English was flawless and unaccented.

Kane nodded to him politely. "I'm good deal cleaner now, Chief."

"I'm not a chief. My name is Sky Dog, a shaman, what you *wasicun* would call a medicine man."

In a respectful tone, Brigid announced, "I am Baptiste. This is Kane. We're here for our friends."

Sky Dog shrugged. "Your friends are trespassers." He pointed to the object topping the pole. "And so was he, as you might recall."

Kane gave the skull an expressionless stare, as if he only looked at it to be polite. He recognized the scraggly beard and shriveled features of Le Loup Garou.

"Our friends aren't roamers," he said. "You know that."

Sky Dog nodded, smiling thinly. "I know it. But my people are just poor, ignorant redskins. They can't tell the difference between all the varied pedigrees of *wasicun*. Even I have trouble."

Kane ignored the sarcasm in the man's tone. He looked past him toward Auerbach, who stared at him with a panicky, pleading light in his eyes. Although tremblings shook his body, they didn't dislodge the heap of tinder at his groin. He called out hoarsely, "I've told them over and over that we meant them no harm, but they don't care!"

Brigid asked calmly, "Why is that?"

Sky Dog jabbed an arm toward the distant bulk of the Darks and grimly stated, "We care very much that the mountains shelter *wasicun*. But as long as you stayed up there, we were content to leave you be."

Kane struggled to control his rising impatience. "As we are you. If our people encroached on your territory, it was accidental. It's not like you posted signs."

Sky Dog's lips compressed. "It is enough that we know the boundaries of our land. We don't make allowances for ignorance. Nor do you, or you would not have blocked the only pass to the mountains."

Kane took a deep breath and exhaled it slowly. Gazing intently into Sky Dog's eyes, he said quietly, "For the trespass, I offer my apologies. I promise it will never happen again."

Sky Dog's mouth stretched in a mocking smile, but he made no reply.

"But," continued Kane, "we will not leave without our people. If you force me, we'll fight for them. Much blood will be spilled. Ours and yours."

Eyebrows knitting together, Sky Dog asked in a low tone, "You threaten us, Gray Ghost?"

"I make promises," Kane retorted sincerely. "If you insist on holding our people, torturing them, then I'll view you as no different than Le Loup Garou and his roamers. Enemies to be chilled."

Sky Dog stared unblinkingly, his eyes locked on Kane's. Kane stared back. By slow degrees, he began tensing his wrist tendons. Then, with a laugh, Sky Dog ended the eye-wrestling contest. He wheeled around, pointing to Auerbach and shouting at the onlookers.

Several of the men glowered at him, one warrior snapping out a stream of harsh, angry consonants. Sky Dog raised his voice, pointing again to Auerbach, then to Kane.

Squinting in concentration, Brigid murmured, "He's telling them to release Auerbach into Gray Ghost's custody, that you are a mighty warrior and a friend. A couple of his people don't think much of it."

Kane nodded. "I figured that out myself." He casually glanced over his shoulder, wondering which declivity in the rolling plain hid Grant.

After a minute of loud shouting and gesticulating on Sky Dog's part, the warriors bent over Auerbach and began cutting through the rawhide thongs binding him to the pole and stakes. The man Kane had hip-tossed cast sullen sidelong glances in his direction, gripping his lance so tightly his knuckles stood out like knobs on his hand.

Auerbach arose hastily, the pile of twigs clattering from his crotch. Rubbing his wrists, gasping in relief, he joined Brigid and Kane. She considerately averted her eyes from his nakedness.

"Thank you," he stammered, "thank you."

Gruffly, Kane demanded, "Where's Rouch?"

Auerbach's fearful eyes flitted around, then settled on the scowling face of the Indian with the lance. "Ask him. His name is Standing Bear."

Kane directed his question to Sky Dog. "Where is the woman?"

The shaman fluttered a dismissive hand through the air. "She stays. Standing Bear claims her as his own. He won her."

Kane faced the bare-chested warrior and said, "Tell him he can't keep her. She's one of us, so she goes with us."

Sky Dog spoke briefly to Standing Bear. The man shook his head with a great deal of vehemence, black tresses whipping around his face. Furious words burst from his lips, accompanied by frequent gestures with the lance.

After a few moments, Sky Dog cut off Standing Bear's oration with a sharp command. Turning to Kane, he said, "Little Willow—the woman—will stay. Standing Bear fought the red-haired man for her and won. He finds mounting her very pleasant because of her enthusiasm."

Auerbach uttered a noise of outrage. Sky Dog continued, "Standing Bear says that if she is your woman, you should not have let her leave your lodge with the red-haired one. She must be dissatisfied with you."

Kane gritted his teeth and was about to say she wasn't his woman. But he thought better of it and instead declared, "The woman goes with us. That is all there is to it."

Sky Dog cast Standing Bear a sideways glance, then stepped closer to Kane. In a conspiratorial whisper, he said, "Gray Ghost, Standing Bear is intractable on this subject. He will not even trade for her, even if you had ten ponies to barter with. If you try to take Little Willow from him, you'll have to fight the entire village. Me included, just so I can keep face."

He paused, then asked, "Is one woman worth it? She's seems very lazy and argumentative to me. Standing Bear may tire of her eventually and let her go."

Kane's mind raced over a series of options, alternatives and courses of action.

Brigid asked, "What if she doesn't want to stay? You'll hold her against her will as a captive? Like the roamers?"

Sky Dog obviously felt uncomfortable by being questioned by a woman, a *wasicun* woman at that. Slowly, as if begrudging each syllable, he answered, "If Little Willow wishes to go with you, that is one thing. We are not slavers. But Standing Bear will oppose it and will fight for her."

He smiled again, hooking a thumb toward Auerbach. "I must point out that he fought Standing Bear for Little Willow. He was about to pay the ultimate penalty for his defeat when you arrived."

Auerbach's hands, clasped over his groin, tightened reflexively.

Kane said, "Bring out the woman. If she wants to stay with you, that's fine."

Sky Dog called out to a teenage girl, who turned and rushed into the village. Auerbach muttered bleakly, "She won't want to stay now that you're here, Kane."

He narrowed his eyes. "What do you mean?"

Unsuccessfully swallowing a shamed sigh, Auerbach replied, "I think this whole deal was part of Beth-Li's plan."

"Plan?" repeated Brigid sharply. "Explain."

Auerbach opened his mouth, but nothing came out except another weary sigh. Faintly, he muttered, "I was a stupe. A triple-dipped stupe."

He had no opportunity to say anything more. The girl returned, trailed by a small, slender woman wearing a fringed smock of bleached doeskin. At first glance, Kane took her for one of the Indian women. Her almond eyes and long hair were no lighter in shade, but her skin was ivory-colored and smooth. Her cheekbones weren't as prominent, but her lips were full and pouting. The smock did nothing to conceal the curvaceous figure beneath. She stared at Kane in a way uncharacteristically bold for an Indian woman.

"Took you long enough," Rouch declared. "I've about had my limit of sour berries and boiled venison." She nodded in Standing Bear's direction. "Not to mention that overstimulated idiot."

Standing Bear, not understanding her words, responded to her nod by stepping up beside her and placing a possessive hand on her shoulder. Rouch glanced at him contemptuously. "See what I mean? Dirty savage."

Sky Dog's lips curled in a silent snarl.

Coldly, Kane asked, "I'm told you belong to that 'dirty savage.' Do you want to stay or leave?"

Rouch's Asian features twisted in a mask of disgust, as if she were scandalized by the mere suggestion. "Do you honestly think I want to stay in this pesthole? Get me out of here."

Brigid said tightly, "It's not that simple."

Rouch flung Standing Bear's hand from her shoulder and made a motion to join Kane. Grasping her roughly by the upper arm, Standing Bear yanked her back, grunting a word in Lakota.

"See?" Brigid asked.

The disgust in Rouch's face instantly became fear. To Kane, she said beseechingly, "Get me out of here—get me away from him!"

Refusing to acknowledge her stricken features and fearful tone, he said flatly, "Auerbach mentioned something about a plan. I want to hear it."

Rouch cast her eyes downward as if she were deeply embarrassed, but Brigid received the distinct impression it was exaggerated, if not feigned completely. She didn't trust Rouch, and her wariness stemmed from more than just jealousy; Rouch had, with Lakesh's blessing, tried to seduce Kane. And she'd wasted no time sharing her affections since then, if Auerbach's admission was true.

Tugging at the fringe on her dress, Rouch said in a halting whisper, "It wasn't a plan, not really. An idea…I was angry with you…I'm sorry."

Her words trailed off, then she said, "I didn't expect to run across these savages."

Sky Dog broke in harshly, "You refer to us as savages one more time, I'll lodge-pole you, Standing Bear and these others notwithstanding."

Kane wasn't sure what lodge-poling consisted of, but he guessed it wasn't pleasant. To the shaman, he said, "She wants to leave. Tell Standing Bear that."

"I will, but it won't make any difference."

Sky Dog spoke tersely, briefly to the warrior, and rage glinted in the man's dark eyes. He thrust Rouch behind him, looked Kane up and down, hawked up from deep in his throat and spit a glob of saliva at his feet. He grated, "*Zuya.*"

Sky Dog rolled his eyes. "It's what I expected. You'll have to fight him for her. In my opinion, she's not worth the effort. Leave her here. Standing Bear is bound to get tired of her and her disrespectful mouth sooner than later."

Kane said nothing for a tense tick of time. Brigid breathed, "I'm leaning toward taking Sky Dog's advice."

So did Kane. He knew he could chill Standing Bear in his tracks, and with Grant as his ace, they stood a decent—not necessarily good—chance of escaping with Rouch. He saw no firearms among the warriors, not even the home-forged muzzle loaders they might have taken from the roamers.

But if he opted for a firefight, a state of war would exist between the tribesmen and the handful of Cerberus exiles. When and if the forces of the villes arrived looking for them, the Indians would eagerly talk all about the dishonorable *wasicun* hiding in the Darks.

Tactically, employing violence to retrieve Rouch might be sound. Diplomatically, it would be a disaster from which nothing could ever be salvaged.

Kane started to speak, but hesitated when he noted the triumphant smirk appearing on Standing Bear's face. Fighting for or leaving Rouch behind was now more than a choice; it had become a challenge. Kane realized if he backed down, knuckled under, he would be branded a coward, not worthy of respect. If he or any of the Cerberus people traveled across the Indian's country again, the warriors would view them as targets.

"Kane!" Rouch's cry was full of desperation, of quivering terror.

Into the trans-comm, Kane muttered, *"Merde."*

He knew Grant would instantly understand the code word, signifying the current situation could be compared to excrement and that he was to stand by.

Kane began to turn away. Standing Bear's patronizing chuckle triggered a hot flash of anger within him, and he spun around on his heel. He struck the warrior across the face with his open right hand. Weighted by the holstered Sin Eater, the impact of the blow cracked like a whip and Standing Bear reeled, almost bowling Rouch off her feet.

Recovering his balance, the warrior stared at Kane in shocked disbelief, the paint designs on his face smeared by the slap. Howling in fury, he lunged forward. Several other men did the same, echoing his cry.

Sky Dog placed himself in front of Kane, speaking curtly and incisively. The men halted, muttering and glaring. The shaman faced Kane, eyes questioning but amused. "You've thought this course of action all the way through?"

"Only the ramifications of not taking it," Kane replied.

Sky Dog shook his head, laugh lines deepening around his squinting eyes. "I'm just an ignorant savage. I don't know big *wasicun* words like that."

He smiled in rueful resignation. "But I know a couple of small *wasicun* words—like, 'you're fucked, dude.'"

The Indians formed a giant circle out on the open floor of the plain. In the center of the circle, a post had been driven into the ground. Rouch stood tethered to it by a length of leather slip-knotted around her right wrist. The wind caught her hair, making it stream behind her like an ebony banner.

Auerbach, once his clothes had been returned to him, had become a bit more talkative, but not cheerful. As he walked with Brigid and Kane toward Sky Dog, he said quickly, "They're doing it just like with me yesterday. Hope you last longer than I did. Not that it makes any difference. The fucking Indians don't play fair—"

"Shut up," growled Kane. "This is their country, and they make the rules."

Auerbach fell silent and dropped back a pace. Sky Dog and Standing Bear stood with two snorting ponies. The animals wore no saddles, only rope halters with a single rein attached to them.

Kane eyed both horses as he approached, studying their withers, their legs, their chests. Though one was dappled and the other a bay, they appeared matched in general size and physical condition. He looked around at the grinning warriors encircling the field in a solid wall of flesh and steel.

Brigid whispered, "I think you'd better call Grant. This isn't just a trial by combat—it's a contest of horsemanship."

"I've ridden horses," he retorted tersely.

She looked at him suspiciously. "For what—all of thirty seconds in Mongolia? You told me you were bucked off."

Kane mentally kicked himself for ever telling her about the incident. He admired horses, but his fondness for them was tempered by his lack of personal contact with them. Bred in Cobaltville, he was accustomed to horses that were dray animals, docile to the point of being comatose. His single experience with a high-spirited steed was during his escape from Kharo-Khoto, when his stolen mount had helped him flee, true enough, but more by accident than design.

He stopped before Sky Dog. The shaman held a pair of rawhide-wrapped wooden staffs, five feet long with the ends curved like blunt-tipped fishhooks.

"You will each take a horse and start at opposite sides of the field," Sky Dog stated in English. Kane figured the smirking Standing Bear didn't need instructions. "You will be armed with the coup sticks. To win, you must remain on the field. The man who rides from the field, is forced from it or unhorsed forfeits the contest. The man who releases Little Willow wins her."

"Sounds simple enough," Kane commented.

Sky Dog chuckled and nodded in Auerbach's direction. "That's what he thought. He learned otherwise."

Kane took a staff, hefting it experimentally. Made of lightweight but sturdy wood, it felt easy to wield, but Kane didn't think it was much of a weapon.

Standing Bear snatched the other staff, twirled it deftly in one hand, tossed it high in the air and caught the butt end on the palm of his other hand. He balanced it there, staring at Kane with a mocking smile. A wave of appreciative laughter rippled among the onlookers.

Kane pretended not to hear it. He asked, "Which is my mount?"

The shaman pulled the bay pony forward. Taking the rope rein, Kane looked into the horse's brown eyes, searching for any signs of a nasty or tricky disposition. Stroking its muzzle, he murmured, "I don't want to ride you any more than you want me to ride you. If you're going to get mad at a human being, get mad at Standing Bear."

The pony snorted and pawed at the ground.

The eager Indians voiced high-pitched ululating cries. Standing Bear nimbly vaulted onto his horse's back, grasping the coup stick in his right hand and looping the rein lightly around his left wrist.

Kane mounted the bay, grateful that the animal didn't shy away from him. He considered stripping off his coat, but decided to keep it on since it concealed his Sin Eater. If matters turned ugly, he wasn't about to fend off Standing Bear or his friends with a stick of wood, rules of conduct be damned. He was a veteran hard-contact Mag— rules wouldn't come between him and survival.

He caught Brigid's eye, and she extended the index finger of her right hand and brought it smartly toher nose. Gravely, Kane returned the one-percent salute. This time, he figured the odds were correct.

The two men kicked their ponies' flanks and trotted out onto the field. Kane watched how Standing Bear guided his horse with the pressure of his knees and heels. He did his best to emulate it. The bay obeyed, even though he jounced painfully on the animal's spine. Without a saddle or even a blanket, it was about as comfortable as riding a fence rail.

He looked toward Rouch, standing at the post. She had her eyes on him, and though her dark eyes shone with fear, they glittered with another emotion—a thrill, an excited anticipation.

She had worn a similar look a month before when she learned he knifed a swampie to death during a mission to the bayous of Louisiana. A cold sickness sprang up in the pit of his belly.

Sky Dog shouted, *"Oh-oohey!"*

Before the echoes of the cry had faded, Standing Bear heeled his pony around and galloped straight at Kane, holding the coup stick like a jousting lance. Kane pressed with his knees, and his pony obediently jumped out of the path.

Standing Bear rode past, almost to the edge of the ring of onlookers. He reined sharply, and his pony reared up on its hind legs. He brought the animal around without its forelegs touching the ground. The crowd shouted its approval. Standing Bear acknowledged the cheers with an arrogant toss of his head.

Kane couldn't help but marvel at the warrior's expertise. He was less a man on horseback than a centaur, the mythical half human, half beast. Standing Bear charged again, riding around Kane in lightning-swift gambados and curvets, swinging his coup stick like a reaper's scythe.

Leaning forward, then backward, Kane barely avoided being struck and hooked. The pony responded to an involuntary squeeze of his knees. It turned and slammed into Standing Bear's mount, drawing an angry whinny from it.

The horse staggered, and Standing Bear swayed on its back. The Indians shouted in approbation, as if Kane's maneuver had been intentional. For a moment, the two animals snapped at each other, then whirled apart. Standing Bear galloped up the field, recovering his balance.

Straightening up, ignoring the spasm of pain in his testicles, Kane patted the bay's neck. "Good boy," he whispered, even though he didn't know if the horse was male or female.

He glanced toward Rouch, still standing tethered. Their eyes met briefly, and he saw her expression of excitement was being supplanted by one of arousal.

Standing Bear thundered back toward him like a sinew-and-muscle typhoon, his long hair whipping around his head. He shrilled the Lakota war cry, *"Hoka-hey!"*

The horses ran at each other, circled, then hurtled around the field, Standing Bear's pony snapping viciously at the bay's rump. Kane's pony shrilled in anger and launched several back-kicks, which nearly unseated him. But the grip of his heels and knees to the rib-slatted sides of the animal was like an iron vise, and his fingers laced about the rein tightly.

Standing Bear flailed at him with his coup stick, and he parried the blows with a loud, castanet-like clacking of wood against wood. One of the blows got through his guard and cracked smartly on his collarbone. Kane tapped with his heels, and the pony lunged away, Standing Bear following closely.

Pounding hooves tore up great clods of turf, and grit and gravel sprayed about. Twice Kane was almost forced from his steed's back by blows from Standing Bear's coup stick. He countered by catching the crook of his opponent's staff, and tried to pull the warrior down.

Standing Bear went with the pull, leaning close and slapping the bay hard on its rump, screaming, *"Dho!"*

Kane had no idea what the word meant, but his pony evidently understood. It exploded beneath him, rearing and bucking. He felt himself slipping off its back and he had no choice but to drop his coup stick and use both hands to grip the rein and the animal's mane.

Standing Bear kept pace, racing by his side, lashing out at him with the wooden staff, raining hard blows on his hip and shoulder.

Pulling hard on the rope rein, Kane managed to slow his pony. Standing Bear rode past and whirled around, his painted face split by a wide grin. His eyes blazed with glee as he kicked his horse into another thundering charge.

Kane knew the obvious option was to turn his pony and allow Standing Bear to pursue him around the field again, but that tactic would only delay the inevitable—and provide more amusement for the Indians. Out of the many things in his life he hated, being pursued, forced into the role of prey, topped the list. It didn't come naturally to him. Also, his arms and shoulders throbbed from the coup-stick blows, and a deep, boring pain radiated out from his crotch into his upper thighs.

Leaning forward, he murmured into the bay's ear, "Screw this."

He reined the pony to a complete halt and slid off its back, sending it trotting away with a slap and a shout. He faced Standing Bear on wide-braced legs, listening to the astonished cries of the onlookers. As the distance rapidly narrowed between the two men, Kane shucked out of his coat, not caring if his Sin Eater was seen. He stood motionless, waiting.

An instant of uncertainty flickered across Standing Bear's paint-masked face, but his warrior's blood beat too hot for him to spare any time wondering what the *wasicun* might have planned. A high-pitched, warbling scream issued from his throat.

When Standing Bear was less than two yards away, Kane flung his coat out toward the horse's head, roaring wordlessly at the top of his voice. The warrior's steed was well trained in the game of combat, but it was still only a horse. It reacted instantly to the flapping, wind-belled coat by digging in its rear hooves and lurching to one side.

With a gargling cry, Standing Bear catapulted forward, over his horse's head, and slammed face-first to the ground. Kane sidestepped to avoid his rolling body. All the oxygen in the man's lungs exploded out in an agonized whoof.

The warrior's pony galloped off, and the assembled Indians raised a great shout. Kane picked up Standing Bear's coup stick and held it over his head in a gesture of victory.

Standing Bear writhed on the ground, mouth opening and closing as he tried to drag in enough air to move his limbs and get him back on his feet. Green grass stains blended with his red face paint. He managed to push himself over onto his back, and Kane planted the blunt end of the staff against his breastbone, pressing hard.

"Stay down, asshole," he snapped, knowing full well the warrior couldn't understand his words. He touched his holstered Sin Eater suggestively. "Stay down for a minute or stay down permanently."

Standing Bear glared first at him, then at the weapon, and comprehension slowly dawned in his eyes. He stayed down. Angling the coup stick over a shoulder, Kane stepped back a few feet, then turned and strode toward Rouch.

Her face was jubilant, her eyes shining like pieces of wet obsidian. "You did it." Her voice was a happy whisper. "You won me!"

Kane said nothing as he reached over and unknotted the tether around her wrist with a single theatrical jerk. The Indians rushed onto the field, waving their arms and shouting. They didn't sound pleased.

Rouch paid them no attention. She was too busy embracing Kane tightly, face tilted up toward his, lips parted. "Oh, Kane!"

Roughly, he disengaged himself. "Keep your mouth shut. We're not out of this yet."

Taking her right hand, he raised it as the angry Indians approached. He didn't see either Brigid or Auerbach among the crowd. Into the trans-comm, he whispered, "Grant?"

"Still here," came the tense response. "I'm watching."

"Keep doing it."

A pair of grim-faced warriors helped Standing Bear to his unsteady feet. Kane saw one of them surreptitiously slip a bone-handled knife into the man's palm. Standing Bear glanced at it, then broke from the crowd and raced at Kane, knife upraised.

Sky Dog's loud, commanding voice brought Standing Bear to a halt a split second before Kane unleathered his Sin Eater.

The shaman approached Kane and Rouch. He looked from one to the other dispassionately. "The contest is over. You have lost."

"I don't think so," Kane said quietly.

Sky Dog shook his head. "You violated the rules, my friend."

"I jumped off my pony intentionally," replied Kane. "I unhorsed Standing Bear and released the woman."

Pursing his lips, Sky Dog said lowly, "Gray Ghost, I am in sympathy with you. You showed great cunning. Yet this was not a contest of cunning, but of skill."

Kane sighed heavily, wearily. He beckoned the shaman to step closer. Eyebrows crooked quizzically, Sky Dog did so and Kane whispered, "This was a rigged contest, and you know it. This was the second time in my life I've been on horseback. We weren't evenly matched."

"True," the man admitted.

"The only way to win a rigged game is to change the rules. Only you can determine whether or not the new rules apply. I suggest—with all respect—that you do so."

Suspiciously, Sky Dog demanded, "Why? You may have a blaster, but you're only one man."

Kane smiled slightly, without humor. "That's where you're wrong and where I'm guilty of a little bit of rigging myself."

Sky Dog's eyes widened, then narrowed. "Just how wrong and how guilty are you?"

"Only a little on both counts. But that little bit can turn into a whole lot of bloodshed. It's up to you."

Sky Dog chuckled, but it sounded forced. "Why do I think this is a *wasicun* bluff?"

Kane shrugged. "A natural assumption. I'd make it myself, if I were in your place. But in this case, it would be a fatal mistake."

Sky Dog glanced over toward Standing Bear, who scowled in fury at Kane. "If I decide in your favor, it will be a great dishonor to Standing Bear. I doubt he'll stand for it—pun intended."

Kane thought a moment, and stated quietly, "I'll apologize to him and offer him compensation. How will that be?"

Sky Dog nodded. "Since Little Willow doesn't want to stay anyway, he might accept your apology. But his idea of compensation might be more than you're willing to pay."

"What do you mean?"

"You'll have to ask him."

Sky Dog walked toward Standing Bear, raising conciliatory hands. Rouch began to speak, but Kane shushed her into silence. Into the trans-comm, he said, "Stand by."

Sky Dog spoke earnestly to Standing Bear for nearly a minute. By degrees, the warrior's posture began to relax, and the wrathful flames in his eyes dimmed, though they didn't gutter out altogether.

At length, Standing Bear grunted a few words, nodded shortly and Sky Dog gestured for Kane to step forward. He faced the warrior as he spoke in a hurried, grim cadence. Sky Dog translated.

"'I accept you have won Little Willow, though not by fair means. However, since she does not wish to stay with me, it would be wrong of me to keep her against her will. But first a price must be paid. I must buy back my honor before I allow you take her. Do you understand?'"

Kane nodded, shifting his eyes over to Sky Dog. "Tell him I regret what happened, that I am sorry."

Sky Dog repeated Kane's words. Standing Bear's lips curved slightly, either in a smile or a moue of distaste. He muttered a question.

"'Will you pay the price for my honor?'" Sky Dog translated.

Kane hesitated, then nodded.

Like the head of a snake with a razor tongue, the knife in Standing Bear's hand flashed up and out.

The point of the knife inscribed a slanting gash on Kane's left cheek. Standing Bear manipulated the knife so deftly and swiftly, Kane had no opportunity to recoil.

As he clapped his left hand over the blood trickling from the cut, the Sin Eater sprang reflexively into the palm of his right. It required a conscious effort of will to keep his finger from pressing the trigger.

The Indians in the immediate vicinity cried out in astonishment at the magical appearance of the blaster in the *wasicun's* hand. Kane surveyed their ruddy, disconcerted faces, baring his teeth, index finger quivering over the trigger. The old Magistrate's pride, the righteous rage fountained up within him. He grappled with the mad urge to chill the lesser breeds who dared to scorn one of the baron's chosen.

After a long, tense moment of internal struggle, he

barely managed to tamp down the volcanic fury. Staring unblinkingly into Standing Bear's eyes, he made a deliberately slow show of pushing the Sin Eater back into its holster.

Standing Bear didn't seem intimidated or impressed. He made a pompous-sounding announcement, then hurled the knife to the ground, where it struck point first. Sky Dog said, "Standing Bear has put the mark of the *unktomi shunkaha* on you…the trickster wolf. From now on, if any our people encounter you, they will know you are cunning like the wolf and just as mean."

Voice pitched low to disguise his anger, Kane said, "Tell Standing Bear I accept the mark. Tell him also that he has no idea how close he came to being marked himself…right between the eyes."

Sky Dog chuckled. "He knows. I think he also knows it takes an honorable man to offer up some of his own honor to buy back that of another."

Standing Bear thrust out his right hand. Kane's eyes flicked from it to the warrior's impassive face. Then he gripped the man's forearm tightly. Standing Bear uttered another imperious proclamation.

"Take Little Willow," Sky Dog translated. "But treat her better from now on. If she returns to me, I will not let her go again."

Kane only nodded, feeling blood trickle down his face and along the side of his neck. The wound stung sharply, but he gave no indication of noticing the pain. Absently, he worried about scarring, but since his body already bore so many, he figured one more wouldn't make much difference.

Standing Bear released his grip, teeth flashing in a broad, slightly mocking grin. He looked past Kane toward Rouch, touched his groin and made a comical frown of disappointment. Rouch averted her gaze. The warrior swaggered into the crowd, and his companions made a path for him, laughing and patting his back.

Kane didn't realize how much tension he had bottled up until Standing Bear walked away. He released his breath in a prolonged sigh of relief and said into the trans-comm, "Situation green. Stand down."

"Standing down." Grant's response came not from the trans-comm but from his right and behind him.

As he heard the words, Kane became aware of a commotion in the onlookers. He whirled around and saw Grant stalking toward him, scowling ferociously at the Indians, who stepped back fearfully. With his dark coat wrapped tightly around him, accentuating his exceptionally broad shoulders, Grant presented the picture of death's black agent. Even Sky Dog's face expressed apprehension. Auerbach and Brigid moved out of the crowd to flank Kane.

"So," said Sky Dog, "you weren't running a *wasicun* bluff after all. Is this the only man lying in wait?"

Kane answered curtly, "You'll understand if I decline to tell you."

"You don't trust us?" Sky Dog challenged.

Kane gingerly touched the shallow cut on his cheek, looked at the blood shining wetly on his fingertips and demanded sarcastically, "Hell, why wouldn't I? You've shown us such wonderful hospitality so far."

The shaman only shrugged.

Grant gave Rouch and Auerbach an appraising stare and inquired mildly, "Are we ready to go home?"

"I am," Rouch declared firmly.

Brigid swept a cold glare over her. Rouch boldly met it, tilting her head at a defiant angle.

Slowly, Sky Dog said, "I would like to know more about your people, about your settlement in the Darks. And why Magistrates are up there."

Kane kept his uneasy surprise from registering on his face. "You recognized my blaster."

"They're called Sin Eaters, as I recall. Which ville are you from?"

Auerbach blurted in angry fear, "We're not telling you anything!"

Without looking at him, Kane intoned, "I'm getting awfully sick of telling you to shut up, Auerbach." Addressing Sky Dog, he asked bluntly, "Why?"

"It may be that we could be of some help to each other. Although you must keep your secrets and we must keep ours, together we may find ourselves engaged in a mutually beneficial situation one day."

Kane weighed the man's words, assessing their sincerity. He stated, "We've already revealed some of our secrets simply by being here. Let's have an exchange. A secret traded for a secret. By my estimation, you owe us about five or six."

Sky Dog smiled slyly. "Actually, that's far more than we have. We only keep one. But it's big."

"How so?" asked Grant.

"Have you wondered why my people have settled so close to the mountains they fear harbor evil spirits?"

"I haven't, no," Kane admitted.

"I have, yes," announced Brigid crisply.

Kane cast her an annoyed, questioning glance.

"Just because I never mentioned it doesn't mean I never wondered," she said a bit defensively. To Sky Dog, she declared, "I've examined the predark maps of this region. The topography hasn't altered all that much since the nukecaust. Only a few miles away is a better water supply and richer grazing land for your animals."

She gestured to the open terrain around them. "This area isn't substandard, but you could do better."

Sky Dog looked at her with a new respect. "I can see I should not have judged you by the same standards I applied to Little Willow."

Rouch's shoulders stiffened, and Kane did his best to repress a grin. Grant just barely managed to turn a chuckle into a throat-clearing sound.

Sky Dog asked, "Gray Ghost, I will trade you a secret, if you promise to keep it as such. I will show you and only you."

Kane shook his head. "No deal." He nodded toward Brigid and Grant. "They have to share in it. I can't exclude them."

"You're not their chief?"

Brigid snapped, "We have no chief." She paused, then amended her declaration. "We do, sort of. But Kane isn't it."

Sky Dog pursed his lips contemplatively. "Will you all make the same promise of secrecy?"

Grant and Brigid nodded.

"Very well." Sky Dog pointed to Rouch and Auerbach. "Go to your lodges. Your possessions will be returned to you. Wait until we return."

Auerbach opened to his mouth to voice a protest, but subsided when Kane gave him a warning glare.

The shaman gestured. "You three will come with me."

He marched away.

Grant, Kane and Brigid exchanged brief glances, then fell into step behind him.

SKY DOG GUIDED THEM away from the village, toward a line of trees sprouting from the plain floor. Shadowy humps of ridges interrupted the flat terrain. The shaman spoke little as he led Brigid, Kane and Grant toward them. "What you will see is our secret and the source of my people's fear of the Darks," he said cryptically.

They crossed a crumbling strip of blacktop road, the ancient two-lane highway that had once twisted its way up through the Bitterroot Range. Aspens, pines and high grasses grew in a tangle on the other side of it.

At the bottom of a shallow slope, a tall tripod shape, like a tepee without its hide coverings, rose from the ground. Colorful feathers decorated the wooden struts and fluttered in the breeze. Unidentifiable bits of rusty metal dangled from rawhide thongs. Hanging from the point where the main braces intersected was a brown human skull with the jawbone missing. As they passed it, they saw a bullet hole perforating its right side. Almost the entire left side of the cranium had been shot away.

Kane asked, "What's this? A warning or a signpost?"

"A bit of both," said Sky Dog. "It has been there for generations. Maintaining it is part of my spiritual responsibilities."

"The skull has been there for a very long time," Brigid observed.

"Four generations at least," Sky Dog agreed. "It once sat on the shoulders of a *wasicun* interloper. According to legend, after killing many of our warriors, he shot himself rather than fall into my people's hands. He fought bravely, but took the coward's path in the end."

"What would have happened if he'd surrendered?" Grant inquired.

"Death by slow torture, probably," the shaman answered.

"In that case," said Kane, "I'd say he showed good sense, not cowardice."

Sky Dog's response to Kane's opinion was a shrug, as if the matter was of little importance.

The four people strode deeper into the wood. Kane realized that no birds sang from the boughs of the trees, and tension began knotting in his stomach. He didn't suspect the shaman was leading them into a trap. Killing them would have been much easier back in the village, if that were his intent. He and Baptiste exchanged uneasy glances. The shade under the towering trees deepened almost to dusk, and anything could be hiding in the shadows.

Sky Dog showed no apprehension as he walked a more or less straight route through the closely growing trees along a faint path that none of them would have noticed as such if they hadn't been following him. Kane estimated they had walked some seventy yards from the roadbed when Sky Dog came to a halt.

At first glance, they stood in a very small, crescent-shaped clearing, with a tall tangle of bushes, shrubs and foliage making up the inner curve. Kane's eyes picked out tree stumps protruding only a few inches above the ground.

Sky Dog gestured. "My people's secret."

Brigid, Grant and Kane followed the man's gesture and saw only the snarl of overgrowth. Sky Dog stepped to it, thrust his arms into the tangled vines and leaves and pulled. He lifted away a large section of a carefully camouflaged shelter made of cross-braced tree limbs interlaced with grasses, weeds and shrubs. The forepart came away in three large pieces. Inside they saw the outline of a long, bulky shape which at first glance was unrecognizable.

Sky Dog waved them over as he stepped inside the shelter. A huge vehicle lay nestled within. The armor plate sheathing the chassis was rust pitted, but they saw how its dark hull bristled with machine-gun blisters and rocket pods, and was perforated by weapons ports. It crouched on flat metal tracks, like a petrified prehistoric beast of prey.

Grant recognized it first. "An old mobile army command post," he announced, trying not to sound impressed. "Predark model, but modified and retooled into a war wag."

Kane's eyes gave it a slow inspection. He gauged its length at around forty feet and its weight at about fifty tons. The fixed, double-thickness steel plates showed deep scoring in places, where armor-piercing rounds had almost penetrated. The juggernaut had seen a lot of action in its day.

He moved to the front, standing on his toes to peer into the cockpit. Since it was eight feet off the ground, all he saw was the bottom portion of a dusty, cracked windscreen. "Is it operational?"

Sky Dog shrugged. "I don't know about the weapons. The wag itself has been out of fuel for a very long time, since my grandfather's day or before."

"Where did you find it?" Brigid asked.

The shaman swept a hand in the general direction of the Bitterroot Range. "According to tribal history, it was found at the foothills. *Wasicun* invaders were inside of it. One group, led by a one-eyed man, went to the plateau of the fog. They never returned."

"Plateau of the fog?" Grant repeated skeptically. "What's that?"

"Our legends speak of a plateau in the Darks cloaked in fog…a mist which killed, rending men apart as if with claws and fangs."

Sky Dog rapped the hull of the vehicle. "The second group of invaders rode in the belly of this steel beast. It carried them down the mountain, then it stopped to move no more. When the *wasicun* left it, my people fell on them. The machine was hauled here and hidden, lest other *wasicun* try to breathe new life into it."

Kane walked to the rear and opened a hatch, the rust-stiff hinges and springs squealing loudly. "Do you mind if we look inside?"

"I brought you here so you could do so," Sky Dog replied.

Kane, Grant and Brigid clambered aboard. The stale air within carried a faint whiff of cordite mixed with the odor of fuel and grease. They moved down the narrow, grate-floored passageway, checking the tiny, cramped sleeping quarters. In one of them, Brigid found a thick notebook. Its plastic covers were torn, and leaves of paper fell out of it. Empty cargo compartments took up most of the interior space. Inside of small side alcoves, they found and inspected the weapons emplacements.

The four-barrel 12.7 mm machine guns were in poor shape, all the moving parts frozen by neglect and time. Grant commented, "Nothing that a couple of days of oiling, cleaning and sanding couldn't fix."

They found sealed crates of many different calibers of ammo and even a few LAW rockets. There were a number of empty gun racks bolted to the walls. In the control compartment, they inspected the instrument panels and were impressed by the array of panels, dials, screens and circuit breakers.

Grant grunted in disapproval, stooping over to inspect the underside of a panel. "The controls were originally designed to be linked by computers. Looks like whoever found this thing bypassed them, rerouting all the circuits to manual-override boards."

Kane nodded, standing between the gimballed driver's and codriver's chairs. He bent down to gaze out the windscreen. The thick bulletproof glass bore ancient starring patterns from projectiles. "This is a hell of a lot of firepower for the Indians to have."

"It's a hell of a lot of firepower for anybody to have," Brigid murmured, pushing past Kane to sit down in the driver's seat. Absently, she thumbed through the notebook.

"What've you got there, Baptiste?" he asked.

"Looks like a log. Nothing much in it but handwritten fuel-consumption reports, weapons and repair status. Here's the only thing of a personal nature."

She handed him a square of coarse wood-pulp paper. The edges were frayed, and it was stained with machine oil and the bottom half bore a smear that looked like either dried ketchup or blood. The hand-printed words on it were faded to almost illegibility. Kane had to lean toward the light peeping in through the port in order to read it.

Hi, Ryan.

If you're reading this, then it means I'm dead. This rad cancer's been eating my guts for months, and I know there's no stopping it. So this is me saying goodbye and the best of luck. If it goes the way I hope, I'll just walk away one night so don't you blasted come after me. Please. That's the Trader talking and not ordering, Ryan, old friend. We've been some places and done some good and bad things. Now it's done. That's all. I thank you for watching my back for so many years. You and J.B. watch out for each other.

There was no signature. Kane handed it back to her. "Mean anything?" she asked.

"Any reason why it should?"

Brigid's lips curved slightly in a patronizing smile. "You're familiar with the *Wyeth Codex*, aren't you?"

"I've heard you and Lakesh mention it enough."

Though Kane's comment was studiedly dismissive, he knew the memoirs of Dr. Mildred Wyeth were indirectly responsible for Brigid's exile from Cobaltville. Some thirty years before, a junior archivist in Ragnarville had found an old computer disk containing the journal of Mildred Winona Wyeth, a specialist in cryogenics. She had entered a hospital in late 2000 for minor surgery, but an idiosyncratic reaction to the anesthetic left her in a coma, with her vital signs sinking fast. To save her life, the predark whitecoats had cryonically frozen her.

After her revival nearly a century later, she joined Ryan Cawdor and his band of warriors. Although the *Wyeth Codex,* as her journal came to be called, contained recollections of adventures and wanderings, it dealt in the main with her observations, speculations and theories about the environmental conditions of postnukecaust America.

She also delved deeply into the Totality Concept and its profusion of different yet interconnected subdivisions. The many spin-off experiments were applied to an eclectic combination of disciplines, most of them theoretical—artificial intelligence, hyperdimensional physics, genetics and new energy sources. In her journal, she maintained that the technology simply did not exist to have created all of the Totality Concept's many wonders—unless it had originated from somewhere, and someone else.

Despite her exceptional intelligence, and education, Wyeth had no inkling of the true nature of the Totality Concept's experiments, but a number of her extrapolations that they were linked to the nukecaust came very close to the truth.

In the decades following its discovery, the *Wyeth Codex* had been downloaded, copied and disseminated like a virus through the Historical Divisions of the entire ville network.

That particular virus had infected Brigid one morning nearly two years ago, when she found a disk containing the *Codex* at her workstation in the Cobaltville archives.

After reading and committing it to memory, she had never been the same woman again.

Brigid declared, "Dr. Wyeth wrote that Cawdor and her lover, J. B. Dix, spent years as members of an organization which traveled the Deathlands, salvaging and dealing in predark artifacts. The leader of the organization went by the name of Trader. So this machine has a certain amount of historical significance attached to it."

Due to her archivist's training, Brigid tried to fit just about everything, no matter how trivial, into a niche in history. Although the exploits of Cawdor, Dix and his band of warriors were still celebrated in folklore and songs in some outland areas, Kane viewed them as just names from the wild old days before baronies were established. He recalled from his Magistrate indoctrination classes that because of the resistance organized by Cawdor, the full institution of the Program of Unification was delayed by several years.

"We know that Cawdor penetrated Cerberus and used the mat-trans unit there," continued Brigid. "So I calculate that this war wag has been here for approximately a hundred years."

Grant pushed himself erect from beneath the instrument board. "All things considered, a pretty good job of jury-rigging. It's not in too bad a shape, given all the time that's passed."

"But it's useless to us," Sky Dog declared. He had entered the vehicle on soundless moccasined feet. "There is no life in it."

"What happened to the handblasters?" Grant asked. "Looks like there were a lot of them."

"My people took them, of course. They are hidden in another place, close by our village."

"Do you have ammo for them?" inquired Kane.

Sky Dog hesitated before shaking his head. "No. What little the invaders had was used on my people long ago."

A sudden suspicion made Kane slit his eyes. "That's one of the reasons Le Loup Garou and his roamers attacked you, isn't it? To get the blasters? He'd heard about them."

Sky Dog sighed sadly. "I fear so. Such a secret can't be kept for so many years among so many people without a few rumors leaking out here and there."

Grant experimentally flicked a switch on a console. Like he expected, nothing happened. "You've got a real prize here, Sky Dog."

The shaman nodded. "I realize that, even if most of my people don't. They still believe it to be a thing of evil, a metal monster symbolizing all the old *wasicun* oppression."

Lowering his voice as if he were afraid he would be overheard and accused of heresy, he added, "But the fact remains if this metal monster had been operational, the roamers would have never been able to attack us and carry off our women and children."

Brigid asked, "You showed us this thing so we can make it operational again?"

"The thought crossed my mind." He pointed to Kane's trans-comm unit. "You have predark tech at your command, wags of your own. And weapons."

"Why should we fix this thing for you?" Kane challenged. "What's in it for us?"

"A simple answer," Sky Dog replied smoothly. "You're all hiding from something up there in the Darks, else you would be living in the villes among your own kind. Nor would you have sealed the pass. Certainly not to keep us or a few roamers out."

Sky Dog looked expectantly from Grant to Kane to Brigid, waiting for either a comment or a denial. When neither was forthcoming, he continued, "I propose an alliance between my people and yours. Provide us with the means to restore life to this machine, train me how to operate it and give us ammunition for the blasters we have hidden. We will be your first line of defense against the enemies seeking you."

He fell silent, folding his arms over his chest. Kane smiled wryly. "You're not asking for much, are you?"

"What if we refuse?" Grant demanded. "Will you have us chilled, now that we know your tribe's great secret?"

Sky Dog made a sound of derision. "Of course not. I already promised you safe passage. Besides, if you do not return to the plateau, more of your people will come. If there's one thing of which I'm positive, it's that where there are a few *wasicun,* more will follow." His lips twisted in a cryptic smile. "And they probably won't be as well mannered as you three."

Kane matched Sky Dog's smile. "What would keep us from returning with more *wasicun* and simply taking this wag from you?"

"Nothing really," the shaman answered mildly. "Except your sense of honor, the same one I saw when you fought Le Loup Garou and wiped out his followers when you could have made it easier on yourself and let him pass."

"Not to mention that you shot Le Loup Garou with an arrow and saved my life."

Sky Dog's smile widened. "I wondered how long it would take you to bring that up."

"Now that I have," Kane said, "I suppose you expect me to repay the debt by agreeing to your proposal."

Sky Dog shrugged. "Follow your conscience, Gray Ghost. Do whatever your heart tells you to do."

Impatiently, Grant said, "Even if we go along with you, it'll take time. We'll have to send techs and mechs to your village. How do we know your people won't invite them to the same kind of wienie roast you planned for Auerbach?"

"My people look to me as expert on *wasicun* ways since I've lived among them." Sky Dog rolled up his right sleeve and thrust out his forearm. Just below the elbow joint was the faded pucker of an old scar. "I lived in Cobaltville until I was fifteen. After my father died, my mother and my sister and brother and I were cast out. A Magistrate used a knife to remove my ID chip so I could never return."

ID chips were tiny pieces of silicon injected subcutaneously into all ville residents, and the chips responded positively to scanners at checkpoints.

"My mother, my sister and my brother wandered for a long time," continued Sky Dog. "My sister was murdered by a roamer gang, my mother died of rad poisoning when we crossed a hellzone. Eventually, my brother and I ended up here. The tribe took us in, sheltered us, accepted us.

You shouldn't wonder that I place their welfare at such a high priority."

Kane didn't wonder, but he couldn't help but speculate about Lakesh's reaction if he accepted Sky Dog's proposal without discussing it with him first. He could easily imagine the blizzard of objections and invective storming from the old man's mouth.

"Something amuses you?" Sky Dog frowned slightly.

Kane realized he was smiling. "Yeah, but nothing to do with what you just said."

He turned toward Brigid and Grant. "What do you think?"

Grant rumbled musingly, "Strategically, what Sky Dog says makes sense. We'd sure as hell have the element of surprise if and when Mags come calling."

Uneasily, Brigid said, "I agree with it in principle. But we should talk this over with our…" She paused, groping for the right euphemism. "Our council of chiefs."

Sky Dog lifted a wry eyebrow. "And do you beat tom-toms and dance around a fire up there in the Darks before you reach a decision?"

Kane laughed. "Only after our animal sacrifices." He put out his hand to Sky Dog. "Deal. My instincts say you can be trusted, though they've been wrong before."

Sky Dog did not hesitate to clasp his hand. "So have mine."

"Good. Then we both know where we stand."

Releasing his grip, Kane moved out of the control compartment, walking toward the rear hatch. "It'll take a few days for us to return, to put together what we need and send some people back."

Sky Dog chuckled. "This monster has waited nearly a century to live again. A little while longer won't make much of a difference."

They left the compartment and the vehicle. While Grant helped Sky Dog restore the camouflage, Brigid took Kane aside.

"You should have consulted Lakesh before making a unilateral decision like this," she said severely.

"And have him back-burner the issue for a month or year?" he countered. "At this point, we can't afford to have anyone but allies at our doorstep."

"What if he overrules your promise?" Brigid asked, lines of worry creasing her forehead. "Then the Indians will think we've broken our word to them and be on the watch for us every time we leave the redoubt."

Kane nodded sagely. "Now you're getting it."

Realization of Kane's reasoning dawned in her eyes. "You've boxed Lakesh into a corner. Now he'll have no choice but to abide by your decision."

"Exactly. Besides, he's always been concerned about our relationship with the Indians. We've just reached our first diplomatic accord with them. He may squawk that the decision was made without his input, but overall he should be satisfied with it."

"And what do you tell Sky Dog when he starts asking questions about Cerberus, about what we're doing there and why?"

"We'll tell him what he needs to know," Kane answered. "I think he's trustworthy."

Brigid wet her lips nervously. "Assuming, of course, your instincts are sound this time."

Kane tentatively touched the knife cut on his cheek. It was already scabbing over. "Sky Dog is worried about the same thing, Baptiste."

"A balance of distrust," she acknowledged quietly. "Diplomacy in its purest form."

By the time they returned to the village, the sun hung a bare handsbreadth above the horizon. At Sky Dog's invitation, they decided to spend the night. After the shaman left them to arrange sleeping quarters, they returned to the knoll to retrieve their packs.

Brigid treated Kane's cut with materials from the first-aid kit. He stood stoically as she cleaned and applied stinging antiseptic to it.

"Superficial," she said, eyeing it critically. "It doesn't need stitches, but you may have a scar."

She started to spray liquid bandage over it, but Kane said, "That stuff itches. Leave it."

As they walked back to the Indian village, Grant asked, "How do we deal with Rouch and Auerbach? Do we take them back as deserters or as captives freed from bondage?"

"That depends on whether they really intended to desert," Brigid answered. "Either way, poor Auerbach was duped by Rouch."

Kane snorted. "You say that because you know he's got the hards for you, Baptiste."

She shot him an icy glare. "And we're all aware of what Rouch has for you, aren't we? She said she was angry with you. It's no mystery about what."

Kane opened his mouth to voice a profane rebuke, then closed it, clamping his jaws tight, his lips compressing in an angry line. He saw no purpose in arguing with Baptiste on the matter of him and Beth-Li Rouch.

Rouch was the newest arrival among the exiles in Cerberus, only a few months out of Sharpeville. Lakesh had arranged for her exile to fulfill a specific function among the men in Cerberus, but he had made it quite clear that Kane was the primary focus of his—and Rouch's—project to expand the little colony.

Her function had yet to be fulfilled, and Kane couldn't help but suspect that Rouch's interrupted cross-country trip had been designed to draw his attention. Auerbach had certainly implied as much.

Uneasily, Grant suggested, "Whatever the reason and whoever is at fault, we need to get to the bottom of it before we start back for Cerberus. If they're not willing to go back with us, we can't just turn them loose on the plains."

Neither Brigid nor Kane needed him to explain. The possibility that Rouch and Auerbach intended to betray the redoubt to their enemies was remote, but could not be discounted completely. One of the reasons behind the injection of the biolink transponders was to monitor the whereabouts of the exiles.

Kane blew out an exasperated sigh. The cut on his face twinged, and he cursed in irritation. "All we can do is question them. If their stories don't match up, or if they stink…" He let his words trail off.

"Then what do we do?" Brigid demanded. "March them out at dawn and execute them?"

Grant grimaced. "Something like that, maybe. Except I won't get up that early."

Brigid didn't smile at the rejoinder. "We don't have the right to do that," she objected fiercely. "Both of you have said there are no loyalty oaths to Cerberus as reasons for doing what you want to do."

"We never put Cerberus at risk," Kane grated. He gestured to the collection of dwellings around them. "These people may be in jeopardy, too. And I don't see how it will benefit anyone to return a couple of traitors to the redoubt and hold them as prisoners forever. We already have one resident captive. We don't need a couple more."

Brigid didn't respond to his reference to Balam, the entity confined in a holding cell for over three years. She declared, "We're making a lot of assumptions. Let's just ask Rouch and Auerbach what the hell they were up to before we start assembling a termination squad."

"Fine," said Kane. "But let me and Grant talk to Auerbach. You'll be too soft on him."

"And I'll question Rouch," Brigid snapped, "woman to woman. I can guarantee I won't be too soft on her."

They sought out Sky Dog, who directed them to the lodges occupied by Rouch and Auerbach. Grant and Kane fetched Auerbach, taking him outside and away from the village proper. The smell of roasting meat wafted to them from a cooking fire, a sharp reminder to Kane how long it had been since he had eaten anything other than the tasteless ration packs.

Auerbach quickly and almost gratefully responded to Kane's questions. His tale was so simple and simple-minded, neither Grant nor Kane doubted its veracity, though they wondered about his sanity. However, they were relieved they didn't have to employ the interrogation techniques they had learned as Cobaltville Magistrates, most of which relied on the physical abuse of a suspect.

Auerbach claimed he had volunteered to check the proximity sensors simply to escape the claustrophobic confines of the redoubt for a little while. He was as surprised as everyone else when Beth-Li Rouch expressed the desire to go with him. Surprised and pleased.

Ducking his head, Auerbach cast his eyes down and started to say something, then broke off, his words trailing off into inaudible mumbles.

"Well?" prodded Grant. "Finish it."

Auerbach tried to look at Kane, but evidently found the ground less intimidating. He was a big man, about Kane's height, but built along heavier lines. Strength-wise, they were probably evenly matched. The main difference between them lay in background—Kane was a blooded killer, while Auerbach wasn't and so he feared him.

"You may not like what I'm going to say," he muttered.

"As if I'm delighted with everything else that's happened in the last couple of days," retorted Kane. "Spit it out."

Clearing his throat, Auerbach nervously shifted his weight from foot to foot. His voice was barely above a shamed whisper. "I've had, ah, relations with Beth-Li.

Only once, about a month ago. I hoped she wanted to pick up where we left off."

Kane stared at him gravely, stone-faced. "Go on."

"It was her idea to strike out cross-country. Just for fun, she said. For the hell of it. When I told her everybody back at Cerberus would be worried, she said that was the idea. She was going to go with or without me, so I went with her."

Grant shook his head in exasperated disbelief. "You two had no destination in mind at all?"

Auerbach fidgeted. "No. Beth-Li claimed that we were doing a recce, you know, for the redoubt. On our second night out, we were captured by the Indians. I guess they saw our campfire."

"You guess," echoed Kane, voice cold with sarcasm. "On flatlands like this, you're lucky Baron Cobalt didn't spot your fire."

Auerbach swallowed hard. "I already said I was a stupe."

"A triple-dipped stupe," Grant reminded him.

Auerbach acknowledged the reminder with a jerky nod. "They came on us so fast, we didn't have time to use our blasters. Standing Bear led the party. Sky Dog wasn't with them, so we couldn't talk, understand each other's languages. On the march to the village, Beth-Li tried to make friends with Standing Bear. By the time we got here, he decided he wanted to be more than friends."

Auerbach's brows knitted in anger and resentment. "When I met Sky Dog, he told me Standing Bear had claimed Beth-Li as his property. He named her Little Willow because of the moves she made. You pretty much know the rest of it."

Grant hissed out an obscenity. "You opposed Standing Bear's claim and ended up dueling him for Rouch."

Auerbach shrugged. "I don't have to tell you that I lost."

Kane ran a frustrated hand through his hair. "This is just idiotic enough to be true. Earlier you said something about a plan. Explain."

Auerbach shrugged again. "Just a suspicion. I think she was testing you, Kane, to see if you'd be the one to come after her." He finally managed to meet Kane's gaze. "I guess you passed it. You not only came after her—you won her from Standing Bear."

"I would have come after any member of Cerberus if they'd gone missing," Kane replied dourly.

"Yeah, maybe, but you wouldn't have fought to win me. Whatever Beth-Li was trying to prove, whoever she was trying to prove it to, I guess she succeeded."

Face twisting in self-loathing, Auerbach dry-scrubbed his red bristle cut with furious fingers. "What are you waiting for? Kick my ass all the way back to the Darks. I'd do it myself, but I'd take pity on me."

"You deserve worse," growled Grant. "And you'll probably get it. From your own conscience."

He eyed Kane quizzically. "Unless you think he needs a blaster-whipping on top of it."

Kane presented the impression of seriously pondering the notion. At length, he said, "Right now, I'm too hungry to waste my time denting his skull. After we find something to eat and after we hear Baptiste's report on what Rouch had to say, I may reconsider."

BETH-LI ROUCH REELED, stumbling the width of the lodge. Only the drum-tight hide walls kept her from falling. The sharp echoes of the slap reverberated inside the tepee.

"I asked you a civil question," Brigid said grimly, resisting the impulse to shake her stinging right hand. "'Fuck off' isn't a civil answer."

Beth-Li touched her reddening cheek. A glint of fear, then anger appeared in her dark eyes. She had yet to change out of the white doeskin smock, and as her face darkened in fury she looked more like an Indian maiden than before.

"How dare you?" she demanded. "Who the hell do you think you are? You've got no right to ask me anything!"

Brigid took a slow, threatening step toward her. "I'm assuming the right and you'll answer me—what were you and Auerbach up to?"

Rouch clenched her fists, then her teeth. "I don't have to tell you anything. You have no authority over me."

"Maybe not in Cerberus. But here, it's just you, me and the walls."

Full lips writhing as if she were going to spit, Rouch demanded, "Get Kane in here. I'll answer his questions, not yours."

Brigid struggled to bottle up the anger the young woman's sneering attitude invoked in her. "This was all about Kane, wasn't it? You duped Auerbach into going with you so Kane might think you two were running off together. But you didn't plan on meeting the Indians or becoming Standing Bear's Little Willow."

Rouch uttered a derisive laugh. "You think you're a genius, don't you?"

"I don't need to be a genius to figure out this stupe scam of yours, Beth-Li. It's so transparent it wouldn't fool a child. And it didn't fool Kane."

Rouch planted her fists on her hips. "He came after me, didn't he? He fought another man for me. That's the important thing, not whether he was fooled."

With a sense of shock, Brigid recognized the emotions boiling within her as jealousy, with a strong undercurrent of humiliation. For a moment, her throat thickened and she couldn't speak.

"Kane won me," Rouch continued. "You don't know what that really means to a man, a warrior like him, do you? No, it's too primal for you to figure out. You're all intellect, sterile and cold." She paused, her smile widening as she added, "And barren."

Brigid groped for a response, first contemplating denying it, then despite herself demanding, "How do you know that?"

Rouch waved a dismissive hand through the air. "I was briefed on everybody in the redoubt."

"By Lakesh?"

"Who else?" Rouch retorted impatiently. "He brought me there. Face it, Baptiste—your profile and Kane's simply don't match up. They never did, not even before your...accident."

Brigid narrowed her eyes, to keep Rouch from seeing the tears suddenly springing to them. Only a couple of months before, she had learned she was infertile, due to exposure to an unknown wavelength of radiation in the Black Gobi. She had suffered chromosomal damage, but to what extent and to what degree of permanency was still undetermined. Although Lakesh knew, as did DeFore, the redoubt's resident medic, Brigid had yet to speak of it to Kane. Finding out that Beth-Li Rouch was privy to her condition not only angered her, but it also grieved her deeply.

"I know Lakesh asked you to stand aside so Kane and I could bond," Rouch went on acidly, "but you didn't. I had to make my own plans. You left me no choice."

Forcing a note of calm into her voice, Brigid asked, "Are you saying this charade of yours—running away, nearly getting Auerbach maimed, putting Kane at risk—is my fault?"

Rouch's lips pursed. "I'm saying that since you refused to cooperate with the breeding program, adjustments had to be made. I made them."

"And part of those adjustments included duping poor Auerbach? You had this in mind for a while, didn't you, when you first seduced him? You used him."

Rouch shook her head in mock pity. "How can a woman who's supposed to be so intelligent be so naive? Of course I used him. Everybody gets used. Fact of life, Baptiste."

"What if Standing Bear had seriously injured Kane—or killed him? What would that have done to your adjustments?"

Rouch's perfect teeth flashed in a grin. "I would've adjusted to that. My life here wouldn't have been too bad. More primitive than I care for, but I already led Standing Bear around by his cock. I'm an adaptable girl."

"So I've been told," Brigid said with undisguised contempt. "That's why you were brought into the redoubt."

Beth-Li Rouch wasn't offended by the observation. Agreeably, she said, "One of the reasons, anyway. Besides, I knew Kane wouldn't let that stupe savage beat him—not with me as the prize."

Brigid's anger slowly faded, replaced by a weary resignation. She wanted to sit down, but the notion of doing so in front of Rouch repulsed her. The dark-haired woman noticed the change in her posture and attitude.

"You think you know Kane," she declared. "But you don't, not really. Underneath it all, he's just as savage as Standing Bear. You're wasting your time trying to convince yourself that he's anything other that what he is—a cold-hearted killer, all iron and ice. Think about all the people he's chilled, all the throats he's cut. You two could never have a future. Deep down, you know it."

Brigid turned away, running her fingers through her tangled red-gold mane. Rouch softened her tone, striving to sound reasonable, if not sympathetic. "I told you before I don't care if you screw him. But stop standing in the way of the program. Let me carry his seed, bear his children. Stop fighting me. There's no way you can win. Trust me on that."

Brigid glanced back over her shoulder. "Are you threatening me?"

Rouch angled a cryptic eyebrow. "More or less. You don't want me as an enemy, Baptiste. Not only do I have Lakesh backing me up—I won't fight fair. I'll get you out of the way one way or the other."

She took a deep breath and whispered fiercely, *"Stop fighting me!"*

Thrusting aside the triangular piece of hide serving as the door flap, Brigid said flatly, "I'm tired of fighting period, let alone you, Beth-Li."

Brigid stepped out into the cool air of early evening. She looked up at the vast canopy of sky, at the fiery colors of sunset tracing the horizon. The gray blue tint of the high sky reminded her of Kane's eyes—a little cold perhaps, but with a hint of passion burning behind them.

Following a burst of laughter, she found Kane, Grant and Auerbach sitting cross-legged around a cook fire with half a dozen warriors. A rabbit turned slowly on a spit over the flames.

Kane talked animatedly, using elaborate hand gestures. Sky Dog translated, and the Indians responded with grins and appreciative laughter. Even Grant's normally truculent expression had softened into a smile of enjoyment. Only Auerbach looked uncomfortable, eyeing the fire apprehensively, no doubt imagining the flames dancing on his groin.

Brigid drew near enough to overhear Kane's account of

shooting down a Deathbird during their escape from Co-baltville. She vividly remembered how the chopper had pursued their old rattletrap Sandcat as Domi desperately tried to avoid the .50-caliber bullets and rockets.

She had no problem recollecting the terror she felt, the almost suffocating sense of doom. Judging by Kane's bright eyes and laughing tones, the ground-to-air duel had been a lark, a grand, exhilarating adventure. The Indians apparently felt the same way, although Standing Bear's face wore a skeptical expression.

Savage warriors all, she thought bleakly. Although she stood only a few yards away from the cluster of men, she felt separated from Kane by a distance that could not be measured. At that moment, she might as well have been looking at a complete stranger.

She couldn't help but wonder what the Indians' reactions would be if Kane provided all the details of their flight, the truth behind it, or at least the truth as they understood it.

Even after all this time, Brigid still couldn't fully accept what she had learned about the nukecaust, or about the Archon Directorate. Until eight months ago, neither Kane, Grant nor Brigid had even the vaguest inkling of the existence of the Archons, let alone the fact that they had influenced the course of history for thousands of years.

On the face of it, Kane seemed the least likely to have stumbled over the evidence of their shadowy existence and presence in human affairs. After all, he and Grant had served for many years as Magistrates, enforcers of the ville laws and baronial prerogative.

All Magistrates followed a patrilineal tradition, assuming the duties and positions of their fathers before them. They didn't have given names, but instead took the surname of the father, as though the first Magistrate to bear the name were the same man as the last.

As Magistrates, the courses their lives followed had been charted before their births. They were destined to live, fight and die, usually violently, as they fulfilled their oaths to impose order upon chaos, obeyed the edicts of the barons who ruthlessly stamped out any sign of rebellion.

The steady course of Kane's life was interrupted by what seemed a simple enough Mag raid. A slagger named Reeth was smuggling outlanders into Cobaltville with bogus ID chips. Their squad's mission was to flash-blast the Mesa Verde slaghole and serve a termination warrant on Reeth.

The simple op turned ugly when Kane realized Reeth's operation was too big, too well equipped for a small-time slagger to pull off. His armament and tech were state-of-the-art, and he even had a computer system, a piece of hardware that was usually reserved for the ultra-elite administrators of Cobaltville.

The Mags' commanding officer, Salvo, served the termination warrant before Reeth could be questioned, but not before Kane saw a strange device the slagger called a gateway. Due to his dislike of Salvo and his rising suspicions, Kane palmed a computer disk.

Back at Cobaltville, Kane found the disk was specially encrypted, designed to defy normal unlocking procedures. Instead of shrugging the matter off, he was consumed by the mystery posed by the disk.

He sought out Brigid Baptiste, a high-ranking archivist in the Historical Division. Despite the common misconception, archivists were not bookish, bespectacled pedants. They were primarily data-entry techs, albeit with high-security clearances. Midgrade archivists like Brigid were editors.

Her primary duty was not to record predark history, but to revise, rewrite and oftentimes completely disguise it on behalf of the ruling elite. Like Kane and Grant, she had believed the responsibility for the nukecaust and its subsequent horrors lay with humankind as a whole. For many years, she had never questioned that article of faith.

As she rose up the ranks, promoted mainly through attrition, she was allowed greater access to secret predark records. Though these were heavily edited, she came across references to something called the Totality Concept, to devices called gateways, to projects bearing the code names of Cerberus and Chronos.

Then one day, over a year before, she was covertly contacted by a secret, faceless group calling itself the Preservationists. Over the following few months, she slowly understood that the Preservationists were archivists like herself, scattered throughout the network of nine villes. They were devoted to preserving past knowledge, to piecing together the unrevised history of not only the predark, but also the post holocaust world.

Whoever the Preservationists were, they had anticipated her initial skepticism and apprehension. To show their good faith, she found an unfamiliar disk in her work area one morning. On the disk was the *Wyeth Codex,* and that began her secret association with the Preservationists.

Though Kane could not have known it, Brigid Baptiste was the perfect person for him to have contacted. She was able to unlock the disk he'd retrieved from Reeth's slaghole, and the digital data held far more questions than answers.

Her curiosity aroused, Brigid didn't devote much time to contemplating the consequences of delving into top secret historical files. The results of her illegal research yielded frightening revelations about the Totality Concept, the Cerberus mat-trans network and the Archon Directorate, which seemed to have been involved in manipulating the course of human history.

Unbeknownst to either Kane or Brigid, Salvo had placed both of them under surveillance. While Brigid was charged with sedition, being a Preservationist and illegally delving into the database, Kane was taken before a tribunal presided over by none other than Baron Cobalt himself.

The baron told him that since the end of World War II, elements within the American, Russian and British governments concealed their covert contacts with a mysterious race of entities known as the Archons. The Archons had a standard operating procedure that they had employed for thousands of years: they established a privileged class dependent upon them, and that elite class in turn controlled the masses of humanity for the Archons.

Kane was further informed that his father was a member of the Trust, and therefore he must accept the tradition, the honor offered to him. Like his father, he would be a member of the elite that ruled society in secret. Other members of the Trust included high officers from all the divisions, including old Lakesh. Henceforth, like them, he would be working for the evolution of humankind.

Though Kane accepted the offer and even agreed when Salvo told him that Brigid Baptiste must be executed, he didn't believe a word of what Baron Cobalt and the other members of the Trust had told him. Nor was he about to allow Brigid Baptiste to be executed because of his own impulsive curiosity.

After he rescued the archivist, Kane, Grant and Brigid fled Cobaltville, aided by Domi, the outlander girl who'd been forced to work as a sex slave for Cobaltville Pit boss Guana Teague.

Though pursued by Magistrates, they managed to make it to the mat-trans gateway at Mesa Verde and transport themselves elsewhere. When they arrived in Redoubt Bravo, once the base for the Cerberus Project, Lakesh was waiting for them with the group of exiles he'd assembled from other villes.

There, Lakesh told them of his history, his great age, and filled in the gaps in their knowledge. He was, in fact, one of the original people who had worked on the Totality Concept projects, specifically Overproject Whisper, which included Chronos and Cerberus. Shortly after the nuke-caust, he spent over a hundred years in cryogenic stasis in an installation known as the Anthill Complex before he was revived to help the Archon Directorate's plans for human-ity reach fruition. He told them how the nukecaust was not supposed to have happened, but the misuse of the Totality Concept projects caused a probability-wave dysfunction.

Horrified, Kane, Brigid and Grant demanded to know why the Archons would allow such cataclysmic events to occur. Lakesh detailed the long-range genetic-engineering program in which all nonessential humans were to be reduced to an expendable minority, existing only to be exploited as slave labor and as providers of genetic material. Lakesh described the Hybrid Dynasty to them, telling them that the previous three generations of barons were human-Archon hybrids under the control of the Archon Directorate.

None of them were convinced by Lakesh's explanation, particularly Kane, until they were introduced to a permanent guest of Cerberus—an Archon named Balam. The creature triggered a primal, xenophobic response in all of them. It communicated telepathically, and according to Lakesh, its mind was somehow linked with all its fellow Archons on a very subtle, unconscious level.

When Lakesh then showed them Nightmare Alley, which offered overwhelming horrific proof of advanced genetic experiments performed by the Archon Directorate, the evidence was undeniable.

Active opposition to the Archon Directorate and the ville network was their only option, since all of them had been reclassified as outlanders. Nonpersons, they could never return to Cobaltville and had been the focus of numerous search parties. Exile had become their way of life.

Brigid's thoughts returned to the present as Kane lifted his hands, index fingers outstretched and made rapid stuttering noises, imitating the reports of autoblasters. In midstutter, he suddenly glanced up and saw Brigid standing there.

His sound effects trailed off, and he said to Sky Dog, "I'll be back in a minute."

As he rose, the warriors groaned in disappointment. "Grant can finish it," Kane said with a grin. "He was there, too."

"Right," Grant drawled. "In my version, *I'll* be the hero."

Kane joined Brigid, taking her by the elbow and guided her away from the fire. "Sorry," she said. "I didn't mean to interrupt the story hour."

He chuckled. "Diplomacy again. These guys judge your worth by how daring you are. I embellished a little, but they expect that."

Brigid gazed up into his face. The knife cut on his cheek was a bright red line, like a streak of war paint. "You're enjoying this, aren't you?"

"It beats sitting around Cerberus waiting for Lakesh to concoct another crisis that only we can deal with."

Brigid didn't reply.

"Did Beth-Li tell you why she and Auerbach did this?"

"Yes. She was trying to get your attention. She took Auerbach along as a pack mule and to make you jealous."

He stood silently even after Brigid had completed the story. "Well?" she prompted.

Kane knuckled his eyes. "Fits with what Auerbach said." He heaved a deep sigh. "Something is going to have be done with Rouch. She's becoming a menace."

"I agree."

"Any suggestions?"

"Cooperate," answered Brigid quietly.

Dropping his hands from his eyes, Kane stared at her incredulously.

"Don't look so astonished," she said crossly. "There's no point to this game any longer. It's getting dangerous, not much different than the macho game you played with Salvo."

At the mention of his mortal enemy and genetic twin, whose driving passion in life was to humiliate and control him, the incredulity in Kane's eyes gave way to anger.

"You're psychoanalyzing again," he snapped. "You know how I hate that, Baptiste."

"Hate it or not, you'd better accept it. You don't find Beth-Li repulsive. The only reason you've been so stubborn is because Lakesh created the project. You don't like the idea of being controlled."

Kane glanced away and cleared his throat. "That's not the only reason, Baptiste. You know that."

She nodded. "Probably not. The other reasons are all mixed up in you—guilt over my exile, feeling responsible for ruining my life, turning me into an outlander. You know that's not true, Kane. Lakesh had already set me up when he slipped me the *Wyeth Codex* anonymously. He had already planned to bring me into Cerberus. You just bumped up his timetable. I would've been part of Cerberus by now even if you hadn't involved yourself."

Pushing out a deep breath, Brigid said, "You spent most of your life taking orders and you'll be damned if you'll obey this one, even if all you have to do is make love to a beautiful woman and impregnate her."

Kane uttered a mirthless chuckle and kicked at a loose stone. "It's nice that everything I do is so simple and transparent."

Brigid shook her head in annoyance. "I'm tired of dealing with this, Kane, of being dragged into a triangle, of talking around it. I'm barren, all right? The radiation I was exposed to in Mongolia damaged my reproductive system, maybe inflicted irreparable harm to my chromosomal structure."

Kane didn't look at her. His gaze was fixed on a faraway point in the lengthening shadows.

"You knew, didn't you?" Brigid demanded.

"Rouch made a comment about it a while back," he answered faintly. "So I asked Lakesh. I figured you'd tell me when you were ready."

The two people stood in silence as twilight deepened around them.

"Thank you for respecting my privacy," Brigid said after a few moments.

"Is your condition permanent?"

"I don't know. DeFore doesn't know, either. She wants to begin a regimen of biochemical therapy, but there hasn't been enough time.

"Now you know, Kane. There's no reason to oppose the program out of misplaced loyalty to me. I promised Lakesh I wouldn't interfere and I'm as good as my word."

She made a move to step around him, but Kane laid a gentle hand on her arm. *"Anam-chara."*

She stiffened, but not to pull away from his touch. Nor did she turn to face him. Both of them had learned the old Gaelic term, which meant "soul friend," during the mission to Ireland. Morrigan, the beautiful, sightless telepath had told Brigid that she and Kane were *anam-charas*, but she had never found out where he had picked up the word. She decided to ask him.

"Did Morrigan teach you that, what it meant?"

"Yes, and other things I never told you about."

She repressed a shiver, but it was not due to the gusting breeze. In a voice barely above a whisper, she asked, "Like what?"

Kane didn't respond for such a long time she wondered if he had heard her. Then in a low, almost embarrassed voice, he said, "You saw Morrigan kiss me on the deck of the *Cromwell*."

"I don't know about that. I know I saw you kissing each other."

Kane uttered a soft, irritated sound. "Whatever. She said you would forgive me because you're my *anam-chara*. I told her there was nothing to forgive because there was nothing between you and me."

Kane took a breath, then said in a rush of words, "Morrigan said there was much between us, much we had to forgive, much we had to understand. Much to live through. And then she said, 'Always together.'"

Brigid didn't move, but she asked, "Did you believe her?"

"I didn't know what to believe, Baptiste. I guess I'm scared to believe it."

"Why?"

He didn't answer and Brigid knew why. Both of them remembered the mat-trans jump to Russia, which had gone very, very wrong. Both of them had suffered from extreme jump sickness, the primary symptoms of which were nausea and frighteningly vivid hallucinations.

But in that instance, they had shared the same hallucination or revelation—that Brigid and Kane were somehow joined by spiritual chains, linked to each other and the same destiny.

Kane was more pragmatic and literal-minded than Brigid, so the concept that their souls had been together for a thousand years or more seemed so unbelievable he feared to consciously examine it. However, he didn't believe in coincidence, either, so the fact they had shared the same hallucination—or revelation—couldn't be ascribed only to jump sickness.

"Why?" she asked again.

He groped for a response that sounded reasonable, but couldn't find one. "Because it might be true."

Carefully, Brigid disengaged herself from his hand, turned and looked levelly into his face. She felt a jolt when she saw the genuine pain, longing and confusion in his eyes. She knew it was only a dim reflection of her own.

"Believe what you want to," she said in a low voice. "But believe it because you feel it. Don't worry about how I enter into it. In the grand scheme of things, we don't owe one another anything. You don't need my permission to participate in Lakesh's plan. You never did, even if Beth-Li thinks otherwise. One thing I don't need is another enemy."

"What makes you say that?"

"Beth-Li told me she'd get me out of the way one way or the other. Like you said, at this point we can't afford to have anyone but allies at our doorstep. Go to Beth-Li or don't go, but remove me from the decision."

With that, Brigid walked away from him. She skirted the cooking fire, then wended her way between the tepees.

Kane watched until her figure was swallowed up by the creeping shadows of dusk. He stood for a long time, despising the painful heaviness in his chest and the quivering in his belly. Then, turning on his heel, he marched through the village.

Beth-Li didn't look surprised when he pushed his way into her lodge. She had changed from the fringed smock to her khakis and greeted him with a knowing smile.

"You talked to Baptiste?" she inquired, gliding toward him on bare feet.

He nodded.

"Good. It took a little doing, but I think she finally saw reason. Is she stepping aside?"

"Yes." Kane bit out the word.

Rouch sidled up against him, sliding one arm around his waist. Her other hand caressed his thigh, then her fingernails dug through the fabric of his trousers, lightly gripping his manhood. She stood on tiptoes, moist lips parting, her dark eyes bright with desire.

"I haven't thanked you yet for rescuing me from that stinking savage," she whispered. "Let me do it now."

Gently, Kane cupped her rounded cheeks between his hands, bending his head to nuzzle the side of her face, touching her delicate earlobe with the tip of his tongue. She leaned her body into his, breathing, "Kane…"

Into her ear, he whispered, "Beth-Li…if you ever threaten Baptiste again, I'll chill you."

His hands clamped cruelly tight on her face, trapping it between them, squeezing her features, distorting her full lips. Drawing back his head, he glared into her eyes, all the desire washed out of them by sudden tears of pain.

Between clenched teeth, voice so thick with fury it sounded like an animal's guttural growl, he said, "I'll break your beautiful little neck."

He gave her head a hard little jerk to the left, dragging an aspirated cry from her. "As easy as that, Beth-Li."

Kane stared at her for a few more seconds, then pushed her aside and stepped out of the lodge. Releasing his breath in a prolonged hiss, he glanced up at the first stars of the evening. He wished he could be up there among them, far and remote from humanity. At that moment, he wished he were anywhere else, even the Tartarus Pits of Cobaltville. At least life there, though brutal, was simple.

He started walking back toward the cooking fire. On the one hand, he regretted terrorizing Beth-Li. On the other hand, he regretted not simply snapping her neck instead of telling her about it. All he had actually accomplished was to make another enemy, but he was used to that.

ICEBLOOD: 07

Grigori Zakat stood on the open balcony, gazing down into the shadow-streaked valley below as light swiftly drained from the sky. The thin air at such a high altitude rendered the transition from day to night startlingly short and abrupt. Only a brief period of twilight marked the demarcation between sunset and nightfall.

Spring took a long time to arrive on the Byang-thang Plateau, and the dry, almost rarefied air was still frigid. Zakat figured his chest was a shade larger from breathing it these past five months.

His wounds had healed completely. Trai's daily application of herbal poultices and tinctures quickly repaired the tissue damage caused by frostbite. The only reminder of his stab wound was a faint scar high on his belly.

Although Zakat had fully recovered, he kept that fact from Dorjieff and the other monks. Only Trai and Gyatso knew he had regained his strength and powers. He had made them his confidants, although Gyatso was more than that. The shaman had sought out Zakat, not the other way around.

Trai was different. She had been ridiculously easy to seduce, pathetically grateful for a man who treated her as something resembling a human being and not as a bipedal mule or as an outlet for lust. Although only a peasant, she was far brighter than she appeared, despite her illiteracy. She was also passionate, an aspect of her personality Zakat recognized and manipulated.

Gyatso had told him not to concern himself with the other monks, especially the Dob-Dobs. They were distrustful of him, but they feared the power of the black shaman even more. Zakat's mission was to ingratiate himself with Dorjieff.

He touched the wood-and-crystal phallus beneath his robe and began his breathing exercise, deepening and regulating his respiration, opening his chakra points in order to receive the summons from Gyatso. Every night for the past month, he stood at the balcony, preparing his mind for Gyatso's signal that all was in readiness. Night after night, he waited, but the signal had not come. He never questioned the Bon-po shaman. Infinite patience was one of the prime articles of Khlysty faith.

After all, Saint Rasputin had not been accepted by the family of the czar overnight. He had waited, performing trivial miracles to earn first the czarina's trust, then her bed.

It always amused Zakat to think about the haughty Alexandra submitting to the unkempt holy man from western Siberia. Rumors of her affair with Rasputin had been one of the triggers for the October Revolution, when the starving Russian masses finally understood that the royal family were flesh and blood, not gods and goddesses.

Of course, those rumors led to Rasputin's assassination by royal retainers, but he had accomplished his mission nevertheless. In Khlysty texts, it was known as the power of causitry—persuasion and seduction to achieve an objective.

Texts, he thought. Zakat remembered prowling the lamasery late at night and how, in a rear vestry, he found ceiling-high shelves sagging beneath the weight of hundreds of crumbling scrolls. Most of them were Buddhist doctrines, but a very few bore odd, unidentifiable cryptograms. There were drawings of geometric shapes such as trapezohedrons, polyhedrons and eye-confusing spiral patterns.

A cold breeze gusted up from below, ruffling Zakat's hair, grown long during his stay in the Trasilunpo lamasery. He pushed a windblown strand back from his high forehead, once more surprised by the wide streak of white that extended from his hairline over the crown of his head to the nape of his neck. Though Zakat possessed no real vanity to speak of, he was a little disconcerted when he noticed the change. He assumed it was an outward manifestation of his physical sufferings out on the plateau. Sometimes, he suspected it was due to Gyatso's assault of *tsal* energy, but either way, he didn't worry about it.

Compared to the journey upon which he and the shaman were prepared to embark, the change in his hair color meant less than a sparrow's tears. He closed his eyes, tightening his long fingers around the balcony's rail, visualizing again the images Gyatso had imparted to him of the vault beneath the lamasery, the "center of the Earth," as Dorjieff had said.

Dorjieff had lived in Tibet for over twenty years, spending the first five of them crushing bandit bands, ragtag revolutionaries and Chinese expeditionary forces. The brutality and utter ruthlessness he employed had earned him the title of Tsyansis Khan-po, the king of fear. But over the course of the past decade and a half, Dorjieff had himself been ruled by fear.

Zakat smiled thinly, recollecting how Dorjieff had been pathetically grateful to have a fellow countryman as first a patient, then as a guest. He still retained a few tatters of patriotism and, when drunk, which was often, would sing the old motherland songs—songs that had ceased to have any meaning nearly two centuries ago when the terrible fire had swept over the face of the planet.

Whatever past accomplishments had earned him a high rank in District Twelve had been drowned in a sea of wine and self-indulgence years before. The king of fear was now a fat, pompous drunkard and, by way of Gyatso's thinking, an utter coward.

Zakat didn't completely agree with that assessment. Cowards were not admitted into District Twelve, and if Dorjieff was fearful of the power pent-up in the vault, it was born of a need to protect Mother Russia and what remained of humanity.

Zakat cared little for Mother Russia and even less for the masses of humankind. The primary reason he had volunteered for duty in the Black Gobi was the opportunity to seize the power that had so obsessed the late Colonel

Piotr Sverdlovosk. He had never learned the source of that obsession, but Gyatso claimed whatever was buried in the ruins of Kharo-Khoto was nothing compared to what lay in the subterranean vault.

After five months, Grigori Zakat still wasn't certain what Gyatso truly represented. The Bon-po religion in which he held high status predated Tibet's conversion to Buddhism by five hundred years. Buddhists sought to exterminate the Bon-po exponents, decrying it as an occult sect that followed the left-hand path of black sorcery, and accusing it of practicing rituals that required human flesh and blood.

He and Gyatso shared a common link there, both adepts and adherents of outlawed religions, both forced to conceal their beliefs and faith.

But Gyatso was something other than a priest, and Zakat was not sure what. Dorjieff had referred to him as an emissary, but had never expanded on the comment. Gyatso dropped only the broadest of hints, promising that all would be revealed once the vault was taken.

The strange, almost empathic bond Zakat shared with the Bon-po shaman did not allow him to receive actual thought images, only emotional resonances. Always those emotions swirled with determination, touched with anger and a sense of betrayal.

Why Gyatso felt that Dorjieff had broken faith with him was never made clear to Zakat, but he entertained his own suspicions. The old Russian had promised to deliver something to Gyatso—an object, a symbol, a birthright—and then reneged. Whatever the object actually was, Zakat always received the confusing impression of a dark, yet somehow shining trapezo-hedron.

Suddenly, a cold cobweb seemed to lightly stroke his mind, then creep down the base of his spine. The touch instantly vanished, leaving the imprint of a single word: *Now.*

Zakat left the balcony, closing and double-latching the door to cut off even the most unlikely means of escape. He strode through the sleep-stilled halls of the lamasery, his yak-skin boots making only the faintest whisper of sound on the stone floor. The cold gray corridor was lit by pine-knot torches sputtering in wall brackets. The overpowering stench of resin and wood smoke had sunk deep into the stonework.

He walked through the assembly hall, keeping close to the bare wall. The roof beams overhead were exquisitely adorned with images of saints and demons. At the right side of the room was a low table at which a dozen lamas sat murmuring over ancient Buddhist texts hand printed on parchment. A monk lifted his face from the scroll and scowled at the intrusion, but said nothing.

Zakat passed through a narrow doorway on the far side of the chamber and into a short stretch of hallway. Turning a corner, he heard a pained, feminine cry and he knew just where to find Dorjieff.

He walked down the gloomy corridor to the closed door at the far end of it. Grasping the handle, he turned it and carefully shouldered the door open.

He saw Trai's fragile frame bent half over the top of an ornately carved oaken desk. Her trousers had been torn away and lay wadded up on the floor. The face she turned toward Zakat showed the first swellings of a welt. Tears glistened on her cheeks.

Dorjieff stood grunting behind her, grasping her buttocks. Though he still wore his silken tunic, his pants were down about his pale hairy legs. On his bearded, drunken face was a dreamy expression.

It took his wine-addled senses a moment to register Zakat's presence. Gazing blearily in his direction, he belched and burbled, "Comrade…be with you in a moment…just a moment…."

Trai uttered a faint cry of helpless rage. Zakat strode toward Dorjieff, giving his right wrist a little shake. The bone-handled knife dropped from his belled sleeve into his palm.

Reaching over with his left hand, he grasped Dorjieff's beard and yanked. The big man had no choice but to stumble in Zakat's direction or have his beard pulled out by the roots. A bellow of pain and rage started up his throat. His foam-flecked lips writhed.

Zakat pressed the flat of the blade against his lips, stifling the cry. The cutting edge sliced into the thick flange of flesh between his nostrils. A thin film of bright red blood sheeted over Dorjieff's face. He gasped, coughing and choking as it sprayed up his nasal passages.

Dorjieff staggered back, clapping his hands to his face, his pants dropping around his ankles. He sat down heavily on the floor, a squeal of shock bursting from his mouth, crimson spraying out in a fine mist.

Trai pushed herself up from the desk, groping for her trousers, but blinded by her tears, she collapsed sobbing against Zakat. He put a comforting arm around her quaking shoulders.

Dorjieff gaped up at Zakat in total incredulity, then with a mounting rage. He managed to sputter, "You Khlysty scum bastard, I'll have you scourged, your skin peeled off, toss you naked and blind out onto the plateau! You're nothing but a filthy *khampa!*"

Mildly, Zakat said, "I am not one of the diseased robbers you drove from this land when you truly were Tsyansis Khan-po. Things have changed."

Dorjieff's bloody face contorted in shame, then fury. At the top of his lungs, he roared, "Gyatso! *Gyatso!*"

Zakat didn't hear or see the Bon-po shaman enter the room. The bio-psionic field in the chamber shifted ever so slightly and subtly, and Gyatso stood flanking Zakat.

Blowing scarlet drops from his lips, Dorjieff blurted, "Gyatso, this man is a viper in our midst. He endangers our pact. Deal with him."

The black-turbaned man didn't blink or even appear to breathe.

Fear began to shine in Dorjieff's eyes. "Gyatso! Deal with him!"

Gyatso inclined his head toward Zakat. "Shall we proceed, Tsyansis Khan-po?"

Dorjieff's mouth dropped open, his labored breathing inflating tiny blood bubbles on his lips. His stricken eyes flickered back and forth between the two men. Terror swallowed up the disbelief. Twice he tried to speak before managing to stammer, "You betrayed me? Gyatso? *Me?*"

"You betrayed yourself," the slightly built man replied in a silky whisper. "Or rather, your fear betrayed you when you allowed it to reign over you. When that happened, you abdicated your title."

Zakat cocked his head to one side, beaming down into Dorjieff's red-smeared face. "The king is dead, Dorjieff. Long live the king."

He gestured with the knife. "On your feet. You still have a service to perform to your monarch."

Dorjieff didn't move, staring glassy-eyed, still grappling with the words spoken by Gyatso. Blood clung to the matted hair of his beard in gummy strands.

Zakat's lips tightened, and he gently pushed Trai aside, transferring the knife to his left hand. He reached inside his robe with his right and withdrew the stubby Tokarev automatic. He loudly cycled a round into the chamber.

Not aiming the pistol, he said, "I won't kill you, old man. But I'll trim that peg of yours for the entertainment of Trai, even though it's a small target."

The threat brought Dorjieff around, and he made a convulsive movement to pull up his pants and conceal his wilted organ. Groaning, he lumbered to his feet, swaying from side to side. Zakat pointed with the Tokarev toward the door. "Take us."

"Take you?" he repeated in a dead voice. "What are you talking about? Take you where?"

Zakat grinned. "Directly beneath the center of the Earth. To the vault."

"The vault where the stone is kept," Gyatso said. "The stone."

The terror of those two words flooded Dorjieff's face. He echoed, "The stone?"

"The stone of Sirius," Zakat said. "The stone of Allah, of Solomon, the stone of the Eight Immortals." He dropped his voice to a whisper. "The key to Agartha. The Chintamani Stone."

With the utterance of the name, Dorjieff's nerve broke. He turned and attempted to dash across the room, tugging desperately at his pants.

Zakat didn't shoot at him. "Gyatso," he stated, his tone chillingly neutral.

There was a splitting, echoing snap, and a plaited length of oiled leather looped like a streak of fire around Dorjieff's ankles. The man fell heavily, face first, to the stone floor. The air went out of his lungs with an agonized grunt.

The man was too frightened to be outraged over the assault to his dignity. He allowed himself to be dragged to his feet by Zakat, then stood motionless as Gyatso uncoiled the whip from his throbbing ankles and hooked it on his belt.

As Dorjieff shambled to the door like a sleepwalker, Zakat turned to Trai. "Stay here until I send for you."

She ducked her head, adoration shining out of her wet black eyes. "As you wish, Tsyansis Khan-po."

Gyatso and Zakat manhandled Dorjieff out into the narrow hallway, pushing him around several sharp curves. The corridor broadened, and at its end stood an immense granite door with a dragon carved in bas-relief coiled across it. Torches in wall sconces flared smokily on either side of it.

With slitted eyes, Zakat studied the recessed lintel, the threshold and the fluted jambs.

"Open this."

Dorjieff's tongue touched his blood-coated lips. "If I do not?"

"Then you will die, as will every monk and serving boy in the monastery."

Dorjieff stepped to the door. He pushed at the stone moulding in a certain place, and a small square of stone flipped open. Beneath it was a small hole, its sharp angles showing it was man-made. Raising his right fist, the bearded man pressed the stone of his ring into it. A loud metallic click echoed in the corridor, as of a hinged spring snapping open.

Very slowly, the heavy slab of stone swung inward at the top. It was precisely balanced on pivots oiled with animal fat. The opening beyond was very dark, shrouded with musty-smelling shadows.

"Lead the way." Zakat prodded the bearded man with the short barrel of the Tokarev.

For a moment, Dorjieff didn't move. "The time is not nigh. The prophecies have not been fulfilled."

"So you have been saying for years," Gyatso said. "The

fact that a new Tsyansis Khan-po has arrived proves the time is indeed nigh."

In a low, scholarly tone, Zakat stated, "From Milarepa's *Hundred Thousand Songs for the Wise*—'That which is held within the heart of the aged king of the East will be taken by the new king fallen from the Western skies.'"

In a hollow, whispery voice, Gyatso said, "And did he not fall from the skies?"

When Dorjieff didn't reply, the black-turbaned man spun him around and pushed him into the gloom beyond the portal. The firelight from the corridor barely penetrated into the murk. Dorjieff walked slowly along the passageway past walls covered with silken, painted *thang-ka*, faded tapestries depicting the lives of various lamas and Buddhas.

With Grigori Zakat digging the bore of the pistol into his left kidney, Dorjieff descended crude stairs hewed out of rock. Ahead and below glowed a dim aurora. The stairway ended in a bowl-shaped chamber. The light shone from a dozen animal-tallow candles in brackets around the curving rock walls.

Drawn on the cavern floor with colored powders was a large *kyilkhor* diagram, a triangular form designed to ensnare Dre, messengers of death. Dorjieff carefully stepped around it. Zakat deliberately scuffled his feet through the intricate lines.

On either side of the cavern, two life-size effigies crafted out of stone faced each other. The statue of a cherubic-faced man squatted cross-legged in the Buddhist attitude of meditation. The image was of Tsong-ka-po, founder of the Trasilunpo monastic order.

The other statue was of a ten-armed monstrosity, wearing a diadem of grinning human skulls above a leering, tusked face. It was Heruka, one of the many wrathful manifestations of the Buddha.

Hanging between the pair of stone effigies was a number of wilted but brilliantly colored tapestries, all bearing twisting *kyilkhor* geometric designs. Gathering a handful of fabric in his right hand, Zakat jerked hard, ripping it loose from the crossbar. The ancient cloth tore easily, and dust puffed up around it in a cloud. In an alcove beyond, a bank of electronic equipment followed the horseshoe shape of the stone walls. Lights flickered on consoles, and the faint hum of power units sounded like a swarm of distant insects.

In the center of the cavern stood a six-sided chamber, all the walls of the same glassy, translucent substance. They had a murky, purplish tint.

The color of twilight, Zakat thought with a half smile.

He turned to face Dorjieff, whose knees had acquired a definite wobble. "A quantum-interphase matter-transfer inducer, part of the old Szvezda Project. The only aspect of the American Totality Concept fully shared with the Soviet Union."

Dorjieff was beyond surprise, but he asked, "How did you know that?"

"How do you think?" Zakat snapped contemptuously. "Have you become so besotted you've forgotten the prime directive of District Twelve, why it was organized over twenty years ago?"

Dorjieff did not answer. With a sleeve, he dabbed gingerly at the blood still flowing over his lips.

"The primary function of District Twelve is to secure any and all predark technology, particularly that related to the Totality Concept," Zakat recited flatly. "Though its parameters have expanded somewhat over the last decade, that was its initial operational protocol. Officially, you may have been dispatched here to keep your eye on China, but you were actually following up on a fragment of damned data. Is that not so?"

Dorjieff blinked in surprise. "Damned data" was a coded reference to predark intel of the highest security classification, less than fact but more than rumor.

"Answer me."

Dorjieff nodded. "Yes."

Zakat gestured with the Tokarev. "Show us what that data led you to."

Dorjieff slowly shuffled past the statue of Heruka. Hidden behind its broad base and draped with a shroud of black cloth rose a stone pillar some four feet in height. The bearded man tugged away the cloth, sending up a scattering of dust motes.

The pillar was covered on each side with crudely incised, bizarre faces. The faces were humanoid, but with oversize, hairless craniums, huge, upslanting, pupil-less eyes and tiny slits for mouths. Eight of the faces were arrayed around the perimeter of the pedestal.

Atop the pillar rested a box of hammered silver, its hinged lid thrown back. The box was lined by a dusty layer of red silk. Inside was an asymmetrical shape, a dark spherical object six inches around.

Both Gyatso and Zakat stepped to the pedestal and stared at the ovoid within the box. It was a nearly black polyhedron, with purplish striated highlights and many flat, pitted surfaces, like the facets of a crystal. It didn't touch the bottom of the box, but hung suspended by eight delicate silver wires extending from the container's inner walls.

Zakat noticed the fascination the stone exerted upon the Bon-po shaman. A smile tugged at the corners of his lipless mouth, and his eyes glittered with an emotion Zakat couldn't identify.

"This is the stone intended to impose order on chaos," said Zakat flatly. "And to hold forth a key to the arcana of the Eight Immortals of Agartha."

"Yes," Dorjieff confirmed.

"This is but a fragment of a larger piece, cut and broken ages ago. It was originally a trapezohedron, was it not?"

"Yes."

"Other than the piece once kept in the Ka'aba of Mecca, this is the largest fragment in the world."

"Yes."

"And there is one other, smaller piece somewhere."

"Yes."

"Where?"

Dorjieff wagged his head, bullishly, from side to side. "That I do not know."

"What do you know?"

Dorjieff bowed his head, his voice a wheezing rasp. "I came to this lamasery in search of something else. I found the stone. And far, far more."

Very slowly, as if his tongue were suddenly heavy as lead, Dorjieff continued, "I was privy to damned data which I'm sure was withheld from you. Some twenty years ago, District Twelve was much smaller, comprising only a handful of officers. A discovery was made among our predark intelligence archives, and District Twelve expanded its duties beyond counterintelligence and parochial concerns."

Zakat bristled at the implication he knew less about the inner workings of his organization than a fat drunkard. Scornfully, he said, "Speak then of this discovery."

"There is a force, a power, if you will, whose entire purpose is to subjugate humanity, regardless of nationality. It is very likely they orchestrated the nukecaust, and they may have been responsible for much of Mother Russia's tortured history."

Dorjieff started to point to the metal box, but dropped his hand. Beseechingly, he said, "Comrade, you must understand. I found more than a key, I found an object of power that transcended my orders, overruled my oath to my country and District Twelve. I stayed here to safeguard it, to stand sentry so it could never be used against us."

"Patriotism is a very thin covering for your own avarice," Zakat sneered.

Dorjieff straightened, his shoulders stiffening, as he tried to draw the tatters of his dignity around him like a cloak. "I speak not of patriotism, but of responsibility for what is left of the human race." He nodded toward Gyatso, adding contemptuously, "That hell-spawn is driven by avarice, by worse than avarice. I knew it the moment he arrived here last year."

Gyatso said softly, "I came here to claim my birthright, to hold within my hands the legacy of Agartha. I am the descendant of the Maha Chohan, the ambassador of the nation of Agartha. All this was foretold by prophecy."

Dorjieff snorted, blowing tiny blood droplets. He winced in pain. "A nation you have never seen, Gyatso, one that is more myth than reality. And what little reality may be attached to it is something we should not inter-act with."

"Why conceal a key which unlocks no door?" Gyatso's question sounded as sharp as the crack of his whip. "Why stand guard over the gates to a kingdom of myth?"

Dorjieff did not answer.

Zakat's smile became a chuckle. "You're a very clever dissembler, old man. You should have been a Khlysty priest. Whether Agartha—the Valley of the Eight Immor-tals—exists or not, this stone certainly does."

He lowered his voice to a mock-conspiratorial whisper. "And why is this lamasery equipped with a mat-trans unit, a gateway? It had to have been installed before the nuclear holocaust."

Dorjieff still said nothing.

"That is why you came here," continued Zakat. "That was the piece of damned data you uncovered. You wanted to learn why this machine from Szvezda had been placed here and to find out if it still worked. Following up on ru-mors of a Chinese incursion was only secondary to your mission."

He paused for a tiny tick of time and declared, "I'm not asking you, old man. You needn't say anything. Your stub-born silence gives assent."

Dorjieff's shoulders sloped in resignation. Bitterly, he said, "You've got it all figured out, don't you? Yes, old

Szvezda documents indicated a gateway here, but not the reason for it. I tortured the abbot here for the information, but either he didn't know or he refused to tell me.

"I cannot be sure if the gateway was placed here by our countrymen or others, but my suspicion is that its installation was meant as an escape hatch for either the guardian of the stone—or its rightful owner, if such a one exists."

Gyatso announced coldly, "He stands before you."

Dorjieff forced a derisive laugh. "You're a complete fool, Gyatso. If the stone is a key, it is also like a bomb waiting for a detonator. As you pointed out, some of its facets are missing. It may be incomplete, but it is by no means inert."

"How do you know that?" Zakat demanded.

Dorjieff dragged in a shuddery breath. "Many years ago, I was foolishly arrogant as you. I dared to touch it. Knowledge of its true nature flooded into my mind. I was illuminated."

"No," Zakat corrected snidely, "you were terrified."

"Terror can be a form of illumination. The terror of finally realizing that what man knows about reality is nothing compared to what he doesn't know—or what he may never know. Damned data indeed."

Dorjieff's bushy eyebrows drew together as he glared at Zakat. "This lamasery was built at least six hundred years ago, a continuation of other lamaseries that had existed here for thousands of years. Its sole purpose is to house the stone, to keep it segregated from the other fragments scattered across the world."

"To keep it from being restored to a full trapezohedron?" Zakat inquired.

"To keep the gates of Agartha forever locked?" demanded Gyatso.

"Yes, on both counts. Though there is far more to it than that."

"You believe the stone is a thing of evil?" the shaman challenged.

Dorjieff shook his head. "It is not evil, but it is not good, either. Those are human concepts and the stone is much older than humanity. In its original form, the stone was fashioned by a prehuman race known in various cultures as the Nagas, the Annunaki, the Na Fferyllt. It was believed to be a spiritual accelerator, used to advance the intelligences and perceptions of the first primitive human beings."

Dorjieff swept his arms around the cavern. "As humanity climbed up the ladder of evolution, the stone was treasured by them, worshiped. It crossed strange lands and seas that no longer exist, it sank with Atlantis and was recovered by the forerunners of the Egyptians. It rested in an underground crypt between the paws of the Sphinx before the Flood. It was found aeons later, split by priests and scattered across the Earth."

"Why?" demanded Gyatso. "If it is not a thing of evil, then why hide it from the sight of man?"

"Because it is a window on Agartha—on the black, forbidden things which no one has ever heard of, not even in whispers. You think Agartha is a magical, fabulous kingdom? No, it is a repository of secrets and the seat of five hundred thousand years of man's hidden history."

Zakat glanced toward the purple-tinted walls of the gateway chamber. "The mat-trans must lead to the other facets of the stone."

"Perhaps," replied Dorjieff. "Perhaps not. The device's destination codes are locked on a specific point and have probably been for two hundred years or more. Where that point might be, if it exists any longer, is something I do not know or care to know."

Zakat chuckled. "And there lies the divide between us."

Dorjieff made a rumbling sound deep in his chest. "The stone must be not be made whole again. If you understand what *I* understand, you would flee shrieking from this place, back to the nest of perverts you call a religion."

"And what do you understand?"

"Assume there are people who have been trained to transcend the accepted laws of physics, who wield wild powers that are called—for lack of a better term—magical. Also assume there are ancient objects and places of otherworldly power that these people can access, using their energies as means of control and as weapons."

"And you're saying," ventured Zakat, "that the black stone is such a weapon?"

"I am saying that the forces flowing through it can be used as such. The forces flow through it unto like a tide. If a tide goes in two directions at once, you have a catastrophe that threatens not only the body, but the soul. The human spirit. That is what I safeguard, not this chunk of rock."

Zakat gestured negligently with the Tokarev. "You are a true martyr, old man, though I doubt Trai would testify you are fixated on safeguarding her spirit."

Dorjieff's face darkened in anger. "You understand nothing of the true nature of the stone."

Zakat smiled mockingly. "I believe I understand enough."

Dorjieff's lips drew away from his red-filmed teeth in a snarling grin. "Then do what I did, if you have the courage. Touch the stone," he taunted.

The smile fled from Zakat's face. He did not move.

"You are afraid," said Dorjieff, a note of triumph evident in his voice. "Not that I blame you for it, but how do you intend to command the forces flowing through it if you fear to touch it?"

Zakat wheeled defiantly toward the pedestal. He extended his left hand toward the open box, keeping the Tokarev in his right pointed at Dorjieff. He caught Gyatso's eye, who looked at him uncertainly.

"My faith," he said, more to reassure Gyatso than to challenge Dorjieff, "will protect me."

Dorjieff gusted out a laugh. "That we will see."

Zakat thrust out his hand, his fingers brushing the surface of the black stone. He felt a distinct tingling rushing up his hand, into his wrist, up his arm. He closed his eyes for a second. When he opened them again, he experienced a vertiginous sensation of seeing in two worlds at once—the world of the senses, and the inner world of the black stone.

With his eyes, he saw Gyatso and the box and the cavern.

In the other world, he saw leagues of endless desert sprouting with black monoliths soaring heavenward. He saw towers and walls in the depths of the Earth, an infinite gulf of darkness, of swirling patterns of force locked forever in a symbiotic contest of order against chaos.

A sudden riot of emotion-fraught images exploded in his mind, triggering a terror so wild it was almost ecstasy, and he became aware of a mindless chittering, as of countless voices murmuring at once.

Zakat felt he was being examined, not by the stone, but by observers that used the black polyhedron as a form of sight more acute than the physical.

A jagged skyline appeared in his mind's eye, in which the hulks of buildings reared from a debris-scattered terrain like broken tombstones. Two monoliths, each at least a hundred feet high, rose from the high tumbles of twisted metal and shattered concrete. The dark windows gaped between tangles of creeping vegetation, but astonishingly, shards of glass still glinted here and there. For a dizzy instant, Zakat felt as if he plummeted through the shockscape of ruins, passing around and over the wilderness of rubble.

Then an animal's snouted face snarled into his, a shocking pink tongue protruding from between great yellow fangs. The brownish silver-tipped fur looked matted and mangy, and Zakat realized it was not the face of a living bear, but an example of the taxidermist's art.

His perspective seemed to broaden, and the bear's face receded. He saw a vast room, almost a man-made cavern. In niches behind shattered glass were elks, elephants, rhinoceros, wolves and other extinct species frozen in eternal postures of stalking or pacing.

Zakat felt a persistent tug. Rather than resist it, he traveled down a broad staircase, past a monstrous, pale blue shape tilting down from the ceiling at a ninety-degree angle. He could not identify it, though its sleek bulk and dimensions reminded him of a wingless Tu-114 fuselage.

At the same time, he became aware of a rhythmic vibration, like the beating of an unimaginably gigantic heart.

He found himself floating through a forest of stone, like a geologist's dream. He passed glittering geodes, clusters of the crystals the size of washtubs, mineral formations of all sizes and shapes.

Hidden somewhere among them he felt the pulsing of energy, black yet bright, beckoning him with a siren song of seduction, whispering to him of power and of the price he must pay—

He blinked, snatching his hand back, almost but not quite giving voice to a cry of primal panic.

Dorjieff laughed. "Come now, Comrade. You barely tickled it. Grasp it as I did, hold it within your hand so you may see and feel what I did. And understand."

Zakat despised the shiver that shook his shoulders as he turned to face Dorjieff. "Like I said, I understand enough."

"And like I said, you know nothing," Dorjieff retorted.

"You have nothing more to say, old man," replied Zakat. "You seem to have a problem accepting that. Your position here has been usurped."

With a speed surprising for a man of such bulk and age, Dorjieff lunged forward. All the memories of his training hadn't been drowned in wine, and with two lightning-swift moves, he disarmed Zakat.

Swinging the barrel of the automatic in short half arcs to cover first Gyatso, then Zakat, then Gyatso again, he growled, "You'll die first, you half-breed hell-spawn. As for you, Father Twilight, I will use you for the same kind of target practice you proposed for me. But my hand is not as steady, nor are my eyes as clear as they once were. There will be many near misses. You'll have to be patient with me."

Zakat only smiled. "I am exceedingly patient, Dorjieff. Get on with it."

Dorjieff aimed the pistol at Gyatso, his finger tightened around the trigger, but he did not fire. The gun, his hand and his entire forearm began to tremble, locked in a muscle spasm. He looked in stunned agony at Gyatso, who gazed unblinkingly, serenely at him.

Softly, Zakat said, "What was it you said to me about this half-breed hell-spawn's power? Oh, yes, 'The secret of Bon training consists of developing a power of concentration surpassing even that of men like yourself, who are the most gifted in psychic respects.'"

The sweat of effort beaded on Dorjieff's forehead and streamed into his eyes. He did not, could not blink them. In a crooning whisper, Zakat continued, "I will allow you a limited freedom of movement. You may turn your wrist and lift your arm. Point the gun at your face, won't you?"

Groaning, his entire body shuddering with the strain, Dorjieff did as Zakat requested.

"Very good, thank you. Now, if you will please open your mouth and place the barrel inside of it...?"

A keening wail of terror issued from Dorjieff's lips, but he obeyed, his arm trembling. His mouth gaped wide as he inserted the short barrel of the Tokarev, and his lower teeth rattled against the metal trigger guard.

Affectionately, as if he were speaking to a lover, Zakat whispered, "Will you please pull the trigger? If you pull it, all of this ends."

Dorjieff's hand convulsed. The Tokarev made a popping sound, like the bursting of a balloon in another room. A tiny twist of smoke puffed from his open mouth, followed a microinstant later by a gushing torrent of scarlet. He staggered, limbs flailing, the pistol clattering to the floor.

Dorjieff hit the ground on his back, fingers and feet twitching. He uttered only a liquidy burble before his body stilled.

Zakat turned away, ruefully rubbing the aching spot on the center of his forehead. He knew that without Gyatso's mind augmenting his own force of will, he wouldn't have been able to induce Dorjieff to commit suicide. The old bastard had not lost all of the strength that had earned him the title of Tsyansis Khan-po.

Gyatso nodded, approving the manner in which Dorjieff had been dispatched. "And now?" he asked.

Grigori Zakat reached out and snapped down the lid of the box. It moved easily on its oiled hinges and closed over the stone, the hasp sliding and snapping into the lock. At that sharp click, Gyatso jumped, a sudden fear visible on his face.

Somehow, Zakat knew it was the first time in the memory of the lamasery that the box had been closed. He was suddenly conscious of a formless presence in the cavern—a presence not in the rock walls, but beyond them.

It was a sense of a faraway inhuman intelligence that had instantly become aware of what he had done. Zakat saw nothing, heard nothing, yet he felt a powerful surging of an icy energy. The aura of the cavern was suddenly oppressive, the very air throbbing with menace.

Zakat kept his left hand on the silver lid of the box as he half turned to face Gyatso. "Now we plan and make our final assessment."

Gyatso cocked his head slightly to one side. "Assessment? I do not understand."

"Of the price we must pay for power." Zakat laughed as he turned to glance at Dorjieff's corpse. "It may be more appropriate to say the price we must persuade others to pay."

Three a.m., Lakesh thought sourly. The midnight of the human soul, when the blood trickles at low tide and the heart beats slowly. He remembered reading that more people with terminal illnesses died at three o'clock in the morning than at any other time.

Lakesh rarely slept more than five hours out of twenty-four, so he often found himself alone in the central control complex of the Cerberus redoubt.

He stared reproachfully over the rims of his spectacles at the image of a slavering black hound filling the monitor screen in front of him. Three snarling heads grew out of a single corded neck, their jaws wide open, blood and fire gushing between great fangs. Because the security cameras transmitted in black-and-white and shades of gray, he couldn't see the garish colors of the large illustration on the wall. He'd seen the crimson eyes and yellow fangs enough times over the years, as well as the word written in exaggerated Gothic script beneath it: Cerberus.

Like everything else in the redoubt, the image of the three-headed hound had weathered the nukecaust, the skydark and all the catastrophes that followed.

Built near the close of the twentieth century, the Cerberus installation was a masterpiece of impenetrability. The trilevel, thirty-acre facility was equipped with radiation shielding, and an elaborate system of heat-sensing warning devices, night-vision vid cameras and motion-trigger alarms surrounded the plateau that concealed it.

Lakesh looked up from the canine heads snarling still and frozen on the screen to the huge Mercator-relief map of the world sprawling across the expanse of the facing wall. Pinpoints of light shone steadily in almost every country, connected by a thin, glowing pattern of lines. They represented the Cerberus network, the locations of all functioning gateway units across the planet.

The installation had been built as the seat of the Cerberus process, a subdivision of Overproject Whisper, which in turn had been a primary component of the Totality Concept. At its height, the redoubt had housed well over a hundred people. Now it was full of shadowed corridors, empty rooms and sepulchral silences, a sanctuary for thirteen human beings. There was one other, a fourteenth, but for him—or it, Lakesh was never quite certain—Cerberus was a prison.

Actually, all the redoubts linked to the Totality Concept became prisons after January 19, 2001. That was why Lakesh hadn't opposed the proposal that he be placed in cryonic stasis. Nor was he the only volunteer among the personnel in the Mount Rushmore installation. The resources of the vast facility were already strained, and it had suffered unforeseen damage during the nukecaust. Some measures had to be taken to preserve the command post.

Constructed inside of Mount Rushmore, to serve as both the central Continuity of Government seat, as well as the coordinating station for the Totality Concept redoubts, the so-called Anthill became more of a tomb every day.

Very few of the contingency plans worked, especially after the desperate military personnel remaining in other installations began to arrive by mat-trans unit. After a few months, there were just too many people to support and the jump lines were blocked so no one else could find refuge from the horrors of the rad-blasted landscape.

Life in the Anthill became an endless interlocking chain of crises, one after the other, coming so fast they seemed to trip over each other. The Overproject Excalibur genetic experiments soured, essential machinery broke down, radiation leaked in, the nuclear winter disrupted not only the local ecosystems, but also all those across America. Lakesh remembered wishing he had refused the evacuation order and stayed behind in Cerberus, known also as Redoubt Bravo.

Lakesh shook his head, trying to drive away the memories. There was no point in dredging them up. When he was resurrected fifty years ago, the handful of people remaining in the Anthill complex didn't even remember those days. Only the present and the future mattered, and essential to those were the Archon Directorate's edicts to rebuild the world in a new image.

The final stage of that rebuilding, the Program of Unification, was well under way when Lakesh was awakened. The rallying cry of Unity Through Action had already spread across the length and breadth of the Deathlands by word of mouth and proof of deed. The long forgotten trust in any form of government had been reawakened by the offer of a solution to the constant states of hardship and fear—join the Unification Program sponsored by the barons and never know want or fear again. Of course, any concept of liberty had to be forgotten in the exchange.

Not every human was invited to partake of the bounty of the barons. Only the best of the best were allowed full citizenship. The caste distinctions were based primarily on eugenics. Everyone selected to live in the villes, to serve in the divisions, met a strict set of genetic criteria that had been established before the nukecaust. The original drafters of the Unification Program had in their possession the findings of Overproject Excalibur's Human Genome Project, as well as actual in vitro biological samples. In the vernacular of the time, it was known as purity control.

After the Program of Unification was established, the in vitro egg cells were developed to embryos. Through ectogenesis techniques, fetal development outside of the body eliminated the role of the mother until after birth. The ancient social patterns that connected mother, father and child were broken, a break that was a crucial aspect of the Unification Program. For the program to succeed, the existence of the family as a unit of procreation—and therefore as a social unit—had to be eliminated.

Sometimes, a particular gene carrying a desirable trait was grafted to an unrelated egg, or an undesirable gene removed. Despite many failures, when there was a success, it was replicated over and over, occasionally with variations.

Kane was one such success, developed secretly by Lakesh. At the thought of him, the furrows in Lakesh's forehead deepened into ruts. He knew he shouldn't worry about Kane, or Grant and Brigid. Too many times in the past, Lakesh had forced himself to accept their deaths, only to see them reappear alive, if not completely whole. They seemed to lead exceptionally charmed lives, but like any other resource, luck had a way of running out.

In his more metaphysical moments, he viewed the three of them as a trinity, the human counterparts of the heads of Cerberus, each one symbolizing different yet related aspects of the soul.

It always surprised and comforted him that such contrasting personalities worked so well together. Even Domi, the least disciplined of the redoubt's staff, displayed a remarkable resourcefulness. But there were two residents of Cerberus who didn't quite mesh with the other parts of the efficient machine Lakesh dreamed of constructing.

One of them was Beth-Li Rouch. Initially, she seemed to be the perfect candidate for his plan to expand their sanctuary into a colony. She was certainly beautiful, young and vital. After Lakesh selected her from the personnel records of Sharpeville, he put into motion a variation of the ploy he had used on Brigid Baptiste, Donald Bry and Robert Wegmann: he framed them for crimes against their respective villes.

Lakesh knew it was a cruel, heartless plan with a barely acceptable risk factor, but it was the only way to spirit them out of their villes, turn them against the barons, make them feel indebted to him.

Beth-Li was the only exile he had chosen not for technical knowledge or expertise, but solely because her genetic records indicated that she and Kane would produce perfect offspring, superior in every way.

He had eliminated the other women in Cerberus for a number of reasons. DeFore, though healthy, had a family history of diabetes. Domi was a genetic question mark due to her upbringing in the Outlands, close to hot spots and hellzones, and he didn't need to conduct medical tests to ascertain if she possessed undesirable traits. Her albinism was the most obvious indicator.

Brigid Baptiste of course had a splendid pedigree, as he had reason to know. However, even if she hadn't suffered the accident in Mongolia, Lakesh would not have wanted her to breed with Kane—or anyone, for that matter. Her gifts were unique, far too valuable to have them diverted by pregnancy and motherhood.

It continued to dismay and distress him how Kane opposed his plan to impregnate Beth-Li. Only recently had his resistance become overt. Before that, his refusal to cooperate had been known in predark psychological terminology as passive-aggressive behavior. Therefore, Lakesh had been pleased when Kane volunteered to go in search of Beth-Li and Auerbach.

When the young woman first proposed the scheme to him, Lakesh had been extremely doubtful it would work, and duping poor Auerbach seemed exceptionally coldhearted. But Beth-Li convincingly argued that the harmless deception would prove Kane's feelings for her one way or the other. At length, Lakesh had been persuaded and gave his grudging approval.

Unfortunately, he couldn't object to Brigid's participation in the subsequent search party without arousing suspicion. Kane had never fully trusted him anyway, particularly after he learned about Lakesh's covert involvement in his upbringing. Lately, even Brigid had expressed skepticism about his plan to create a colony.

He ran a hand through his hair, which was the color and texture of ash. Her doubt had disappointed him. Kane, despite his high intelligence, tended to view situations in black-and-white, no doubt a carryover from his life as a Magistrate.

Brigid on the other hand, could swiftly meld thesis, antithesis into a synthesis of diverse, sometimes contradictory concepts. Or at least, she had been capable of that until Kane's simplistic approach to life's vagaries infected her.

The breeding program was a stopgap measure anyway. Lakesh had feverishly held on to the hope that the path to reversing the postnukecaust horrors lay in reversing the probability-wave dysfunction triggered by Operation Chronos in the late twentieth century.

It had proved to be a hope so vain, so futile that he could not think of a word in the several languages he spoke fluently to describe it. The very fabric of space-time itself had been deliberately folded, time squared to prevent any change made in the past from affecting the present.

Lakesh never spoke of his profound despair over the failure of the Omega Path program to anyone. Outwardly, he adopted a cheery demeanor, but inwardly he often wished he was still deep in cryo-sleep, blissfully unaware of what the world had become. His wellspring of hope had run dry, the bucket filled only with the dry dust of defeat.

More than once over the past couple of months, he railed at himself to accept the inevitable, to live out the rest of his life among the Cerberus exiles, taking what joy he could find. With the replacement parts surgically bequeathed to him upon his resurrection in the Anthill, he might have another twenty years of life, thirty if he took care of himself.

But he knew Cerberus couldn't remain hidden for that long. In rare, maniacally optimistic moments, he calculated that the redoubt could be concealed for two years. In his more common, pessimistic moments, he figured it would be fortunate to escape discovery for another six months.

Despite the fresh memory of the tortures inflicted upon him before escaping from Cobaltville, Lakesh couldn't repress a smile at the irony. Salvo had been convinced of the existence of the underground resistance movement called the Preservationists. But the group was an utter fiction, a straw adversary crafted for the barons to fear and chase after, while his true insurrectionist work proceeded elsewhere. Lakesh had learned the techniques of mis- and disinformation many, many years ago while working as Project Cerberus overseer for the Totality Concept.

Salvo had believed that Lakesh was a Preservationist and that he had recruited Kane into their traitorous rank and file. When Baron Cobalt had charged Salvo with the responsibility of apprehending Kane by any means necessary, he presumed those means included the abduction and torture of Lakesh, one of the baron's favorites.

Kane, Grant, Domi and DeFore had rescued Lakesh and taken him back to Cerberus, but in the process increased the odds the redoubt would be found. Although the installation was listed on all ville records as utterly inoperable, and the Cerberus mat-trans unit was slightly out of phase to prevent detection, Lakesh extrapolated that Baron Cobalt would leave no redoubt unopened in his search for him, conducting a hands-on, physical search of every redoubt. Other than rescuing Lakesh, his trusted adviser, from the grasp of people he believed to be murderous insurgents, Baron Cobalt's monumental vanity and ego were at stake. Kane had twice humiliated the baron, and that was two times too many for a creature who perceived himself as semidivine.

Despite recent efforts to lay false trails in other redoubts, Lakesh knew the search would eventually narrow to the plateau in the Bitterroots. His options were limited. If he returned to Cobaltville with a tale of having escaped the Preservationists, he feared the baron's suspicions would turn to him. Even if the baron pretended to believe him, he would certainly mistrust him.

Too many things had happened since the rescue. Kane had mortally wounded Baron Sharpe, and Brigid was suspected of assassinating Baron Ragnar. Baron Cobalt would never accept that a doddering old pedant had managed to wriggle out of the clutches of such ruthless revolutionaries.

Another option, often discussed but never implemented, was to relay ransom demands to Baron Cobalt for Lakesh's safe return. There had not been enough time over the past couple of months to work out the fiendishly complicated details of such a plan.

Lakesh took off his thick-lensed spectacles with the hearing aid attached to the right earpiece, and massaged the bridge of his nose. Everything seemed complicated lately, even getting a decent night's sleep.

Tapping a button on the keyboard, he transferred the vid network to another camera, one trained on a stretch of empty corridor and the door leading to Balam's confinement facility. The creature behind the electronically locked door couldn't be considered as a member of the redoubt. He—or it—was a prisoner, a specimen to be studied, not that more than three years of observation had provided any useful data beyond what had been theorized in the twentieth century.

A sudden flicker of movement on the screen commanded his attention, dragging his thoughts back from the past. Squinting, Lakesh fumbled for his eyeglasses, seating them on his face. He stared at the figure on the screen first in surprise, then with a growing alarm.

Banks, the warder of Balam, shuffled down the corridor. That in itself would not have been an unusual sight except it was 3:30 a.m. and the youthful black man was clad only in his underwear.

As he came closer to the vid lens, Lakesh noticed how his normally trim blocked hair was pushed out of shape on the right side and how his characteristically bright, alert eyes were almost closed, surrounded by puffy bags.

Obviously, Banks had just risen, awakened from a deep slumber. Lakesh expected him to stop before the door leading to the confinement area, punch in the code and enter. The young man's sense of responsibility toward the imprisoned entity always amused and bemused him. He hadn't been selected for the assignment because of his compassion, but because he possessed the psychic strength to block Balam's telepathic influence.

Lakesh assumed that after three years of looking after Balam, of preparing his cattle blood and chemical nourishment, Banks looked at him as something of a pet. Lakesh had never cautioned him about adopting that attitude, inasmuch as no one else in the redoubt could stand to be in Balam's presence for more than a couple of minutes.

Dread rose in Lakesh as Banks passed the door and continued on down the dully gleaming vanadium-alloy corridor. He lifted his bare feet scarcely an eighth of an inch above the floor. He walked out of range of the vid camera.

Lakesh realized there could only be two places for him to be going—the main sec door or the control complex in which he sat. He doubted Banks had the overpowering urge to step outside for a breath of fresh, predawn air, especially in his underwear. The temperature on the plateau, despite the springtime warmth below, hovered only a degree or two above freezing.

Lakesh swiveled his chair around as Banks appeared in the doorway, looking at him dully from beneath half-closed eyelids. Swiftly inspecting his slack-jawed face, Lakesh wondered if the young man was sleepwalking.

Softening his normally reedy voice, Lakesh said, "Good morning, Banks. What gets you up so early?"

Banks remained standing in the doorway, listing slightly from side to side. A half hiss, half whisper passed his lips like steam escaping from a valve. *"Kayyy-nuh."*

Icy fingers tapped the buttons of Lakesh's spine. "What?"

Banks drew in a soft breath and expelled it in another hiss. "Kayyy-nuh. Where…is…Kayyy-nuh?"

The timbre of his voice sounded utterly flat, totally devoid of any emotion whatsoever, which matched the blank expression on Banks's face. Despite his growing apprehension, Lakesh maintained a quiet, level voice. "Do you mean Kane?"

"Where?" came the rustling question.

"He's not here, Banks. You know that."

Lakesh wet his suddenly dry lips and inquired conversationally, "Why do you ask?"

Banks's eyelids drooped lower. "Must Kane speak. Must stone warn. Must warn about."

Lakesh listened, feeling the short hairs on the nape of his neck tingle and lift. Banks spoke slowly, as if he were feeling his away around verbal communication, not quite grasping the rules of grammar and syntax.

With a surge of both fright and fascination, Lakesh used the armrests of his chair to lever himself to his feet. He blurted, "Balam! *You're Balam!*"

Banks didn't react, the blank expression remaining steady. "Kane only. Tell must Kane. Danger in stone. He go. He stop. Only Kayyy-nuh."

The last word stretched out like taffy from between Banks's slack lips. His knees buckled, and his lean body sagged and would have collapsed had he not fallen against the door frame. Lakesh rushed around the computer station and caught him, manhandling him into a chair.

Banks shivered uncontrollably, hugging himself. He lifted his head, looking around in bewilderment, eyes blinking rapidly. They focused on Lakesh. "What's going on? What am I doing here?"

He made a move to rise from the chair, but Lakesh pushed him back gently. Soothingly, he said, "Settle down. You were sleepwalking."

Banks raised questioning eyebrows. "Me? I've never sleepwalked in my life."

"There's a first time for everything," Lakesh replied inanely. "What's the last thing you remember?"

"Going to bed," Banks retorted impatiently.

"No dreams that you recall?"

Lines of concentration crossed the young man's forehead. "Not a dream exactly. I remember waking up for a second, thinking there was a bird in my room. Then I went back to sleep. That must have been hours ago."

Lakesh struggled to keep his voice steady. "What kind of bird?"

Banks frowned. "A big one...not an eagle...all gray feathers. I think it was an owl. Yeah, a great big owl, flying right at my head. Staring at me."

His shoulders shook in a shudder. "I remember waking up. Or at least, I *think* I remember waking up."

"What do you remember most about the owl?"

Banks's expression went vacant. "Its eyes. It had great big black eyes. Huge and slanting. But owls don't have black slanting eyes, do they?"

"Ornithology isn't my field," answered Lakesh, "but no, I don't think they do."

He waited a moment before inquiring, "By any chance, did the owl's eyes remind you of Balam's?"

Banks chewed his lower lip, then ducked his head. His "Yeah" carried a note of anxious realization.

Banks knew almost as much as Lakesh did about Balam and the race he represented, which was very little. The biological studies performed back when the Archons were referred to as PTEs—Pan Terrestrial Entities—were frustratingly incomplete.

At first, the entities were classified as EBEs—Extraterrestrial Biological Entities—but that designation was later amended, since it may have been premature if not erroneous. When everything known about the Archons was distilled down to its basic components, all the scientific minds devoted to the subject could agree on only one thing—they knew very little.

Autopsies performed on bodies recovered in the New Mexico desert in the 1940s proved they were composed of the same basic biological matter as humans, although their blood was of the rare Rh type. They were erect-standing bipeds, with disproportionately long arms and oversize craniums.

The possibility that they originated on another planet was only that, a possibility. Certainly the Archons had never made such a claim, but they never disputed it, either. Nor did they object to being called Archons. The term derived from ancient Gnostic beliefs referring to a parahuman force devoted to imprisoning the spark of the divine in the human soul. Recently, Lakesh began to suspect that an Archon race as such did not exist any longer.

No clear-cut answers about the Archon Directorate had ever presented themselves. Only its agenda was not open to conjecture; it had been the same for thousands of years. Historically, they made alliances with certain individuals or governments, who in turn reaped the benefits of power and wealth. Following this pattern, the Archons made their advanced technology available to the

American military in order to fully develop the Totality Concept. It was the use of that technology, without a full understanding of it, that brought on the nuclear holocaust of 2001.

The apocalypse fit well with Archon strategy. After a century, with the destruction of social structures and severe depopulation, the Archons allied themselves with the nine most powerful barons. They distributed predark technology and helped to establish the ville political system, all to consolidate their power over Earth and its disenfranchised, spiritually beaten human inhabitants.

The goal of unifying the world, with all nonessential and nonproductive humans eliminated or hybridized, was so close to completion there was no point in wondering what the Archons actually were.

Lakesh was no closer to solving the enigma than his ancestors had been thousands of years before when they wrote the *Mahabharta* and the *Ramayana,* which described the coming of the "Sons of the Moon and the Sun" in flying machines called *vimanas.*

He had once believed the solution to both the riddle of the Archons and humanity's mysterious origins lay in ancient religious codices. Now he had come to accept that he could not penetrate a conspiracy of secrecy that had been maintained for twenty thousand years or more.

The few surviving sacred texts contained only hints, inferences passed down from generation to generation, not actual answers. Millennia-old documents that might have held the truth had crumbled into dust or were deliberately destroyed.

Or perhaps no clear-cut truth existed.

Perhaps the so-called Archon Directorate was simply part of humankind's existence, forever and always, not a curse, not a blessing, not a friend or a foe.

Lakesh had seen his first representative of the Archons in the Dulce installation, in the early 1990s. Although he watched the entity for less than a minute, lately he had begun to wonder if that Archon might not have been Balam himself. On their mission to Russia, Brigid, Kane and Grant had learned about the discovery of a creature sealed within a cryonic-stasis canister at the site of the Tunguska disaster. According to their source, he had lain buried for over three decades, until the end of World War II. He was revived, spending several years as a guest of the Soviets before being traded to the West. His name was Balam.

On the British Isles, the self-proclaimed Lord Strongbow confided to them that in the performance of his duties as a liaison officer between the Totality Concept's Mission Snowbird and Project Sigma, he dealt directly with a representative of the Archons, a creature called Balam.

Obviously, Balam had acted as something of a liaison officer himself, an emissary of the Archon Directive throughout the latter half of the twentieth century. In light of that information, Lakesh was working on the hypothesis that Balam might be the only and perhaps last Archon on Earth.

And if Balam was indeed the last of his kind, then there was no Archon Directorate, just like there was no real group called the Preservationists.

Lakesh suppressed a curse. At three o'clock in the morning, all sorts of bleak concepts occurred to him.

However, one empirically proved element about the Archons was their great psionic abilities. Each of the entities was connected to the others through some hyperspatial filaments of mind energy, similar to the collective consciousness of certain insect species. Judging by Balam's distressed reaction when Baron Ragnar was murdered, those filaments even included the hybrids, the Directorate's plenipotentiaries on Earth.

Banks said slowly, "According to the abduction literature you had me study, one of the hallmarks of Archon telepathic contact and control was the mental transmission of a terrestrial animal with unusually large dark eyes."

Lakesh nodded. "Using an owl is a classic."

Voice quivering, Banks stated, "Balam took me over. Possessed me."

"Another term might be *channeled*," Lakesh suggested. "You were asleep, your mental defenses down. We've always wondered about the extent of Balam's psionic abilities—now we know a bit more."

"Why do this to me, after all these years?"

Lakesh tugged at his long nose absently. "The first question is easy to answer. You've been in close proximity with Balam every day for the past three and a half years. He probably knows your thought processes better than anyone else's in the redoubt...perhaps better than any other human being's on Earth. It was child's play for him to insinuate himself into your sleeping mind."

Almost unconsciously, Lakesh began to pace back and forth in front of Banks. "As for why now, he never had a reason before. Through you, he made an effort to initiate communication, something the little bastard has never done."

"Communication?" echoed Banks. "With you?"

Lakesh shook his head. "Oddly, no. With Kane. That's who you—he—asked for."

"How come he didn't know Kane is gone? I knew it."

"Balam didn't, which indicates his psionic manipulation of you was superficial. Which also indicates his abilities have definite limits."

Banks didn't look particularly relieved to hear that. Doubtfully, he said, "So either he can't go very deep or he didn't need to."

His eyes narrowed. "But why ask for Kane? If there's anyone in the redoubt who would pay hard jack for the privilege of breaking Balam's neck, it's Kane."

"True, but Kane is also the only person who ever shook up Balam enough for him to deviate from his patented speech about how superior he and his kind are."

Banks nodded, recollecting his astonishment when Lakesh informed him of the telepathic exchange between Kane and Balam a couple of months before. *Humanity must have a purpose,* Balam had said. *And only a single vision can give it purpose…your race was dying of despair. Your race had lost its passion to live and to create. We unified you.*

"Obviously," Lakesh continued, "something agitated Balam greatly, similar to when he reacted to the murder of Baron Ragnar."

Banks rose quickly to his feet, ruefully eyeing his state of undress. "I should probably check on him, then."

"I'll do it. He got to you once already. He won't get to me."

"I wasn't expecting it," Banks argued. "I'll have my defenses up now."

"Just the same, you shouldn't expose yourself to another opportunity. As it is, I'll wager you feel enervated, have a headache and a great thirst."

Banks glanced toward him in surprise. "The headache is going away. I feel exhausted and I'm parched, though. How'd you know?"

"Standard postabduction symptoms, reported by contactees throughout the twentieth century. You're still too weak to completely screen out Balam's influence if he wants to make a second try at speaking through you."

They left the control center and walked down the corridor to the door of Balam's facility. Banks eyed it anxiously as Lakesh punched in the six-digit code on the keypad. The confirmation circuit buzzed, and the lock clicked open.

"Sir—" Banks began.

"Don't worry," Lakesh said reassuringly. "Go back to your quarters, get dressed, drink a jug of water. If you feel up to it, come back here."

Banks nodded. "Yes, sir."

Lakesh watched him walk away and turn the corner, then he pushed open the door. He stepped cautiously into the large, low-ceilinged room. He saw computer keyboards and medical monitors on their own individual desks. A control console ran the length of the right-hand wall, the multitude of telltales and readouts glowing green and amber.

Lakesh's nostrils recoiled from the astringent smell of chemicals. The room always smelled vaguely of antiseptic and hot copper as a result of the trestle tables loaded down with glass beakers, Bunsen burners and chemical-filtration systems.

The left wall of the room was constructed of heavy panes of clear glass, behind which was a deeply recessed room dully lit by an overhead neon strip, glowing a ruddy red. Balam's optic nerves were very sensitive to light levels much above twilight.

Lakesh stepped to the wall and peered in. He saw nothing but the crimson-tinged gloom.

"I know you're awake in there," he announced. "Otherwise, you wouldn't have pulled your ventriloquist act on Banks. You're not Edgar Bergen and he's not Charlie McCarthy. If you have something you want to communicate, then do it straight out."

Lakesh watched the blurred shape, a darkness within a darkness, shift like twisting mist in the hell-hued murk. He was able to catch only a glimpse of the entity's fathomless, tip-tilted eyes and narrow features before Balam erected his hypnotic screen, a telepathic defense that clouded human perceptions and concealed his appearance from the ape kin who held him captive.

When the nonvoice slid into his mind, he expected to sense the same message Balam had been imparting for over three years: *We are old. When your race was wild and bloody and young, we were already ancient. Your tribe has passed, and we are invincible. All of the achievements of man are dust—they are forgotten.…*

We stand, we know, we are.

The words were less than rhetoric, more than a threat. It was the arrogant, scornful doctrine of a race so old that the most ancient civilizations on Earth were only a yesterday beside it. The underlying psychological message was always the same, stimulating panic, fear and despair in those exposed to it—you cannot win, we are undefeatable, bow to the inevitable. Surrender.

Instead of words, an image flashed into Lakesh's brain, so vivid it was almost a three-dimensional projection. He saw Kane as Balam had first seen him, nearly a year before, pale eyes glinting with hatred, face twisted by revulsion. A jumbled flood of emotions accompanied the vision of Kane—with fear, anger, respect and overlying it all, an almost desperate sense of need.

"Why do you need Kane?" Lakesh asked aloud, shocked almost into speechlessness.

For a chaotic instant, through Balam's mind he caught a flash of black malignity, an impression of something fearsome in a secret place, now spinning a vast web of great menace.

He realized the entity showed him this deliberately, to impress upon him the urgency of his need. Within Lakesh's mind, a series of separate geometric shapes appeared, then rushed together, interlocking to form first a polyhedron, then a trapezohedron.

The image vanished and Lakesh reeled, lungs laboring for air. Cold sweat filled the furrows on his forehead. For a very long moment, he could only stare, feeling fascination, incredulity and fear warring for dominance within him.

For the first time in over three years, Balam had actually communicated a desire and an emotion other than a cold, arrogant superiority. The creature conveyed a sense of a terrible lurking danger and at the same time requested—no, *pleaded*—for help. And not just anyone's help, but that of Kane, a human who loathed and despised him and everything he represented.

"Kane is not here at present," Lakesh croaked. "I hope he will return shortly. I will bring him to you when he does."

The mist faded, as if sucked back to the far end of the cell. The communication ended as suddenly as it had begun. Lakesh turned away from the glass wall, limbs trembling, but not in reaction to the telepathic exchange. His mind wheeled with conjectures. He couldn't understand what had chipped through Balam's armor and evoked such fear in him he would beg for help from one of the lowly ape kin who held him captive.

On a deep, visceral level, Lakesh knew if the haughty Balam was afraid, then he should be terrified.

And he was.

Domi punched in 3-5-2 on the keypad next to the vanadium sec door, grasped the lever tightly and pulled it up. Immediately came the whine of buried machinery, the prolonged squeaking hiss of hydraulics and pneumatics. With a grinding rumble, the multiton sec door opened, the massive panels folding aside like an accordion. She had been told that nothing short of an armor-piercing antitank shell could even dent the six-inch-thick slabs of metal.

She squeezed her slight body between the frame and the door and stepped out onto the plateau. The ragged remains of a chain-link fence clanked in the breeze that gusted up over the edge of the precipice. A telemetric communications array, uplinked to the very few reconnaissance satellites still in orbit, was nestled at the top of the mountain peak.

Domi raised her right hand to shield her sensitive ruby eyes from the dazzle of the noonday sun, wincing at the twinge of pain from her shoulder. Less than three months before, a bullet had damaged the joint, and DeFore had replaced it with an artificial ball-and-socket joint. Long, painful weeks of physical therapy followed the reconstructive surgery, but she had regained the full use of her arm in a remarkably short time. DeFore attributed her recuperative powers to her near feral upbringing in the wild hinterlands beyond the villes, where the victim of an injury either made a full recovery or died.

Scarcely topping five feet in height and weighing a hundred pounds, she looked too frail to have been born in the Outlands, the untamed wildernesses beyond the cushioned tyranny of the villes. Her ragged mop of bone white hair framed a piquant, hollow-cheeked face. Her sleeveless red tunic was belted at the waist, which left her porcelain-colored arms and legs bare and accentuated the insolent arrangement of her curves.

The average life expectancy of an outlander was around forty, and the few who reached that age possessed both an animal's cunning and vitality. Domi was nowhere near that age; in fact, she had no true idea of how old she actually was, but she possessed more than her share of wits and vigor.

She didn't miss the short and often brutal life in the Outlands. She had quickly adapted to the comforts offered by the Cerberus redoubt—the soft bed, protection from the often toxic elements and food that was always available, without having to scavenge or kill for it.

Domi had enjoyed similar luxuries during her six months as Guana Teague's sex slave. The man-mountain of flab had been the boss of the Cobaltville Pits and he showered her with gifts. He didn't pamper her, though, since she was forced to satisfy his gross lusts.

Domi rarely dwelled on the past, but she often replayed how she had cut Guana's throat and how the blood had literally rivered from the deep slash in his triple chins. She always smiled in recollection of kicking his monstrous body as it twitched in postmortem spasms.

The only possession she had kept from those months spent in Teague's squat was the long, serrated knife that had chilled him.

Beneath her shading hand, she gazed at the mouth of the road opening up on the far side of the plateau. The trans-comm message from Grant had been received only a few minutes ago. She was less interested in learning that Auerbach and Rouch had been found than in hearing Grant's lion growl of a voice announcing their return.

Domi didn't list patience among her virtues, and waiting in Cerberus for the past five and a half days for word had been difficult to endure. The reasons why she had to stay behind in the redoubt were sound, and she tacitly agreed with them. The other exiles were ville-bred academics, and few of them dared to venture very far from the sec door.

If Grant and the others didn't return after seven days, her instructions were to come after them. A journey on foot down the rugged road leading down from Cerberus to the foothills would have been a hardship, but she knew how to live off the land. She also knew how to kill, quickly, efficiently and without remorse.

Faintly, borne on the wind, came the muted roar of laboring engines. Within moments the six-wheeled Hussar

Hot Spur Land Rover hove into sight, followed a few seconds later by the armored, tank-treaded Sandcat.

The Sandcat's low-slung, blocky chassis was supported by a pair of flat, retractable tracks. Its gun turret, concealed within an armored bubble topside, held a pair of USMG-73 heavy machine guns. The hull's armor was composed of a ceramic-armaglass bond, which served as protection from not only projectiles, but went opaque when exposed to energy-based weapons, such as particle-beam emitters.

As the two vehicles rumbled onto the plateau and toward the redoubt's entrance, she saw Auerbach and Rouch in the Hotspur. Their faces locked in grim, unsmiling masks, neither of them seemed to see her. Domi was forced to step aside to keep her feet from being run over. She resisted the urge to give them an obscene gesture as they rolled past.

Through the open ob port of the Sandcat, she saw Kane behind the wheel. Grant leaned over from the codriver's seat to call out, "We found 'em." He spoke loudly in order to be heard over the steady throb of the 750-horsepower engine.

"Nobody hurt?" Domi called back, walking beside the vehicle.

"Nothing serious," Kane said. "The usual."

Domi saw the thin, scabbed-over dark red line on his cheek and grinned. "Yeah, so I see."

Glimpsing Brigid's outline in the rear passenger compartment, Domi stated, "Lakesh big-time wants to talk to all of you. Attendance as in mandatory."

Kane eyes flashed. "Good. I big-time want to talk to him, too."

He drove the Sandcat into the redoubt and braked as Auerbach stopped the Hotspur long enough for Rouch to disembark. Grant and Brigid climbed out while he was stopped, then he followed the Hotspur down the twenty-foot-wide main corridor to the vehicle depot, adjacent to the armory.

Wegmann waited for them to park the wags in their designated stations, on either side of the fuel pump. He eyed Auerbach sourly as the man climbed out of the Land Rover.

"How was your holiday, Auerbach?" he asked snidely. "I wish I could go off for five days with Rouch—or any woman, for that matter. But no, I've got to hang out here, servicing the air circulators, mopping up grease, fixing toilets. As if I didn't have enough to do, now I've got to service both these wags. Thanks a lot."

"Fuck off, pissant," Auerbach snapped.

Wegmann widened his brown eyes in mock hurt. "I thought you'd come back all fit and rested, but hey, you're just as obnoxious as the day you left. What happened, Auerbach? Rouch wasn't as much fun as you hoped? Or was it the other way around?"

Peeling his lips back from his teeth in a snarl, Auerbach lunged for the much smaller Wegmann. Kane managed to insert himself between the two men. He elbowed Auerbach to one side. "Enough."

The red-haired man strained against Kane for a moment, then stepped back. "I'm not gonna take shit from that little asshole."

"You don't have to," Kane replied. To Wegmann, he said, "It'd be a real wise move for you to apologize before you start servicing the wags. I've got other business to attend to, and I won't be here to protect you."

Wegmann glared, not in the least intimidated by either man. In his mid-thirties, he was no more than five and a half feet tall, weighing maybe 140 pounds. He might look slight physically, but he was a scrapper and a mechanical genius. He also claimed to be a musician.

Heeling around toward the Hotspur, he snapped an insincere "Sorry" over his shoulder.

Kane guided Auerbach out of the depot with a hand pressed against the small of his back. "Go to the dispensary. Have DeFore take a look at that shoulder."

Auerbach nodded glumly, his anger replaced by shame. "I guess I'd better get used to that treatment. I'll be the laughingstock of Cerberus once the story gets around."

"You made a mistake," Kane said, slightly surprised by how sorry he felt for the man at the moment. "A time will come when you can make up for it."

Auerbach nodded again and walked away, head hung low, posture slumped, a defeated and weary man.

Kane entered the armory, pressed the flat toggle switch on the door frame and the overhead fluorescent fixtures blazed with a white, sterile light.

The big square room was stacked nearly to the ceiling with wooden crates and boxes. Many of the crates were stenciled with the legend Property U.S. Army.

Glass-fronted cases lined the four walls. Automatic assault rifles were neatly racked in one, and an open crate beside it was filled with hundreds of rounds of 5.56 mm ammunition. There were many makes and models of subguns, as well as dozens of semiautomatic blasters, complete with holsters and belts. Heavy-assault weaponry occupied the north wall, bazookas, tripod-mounted M-249 machine guns, mortars and rocket launchers.

All the ordnance was of predark manufacture. Caches of matériel had been laid down in hermetically sealed Continuity of Government installations before the nuke-caust. Protected from the ravages of the outraged environ-ment, nearly every piece of munitions and hardware was as pristine as the day it rolled off the assembly line. In the far corner, his and Grant's Magistrate body armor rested on metal frameworks, standing like grim black sentinels.

Kane went to a gun case and unstrapped his Sin Eater from his forearm. He felt a distant wonder when he real-ized he hadn't had to fire a shot or chill anyone on this mission. He had returned to the armory with the same full clip as when he'd left it.

However, he had been tempted to fire a few rounds during the three-day journey back to the foothills. Auer-bach was silent and sullen and Rouch responded with spits and snarls whenever Kane or Brigid spoke to her.

He hadn't apprised Brigid of what passed between him and Rouch at the Indian village. If she was mystified by the open hostility Beth-Li directed at both of them over the past couple of days, she didn't comment on it.

Kane repressed a snort as he replaced the grens in their foam-cushioned cases. Life was becoming far too compli-cated in Cerberus lately, and he laid the blame squarely on Lakesh. The situation with Beth-Li had its amusing as-pects, but all the entertainment value was squeezed out of it. He was honest enough with himself to be flattered by the young woman's attentions and intents. No man could be otherwise.

Grant and Domi shared a superficially similar relationship. Domi claimed to be in love with Grant, viewing him as her savior from the chains of servitude forged by Pit boss Guana Teague.

From what Grant said, Domi had saved him when Guana was literally crushing the life out of him. Regardless, Domi had attached herself to Grant and for a time her blatant attempts to bed him made Beth-Li's actions seem cold and standoffish.

Although expressing jealousy of other women, it was obvious Domi loved Grant fiercely. Kane did not know if his friend had ever tired of resisting the albino girl's charms and surrendered to them, but he tended to doubt it. Domi could be sixteen or twenty-six. Grant was pushing forty and if he involved himself with Domi, he said he'd feel twice that.

He had spoken in jest, but Kane suspected the emotional wounds inflicted by his ruined affair with Olivia years ago in Cobaltville had yet to fully heal. Kane had never asked Grant about Olivia. The two men observed an unspoken understanding that it was a forbidden topic.

Kane stepped into the corridor and made for the central control complex. He was sure he would find Lakesh there, but he forged a mental resolution not to be distracted by the old man's crisis of the day. He intended to have a final discussion on the matter of Beth-Li, then inform him of the pact he had struck with Sky Dog. He would not allow anything—no matter how urgent—to interfere with it.

His resolve faltered when he entered the huge chamber. Brigid and Grant stood over Lakesh at the main computer station, listening with rapt expressions as the old man spoke earnestly, gesturing with his hands.

When Lakesh caught sight of Kane, he waved imperiously. "Didn't Domi give you my message?" he demanded impatiently. "You were to report to me immediately."

Kane increased the length and speed of his stride. He saw Grant glance his way and distinctly heard him mutter "Shit" before discreetly sliding away from Lakesh and Brigid.

Lakesh was too caught up his agitated excitement to take notice of the expression on Kane's face or the icy gleam in his pale eyes. "As I was telling dearest Brigid and friend Grant, something unprecedented happened early this morning—"

Placing his hands on the back of the chair on either side of Lakesh's shoulders, Kane thrust his face down and close to Lakesh's.

"Something unprecedented is about to happen right now," he said in a low, deadly tone. "A sneaky old fart is about to fly across this room with only a boot on his scrawny ass as the propellant."

Lakesh blinked at him from behind the lens of his glasses, completely baffled by Kane's words. Then annoyance replaced the confusion.

"You're angry with me again," he said waspishly. "Nothing new about that. But a situation developed here that is so extraordinary—"

"Nothing new about that, either," Kane interrupted.

"He's not exaggerating, Kane. Hear him out," Brigid urged.

Kane straightened up, scowling down into Lakesh's deeply seamed face. "What is it this time? Have you located a new bunch of freaks to shoot at us? Another space station you want us to visit? Just tell me—we live only to risk our lives for you, you know."

Lakesh wisely chose to overlook the sarcasm. "It has to do with Balam. He asked to speak to you."

Kane was shocked into speechlessness for a long moment. All he could think of to say was a faint "What?"

Swiftly, curtly, Lakesh related his brief communication with Balam and how it had come about through Banks.

"A stone?" rumbled Grant. "What the hell is so dangerous about a stone?"

"Not just a stone, but one in the shape of a trapezohedron." Lakesh used his gnarled fingers to trace a geometric form in the air. "That was the image Balam imparted."

"Does it mean anything to you?" Brigid asked.

"It didn't at first."

"And now?" inquired Kane.

Contemplatively, Lakesh answered, "Certain ancient cultures attached mystical significance to a kind of very rare rock—tektites."

"I thought tektites were meteor fragments," Brigid said.

"That's the standard mineralogist's view, yes. But actually, nobody was ever certain where tektites came from. More than one contained isotopes of untraceable radioactive material and had very unusual magnetic readings."

"How unusual?" Kane demanded.

"They were antimagnetic, with a polarity capable of suppressing gravity...or affecting the electromagnetic field of the human brain."

"That still doesn't sound like anything to scare anybody," Grant argued. "If Balam is an anybody."

Lakesh heaved himself out his chair. "I concur. So let us pay him a visit and settle the question."

Kane lifted a hand. "Hold on. I'm not about to let that little gray bastard crawl around in my head just so he can tell me about some scary rocks."

"Kane," Brigid began, "you're missing the point as usual. Whatever Balam wants to talk about, this is the first time he's ever initiated a communication. And he wants you, not Banks—whom he knows best. Not even Lakesh—whom he blames for his captivity. Only you."

Lakesh's head bobbed in vehement agreement on his wattled neck. "Precisely, friend Kane. This is the kind of breakthrough we've been waiting for, hoping for. Balam is our only direct feed for data about the Directorate."

"You'll understand if I'm less than honored by his request," he retorted.

Lakesh and Brigid stared at him expectantly.

Kane drew in a slow, thoughtful breath. "How do you know he doesn't want to take me over, make me his slave? Or fry my brain?"

"If he had that ability and intent, he would've done it long ago." Lakesh adopted a reasonable, persuasive tone. "He was only able to gain control of Banks when he was at the deepest stage of sleep and he didn't—or couldn't—read his mind completely. Otherwise, he would've known what Banks knew—that you weren't here."

Kane cast a questioning glance toward Grant. The broad
yoke of the big man's shoulders lifted in a shrug. "Makes
sense to me. Just talking to it—him—is important, even
if all he wants is to discuss his rock collection."

Turning to Brigid, Kane asked, "What about you, Baptiste? What do you think?"

Surprise that he had solicited her opinion flickered in
her eyes. "I agree with Lakesh and Grant. We've been trying to establish a dialogue for months. I doubt there's
much risk involved."

Grant patted the bulge of his holstered Sin Eater beneath his coat sleeve. "We'll all go with you. If he gets out
of line, I'll shoot through the glass and blow his oversize
brains out."

Lakesh muttered tensely, "Friend Grant, I don't think
such an extreme action will be at all necessary."

Grant grunted. "I don't think it, either. But since I'm not
sure, the blaster goes with us."

Kane peered through the glass wall, seeing only his distorted reflection and dripping beads of condensation. "I'm here, you little prick," he announced. "Show yourself."

Standing in a semicircle behind him, Lakesh, Banks, Grant and Brigid shifted uncomfortably. Banks admonished quietly, "You don't have to insult him."

Kane looked toward him, eyebrows angled quizzically. "You think I'll hurt his feelings? You don't really believe he has any to hurt, do you?"

"I don't know," Banks retorted. "But if he can feel fear, it stands to reason he can feel humiliation. And if he can feel humiliation, he can feel anger—"

The young man's words suddenly blurred into an articulate cry, half alarm, half pain. He staggered back a pace, catching himself on the edge of a trestle table.

Lakesh was instantly at his side. "What is it?"

Simultaneously, Kane became aware of a fluttering movement on the periphery of his vision, behind the glass pane. He whipped his head around, seeing the suggestion of a billowing mist in the far recesses of the cell.

In a groaning voice tight with effort, Banks said, "It's Balam—he wants to speak through me."

With a click and whir, Grant's Sin Eater sprang into his hand. Eyes slitted, he aimed it at the transparent panel, finger hovering over the trigger. Shifting the barrel back and forth, he grated, "I can't see him."

"*No!*" Banks's voice was an anguished bleat. "No, he's not forcing me. He's asking my permission."

Lakesh put an arm around the technician's shoulders. "It's up to you, Banks. At least he's asking."

A dew of perspiration filmed his forehead. Squeezing his eyes shut, Banks said, "It's not like this morning…he's not trying to take me over, animate me. He's requesting a melding of…of perceptions, of intellectual resources."

Grant looked back and forth from Banks to the cell. A shudder racked Banks's body, and he uttered a faint, strangulated cry. He bowed his head for an instant, then slowly lifted it, pushing himself to his full height. Opening his eyes, he swept everyone in the room with a calm, dispassionate gaze that finally fixed on Kane.

He met the gaze and he felt his flesh prickle as if a thousand microscopic ants marched over his skin. Somehow, he glimpsed Balam's huge, slanted black eyes superimposed over those of Banks.

"Kane," Banks said mildly. "Balam is here with me, speaking with my voice, drawing on my knowledge of language and his familiarity with all of you."

Lakesh, Grant and Brigid drew back from him.

Feeling a little foolish but more than a little enthralled, Kane asked, "What do you want from me?"

"Your intervention."

"In what?" inquired Brigid.

Banks-Balam didn't remove his eyes from Kane's face. "Please, don't distract me. This binary state is difficult to maintain. My mental equilibrium must not be disturbed, or the meld will be lost. I must stay focused."

Brigid frowned at the rebuke, but said nothing more.

"You have often speculated about me and my kind," Banks-Balam stated. "It would not be an exaggeration to say that questions about the so-called Archon Directorate have consumed you."

Kane nodded. "It's not an exaggeration. You have no idea how many times I thought about beating the truth out of you—him."

Banks-Balam returned the nod, graciously inclining his head. "Actually, I *do* have an idea. Somewhere on the order of five hundred separate desires, and twice that many passing whims."

"Then you should be grateful I never acted on them," Kane said harshly.

"Such tactics would have availed you nothing. You would not have learned anything."

"Am I going to learn something now?"

"Yes. You believe that the Archons are all part of a collective hive consciousness, all linked mentally in this fashion."

"That's not true?" Kane inquired.

"As far as your limited perceptions can be expanded, it

is true enough. However, if we so-called Archons were truly products of one linked group consciousness, all the individual components would be as mindless and interchangeable as ants and bees. Drones driven only by instinct."

"If you say so," muttered Kane.

"As in any form of electromagnetic energy exchange, there are broadcasters and receivers. And conductors."

Lakesh stiffened, eyebrows climbing toward his high hairline, over the rims of his spectacles. He opened his mouth to speak, then closed it again.

Banks-Balam apparently guessed—or sensed—the question he wanted to ask. "No, I am not a conductor. If you will relax, Kane, close your eyes and open your mind, I will show you what the conductor is."

Kane hesitated, glancing from one face to another. Grant scowled, Brigid looked doubtful and Lakesh smiled encouragingly. With a mental shrug, Kane slowly exhaled and let his lids drop over his eyes. Nothing happened. He was very aware of the electronic sounds from the control console, even his own breathing. He waited for a few seconds and was on the verge of opening his eyes when an image crowded into his mind.

He saw floating geometric patterns, orbiting one another. They rushed together and locked in position to form a black trapezohedron, a stone with glowing striations.

"Do you see it?" came the soft query.

"Yes. A black rock or an ore."

"It is that, yes, but it is far more—or less. It does not fit atomically with any of the tables your science understands. You would be unable to study it because only part of it exists within your concept of matter in space."

Kane opened his eyes, but disturbingly, the vision of the black yet somehow shining trapezohedron remained fixed in his mind. He saw it vividly every time he blinked.

"It was brought here so long ago that it would far exceed your conception of time."

Kane asked coldly, "Back when our race was wild and bloody and young?"

A slight smile creased Banks-Balam's face at the ironic reference. "Exactly."

"Exactly," repeated Kane impatiently, icily. "Exactly what is it? You called it a conductor. Is it a device disguised as a rock or the other way around?"

"It is both and it is neither. It is a creation, pure matter crafted from scientific principles understood millennia ago, then forgotten. Through it, the pulse-flows of thought energy converge. Through it, the flux lines of possibility, of probability, of eternity, of *alternity* meet."

"Which," Kane said flatly, "tells me absolutely nothing."

As if Kane had not commented, Banks-Balam continued, "It is more than an artifact—it is a key to doors that were sealed aeons ago. They were sealed for a good purpose. Now they may be thrown wide and all the works of man and non-man will be undone. Time and reality are elastic, but they are in delicate balance. When the balance is altered, then changes will come—terrible and permanent."

Kane listened, not to the words themselves but to the sense of urgency and conviction behind them, to the implications of vast dark forces flowing like an inexorable tide—a tide even Balam feared.

"What is it you want me to do?" he demanded.

Banks-Balam blinked and wiped at the perspiration on his face. A tremor shook his hand. His voice sounded hoarse. "The meld is weakening. I do not wish to inflict further strain on this vessel of communication. He has always shown me kindness and compassion."

The remark startled Kane, startled them all, but he snapped, "Get to it, then."

"The form in which the stone was crafted was not arbitrary. It served a function. It was altered over the centuries, facets of it removed and scattered across the face of the Earth. Each fragment acts as a lodestone for the others. They will always lead to one another. One of the fragments has been seized by a thief, and will draw the thief to the others. He thinks he has found a prize, a means to power. You must prevent him from reaching his objective, Kane. I trust only you."

Kane's eyes widened in astonishment. "Me? You trust *me*?"

Banks-Balam drew trembling fingers over his sweaty brow. His breathing came in short, labored rasps. "I trust a predator to know what to do against another predator. Fang pitted against claw, blood spilled for blood. Violence met with violence. Your father possessed these same instincts, else I would not be here.

"I know your hatred of me is deep, and I understand how you blame me for what was done to this world, to your race. I am content to accept your hatred and blame, regardless of how misplaced it is. However, if you wish to help this world and your race, you will do as I bid."

Kane clenched his teeth, then tightened his fists as the memory of his father—frozen forever in cryo-sleep, unaware of the vile uses to which his body was put—drove away the image of the black stone. He took a threatening half step forward, momentary rage blotting out the realization that he could not harm Balam without harming Banks.

It was all very convenient, very strategic.

"Where are these fragments?" he demanded, pitching his voice low to disguise the vibration of fury in it. "Who is the thief?"

"That will be made clear to you in short order, as the thief attempts to recover the piece in this hemisphere, on this continent."

"Where is it?"

"The place of the dead animals," Banks-Balam replied faintly. "In the Hall of the Frozen Past."

In angry bafflement, Kane growled, "Talk sense, you little son of a bitch. Where the hell is the Hall of the Frozen Past?"

Banks's body abruptly slumped, his knees buckling. Lakesh and Grant secured grips on the young man's arms and kept him upright. A rattling, protracted gasp tore from his throat, and for a moment he shook so violently it was almost a convulsion.

He managed to get his legs under him and stand up, leaning heavily against the edge of the trestle table. His sweat-damp face glistened in the dim light, and his eyes were dulled by fatigue. He stared around without focusing for a few seconds, then put a hand to the left side of his head, wincing in pain.

"Feels like my brain is about to pop out of my skull." He cleared his throat noisily. "I need a couple of gallons of water to drink, too."

Brigid eyed him keenly. "How much do you remember?"

"All of it. I felt like I was an observer, standing in the wings on the stage of my mind." His lips twitched in an uncertain, wry smile. "I coached Balam whenever he needed help with his lines, when he wasn't sure of the right words. He doesn't care for verbal communication. He thinks it's inefficient."

Kane swung around to stare at the glass-fronted cell, eyes trying to pierce the red gloom. "The little bastard learned fast. The question is, do we believe him?"

"Of course!" Lakesh exclaimed, sounding slightly scandalized. "Why wouldn't we?"

"No reason," Grant said tonelessly. "Except that he's a deceiver, an inhuman manipulator who helped to orchestrate the nukecaust and the death of 99.9 percent of the human race, and that his kind tried to hybridize or enslave the remaining one-tenth of a percent. Other than that, I guess his word is unimpeachable."

Banks pulled away from Grant and Lakesh and half stumbled over to the sink. Ignoring the cup on the countertop, he turned on the faucet and bent over it, allowing the stream of water to flow directly into his mouth. All of them watched as he swallowed and swallowed, drinking mouthful after mouthful. Finally, he pushed himself up, wiping his mouth with the back of his hand. "That's better."

"I suppose," ventured Brigid, "we can try to cross-reference what Balam said about black stones with the historical records in the database. That might yield some results, give us a better idea of what he was talking about."

"If he wants my help," Kane declared, "he's going to have to offer something substantial in return."

"He claimed by helping him, you'd be helping humanity," Lakesh argued.

Kane scoffed. "That old saw."

Addressing Banks, Brigid asked, "If your thought processes were melded with Balam's, then you must have sensed what he was feeling and thinking. Was he trying to deceive us?"

Banks shook his head. "I don't think so. He's legitimately afraid of the black stone. The fear was very close to the surface."

"Did you pick up anything about the Archons?" Lakesh nearly quivered with excitement. "Anything, no matter how trivial?"

Banks frowned in concentration. "No, not really. Balam has a very regimented, compartmentalized mind, locked into specific channels. I don't know if he was deliberately shielding that information from me or just completely focused on the main topic."

He inhaled a weary breath. "I did pick up scraps of feelings, like emotional echoes." Nodding toward Kane, he said, "He has a great respect for you, an admiration almost. And a trust."

"Anything else?" Brigid asked.

Banks closed his eyes. In a husky half whisper, he replied, "Sadness. A deep, terrible sadness."

Grant snorted. "I'll bet. For himself."

Banks shook his head. "No...for all of us."

"Don't you understand, Kane? Humanity is vanishing. Every passing day marks one more step toward our extinction."

Lakesh paced his small office, thin arms locked behind his back. "The hybrids multiply while our own procreation is circumscribed either by the laws of the barons or environmental conditions."

Leaning against the wall, arms folded over his chest, Kane said darkly, "We've had this discussion before."

After shaving, showering and changing into a white bodysuit, the duty uniform of Cerberus personnel, Kane had cornered Lakesh in his lair, determined to settle the issue of the old man's breeding program once and for all.

Lakesh didn't acknowledge Kane's observation. "If we had access to artificial-insemination techniques, if De-Fore had the knowledge of how to perform them, if we had prenatal-manipulation technology here, I would have never conceived the plan."

Kane stretched out a leg, blocking Lakesh's pacing path. "You're going to have to *un*conceive it, at least as far as Beth-Li and I are concerned. Have you spoken to her since we got back?"

Lakesh shook his head. "No, nor do I know the details of where and how you found her and Auerbach." He tilted his head, eyeing the cut on Kane's cheek. "Would my assessment that bloodshed was involved be incorrect?"

"Not at all," Kane answered. "Nor would it be incorrect if you placed the responsibility for it on Beth-Li."

"Explain."

"That's why I'm here."

Crisply, Kane told him everything that had transpired at the Indian settlement, what Auerbach and Rouch had said and the details of Sky Dog's proposal to repair the war wag.

Lakesh's reaction was mixed; while he was angry, he seemed the most incensed about the agreement struck with Sky Dog, but he was intrigued about the war wag.

As Lakesh began to upbraid him for making the pact without consultation, Kane cut him off with a stern voice. "It's done. We have to abide by it now. Let's move on to Beth-Li. Her stunt put all of us at risk, and she threatened Baptiste. She can't be trusted, and you're going to have to do something about her."

"Like what?" challenged Lakesh. "Exile her from exile? Return her to Sharpeville so she can be executed? Lock her up in a holding cell, confine her permanently like Balam?"

"Don't ask me—she's your problem," Kane said flatly. "You brought her here, so you deal with her. How you have the balls to accuse me of making unilateral decisions after what you pulled is beyond me."

"And why you refuse to cooperate is beyond me. I'm not asking you to pull sewer maintenance."

"As corrupt as she is," replied Kane coldly, "you might as well be."

"*Corrupt?*" Lakesh rolled the word on his tongue contemptuously. "Since when did you decide to become a paragon of virtue? She's a splendidly healthy young woman, with remarkable genes, and with the very strong female drive to pass them on. How does that make her corrupt?"

"She's a little more than that. If you weren't blinded by your ego, unable to see your own errors, you'd acknowledge it. Beth-Li is underhanded, self-centered, manipulative and arrogant." Kane slitted his eyes. "Maybe that's why you're so fond of her…kindred spirits, that sort of thing."

Sudden rage glittered in Lakesh's rheumy blue eyes. Kane stared at him, stone-faced.

Then, bit by bit, the anger burning in Lakesh's eyes ebbed away. Kane knew the old man realized there was a good deal of truth in his charges, and being an essentially honest man, he wasted no time on sputtering denials.

Heavily, he admitted, "I don't suppose I'm really much of a manipulator, since you see through all my attempts so easily."

"I've been manipulated since the day I was born— even before I was born. I ought to be able to recognize it by now."

Lakesh winced as if he had been stung. He knew what Kane was alluding to. Some forty years before, when he first determined to build a covert resistance movement against the baronies, he riffled the genetic records to find the qualifications he deemed the most desirable. He used the Archon Directorate's own fixation with purity control against them. By his own confession, he was a physicist cast in the role of an archivist, pretending to be a geneticist, manipulating a political system that was still in a state of flux.

Kane was one such example of that political and genetic manipulation.

Lakesh said quietly, "I have already expressed my remorse about that—and offered my apologies."

"Yet you still want to improve the breed, by any means you think are necessary." Kane blew out a long, weary breath. "I've cooperated with the missions you've concocted because you convinced me of their importance. I'm not convinced of this one. The timing is all wrong, for one thing. Our situation here in Cerberus is too chancy. We could be under a full assault at any time. We don't need to complicate it with pregnancies or infants."

Lakesh sat down behind his tiny desk, propping his chin beneath a hand. "I can't debate you on that, but I maintain you are refusing to understand my point of view," he said, his voice petulant.

"Wrong again, Lakesh," replied Kane. "I understand you're trying to atone for the sins you committed when you were part of the Totality Concept and worked unknowingly for the Archons. I admit I've blamed you for your part in all of it, in the nukecaust, in the formation of the baronies. Maybe that blame is misplaced, maybe it isn't.

"Maybe your own guilt is misplaced. I haven't made up my mind yet. But one thing I'm certain about—you can't buy back all the people who died in the nukecaust and after by turning this redoubt into a breeding farm."

Lakesh grunted softly. "Whether you're right or wrong, I will accept your decision not to participate. Which still leaves us with the question of what to do about Beth-Li."

Kane smiled wryly. "Another place where you're mistaken. It leaves *you*—not 'us'—with the question of what to do."

The intercom on Lakesh's desk buzzed, then Bry's strident voice blared out of it. "Sir, are you there?"

Lakesh poked at the key. "I am. What is it?"

"Activity on the mat-trans network. An anomalous signature—again." Bry's voice held more annoyance than agitation.

"I'll be right there." Lakesh rose from the desk, murmuring, "This is getting to be a rather tedious routine, isn't it?"

Kane didn't answer as he followed him out into the corridor. He presumed the question to be rhetorical. Over the past few months, the sensor link of the Cerberus network had registered an unprecedented volume of mat-trans traffic. Most of it was due to the concerted search for the renegades from Cobaltville, who had, in the space of a few short months, kidnapped a senior archivist, seriously injured one baron and assassinated another.

Lately there had appeared anomalous activities, or signatures of jump lines that couldn't be traced back to their points of origin.

The madly ambitious Sindri had been the first, making an excursion on Earth from his base on the *Parallax Red* space station. After the threat he presented had been neutralized, the ingenious dwarf had sent them, via the Cerberus mat-trans unit, a taunting message that he was still alive and could overcome their security locks. Sindri's theatrical gesture had consequences. Although the Cerberus mat-trans computers analyzed and committed to their memory matrixes the modulation frequency of Sindri's carrier wave, and set up a digital block, if he could overcome one measure, it stood to reason he could overcome another.

Certainly there were any number of unindexed, mass-produced, modular gateway units. After the initial success of the quantum-interphase matter-transfer inducers, the Cerberus redoubt had become something of a factory, turning them out like an assembly line.

Years ago, when Lakesh had used Baron Cobalt's trust in him to covertly reactivate the Cerberus redoubt, he had seen to it that the facility was listed as irretrievably unsalvageable on all ville records. He also had altered the modulations of the mat-trans gateway so the transmissions were untraceable, at least by conventional means. Sindri had proved there were ways of circumventing those precautions, although Lakesh still had no idea of how he managed to do it.

After he entered the control complex, Kane's gaze went automatically to the Mercator-relief map spanning the wall. A yellow pinpoint of light glowed steadily in the northeast region of the United States. Bry, from his station at the main ops console, said, "Manhattan Island, in case you're wondering."

A thin man with rounded shoulders, a headful of coppery curls and a perpetual expression of wide-eyed consternation, Bry acted more or less as Lakesh's scientific apprentice in the intricacies of the mat-trans gateways. "It's not the one in Redoubt Victor, in the South Bronx."

From a computer terminal, Brigid stirred. Kane hadn't seen her when he first entered. "Then it's got to be the one beneath the Twin Towers, the World Trade Center. The only other redoubt in New York State is up in the Adirondacks."

She should know, inasmuch as she had memorized the locations of all the Totality Concept–connected redoubts.

Kane set his teeth against a groan of dismay. The best known hellzone in the continental United States was the long corridor between D.C., New Jersey and Newyork, a vast stretch of rad-rich ruins. Not too long before he had visited the vicinity of Washington Hole, and although miles away from ground zero, he had still undergone a prolonged and unpleasant decam process upon his return to Cerberus.

"No registered origin point?" Lakesh asked briskly.

"No, sir," answered Bry laconically. "Just like the last time."

Bry's drawled reference to the last time made both Kane and Brigid nervous. Lakesh, too, but he hid it well.

"Could it be Sindri again?" Brigid asked, adjusting her wire-framed, rectangular-lensed eyeglasses. Though primarily a means of correcting a minor vision impairment, the spectacles also served as a badge of her former archivist's office.

Lakesh shook his head. "I hope not. We don't need to contend with him again."

"If it is him," Kane said, "and he's still looking for a place to transplant the Cydonia colony, he'll find Newyork less appealing than Washington Hole. He and his trolls won't stay long. We can leave them be."

Lakesh's mouth turned down at the corners in a moue Kane couldn't read. Though he was consumed with guilt by his long association with the Totality Concept, his ego was still tied up with his history-making breakthroughs on Project Cerberus. The notion of someone else tinkering with the gateways was an affront to his vanity.

Turning to Brigid, he asked, "What results has the database yielded about Balam's black stone?"

"Too damned many," she replied dryly. "I've compiled the most detailed, most substantiated and least contradictory of the reports into a briefing jacket."

Slightly surprised, Kane asked, "There was a lot about the black stone in the historical records?"

"Not exactly the historical banks. *Esoteric* may be a more accurate description. Another word might be—" She trailed off, groping for the right word.

"*Crazy?*" Kane inquired helpfully.

"That," she agreed. "And *scary.*"

"I presumed it would be," Lakesh stated tersely, "judging by Balam's attitude. Let's round up Banks and Grant and whoever else wants to be in on this and convene in the cafeteria."

"*I* don't want to be in on this," muttered Kane. "But I don't think that'll matter much."

The Cerberus redoubt had an officially designated briefing room on the third level. It was big and blue-walled, with ten rows of theater-type chairs facing a raised speaking dais and also had a rear-projection screen.

The briefing room was never used except to watch old movies on laser disks in storage. Most of the movies were instructional aids, addressing questions about hygiene, routine maintenance of the nuclear generators and what to do in case of an enemy incursion. The latter was intercut with footage from a film made in the 1980s entitled *Red Dawn*, wherein a group of high-school students waged a guerrilla war against Russian invaders.

Kane found the films *The Day the Earth Stood Still* and *Independence Day* silly, too, but a bit more relevant. He especially enjoyed the scene in *The Day the Earth Stood Still* where a dignified English actor playing an alien reamed out the military for acting foolishly with atomic weapons. He laughed out loud when the alien threatened to turn his invincible sec droid loose on them if they didn't change their ways. He couldn't help but take a bitter pleasure in the irony.

At any rate, since the briefings rarely involved more than a handful of people, they were always convened in the more intimate dining hall. Lakesh, Brigid, Banks, Grant and Kane sat around a table, sharing a pot of coffee. Access to genuine coffee was one of the inarguable benefits of living as an exile in the redoubt. Real coffee had virtually vanished after the skydark, since all of the plantations in South and Central America had been destroyed.

An unsatisfactory synthetic gruel known as "sub" replaced it. Cerberus literally had tons of freeze-dried packages of the authentic article in storage, as well as sugar and powdered milk.

Brigid passed out illustrations, downloaded and printed from the historical database. Most of them depicted uninteresting chunks of dark stone, some of them balanced atop obelisks or resting on altars.

Without preamble, she stated, "Many cultures, separated by time and distance, held certain black stones in a kind of respect, fear or veneration for a number of reasons. Apocryphal religious texts tell of Lucifer coming from the sky bearing a black stone that was then split into fragments and scattered among humanity.

"One ancient South American legend relates that the god Tvira built a temple on an island in Lake Titicaca to hold three holy stones, called the *kala*.

"Similarly, three black stones were venerated by Moslems in the Ka'aba at the great mosque of Mecca. There are several traditions associated with these stones, but all agree they are of celestial origin. Moslems say the stones were white at first, but had the property of absorbing black or sinful thoughts."

Brigid pointed to a black-and-white line-scan photograph depicting a dark octagonal shaft of stone with indecipherable characters spiraling around it, leading up to a small black polyhedron.

"In Hungary," she said, "near the village of Stregoicavar, there was a black monolith that nineteenth-century occultists spoke of as one of the keys."

Banks picked up the illustration, studying it intently. "Keys. The same phrase used by Balam."

"What does it mean?" Grant asked.

"I'm getting to that," replied Brigid. "There were a lot of superstitions regarding the stone and the monolith, especially the assertion that if anyone slept in its vicinity, they would be haunted by monstrous nightmares of another world forever after. There are legends of people who died raving mad because of the visions the stone evoked."

Kane looked at the stone balanced atop the shaft. "The shape I saw was a trapezoid."

"A trapezohedron," Lakesh corrected him. "Evidently, that was the original shape of Lucifer's stone."

"And referred to in many ancient documents as 'the shining trapezohedron,'" Brigid interjected. "Which makes sense, since Lucifer's name is derived from *lux* and *fero*...'bringer or carrier of light.'"

"I thought Lucifer was just another name for the devil," commented Grant.

Lakesh smiled impishly. "In revised mythology, his name became synonymous with Satan. He was actually an angel of Heaven, but a fallen one. Like Prometheus, he was punished because he brought mankind the light of knowledge. Something to which I can relate."

"I'll bet," Kane drawled blandly.

Brigid glanced at him in irritation before declaring, "A number of esoteric and suppressed volumes dating back to the Gnostic tradition mention the original form of the stone as a trapezohedron. An Arab scholar who went by the name of Abdul al-Hazred wrote of it in his eighth century manuscript, *Kitab al-Azif*. Von Junzt alluded to it in his *Unausprechlichen Kulten,* as did the Ponape Scripture and Prinn's *De Vermiis Mysteriis.*"

The difficult pronunciations rolled easily off Brigid's tongue, which Kane found more annoying than impressive. Due to her eidetic memory, she could memorize almost anything instantly, even words in foreign languages.

"The most recent mention of the stone," she continued, "is from the 1920s and directly reference the reason why the fragments of the black stone were called keys.

"In Buddhist and Taoist legends, there is the tradition of the Eight Immortals, eight masters who reside in a secret city beneath a mountain range on the Chinese-Tibet border. The city, known as Agartha in some legends and Hsi Wang Mu in others, is possibly underground and has been said by many to be near Lhasa. There have been numerous and dubious reports of explorations of tunnels leading to the city, but the most convincing came from Nicholas Roerich, a Russian artist and mystic.

"During his travels through Asia in the first decade of the twentieth century, Roerich heard of the Eight Immortals and their abode in the mountains. He was told, 'Behind that mountain live holy men who are saving humanity.' A native guide told him of huge vaults inside the Kun Lun Mountain Range where treasures had been stored from the beginning of history, and of strange 'gray people' who had emerged from those rock galleries throughout history."

Brigid paused to take a sip of coffee, then went on. "In the 1920s, a high abbot from the Trasilunpo lamasery entrusted Roerich with a fragment of a 'magical stone from another world,' called in Sanskrit the Chintamani Stone. Alleged to have come from the star system of Sirius, ancient Asian chronicles claim that 'when the Son of the Sun descended upon earth to teach mankind, there fell from heaven a shield which bore the power of the world.' Perhaps it was a meteorite, or possibly an artifact brought by visitors from another solar system.

"Roerich's wife wrote that the stone possessed a dark luster, like a dried heart, with four unknown letters. Its radiation was stronger than radium but on a different frequency.

"Asian legends state the radiation covers a vast area and influences world events. The main mass of the stone is kept in 'a tower in the City of the Starborn.'"

Kane murmured, "I'm starting not to like the sound of this."

Brigid paid his comment no attention. "According to ancient chronicles, the stone was sent from Tibet to King Solomon in Jerusalem, who split the stone and made a ring out of one piece. Centuries later, Muhammad took three other fragments to Mecca. A smaller fragment of the stone was sent with Roerich to Europe to help aid the establishment of the League of Nations. With the failure of the league, Roerich returned the fragment to a Trasilunpo lamasery in Tibet. Supposedly, the thirteenth Dalai Lama decreed the fragments were to be kept in separate places for safekeeping. During Roerich's journey to Tibet, he reported that he saw a flying disk, over two decades before the term 'flying saucer' was coined. He was told by his guide that it was an airship from Agartha, leading them to the hidden city."

Lakesh looked completely enthralled. "Did Roerich speculate on the physical composition of the stone?"

Brigid nodded. "He speculated the stone was a form of moldavite, a magnetic mineral said to be a spiritual accelerator. Also, some historians have stated that a fragment of the Chintamani Stone can act as a homing beacon, leading to the main piece and therefore to the abode of the Eight Immortals."

"What about the unknown letters inscribed on the stone?" Banks asked.

"Roerich recognized them as Sanskrit and translated them as reading, 'Through the stars I come. I bring the chalice covered with the shield. Within it is a treasure— the gift of Orion.'"

"And the so-called Eight Immortals?" Kane inquired. "What are they supposed to have been—or be, since they're immortal?"

"Roerich asked the same question," answered Brigid. "The abbot told him how the immortals were made of air and clay, formed by Mu Kung, the sovereign of eastern air and Wang Mu, queen of the western air."

She paused, and with a crooked half smile, added, "Or if you want a post-Taoist spin on it, they came from a planet in the solar system of Sirius and established a stronghold in Asia to conduct their genetic and hybridizing programs."

Kane pressed the heels of his hands to the sides of his head. "I should've known."

Grant pursed his lips. "I still don't see how the stone relates to any of this. What's the connection?"

"Roerich's theory about the stone is that it's charged with *shugs*, currents of psychic force. He speculated it resembled an electrical accumulator and may give back, in one way or another, the energy stored within it. For instance, it will increase the spiritual vitality of anyone who touches it, infusing him with knowledge or enhancing psychic abilities that allow him to glimpse Agartha, the Valley of the Immortals."

Brigid touched her lips with the tip of her tongue and said hesitantly, "There's something else."

Kane groaned. "I *knew* there had to be."

"I cross-referenced Agartha and came across something else in the database." She took a deep breath and declared, "In 1947, the same year as the Roswell crash, a mysterious man who called himself the Maha Chohan, Regent of the Realm of the Agartha, visited France. Not only did he describe the underground kingdom of Agartha, claiming its origins dated back fifty thousand years, but he made allusions to a system of physics that transcended what the scientists of the day understood.

"He was quoted as saying, 'All the sacred sciences are still preserved in Agartha.' He also hinted that it was more than a city, but a sanctuary for the superior ancestors of humankind."

"Hmm," Lakesh said meditatively. "So far, it all fits with what little we know of the Archon presence on Earth. If Agartha is a sanctuary for Archons, it is little wonder that Balam became so agitated, particularly if the fragments of the black stone are keys that lead to it."

"Do we have any idea where any of these fragments might be?" asked Banks.

Brigid slid a sheet of paper across the table to him. On it was a photographic reproduction of a dark stone, one side of it smoothly angled and faceted. It rested inside of a glass case, bracketed by other, smaller chunks of rock. A metal plate affixed to the base of the case bore the word Tektites.

She said, "This picture shows part of the permanent mineral exhibit at the Museum of Natural History in Newyork."

She swept an expectant gaze back and forth across the faces of the four men.

"Where the anomalous mat-trans signature registered," Lakesh muttered apprehensively.

Banks, in the same low, anxious tone said, "The Hall of the Frozen Past."

"That's as accurate a description of the museum as I ever heard," Lakesh replied.

Kane tapped the illustration with a forefinger. "You're saying this is a fragment of the Chintamani Stone, Lucifer's stone? The shining trapezohedron?"

Brigid shrugged. "What else could it be? Combined with the gateway materialization in Manhattan, and the clues Balam fed us, the conclusion is fairly obvious."

"Maybe too obvious," Grant rumbled suspiciously.

Banks shot him an accusatory glare. "He wasn't lying. I would have sensed it."

"Then why didn't he just tell us where the fragment could be found?" demanded Kane. "Hall of the Frozen Past, my ass. That could just as easily refer to the cryogenic-suspension facility in Dulce."

"I have a theory about his choice of words," Lakesh ventured.

Grant and Kane snorted disdainfully at the same time.

Lakesh ignored them. "During his communication with us, Balam was limited in his descriptive language by Banks's easily accessible store of knowledge." He addressed the young man. "What do you know about the museum?"

Banks shrugged. "Almost nothing. I've heard of it, I guess, but it's not at the forefront of my mind. I usually get it mixed up with the Smithsonian. All I have are impressions of what it was supposed to be."

"Exactly. Balam more than likely drew on your inchoate impressions, and the closest approximation he could come up with was Hall of the Frozen Dead."

Kane swallowed a mouthful of coffee. "Balam also mentioned a thief. Do you figure that's who made the jump into the Manhattan gateway?"

"I would presume so," Lakesh answered. "On his way to the museum to recover the piece of the stone, drawn by the fragment already in his possession."

Thoughtfully, Grant knuckled his heavy chin. "Best as I recall from old Intel reports, Manhattan Island is a flat zone—not part of any baronial territory. It's supposed to be overrun with slagger gangs and muties. All the bridges are down, so there's no way off it…kind of like a giant, open-air prison. There's no escape from Newyork."

"Which doesn't make it that much different than your average ville," Brigid interjected wryly.

Kane leaned back in his chair, frowning at the picture of the tektites. "So because Balam suddenly gets a hair up his ass—if he has an ass—we're expected to jump to Manhattan on a rock-collecting expedition?"

Lakesh drummed his fingers on the tabletop. "Yes, but not simply because he wants us to do it. This is a way to establish a rapport with him, and perhaps to others of his kind."

"And," Grant argued, "it may be a trap, to get as many of us chilled as he can, reduce the number of the opposition so others of his kind can break him out of here."

Lakesh nodded grimly. "There's that possibility, too."

"I believe Balam is sincere," Banks declared vehemently.

Gently, Brigid said, "Don't take this wrong, but you can't trust your perceptions. He may have altered them."

"Don't you think I'd know it?" he argued.

"Not necessarily," Kane said. "You yourself told me that you didn't know the extent of Balam's mental influence on the human mind."

Lakesh shook his head in weary frustration. "Regardless of the risks, this is a mission we must undertake, for diplomacy's sake if nothing else. We must try to establish a bond of trust and channel of communication with Balam—not just for our benefit, but for what remains of mankind."

"Diplomacy?" repeated Kane skeptically. "With the Archons?"

"How is it any different than the way you dealt with the Indians?" Lakesh challenged.

"A bond of trust stretches both ways. What if it *is* a trap Balam has laid for us?"

No one spoke for a tense moment, then Banks pushed his chair back noisily from the table. "I'll go if the rest of you are afraid."

His announcement was hard with conviction.

Kane's eyes flashed with anger, then an amused smile played over his face. "There's a difference between caution and fear, kid. This is a percentage play, calculating the odds, figuring if what we might gain outweighs what we might lose."

"I think it is," Banks stated dogmatically.

"No surprise," observed Grant. "But since you don't know a blaster from a blister, you'll stay here."

Brigid glanced at him in surprise. "You're volunteering?"

Grant nodded. "Under one condition."

"Which is?" inquired Lakesh.

"If it's a trap, and if I manage to make it back, I get to chill Balam. As slowly and as painfully as I can."

Banks squinted toward Grant, trying to ascertain if he was serious.

"Whoever makes it back earns that honor," Kane said smoothly. "At least we'll have more to look forward to than another cup of coffee."

Lakesh stressed urgency and expediency, so an hour after the briefing, Kane, Grant, Domi and Brigid met him in the ready room adjacent to the central control complex. It held only a long table and the Cerberus gateway chamber.

Enclosed on six sides by eight-foot-tall slabs of brown-tinted armaglass, the Cerberus unit was the first fully operable and completely debugged mat-trans unit constructed after the success of the prototype in the late twentieth century.

All of them understood, in theory, that the mat-trans units required a dizzying number of maddeningly intricate electronic procedures, all occurring within milliseconds of one another, to minimize the margins for error. The actual conversion process was automated for this reason, and was sequenced by an array of computers and microprocessors. Though they accepted at face value that the machines worked, it still seemed like magic to Brigid, Kane and Grant.

Intellectually, they knew the mat-trans energies transformed organic and inorganic matter to digital information, transmitted it through a hyperdimensional quantum path and reassembled it in a receiver unit. Emotionally, the experience felt like a fleeting brush with death, or worse than death. It was nonexistence, at least for a nanosecond.

Their first jump, made some eight months ago, from Colorado to Montana, had been marked by nausea, vertigo and headaches, all symptoms of jump sickness. Lakesh had explained that the ill effects were due to the modulation frequency of the carrier wave interfacing with individual metabolisms. It had since been adjusted and refined, but Kane wondered how the few hardy souls who had used the devices after nukecaust could have tolerated the adverse physical effects.

Grant and Kane wore their full suits of Magistrate body armor. Though relatively lightweight, the polycarbonate was sufficiently dense to deflect anything up to and including a .45-caliber projectile. The armor absorbed and redistributed a bullet's kinetic impact, minimizing the chance of hydrostatic shock.

The armor was close-fitting, molded to conform to the biceps, triceps, pectorals and abdomen. The only spot of color anywhere on it was the small, disk-shaped badge of office emblazoned on the left pectoral. In crimson, it depicted stylized, balanced scales of justice, superimposed over a nine-spoked wheel, and symbolized the Magistrate's oath to keep the wheels of justice turning in the nine villes.

Like the armor encasing their bodies, the helmets were made of black polycarbonate, and fitted over the upper half and back of their head, leaving only portions of the mouth and chin exposed.

The slightly concave, red-tinted visor served several functions: it protected the eyes from foreign particles, and the electrochemical polymer was connected to a passive night-sight that intensified ambient light to permit one-color night vision.

The tiny image-enhancer sensor mounted on the fore-head of the helmet did not emit detectable rays, though its range was only twenty-five feet, even on a fairly clear night with strong moonlight.

Their Sin Eaters were securely holstered to their right forearms. Attached to their belts by magnetic clips were their close-assault weapons. Chopped-down autoblast-ers, the Copperheads were barely two feet in length. The magazine held fifteen rounds of 4.85 mm steel-jacketed rounds, which could be fired at a rate of 700 per minute. Even with its optical image intensifier and laser scope, the Copperhead weighed less than eight pounds. The two-stage sound and muzzle-flash arrestors screwed into the blasters' bores suppressed even full-auto reports to mere whispers.

Fourteen-inch combat knives were scabbarded on the sides of their boots. Honed to razor-keen cutting edges, the titanium-jacketed, tungsten-steel blades were blued so as not to reflect light.

Brigid and Domi wore long coats and dark clothing of tough whipcord, with high-laced boots enclosing their feet and calves. A mini-Uzi hung from a strap beneath Brigid's coat, and Domi's Detonics .45 Combat Master was snugged in a shoulder holster. A flat, square case containing medicines and dehydrated foodstuffs lay on the table, next to a small packet of precision tools. Other odds and ends of equipment, like Nighthawk microlights, rad counters and the motion sensor lay scattered on the table.

Lakesh swept all of them with a searching, penetrating gaze. "Are you all aware of what you're to do?"

"Other than making our way to the museum," Brigid said, touching the tool packet, "you want us to remove and return with the Newyork gateway's molecular-imaging scanners."

Lakesh nodded. "As you know, every record of every gateway transit is stored in the scanner's memory banks. We need to download and review them in order to trace the point of origin of our interlopers."

Kane snorted. "They're no more interlopers than we are. I'm more concerned with finding the museum. Manhattan is dark territory, has been since the nukecaust."

"I found a New York City street map in the database," Brigid asserted. "I memorized the shortest route to the museum from the World Trade Center...though I imagine there have been some changes since the map was made and since we were last there."

Lakesh acknowledged her oblique reference to the disastrous time-travel mission with a wan smile. A couple of months before, Brigid and Kane had been temporally phased to December 31, 2000, in a desperate bid to change the future in the past. They had arrived in *a* past, but not *their* past, so any action they undertook had no effect on their present.

"You'll materialize in the same gateway as you did on that occasion," Lakesh said. "Or rather a duplicate of it, so you should have no trouble finding your way around."

He picked up the packet of tools and handed it to Brigid. "I've already shown you the procedure for removing the scanner's hard disk."

As she stowed it in a coat pocket, he asked, "So we're clear on everything?"

"Except," Grant stated, "the reason for this op. I'm still fuzzy about the importance of this rock."

"That makes two of us," said Kane.

Domi held up three fingers. "Three of us."

Brigid eyed her dourly. "You weren't at the briefing."

Grant tapped his breastplate and hooked a thumb toward Kane. "*We* were and we still can't figure it out. Balam hinted that it was a conductor of some kind, you gave us a history lesson and I'm no closer to understanding the point of this than I was two hours ago."

Brigid smiled wryly. "To be frank, neither can I, not completely. But I remembered something I was shown in Ireland, in the Priory of Awen's citadel—the so-called speaking stone of Cascorach."

Lakesh stiffened in surprise. "You're right. I didn't make the connection."

"It was a dark stone," Brigid continued, "and when touched by Morrigan's mind energy, it activated something like a recording, a psionic message implanted within the designs cut into its surface. Morrigan told me that ancient people knew that certain stones and metals could be charged with a memory, like a storage battery. She also mentioned that quantum theory dealt with such an electromagnetic effect."

Kane nodded. "I remember you telling me about it. So you suspect this black stone of Balam's is the same thing?"

"It's possible," she replied. "Perhaps it holds all the hidden information about the Archons and that's one reason he's so terrified."

Thoughtfully, Grant said, "And some of that information might be about their weaknesses, their vulnerabilities and he doesn't want us apelings to access it."

"Exactly," stated Brigid.

"Even if that's true," Kane interposed, "won't we need a psi-mutie like Morrigan to tap into it?"

"Worry about that later," said Domi impatiently, picking up the equipment case, a microlight and a rad counter. "Let's jump."

Grant slipped the motion sensor over his left wrist, and the four people crossed the anteroom and entered the gateway jump chamber. Right above the keypad encoding panel was imprinted the notice Entry Absolutely Forbidden To All But B12 Cleared Personnel. Even after all this time, they still had no idea who the B12 Cleared Personnel were and what had happened to them.

Grant pulled the heavy, brown-tinted armaglass door closed on its counterbalanced hinges. Manufactured in the waning years of the twentieth century, armaglass was a special compound combining the properties of steel and glass. It was used as shielding in jump chambers to confine quantum-energy overspills.

The lock mechanism clicked and triggered the automatic initiator. A familiar yet still slightly unnerving hum began, climbing in pitch to a subsonic whine. The hexagonal plates on the floor and ceiling exuded a shimmering silvery glow that slowly intensified. A fine, faint mist gathered on the floor plates and drifted down from the ceiling. Thready static discharges crackled in the wispy vapor. Lakesh had explained that the vapor was actually a plasma form, a side effect of the inducer's "quincunx effect"—the nanosecond of time when lower dimensional space was phased into a higher dimension. The mist thickened, curling around to engulf them.

Kane watched the spark-shot fog float before his visor and he closed his eyes. He plunged through a kaleidoscope that constantly shifted into patterns of colors he couldn't name, somersaulting over a never ending series of contrasting textures, hues and shapes.

HE OPENED HIS EYES and saw nothing but mist, but he heard the emitter array beneath the jump platform winding down from a hurricane howl to an electronic whine. Kane didn't move, waiting for the world to stop spinning. The vertigo and nausea slowly seeped away, as did the vapor. He heard his companions stirring around him, taking in shuddery breaths.

Raising his head, he blinked blearily and looked around. Through the transparent armaglass walls, he saw a small chamber with a control console running the length of one wall. To his left, a ten-foot-high passage, walled with dully gleaming metal, led straight ahead.

Carefully, all of them got to their feet. Grant said hoarsely, "This unit has clear walls."

"It's not a redoubt, not exactly," Brigid told him.

Lakesh had once said that many of the armaglass walls were color-coded to differentiate all the Totality Concept–related redoubts. Inasmuch as use of the gateways was restricted to a select few personnel, it was fairly easy for them to memorize which color designated what redoubt.

They peered through the wall of the jump chamber. The only light was provided by the red and green blinking telltales on the console. The control room was covered by a carpet of dust. They saw faint imprints of feet in the dust of broken plaster that had fallen from the cracked ceiling. Splits high in the walls showed where the vanadium-alloy shielding had buckled.

"A little less tidy than I remember," Brigid murmured.

Kane chuckled uneasily. He still had difficulty sorting out what had happened when they attempted the temporal dilation on the final day of the twentieth century. They had successfully traversed the time stream, true enough, but they arrived in an alternate past, a probability branch almost but not quite identical to their own.

He experienced a momentary disorientation as he tried to reconcile the fact that this was, yet was not, the same subterranean installation they had visited before.

Extending his left hand, Grant made a sweep with the motion detector. The faintly glowing LCD on its face registered no movement within the radius of its sensor beams.

Taking the point as always, Kane lifted up the door handle and stepped out carefully and quietly into the control room. His companions followed, Domi double-fisting her Combat Master. Brigid swiftly moved toward the master console. Removing the tool kit from her pocket, she spread it open and selected a tiny, almost delicate screwdriver.

"You're sure you know how to do this?" Kane asked.

"I went over it step by step with Lakesh after the last time," she retorted a bit peevishly. "Even if I make a mistake, what's the worst that could happen?"

"You could short out the mat-trans," Grant responded gruffly. "And strand us here."

She shook her head in annoyance. "This is a dedicated system. It has nothing to do with the jump cycles. Domi, come over here and give me some light."

Obligingly, the albino girl stepped over beside her, turning on her small Nighthawk. Grant and Kane moved to the six-foot-tall open doorway to peer into the dark passageway beyond. They activated the image enhancers on their helmets. Even through their night-vision visors, they saw nothing but shadows and dust.

They waited quietly while Brigid kneeled beneath the console, removing the protective plate and making all the necessary disconnections. After ten minutes, she held an ovular disk in her hand, about a quarter of an inch thick.

"Done," she announced, slipping it into her pocket.

"Let's get the rest of this mission over," Grant said in a tense whisper. "Triple red."

They entered the corridor, the amber-colored beams from Brigid's and Domi's microlights illuminating their path. The hallway stretched for a hundred feet then reached a junction, where four passages radiated off like the spokes of a wheel, just as Kane and Brigid remembered. It was a very unsettling sensation, to retrace steps through a place they knew they had never actually visited.

At the mouth of each side-branching corridor, red numbers, one through four, were just visible through the patina of dust. The set of tracks drifted off to the opening on their left. Kane led them to the one to their far right. The passage was short and opened into a reception room furnished with armchairs, a couch, a low table and a coffee machine. A television set supported by a metal framework was positioned in a corner just below the ceiling. All of the items showed their age, speckled with rust and covered with a film of dust.

Kane pointed to a double set of doors. "The elevator. Think it still works?"

Brigid stepped forward. "Only one way to find out."

The elevator doors were opened by a proximity sensor, but it didn't respond when she waved her hand in front of the grit-encrusted control plate. She cleaned it of its accumulation of dust and tried again. The doors slid apart with a grinding creak. The car was large, with verdegris-coated brass handrails, and easily accommodated all four of them.

"Whoever arrived before us may still be wandering around down here," Grant observed. "They didn't find the lift."

As soon as the doors slid shut, the car ascended with ominous groans and shudders. The noise didn't decrease as they rose higher, but the ascent lasted only a handful of seconds. When they squealed to a lurching stop, the doors opened on a large square room. The floor was thickly layered with concrete dust. The walls were black-speckled marble and showed ugly crisscrossing cracks.

A long, horseshoe-shaped console occupied the facing wall, but it was half-buried by fallen stone and metal conduits. An ornate, gilt-faced clock lay on the floor, its glass face shattered, the hands frozen at 12:32. On the right side of the room, a hallway stretched away, lined on both sides with wooden doors. On their left they saw a glass-and-chrome door that led to a murky semidarkness. Though the heavy glass bore cracks, it was still intact.

Kane crept out of the lift, followed by Grant, who swept the motion detector back and forth. Domi and Brigid followed them cautiously. The dust was much thicker here, and they moved slowly to avoid stirring it up any more than necessary. Kane paced over to the door and peered out into what was once an underground parking garage.

Now it was a graveyard for scores of rusting vehicles, almost all of them squashed beneath tons of tumbled rubble. Huge chunks of brick and massive slabs of concrete, bristling with shorn-off reinforcing rods, filled the area within and beyond his range of vision. A cold and bleak daylight filtered in from an opening somewhere.

Putting his shoulder against the door, Kane gave it a shove. The electronically controlled solenoids had long ago been burned out and it opened, though not easily. The bottom of the metal frame dragged loudly against small particles of rock.

Stagnant water lay in algae-scummed pools on the floor, and the cool, dank air tickled their nostrils. Kane started walking toward the source of the light. He saw no sign of habitation, recent or otherwise, and Grant's periodic motion detector sweeps caught nothing, either.

The four people picked a path over the heaps of debris on their way to the light, speaking little. The longer they walked, the more repulsive became the odors; an effluvia of urine, rotting meat and mildew hung over the garage like a shroud. The piles of rubbish rustled when small animals darted into them at their approach.

As they strode beneath a roof overhang, a faint click of stone against stone reached their ears. Domi whirled in the direction they had come, leading with her blaster. Her delicate nostrils flared.

All of them stopped, turning to look where she had her Combat Master pointed. They were more unnerved by her stance, like that of a snow leopardess preparing to pounce.

"Just a loose rock," Grant said quietly.

Domi whispered fiercely, "Not just sound—smell."

She had reverted to the terse, broken mode of speech of the outlander, as she always did when under stress.

Kane and Brigid sniffed the air experimentally. Grant didn't bother, inasmuch as his sense of smell was seriously impaired due to having his nose broken three times in the past.

At first, neither Brigid nor Kane smelled anything more noisome than the blended varieties of stench they had already detected. Then a faint miasma inserted itself into Kane's nostrils, and he realized it was an odor he had encountered twice before in his life.

The first time had been a number of years before, when he and Grant stumbled on a snake pit in a hellzone. The second time was far more recent, when the mutagenically altered Lord Strongbow broke a sweat. The musty reek was the same—the cold, repulsive taint of reptiles.

At the same time the memory registered, the scalie dropped from the ceiling.

Out of the four of them, only Domi had ever seen a scalie before. Most of the obviously mutated human breeds had been on the road to extinction for a long time. Some, like the swampies, managed to survive, due in part to their isolation. Others, like the once fearsome stickies, had been the target of a concerted campaign of genocide on the part of the villes. Since they tended to congregate in clans and form settlements, they weren't hard to find and exterminate. Scalies, on the other hand, reportedly haunted the shadows, often in the shunned ruins of predark cities, more legend than reality.

As his Sin Eater sprang into his hand, Kane caught only a brief impression of a small yet very broad and squat figure dressed in a collection of rags. The hairless, blunt-featured head was coated in thick, overlapping scales, as were the talon-tipped hands it swept toward Domi. They gripped a foot-long sharpened shard of metal.

She squeezed the trigger of the Combat Master before the scalie had fully regained its balance. The .45-caliber round caught the creature dead center, smashing through the sternum and bursting both lungs. The scalie flailed backward, blood spewing in a liquid banner from its chest, clawlike toenails scrabbling loudly on the concrete floor.

It fell with a wet, slapping sound. The scalie's pendulous lips writhed back over yellow pointed teeth, and a geyser of blood fountained up over them. Its dark-rimmed eyes glittered with hate before it gasped and died.

The booming echoes of the blaster's report rolled throughout the garage. Domi's face twisted into a porcelain mask of revulsion, but she stepped closer to the scalie, drawing a bead on its head.

Grant slapped down the barrel of her blaster, saying, "I think you got him."

Domi swung her head up and around, ruby eyes bright with rage, but she didn't aim at the mutie again. "Reminds me of Guana," she muttered in a guttural voice.

Grant remembered the faint greenish tint of Guana Teague's skin and its odd, faintly scaled pattern. A lot of people had suspected that Guana had a scalie in the family woodpile—hence his nickname. The loathing Domi felt for her former master still ran deep, even after all this time, and Grant didn't blame her for it.

Brigid moved closer to the scalie, inspecting it visually, noting its deep-set eyes and the brachycephalic contours of its skull. She didn't bother suppressing a shiver of repulsion or speculate on what bizarre combination of warped DNA could have created such a mixture of reptile and human.

"Let's keep moving," Kane said. "If we have to face more of those things, I'd rather do it in the open."

Taking the point again, he led them to wide concrete steps stretching upward. Painted on the wall beside them, faded almost to illegibility, were the words Exit To Street Level. The feeble shafts of sunlight angled down the throat of the stairwell.

He easily recalled the last time he climbed these stairs, how he, Brigid and Salvo emerged into a courtyard between the Twin Towers and stared in stunned silence at the majesty of prenuke New York City.

He climbed out into the same courtyard and once more stood dumbfounded. Not, however, at the vista of the thriving metropolis, but rather at its ruins, the hecatomb of a vanished civilization. The fields of devastation stretched almost out of sight. The few structures still recognizable as buildings rose at the skyline, then collapsed with ragged abruptness.

The courtyard itself was buried beneath tons of rubble that had fallen from the ramparts of the two skyscrapers. Tilting his head back, Kane saw that both buildings looked as if they had been broken by titanic blows combining shock and fire. The sky was a canopy of pewter-colored clouds, and what little sunlight pierced them had an unearthly, diffused quality to it.

All four people stood for a moment, silently appraising the panorama of desolation. Consulting her rad counter, Brigid said in a hushed voice, "Green. Whatever kind of explosives caused this destruction had an exceptionally low rad yield. Maybe missiles with short-term 'squeeze' yields."

"Which way?" Kane asked.

She pointed eastward. "That way."

Clambering over massive chunks of concrete, scattered shards of glass and twisted girders of steel, they reached the Avenue of the Americas and began walking. Brigid cryptically warned them to stay away from the black maws of subway-tunnel entrances and open manholes. No one questioned her, assuming she drew on information about Manhattan gleaned from the *Wyeth Codex*.

As they passed through the shadows cast by the shattered monoliths, they heard, far in the distance, a rhythmic thumping, as of a metal drum being pounded repeatedly by a mallet. The sound was too regular to be the product of the wind.

Kane's pointman senses rang an alert, and he cast a grim glance toward Grant. The man's lips tightened beneath his mustache. "I think we've been formally announced."

Gaping rents in the crumbling masonry and the dark windows leered down at them, like monstrously distorted, mocking faces. They strode down the broad avenue, turning onto Columbus. On some of the city blocks, the breadth of rubble was so widespread, they could see no discernible difference between the street and the ruins. The roadbed itself had a ripple pattern to it, a characteristic result of earthquakes triggered by explosive shock waves.

As they reached a corner obscured by a great pile of debris and broken stone, they heard a raucous chorus of high-pitched shrieks and squawks. A swarm of small black shapes held aloft by furiously beating wings darted over a pair of bodies sprawled on the ground. They dived and dipped and banked at such a blurring speed, Kane couldn't get a good look at them.

"Scream-wings," Domi declared quietly.

All of them had heard of scream-wings, but like scalies, the bat-winged predators had been relegated to the status of legend. Barely six inches long with a two-foot wingspan, the creatures were equipped with serrated razor teeth, curving claws and whiplike tails. Rare even in the wild old days before the Program of Unification, scream-wings traveled in flocks.

Several of them circled overhead, clutching bloody chunks of flesh in their talons, chewing on them as their leathery wings beat the air.

Domi looked around, then approached the edge of the debris and pulled a rusty length of reinforcing steel from beneath a heap of bricks. As the others watched, mystified, she slowly approached the bodies, swishing the metal rod through the air over her head, producing a deep hum.

Almost at once, the scream-wings stopped screeching and in a black, flapping cloud, flew up and away from the bodies. Although they didn't go far, the flock maintained a safe distance overhead, circling clockwise.

Still whipping the rod around and around, Domi explained, "They're deaf, but they feel vibrations in the air. They think a big bird is down here."

Keeping uneasy eyes on the fluttering, banking scream-wings, Brigid, Grant and Kane strode to the bodies. Though it was partially eaten, they recognized one of the corpses as a scalie. A bullet had punched a small hole in its forehead and a much larger one through the back of its head. A slop of blood and brain matter oozed across the street.

The other body was human enough, the face still unmutilated. A thick metal spike protruded from his chest. His clothing consisted of a short dark jacket, baggy, coarsely woven trousers and boots of animal hide. A heavy iron cudgel, shaped like an oversize, old-fashioned door key hung from a thong about his waist.

Despite the black soot smeared over his round face, Brigid noted the epicanthic fold of the glazed eyes. "An Asian. Maybe a Mongol," she said.

Domi, still wielding the length of steel in a circle over her head, said impatiently, "Let's go. My arm is getting tired."

They moved on down the street. After a few yards, Domi dropped the rod to the ground. Almost immediately, the clot of scream-wings swarmed down and covered the corpses again.

"They managed to find another way out of the installation," Grant commented. "We'll be contending with one blaster at least. Fairly small caliber, I'd judge."

"For some reason," replied Kane, "that doesn't make me feel a whole lot better."

They passed between silent shells of buildings and then into an expanse of tangled overgrowth. High grass and rank weeds sprouted between paving stones that had once been sidewalks. From all sides, foliage crept in, making a snarl of thorns and vines.

"This used to be Central Park," Brigid panted, disengaging her coat from a briar bush.

They struggled through the dense thicket until they reached a deeply furrowed avenue. On the other side was a series of huge pillars, thrusting their jagged, sheared-off pinnacles into the sky. The sprawling complex of buildings was overgrown with vines and creepers, masking the facade and the windows. The edifice was staggering in size, and one whole wing had tumbled into a featureless mass of moss-covered stone.

Mammoth blocks of granite lay in the overgrowth. The statue of a man on horseback, his features obliterated by the passage of centuries and acid rain, rose up from a skein of thorny brush.

Carved on a pediment above a huge arched entranceway, the inscription Knowledge was barely visible. It was bracketed by two other words, but the letters had long ago been erased by the hand of time. Behind a wavering line of crumbling walls, they saw a vast, stained dome.

Brigid pointed to it. "The Hayden Planetarium."

Kane crossed the avenue, moving toward a wide expanse of cracked, grass-grown stone slabs leading up to the archway, flanked by crooked columns. He paused at the dark door, waiting for the others to join him. Grant made a motion-sensor sweep, which registered nothing, and they stepped in.

The foyer led directly into a long, broad hall that ran away until its nether end grew indistinct in the distance. Skylights were set in the lofty, vaulted ceiling, allowing weak sunlight to flow through the broken glass and wire mesh. Dead leaves covered the tiled floor in an ankle-deep layer. Here and there, the marble walls showed blackened soot streaks from ancient cooking fires. Moldering rubbish was heaped in the corners.

Grant and Kane had seen wrack and ruin before in their missions as Magistrates, but nothing like the chaos within the walls of the museum. As they strode down the hall, they beheld the fantastic at every turn. On one side was the heaped clutter of a pharaoh's treasure. On another, through shattered glass, they glimpsed the stuffed remains of animals not seen since before the nukecaust.

A massive heap of huge bones lay on the littered floor, and they were forced to pick their way around them. A huge skull, displaying fangs like six-inch daggers, grinned at them as they walked by. Domi gazed at the scattering of bones apprehensively, noting that just one of the ribs was almost the size of her entire body.

"What kind of animal is that?" she murmured. "Mutie? What kind of animal chilled it, ate it?"

Brigid's chuckle sounded forced. "It's the skeleton of a tyrannosaurus, a carnivorous dinosaur. Whatever killed it has been dead for at least eighty million years, so don't worry that we'll meet up with it."

They passed exhibit after exhibit, the litter of treasures from every possible time, the stuff of myth and legend.

The four people turned into an open archway and traversed yet another broad hall lined on either side by all varieties of animals, faces and bodies frozen forever. Many of the beasts were posed within dioramas that portrayed them in their natural habitats.

Lions crouched, antelope frolicked, elephants lifted their trunks to trumpet, a mountain gorilla rose from African foliage to drum on its chest.

All of them had seen pix at one time or another of most of the animals on display. Brigid in particular retained a vivid memory of the collection of preserved and mounted beasts in the archives of Cobaltville's Historical Division.

Bleakly, Kane thought of the astonishing variety of wildlife that had existed in the world before the nukecaust, although he had been taught that many species were only years away from extinction before the first bomb detonated.

The mutant descendants of some of these animals had very limited life spans and most, if not all, of these were extinct now, too. He wondered absently if a giant mutie variety of gorilla might not live still in the forested vastness of Africa. He couldn't help but smile at the possibility.

The hall ended at a flight of wide steps that pitched downward into a darkness the illumination provided by the skylights could not reach. A gargantuan, streamlined shape, nearly a hundred feet long, blocked the center of the stairwell. By looking up, they saw the giant fluked tail anchored to a steel cable stretching down from an eyebolt in the ceiling.

"What the hell is this thing?" Grant asked, his eyes running from its blunt snout and up along its pale blue surface.

"A blue whale," Brigid replied. "The largest mammal on Earth—a long time ago."

Kane observed where the cable supports had snapped on the leviathan, so it hung down at a ninety-degree angle. "What must a mutie version of it been like?" he murmured in awe.

With a touch of bitterness, Brigid answered, "I imagine they were extinct before the nukecaust. Maybe they were the lucky ones."

The four people sidled around the whale's suspended body, Kane assuming the point. The image enhancer mounted above his helmet's visor lit up his path, amplifying the beams from Brigid's and Domi's microlights and thus dispelling some of the gloom.

"Where to now?" Domi asked.

"The Morgan Memorial Hall of Minerals and Gems," Brigid replied. "It's the most likely place in the museum to find the stone."

They reached the foot of the stairs and waited as Brigid glanced around, trying to get her bearings. Suddenly, they were galvanized by a sound ahead of them, a faint but distinct scraping. Grant and Kane automatically dropped into crouches, Sin Eaters aimed at the shadows. The noise came again, this time overlaid by the jangle of breaking glass.

The two men moved forward, walking heel to toe, carefully placing their feet so as to not raise rustles from the debris on the floor. Brigid and Domi followed them, allowing the men's armor to act as a protective buffer.

As they turned a corner in the corridor, hugging the wall, they saw a white spike of light piercing the darkness. They could hear the murmur of voices, but couldn't make out the words.

Ahead of them lay a maze of tables, display cases and platforms. The sweeping beam of the flashlight struck brief, glittering highlights from the collection of stone, gems, geodes and crystals that filled the large room. They were dizzying in number, of all shapes, sizes and colors, far too much to absorb in a single glance.

A man's voice echoed in the shadow-shrouded semi-darkness, an exclamation of excited triumph. Kane didn't recognize the language, but it sounded familiar.

"Russian," Brigid breathed from behind him. "He said, 'Here, this must be it.'"

Kane knew she spoke Russian, so he wasn't surprised by her translation. He was more surprised that they had encountered Russians. "What the hell are they doing here?" he whispered to no one in particular.

"Evidently, the same as what we're doing," Brigid replied evenly.

Grant grunted softly in disgust. Although he had learned like the rest of them that Russia was only indirectly responsible for the nukecaust, the prejudices of a lifetime weren't easily cast aside.

"So the thief came from Russia," he said slowly. "Not from the Peredelinko unit, or we could have traced the jump line. There must be another unindexed gateway somewhere in the country."

Brigid knew scientists had built on Project Cerberus technology and created their own project called Szvezda, but she didn't mention it. "We can't let them take the stone back to Russia," she stated.

Kane nodded curtly in silent agreement. Their prior visit to that country some five months before had scarcely been a pleasure jaunt. To Grant, he whispered, "Flank 'em. I go right, you go left."

"Right."

They bent over in crouches, bodies tensed. Kane murmured, "Set."

"Go," Grant responded.

The two men moved out into the hall, drawing on their long years of service together and their shared heritage as Magistrates. They crept forward slowly to avoid stepping on pieces of glass, alternating their attention from the floor to the wavering glow of the flashlight.

Kane heard two voices now, exchanging words in Russian. He pictured a squad of AK-toting Internal Security Network troopers wearing dun-colored greatcoats, jodhpurs and fur caps with silver disks pinned to them.

Circling a long display table, Kane duck-walked at an oblique angle toward the mutter of voices. He stopped at its corner, eyes widening behind the visor. He saw four figures standing before the shattered remains of a glass case, and they were nothing like the images his imagination had supplied.

All of them were garbed in shaggy fur coats and vests, high boots laced with colorful strips of cloth. One man was short and rather stout, with a shaved head and swart Asian features smeared with soot. Like the corpse they had found on the street, a crudely fashioned, key-shaped cudgel hung from his waist. He held a flashlight in his right hand.

A woman—a girl, really—stood near him. A bright red scarf was wound about her neck, contrasting sharply with tumbles of glossy black hair. The cast of her eyes, and the fullness of her lips put him in mind of Beth-Li, though this woman wasn't as slender.

A man wearing a high black turban of dark leather spoke in a lilting, whispering voice, and Kane felt a cold hand of fearful recognition stroke his spine. His build was slight, graceful and his face seemed to consist primarily of delicate brow arches, prominent cheekbones and a very long, pointed chin. The large eyes behind the round-framed spectacles were jet-black. Although the eyes were slanted, they didn't possess the Asian epicanthic fold. The fingers loosely holding an AK-47 looked excessively, almost inhumanly long.

Kane did not recognize the turbaned man as an individual, but as a type. Although he was more darkly complexioned than others Kane had seen, Kane was certain the man was a hybrid, a mixture of human and Archon genetic material. He noted the bloodred baldric extending across his torso from left shoulder to right hip and the short, curving sword hanging from it.

The third man commanded most of his attention for a number of reasons. He was a head taller than his companions, topping even the black turban by several inches. His black hair fell to his shoulders and bore a wide streak of white. His lean body was clothed from neck to ankle in a long fur coat.

He stood motionless, holding a chunk of stone resembling onyx in both hands. His deep-set eyes seemed to gleam with lights that floated up slowly through pools of darkness.

His aquiline profile rang a distant chord of familiarity within Kane. He was sure he had seen the man before, but he wasn't sure of when or where.

The man cupped the stone in his hands, head bowed over it, as if he were drinking some liquid force that flowed from it. The turbaned man spoke to him in an impatient, challenging tone.

With one hand, he reached for the black stone, but the Russian checked his movement with harsh, peremptory words. The bespectacled man turned, handing the auto-rifle to the girl.

In the brief of tick of time between the girl firmly gripping the weapon and the man relinquishing his hold on it, Kane swiftly rose to his feet.

"Freeze!" he roared, using his well-practiced Mag voice at a volume that intimidated malefactors and broke violent momentum. He knew he should have apprised Grant over the helmet comm-link of what he was doing, but there wasn't time.

He bellowed in English, so he wasn't sure if any of the four people would understand him, but they did freeze in midmotion. They stared at the black-armored apparition in silent surmise, and Kane couldn't help but feel impressed by their rigid self-control.

The tall man's lips curved in a smile. In English, with only the slightest trace of an accent, he said, "I am afraid the museum is closed for renovation."

Kane's eyes swiftly swept his surroundings, searching for Grant. His partner's disgruntled voice filtered through the helmet comm-link into his ear. "I'm not in position. Keep them covered."

The four people continued to regard Kane with a bone-chilling calm. They didn't move, but the Russian asked, "What do you intend to do?"

Kane didn't respond to the question. Instead, he ordered, "Tell the girl to drop the blaster."

The Russian spoke to her in an indecipherable conglomeration of consonants, and she carefully laid the AK down on the floor.

Kane said, "I've seen you somewhere before."

The Russian's eyes flickered with surprise. "I confess your voice has a familiar ring, and since I've only met three Americans in my life, by a process of elimination you must be one of them." He paused for a second, as if ransacking his memory. "You were dressed less formally when I last saw you, but I believe your name is Kane."

Kane's mind provided a silver-disked cap, a greatcoat and gave the man's long locks a shearing. He bit back a curse of surprise. He was one of Colonel Sverdlovosk's District Twelve troopers who had accompanied them on the flight from Russia to the base in Mongolia.

"The colonel didn't make introductions," Kane said. "What's your name?"

The man inclined his head in a short bow. "My name is Grigori Zakat, once a major in the ISN. I now go by the title of Tsyansis Khan-po. As far as I am aware, I am the only survivor of the massacre of the Black Gobi garrison. Do you know Colonel Sverdlovosk's fate?"

"He'd dead." Kane waggled the barrel of his Sin Eater. "I chilled him with this blaster."

Zakat's eyebrows rose as if he were impressed. "Ah. And the Tushe Gun?"

"He'd dead, too," Grant rumbled from behind him, his Sin Eater on a direct line with the back of the Russian's head. "I chilled him with *this* blaster."

Zakat didn't even glance in his direction, nor did his companions. They maintained a steady gaze upon Kane. "Our paths haven't crossed again by mere happenstance."

"Very perceptive," Kane replied. "It appears we have the same goal."

Zakat's lips quirked in a smile. "Which is?"

"That chunk of rock in your hands."

The black-turbaned man said in a sibilant voice, "I

represent its true owners. We are returning it to where it belongs."

"Who are you?" Kane demanded.

The man squared his shoulders, raising his chin, cocking his head at a defiant angle. "I am Gyatso Chohan, direct descendant of the Maha Chohan, first ambassador from the nation of Agartha and keeper of the key."

"And this," Zakat offered mildly, pointing to the woman, "is Trai."

"And the guy in blackface?" Grant asked.

"Shu," replied Zakat.

"Is that a name," Grant growled, "or a sneeze?"

Zakat chuckled. He was the only one who did.

Impatiently, Kane declared, "Ownership issues can be worked out later. Right now I want you to put the rock on the floor and kick it over to me."

"No!" Gyatso's voice hit a high note of outrage. "It is not yours, outlander dog!"

"Calling me an outlander dog when we're in my own country is a pretty piss-poor insult. Do as I say, Zakat."

The Russian did not move, but continued to cup the stone in his hands. "What do you know of this stone? Why do you need it?"

"My business," Kane grated. "Do it and live, Zakat, or don't do it and die. Your choice."

Zakat continued to stare expressionlessly. Kane's finger hovered over the trigger of his pistol, lightly brushing it.

The sound of the shot was an explosive, ear-knocking crack! For an irrational half instant, Kane thought he had unintentionally fired the Sin Eater. He jumped and he heard Grant cursing. Reflexively, his head jerked around to where the sound had come. He recognized the report as made by Domi's Combat Master.

"Kane!" Brigid's trans-comm accurately transmitted her fear into his ear. "We've got company. Has to be scalies."

"How many?" he asked into the transceiver built into the jaw guard of his helmet.

"A lot. At a bare minimum, a dozen. Probably more."

"Hold them off," he told her. "Stand by."

Grant demanded, "What the hell's going on back there?"

"Scalies," Kane replied grimly. "The bastards tracked us here."

Zakat shifted his feet slightly. "We encountered a group of them. Shu's brother Chu was killed. I feared they would lay in wait for us."

Kane didn't respond, mind racing over dozens of plans and discarding most of them.

In a bland, colorless tone, the Russian said, "I submit we have no choice but to agree to a truce, an alliance of convenience—at least until we have dealt with the most immediate threat. As you said, issues of ownership can be worked out later."

Kane examined the man's proposal from several angles and realized it was the only short-term solution that made sense. "Agreed," he stated.

Zakat made two swift motions with his hands. He slid the chunk of rock into a voluminous inner pocket of his coat while simultaneously drawing a stubby Tokarev automatic from his belt. He spoke to Trai, and she bent down to pick up the AK. Shu removed the key-shaped cudgel from his waist, holding it by its leather thong. Gyatso unsheathed his sword with a rasp of steel against leather.

"Stay here with them," Kane said to Grant as he stepped into the murk.

He retraced his path through the display cases and tables, reaching Brigid and Domi at the corner. Both women had their blasters in hand and peered anxiously down the corridor. Faintly, he heard the shuffling of feet, the clatter of claws on the floor.

"Do you know another way out of here?" he asked Brigid.

She shook her head. "I memorized only the way to the Hall of Minerals and Gems."

Kane set his teeth on a groan. "It's a safe bet the scalies know their way around this place. Come on."

Domi and Brigid followed him back to the others. Kane didn't waste time on introductions. He stabbed a hand toward the farthest end of the exhibit hall. "That way."

No one questioned his choice of routes, since it stretched in the opposite direction from the way the scalies had to come. Due to the broken glass carpeting the floor, stealth wasn't an option, but the muties knew where they were anyway.

The hall of minerals ended on a wide transverse corridor, running to the right and to the left. On impulse, Kane chose the right. The glow from the Nighthawks and the flashlight in Shu's hand cast an eerie twilight over the passageway.

Narrow arches opened occasionally on either side, but they kept to the corridor. A worry that they had taken the wrong branch grew in Kane. Though the silence seemed absolute, his pointman's sixth sense told him they were not alone. More than once, passing one of the dark arches, he felt the glare of unseen eyes. He suspected they were being played with, herded into a trap.

Ahead of him in the darkness sounded scuffings and slidings not made by human feet. Gesturing sharply behind him, Kane came to a halt. Far too late, he sensed the rush of bodies. At that second, scalies poured from the doorways on both sides of the corridor behind them, toe claws clicking like castanets, giving tongue to guttural yowls.

Kane instantly realized the mechanics of the trap: while one small group of muties pursued them through the hall of minerals, a far larger group lay waiting in adjacent chambers and ahead of them. He had blithely led everyone right into the ambush.

There wasn't time to make a head count. The scalies rushed like shadows, affording Kane only nightmarish glimpses of them. He raised his Sin Eater and pressed the trigger. Flame wreathed the muzzle, smearing the gloom, casting an unearthly strobing effect on the inhuman faces snarling before him. The corridor became a babel of shouts and screams, punctuated by the stuttering roar of the Sin Eater. He heard Grant open up with his own blaster, and Zakat's Tokarev snapped out steady, hand-clapping bangs.

Bodies slammed into Kane, nearly bowling him off his feet, fetching him up hard against the wall. The quarters were too confined to safely hose bullets around without hitting one of his own people, so he used the Sin Eater as a bludgeon, clubbing away taloned hands clawing for the unprotected portion of his face.

Lit by the Nighthawk microlights, the battle in the corridor took on an unreal, almost hallucinatory quality.

The scalies were armed with crude spears made of sharpened steel rods, poleaxes and daggers forged from metal shards. They stabbed and thrust at the human interlopers, howling and hissing in liquid fury. Kane felt the impacts on the breastplate of his armor as if multiple fingers poked him repeatedly.

Gyatso swung his short sword in a fast, glittering arc, wheeling on the balls of his feet. The blade slashed through scaled throats, plunged into bellies, withdrew to chop at arms and hands. A keening cry issued from his lips.

Using the wall at his back as a brace, Kane kicked out, sending a scalie sprawling into one of its comrades. Taking advantage of the momentary respite, he shoved the Sin Eater back into its holster and reached down for the combat knife in its boot scabbard. His fingers pressed the quick-release button, and he whipped up the long blade just in time to parry a spear thrusting for his face. His knife whirled down to strike the shoulder of his attacker, gashing the chest and driving the hissing monster back.

The same strategy occurred to Grant when he found himself backed to the wall. He leathered his Sin Eater, drew his knife and leaped to the attack even as a dagger point raked along his ribs. He was no defensive fighter. Even in the teeth of overwhelming odds, Grant always carried the battle to the enemy.

His blade chopped out and dropped a scalie, severing a shoulder, while a whistling backhand stroke sank into the skull of another. The scalies crowded him fiercely, raining blows blindly but hampered by their own numbers and lack of strategy.

Domi was reluctant to holster her Combat Master, but she drew her long serrated knife, the one with which she had cut Guana Teague's throat. She sank the point into an arm. She used the blaster barrel to block blows whistling her way. Metal clashed loudly against metal, blue sparks briefly lighting up the darkness. She moved in a blur of speed, dodging, ducking and sidestepping. She slashed the blade in a flat arc, the point tearing through the tough flesh of a scalie's forehead. It uttered a croak of horror as blood rivered into its eyes. As it lifted its hands to staunch the flow, she drove the knife halfway to the hilt into the side of its throat.

Brigid drew her own blade, a Sykes-Fairbairn commando dagger, but it was slapped down by a thrust from a poleax. The blunt end of the shaft rammed into her stomach, and the air shot from her lungs and tears sprang to her eyes. She allowed herself to fall forward against her assailant, smelling the musty reek of its muscular, scale-covered body. As she fell, she stabbed savagely with the dagger, feeling the point meet a second of resistance before sinking deep into yielding flesh. The howl of surprised pain bursting from the scalie's throat nearly deafened her. Hissing and snapping, her foe fell atop her, bearing her to the floor.

Shu lashed out with the key-shaped cudgel, the heavy iron crashing against a skull and shattering it. The scalie yelped, hands clasped to the bleeding split in its scalp and bone, then fell to the floor and rolled in agony.

He struck another stickie with his iron key, smashing it into the mutie's temple. The creature's blood and brains spattered in its face.

Trai wielded the AK like a quarter-staff, blocking knife thrusts on the wooden stock and driving the butt full into faces, breaking noses and teeth, fighting as savagely as the muties.

Only Grigori Zakat did not resort to a weapon other than his firearm. He squeezed off shot after shot, always striking a scaled target. Kane caught fragmented glimpses of him moving swiftly and skillfully, weaving and dodging all blows that came his way.

A crude knife blade flicked out of the shadows, caught the gun and knocked it from the Russian's hand. Zakat skipped to one side, avoiding the sharp point, and his arms whipped out, trapping a scalie's head between them, one at the neck, the other at the rear of the skull. Zakat performed an odd twisting and sliding dance step. The mushy snapping of bone was easily audible even over the cacophony of grunts and growls. When Zakat's hands relaxed their grip, the scalie sprawled motionless to the floor.

Kane's knife ripped open a belly, but he took a hammer blow across his shoulders, which nearly drove him to his knees. A spearhead jammed hard into his solar plexus. He latched on to a scaled wrist and kicked the mutie's kneecap loose with the metal-reinforced toe of his boot.

Screaming and plucking at its leg, the scalie fell into the path of two muties. All three went down in a tangle of thrashing limbs. As one of them tried to get up, Kane kicked it in the head as hard as he could. A hand clapped onto the back of his neck, and he whirled, his razor-edge blade slashing in a flat arc.

The shock of impact jarred up his right arm into the shoulder, and a scalie reeled away, hands at its deeply gashed throat, blood bubbles bursting on its lips and squirting from between its fingers. Crimson droplets splashed over Kane's visor, obscuring his vision.

Back and forth, the battle rolled, blades slashing and chopping, scarlet streams spurting, fanged mouths screaming, feet stamping the fallen underfoot.

Finally, the scalies engaged in a reluctant, stubborn retreat, snarling and spitting in rage. The wounded backed away, whining. Many mutie bodies lay on the floor in widening pools of blood. Blood splattered the walls, smeared the floor and almost everybody in the corridor. Only Zakat seemed untouched. With Grant's help, Brigid heaved the heavy body of the dead scalie away and sprang to her feet.

Now that there were fewer muties to crowd around and impede each other, the danger for the humans was greater. There was room for the scalies to throw knives and their crude spears.

One of the withdrawing scalies drew its arm back, but the red kill dot projected from the laser autotargeter of Grant's Copperhead bloomed on his chest. A ripping triburst stitched holes in its torso, slapping the mutie backward, the knife clanging to the floor.

"Let's go," Kane husked out, starting a shambling run down the corridor. He unlimbered the Copperhead from his belt and stroked the trigger, directing a prolonged burst into the murk ahead of him, not certain if any of the

4.85 mm steel-jacketed rounds found targets. Ricochets whined and buzzed like angry insects.

Guttural voices bellowed behind them, and he heard the others begin sprinting after him, following his lead. Ahead of them glimmered a faint wedge of light, briefly limning the scuttling figures of the fleeing scalies.

Kane palmed away the blood spatters on his visor and increased his speed, not wanting to give the muties time to stage another ambush. He heard a smacking thud behind him and he risked a quick over-the-shoulder glance. Shu stumbled forward, clawing at the three-foot-long rod of rusty metal sprouting between his shoulder blades. He hit the floor heavily on his face, making no attempt to break his fall.

The girl, Trai, slowed her pace a trifle, but Zakat's clipped voice blurted a string of syllables and she began running again, ignoring the impaled Shu.

The wedge of dim light was another archway, and when Kane sprinted under it, he saw four scalies dashing pell-mell for the stairwell that led to the upper level. The corridor branch he had chosen evidently angled around the below-ground floor, ending on the opposite side of the exhibit hall.

Zakat caught up to him. He had taken the AK from Trai and cradled its knife-nicked stock in his arms. "We must not allow the misbegotten lizards to gain the high ground," he panted.

Kane wheezed, "My thoughts exactly."

Zakat triggered the AK as he ran, shifting the barrel in short left-to-right sweeps. Flinders of stone exploded from the stairwell's balustrade, and bullets punched a series of dark holes in the back of one of the scalies. Flinging up its arms, it staggered for a few feet before falling facedown at the foot of the stairway.

Bleating in fear, the other three muties bounded over the body and took the stairs two at a time. Zakat and Kane reached the base just as the scalies struggled to squeeze past the massive head of the blue whale, forced to climb the steps in single file.

The two men opened up at the same time, the drumming roar of the AK-47 drowning out the silenced reports of the Copperhead. There was nothing silent about the reactions of the scalies as the double hailstorm of lead battered them.

They screamed, jerked, flailed and spasmed. Blood and brain matter sprayed the sleek surface of the whale, and its pale blue surface acquired several punctures from wild bullets.

The trio of muties slammed down on the stone risers and, after a few twitches, made no further movement.

Gusting out a sigh, then inhaling, Kane coughed from the acrid cordite fumes. He turned to face the panting Grant, Brigid, Domi, Trai and Gyatso. All were daubed with liquid crimson, but it was impossible to differentiate scalie blood from their own.

He asked, "Is everyone all right?"

All but Gyatso and Trai responded with affirmatives. The girl eased past them to stand beside Zakat, looking up at him in adoration.

Grant hooked a thumb over his shoulder. "I don't think we're being followed, but they can always circle back around through the hall of minerals and come up behind us again."

Before Kane could respond, Zakat announced, "In that case, I suggest our truce continue until we reach the gateway installation. There may be a mob of the monsters waiting to waylay us on the streets."

Kane nodded tersely. "Only until then."

Zakat started up the steps, but Kane restrained him. "I'll walk point."

The Russian smiled thinly. "As you wish, Comrade."

Kane went first, followed by Zakat and his party. Grant brought up the rear, continually checking their backtrack out of habit. There were no signs or sounds of muties who may have regained their courage.

To get past the whale, Kane had to step on the bullet-riddled corpses of the scalies, and blood squished loudly beneath his feet. Zakat's shoulders heaved in an exaggerated, theatrical shudder as he crossed them, murmuring, "Filthy, wretched things."

At the top of the stairwell, they waited for the others to join them. As Brigid struggled over the bodies, one hand on the whale and the other on the balustrade, Kane said to Zakat, "Since you didn't know what happened to Sverdlovsk, I'm assuming the Mongols weren't answering any of Russia's questions."

"You assume correctly," Zakat replied smoothly.

Then, in an eye-blurring burst of speed and coordination, he whipped up the stock of the AK autorifle, crashing it into the side of Kane's jaw.

The brain-jarring impact of the unexpected blow caused Kane's surroundings to wink out for an instant.

When they returned, he became aware of two things more or less simultaneously: a sickening pain in his head and the realization he was falling down the stairs, his back bumping violently against the risers. The cut on the tender lining of his cheek filled his mouth with blood.

He heard Brigid cry out a nanosecond before he caromed into her. She clawed out for the balustrade and managed to keep her footing, but Domi wasn't so fortunate. He clipped her ankles with his head and sent her tumbling over the corpses of the scalies. She uttered a piercing shriek of anger and fear as she fell.

Kane heard the staccato stuttering of the AK-47 and he frantically tried to bring his Copperhead to bear. No bullets came near him, however. He heard semimusical twangs, as of giant guitar strings being plucked, then a pair of whiplike cracks.

He had a fragmented glimpse of Zakat, Trai and Gyatso at the head of the stairwell, right before the vast body of the blue whale began a roaring tobogganing slide down the granite steps.

The Russian had shot away the leviathan's few remaining support cables, and it cannoned down the stairwell like a runaway locomotive. Kane pressed his body tightly against the stone pedestals of the balustrade, and a giant fin missed his head by a finger's width.

The whale rocked slightly from side to side, its pale underbelly bouncing off each riser with nerve-racking screeches. It rumbled past Kane and Brigid, then its snout smashed into the floor below with a hollow thunderclap.

Kane elbowed himself to his feet, glanced toward Brigid to make sure she was all right, then looked down the stairwell. Over the rolling echoes of the crash, he faintly heard a voice lifted in mocking laughter and Zakat calling out, *"Dasvidanya, idiotisch!"*

The passage of the gigantic whale body and its impact had raised flat planes of dust, and Kane didn't see either Domi or Grant. Torn between running up the stairs after Zakat or running down to check on his team, he spit out blood then called, "Grant! Domi!"

For a long moment, he heard nothing. Then, in a voice tight with strain, high and wild with fear, Domi cried, "Help him!"

Spitting out more blood and a curse, Kane lunged down the steps, Brigid on his heels. He followed the streamlined contours of the blue whale and cautiously approached the massive head. Domi, a white wraith in the murk, lifted a tear-wet face and repeated in a forlorn whimper, "Help him."

Icy fingers of fear seized Kane's heart. Domi knelt beside Grant, trying to cradle his head in her lap, which was all that was visible of him beneath the sweeping, furrowed curve of the whale's underjaw.

Grant was in a great deal of pain and as angry as Kane had ever seen him, which probably kept him conscious.

"Do you fucking believe this?" he raged through mashed and bloody lips. "I'm probably the first bastard in three hundred years to be crushed by a whale!"

"You're not crushed," Kane told him, kneeling down, although he had no way of knowing. "Maybe a little compressed."

The preserved carcass of the animal had caught Grant broadside, steamrollering him down the stairs. The weight of the whale had to be gauged in tons and if Grant hadn't been wearing his armor, he most definitely would have been crushed. Only his left arm and his head were free. Domi, on the verge of hysterics, tried to hold him up. Neither Brigid nor Kane had ever witnessed such an emotional reaction in her, not even when she learned the grisly fate of her people in Hell's Canyon some months back.

Out of the corner of his eye, Kane saw Brigid kneading her midsection and grimacing. "You sure you're all right?"

She nodded. "More or less. You?"

Kane gingerly probed the laceration on the inside of his cheek with his tongue. The bleeding seemed to be tapering off, but his facial muscles throbbed fiercely. "More or less."

To Grant, he said, "Don't go anywhere."

He and Brigid hunted through the lower levels for anything they could improvise as a fulcrum. After what seemed like a maddeningly long time, they came across a storage room holding the remains of some long-ago and forgotten construction project: disassembled scaffolding, concrete blocks, sturdy planks and timbers.

They had to make two trips, staggering under the weight of a square timber and several concrete blocks, alert for any sign of scalies who might have lingered.

Balancing the wooden beam on a concrete block, Kane jammed and worked and nudged one end beneath the whale's jaw, as close to Grant as he could manage. Brigid combined her strength and weight with Kane's on the timber. After a long moment of grunting exertion, they were able to lever up the whale's head just far enough for Domi to shove in a concrete block to act as support. Grant swore, wrestled, strained and managed to free his right arm.

"Can you feel your legs?" Brigid asked him, green eyes bright with worry.

"Yeah," he rasped. "They hurt like hell."

"That's a good sign," said Kane.

"I know," Grant snarled. "That's why I'm so goddamn happy at the moment."

Kane stated, "Domi, Baptiste, I'll need you to work the timber while I try to pull him out. Neither one of you are strong enough for that."

They acknowledged his instructions with grim nods. Domi took Kane's place at the fulcrum as he stooped over

Grant, securing firm grips on his forearms. Grant clasped him about the wrists.

"I'm going to pull hard," Kane warned. "If it starts to hurt too much, sing out."

He knew Grant wouldn't, even if he experienced the agony of the damned, but he figured he'd give the man the option.

Kane counted backward from three, bracing his legs, planting his feet solidly. At his shouted "One!" Domi and Brigid hurled their bodies against and over the timber. With a creak of wood and grate of stone, the whale's jaw shifted upward.

Kane catapulted backward. For an eternal moment, he strained against Grant, muscles quivering with tension. Adrenaline surged through him, and with a scraping, slithery sound Grant slid free. Kane saw he used his left leg to kick himself out from under the pinioning weight, so he wasn't paralyzed.

Breath coming in harsh, labored gasps, Grant hiked himself up to a sitting position and took off his helmet. Perspiration sparkled against his dark skin. His lips were swollen and lacerated, but only a cut at the corner of his mouth looked deep enough to require stitches.

Brigid examined his legs as best she could through the polycarbonate sheathing. She guessed the right ankle was broken and suggested removing his boot.

Grant took a sip from the water bottle Domi handed to him and shook his head. "Big neg on that. You'd have to have cut it off. With the metal bracings in it, it's the next best thing to a splint."

He washed down a painkiller, coughed and winced. "Pain in my chest. Hurts when I breathe too deep or swallow."

"Cracked ribs maybe," Kane said. "You got off lucky, though."

"Why is it," Grant asked between clenched teeth, "that whenever I get hurt, you always tell me that?"

Kane tried to grin, despite the pain in his jaw. "I just don't want you to feel sorry for yourself."

Domi dabbed at the blood streaking Grant's chin with a square of gauze taken from the equipment case. "Got to get out of here before sundown. Muties may come back with reinforcements."

Brigid cast an anxious glance up the stairwell. "It won't be easy getting out of here."

"Hell," Kane snapped, "what is?"

She ignored the observation. "One or two of us could make it back to the gateway. Go back to Cerberus and return with DeFore and a stretcher."

"That could take hours," Grant said. "By then, we could be contending with an army of scalies. Let's just go."

With Domi's and Brigid's help, Grant rose to his feet. He draped an arm over Kane's shoulders, leaning into him, balancing on his left foot.

"Just like old times," Kane grunted as Grant sagged into him. "Except you've put on weight since then. I hope I'm in shape for this."

Grant understood the reference to the time a dozen years ago when he had been wounded in the Great Sand Dunes hellzone and Kane had lugged him for days through appallingly rugged terrain.

Sarcastically, he replied, "If it starts to hurt too much, sing out."

Climbing the staircase wasn't quite the ordeal Kane had feared. The risers were broad, not particularly high, and Grant was able to relieve him some of the burden by bracing one arm against the balustrade. Though they staggered and swayed a bit, they managed to make it to the top without falling or stopping for a rest.

They shuffled through the vast exhibit halls. Domi took the point while Brigid walked beside Grant and Kane, steadying them.

"Did the Russian and his crew make off with the rock?" Grant asked.

"Afraid so," Kane answered curtly, boots crunching loudly on shards of glass.

"You should've gone after them," Grant said reproachfully. "I would've been all right."

"Now you tell me," Kane retorted. "Fuck it. If Balam wants that rock so much, he can go after it himself."

By the time they reached the museum entrance, the pewter-colored sky had darkened to the hue of old lead.

"If we're really lucky," Brigid commented dourly, "we'll get back to the installation just as the sun goes down."

They weren't lucky. Fighting through the tangled green hell of Central Park was slow, exhausting work. Thorny vines constantly snared Kane's legs, and twice he nearly tripped and dropped Grant. After they made their way through the park, they were forced to stop and rest for ten minutes.

Despite the pain pill Grant had taken, he winced constantly and was barely able to bite back groans. Brigid and

Domi took turns supplementing the support Kane provided for him, although he protested, claiming two blasters were needed to adequately cover the zone. However, only once did they catch sight of a darting, indistinct figure that might have been a scalie. It maintained a safe distance from them. They came across the corpses of Chu and the scalie still lying in the street. The scream-wings had stripped almost all the flesh from them, and it was impossible to tell by the bloody, skeletal carcasses which had been mutie or human.

By the time the jagged tops of the World Trade Center came into view, full night had fallen. Nearly two hours had passed since they left the museum. All four people were too tense and weary to celebrate. The scalie Domi had shot floated in a pool of drying blood in the parking garage.

"About there," she chirped, striving to sound cheerful.

Kane glared at her. His legs wobbled, his jaw throbbed and his shoulders and back ached with a constant, bone-deep pain.

"Another one-percenter to add to our scorecard," Grant husked out faintly. "That's something."

WITHIN MINUTES of rematerializing in the Cerberus jump chamber, Grant was wheeled off in a gurney to the dispensary. Domi ignored all of DeFore's instructions to remain behind. She distrusted the "fat-assed doctor lady," as she referred to DeFore, because she suspected the older woman had designs on Grant.

Lakesh was full of questions, and his seamed face collapsed into a scowl of disappointment and anger when Kane tendered his report.

"So," he said, his reedy voice pitched low, "you got nothing but hurt?"

Brigid removed the imaging scanner's hard disk from her coat pocket and handed it to him. "We can find out where Zakat and his people came from and jumped from, at least."

Lakesh said nothing, but judging by the set of his lips, he didn't think the disk was much of a prize.

Kane tugged off his helmet and fingered the swelling at his jaw hinge. "When Balam mentioned a thief, he didn't mention that he was a District Twelve officer. A professional."

Lakesh peered at him over the rims of his eyeglasses. "You said he was in the company of Asians?"

"And one hybrid, as far as I could tell."

Lakesh blinked in surprise. "A hybrid?"

Brigid nodded. "I didn't have the chance to get a really good look at him, but he had all the primary physical characteristics."

"More than that," interjected Kane, "he claimed his name was Gyatso Chohan, direct descendant of the Maha Chohan, the Agarthan ambassador."

Both Brigid and Lakesh stared at him in astonishment. Brigid was the first to recover sufficiently to speak. "Then there could be a direct link between the Chintamani Stone, Agartha and the Archon Directorate."

"Which means," Kane declared coldly, "Balam isn't telling us everything he knows about the stone—which should come as no great surprise."

Lakesh shook his head in furious negation. "You don't seriously suspect Balam sent you into a trap, do you?"

"At this point, I seriously suspect everything Balam told us—or didn't tell us, particularly about a hybrid with a connection to this Agartha place."

"The only way to settle the matter," Brigid said crisply, "is to question Balam. Do you think Banks feels up to another ventriloquism session?"

Kane eyed Brigid's face, which was crusted with speckles of scalie blood. "Whether he is or isn't, I know I don't feel up to it at the moment. We should clean up before we do anything."

Lakesh slapped the hard disk against the palm of one hand. "And I should trace the jump line used by Zakat and his people. Let's meet at Balam's holding facility in an hour or so."

Kane and Brigid crossed the control complex to the main corridor. Since the rad counters registered negligible levels of radiation, they saw no need to visit decam. Kane said to her quietly, "You handled yourself well back there, Baptiste."

Dryly, she replied, "If I hadn't, I'd be dead. Later I'll have a nice case of delayed reactions."

"I'll slap you if you really need it."

She turned a bend in the corridor, heading toward her quarters. "And I'll do the same for you."

Kane went to his own suite of rooms, shucked out of his armor and took a long, hot shower. After pulling on the one-piece white bodysuit, he took ice from his small refrigerator, wrapped it in a towel and applied it to the side of his face. He sat down and tried not to dwell on dark thoughts, but they crowded into his mind. It was always difficult to reconcile the present with the past.

Shortly after skydark, a group of families who had taken measures to survive a nukecaust and its resulting horrors emerged from their shelters, their caves, their refuges. The North American continent was now the Deathlands, but they believed they had inherited it by divine right—they had survived when most others had not.

The families and their descendants spread out and divided the country into little territories, much like old Europe when it had been ruled over by princes and barons. Though the physical world was vastly changed, they were determined to bend it to their wills, to control it and the few people still struggling to live upon it.

At first the families half-jokingly referred to themselves as barons, but as the years crawled by, the title no longer had a fictitious origin. The families instituted a tradition and bestowed upon their descendants the title of baron, and the territories they conquered became baronies. Though these territories offered a certain amount of sanctuary from the anarchy of outlying regions, they also offered little freedom. In the beginning, people retreated into the villes ruled by the barons for protection, then as the decades went by, they remained because they had no choice. Generations of Americans were born into serfdom, slaves in everything but name.

After nearly 150 years of barbarism and anarchy, humankind reorganized, coalescing from the ruins of the predark societal structures. Many of the most powerful, most enduring baronies evolved into city-states, walled fortresses whose influence stretched across the Deathlands for hundreds of miles.

In decades past, the barons had warred against one another, each struggling for control and absolute power over territory. Then they realized that greater rewards were possible if unity was achieved and common purpose exploited.

Territories were redefined, treaties struck among the barons, and the city-states became interconnected points in a continent-spanning network. The Program of Reunification was ratified and ruthlessly imposed. The reconstructed form of government was still basically despotic, but now it was institutionalized and shared by all the formerly independent baronies.

Control of the continent was divided among the nine baronies that survived the long wars over territorial expansion and resources. With this forward step in social engineering came technical advances. Technology, most of it based on predark designs, appeared mysteriously and simultaneously with the beginning of the reunification program. There was much speculation at the time that many previously unknown stockpiles were opened up and their contents distributed evenly among the barons. Though the technologies were restricted for the use of those who held the reins of power, life overall improved for the citizens in and around the villes. To enjoy the bounty offered by the barons, all anyone had to do was to first accept responsibility and then to surrender it.

It had all seemed so simple. Irresponsible humanity had allowed their world to be destroyed by the irresponsible people they had put in charge; therefore humanity would no longer be permitted to have responsibility, even over their own lives. The barons accepted the responsibility, or rather had it ceded to them.

The populations of the villes and the surrounding Out-lands cooperated with this tyranny because of a justified fear and an unjustified guilt. For the past eighty years, it had been bred into the people that Judgment Day had arrived and humanity had been rightly punished. The doctrines expressed in ville teachings encouraged humanity to endure a continuous punishment before a utopian age could be ushered in. Because humanity had ruined the world, the punishment was deserved. The doctrines ultimately amounted to extortion—obey and suffer or disobey and die.

The dogma was elegant in its simplicity, and for most of his life, Kane had believed it, had dedicated his life to serving it. Then he stumbled over a few troubling questions, and when he attempted to find the answers, all he discovered were many more troubling questions.

However, the most important question, the guiding mystery of his life was to learn who—or what—was actually responsible for the nukecaust and for implanting these mistaken beliefs in humanity.

Intellectually, he knew all the conditioning was a sham, psychological warfare practiced on a national scale. Dealing emotionally with the realization was a different matter altogether. Breaking away from a lifetime of indoctrination, of believing in certain things in certain ways, sometimes seemed an insurmountable problem.

Conditioning.

Kane turned the word over in his mind a few times, then removed the ice pack. His jaw was numb, but the swelling had been reduced. He left his quarters and walked to the dispensary.

Grant lay on one of the beds within a screened partition. DeFore hovered over him, elevating his right leg. It was swathed in bandages and encased in a metal splint from instep to knee. An IV drip was attached to a shunt on the inside of his left elbow. Black stitches showed at the corner of his mouth. Domi stood at the head of the bed, crusted blood showing stark against her white face.

"What's the diagnosis?" he asked, attempting a bantering tone.

He had directed the question at Grant, but DeFore answered curtly, "A closed fracture of the tibia and talus bones. A number of strained ligaments, abrasions and some internal bruising."

DeFore, a stocky, buxom woman with bronze skin, ash-blond hair and deep brown eyes, made no secret of her dislike of Kane—or rather, her distrust of him. In her medical opinion, he displayed unstable tendencies and exhibited symptoms of post-traumatic stress syndrome. In the recent past, she had tried to order Kane confined to the redoubt so he could be treated, but she had been overruled.

"And the prognosis?" he inquired, this time asking her directly.

Grant answered before she could. "At least a week flat on my back."

"Could be worse," remarked Kane. "Not everybody who's gone one-on-one with a blue whale got off so lucky."

"I'll chill that scrawny Russkie rat-bastard next time I see him," Domi asserted fiercely. "Big time."

"You'll have to get in line," Grant rumbled.

DeFore finished propping pillows beneath Grant's leg and turned to face Kane, full lips pursed in disapproval. "Thanks for bringing me another casualty, Kane."

"Don't start," Grant said sharply. "This wasn't his fault. Blame Lakesh for buying into Balam's wild-rock chase."

DeFore looked to be on the verge of saying more, but she addressed Domi. "You need to clean up. We don't know that scalie blood might not have toxic bacteria swimming around in it."

Domi glowered at her, but Grant side-mouthed to her, "Do as she says or you'll be on the receiving end of a sponge bath."

The girl reluctantly moved away from the bedside. Grant met Kane's eyes. "You figure what happened was part of Balam's plan to get us chilled?"

"I don't know. I doubt it. I *do* figure he knows more about all of this than he let on. I intend to get the answers out of him."

Grant snorted scornfully. "What makes you think he'll be straight with you the next time?"

Kane showed the edges of his teeth in a hard, humorless grin. "Because next time, I'm making the rules."

Kane, Banks, Lakesh and Brigid stood before the glass walls of Balam's cell. All eyes were fixed on Kane, and they reflected incredulity and skepticism in equal measure.

"No," Lakesh declared, shaking his head vehemently. "Absolutely not. I forbid it."

Kane bristled at Lakesh's autocratic tone, but he kept his anger in check. "I'm not suggesting this for the hell of it. We've got to try a new approach in dealing with Balam. We all troop in here like we're requesting an audience with a goddamn baron, communicating through a second party while he's safe and smug behind glass. He won't even allow us a good look at him."

"He's a prisoner," Banks protested.

"But he doesn't act like one," Kane countered, "and most of the time he's not treated like one. You in particular treat him like a foreign dignitary or a diplomatic envoy instead of what he really is—an arrogant, conniving, inhuman monster who wants something from us."

Although her expression showed doubt, Brigid said, "You've got a point. The only time we've ever achieved any kind of exchange was when you behaved disrespectfully toward him."

Lakesh squinted toward the cell, swallowing hard. "But to release him after all this time…it's dangerous."

"That's what he's conditioned us to believe," Kane declared. "Psy-war tactics, just like the conditioning perpetrated by the unification program. We know now it was all bullshit, nothing but control mechanisms. That's what I think Balam's standard 'we stand, we know, we are' message is.

"He's been a prisoner here for over three years. That's the hard reality. We can keep him here forever or let him go. We have the power to do that. Not him. Past time we let him in on that fact."

No one spoke, but they eyed each other questioningly, nervously.

"We've got to knock him off his pedestal," Kane argued. "Stop segregating him from the apekin. Prove to him once and for all who is the prisoner and who are the warders. If he wants favors from the warders, then he's got to give something in return. Like the truth."

Brigid clicked her tongue absently against her teeth, swiveling her head to stare at the red gloom within the recesses of the cell.

Contemplatively, she murmured, "You're right. We did what he asked us to do and nearly got killed. If he had told us a hybrid was involved, we could have taken measures."

"Maybe he didn't know a hybrid was involved," Banks protested, though he didn't sound convinced of his own words.

"You told us he had an extreme reaction to Baron Ragnar's assassination," Brigid reminded him. "That proves the existence of a mind-link between Archons and hybrids."

Banks shrugged. Kane gazed levelly at Lakesh. "Well?"

The old man sighed and tugged at his long nose. "I don't know. I simply don't know. I traced the jump line Zakat and his people used. The transit path didn't track back to Russia but originated from an unindexed unit, not part of the Cerberus network."

"Did you get a fix on the unit?" Brigid asked.

"Tibet, somewhere in the Himalayas. By cross-referencing the coordinates with the geographical database, it locked in on the Byang-thang Plateau."

"The Byang-thang Plateau?" echoed Kane, stumbling over the pronunciation. "What the hell is there?"

"An old Russian or Chinese military installation, perhaps."

"Or," Brigid ventured, "the Trasilunpo lamasary I found mentioned in the historical records—the same lamasery where the Chintamani Stone was reputedly sheltered. A modular gateway unit could have been installed there before the nuke."

Lakesh nodded. "I considered the same thing. The autosequencer shows a live transit line, so our unit can lock in on it."

Kane's lips compressed. "Waste of time."

Lakesh looked at him quizzically. "Why so?"

"Because none of us will be following that line unless you agree to release Balam."

The old man's blue eyes flashed with sparks of anger. "Blackmail is beneath you, friend Kane."

"It's not blackmail, it's negotiation. You want something from me, I want something from Balam, Balam wants something from us. We all get something or nobody gets anything."

Lakesh scowled ferociously, but Kane maintained a composed, neutral expression. He noticed Brigid doing her best to repress a smile.

Kane guessed the kind of thoughts wheeling through Lakesh's mind. The cooperation among the Cerberus exiles was by agreement; there was no formal oath or vows like those he and Grant had taken upon admission into the Magistrate Division. There was no system of penalties or punishments if cooperation was withheld, nor was there a hard and fast system of government within its vanadium walls.

There were security protocols to be observed, certain assigned duties that had to be performed, but anything other than that was a matter of persuasion and volunteerism. Lakesh really didn't have the power to forbid anyone to do anything, so Kane had him over the proverbial barrel and he wasn't ashamed of it.

Finally, Lakesh spit a wordless utterance of frustrated disgust and gestured toward the control console. "Do it, Banks. Open the cell."

Banks opened his mouth as if he were about to protest, closed it and stepped over to the panel. He touched a knob, and the overhead lights dimmed to dusk level. "We don't want to cause him discomfort."

"Like hell we don't," Kane snapped. "Bring them up a bit more—not enough so he's blinded, but enough so we can get a good look at him for once."

Banks hesitated. Dolefully, he said, "Has it occurred to you that we may be doing exactly what Balam wants us to do? Maybe he implanted this suggestion in your mind so he can escape."

Kane thought that possibility over for a few seconds. "If the little bastard can get through all of us, out of this locked room and somehow out of the redoubt, then he's more than welcome to escape. Good riddance to a bad alien."

As Banks manipulated the knob again, the lights brightened. He reached out to a row of keys on the console and depressed three of them in a certain sequence. Electronic chimes rang from the vicinity of Balam's cell, then one entire pane slowly rose, sliding into a double-slotted frame. A puff of air wafted out, carrying with it the faint scent of wet cardboard sprinkled lightly with cinnamon and bleach. The mingled odors weren't repulsive, but they were certainly odd.

Facing the open portal, Kane announced loudly, "Recess time, you little hell-spawn. After three and a half years, you should be happy to stretch your legs."

Nothing stirred or shifted within the gloom of the cell. Kane took a threatening step forward. Sharply, he commanded, "Come out or I'll drag you out."

He half expected his mind to be clouded by the quasi-hypnotic mist that Balam projected to mask his true appearance. Instead, he heard a soft footfall, then another and another. A figure loomed in the crimson-hued murk, stepped to the open portal and paused, looking around curiously.

Always before, Kane had received only a fleeting impression of Balam's physical appearance, and then it was overshadowed by an image of his huge, penetrating eyes. He sensed Brigid tensing beside him.

She had seen the mummified remains of an Archon in the Black Gobi, and both of them had encountered a horde of hybrids at the Dulce installation. They had been shown the preserved corpse of an Annunaki, purportedly the root race of the Archons. There had been a suggestion of the monstrous about all of them.

Balam did not resemble a monstrosity. He reminded Kane of a work of art, as crafted by a minimalist sculptor. He was very short, barely four feet tall, and excessively slender, his body like that of a half-grown boy.

He wore a dark, tight-fitting suit of a nonreflective metallic weave. The one-piece garment covered him from throat to toes, leaving only his hands and head bare.

His high, domed cranium narrowed down to an elongated chin. His skin bore a faint grayish pink cast, stretched drum tight over a structure of facial bones that seemed all cheek and brow, with little in between but two great upslanting eyes like black pools. His nose was vestigial and his small mouth only a tight, lipless slash. Six long, spidery fingers, all nearly the same length, dangled at the ends of his slim arms.

"Polydactyl," Brigid murmured.

"What's that?" asked Kane.

"An extra digit on his hands, probably his feet, too."

Balam stood swaying like a reed before a breeze. Kane had seen the movement before, when the hybrids in Dulce addressed Baron Cobalt. He had guessed it was a form of ritual greeting.

Kane stepped closer, close enough to be aware of Balam as a living creature, smelling his unearthly, musky perfume. He saw the faint rise and fall of respiration and the tiny pores in his finely textured skin.

The huge, tear-shaped dark eyes regarded him, alert but not frightened. Thin membranes with a faint crisscrossing pattern of blue veins veiled them for an instant. Balam breathed, moved, blinked and reacted to his presence.

Kane gestured grandly. "No need to stand on ceremony. Join the apekin in our jungle."

Balam stepped into the room with the same kind of bizarrely beautiful danceresque grace possessed by the hybrids. He didn't seem intimidated, even by the three humans towering over him. He looked around, and his slit of a mouth parted. A sound issued from it, faint, hoarse, but far deeper in timbre than any of them expected.

Balam asked, "Why?"

"SO YOU CAN SPEAK," Kane declared, smiling mockingly. "Why were you using Banks here as your mouthpiece?"

One of Balam's bony fingers unfolded, touching the base of his throat. "Difficult," he said in a scratchy, strained whisper. "Structure here different. Verbalizing thoughts difficult."

"Atrophied vocal cords?" Lakesh murmured.

Banks dragged a stool over. "Do you want to sit?"

Balam shook his head. Again he rasped, "Why?"

"Because you're no longer of value as a captive," Kane replied flatly. "Or a hostage. It doesn't seem like the Directorate knows you're here. And if they do know, they don't care."

"You…" Balam paused to cough, a shockingly human sound. "You set me free?"

Kane eyed him coldly. "Not yet. But if we did, where would you go?"

Balam responded to the question with one of his own. "Stone…did you find stone?"

"We found it, but we didn't recover it," Brigid stated. "And here's why."

She launched into a terse, blow-by-blow recounting of the events in New York. Balam's placid, masklike countenance didn't alter. Kane wondered if it could.

"A hybrid was one of the thieves," Kane said. "He claimed descent from the Agarthan ambassador. What do you know about that?"

Balam only blinked.

"This is all tied up with the Archon Directorate, isn't it?" Kane pressed, a note of anger apparent in his voice. "What's it about?"

"You must get stone, Kay-nuh."

"Why must he?" Lakesh asked.

"Key," Balam replied. "Key to all futures. Key to all our destinies."

"*Our* destinies?" Kane repeated derisively. "Humans and Archons share a destiny other than master and slave?"

Balam swallowed hard and painfully. His tissue-thin eyelids dropped over his eyes for a moment, then his fathomless black gaze sought out Banks. He stretched out a beseeching right hand toward him.

"Meld me," he whispered. "So may explain."

"I don't think so," snapped Kane.

"It's my decision," Banks countered. "I'll do it so we can get this over with."

Balam kept his hand out. "Touch. Make meld more strong. Explain more."

At that, Banks's determination wilted a bit, his brow knitting in consternation. But he firmed his lips and stepped forward, reaching with his left hand. Their fingers touched, then intertwined.

"Relax," whispered Balam. "Like before. Empty mind."

Perspiration suddenly sprang to Banks's forehead, then ran down his face in large drops. His lean body quaked in a seizurelike shudder, his sweat-sheened face contorting.

"Banks?" Brigid questioned, putting a hand on his shoulder.

In a barely audible whisper, he said, "Now we may proceed."

Kane saw Balam's lipless mouth move slightly, synchronized with Banks's voice, forming the words he wanted vocalized. The ventriloquist-and-dummy analogy had more foundation than ever before, and it made Kane shiver.

"I was not aware of the new human's presence," Banks-Balam said, voice growing louder and stronger.

Kane quirked an eyebrow, remembering "new human" was Baron Cobalt's choice of euphemisms for the hybrids.

"I sensed only the man you call Zakat because he touched the fragment of the trapezohedron sheltered in the lamasery. He now has two of the pieces, which will lead him to the third and prime facet."

"Which lamasery?" Lakesh demanded.

"You know it as the Trasilunpo in the nation called Tibet."

"You still haven't explained the importance of the stone," challenged Kane. "Or at least why *we* should consider it important."

Banks shifted his gaze toward Lakesh. "*You* know, Mohandas Lakesh Singh. The knowledge is buried within your mind, but you have yet to make the connection."

Lakesh's face acquired a new set of seams. "I see no reason to speak in riddles."

"I described the stone as a creation through which the flux lines of possibility, of probability, of eternity, of *alternity* meet."

Lakesh stared first at Banks, then at Balam in bewilderment. Then his head snapped up, eyebrows crawling above the rims of his glasses, toward his hairline. "The trapezohedron is a point of power, a nontechnological quantum vortex?"

"Vortexes which you once tried to locate and access by technological means."

Brigid demanded, "Are you saying the Chintamani Stone, the trapezohedron is a naturally occurring hyperdimensional vortex point like the one we found in Ireland?"

"It is a key," Banks-Balam stated simply.

Kane thrust his head forward, eyes glittering in predatory anticipation. "A key to the home of the Archons?"

Banks-Balam did not respond for such a long time Kane almost repeated himself. Finally, the soft answer came, "Those you call the Archons cannot be found with any key."

Crossly, Brigid asked, "Why do you keep qualifying every remark about the Archons? What do you call yourselves?"

The word passed the lips of Banks in a rustling whisper. "Humans."

Everyone gaped at Balam in outraged disbelief. Kane snarled, "You're not human, you little son of a bitch. We learned all about you, how you're the result of a crossbreeding program between a reptilian species called the Annunaki and the Tuatha De Danaan—who, though humanoid, weren't human."

The sound that floated from Banks was so unusual, it took them several seconds to recognize it. Balam was forcing Banks to laugh.

"You learned only a small, oversimplified bit of my people's origins, our history, and even that was distorted by myth and legend. But it does not change the fact that the so-called Archons are still human, native to this world.

"Yes, what you believe to be mankind is old, but they were not the first on Earth. My race is far, far older, but it was your folk who so long ago cut the thread that bound us to one another. We had no choice but to draw apart. Far, far apart have we drawn, we who might have shared this world with you but for the slings and swords and spears of your ancestors. We who were not aliens, yet alienated."

Banks-Balam spoke with bitterness, but a note of pride underscored his words. "It is we who gave you the legacy of science and spirit, yet you allowed it to drift into madness."

Kane felt rage building in him, and it required all of his self-control to contain it. "We've heard variations of this speech before," he said. "We know all about how your kind raised us from the ape, how fucking superior you are to us, how you're reducing us to the ape again. If the stone doesn't lead to the Archon Directorate, then where can they be found?"

"They cannot be found."

The response came so quickly, Kane felt his nape hairs prickling with suspicion. "You're lying."

Balam cocked his head at him, a movement that was reminiscent of a praying mantis trying to figure out the nature of a new prey. "You have been misled by your people, trained to think in rigid channels. They created the Archon Directorate appellation for the sake of simplicity, to ease clerical chores."

"Are you saying," Brigid ventured haltingly, "that there is no such thing as the Archon Directorate?"

Banks and Balam shook their heads slightly at the same time. "This is not the topic of the discussion."

Lakesh suddenly hugged himself, shivering, but not from fear. His eyes shone with a jubilant light. In a thrilled whisper, he declared, "The Oz Effect. I was right. By God, I was right."

"What?" Brigid and Kane demanded in unison.

"A theory I've been toying with. Balam, we know more about you than you realize. Once there were many of your kind. You mastered space and hyperdimensional travel aeons ago, probably using the quantum-pathway technology left by your forebears. Your people served, either by accident or design and sometimes both, as the source of myth cycles, religions and secret societies.

"Revelations about your people, our cousins, were kept hidden for thousands of years. Why? Because they may have accelerated the spiritual evolution of mankind. But your scientific secrets were doled out piecemeal until humanity's fixation with technology reached critical mass and plunged us into a cataclysm."

"One of many cataclysms," Banks-Balam said softly. "This last one was the ultimate baptism of fire for humankind to overcome—to forge your spirits in a crucible and have them grow strong or to shatter forever."

Lakesh acknowledged the observation with a dry chuckle. "A baptism for your people, as well, wasn't it? A last-ditch solution to the final curtain of extinction."

The old man took a step forward, bending down, hands on his knees so he could stare unflinching and unblinkingly into Balam's huge eyes. "Over two hundred years ago, I saw you at the installation in Dulce, New Mexico. Since then, I have learned you acted as the liaison between the American government's Overproject Majestic and the so-called Archon Directorate.

"Before that, you were a guest of the Soviets. They dug you out of the crater at the Tunguska blast where you'd been in cryostasis for thirty-some years when your vessel crashed."

"What's all that got to do with the home of the Archon Directorate?" Kane asked, not trying to disguise the angry impatience in his voice.

Lakesh grinned broadly. Without removing his gaze from Balam, he said, "Friend Kane, dearest Brigid, the Archon Directorate stands before you."

Balam's blank face registered no emotion whatsoever, but he jerked his hand free from Banks's grasp as if scalded. The young man gasped, his features squeezing together like a fireplace bellows. He staggered and pressed his fists against his temples, and would have collided with a trestle table if Brigid hadn't caught him.

All of Kane's anger was washed away by icy floodwaters of shock, incredulity and denial. He was too dumbfounded to speak.

Banks steadied himself, massaging the sides of his head. He glared at Balam and said accusingly, "You might have told me you were going to do that."

Lakesh laughed, a harsh sound without mirth. "He might have told us a lot of things."

"Lakesh, you're going to have explain what you mean," Brigid declared.

Lakesh kept his eyes on Balam's. He crooned, "You gave us enough clues to put the puzzle together—I grant you that. Not to mention an equal number of diversions, false trails and pieces that almost fit but didn't quite. But now we know the truth, Balam—you're the only one of your kind. The last Archon, or whatever you prefer to call yourself."

Kane and Brigid were stunned speechless, grappling with the enormous implications of Lakesh's confident assertion.

"The Archon Directorate was protective coloration," he went on, "an art your people were masters of over the long, long track of centuries and civilizations."

Brigid finally found her voice. "You mean the Archon Directorate is only him?" she questioned. "All along, only one of them?"

"At least over the last couple of hundred years." Lakesh's tone held a gloating note. "The Oz Effect, wherein a single, vulnerable entity created the illusion, the myth of an all-powerful force as a means of manipulation and self-protection. My compliments, Balam. Over the last four millennia, you kept the entire human race guessing.

"You allowed us to suspect you were gods, demons, fairies and finally extraterrestrials, always fitting your presence into the current frame of reference. You let us believe you were everything but what you really were—a dying people, racing inexorably to the finish line of extinction.

"That was the reason for the hybridization program, so your people would live on in one form or another, a form you chose. I don't think I'd be too far off the mark to suggest that most, if not every molecule of Archon genetic material in the hybrids derives solely from you.

"Thus, you are both the last of your kind and the father of a new race. A bridge between the old and the new. Hence the reality of the psionic threads supposedly linking all of the so-called Archons to each other and to your half-breed spawn."

Lakesh straightened up swiftly, face flushed, eyes shining brightly. "And for the first time in thousands of years, a race of beings that carry the genetic characteristics of your folk may at last win the game of the survival of the fittest. A contest your people knew they had lost probably twenty thousand years ago."

Kane tried to speak, but he felt numb, dislocated, as if his brain were immersed in soggy cotton wadding. "He—Balam...he's it? He and he alone orchestrated the nukecaust, the unification program, all of it? Just so *his* genes would be the ones in the majority?"

"Every father wants the best opportunities for his children," Lakesh said. "Balam—whether he had hands-on control of events that led up to the nukecaust or not—was simply eliminating the competition. He stacked the deck, and if a few hundred million of us had to die in the process, that was all part of the game."

Kane stared at the fragile creature, recalling all the equally fragile hybrids he had seen. He remembered what Baron Cobalt had told him: "The humanity you know is dead. The new humanity is taking its place. All a matter of natural selection. Nature taking its course.... We are a highly evolved breed, and our numbers are growing.... This is our world now, and nothing can be done to arrest the tide.... Accept our kind as we have accepted *your* kind."

A roaring red madness shredded Kane's soul. He lunged forward, shouldering Lakesh aside, his hands encircled the slim, short column of Balam's throat. His flesh felt slick, but warm with life. Kane snatched Balam up, swinging his feet clear of the floor. The slender creature weighed no more than a child's doll.

Dimly, he heard Brigid, Banks and Lakesh shouting his name. He squeezed, staring straight into Balam's fathomless eyes, silently daring him to fight for his life. Banks and Brigid latched on to his arms, beating at his wrists, trying to prise his fingers from Balam's neck.

The pain of their blows was drowned in his hatred, so intense it in turn became pain. Kane felt as if his body had turned to steel, and his hate flowed like electrical current out along the line of his vision, pouring into Balam's eyes to shrivel whatever imitation of a soul he possessed.

With appalling suddenness, the expressionless face of Balam dimmed, blurred and all Kane could see were the huge eyes, engulfing everything. First there was an utter blackness, then vague, evanescent shapes wavered within it before taking shape.

Like storm clouds dispersing, the blackness rolled away and Kane saw a huge city of dark stone rising at the base of towering, snowcapped mountain ranges. A massive, round column of white rose from the center of the city, jutting at least three hundred feet into the sky. With a faraway sense of shock, he recognized it as a prototype of the Administrative Monoliths in all of the villes. On a subliminal level, Kane understood the city was more of a symbol, representing many similar settlements scattered over the world.

A thready nonvoice whispered, *This was who we were.*

Kane floated over the buildings, receiving an impression of odd angles and immense green-black blocks. Though the lines of the structures looked simple, they possessed a quality that eluded real comprehension to their size and shape, as if they had been built following architectural principles just slightly apart from those the human brain could absorb.

From the city, silvery disks like polished coins seen edge-on rose and flitted across the sky. Some were very small and delicate, while others were gargantuan spheres, like moons given the power of flight.

Through the streets of the city moved beings cast in the mold of humanity, but they were not human as Kane defined the term. They were dome-skulled, slender creatures, very tall and graceful. Their tranquil eyes were big and opalescent, their flesh tones a pale blue.

Somehow, Kane understood that they were a branch on the mysterious tree of evolution, yet the twigs of humanity sprouted from their bough. In physical appearance, they were as separate and as apart from Balam as humanity was from his Neanderthal progenitors. In spiritual and intellectual development, they were as superior to mankind as a Neanderthal was to an ape.

Kane knew that they existed, much less thrived, as part of a pact between two root races that had warred for possession of Earth. They were a bridge, not only between two races, but flowing within them, mixing with the blood of their nonhuman forebears, was the blood of humanity.

These beings were mortal, though exceptionally long-lived. Like the humanity to which they were genetically connected, they loved and experienced joy and sadness. Their cities were centers of learning, and the citizens didn't suffer from want. They knew no enemies; they had no need to fight for survival. As the end result of a fight for survival between their ancestors, the beings had been born to live on the world of humans and guide them away from the path of war that had nearly destroyed Earth.

Their duty was to keep the ancient secrets of their ancestors alive, yet not propagate the same errors as their forebears, especially in their dealings with mankind, to whom they were inextricably bound.

Humanity was struggling to overcome a global cataclysm, striving again for civilization, and the graceful folk in the cities, the outposts, did what they could to help them rebuild. They insinuated themselves into schools, into political circles, prompting and assisting men into making the right decisions.

They sought out humans of vision, humans with superior traits. They mingled their blood with them, initiated them into their secrets, advised them. On many continents—Mu, Gondawara, Hyberborea, Atlantis—new centers of learning arose, empires and dynasties spread out carrying the seeds of civilization.

The folk had no god, no true deity they worshiped, but they valued a relic, a totem, an oracle. Kane saw it in a vast space. He couldn't see the roof or the walls, but had the impression of an enormous chamber. In front of him, a strange radiance played about an altar made of six sharply cut slabs of stone.

The source of the glow he couldn't see, but on the altar lay a night black, yet shining object. He inspected it from

all sides, but its confusing lines looked different from
every angle. Its facets were highly polished, and it didn't
resemble a stone. It was a sculpture, incorporating much
of the same geometric principles as the city itself.

It pulsed with life, yet it wasn't alive. It exuded an im-
measurable intelligence, but it wasn't sentient. Kane only
vaguely understood its nature. The trapezohedron was the
sum-total of all that the root races knew and believed. It was
a teacher, a means of communication, a key to parallel casements. Kane wasn't quite certain of what that meant, but it
didn't matter. He was only an observer of the panorama of
a prosperous, self-satisfied civilization, of the accomplishments of a prideful people who had tamed a savage world.

The trapezohedron wasn't the deity of their civilization, yet it was their heart.

Then, after uncounted years, came the new cataclysms.
The magnetic centers shifted, the great glaciers and ice
centers at the poles withdrew toward new positions. Vast
portions of the ocean floor rose, while equally vast land
masses sank beneath the waves. The configuration of the
Earth altered.

Convulsions shook mountains and the nights blazed
with flame-spouting volcanoes. Earthquakes shook the
walls and towers of the city made of green-black stone.
Many of the folk died quickly, while others lingered in a
state of near death for years. The vast knowledge of their
ancestors, the technical achievements bequeathed to
them, became their only means of survival.

The survivors consulted the stone, the shining trapezohedron, desperate to find a solution to their tragedy
within its black facets. It showed them how to build

thresholds to parallel casements. Over the stone appeared
what seemed to Kane to be an archway surrounded by
fireflies, strung around it in a combination of glimmering colors.

In ages past, the root races had used such thresholds,
knowing that Earth was the end of a parallel axis of these
casements. Kane only dimly realized what all of it meant,
but he understood the basic principles of the mat-trans
units were in use, although expanded far beyond linear
travel from place to place.

The stone also suggested that they changed themselves
with the world, to alter their physiologies. Using ancient
techniques, the race transformed itself in order to survive.
Muscle tissue became less dense, motor reflexes sharpened, optic capacities broadened. A new range of abilities
was developed, which just allowed them to live on a
planet whose magnetic fields had changed, whose weather
was drastically unpredictable.

Their need for sustenance veered away from the near
depleted resources of their environment. They found new
means of nourishment other than the ingestion of bulk
matter. They had no choice.

The proud, unified race of teachers and artisans degenerated, scattered, a lost tribe skulking in the wilderness.
The survivors had no choice but to spread out from the city.

A few of them stayed, trying to adapt, the land changing them before they changed the land. Their physical appearance altered further as they retreated. The changes
wrought were subtle, gradual. In adapting themselves to
the changing conditions of the planet, they who had been
graceful neogods became small, furtive shadow dwellers.

Only a handful of the folk remained among the lichen-covered stone walls of their once proud city. The new generations born to them were distortions of what they had been. The weak died before they could produce off-spring, and the infant-mortality rate was frightful for a thousand years. They did not leave the ruins to find out how humanity had fared in the aftermath of the changes.

Humankind adapted much faster to the postcata-strophic world, and new generations began to explore, to conquer. They conquered with a vengeance and ruthless-ness and spilled oceans of blood. In their explorations, they found their way into the city—men in leather har-ness, helmets of bronze, bearing bows, spears and swords.

They brought war to the stunted survivors of the catas-trophes, viewing them not as their progenitors had, as mentors or semidivine oracles, but as *things*—neither man, beast nor demon, but imbued with characteristics superior and inferior to all three.

Scenes of screaming chaos and confusion filled Kane's mind, bloody sequence following bloody sequence, com-ing so swiftly they melded into one long tapestry of atroc-ity, murder and theft. He glimpsed a bearded man working the blade of his sword between the facets of the stone, pry-ing them out, putting them in his cloak and fleeing.

The men pursued the small folk through the vast ruins of their city, slaughtering and butchering until they had no choice but to fight back. The farther they had retreated from the world, the greater had grown their powers in other ways. The humans fled in blind panic, but the folk knew others would inevitably return, perhaps to steal the rest of the trapezohedron.

They had not been defeated, only beaten back. They knew they couldn't hope to defeat humans, but they determined to control them. If nothing else, they still possessed the monumental pride of their race and devotion to the continuity of their people. To accomplish that, they knew they had to retreat even further.

Kane glimpsed a mountain and a cavernlike opening hidden between great boulders. He groped through a long, narrow tunnel built of heavy joined stones. Small worn steps, too small for human feet, led downward out of sight, into clinging blackness. He came to a round, low chamber with a domed ceiling.

In its center, on an altar sat the black stone, incomplete yet still pulsing with power. The small, stunted folk clustered around it, caressing its dark surface with their six-fingered hands, drawing on its wellspring of knowledge, projecting their own experiences into it, using it as a means of broadcasting to any of their brethren who might still live on the face of the world. The message was simple: "We are here. Join us."

A pitifully small few did, descending into the bowels of the Earth to live and plan. One who came was the last of the parent race, still alive and unchanged. The name Lam entered Kane's mind. He rallied his people, becoming a spiritual leader, a general, a mentor. He knew his folk could not stay hidden forever, nor did they care to do so. The human race could not be influenced without interaction.

Under Lam's guidance, he and some of his people ascended again into the world of men, to influence the Phoenicians, the Romans, the Sumerians, the Egyptians,

the Aztecs. Lam was known throughout human historical epochs, but by names such as Osiris, Quetzacoatal,
Nyarlthotep, Tsong Kaba and many others.

Lam and his people watched many nations and tongues
be born and die, and they were proud that they survived
while so many human civilizations did not.

The visions came faster now, images whirling through
Kane's mind, then vanishing.

Legends filtered out among holy men about the underground city beneath Asia. It was called many things, Hsi
Wang Mu, Bhogavati, Shamballah, Agartha. Myth and
yearning built Agartha into a noble and beautiful metropolis with streets paved with mosaics of emeralds, rubies
and diamonds. It was, of course, nothing but a refuge for
the pitiful remains of a once proud people.

Though their life spans had been reduced over the pre-
ceding centuries following the changes, they were still
long-lived. But they weakened and died while the human
race was still young and virile. Within humans lay their
salvation.

As they were themselves the product of genetic manipulation, Lam turned to humankind, first to restore their
own flagging vitality, then to carry the seed of his folk onward so it wouldn't vanish.

Most of the bioengineering experiments took place in
Asia, and there were many, many failures. Sterility was the
common defect in the hybrids birthed in Agartha.

Finally seven hybrids were born who could reproduce.
The seed of Lam's once proud race lived, albeit in diluted
form. If there were such a thing as pure-blooded hybrids,
these seven creations were it. Kane saw them, slender and

compact of form, amber skinned, wearing simple draper-
ies, huge eyes displaying wisdom but little passion.

They were attuned to the trapezohedron, the Chintamani Stone. They used it to manipulate the properties of the
stolen facets, to lead those humans seeking Agartha away
from it.

With Lam as their guide, the seven ventured out into
the world, visiting the lamaseries, teaching lessons as their
forebears had done. Legends collected around them, and
they became known as the Eight Immortals.

But they were not truly immortal, and even long life
spans have their limitations. Eventually they died, but
not before spreading the concept of Agartha, the mystical
community that guided the evolution of humanity. In reality, Agartha was a refuge for Lam's people, drawn there
by the beacon of the stone.

In the centuries that followed, Lam and his people continued to interact and influence human affairs, from the
economic to the spiritual. They allowed things to happen
they could have stopped, or nudged events in another direction. Employing the technology left behind by their
forebears, they visited their ancestors' bases on the Moon
and the other planets in the solar system.

Balam himself was returning from a mission in space
when his vessel malfunctioned and exploded over the
Tunguska River region in Siberia. He lay in cryosuspen-
sion for over thirty years until discovered and revived by
a Russian scientific expedition.

After another accident involving one of their flying vehicles in the late 1940s, an Agarthan emissary was dispatched to war-weary Europe for a twofold purpose: to

sprinkle fanciful tales about the hidden city of Agarthans with its perfect beings with diplomatic ties to extraterrestrials, and to make certain the Roswell incident was properly covered up.

The ambassador, who went by the title of the Maha Chohan, was one of the most human appearing of the hybrids, and possessed a glib tongue and pronounced psionic abilities. He was instrumental in negotiating the release of Balam from the Soviets.

By the middle of the twentieth century, the number of Lam and Balam's people had dwindled as humanity's population had exploded. They had inbred the same gene pool too often, replicating it over and over, until the bloodlines had degenerated, and only pale, disease-prone imitations of their people were born.

Now, Balam's nonvoice whispered, *see us as we are.*

Once more, Kane saw the altar room of the trapezohedron, but the chamber had become a catacomb. Around the altar reposed bare bones, the skeletal remains of the seven immortals, hollow eye sockets staring at the roof for eternity.

Lam stood at the altar, eyes wide open and seeming to stare straight into Kane's soul. Within his long fingers rested the cube of dark stone.

Spare him his pitiful immortality, sighed Balam.

WITH A SAVAGE EFFORT, Kane tore his gaze away from the obsidian depths of Balam's eyes, glimpsing for an instant a reflection of his face, drawn in a bestial snarl.

Immediately, his ears rang with shouts, and he felt fists battering at his arms, hands wrenching at his fingers. He released Balam, and the small figure alighted on the floor without a misstep.

Kane allowed himself to be borne backward by Brigid, Banks and Lakesh. Banks cried out angrily, "What the hell are you doing?"

Bewilderment was in the stare Kane cast him. "How long?"

"How long what?" Lakesh demanded, breath coming fast and frantic.

Kane yanked his arm away from Banks's grasp. "How long was I holding Balam?"

"I wouldn't call it holding," Brigid snapped. "You were trying to strangle him."

"I know what I was doing," Kane retorted. He winced as a needle of pain stabbed through the left side of his head. "How long was I doing it?"

Banks scowled. "Only a couple of seconds, thank God. We kept you from getting a good grip on him."

The strangeness of Kane's question finally penetrated Banks's anger, and he looked at him curiously. "Why do you ask that?"

Kane probed his temple with fingers. The pain was already ebbing. "I think I learned more about Balam in those couple of seconds than you learned in the last three years."

Balam stood and blinked calmly at them, completely unperturbed by his brush with violent death.

"He telepathically gave me a history lesson," continued Kane. "He didn't answer all the questions, but he answered a good deal of them."

Brigid, Lakesh and Banks stared at Balam in silent wonder. Kane did, too, and for the first time realized Balam's pride and dignity had foundation.

He said to him quietly, "You never tried to escape because you have no place to go. There's nothing for you in Agartha. Your work is done, you've accomplished the mission to keep your race alive."

He did not ask a question; he made a statement. Balam inclined his head in a nod.

"And you fear that if Zakat returns the facets of the stone to the trapezohedron, he'll accidentally tap into these 'parallel casements' and undo everything you have achieved."

Again came the nod.

"What are parallel casements?" asked Lakesh, sounding mystified and intrigued.

Kane shrugged. "I don't know. Some phenomena associated with the stone. Phenomena that Balam fears."

"Why?" Brigid asked, enthralled yet disturbed.

Kane shook his head, still trying to reconcile the history Balam had imparted with his own hate-fueled prejudices. "He wasn't clear about it."

He forced himself to lock gazes with Balam, mentally comparing the small, pale, big-domed entity with the images of his parent race. It was like seeing a reflection in a distorted mirror, a cruel reminder of what might have been. As his people had risen higher than humanity's aspirations, so they also sank lower than mankind's nightmares.

But for humanity, Kane felt even worse—he had no sense of the mighty brought low by an indifferent cosmos. Compared to Balam and his people, mankind was always low, not the first lords of Earth at all. They only arrogantly imagined themselves that they were ever really its lords, but older and more enduring races preceded them.

Balam met his gaze dispassionately, but Kane sensed the loneliness and pain radiating from him like an invisible aura. But regardless of his reasons, Balam and his kind had conspired against humanity for uncounted centuries. A natural cataclysm had decimated their civilization, so in turn they had orchestrated an unnatural one to bring mankind in line with their concepts of unity.

He remembered what Balam had said to him: *Humanity must have a purpose, and only a single vision can give it purpose.... We unified you.*

Now he knew part of the reason why, but it didn't erase the sin.

"You unified us, all right," Kane said grimly. "You gave us a purpose—to reclaim our world from those who carry your blood."

Balam whispered, "And yours."

Kane felt the anger build in him again, but it was a weary kind of anger, an afterthought to the bleak realization that the so-called Archon Directorate hadn't really conquered humanity—it had tempted humanity with the tools to conquer itself.

Naked greed, ambition, the thirst for power over others, those were the carrots snapped up gleefully by the decision makers. Yes, in order to survive Balam and his people had tricked mankind into living down to its most base impulses, but always the choice of whether to do so had been man's.

"Kane?" Brigid stared at him keenly, quizzically.

Kane shook himself mentally and said to Balam, "You want our help?"

"*Must* help," Balam corrected.

"We apekin have done enough of your dirty work over the centuries," he declared flatly. "So, whatever must be done, you'd better roll up your sleeves. You're going to be right on the firing line with us."

Nausea and a blinding headache kept Kane on his back. He was aware of nothing for a long time, except for the blanket of pain and weakness that covered him.

Just how long it was before he opened his eyes he couldn't say. He forced himself to roll over, gathered himself and rose on shaking hands and knees. He squinted at the purple-tinted armaglass walls, feeling the pins-and-needles static discharge from the metal floor plates even through his gloves.

Brigid groaned and stirred.

"Lie still. Sickness go away soon."

The scratchy, whispery voice carried no tones of friendliness, only an appreciation of reality. Kane looked up at Balam standing near the chamber door, his small form swathed by a fleece-lined, hooded parka. The light from the ceiling fixture struck yellow pinpoints in his ebony eyes.

Brigid pushed herself to a sitting position, briefly sinking her teeth into her underlip. "Rough transit," she murmured. "The matter-stream phase lines must not have been in perfect sync."

Kane forced himself erect, stumbling slightly as he stepped on the hem of his coat. "Piece of Russian shit. Should have known what to expect after our jump to Perdelinko."

Brigid smiled wanly and took Kane's proffered hand, allowing him to hoist her to her feet. The mat-trans jump to Russia was always held up as a standard for bad transits, especially by Grant. So, in a way, it was good that he had been physically unable to accompany them.

Kane and Brigid were dressed similarly to when they had jumped to Russia. She wore a long, fur-collared leather coat over a high-necked sweater, whipcord trousers and heavy-treaded boots. The mini-Uzi hung by a strap around her shoulder.

Kane had decided against wearing the armor since their destination was a cold one. He had borrowed Grant's Magistrate-issue coat, since its Kevlar weave not only offered protection from weapons, but was also insulated against all weathers. However, it was a bit too big for him, and the coattails fell nearly to his heels.

The Sin Eater was snugged in its forearm holster beneath the right sleeve, and he wore a gren- and ammo-laden combat harness over his sweater.

Brigid picked up the pack containing emergency medical supplies, concentrated foodstuffs and bottled water. She started to shoulder into it, but Kane said, "Give it to Balam. Let him do his share."

Brigid glanced quickly at the creature. He gazed placidly at her, then extended his hands. She gave him the pack, and he struggled to slip it on. Bending over him, she adjusted the straps, feeling foolishly like a mother helping a child get dressed for school.

She had to forcibly remind herself Balam was as far from a child as it was possible for even a semihuman to be. After Kane had recounted the details of Balam's telepathic history lesson, she speculated that he might be as old as fifteen hundred years, born around the time the tales of Agartha began circulating throughout Asia.

After snugging the pack straps, she turned on the motion detector and swept it toward the door. No readings registered, so she nodded tersely to Kane.

Stepping to the door, Kane grasped the handle, lifting and turning it. Lock solenoids clicked open loudly, and he toed open the door, a few inches at a time. Through the armaglass, he saw dimly what lay beyond.

The jump chamber nestled inside an alcove with a bank of electronic equipment curving in a horseshoe shape along the stone walls. Like Kane had expected, lights flashed on consoles and he heard the faint hum of power units.

Past the bank of electronics, he saw what he didn't expect. Two life-size statues faced each other, one with ten arms and a demonic face, and the other a likeness of a cherubic man squatting cross-legged on a stone block.

Blended with a musty, dusty odor, another stench permeated the rock-walled vault, one Kane had smelled many times in his life but never grown accustomed to. He saw a humped shape covered by a black cloth behind the ten-armed statue. Striding over to it, he snatched the fabric away.

The bearded face of a man gaped up at him. His face was layered by a thin crusting of blood that had stiffened and discolored his beard. A brownish puddle surrounded his head. His eyes possessed the opaque film of a corpse in the first stages of decomposition. Brigid and Balam came closer, although Balam seemed disinterested.

"Shot through the mouth at close range," Kane said quietly. "Three, maybe four days ago."

Balam padded over to a stone pillar nearly as tall as he was. He fingered the pedestal topping it. The surface bore a vague square outline, as if something that had rested there for many years had been removed.

"Here was stone," he said.

Kane glanced toward him, noting how the pillar was covered on each side with crudely incised faces. The eight faces were humanoid, but with oversize hairless craniums, huge, upslanting, pupil-less eyes and tiny slits for mouths. They were stylized representations of Balam's own face.

Kane looked around at the vault, sensing its vast age. Only the gateway unit and its control systems struck a discordant note in the overall atmosphere of antiquity. "Why is there a mat-trans unit here?"

Brigid shrugged. "Any number of reasons. If this is a Szvezda unit, then it may have been installed here so Russian intelligence could keep their eye on Red China. If Szvezda was anything like Cerberus, then all military or government officials had to do was say they needed a unit for security reasons."

"I have a feeling there was more to it than that," Kane replied, glancing sharply at Balam. "Am I right?"

Balam didn't answer. He moved toward the shadowy, far end of the bowl-shaped vault. After a moment, Kane and Brigid followed him. In the eight hours since his communication with Balam, Kane's natural suspicion had risen. Despite the information Balam had imparted, Kane wasn't convinced that he had been given the truth, or if he had, that he'd been given the whole truth.

When he presented his uncertainties to Lakesh, the old man had said sadly, "As a species, perhaps we can retain a semblance of sanity only by *not* understanding our frightfully shaky position in the scheme of things."

Kane grudgingly admitted that possibility, but he also didn't believe that Balam had withheld certain truths simply to spare his fragile human brain.

They followed Balam up a flight of stone steps and into a passageway with walls covered by silken, hand-painted tapestries. They came out into a corridor, through an open door crafted from granite. Kane barely glanced at the ornate dragon bas-relief carved over it. His pointman's instincts rang an alert, and the Sin Eater filled his hand.

Balam turned to the left. The corridor narrowed, turning and bending sharply several times. They passed several closed doors, but Kane heard no sound from behind any of them, so he didn't bother to see where they might lead.

Turning a corner, he heard a faint humming from behind him. He whirled and saw a shaved-headed, black-faced man spinning a key-shaped cudgel over his head by a leather thong. Before he could press the trigger of the Sin Eater, the heavy metal bludgeon snapped out.

Kane shifted position, slamming into Brigid with a shoulder, and the key crashed loudly against the wall, passing through the space that had, a microsecond before, been occupied by his head. The cudgel struck sparks from the stone, chipping out a finger-sized splinter.

As Kane aligned his red-robed form with the bore of the Sin Eater, Brigid shouted, "Don't!"

The man yanked back on the thong, the key clattering on the flagstoned floor. Kane lunged in the same direction. He stamped down on the cudgel, and the man stumbled, the length of rawhide slithering from his grasp. Kane swept the barrel of the blaster across the base of his skull.

Kane didn't put all of his strength into the blow, assuming Brigid not only wanted him alive but conscious so he could be questioned. With a grunt, the shaved-headed man fell to his hands and knees.

Gathering a fistful of soiled robe in his left hand, Kane wrestled him to his feet. The man's small eyes blinked back tears of pain, and he looked at Kane dazedly. Brigid came forward, putting questions to him in a halting, singsong language that sounded like utter gibberish to Kane.

The man didn't reply, his soot-smeared features settling into a stubborn mask. Annoyed, Brigid said, "I don't know if I speak Tibetan with such an accent he doesn't understand or if he's just being uncooperative."

Kane shoved him against the wall. "Is he a priest?"

"A warrior monk, a Dob-Dob. The lamasery's version of a sec man. Traditionally, Dob-Dobs are drawn from the ranks of condemned criminals."

"Slaggers with religion," muttered Kane, planting the bore of his Sin Eater under the monk's chin and forcing his head back. "Tell him we offer him the chance to join a new religion—the Holy Order of Talk or Die."

"That's pretty much the first thing I said to him," Brigid retorted. "He doesn't fear death."

At the periphery of her vision, she noticed Balam edging closer. He pulled back the hood of his parka. The Dob-Dob's eyes darted toward him, then widened as far as the epicanthic folds would allow. A high-pitched yammering burst from his lips, and a jet of urine streamed down and collected in a noxious pool at his feet. His body was consumed with shudders, then seemed to turn to melted wax and flow down to the floor.

Mystified, Kane allowed him to sink down, watching him press his forehead against the flagstones, hearing him speak rapidly in an aspirated voice. Then he realized the Dob-Dob's reaction to the sight of Balam didn't stem necessarily from terror, but from an awe so intense it was almost ecstasy.

Kane stepped to Brigid's side. "What the hell is he saying?"

She narrowed her eyes in concentration. "It's a dialect, Sanskrit words mixed with Tibetan. A prayer language, I think. He believes Balam is one of the eight immortals."

Bleakly Kane thought that Balam very well could be.

Balam dammed the flood of words by interjecting questions in the same babbling tongue.

The Dob-Dob responded quickly, face still pressed against the flagstones. Kane experienced a wave of disgust at the way the man abased himself, wallowing in his own waste. He saw him as a symbol of what Balam's folk had been trying to achieve with humanity for thousands of years. In place of knowledge, they implanted superstition, and in place of truth, fear.

Balam spoke again, and the Dob-Dob ceased gibbering. Turning to Kane and Brigid, he said, "The thief we seek departed this place at dawn."

Kane demanded suspiciously, "That's all he said?"

"He prayed to the eight kings who walk in the sky and thanked me for leaving the illuminated abode of Agartha to speak to him. He also begged forgiveness for failing to protect the stone as this sect had been charged with doing."

Balam's voice grew strained, and his last words were so faint and hoarse they had difficulty understanding him.

"How did the thief leave here?" Brigid asked.

Balam tapped the prostrate Dob-Dob on the top of his head until he reluctantly lifted his face. Tears cut runnels through the black soot smeared over his cheeks. Balam pointed to Brigid and whispered a few words.

The monk slowly climbed to his feet and bowed deeply, respectfully toward her. Brigid asked him questions in Tibetan, and the man responded promptly.

After a couple of minutes, she said to Kane, "They left on horseback. Tsyansis Khan-po, as he calls Zakat, carried a metal box. Gyatso, the girl and another Dob-Dob by the name of Yal went with him. He claims he was corrupted."

Recalling how he used the term to describe Beth-Li Rouch, Kane echoed, "Corrupted? How?"

"Leng—that's his name—wasn't really clear on that. He calls Zakat and Gyatso *dugpa*s, or black magicians who can reflect their images on weaklings. I take that to mean they have the ability to impose their wills on others."

"Since Gyatso is hybrid, I'm not surprised. But what about Zakat? Is he a psi-mutie?"

The only breed of human mutant that had increased dramatically since skydark was the so-called psi-mutie—otherwise normal in appearance, they possessed advanced extrasensory and precognitive mind powers.

"It's possible," she admitted. "But not everybody in the lamasery was corrupted. My guess is that Zakat and Gyatso, working in tandem, were able to zero in on the most impressionable minds. Maybe their powers were augmented by the stone."

Kane glanced toward Balam. "Is that likely?"

Balam nodded once.

"Do you know where they're going?"

Balam nodded again, evidently wishing to save his voice.

"And can it be reached overland?"

Balam nodded once more, then turned away. To Brigid, Kane said, "Ask Leng if he can provide transportation for the immortal and his party so the thieves can be caught."

Brigid did as he directed and after Leng replied, she said, "Yes, and we're more than welcome to them."

They followed Leng along the hallway, through several large chambers and out into a courtyard. A bitter wind whistled over the walls. The sun sank behind far-off mountain peaks that looked like gray shadows. The cold, rarefied air made their lungs ache with the effort of breathing.

"We're going to have to wait until sunrise," Kane said. "Ask Leng to show us around."

Other than Leng, there appeared to be only a few people in the lamasery. Most of the monks and other Dob-Dobs had fled after the murder of the high lama, whom

Zakat had not only killed but whose title, the king of fear, he had appropriated. They had left his body where it fell, too frightened to enter the vault of the stone.

Leng showed them around the monastery and to its library, which was underneath the main building. The majority of the manuscripts were scrolls as much as fifty feet long; others were sheets of ancient parchment tied between wooden blocks.

Brigid looked at the shelves, entranced. "There are enough ancient manuscripts here to keep a hundred translators busy for a lifetime—but there's probably not five people alive who could read the script."

Kane nodded toward Balam. "I'll bet he could."

Balam didn't confirm or deny the observation.

Leng led them back upstairs and served them an unsatisfactory meal of yak butter, grain porridge and a bitter green tea. Both Kane and Brigid were a bit surprised to see Balam consume it, apparently with relish as if he considered it a delicacy.

Unaccustomed to the thin air, Brigid and Kane tired quickly. After eating, they both did their best to stifle yawns. Leng escorted all three of them to a cell. Kane glanced out the solitary window and saw a view of snow-clad peaks. Looking down, he saw a sheer drop of at least a thousand feet.

Leng built a fire in the stone hearth in the middle of the floor, and since there was no chimney, they had to keep the wooden shutters of the window open to allow the smoke to escape.

The temperature dropped quickly after the sun went down, and they tried to find a balance between asphyxiating and freezing. The cell came furnished with only one cot, and Leng made it obvious that it was reserved for Balam. He did fetch piles of quilts and fur robes for Kane and Brigid to burrow in. To conserve body heat, they lay together. In order to breathe, they lay near the window. Balam simply draped himself in a number of blankets and quilts and apparently dropped off to sleep as soon as he lay down.

Quietly, Kane asked Brigid, "What was the word Leng used for Zakat and Gyatso? *Dugpas*?"

"Yes," she replied. "Gyatso is a practitioner of the old Bon religion. They're thought to cultivate evil for evil's sake. Supposedly, they're hypnotists and just as keen on getting control of humanity as, for instance, Balam's people were."

Kane shivered. He was too cold and tired to listen to another history lesson. The acrid smoke of tamarisk roots smoldering in the hearth made his throat feel raw and abraded.

"If Gyatso truly considers himself the Agarthan ambassador," Brigid continued drowsily, "he's in one deep psychological quandary."

"How so?"

"As a Bon-po shaman, he is as much Agartha's enemy as the law of gravity is the enemy of people who think they can fly."

Kane found the simile funny due to his oxygen-starved brain. He couldn't help but laugh. Brigid's teeth chattered, and she snuggled close to him, resting her head on his shoulder. "I'm glad somebody finds something amusing about this."

"An hour from now, after I suffocate, I probably won't."

He briefly wondered how she would react if he kissed her, but decided not to risk it. Balam's presence in the room was a definite ardor-squasher. He drifted off into a surprisingly deep and thankfully dreamless sleep.

He awoke at dawn, when the first rays of daybreak shafted in through the window. He felt stiff and sticky, as he always did after sleeping in his clothes. He was also very cold and thirsty. Brigid awoke when he pushed himself up, and groaning, she hiked herself to a sitting position.

Balam perched on the foot of the cot, gazing out the window, the golden light of the sun casting amber shadows over his pale flesh, his eyes half-closed. He paid them no attention as they stumbled to their feet, kicking away the quilts and robes.

Balam rasped, "We go now."

"We go later," Kane stated in harsh tone that brooked no debate. "After we apekin have attended to a few wake-up traditions. I *do* hope you'll be patient with our primitive customs."

Balam ignored the words and sarcastic tone in which they had been delivered.

Leng arrived with more bowls of porridge and cups of tea. He directed Kane and Brigid to a bathroom, which was more of a latrine. They took turns relieving themselves and splashing water on their faces from basins that were filmed with ice. If nothing else, the freezing water helped Kane come to full alertness.

Leng took them outside to a shed where half a dozen sturdy, shaggy ponies were stabled. They all looked very tough, bred in the Tibetan wilderness and used to hardship.

Knowing which horses were the best, Leng carefully selected three. Kane helped him saddle and bridle them. Balam stood apart, watching the process with what seemed like trepidation.

Kane gestured for him to come near the smallest of the animals, and when he did, it squealed and snapped its teeth viciously at him. Kane couldn't help but grin. "He's a good judge of character, at least."

Balam gazed at the pony impassively, and Kane received the distinct impression he had no idea of how to mount it. Putting his hands under Balam's armpits, he swung him up and planted him firmly in the saddle. He held the bridle, restraining the pony until it grew accustomed to the smell and feel of its rider. Kane stroked the animal's neck and crooned soothing words to it until it calmed down.

Leng adjusted the stirrups, and Kane inserted Balam's tiny feet into them. He whispered, "Thank you."

Kane looked at him in surprise, a bit startled by the acknowledgment of help. Biting back a sarcastic rejoinder, he said simply, "My pleasure."

They rode the trail with one leg dangling over the edge of a precipice and the other scraping against the cliff face. The rock-ribbed slant pitched downward at an ever steepening angle.

Above them were snow-gilded peaks glimmering like powdered diamonds, but the trail beneath them was cast into cold, silent shadow. It wound around and down, ever down, skirting gorges and ravines littered with house-sized boulders.

Since Brigid and Kane assumed Balam knew where he was going, they didn't question him as he took the point. The trail led in only two directions—back and up to the Byang-thang Plateau, and down, ever down.

Around noon, they reached a windswept level place on the path, and Kane pointed out the remains of a cold camp and scatterings of horse dung. After the discovery, his pointman's sense was nervously alert, his eyes scanning crags and outcroppings for any sign of life.

Less than an hour past the campsite, a wind sprang up and began blowing powdery snow in swirling, eye-stinging clouds. The ponies lowered their heads and trudged through it. Balam bowed his head likewise, wrapping the lower portion of his face in a woolen scarf.

For what seemed like a chain of interlocking eternities, they marched through the thickening curtains of snow, which revealed only glimpses of fissures and chasms when the howling wind tore momentary rents in it.

The billowing clouds of snow reduced their range of vision to only a few yards, and the moisture froze on their eyelids. Their faces, hands and legs grew numb, and ears and teeth ached fiercely.

Over the keening wail of the wind, Kane thought he heard the frightened neighing of a pony and he cautiously squinted directly into the wind. He caught only a blurred fragment of Balam's pony disappearing over the edge of the trail.

Reining his own mount in sharply, Kane slid from the saddle. He shouted to Brigid, "Stay there! Something's happened!"

He could barely see her on her horse and he wasn't certain if she heard him, but she remained in the saddle.

Kane made his way slowly to the point where he thought the pony had fallen, the wind setting his coattails to flapping like the wings of an ungainly bird. The snow burned his eyes, so he closed them, dropping to his knees and inching forward, calling for Balam.

He reached the ledge rim and shouted over it, but he

scarcely heard his own voice. He started to back away when fingers clutched desperately at his right hand and wrist. Groping down, Kane felt Balam's arm and he pulled him up from the rock knob where he had been dangling.

Balam lay in Kane's arms like a child, trembling violently and once or twice he tried to speak. Cautiously, Kane worked his way backward until he felt the cliff pressing into his back, and then he sidled over to his horse. He knelt beneath the animal, using it as an unsatisfactory windbreak, and put Balam on his feet. "Are you all right?"

Balam nodded, vein-laced eyelids squeezed shut. He still shivered, and Kane had no way of knowing if it was from fear or cold, but he didn't blame him either way. After spending three and a half years in a twenty-by-twenty cell, Balam was experiencing a very unpleasant reintroduction to the world.

He hoisted him onto the saddle of his pony and led it by the bridle past the point where Balam's mount had plunged into the ravine. He climbed on behind Balam, heeling the pony forward.

The trail entered a gash in the cliff face and descended through a tunnel that had been enlarged out of a natural cave. Sheltered from the merciless lash of the wind, they reined up and dismounted. Now at least they could speak without shouting.

"What happened back there?" asked Brigid, her heavy, disheveled mane of hair glistening with snow, her face reddened by the scouring of wind-driven sleet.

"Balam's horse missed his step," he answered. "Nearly took Balam with him."

"Good thing you were paying attention." She made the comment between chattering teeth.

Balam husked out, "Thank you."

Kane tried to grin derisively, but his lips were too chapped. "My pleasure. How far now?"

Balam made an odd gesture with one hand, languid and diffident. "Not long now."

"You're not sure?" demanded Brigid.

"Long time since I came this way. Landmarks change."

"How long?" Kane inquired.

Balam performed the hand gesture again, and Kane wondered if it was the equivalent of a shrug. "Not sure. Around time when we aborted Norse colonization of the North American continent."

Brigid's eyes widened in astonishment. "That has to be eight or nine hundred years ago."

"Long time," Balam whispered agreeably.

After resting for half an hour, they continued on their way. The storm was gradually blowing itself out, and there were longer lulls between the freezing, gale-force gusts.

The trail led for two miles along a fairly level parapet of basalt until it turned sharply and began to zigzag downward. Kane could see that it was largely hand-hewed and in some places it looked as if demolition charges had done the work. Regardless, the construction work was obviously ancient.

The snow became little more than intermittent flurries the longer and deeper they rode. As sunset approached, the flurries ceased altogether and Kane saw more horse droppings on the path.

The trail flowed seamlessly into relatively flat, stone-littered ground. Balam's slender frame stiffened in the saddle, as though he was excited or apprehensive.

They followed a dry, boulder-filled streambed that wended its way through a sheer-walled ravine. Kane had visited some wild places before, but this piece of Tibet had to be one of the most inaccessible regions on the face of the Earth.

The sky purpled with twilight when they marched out of the ravine into a box canyon. Bulwarks of granite stood like huge tombstones all around them. In the rock face fifty yards beyond the ravine, they saw a black cleft, partially hidden by clumps of tall, dry grass and slabs of limestone.

Balam inclined his head toward it. "There."

"That?" demanded Kane. "That hole in the wall is the door to your magic city of immortals?"

Wriggling impatiently, Balam tried to dismount, so Kane reined the pony to a halt. He jumped to the ground and stood with his eyes fixed on the dark gap. His body swayed slightly, gracefully to and fro like a reed touched by a gentle wind.

It occurred to Kane that Balam might be experiencing a deep emotion, so he said nothing. At the same time it had occurred to him that although he had seen horse manure on the trail, he saw no sign of horses anywhere in the vicinity. The ground was far too hard and stony to take tracks, but he scanned it anyway.

Then he heard the flat cracking snap of a rifle, followed a shaved slice of a second later by a little thump of displaced air next to his left ear.

Kane lunged off the saddle, Sin Eater springing into his hand. Another shot split the heavy silence of the canyon, and the gravel gouted in front of Brigid's pony. It shrilled a frightened cry, rearing up on its hind legs. She managed to kick free of the stirrups and slid over the horse's rump, alighting on her feet. She fumbled to bring her mini-Uzi to bear.

Grigori Zakat's disembodied voice floated on the air, the echoes distorting it as to the direction from which it emanated. "I did not kill you before when I had the chance, Kane. I prefer not to kill you now."

Kane looked wildly around, assuming a combat stance, eyeing every boulder, declivity and decent-sized bush in the zone. "Then why are you shooting at us?"

"To illustrate my preference that you stay alive. I hope you don't hold my actions in the museum against me."

"You hope wrong," Kane replied, crouching down behind his pony, pulling Brigid to him.

A note of laughter twisted through the canyon. It held an odd, high note. "You are the grudge-holding type. I'd hoped you were more emotionally mature than that. How did your friends, the black man and the white girl, fare?"

"They had a whale of a time," answered Kane, ignoring the sour look Brigid cast in his direction. "What do you want?"

"Obviously, the same as you. The Chintamani Stone, the shining trapezohedron. I have two of its facets in my possession, and they have led me here, to Agartha, to the Valley of the Eight Immortals, to claim the primary piece."

"What makes you so sure this is Agartha?"

"Call it intuition. Besides, I have the ancestral ambassador with me. He should know."

"If that's true, what's keeping you from strolling in and taking it?"

Balam behaved not only as if he were oblivious to the gunshots, but to the conversation. He continued to stare at the cleft, body still swaying.

"I intend to wait until morning. Now, however, with you here—by the way, what is wrong with your small friend?—I propose another alliance of convenience. Safety in numbers and all that."

"We've already had an example of your version of a truce, Zakat."

The Russian laughed again. "I understand your point of view is different from mine, but what harm will it do to cooperate? I have you pinned down—you can't go anywhere. It won't cost you anything to go along with me. I know you think I handed you a raw deal in Newyork, but I'll make it up to you. Are you a religious man, Kane?"

Out of all the threats and boasts he expected Zakat to taunt him with, that question took him aback. "I've never thought about it. Why?"

"Because I am. In fact, I am an ordained priest. The deity of my religion is power, and the way one communes with such a god is to recognize and accept one's destiny. We are all agents of it. What is happening now is supposed to happen."

"What are you going to do next?" Kane asked sneeringly. "Read my fortune?"

Zakat laughed again, as if he found the question truly funny. "Once I retrieve the prime piece of the trapezohedron, I can probably do far more than that. My point is, if you obey the law of power, you therefore shall gain more. It is a cumulative effect, known in my religion as causitry."

While Zakat spoke, Kane scanned every inch of the area. Because of the deceptive echoes, Zakat and his people could be behind them. He felt ridiculously vulnerable, hunkering down behind a shaggy pony. He knew he had been in tighter spots in his life; he just couldn't recall them offhand.

"Therefore," Zakat continued reasonably, "causitry is part of destiny and my actions caused your destiny to interact with mine."

"Oh, shut up," Brigid muttered.

Zakat continued to wax eloquent on subjects metaphysical. Kane listened to the man's blandishments and with a start he realized he was actually considering the man's proposition. He was a masterful persuader. He couldn't help but suspect that the fragments of the stone in his possession were augmenting Zakat's psionic abilities.

Balam suddenly commanded Kane and Brigid's attention. He strode deliberately toward the opening in the cliff wall, unzipping his parka as he did so.

"Tell the midget to stop, Kane," Zakat commanded sharply. "All of us enter together when the time is right."

"Do as he says, Balam," Brigid called.

Balam kept walking, shrugging out of his coat, dropping it on the ground behind him. The rifle cracked again, and a column of dirt spouted less than two feet in front of him. His measured, single-minded stride didn't falter.

Kane watched, completely dumbfounded as Balam began peeling off his dark one-piece garment, stripping naked. He stopped only to step out of the leggings and then continued on, padding over sharp-edged pebbles on bare, six-toed feet.

A voice burst out with a stream of agitated consonants, and black-turbaned Gyatso squeezed out between two boulders. He raced toward Balam, shrieking frenzied words, waving his arms over his head. Zakat bellowed something in Russian, and Kane figured it was an order to stop.

Kane sprinted after Balam, firing a triburst in Gyatso's direction. The light was poor, the man's clothing was dark and he reacted with inhumanly swift reflexes. He bounded straight back, and the9 mm rounds dug gouges in the dirt and ripped white scars on the rocks behind him.

Two blasters opened up from behind the bulwark of stone, one obviously the Tokarev. The canyon walls magnified the staccato reports. Brigid fired her autoblaster, spraying Zakat's basalt shelter with a hailstorm of lead, driving Gyatso back behind them.

Kane didn't divert his attention from the rocks and so caught only brief glimpse of the darkness of the cleft swallowing Balam's pale body. He continued firing round after round until he reached the gap. It was just wide and high enough for an adult to slip through on all fours. He knew the gap was not a shallow depression but a tunnel. His flesh tingled at the prospect of crawling headfirst into a pitch-dark passageway, but it tingled even more at continuing a firefight with enemies who probably outgunned both Brigid and him and had good cover.

As Brigid joined him, he snapped, "Get in there. I'll cover you."

She looked at the opening fearfully, then flinched as a bullet struck the cliff over her head and sprinkled rock chips in her hair.

Grabbing her by the collar, Kane forced her down in front of the opening. "*Go*, goddammit!"

With a fatalistic shrug, Brigid wriggled into the cleft.

The rough-edged tunnel narrowed from a four-foot diameter to three within the first yard. The little light peeping in from outside vanished quickly, and Kane stared straight ahead into unfathomable darkness. If not for the sound of Brigid's scuffling on the stone, he wouldn't have known she was there. He resisted the urge to unpocket and turn on his microlight.

The sound of voices from ahead of him was such a surprise he nearly stopped dead. A second later, he realized he had heard the echoes of Grigori Zakat's voice, but he wasn't comforted. He glanced behind him. Outlined against the hazy, irregular opening, he could just barely make out the Russian's head.

He crawled faster and could only pray the tunnel would curve or drop before it occurred to Zakat to open fire into the cleft. He crawled as rapidly into the blackness as his hands and knees could move. His head bumped into knobs, and loose pebbles dug into his knees. His coat might turn a 7.62 mm bullet, but he didn't want to find out.

At the sudden crack of the triggered AK, he dropped flat, hoping Brigid did the same. He heard a soft zing over his head. The whine of a ricochet instantly followed.

He whispered, "Baptiste, are you all right?"

"More or less," came the pained reply. "I bumped my head."

"Belly crawl or you'll have more than a knot up there."

They wormed forward on their bellies. There came the crack of another shot, and rock chips sifted down on the back of his neck. Kane and Brigid slithered and scraped along. The tunnel narrowed even more, and the walls caught at Kane's shoulders, but he kept clawing and scrabbling onward, sweat stinging his eyes.

The click of a firing-rate selector reverberated throughout the darkness. He knew Zakat had switched from single shot to full-auto.

He heard a frightened cry from Brigid an instant before the tunnel floor vanished under his hands. He dived headlong into a sepia sea. Just as he fell, a stream of bullets tore through the tunnel and passed over his plunging body. They bounced off rock with a series of eerie screams.

Kane wasn't listening. He was too busy clawing at empty air, groping for a handhold. He didn't grope for very long. A breath-robbing crash numbed his body, and he was only dimly aware of tumbling head over heels down a slope. By the time a rock stopped his thrashing descent, the burst of autofire had ceased.

When his senses returned, he found he had fetched up against the base of a boulder in a half-sitting position. He heard a deep groan from Brigid, somewhere nearby.

He thrust his hand into his coat pocket and removed the Nighthawk microlight, flicking it on and shining the amber beam around. Brigid was pushing herself up from the rocky ground, teeth clamped tight on groans of pain.

"Don't ask me if I'm all right," she said lowly. "I'm liable to hit you."

Kane cast the light upward, and it haloed a set of small, worn steps leading downward from the tunnel opening, nearly ten feet above them. Now he knew how Balam had kept from breaking his neck. He heard sounds from the tunnel, scramblings and murmurings.

He forced himself erect, wincing at the flares of pain igniting all over his body. "Can you walk, Baptiste?"

She wobbled to her feet, gingerly dabbing at the blood flowing from a cut on her scalp, right at the hairline. "Guess I have no choice."

Pulling off the glove from his left hand, Kane wetted a forefinger and tested the air currents that swirled around unseen obstacles. He detected a movement of air to their left and, taking Brigid by the hand, began a shambling run in that direction. Chunks of rock clattered at their feet as they threaded their way between outcroppings of granite and basalt. He kept listening for the approach of Zakat and his crew or the sound of their fall when they reached the point where the tunnel opened into empty space.

After a couple of minutes, when the sound had still not come, Kane and Brigid set out along a narrow corridor of stone. Holding the microlight out before him, Kane led the way quickly, occasionally confused by his own writhing shadow.

"Balam didn't have that much of a jump on us," he said. "We ought to come across his tracks or something."

Brigid patted her pockets and said grimly, "My Nighthawk is gone. It must have fallen out of my coat when I fell."

Kane nodded, but said nothing. The microlights emitted a powerful beam, and therefore the batteries didn't last very long. Relying only on one source of light in an environment like this didn't do much for his sense of optimism.

The corridor widened and the ceiling grew higher. Irregular stalactites hung from above, and they wended their way around stalagmites thrusting up from the floor. The light beam glinted off mineral deposits embedded in the rough walls—silvery mica, brilliant quartz and soapy limestone. A brooding, unbroken silence bore down on them, like the pressure of a vast, invisible hand. Then they heard the scuff of footfalls.

Cursing under his breath, Kane set off at a trot with Brigid beside him, both of them trying to move as quietly as possible. The passage they walked branched into a Y. They chose the opening on the left, because it had the strongest current of air.

They strode along it for only a short distance, then stopped. The movement of air was almost a breeze, wafting up from below. The cavern floor dropped straight down into utter darkness. Brigid kicked a pebble over the edge and counted quietly. She got to five before they heard it strike far, far below.

Shuddering, Brigid and Kane backed away. They heard the sound of voices and saw the glow of a flashlight, dimly illuminating the branching-off point of the tunnels. They ran noiselessly, on the balls of their feet, toward the Y. They paused a moment at the junction to make sure they couldn't be seen, and then darted into the right-hand shaft. They flattened themselves against the wall. Kane turned off the Nighthawk and double-fisted his Sin Eater. They watched the halo of light grow brighter.

Framed by the aura of two flashlights, Zakat, Trai, Gyatso and a black-faced Dob-Dob—the man Leng had called Yal—appeared at the junction. They looked warily around. If any of the four had taken the tumble out of the tunnel into the cavern, they looked none the worse for it.

Though he knew he was nearly invisible in his black coat, Kane pressed himself harder against the side of the tunnel. He watched Zakat check the air movement with a wet fingertip and, as he and Brigid had done, they turned down the left-hand tunnel.

Kane removed a concussion gren from its clip on his combat harness.

Because of the darkness, Brigid couldn't see what he had done, but she heard the faint clinking of metal. In an alarmed tone, she whispered, "What are you going to do?"

"I hate being chased," he grated.

He soft-shoed back to the junction and heard Zakat and Gyatso speaking in low tones. Peering down the tunnel, he saw they had reached the end. Kane unpinned the gren and lobbed it down the shaft with a gentle, under-handed toss.

Zakat heard it bouncing and silenced Gyatso with a sharp hiss. Kane stepped back swiftly and turned, but he saw the Russian bounding forward with inhuman speed.

He kicked the gren like a football, propelling it down the tunnel into the branching-off point, back toward him.

A blaze of light illuminated the junction with a yellow-white glare. The detonation was a brutal thunderclap, which instantly bled into a loud rumble, as if a great wheeled machine were approaching. Bits and pieces of rocks pelted down from overhead, and Kane moved back to the right-hand tunnel, glancing behind him. Chunks of stone fell into the branching-off point of the passageways. Rocks and debris rained down with splintering cracks and crashes. The entire cavern roof seemed to be in motion.

Kane grabbed Brigid by the sleeve and pulled her farther into the shaft as a small rockfall filled the junction with heaps of stone. The floor trembled under their running feet, riven with ugly, spreading cracks.

With an earsplitting roar, an entire section of cavern floor collapsed, plunging downward and carrying Brigid with it. Kane still had a tight grip on her sleeve, and her unsupported weight caused him to fall flat on his stomach.

She dangled at the end of his arm over a void of impenetrable blackness. There was a crack of splitting rock, and her weight abruptly increased. Kane felt himself slipping forward, and he fought to dig the toes of his boots into the hard ground. He heard Brigid's boots groping for purchase.

"Grab me with your other hand," Kane directed through clenched teeth.

Brigid's other hand grasped his forearm, just below the elbow, and Kane was dragged forward a few frightening inches. Straining every muscle in his shoulders, arms and back, he wormed backward, pebbles pressing cruelly into his thighs, groin and chest. He ground the side of his face into grit and dirt. Sweat slid down into his eyes, and his limbs quivered with the strain.

Finally, he lifted Brigid to the level where she was able to swing up a leg over the edge of the rockfall. For a long minute, they lay on the cavern floor, panting and gasping. Finally, Kane pushed himself into a sitting position and turned on the Nighthawk.

When the microlight illuminated Brigid's face, Kane almost wished they were in darkness again. The woman's face was clotted with dried blood from her scalp wound, and her emerald eyes were dulled with fatigue and pain and surrounded by dark rings. Even her curly mane of hair drooped listlessly.

She looked at him and said, "You look terrible."

"Thanks to you," Kane retorted angrily. He scowled at her, then forced a laugh. He stood up slowly, silently enduring the spasms of pain igniting in his back and legs.

"Well," he said after a moment, "Zakat and his crew are behind us, so we can't go back. Balam is somewhere ahead of us. So we have to go out."

"And down," said Brigid gloomily. Gingerly, she stepped forward and peered into the yawning blackness below.

She took a deep breath and inched out onto the ledge, flattening herself against the rock wall, digging the fingers of her hands into the fissures and crevices. After a moment of hard swallowing, Kane stepped out after her, strapping the microlight around his left wrist.

The ledge made a sharp turn to the right after a few steps, and its pitch descended at an increasingly steep angle. Kane and Brigid were forced to edge along it with their hands gripping the wall tightly. Kane wondered how deep beneath the surface they were. He couldn't hazard a guess, but he suspected the ledge beneath their feet wasn't natural. Its smoothness spoke of craftsmanship, though whether it was carved by human hands, he had no way of knowing. Nor did he particularly want to know.

It was slow, laborious work and it was perilous, for ominous cracklings at the lip of the ledge warned that their combined weight might start a slide, sending them both plunging into the blackness.

Kane worried that the batteries of the Nighthawk were dangerously low, but he didn't turn it off. The ledge gradually widened into a true path. Both of them breathed easier when they no longer had to inch sideways, but the dim glow of the microlight diminished their relief. The flashlight offered little more than a firefly halo where the ledge met and joined with a rocky floor.

A faint rumble sounded to their right, and they halted, expecting another downpour of stones. A few seconds of hard listening told them the noise was that of an underground stream or river. Kane was suddenly, sharply aware of how thirsty he was.

They moved along the path, beneath ponderous masses of stone. The Nighthawk abruptly went out. The echoes of Brigid's despairing groan chased each other through the impenetrable blackness.

The two people stopped walking, hearts trip-hammering within their chests as they stood motionless in the stygian darkness. Kane's breath came in harsh, ragged bursts as he struggled to control his mounting terror. The mission priority was the spur that drove him to start walking again, taking Brigid by one arm and feeling his way along the rough walls. Then, far away, he saw a tiny blue-yellow flicker of light. He pointed it out to Brigid, and they increased their pace. The crunch of their footfalls sent up ghostly reverberations.

The path suddenly debouched into a gloomy underground gallery with walls of black basalt. Stalagmites and outcroppings thrust up from the floor. To both Brigid's and Kane's dismayed surprise, they saw that the source of the ectoplasmic light came from a small square panel of a glassy substance inset in the gallery wall.

Walking over to it, Brigid eyed it curiously, reaching out a tentative hand to touch it. "I've never seen anything like this before."

"I have," declared Kane grimly.

She jerked her hand away and turned to face him. "Where?"

"In the Black Gobi, in the tent of the Tushe Gun. I guess there isn't any need to wonder where he got them…or where this one came from."

Brigid nodded and stepped away from the glowing panel. The self-styled Avenging Lama had made the ancient Mongolian city of Kharo-Khoto his headquarters. Beneath the black city lay an even more ancient structure, a space vessel. The Tushe Gun had looted much Archon technology from it, without understanding what it was.

Softly, Brigid said, "And I guess there's no more need to wonder why Balam was drawn to this place."

They strode through the gallery, accompanied by the ever present echoes of their footsteps. Every few yards, they came across more of the light panels. They provided a weak, unsatisfactory illumination, but they were grateful for them nonetheless.

The gallery narrowed into a crevasse, which they squeezed into, clambering over fallen masses of stone. The splash of rushing water grew louder as the fissure turned to the left. After a few steps, they found themselves standing on a stone shelf a foot or so above the surface of a river. The opposite bank was about seventy feet away, butting up against a wall of basalt.

The water looked black, but Kane rushed to it anyway, lying flat and plunging his head into the icy current. Brigid kneeled beside him, taking off her gloves before cupping handfuls of water to her mouth.

The water had a peculiar tang to it, a sour limestone aftertaste, but they drank their fill anyway, washing away the blood and grime on their faces. When Kane blunted the edge of his thirst, he became aware of a gnawing hunger and he wondered aloud if there were any fish in the stream.

Brigid didn't reply. She peered in the direction of the river's current. "There isn't a path. If the river leads to a way out, we'll have to swim. Or go back."

Kane raked the wet hair out of his eyes. "There's nothing to be gained by that. Zakat and his crew are better armed than we are."

Brigid nodded. "Yeah, but I'm not up to swimming. The river is cold, probably fed by meltwater. We'd both succumb to hypothermia inside of a couple of minutes."

Kane rose, looking past Brigid to the other side of the stream. Though the light was uncertain, he was sure he saw a long object bobbing on the surface, almost directly across from their position. Leaning against the rock wall, he tugged off his boots, shucked his coat and slid into the water.

"What are you doing?" Brigid demanded.

"Wait and see, Baptiste."

His feet touched the gravelly bottom. The water was shockingly, almost painfully cold, and it took all of his self-control not to curse. He started wading across, moving as quickly as he dared. After a few steps, the icy water lapped at his thighs, then up to his waist. He kept walking, fighting the strong current. A time or two, loose stones turned beneath his feet and he nearly fell.

When he reached the other side, he was gasping and out of breath. From the hips down he was completely numb, but the bobbing shape was what he had hoped it would be. A six-foot-long boat made of bark and laced yak's hide was tethered to a boulder by a length of leather. A wooden pole about ten feet long lay on the bank.

Pulling himself ashore, Kane snatched the tether free and took the pole. Tentatively, he eased into the little boat. The craft sank a bit, the hide-and-bark hull giving a little, but it seemed river worthy.

With pushes of the pole, he propelled the boat across the river. He had difficulty crossing it because of the current, but the pole always touched bottom. When the prow bumped against the opposite bank, Brigid handed him his boots and coat. She hesitated only a moment before gingerly climbing into it.

Hastily, Kane put on his coat and boots. He shivered as he did so. Taking the pole again, he pushed off and the boat slid out into the river, rocking a bit. He poled the craft so it hugged the right-hand wall, close to the light panels, not voicing the host of new fears assailing him.

He was afraid the river might debouch in a dozen different directions, or lead to a waterfall or that the boat might spring a leak. But after twenty minutes of steady poling, with none of his fears bearing out, he tried to relax. When his strained shoulder muscles couldn't take any more abuse, he turned the task of poling over to Brigid.

Kane sat down while she expertly directed the craft. She said, "This used to be a form of recreation. It was called punting."

"Offhand I can think of a dozen recreational activities I'd rather be doing."

"All with Rouch, I'll bet," she replied with a studied nonchalance.

Kane glowered at her, but didn't respond. Linking his hands behind his aching neck, he inquired, "What do you think, Baptiste?"

"What do I think about what?"

"Is this Agartha, the Valley of the Eight Immortals Zakat is so crazy to reach?"

Brigid pushed her shoulder against the pole. "If it is, it's a far cry from the way the city was described in legend. I haven't seen a speck of gold or a chip of diamond yet. If there ever were Agarthans, they came down here ages ago to die."

Brigid paused, started to say something else, then stopped talking and poling. Kane straightened up. The waterway opened into a huge, vault-walled cavern. It was immense, most of it wrapped in unrelieved darkness. Black masses of rock hung from its jagged roof.

The river narrowed down to a stream, and the current carried the boat beneath an arching formation. A constant sound of splashing beyond it indicated a waterfall.

Brigid pushed the craft toward the nearest bank. She poled them aground on the pebble-strewed shore. They climbed out of the boat and looked around at the city of stalactites and stalagmites rising all around them. Illuminated by dozens of light panels, they saw towers of multicolored limestone disappearing into the darkness overhead, flying buttresses and graceful arches of rock stretching into the shadows.

Kane and Brigid moved forward uncertainly, struggling not to be overcome by awe. Then Brigid stabbed out an arm, pointing ahead. They stopped and stared, surrendering to astonishment.

The figure was a statue, standing in erect position. At least fifteen feet tall, it represented a humanoid creature with a slender, gracile build draped in robes. The features were sharp, the domed head disproportionately large and hairless. The eyes were huge, slanted and fathomless.

The stone figure pointed with one long-fingered hand toward the farther, shadow-shrouded end of the cavern. There was something so strikingly meaningful about the pointing arm and the intent gaze of the big eyes that the statue seemed not crafted out of stone at all, but a living thing petrified by the hand of time.

"Somebody lived down here," Kane muttered.

Brigid nodded thoughtfully. "A long, long time ago."

They started in the direction of the statue's solemnly pointing arm. It led them across the cavern, to a crevasse that yawned at the far end. A worn path was still discernible, and they followed it toward the black opening.

Kane suddenly tugged Brigid to a stop. "Are you sure nobody's lived down here for a long, long time?"

Nettled by the hint of sarcasm in his tone, she followed his gaze downward.

In the fine rock dust on the cavern floor, they saw the clear, fresh print of a small foot with six delicate toes.

In the wavering glow of the light panel, Kane and Brigid looked at each other, at the footprint, at the solemn statue and back to each other.

"If Balam made this footprint, then he's not too far ahead of us," Kane said, unconsciously lowering his voice to a whisper.

"That print could have been here for ages," replied Brigid. "There's nothing down here to disturb it."

She studied the looming sculpture. "There must have been a migration down through these caves. Balam's people set up that statue as a marker, a guidepost so that they would know the way to follow."

Kane stepped forward. "I think we should do the same thing."

They followed the worn, broad path that led into the cavern and to a fissure at the far end. Another light panel illuminated a very narrow, winding stair hewed out of stone, a route taken by a doom-driven race. The stairs angled steeply into darkness.

When Kane and Brigid started down, they discovered its downward angle was not quite as sharp as they feared. The stairs led to a wide, vault-walled space from which many other fissures radiated. A square light panel shed a feeble glow over one of the cracks.

They didn't speak as they entered the passage, but Kane's mind was in a fever of speculation and conjecture. He understood now why Balam and his kind had such huge eyes, why they were most comfortable in low light levels, why historically they had been slandered as hell-spawn. They had no choice but to shun the light, lurk in the shadows, and early man had viewed them as demons, scuttling up from the bowels of the Earth to practice devilment.

Perhaps the myth of Agartha was a long-range public-relations campaign, to plant in human consciousness the concept of a semidivine race living in a subterranean city, not a horde of inhuman devils.

Kane and Brigid forged their way through a bewildering labyrinth of fissures, galleries and small caves. Every few hundred feet, the path was marked by the blue radiance of a light panel.

They squeezed into another crack in the rock and were plunged into complete darkness. They felt their way for a few minutes, then in the black void ahead of them, Kane saw a filtered, pale blue glow. The scope of the illumination was far wider than one of the light panels.

"Do you see that?" he asked over his shoulder.

"I do," Brigid answered. "Maybe it's a natural phosphorescence given off by fungus and lichens."

Their ears detected a distant, almost inaudible reverberation. The regularity of its throbbing rhythm instantly gave them both the knowledge of its nature.

"Archon power generators," blurted Brigid. "Like the ones we saw in Dulce, and in the spacecraft beneath Kharo-Khoto."

The passage ended on a broad shelf of basalt, thrusting out over a cavernous space so vast their eyes could only dimly perceive its true proportions. Their first stupefied impression was of an alien underworld, occupying the entire center of the Earth. As their eyes adjusted, they gained a sense of perspective on the vista spread out before them.

From the stone shelf, the ground sloped gently downward toward a collection of structures. The buildings were of black basalt, quarried from the cavern walls, and Kane realized they were built in the same odd architectural style as the surface cities Balam had shown him.

The structures were low to the ground, windowless and some of them sprouted fluted spirals. A tower identical to the Administrative Monoliths, but less than half the height, jutted up from the center of the settlement. Like the villes, the city plan was a wheel, radiating out from the central tower.

The roof of the enormous cavern was tiled with the light panels, every square inch completely covered by them, except for where jagged stalactites thrust down.

The area wasn't quite as gigantic as their first stunned impression, perhaps only half a mile in circumference.

They saw and heard no signs of people in the streets, only the rhythmic drone.

"Agartha," Brigid murmured. "Shamballah. Bhogavati. The source of all the myths about underground kingdoms."

Kane swept his gaze over it, mentally comparing it to the visions of the mighty cities Balam had imparted to him. It had a desolate, abandoned look to it, evoking more sadness than awe.

"No one has lived here for a long time," he said quietly.

As they walked down the slope, Brigid sniffed the air and detected the faint whiff of ozone. "The power generators are probably hooked up to an air-circulation system, either recycling the oxygen trapped down here or pumping it in from the surface."

They approached the city cautiously, alert for any signs of habitation. Brigid gestured with her left hand toward the tower, opening her mouth to point out a detail to Kane. The motion detector on her wrist suddenly emitted a discordant beep. Both of them came to sudden halts.

She raised the LCD to eye level. Three green dots marched across the window in a more or less straight line. At the bottom edge of it, a changing column of digits flickered.

"Three hits," she breathed tensely. "About ten yards ahead of us."

"Zakat and his people?"

Brigid shook her head. "If they survived the cave-in, they couldn't have gotten ahead of us."

The two people stood out in the open, and the only available cover was the nearest building. To reach it, they would have to run in the direction of the approaching contacts.

Kane double-fisted his Sin Eater. "We've got no choice but the old brazen-it-out strategy."

Brigid hefted her mini-Uzi, remarking sourly, "Your favorite."

They stood stock-still as three figures appeared around the corner of a building. At first glance, they looked like Asians, but when they drew closer, Kane drew in his breath sharply and he sensed Brigid stiffening beside him.

Clothed in flowing garments of a saffron hue, their bodies were short and stocky, and their hairless heads unusually round. Their skins were pale, but with a bluish pallor, perhaps due to the illumination cast by the light panels. They looked like human beings except for two details—their huge, large-pupiled dark eyes and their six-fingered hands and feet.

They didn't appear excited at the sight of Kane and Brigid, almost as if they were a welcoming committee sent to meet them at the city limits.

"Don't make a move," Brigid said. "I don't think they mean us harm."

She held up her right hand, palm outward in the universal sign of peace. The Agarthans—if that was who they were—showed no signs of recognizing it. Their blank expressions didn't alter.

Brigid spoke a few words of Tibetan to them, and still they didn't react. Kane noticed the strange, sluggish uniformity in the way they walked. Alarmed, his finger rested lightly on the trigger of his blaster.

"If they don't stop," he side-mouthed to her, "I'm going to fire a warning shot."

"They don't appear to be armed."

"And they don't appear to be friendly, either."

"Maybe they just don't understand."

As three figures drew closer, Kane suddenly realized why they didn't understand, and his stomach lurched sideways. Not only did the three men appear identical in shape, form and clothing, but also they all wore the same slack-mouthed, vacant expression. Their staring eyes were dull, and the look they gave Kane and Brigid was the same one a cow might give to a passerby. Spittle flecked their lips, and their chins glistened with drool.

Kane felt a surge of horror and didn't know why. Mental retardation is pitiable, pathetic, not horrible—but the three men were.

"Oh, my God," Brigid breathed. "They're idiots."

The triplets halted a few feet in front of them, gazed at them in impersonal silence, then simultaneously pointed to the tower.

"An invitation," muttered Kane, "or a command?"

"Whatever," Brigid said, "I think we'd better accept. It's where we were going eventually, anyhow."

The Agarthans turned and marched back in the direction they had come, not looking back to see if the outlanders were following them or not. Kane and Brigid fell into step behind them.

"It'd be nice to know if we're guests or prisoners," Kane remarked.

"They probably don't care one way or the other," she declared. "They were assigned the task of meeting us, they're fulfilling it and that's all there is to it."

"Who assigned it?"

Brigid shrugged. "I'm sure we'll find out."

They passed windowless dwellings that reminded them both more of mausoleums than homes. The streets were completely deserted, and the silence was absolute except for the tramping of their feet.

They followed the three men to the base of the tower, through a low-arched doorway and into a corridor. The hallway curved around, then abruptly became a flight of stairs—small stairs, exactly like the image Balam had implanted in Kane's mind.

"Seems a little redundant," Brigid commented wryly, carefully balancing herself on the small, irregular risers.

"What does?"

"They live in the cellar of the planet, yet they build another cellar beneath it."

Kane felt too tense to chuckle. A dim light shone below, its radiance peculiar, suggesting an electric arc light as seen through a milky mist. The throbbing drone grew louder as they descended, like the murmur of a far-off crowd.

When the steps ended at another archway, they saw a pair of generators. Twelve feet tall, they resembled two solid black cubes, a slightly smaller one placed atop the larger. The top cube rotated slowly, producing the drone. The odor of ozone was very pronounced.

Past the generator-flanked door, they entered an oval gallery whose walls, floor and ceiling seemed coated by a lacquer of amethyst, reflecting the light cast by flames dancing in a huge bowl brazier.

At the very center of the gallery, in a stone-rimmed depression, stood a stone altar, with a figure behind it. Kane caught his breath. The scene was exactly the same as

Balam had shown him. Around the altar reposed bare bones, hollow eye sockets staring into eternity.

Lam stood at the altar, eyes wide open and seeming to stare straight into Kane's soul. Within his long fingers rested the cube of dark stone.

At first glance, the figure appeared to be a life-size statue, crafted with marvelous perfection. The high-boned face exuded a dignified calm, aware of all the immensity of time. The two big eyes were veiled by heavy, shutterlike lids.

Kane forced himself to step closer, heart hammering within his chest, focusing on the black yet somehow shining stone gripped in the six long fingers.

A hoarse, disembodied voice echoed through the gallery. "This is who we are."

BALAM STEPPED from the wavering shadows cast by the flames in the brazier. Like their escort, he wore a simple, draping robe of saffron. He gestured around him with one hand.

"Thousands of years ago was our migration. This is all that remains of the exodus. This is the nest of the Archons you sought in order to destroy. This is the home base of your enemies."

Balam nodded to the three men who stood shoulder to shoulder, eyes and expressions uncomprehending. "They are the last of the original hybrids created here, birthed to command the future. They are the immortal kings sung about in Agarthan legend. They bear the mingled blood of both our peoples."

His whispering voice held no emotion, no heat, but both Brigid and Kane sensed a grief so deep it was almost a despair. "We had no choice but to expand our breeding stock, our gene pool. To purify our impure blood."

Kane could not find words, but Brigid inquired quietly, "More and more genetic irregularities began cropping up, congenital defects became commonplace?"

She indicated the triplets with one hand. "They appear to be suffering from a form of myxedema."

Balam nodded, but did not speak.

Kane tried to dredge up anger, even pity, but all he found within him was a cold, weary resignation. "You misled, tricked and nearly obliterated humanity because of birth defects?"

Balam whispered, "One avoids disease by living in accordance with the laws of health. If not, one is at the mercy of those who spread disease."

"What's that supposed to mean?" Kane demanded.

"We set for ourselves the goal of not being affected by the disease spreaders. So we manipulated them to infect their own kind."

"Disease spreaders," Brigid repeated bitterly. "You mean humanity."

"Humankind had as many opportunities to check the disease, to cure it, to immunize themselves as they did to spread it. The final choice always lay with them. What you know as the Totality Concept could have accelerated man's development. Instead, it was used to accelerate the disease."

Kane wished he could squeeze the trigger of his blaster and so blot out Balam, but he knew it wouldn't blot out reality.

"You could have had the stars by now," Balam continued. "You chose the slag heap instead."

"We're nothing but savages to you," Kane said lowly. "Like you said, you will reign when man is reduced to the ape again. So it's all over, isn't it? The human race has come to an end."

He didn't expect a response, but if Balam did, he figured he would agree. Instead, Balam husked out, "Nothing ever ends, Kane."

Balam stepped down gracefully into the depression, walking among the bones, standing beside the stiff figure with the black stone in its hands.

"This is Lam. My father. Within his hands, he safeguards our forebears' archives, the keys to what might have been and what yet may. His vigil is almost done."

Brigid frowned. "Explain."

Balam's mouth quirked in an imitation of a smile, which was almost as startling as his reply. "Would you have me explain the workings of one of your primitive aircraft if you did not first have a grounding in all the mechanics of its operations—the laws of friction, aerodynamics, electricity? Do you expect me to explain with a single sentence the nature of the trapezohedron?"

He paused to cough, then stated, "When my people first determined the course of their future, they consulted the trapezohedron. Through it, they saw all possible futures to which their activities might lead. From the many offered to them, they chose the path that appeared to have the highest ratio of success."

"What are you saying?" Brigid asked impatiently. "That

the stone is some kind of computer, extrapolating outcomes from data input into it?"

"It does more than extrapolate. It brings into existence
those outcomes."

Brigid's eyes suddenly brightened. "You're talking about
alternate event horizons."

"That is one description," replied Balam. "You experienced something similar recently. Time is energy. A flow
of radiation particles your science has named chronons.
Chronal radiation permits objects in sync with its fre-
quencies to go up or down. This is the basic underpinning
principle of what was called Operation Chronos."

"But we didn't go up or down," Brigid objected. "It was
almost as if we went…" She paused, groping for the right
word. "Sideways."

"Side-real space, where there are many tangential points
lying adjacent to each other."

"Parallel casements," murmured Kane.

Again came the ghost of an appreciative smile. "You
remembered."

"But I don't understand what it means."

Balam beckoned to him. "I will provide a small demon-
stration, so perhaps you may glean a faint comprehension."

Hesitantly, Kane stepped down into the depression,
eyeing the motionless figure of Lam apprehensively. "Is
he dead?"

Balam said only, "Touch the stone, Kane."

He didn't move. "What will happen?"

"That only you can say. Touch it."

Tentatively, Kane reached out with a forefinger, placing
the tip on the cold surface of the black stone so as not to

come in contact with the flesh of Lam. He waited for something to happen. Then it did.

Light, sound, vibration and solidity flared up through him, and the circuitry of his nervous system seemed to fuse as awareness and perception multiplied.

He saw himself dying on the street. He leaned against a lamppost with one hand, with the other pressed over his stomach, blood oozing between his fingers. His body wore tight black breeches and high black boots, an ebony uniform jacket with silver piping tight to the chest and shoulders. He saw an insignia patch on the right sleeve, worked in red thread, a thick-walled pyramid enclosing and partially bisected by three elongated but reversed triangles. Small disks topped each one, lending them a resemblance to round-pommeled daggers.

A broad black belt held half a dozen objects sheathed in pouches. Between his feet lay a Sin Eater and a peaked uniform cap.

As Kane watched, he saw himself sag to his knees, toppling sideways and down, sprawling across a cobblestoned gutter. Another figure slid into his frame of vision. It was a tall man, almost cadaverously lean, wearing an identical uniform.

Kane instantly recognized his narrow, sunken-cheeked face with its odd, flat complexion. The dark curved lenses of sunglasses masked his eyes. Before holstering his own Sin Eater, Colonel C. W. Thrush nudged his body with a booted foot.

Kane jerked his hand back, stumbling as if from a blow. Present and future mingled in his mind for an instant of utter chaos. Sounding half-strangled, he gasped, "I saw myself. I was wounded, dying. Is that my future?"

"No," Balam replied. "Your present on a parallel casement. On a lost Earth."

Kane blinked, desperately trying to rid his memory of what he had just seen, snatching for some straws of comprehension. "I don't understand."

"If you seek hard enough, to every question you shall know the answer." He paused, and added cryptically, "There are others who seek answers."

At that moment, Grigori Zakat, Gyatso and Trai stormed in.

Zakat wielded the AK automatic, his face streaked with blood that trickled from a laceration on the side of his head. Gyatso's turban and spectacles were missing and a bruise purpled his forehead. Only Trai appeared unhurt by the rockfall. Kane assumed Yal had been seriously injured or killed, but he didn't figure on asking about him.

Zakat swept the barrel of the autorifle back and forth in jerky arcs, covering the triplets, then Brigid, then Kane and Balam.

His eyes widened when he saw the figure of Lam and widened even more when he got a good look at Balam. He seemed to be struck speechless, tongue glued to the roof of this mouth.

Gyatso's reaction was similar to when Leng first saw Balam. A torrent of words spilled from his lips and he dropped to his knees, bowing his head. Balam regarded him disdainfully, then coldly turned his back on him.

"Nobody move," croaked Zakat, his face shocking pale beneath its layer of dirt and blood. He had to forcibly wrest his gaze away from Lam and the black stone. "Disarm yourselves."

Kane and Brigid exchanged glances, and Kane growled, "Screw you. You're the one who's outgunned."

Zakat laughed, a wild, high tittering with notes of hysteria running through it. "Ah, but I have more targets."

He stepped swiftly behind the triplets, who looked his way disinterestedly. "Who are these cretins?"

"They have the minds of children," Brigid stated with a forced calm. "They're harmless."

"But you force me to use them to prove to you that I am not."

The shot sounded obscenely loud in the gallery, thunderous echoes rolling. The little man in the center arched his back, as if he had received a fierce blow between his shoulder blades. A wet crimson blossom bloomed on the front of his robe, the fabric bursting open in an eruption of blood. He toppled forward into the depression, bones clattering and rattling with the impact.

The other two men clapped their hands over their ears, eyes wide in wonder, drooling mouths each forming an O of wonder.

"You sick bastard!" Brigid shrilled, bringing her Uzi to waist level.

"To save the others," Zakat replied mildly, "all you have to do is disarm."

Kane holstered his Sin Eater, unbuckled it from his forearm and dropped it to the floor. He unscabbarded his boot knife and laid it next to the blaster. Reluctantly, Brigid unslung her Uzi, holding it by the strap. Trai rushed forward, snatching the weapons, frowning uncertainly for a second at the Sin Eater.

"What is it you want?" Kane demanded angrily.

Zakat stepped from behind the Agarthans and nodded toward the kneeling Gyatso. "What he wants."

"Power?" challenged Brigid.

Zakat smiled a pitying smile. "About three hundred years ago, an English novelist wrote, 'We seek power entirely for its own sake. We are not interested in the good of others; we are interested solely in power…the object of power is power.'"

He walked closer to Gyatso, who appeared to be mumbling a prayer. "The power locked up in the stone is the key to achieving that object. It is Gyatso's legacy, his by right of birth."

Balam spoke for the first time since Zakat and his people entered. In his scratchy, whispery voice he said, "He is the end result of many experiments conducted on this continent over a period of many centuries. His only legacy is that he exists at all."

Gyatso's expression slid from one extreme to another— shock, hurt, betrayal and finally outraged anger. Because Balam had spoken in English, he responded in the same language.

"I have heard all the tales about my ancestor, the Maha Chohan. I strengthened my will to find his nation and take my place in it. I did not allow myself to fail at any task, no matter how trivial. I devoted myself to learning the old ways of Agartha. I studied my entire life for this moment. I abase myself before you."

Balam's tone was flat, but it carried a contemptuous undercurrent. "You debase yourself, rather." He nodded toward Zakat. "You are but a foil for that man, and that is the true goal of all your ambition. To be used."

Gyatso sucked in a deep, shuddery breath, then released it in an enraged roar, *"I demand my legacy!"*

Balam gestured diffidently with a six-fingered hand. "Take it."

Blinking at him in astonishment, Gyatso stammered, "You grant me permission to claim my birthright as the descendent of the Maha Chohan?"

Balam's retort was a whisper. "I grant you nothing."

With a rustle of his coat, Gyatso bounded to his feet. He stepped down into the depression, pushing Kane aside. He stopped before the figure of Lam. His eyes widened until his jet-black irises were completely surrounded by the whites. His lips moved, and a whispering, altered voice came forth. He spoke quickly, the syllables tripping over each other so rapidly the words were unintelligible.

Gyatso grasped the stone, first with his left hand, then his right, covering Lam's fingers with his own. He bent forward, head touching it. Kane felt his nape hairs tingling when the man crouched over as if drinking an invisible radiation into his soul.

Then Lam's eyes opened.

For an instant, there was a movement in the air about him, such as the ripples made in water when a fish swims close to the surface.

Gyatso's body spasmed violently, writhed and he threw back his head and howled, a scream ripped from the roots of his soul. His mouth gaped open, but no words came out. He croaked a sound of pain and terror and despair.

His back arched violently, and the sharp cracking of cartilage and bone seemed to fill the gallery. From the corners of each bulging eye squeezed droplets of blood. Then those eyes burst in gelatinous, watery sprays. He collapsed onto his back, arms and legs kicking and contorting.

Trai screamed long and loud in horror, and the shriek broke the invisible bonds weighing down the limbs of Brigid and Kane.

Kane sprang out of the depression directly for Zakat. The stunned Russian just managed to catch Kane's streaking movement in time to bring the AK around, but his motion was impeded by the two men standing around him.

Kane changed direction in midleap, diving low, bowling the men off their feet, knocking them into Zakat. All of them went down in tangle of thrashing limbs and hooting calls of confusion and distress.

Simultaneously, Brigid lunged for Trai, who stood and shrieked, hopping up and down in her terror. Because she bore a slight resemblance to Beth-Li, Brigid had no compunction about punching the girl as hard as she could on her rounded chin.

Trai spun almost completely around, stumbling over the kicking legs of the men, and went down, sprawling awkwardly.

Kane crawled over the twins, backfisting the barrel of the AK aside. Zakat's finger closed over the trigger at the same time, and he fired a stuttering burst into the ceiling.

Ricochets screamed, and rock chips and fragments sifted down. The bolt of the autorifle snapped loudly against an empty chamber.

Kane gripped the barrel and the stock, throwing his weight downward, pressing the frame against Zakat's throat. The Russian wrenched and heaved for a frenzied instant, straining to keep the rifle from crushing his windpipe.

He flung up his left leg, twisting with surprising agility, slamming the back of his heel against Kane's collarbone and tossing him aside.

Zakat rolled to his feet immediately, giving his right hand a little shake. Kane saw the bone-handled knife with the six-inch blade slide from his sleeve into his palm.

The Russian cast a single, feverish glance in the direction of Gyatso, then spun around and ran.

Kane spared a moment to snatch up his holstered Sin Eater before he raced in pursuit. Brigid called out after him, "He has two facets of the stone, remember."

Kane didn't waste time or breath to tell her he was well aware of that. He stumbled up the small steps, cursing when he banged his knee against a riser. Grigori Zakat was already out of sight, in the corridor above, but his running footfalls echoed back to Kane.

He followed Zakat by sound alone, out of the tower and through the silent streets of the eerily illuminated city. The Russian was amazingly fleet of foot.

As Kane scrambled up the slope that led to the tunnel, he heard faintly, over the sounds of his scrabbling ascent, a swishing hum. The Sin Eater, still in its holster, was torn from his hand by a blow from a key-shaped cudgel. Pain stabbed through his metacarpal bones, into his wrist. He skipped around just as Yal appeared from behind a clump of boulders, snapping the key back into his hand by the leather thong.

Kane rushed him, legs pumping furiously. Yal swung out with the cudgel again. Kane dodged, felt it smack along his left shoulder and kept running. He delivered his boot full into the Dob-Dob's groin.

Yal uttered a strangulated screech of agony and bent at the middle. Kane drove him half-erect again with a knee to the chin, and his fist flattened his nose, knocking him unconscious.

Retrieving his blaster, Kane noted with a grunt of disgust that the spring-release-cable mechanism in the holster was knocked askew. He knew from past experience it couldn't be repaired quickly or easily, so he raced into the tunnel opening.

He bumped and bounced from wall to wall and when he exited it, he caught just a fragmented glimpse of Zakat darting into one of the side passages. Kane went in after him.

The shaft was narrow, lit by the pale blue astral glow from overhead light panels, which turned complete darkness to twilight. He moved stealthily, somehow sensing that Zakat had stopped running and lay in wait for him.

The Russian's voice drifted through the passageway, from the murk ahead. "Why do you chase me, Kane?"

The unexpected question confused him, threw him off balance. "You have two pieces of the trapezohedron."

"So? Is that a reason to hound me, to murder me? If I give them to you, will you spare my life?"

Kane ignored the query, creeping on down the shaft, trying to make as little noise as possible.

Zakat chuckled, his voice a sepulchral echo. "You don't know the answer to that, do you? You believe you can kill me and suffer no consequences. Such arrogant simplicity."

Kane snorted. "Look who's talking, King of Fear. You murdered a mentally retarded man just to make a point. You think you're free of those consequences?"

"As you said," came Zakat's reply, "I had a point to make. His death was not gratuitous. I was obeying the law of power. All power has its price, whether in blood or dignity. Depending on the market value of the power sought, the price goes up. If you murder me out of revenge, you are squandering spiritual coin. You gain nothing."

"Except," Kane grated, "a crazy dead Russian. I'll settle for that."

The tunnel opened onto a broad, curving sweep of shelf rock. By the feeble glow shed by a light panel over the shaft mouth, Kane saw an outcropping of flint to his left. It was large enough for a man to hide behind.

Cautiously, Kane circled it, glancing over the rim of the ledge, seeing nothing but a pitch-black abyss below. The Russian hadn't concealed himself behind the rock formation, so he paced around the shelf, returning to the edge, wondering if the man had found a way to climb down into the chasm.

A rasping, scraping sound reached him, and he pivoted on his heel just as Grigori Zakat dropped lightly from a shadow-shrouded fissure above the tunnel mouth.

Zakat took a step forward. Kane backed up carefully so as not to slip on a loose stone and plunge over the precipice. He tossed his Sin Eater to one side to keep both hands free. The Russian took another slow, deliberate step, then leaped forward, knife held for a disemboweling thrust.

Kane kicked off the rock shelf and dived for Zakat's groin, but the slender man was ready. His knee came up hard against Kane's head, and at the same time, the edge of the knife slashed down at the base of Kane's skull.

Kane rolled frantically, feeling the dagger sink into the collar of his coat. Only the tough, Kevlar-weave fabric prevented it from biting deep into the back of his neck.

Springing to his feet, he faced Zakat, who now had his back to the abyss, but the Russian had no intention of staying there. Rushing to the attack, he wove a whistling web of steel with the dagger blade held before him. Kane stood his ground, balanced lightly on the balls of his feet, leaning back from the waist, batting Zakat's knife hand aside as the blade menaced his neck and chest.

For a long moment, they exchanged a flurry of knife strokes and hand slaps, the point of the blade missing Kane's midsection and throat by fractional margins, once dragging along the front of his coat.

Grigori Zakat's breath came in labored rasps, and his face darkened in exertion and frustrated fury. He stumbled slightly from the force of one of Kane's open-hand blows against his forearm. As he regained his balance, he lashed out with the knife in a backswing.

Kane turned with him, locking the man's right wrist under his left arm and heaving up on it with all his upper-body strength. Zakat cried out in pain and jacked up a knee, seeking to pound Kane's testicles, but Kane shifted so the impact was on his upper thigh.

Zakat's free hand darted out, locking around Kane's throat, fingers clamping down like a steel vise. Kane maintained the pressure on the captured arm, and the knife dropped from nerve-numbed fingers, chiming against the stone.

Zakat's hand tightened, and Kane fought for air, blackness closing in on the edges of his consciousness. Releasing the Russian's arm, he lunged backward, at the same time raising both hands above his head. Pivoting violently at the waist, he used the well-developed wing muscle at the base of his shoulder as a fulcrum, prying away Zakat's stranglehold.

The Russian snarled as his hand lost its grip, and he ripped strips of Kane's skin away beneath his long fingernails.

Kane inhaled deeply, repressing the cough reflex. He knew if Zakat had latched on to him with both hands, the man would even now be choking him to death.

Zakat swung at his face with a knotted fist. Kane dodged back and then in, ramming into him with a shoulder, carrying him back to the rim of the ledge, hand full of the man's coattails.

Digging in his heels, feet gouging shallow channels through the scattered pebbles, Zakat pounded his fists into Kane's kidneys, sending waves of pain-induced nausea through him. The Russian wrenched his body back and forth, heaving from side to side as he wriggled out of his coat, slipping away from Kane's rush. Kane tripped over his out-thrust leg and sprawled on his hands and knees within a couple of feet of the shelf lip. He caught a glimpse of the facets of the black stones falling from the coat's pocket and bouncing into the shadows of the outcropping.

Uttering a cry of dismay, Zakat lunged for them, and Kane swept out his legs in a slashing kick, catching the Russian just behind the knees. He fell, half on top of Kane. They thrashed in a limb-flailing whirl, Zakat clawing for Kane's eyes.

Kane stiffened his left wrist, locking the fingers in a half-curled position against the palm, and drove a killing leopard's-paw strike toward the man's face, hoping to crush his nose and propel bone splinters through his sinus cavities and into his brain.

The struggling Zakat lowered his head, and Kane's hand impacted against his skull. Needles of pain lanced up his forearm and into his elbow joint.

Face contorted in a bare-toothed snarl, Zakat punched him in the jaw, bouncing the back of his head against the unyielding surface of the ledge. Little multicolored pin-wheels spiraled before Kane's eyes. He thrust up his right leg, pounding the knee into Zakat's rib cage. The Russian grunted, cursed and slid to one side. Kane rolled, bucking the man off of him.

Zakat leaped onto Kane's back, arms quickly curving under and up, hands linking at the back of Kane's neck in a full nelson. Kane's head went down under the relentless pressure of the Russian's arms. With a thrill of horror, he heard the faint creak of vertebrae.

"Not the first time," Zakat grunted breathlessly into his ear, "I have broken a man's neck."

Kane had no reason to doubt it as his face flattened against the unyielding surface of the stone shelf. Zakat used his toes, the balls of his feet to muscle Kane forward. Sharp-edged pebbles bit into his knees, cut into his hands as he resisted the Russian's efforts to manhandle him off the ledge. Zakat strained against him, trying to snap his neck and propel him into the abyss.

Levering with his arms, bucking with his hips, Kane shoved himself sideways. Zakat twisted to keep from being pinned beneath him. He steadily applied the full nelson, driving Kane's chin against his collarbone.

Clawing up a fistful of grit, Kane thrashed and kicked, getting his hand up behind his head. He mashed and ground the rock particles into Zakat's face, ruthlessly scouring his eyes.

The Russian didn't cry out, but he inhaled sharply, tossing his head, and for an instant the pressure against Kane's neck lessened. In that instant, Kane tightened his body like a bowstring, arching his back, planting both boot soles firmly on the ground and slamming the back of his skull against Zakat's forehead.

The Russian uttered a growl, bearing down again, and Kane head-butted him a second time. The distance was too short for maximum effect, but Zakat's grip loosened even more.

Kane's legs levered like springs, powering him up and over in a somersault, breaking the full nelson. Zakat spit an oath in Russian and flailed around for the knife, fighting to get to his feet at the same time.

Kane made it a full half second before Zakat did, and as the Russian's fingers touched the handle of the dagger,

Kane swept his left leg up in a fast, powerful kick. He delivered the metal-reinforced toe of his boot against the underside of the Russian's jaw.

Head snapping back, Zakat fell heavily to the shelf edge, his body dislodging a few loose stones. They clicked as they bounced against the chasm wall, disappearing into the blackness.

Despite glassy eyes, the slender Russian bounded to his feet and launched several roundhouse punches at Kane's face. Kane ducked one fist, blocked the other with a forearm and caught Zakat in the face with a lightning-swift double hammer blow. Blood sprayed from the man's nostrils, and he swayed, clumsily trying to return the punches.

Zakat was deceptively strong, with years of experience as a back-alley fighter, but as Kane evaded the man's fists, he knew he had never stood toe-to-toe with an opponent and fought it out—at least not against an opponent with Kane's training, instincts and reflexes.

Zakat thrust his arms forward, hands seeking another stranglehold. Kane knocked both arms aside with his elbows and whipped his right fist into Zakat's temple. He drove a pile-driver punch deep into the man's belly, fancying he could feel the his backbone press against his knuckles.

The Russian jackknifed at the waist, a strangulated wheeze bursting from his lips. Zakat staggered to one side, boots grating loudly on rock as he fought to keep erect. Measuring him off, Kane bent diagonally at the waist, arcing his left leg up and around in a spinning crescent kick.

The toe of his boot slammed against the side of Zakat's jaw, turning him completely around in his tracks. It was a fast move, deftly delivered, but nothing his Mag martial-arts instructor would have cheered about.

Zakat stumbled, arms windmilling, and he stumbled off the rim of the ledge. He didn't plunge into the darkness. His hands shot out, fingers securing a grip on the stone lip. Kane heard him kicking frantically for a foothold.

Kane stepped to the outcropping, groped around its base for a few seconds and his hands closed over the facets of stone. He moved to the edge of the shelf. Towering over him, Kane gazed down into Grigori Zakat's blood-wet face. Panting, he bared his red-filmed teeth at him in either a grimace or a grin, eyes darting to the two black rocks in Kane's hand.

"You don't dare let me die," he half gasped. "You need me, need my abilities to channel the energies of the stone."

Kane stopped himself from massaging the deep, boring pain at the back of his neck. He rasped, "What makes you think I give a shit?"

Uncertainty flickered in Zakat's pale eyes. "You have the stone, but you don't know how to use it. Its power is useless to you without me."

Kane said nothing, but upon glancing down he saw a small object glinting against the dark rock. Slowly, he eased to one knee and picked up the tiny wooden phallus with the stylized crystal testicles by its leather thong.

Zakat stared at it in hungry shock.

"What about the power of this?" Kane asked in a soft, rustling tone.

With his right hand, Zakat made a grab for the amulet. He missed it by inches, and the fingers of his left hand slipped. Frantically, he scrabbled to regain his hold. In a high, aspirated voice, he shrieked, "Useless! You'll have a key, but no idea of how to find the lock!"

Zakat's forearms trembled with the strain of resisting the irresistible drag of gravity. His wild eyes followed the pendulum-like movement of the Khlysty cross dangling from Kane's hand.

"You need me!" His scream slashed through the darkness, echoing repeatedly.

Kane dropped the wood-and-crystal emblem between Zakat's hands. "And you need this," he said quietly, flatly. "Use it as a key."

Zakat made a frantic grab for it. After an instant of mad clawing, he snatched it up and then disappeared over the edge of the shelf. He pitched down into the impenetrable blackness, and Kane heard his body slithering against the rock wall, then nothing, not even a scream.

He kneeled at the rim of the ledge, waiting for the faint sound of Grigori Zakat's body striking the floor of Hell. When it didn't come, he slowly pushed himself to his feet. Tension drained out of him, leaving him weak and trembling.

Hefting the fragments of stone in his hand, he tried to sense something special in the way they felt or looked. They appeared to have properties no different from the rocks that surrounded him.

"Doesn't that just figure," he muttered to the abyss. He slipped the rocks into a pocket, then turned and shuffled into the tunnel.

The first thing Kane heard upon returning to the gallery beneath the tower was a woman weeping piteously. Trai sat on one of the paving stones at the rim of the depression, huddled in a little ball of grief, hugging herself, rocking back and forth. To his surprise, Brigid sat beside her, patting her back, speaking to her soothingly in her own language. They were alone, the bodies of Gyatso and the slain triplet nowhere in sight.

"What's with Zakat's bitch, Baptiste?" he demanded. "She'll have more to cry about once she hears about where he ended up."

Brigid glanced at him reproachfully. "She knows already, somehow. She felt the link she shared with him disappear."

"Good. I wasn't sure if the son of a bitch was dead or not."

"What about you?" she asked.

He rubbed the back of his neck. "Just don't ask me to stand on my head for the next couple of days."

Brigid got to her feet, a hand on Trai's shoulders. "She's just a child, not really to blame. She was a servant in the monastery, and the monks, particularly the high lama, treated her badly. Zakat seduced her with kindness—and probably his psi-abilities."

Kane shrugged disinterestedly. "Where's Balam?"

"Attending to the body of his son."

"His son?" Kane echoed, startled.

"The triplets are his children, born of a human woman nearly four hundred years ago. Like he said, they are the last of their particular breed."

Kane shook his head and covered his eyes for a moment. He tried to loathe Balam again, even tried to pity him, but he could find neither emotion within him.

"Kane."

At the hoarse whisper, he dropped his hand and saw Balam, flanked by the drooling twins, stepping down into the depression. "You recovered the facets of the trapezohedron."

Balam wasn't asking; he was stating. Kane removed them from his pocket and held them out. Balam made no indication he even noticed. He inclined his head toward the ebony cube laced within Lam's fingers.

"Take it and go."

Kane's blood ran cold and his flesh prickled. "And end up like Gyatso? Offhand, Balam, I can think of a hundred easier ways to check out."

"The new human was responsible for his fate. The energy he directed into the stone was strong, but it was of an incompatible frequency. It was deflected, turned inward and it destroyed him. Take the trapezohedron, Kane."

He looked into the face of Lam, eyes closed again in placid contemplation. He stepped down into the depression.

"Kane!" Brigid spoke warningly, fearfully. "What if—?" She bit off the rest of her question.

He replied, "If the 'what if' happens, you know what to do."

He heard the clicking of the overhung firing bolt on her Uzi being drawn back, and he threw Balam a cold, ironic smile. It wasn't returned.

Reaching out, he touched the black rock in Lam's hands, feeling his pulse pound with fear. He tugged gently, experimentally. The trapezohedron came away easily, and without resistance it nestled in Kane's hands.

Almost as soon as it did, the flesh on Lam's face and limbs dried, browned and withered. His eyes collapsed into their sockets, and his body fell, his robe belling up briefly as he joined the skeletal remains around the altar.

Kane froze, the hair lifting from his scalp, his mind filling with primal, nameless terror. He gaped wild-eyed at Balam.

"His vigil is complete. Yours begins."

Kane despised the tremor in his hands and voice. "My vigil for what?"

"To find a way for your people to survive, as mine did."

Kane swallowed with painful effort. His throat felt as if it were lined with sandpaper. "The only way is to displace the barons—you know that."

Balam nodded.

"What do you want in return?"

"Nothing in return. I have returned to the old, old ways of our forebears when we passed on truth rather than burning it."

"But you *did* burn it," Brigid spoke up accusingly.

"To preserve ourselves," Balam replied. "A sacrifice made for an appointed period of time. That time is over. Our blood prevails."

Kane shook his head in frustration. "I don't— Are you *betraying* the barons, blood of your blood?"

"They are blood of your blood, too, Kane. I no more betray them than you do."

"A state of war will exist between our two cultures again," Brigid noted. "Rivers of that mixed blood will be spilled."

"If that is the road chosen," Balam said faintly, "then that is the road chosen. Blood *is* like a river. It flows through tributaries, channels, streams, refreshing and purifying itself during its journey. But sometimes it freezes, and no longer flows. A glacier forms, containing detritus, impurities. The glacier must be dislodged to allow the purifying journey to begin anew."

Quietly, Brigid asked, "And what of you? What will you do?"

Balam stood, swaying slightly, his huge, fathomless and passionless eyes fixed on them. Then he flung up one long, thin arm in an unmistakable gesture, pointing to the entrance to the gallery. "I will do nothing, and you must do what you can. Go."

Then he turned and walked away, trailed by his sons.

For an instant, Kane grappled with the desire to go after him, but he knew there was no point to it. Taking

Balam back to Cerberus served no purpose. What Balam actually was, Kane could not know, but a strange, aching sadness came over him as he watched the creature stride gracefully away.

He didn't know why he felt such a vacuum within him; then he realized he was reacting to an absence of hate.

Kane turned toward Brigid, and she saw the confusion, the uncertainty in his eyes. Softly, he asked, "Now what do we do?"

Brigid looked from Kane to Trai and to the black stone nestled between his hands. "We wait for tomorrow."